THE RISING

UNLAWFUL MEN BOOK 4

JODI ELLEN MALPAS

Jodi Ellen Malpas

Editing by - Marion Archer

Proofing by - Karen Lawson

Cover design by – Hang Le

PRAISE FOR JODI ELLEN MALPAS

"Malpas's sexy love scenes scorch the page, and her sensitive, multilayered hero and heroine will easily capture readers' hearts. A taut plot and a first-rate lineup of supporting characters make this a keeper." —*Publishers Weekly* on *Gentleman Sinner*

"This book is JEM at her best, the secrets, lies, enemies... and tongue it cheek humour. It's all there on every single page! I had no idea where this book was going or how the book would end. The journey was as captivating as it was enigmatic." - *Kindle and Koffee Book Blog* on *Wicked Truths*

"It's just twist after dark and delicious twist; a completely, unquestionably unpredictable ride from start to finish. This is the kind of book where every page is important, because there is just SO MUCH going on, and it's an intricate dance from loathe to love for this couple." - *Jeeves Reads Romance* on *The Brit*

"So it's safe to say, Jodi has once again completely smashed it with another sensation making it the best read of 2021! Hold on tight your about to be enthralled." - *Booksobsessive* on *The Enigma*

"A magnetic mutual attraction, a superalpha, and long-buried scars that are healed by love. Theo is irresistible." —*Booklist* on *Gentleman Sinner*

"Filled with raw emotions that ranged from the deepest rage to utter elation, Jodi Ellen Malpas wove together an incredible must-read tale that fans will certainly embrace." —*Harlequin Junkie* on *Gentleman Sinner*

"The characters are realistic and relatable and the tension ratchets up to an explosive conclusion. For anyone who enjoys *Sleeping with the Enemy*-style stories, this is a perfect choice."—Library Journal on *Leave Me Breathless*

"*The Controversial Princess*, told from Adeline's POV, is thick on plot, rich in character development with Kindle-melting sex and the perfect blend of twists and turns, shockers and villains!" — SueBee, Goodreads Reviewer

"*The Controversial Princess* is an all-consuming, scorching hot, modern royal romance with twists, turns and a jaw-dropping cliff-hanger that will leave you begging for more." —Mary Dube, *USA Today HEA*

"*The Controversial Princess* provided us with the romance our hearts needed, the passion our hearts craved, with jaw dropping twists and turns that kept us guessing and eagerly flipping the pages." — TotallyBooked Blog

"A brave, cutting-edge romance...This is a worthwhile read." —*Library Journal* on *The Forbidden*

"Unpredictable and addictive."—*Booklist* on The *Forbidden*

"*The Forbidden* proves that Jodi Ellen Malpas is not only one of the romance genre's most talented authors, but also one of the bravest. In this raw and honest portrayal of forbidden love, Jodi delivers a sexy and passionate love story with characters to root for. *The Forbidden* is easily my favorite read of 2017!"—Shelly Bell, author of At His Mercy, on *The Forbidden*

"*The Forbidden* is a gut-wrenching tale full of passion, angst, and heart! Not to be missed!"
    —Harlequin Junkie on *The Forbidden*

"Every kiss, every sexy scene, every word between this pair owned a piece of my soul. I could read this book a hundred times and still react as if it was the first time. *The Protector* is a top 2016 fave for me." —Audrey Carlan, #1 bestselling author of The Calendar Girl series on *The Protector*

"4.5 stars. Top Pick. Readers will love this book from the very beginning! The characters are so real and flawed that fans feel as if they're alongside them. Malpas' writing is also spot-on with emotions."—RT Book Reviews on *The Protector*

"*With This Man* took this already epic love story to a whole new, unthinkable height of brilliance." – Gi's Spot Reviews

"Super steamy and emotionally intense." –The Library Journal on *With This Man*

"Jodi Ellen Malpas delivers a new heart-wrenching, addicting read."—RT Book Reviews on *With This Man*

"We really don't have enough words nor accolades for this book! It had everything and MORE with added ghosts from the past as well as a surprising suspense. But mostly, it was about a love that proves it can conquer anything and everything placed in its way. A beautiful addition to one of our favourite series!"—TotallyBooked Blog on *With This Man*

For Danny & James.
Thank you for tempting me into the darkness.

THE
RISING

JODI ELLEN
MALPAS

1

DANNY

I'd rather be dead. It's got to beat constantly dodging death, and the many men out there who want to put an end to me aren't the only ones I need to be wary of. I'm more concerned about what my wife is capable of.

I look up at our villa as I exhale and drop my arse to the sand, fucking exhausted. Exhausted of running. Exhausted of fighting with Rose. Plain fucking exhausted. I grab the bottle of Scotch and swig some more—it's probably unwise, I need my wits about me while my wife is on the war path, need the ability to duck speedily —but . . . fuck it. Let her at me. Like I said, I'm too exhausted to fight, and the weightless sensation coming over me is a brief respite.

I fall to my back on the sand and stare at the black, twinkling sky, taking another drag of my cigarette and another glug of Scotch, spilling some of it over my face as I do. For fuck's sake. It was such a lovely evening—my little boxing match with Otto aside. What the fuck's with that, anyway? Him? My mother? I snort, sucking back another hit of nicotine, followed quickly with another shot of the hard stuff. "Not fucking happening," I say to the sky. "Over my dead body." Which might be a distinct possibility if Rose gets her hands on me.

I lift my head a fraction, looking back up at the villa. I hope Mum's managed to reason with her because I certainly couldn't. In fact, I was like a red flag to a bull. I left the room on numerous occasions to let her calm the fuck down, and the moment I entered again, hearing she'd quietened, she'd flown at me, either with words or deranged, flailing, desperate arms. I restrained her more than once, since I couldn't fuck her into submission with my mother and Otto there. So in the end, I forced myself to leave the house before she did any damage to herself or our baby. I feel like a man on the edge of heaven and hell, and some unknown fucker out there will dictate which way I fall.

My wife might save him a job soon, though. And yet, I can't be angry with her. Can't be pissed off. I can't blame her for flying off the handle. For throwing the vase at the wall. She's pregnant and her emotions are all over the place. Next to that, I've promised that woman peace and failed to deliver it one too many times. I feel fucking hopeless. Useless. I know my wife better than anyone, and when she feels threatened, she fights. And as always, I'll let her take her anger out on me.

I flick my cigarette away and finish the bottle, dropping it clumsily to the sand. The sky's starting to spin. My thoughts are getting all tangled, telling me to go back to her. Deal with this mess. But I'm pretty sure she screamed clear instructions to *never* go back.

Unlucky for Rose, I can't live without her.

I lift my head as far as I can manage and scowl at our villa. "And you love me too, woman, so stop being so f-f-fucking ridiculous." My head hits the sand on a soft thud that feels anything but soft. "Bastard," I grumble. Fuck me, I haven't been this drunk in years. Not since Dad's funeral. Not since I realized I'd fallen in love with the ice princess. "Why'd y-you have t-to be such a bitch?"

A face appears above me, and I squint hard, trying to get some focus. "Found him," James calls.

"For fuck's sake." Brad appears, lifting his mobile to his ear.

"We've got him." He hangs up and gives me a nudge with the toe of his shoe. "You think this is gonna solve all our problems?"

"Fuck you," I spit. "And go get laid. You're a miserable fucker recently."

"Well, there's been no in-house whore for a while," James says, and I chuckle, getting another nudge from Brad, this time significantly harder.

"I'm going before I beat him to death."

"I'd like to see you try," I yell to his back as he stomps off up the beach. "Don't you know who I am? Be afraid, Brad. Be very af-f-raid."

"What the fuck are you doing?" James mutters tiredly, bending to get closer, bracing his palms on his knees.

"What the fuck does it look l-l-like I'm doing?" I pat about on the sand and find my bottle, lifting it to my lips and swigging. Nothing comes out. I snarl and toss it aside. "I'm getting shitfaced. Get me another bottle."

"No."

"What do you mean, no?" I scramble to sit up, swaying something terrible. *Fucking hell, just shut the fuck up, Black, and lie the fuck down before you throw up.* "Don't you know who I am?"

James laughs. Why's he laughing? "Yes, I know who you are. You're a man who's in the doghouse. Come on, you prick." He moves in behind me and hooks his arms under mine, getting me up with relative ease, considering I'm fucking legless. "Rose is upset."

I laugh loudly. "Upset? Is that what we call fucking psycho these days?" I shrug him off and stagger a few paces, but quickly steady myself. I look down. My feet are in the water. And my arse feels a bit damp. "You know what I'm going to do?" I ask. "To fix this fucking mess?"

"Sober up?"

"I'm going to kill The Bear." I start trudging up the sand toward my villa. "This is all your fucking fault, anyway." Why's that only just occurred to me? This shitstorm is all James's doing, because he's the fucker who resurrected me. I was quite happy being dead.

I stop. Turn. Sway. Blink. His eyebrows are nearly touching his hairline. "I should kill you too." Or at least punch his fucking lights out. That'll make me feel better.

James's arms open up invitingly, and I clench my fist. He's goading me. I'm not so drunk I don't recognize that.

"I've always wondered who'd come out on top between The Brit and The Enigma." His head tilts. "So let's find out."

He has? I thought we were friends. *The fucker.* I draw back my fist, narrow my eyes, and swing, intent on planting a precisely placed fist on his jaw.

But it hits precisely . . . nothing. "Fuck," I mutter, spinning on the spot before face-planting the sand. I roll to my back and find James looming over me.

"You done?" he asks as I spit out endless grains of sand. "Or do I have to knock you out and drag you back to your wife?"

"I'm staying at yours."

He laughs. "You've got more chance of digging a hole here on the shore and finding The Bear." He offers a hand. "I'm not joining you on the wrong side of your wife. Give me your fucking hand, you dick."

I huff and throw out a disorientated arm, taking a firm hold, and James hauls me up, but this time he doesn't let me go, supporting me as I stagger up the beach. "How'd Beau take the news?" I ask, hoping James is in the doghouse with me.

"You mean the news that the man who ordered the death of her mum and my entire family is, in fact, alive when we all thought we'd just executed a pretty fucking seamless plan and killed the fucker?"

"No, I mean the news that you're a sarcastic knob." I shove him away. I can walk on my own. "Yes, that news," I grumble. "I was having a lovely evening until he called to let us know we killed the wrong man."

"Me too," James muses, and I look at him, albeit through drunken eyes, but I see the lost man who's still lingering. For a brief moment, he and Beau had their peace. For a brief moment, it was sunshine and smiles. For a brief moment, we all thought that part of the story was over.

But when you're me and James is James, it's never really over.

So, yeah, we're all shook up. Some of us—like my wife—are fuming. Some of us, like Beau, are quietly contemplative. Others, like Brad, Otto, and Ringo, are thirsty for blood again.

And then there's me.

Drunk.

But the alternative is a bloodbath, and I've not quite recovered from my most recent rampage in Miami. I need a rest.

There's no rest for the wicked, kid.

"Oh fuck off," I slur, making James recoil. "I'm not talking to you." I stagger away, willing my dead father to leave me the hell alone. I do not need his input right now. "Call the men," I order, throwing a hand in the air, as if all of them might see me beckoning them. "We need a mee-ee-ee-ting." Let's figure out some shit, make a plan, and kill that fucking bear.

Again.

"For fuck's sake," James breathes.

"Fuck." I trip up nothing and land face first, getting another mouthful of sand. I start to spit and splutter as I get myself back to my feet again, marching on, determined. "I want meetings with . . ." I frown and turn to find James. "Who's still alive?"

He shakes his head, in despair, I think, but he doesn't get a chance to answer. Mum appears from nowhere and seizes me. "Where the hell have you b—" Her nose wrinkles. "You're drunk."

I roll my eyes. Or try to. "Just trying to numb the pain."

"You're hurt?"

"Yes, I'm fucking hurt. Didn't you see my wife's fist meet my fucking nose?"

"Oh, that."

"Yes, th—"

"Oh good, you found him," Otto grunts, and isn't he like a red fucking flag to an angry bull? I don't want to see that fucking fuck head. I watch as his hand meets my mother's arm. "Where the fuck have you been?" he asks.

I look up at his bearded, pierced face. "Plotting your death." I lunge, Mum cries out, and James yells, tackling me from the side and taking me down. I land with a grunt. "Let me at him," I demand.

"Fucking hell," James breathes. "You'll be telling him to *put 'em up, put 'em up* soon. What are you, the fucking lion who found his courage?" James stands and hauls me up, walking me back from my target.

I scowl, fighting his hold. Obviously, I get nowhere. "My mother is off fucking limits," I yell. "You even *think* about touching her again, you'll have *me* to deal with."

"I'm trembling in my fucking boots, Black," Otto grumbles, earning a smack from my mother and undoubtedly a plead not to goad me.

"Okay, I think it's bedtime." James directs me toward the villa. "We'll have our m-m-meeting tomorrow." I'm shoved through the door where I find my wife, my fucking *wife*, the woman who is supposed to love me unconditionally, looking at me like she's about to slap some conditions *on* me. I scowl. Or I try to. And then my eyes drop to her tummy. And I smile. I can't help it. But I quickly remember . . .

We're not talking.

"I hate you," I hiss, jabbing a finger in her face. Her gorgeous, *lovely* face. "I hate you so fucking much." I may be steaming, but I see her shoulders drop, all fight leaving her. She's calm. I'm plastered. And as if to prove exactly how plastered, I start rocking back on my heels, forcing James to catch me.

"Can I have a cuddle?" I ask, pouting. "Please?" I ignore the chuckles behind me and open my arms, walking to her, my efforts to remain in a relatively straight line quite feeble. "I don't want to fight."

"You always say that after we've had a fight, but you seem quite set on fighting while we're fighting."

"What am I supposed to do, baby? Hide everything from you?" I take her chin and lift her face to mine, closing one eye to focus. Perhaps I should hide it all. Leave her here, go back to Miami, deal with it all, and come back. Hopefully in one piece. I feel like I've been tossed back to the beginning of this shitshow and have to sit through the entire crappy performance all over again. Except this time, I have no fucking popcorn. Or any fucking leads. And my wife's fucking pregnant. *Fuck my life.* I rest my hands on her shoulders and she exhales heavily, taking my wrists.

"I don't want you to hide anything from me," she says.

"Then I won't." *Bullshit, Black.*

"How's this happened?"

I squint, thinking hard, like I might find the answer. Of course I won't fucking find the answer, and in this moment, actually, I don't want to. I just want to go to bed and cuddle her to death. Fuck the men. We'll meet in the morning.

I turn, ready to instruct them all to fuck off, with the exception of my mother, of course, but find everyone has gone. "Where did they go?"

"Home, I expect." Rose snakes an arm around my waist, and I start walking us to the bedroom. Leaning on her. Just a little. "Everyone's been looking for you for hours."

"I was on the beach getting drunk."

"No shit."

"No, really, I was." I dip and push my mouth into her hair, just before we reach the bed, and she releases me. I fall onto the mattress. Room spin finds me immediately. "I'm rea"—*hiccup*—"...lly drunk."

"You're really fucking annoying, that's what you are." She unfastens my trousers and I look down on what I expect is a lopsided grin. *Oh, yeah?* I had hoped but didn't want to assu—

"Forget it, Black," she mutters, yanking my trousers down my legs and casting them aside before starting on my shirt.

"Did you say no to me?" I seize her wrist and still her, looking at her for an answer. The right answer. "I'm a mafia boss, baby."

"I know," she purrs, dropping her lips to mine and kissing me softly. I sigh happily, opening up to her. "But tonight, you're not a hard one." She pushes into my soft dick as she bites my lip. "And this moll is too tired after stressing out over where her mafia husband had disappeared to."

I scowl. "I was on the beach."

"Yes, but I thought you'd left for Miami."

I snort. "Without James and Brad?"

"And Otto and Ringo and Goldie."

"Otto can fuck off." I slam my head onto the pillow. "He's banished."

"Tell your mother that."

"I will." I grab Rose and yank her onto the bed, wrapping every arm and leg around her. Or try to.

"Still hate me?" she whispers, kissing my forearm where it's curled around her neck.

"Always, baby," I murmur. "And forever."

～

Fuck. Me. To. Hell.

"No, no, no," I mumble, rolling over, trying desperately to find a cool spot on my pillow.

"Yes, yes, yes," a sweet, feminine voice sings back.

I still and scowl. Pout. Roll my eyes. I'm never going to live this down. Only twice in my life have I been drunk beyond drunk. It's not me. I'm vulnerable under the influence. At risk. But the truth is, if I hadn't drunk last night, I would have headed straight to the hangar, got on my plane back to Miami, and . . .

And blown the whole fucking city up.

It was a terrible idea. Worse than getting so drunk I feel like a few grenades have gone off in my skull.

My face squished in the pillow, I listen as the sound of her bare feet padding the floor gets closer. Her face appears, looking all too fucking smug. "You're dribbling," she whispers, leaning in and licking my lips. Naturally, everything inside lights up like fireworks and my blood starts pounding instead of my head. She smells so good. Tastes incredible. Feels like heaven. I find it in myself to push my hands into the covers and roll to my back, grabbing her wrist as I do and yanking her on top of me. But just as I'm moving in for a kiss to get us started, to get what I know is going to be a challenging day off to the best start, I detect a wave of worry fly across her face.

I withdraw. "What's up?"

Her cheeks balloon, her hand slaps across her mouth, and she flies up from the bed, dashing across the bedroom. She doesn't bother shutting the door—time is obviously of the essence—and a second later, the retching starts. I pout. "You okay, baby?" I call, dragging myself up, my hangover back with a vengeance. Self-inflicted, mind, so I'll keep my gob shut. I make it to the door just as she brings up last night's dinner, her body jacking, her arms braced on the seat.

"Fine," she heaves, jolting again, bringing up dessert.

I wince, crouching behind her and rubbing her back, tucking some stray strands of hair into her hair tie. "It's definitely a girl," I say, pulling some tissue from the holder and passing it to her.

She inhales heavily and exhales even more so, dropping to her arse and slumping back into me, exhausted. I shuffle back until I find a wall, taking Rose with me, and settle against it, holding her between my legs, my arms wrapped around her chest. "How do you know?"

"Because only a woman could be this difficult." I lean in and have a nibble of her ear as she chuckles weakly, snuggling into me anywhere she can. This is my Rose. Peaceful. "Feel any better?"

"Not really," she whispers. "You?"

"Not really," I admit, sighing into her hair. I don't know what to say to her. I don't know what happens from here. Returning to Miami was always on the cards, but we both—and by both, I mean James and I—felt a fuck load better about it with The Bear dead. Trying to sort business while ensuring Rose and Beau were safe was too fucking stressful. I don't want to return to that. Dodging bombs, looking over my shoulder, arguing constantly with my wife.

Problem is, I don't appear to have a choice in the matter, and Rose doesn't react all too well when choices are taken away from us.

"What happens now?" she asks, and it's hesitant.

Now, we go back to Miami and fix the fucking problem. Simple. But simple isn't going to be easy, not on my health, and definitely not on my marriage. "Now," I say, moving my hands to her belly, "you will do what you're told and concentrate on this."

Her hands land on mine, circling. "While you go back to war," she whispers, the statement almost accepting. But what choice does she have? What choice do *any* of us have? His contact last night wasn't just a courtesy call to let us know we'd failed to eliminate our biggest enemy. It was a warning.

And the mystery is reignited.

"Come on," I say, encouraging her up. I sling an arm around her and walk us to the kitchen, placing her on a chair and collecting some of that green shit from the fridge she's drinking a lot of lately. James got her onto it, and now I'm pretty sure she must be pissing the stuff. I pour some into a glass and pass it to her, setting the jug down and glancing around, listening. Something's different. "Where's the kid?"

"He stayed at your mother's." She takes a sip, her eyebrows high. I know what she's thinking. She's thinking I would hate for Daniel to see me drunk. She would be right.

"What are you doing today?" I ask.

"While you plot death?"

I give her a tired look and get myself some water, popping a few painkillers. "Rose, baby, I don't want you stressing out."

"Oh, Danny, please." Her glass hits the table a little heavily, but I'm not concerned about having any breakables hauled at me. She's too exhausted and can hardly hold herself up, let alone find the strength to chuck things around with any kind of force. This sickness is dragging out, but Doc's happy, and if Doc's happy, I'm happy. "Are you telling me not to worry about you?" she asks.

"Yes, that's exactly what I'm telling you." I get some pastries from the cupboard and load them onto a platter with some butter and jam. "Your worry is wasted because it's all going to be fine." I set everything on the table and take a seat beside her.

"Is that why you got roaring drunk last night, huh?" She accepts the Danish I slide in front of her and has a safe nibble.

"I was letting off some steam." I point my butter knife at her. "It's cheaper than smashing vases and bowls."

Her scowl is half-hearted as she chews slowly, but I see her remorse. She's a fiery fucker when she wants to be, and I know it's pretty fucking sick that I love her fire. But she needs it being married to me.

"So what are you doing?" I ask again. Conversation done.

"Beau and I are going shopping, and I wanted to pass by the market and pick up some ingredients for that curry I mentioned, but now—"

"Now, what?"

"Well, now . . ." She tilts her head, her expression expectant. "What are *you* doing?"

She knows what I'll be doing. I lick some jam off my fingers and sink my teeth around a croissant, filling my mouth and relaxing back in my chair. Her eyes drop down my bare chest. She pouts. Then leans over and gives my pec a little stroke. I watch her hand work over my flesh, across the small scar below my collarbone. "Feel better?" I ask, looking up at her, my voice low.

Her eyes jump up to mine. Her demure smile is my answer.

I'm up fast, grabbing her from the chair and getting her quickly but gently over my shoulder. Her squeal barely stabs at my brain. "You want to know what I'm doing? I will start by fucking my wife ferociously." I drop her on the bed, and she immediately starts pulling off the T-shirt and wriggling out of her knickers as I kick my boxers off. I seize my dick and start working myself to full hardness, and Rose watches me, her hands falling to her boobs and massaging. My wife's a walking sex bomb, but I can't say I've ever found her *this* sexy. Her boobs a bit bigger, her stomach a little rounder, her arse getting curvier. And the look in her eyes.

The mother of my baby. Keeping my hands off her has always been a challenge. Now it's plain painful.

I look down at my weeping dick, my teeth clenching, and walk on my knees up the bed, still working my cock. I knock her hand away, smiling when her back arches, and dip, taking her boob in my mouth. Her groan is long and low. My heartbeats are hard and fast. "Oh, yes," she breathes as I suck her nipple, relinquishing my hold of my dick and walking my fingers up her inside thigh, smiling when she spreads her legs farther.

"You want me to fuck you with my fingers, baby? Or my tongue?" I sink two fingers into her pussy and watch in fascination as her face contorts, her hands flying up to grip the headboard. "Or my big, hard, throbbing cock?"

"Yes," she whispers, flexing her hips to meet my fingers' drives. "All of it."

All morning sickness and hangovers are forgotten. As is—*I fucking hope*—all thoughts of the sadistic, sick fucker that's after us. I crawl down her body, shove my tongue past her pulsing, wet lips, and eat her pussy like it's my last supper.

"Shit, Danny!"

Her constant yells push me on, encourage me, my eyes closing, my mouth ravenous.

And just when she's about to come, I withdraw, flip her over, and ram my dick into her, fucking her hard, fast, and brutally. My roars and her screams must be heard across the island.

But still, I pump faster, grind harder, trying to pound my previous thought away.

My last supper.

2

_____

ROSE

He's smashing into me like a madman. I'm fighting to find my breath. He's taken me violently many times, made me wonder how much more of his power I could sustain, but never have I been in this situation before.

I need him to stop. He's out of control. Yelling constantly, his fingers clawed into my hips, his flesh slapping against my ass loudly. The soreness between my thighs is raw. My head is ringing. "Danny," I mumble into the pillow, grappling at the sheets. "Danny, please."

He pounds on, deranged and oblivious to my discomfort. "Come on, baby," he bellows, following it up with a bark of pleasure. "Come on!"

"Danny, stop." I choke over my words, feeling him hitting me deeply, so deep I'm in pain.

"Tell me when, Rose."

"Danny, I can't."

"Come on, baby!"

"Danny, please, stop." *Fuck, this hurts.* "Danny," I mumble, without breath or energy to yell, my body limp, at the mercy of his ruthless taking.

Stop!

And then I feel him jerk on a choked cough and he collapses onto me, panting, sweating, pushing me into the mattress, his hips grinding, his seed spilling into me, hot and endlessly as he groans into my neck. I lie still, completely dazed. And not for the right reasons. "Get off me," I say, my throat hoarse, my body not my own. It's a feeling I never thought I would have again. An empty, hollow, helpless feeling. Nothing. I feel nothing.

"Rose?" He strains my name past his fitful breathes, shifting slightly.

"Get. Off. Me," I order, my voice brittle. I wince when he slides out of me, leaving his cum trickling down my leg.

"Baby, what's up?"

I push my hands into the mattress and get off the bed, jarring when he catches my wrist, stopping me from walking away. "Let go, Danny." I know what he's expecting here. He's expecting me to lash out. I'm too numb. Too shocked. He has never violated me. He's always sought permission in his own fucked-up way. I turn my eyes up to his, and he recoils the moment he sees the emptiness of my expression, dropping his hold. "I told you to stop. You didn't stop." I walk away, numb, and lock myself in the bathroom. I immediately turn on the shower and step in, a familiar sense of detachment creeping through me, a shield that's been broken for years seeming to fix itself. I look down my body. I don't see my small bump.

I see an object.

I swallow and sink to the floor, dragging a washcloth over, sobbing as I clean myself, scrubbing between my legs. Scrubbing my husband off my body.

Because today he's not my husband.

Today, he's just another man who didn't listen when I told him to stop.

. . .

It's the only time I can recall when he's not come after me. I can't say I'm sorry. Once I've got myself together, I leave the bathroom. The bedroom is empty, and I dress in silence, pulling on a long blush skirt and a sleeveless white shirt, knotting the ends. I quickly rough dry my hair, put some sunscreen on my face and arms, and my gold-jeweled sandals on my feet. I grab my cell off the nightstand, my purse off the back of the chair, and a hair tie off the bed. The hair tie that unraveled from my hair while he took me like an animal. I stop and stare at the strewn sheets, then look over my shoulder when I hear the door to the villa slam shut. He's gone. Can't face me.

Good. I can't face him either.

I start pulling my hair up as I head to the kitchen but come to an abrupt stop when I enter and see Danny sitting at the table, dressed in a white shirt and blue chinos, spinning his cell in his grasp. I disturb his deep thoughts and he looks up, the fiddling of his phone stopping. I stare into his icy eyes that are far from cold at the moment. They're worried. I have no idea what to say to him.

I look away, grabbing my keys off the console by the door and leaving. "Rose," he calls, coming after me. "Baby, please, don't walk away from me."

I keep up my pace, pulling my cell from my purse and dialing Beau to find out how long she'll be. I don't even make it to my contacts. I hear wheels on gravel and see her yellow Jeep driving through the villa gates.

"Rose," Danny breathes, rounding me and putting himself in front of me. I sidestep him and wave to Beau, seeing James in the passenger seat.

As soon as she pulls to a stop, James gets out and I take his place, setting my purse on my lap.

"Morning," he says, his body still dipped for me to kiss his cheek.

"Let's go," I say, unable to appreciate the significance of such a simple moment—a moment when Beau and I can hop in a car and go out for the day without the Vikings guarding us or Danny and James fretting. But is that going to change now?

Beau doesn't pull away, her eyes on me. "You two still haven't made up?" she asks, turning her eyes onto Danny. I peek at him too, seeing half the man I know. An unsure man. A lost man.

"Rose," he murmurs softly, his eyes beseeching.

I return my attention to the road, and Beau finally pulls away. I look in the side mirror, seeing James with his hand on Danny's shoulder.

"What's going on?" Beau asks, splitting her attention between me and the road. She knows this is more than an extension of last night's drama. Of course she does. And because she is my best friend, I want to tell her. And because Danny is my husband and I don't want her to think bad of him, I don't want to tell her. I wonder if I'm overreacting. I wonder if I'm being unreasonable. I wonder if I have the right to feel this hollow. Our sex life has always been color- ful. It's always been very physical and sometimes violent. The nature of our relationship has always dictated that. Who Danny is. Who I am. Two people like us coming together was always going to be . . . volatile.

But today?

Perhaps it's my emotions. Perhaps my frame of mind, consid- ering the recent bombshell. I don't know. I sigh and look across to my friend. She looks together. What I don't know is whether it's a front because Beau has certainly played me before. Shown perfect serenity and felt utter despair. "Are you okay?" I ask, turning in my seat to face her. I reach for her sunglasses and pull them off, and she lets me. She knows what I'm doing. There's no evidence of tears. No squinting eyes from a headache. Perfectly together.

"No, I'm not," she says, making me recoil. She plucks her shades from my hand and slips them back on before bracing her arms against the wheel. "None of us will be okay until a certain someone is dead, and since we're back to wondering who the fuck that certain someone is, we'd all better buckle up."

On those words, I reach for my seat belt and pull it on. "Have you got sunscreen on?" I ask, eyeing her bare arm where her scar is visible. I would smile if I was confident her wound was out loud and proud with no underlying reason. Like trying to fool us all that she's fine.

"Yes, Mom, I have sunscreen on." Beau grimaces at the road. "You know he won't let me leave the house without smothering me in it."

"Good." I get my cell out and text Esther, asking what Daniel's plans are, since he's developed a habit of not answering me. Then I drop it in my lap and rub at my head. "Of course The Bear couldn't be Perry Fucking Adams," I blurt at the windshield. "And do you know what's most fucking annoying?" I ask, not giving her a chance to answer. "If I had known what was going on in my husband's head, if he had bothered to share anything, I would have fucking told him Adams wasn't capable." I spent weeks with the idiot, seducing him, stroking his ego. He was bent, corrupt, a liar, and a cheat, but he didn't have crime on *that* level in him. I wince, looking down at my cell when it rings. Like Daniel can't answer my texts, Esther can't seem to either, but unlike my son, at least she calls me in answer. "Hi," I say, clicking her to loudspeaker as Beau takes a left toward town.

"He's just left with Tank and Fury. Fury's taking him out on the water, Tank's had an order from the men to catch up with you two."

I turn my tired eyes onto Beau. I knew it. *Goodbye freedom.* Beau smiles, but it's small. She feels the same, and Esther knows she will have been telling me something I absolutely don't want to hear, but she's bracing me. "Thanks."

"How's the drunken idiot?"

"Probably getting drunk again." I reach into my purse and pull out my sunglasses, slipping them on, feeling tears biting at the backs of my eyes.

"What's happened now?" she asks, exasperated.

I can hardly tell her that I said no and he didn't listen. "Nothing," I sigh. "We're going shopping. Need anything?"

"Nothing," she says, refraining from questioning me. I bet she grills Danny, though. And, like me, he will lie.

"See you later." I drop my cell into my purse and sink into my seat. "How did James take the news?" I ask, turning my head, just catching Beau's shrug.

"Quietly. You know James. He doesn't say much, but he thinks lots."

I laugh but not with humor. While my husband brandishes his reputation like a weapon, James keeps his off the radar. The deafening killer and the silent killer. They're quite different like that, and yet scarily similar.

"I don't want him to worry about me," Beau goes on, and this time I am laughing with humor. What planet is she on?

"Next to killing, Beau, worrying about us is what our husbands do best." I frown at the windshield. "Actually, given they killed the wrong man, I think they worry better than they kill."

Beau lets out a bark of laughter, and it's so great to hear, even if our humor is warped. "Do not let him hear you say that."

I scoff. "What will he do? Kill me? We just established our husbands are terrible murderers." I'm talking shit. They're frighteningly talented at ending lives. They just got the wrong life on this occasion.

"Anyway," Beau goes on. "Husbands? I've not married my killer." She smirks at the road.

"Why don't you just say yes?" I know he's asked, *more* than once.

"Because he killed Lawrence's husband," she says on a shrug.

What? I stare at her, my mouth open. "Why didn't you tell me?"

"I only found out last night before dinner, and in case you missed it, a lot of shit has hit the fan since then." She gives me a high eyebrow, and I sigh. "It's going to be okay, you know that, right?" Reaching for my hand, she gives it a comforting squeeze. I don't know what Beau's had, but I want some.

"How do you know?" This is like an unbearable, spinning merry-go-round, everyone's emotions constantly being tossed from exhilarated to despair.

"Because you're married to The Brit, and I am with The Enigma." She takes her hand back to the wheel, smiling.

"Did *you* miss the shit hitting the fan last night?" I ask, completely bemused.

"I'm meditating. Lawrence insisted."

"What, and now you're all up for war?" I ask, sarcasm rife in my tone.

"Not up for it. Perhaps just accepting. You should try it."

"Accepting?"

"Meditating. It might lead to acceptance."

"I cannot accept raising my baby in the criminal underworld. I'm not becoming a mafia family."

"Rose," Beau sighs, reaching over and giving my belly a rub. "I hate to break it to you, but we're already a mafia family."

I pout and clench her hand, hoping one day I can feel my friend's tummy and know there's life in there again for her too. Family. We're one big fucked-up family. Fucked up, yes, but we all have each other.

"What do you think it is?"

"What *what* is?" I ask, confused.

"The baby." She laughs. "Boy or girl?" Her curiosity endears me and pains me. How happy she is for me, and yet so deeply sad for herself and James.

"I hope it's a boy, because—"

"Imagine Danny with a girl."

"Exactly." We both shiver at the thought. He would never cope.

"What are we shopping for anyway?" she goes on.

Shaking my head, back to bemused, I pull out my cell. "I'm making that curry I told you about." I show her the screen and the recipe I saw on TV the other day. Just watching TV. Chilling out. Being a vegetable. Eating. Drinking broccoli juice. *Bliss.* "I need every vegetable known to man and some goat."

"And will you be talking to your husband by this evening when we all descend on you for dinner?"

"Tonight's cancelled," I mumble. "I can't imagine everyone is up for it after last night, anyway. I'll eat the curry myself."

"Okay," she breathes, sounding as convinced as I feel. Not about the curry. I'll eat it all, no problem.

3

JAMES

I knew there wouldn't be a meeting today. Not after the state of Danny last night, and definitely not after turning up at their villa this morning and seeing both of their faces. All is not well in the Black residence. So I took him out on the water, hoping to shake some life back into him. He managed to pull his head out of his arse briefly in front of Daniel before Fury took the kid back to the villa to do some studying with his private tutor.

Then . . . back to brooding. I let him be. I've learned during the short time Danny and I have known each other not to disturb him when he's sulking like a brat. He'll talk when he's ready.

"I'll see you later," I say as he trudges off up the beach toward his villa, raising a hand in acknowledgment. I frown at his back. "Is now a good time to talk about the next shipment from Chaka?"

"No."

"What the fuck have you done, Danny?" This despondency, Rose's face, neither are a result of too much alcohol on his part and a meltdown on hers. Something's happened.

"I'll see you later for dinner," he calls, ignoring my question. "And get some fucking sunscreen on your back."

I rake a hand through my wet hair and roll my shoulders, feeling my skin becoming tight, just from a few minutes' exposure. I pull my wetsuit back up my chest and call Otto.

He answers immediately. "I was just going to call you."

"Why?"

"Click the link I just sent."

My phone dings in my ear, and I pull it away, doing as I'm told, knowing before I've seen what Otto's sent me that I'm not going to like it. But I massively underestimate how much. "The fuck?" I whisper.

"Yeah."

I stare at the online article, my eyes scanning the headline. "Who rules Miami?" I say, my blood getting hotter with every word I read about The Brit and The Enigma, and the FBI, who is power-less to stop them running amok in Miami. I finally get to the reporter's name. The reporter who clearly has a fucking death wish. "Who the fuck is Natalia Potter?" I ask. And where the hell has she got this information from?

Have I ever asked such a stupid question?

It'll never be over. We know that, which is why the boatyard has been repaired after we blew it up. It goes unspoken, but the girls know we're not out. We need control of Miami. So long as we main-tain control, we're *in* control. Power equals safety. Keep a presence to keep a life outside Miami. Disappearing isn't an option because we'll always be found, so we must keep a finger on the pulse to keep our lives. Simple.

"I'm working on it," Otto says, hanging up before I can bark my order to take her down. *A reporter, James. A female* reporter, who clearly has no fucking idea who she's dealing with.

I take a few breaths and dial Chaka.

"Is he dead?" he asks in answer.

I look at Danny in the distance, my frown returning. *What the fuck has happened?* "I'm afraid not." I start heading back to our beach hut. The beach hut that is far from a *hut*. "Just a bit distracted at the moment."

"Ah, Daddy Black," Chaka says, a little laughter in his tone.

I slow to a stop, surprised. News travels fast, but not all the way to fucking Africa, and definitely not when everyone has purposely been keeping Rose's pregnancy under wraps, for obvious fucking reasons. I hum a noncommitted reply and look back up the beach, seeing Danny in the distance. How the fuck does Chaka know? "We still good for the delivery on the nineteenth?" I ask.

"We might have a problem."

"I'm sure we don't, Chaka," I say, watching as my toes sink into the silky sand with each step I take. The problems are piling. "Because we've stepped on a few Russian toes and promised the Mexicans a really fucking great deal, and not delivering on the deal isn't going to look good. Could cause some bad feeling, if you know what I mean." Or have them turning back to the Russians for their supplies. *Do not make me threaten you.*

"I'll express your concerns."

"To whom?"

"The person in charge of the Coast Guard training course happening the day of our scheduled delivery."

I look to the beautiful blue sky. *Fuck it.*

"We'll need to deliver on the Monday."

"That's three days late, Chaka."

"You want me to deliver on a weekend?" he asks on a laugh.

He's right. The area is heaving on a weekend. "I'll confirm." I hang up and kick the sand on a curse.

"Something up?"

I still.

Smile to myself.

That voice.

I drop my head and find her on the veranda. In a bikini. A small one. Her blonde hair wild, her dark eyes shimmering. She has a piece of mango in her hand, her lips wet with the juice. And all of my problems melt away. I hear music coming from inside, and I cock my head when London Grammar's *Lose Your Head* registers. Our track. Her smile is fucking everything. So is the fact that she *hasn't* ripped strips off me for something that is way out of my control. She's affected, of course she's affected. Quiet, contemplative.

Clingy.

Needy.

Can't say it's unwelcome.

But I see acceptance. It's so fucking stunning on her. She knows I'll end this eventually. Whether today or tomorrow, I'll end it. I won't stop until I find him and kill him. It's just life now. Our life.

I walk toward her, the music getting louder, and she drops her mango, backing up slowly, smiling knowingly. I follow her through the beach hut, stopping to get out of my wetsuit—which takes much longer than I want—leaving it on the lounge floor as Beau drops her bikini top. I follow it to the tile. Peek up. Oddly, it's not the vision of her perfect boobs that holds me rapt, but the sight of her eyes sparkling wildly. *Alive.* Even now when we're once again facing uncertainty, she's alive.

Light.

It's been four weeks since her last period. It's gone unspoken but is screaming loudly. As are her words last night before the shit hit the fan at dinner. She wants to try. She wants a baby. I was hesitant *before* we got the call that's going to take us back to Miami—she's still delicate. But at the same time, I want that with her. A beacon of peace. Light in our darkness.

For Beau to find that sense of tranquility again.

But is she ready? Is her body ready? Her mind? And, more painfully, after everything her body has been through, is it capable of carrying a baby? I know Beau is terrified it isn't. She needs to know she's not physically broken. I need to give her that.

Do.

Don't.

Fuck.

I prowl forward again, my body temperature rising with every step, following her until we're in the bedroom. She stops at the end of the bed. One nudge has her falling to the mattress. The way she gazes up at me could break me. With so much trust. So much love. I plant one fist into the sheets by her leg, the other on the other side, and crawl up, settling just right so my face is in line with her stomach. And I worship every inch of her skin, kissing her from one side to the other, over and over, inhaling her scent, kissing her scar, as she weaves her fingers through my hair, humming happily. Sometimes, just being like this, so fucking close, so fucking in love with her, is as good as being buried inside of her.

Sometimes.

I kiss my way up to her face, tasting and smelling the sweet mango, and roll my hips, slipping into her easily. Her legs circle me, her arms hold me, her mouth adores me. Her breathy whimpers, my low grunts, her shallow cries, my extended moans, all mingle and meld together, creating the most beautiful music to make love to. My lips never leave hers. My groin grinds constantly. Her hips meet every roll. And when her short nails sink into my shoulders and she stiffens all over, I kiss her harder, pump firmer, groan louder.

Her yell of release triggers mine, and I come with force, groaning into her mouth as she whimpers into mine. And our eyes open at the exact same time. Meeting.

Love colliding.

I smile, inhale, and bury my face into her wet neck, tasting the salt of the air and of her sex sweat. "I missed you today," I whisper, wondering why today more than any other day. Perhaps because after the call I took last night I know our time here with the sunshine constantly on our faces is coming to an untimely end. Life in St. Lucia is unbeatable. In fact, before last night, I was considering suggesting we buy a place here. Although I know that was already happening without saying.

"What's going on with Danny and Rose?" Beau asks quietly, stroking soft circles across my back, making my shoulder blades pull together, my teeth gritting.

"You noticed something too, huh?"

"Yes, but she was cagey."

"So was he."

"So you don't know what's happened?"

"Not a clue. He hardly spoke a word the whole time I was with him." I lick her skin, bite at her flesh, kiss her throat, and she writhes beneath me, sighing.

"So you didn't discuss the fact that you both killed the wrong man?"

I smile into her skin before pulling out. "Actually, *you* killed the wrong man."

Her nose wrinkles. "I was getting fed up with you two toddlers arguing about who was going to get the honor and pull the trigger."

"Us two toddlers?" I ask, subtly laying my arm over hers above her head, effectively trapping them. She stiffens everywhere, which means her internal muscles squeeze my softening dick. It's a fight to resist recharging and going again. "You want to recant that?" I walk my fingers down to her ribs, my look expectant, and she's laughing before I even start tickling her. The sight is nothing short of perfection.

"Nope," she says, and suddenly she's moving. So fast, I don't have a moment to consider what the fuck is happening and *how* the fuck it's happening. I land on my back with a thud and Beau is straddling me. I look around, seeing I'm on the floor. "Do you submit?" she asks, making me grin, my mind invaded with a million flashbacks of the very first time I had her pinned to a floor.

"Never," I breathe.

"Good." She slams her lips on mine and kisses the daylights out of me, her tongue violent in its swirls, her mouth insatiable. This. *Fuck . . . me.* I once told Beau I was scared of *us*. Terrified. And I still am, because loving this hard, loving this intensely, has got to be dangerous.

I roll us, going at her with equal ferocity, fisting her hair, our mouths mad and clumsy.

I hiss. "Fuck."

Beau pulls away sharply, panting. "What?"

"Nothing," I say through gritted teeth, pain searing me. I go back to her mouth, but she turns her head, denying me.

"I'm fine."

"Sure, Rambo," she mutters, forcing my torso up and looking at the dressing on my shoulder. "It's wet." Unimpressed eyes land on me. "Why didn't you put a waterproof dressing on it?"

"Salt water will do it good." My chin hits my chest as I peek down, and Beau starts picking at the edge and peeling away the soggy dressing. She reveals a tidy round wound. Doc did a good job. I pluck the bandage from her fingers, toss it aside, and get us back to business, claiming her mouth again, ready to reload and go again.

"James? Beau?"

I withdraw, startled. "Did you hear that?"

"Hear what?" she asks, trying to pull me back onto her mouth. Of course, I oblige, kissing her again, but my ears are listening. Yet all I can hear are Beau's indulgent moans.

Bang!

The sound of the door flying open and hitting the wall makes me jump and Beau squeal.

"Oh, shit," Brad says, as I look over my shoulder, finding him standing in the doorway. "Sorry." But he doesn't move, just fucking stands there like a plum, while I ensure every part of me is covering every part of Beau. "Nice ass."

"You better be talking about mine," I warn, trying to gage exactly what of Beau's is on display. She laughs, wrapping her arms and legs around me as I drag down a sheet from the bed and work on covering her. "I hope for your sake this is an emergency, Brad." I fight back the blood flowing into my dick and leave Beau with all the covers, standing, bollock naked. Brad's eyes fall to my semi-erect cock, and I lay a hand over it protectively as I walk across to the chair, grabbing some boxers.

"It *is* an emergency." He turns and leaves the room. "Something's wrong with Danny."

My head drops back, my face pained, part discomfort—my dick

aching—part exasperation. I yank on my boxers and go to Beau, pulling her up from the floor and kissing her hard on the lips. "Get a shower."

"No, thanks." She slips past me, tucking the sheet in. "I want to know what's up with Danny too."

I'd like to tell everyone that he's simply got a bastard hangover, that they're all worrying over nothing, but I know as well as anyone that there's more to it. I follow and find Beau pouring juice out of the blender into glasses. Her mobile rings, and she looks at the screen. I see a shift in her stance.

"Who is it?" I ask, trying not to sound accusing.

"My dad. I'll call him back." She refuses to look at me. Her fucking father. *Prick*. He's the only bit of Beau I don't like.

"Have you seen Danny?" Brad asks me, getting comfortable on a stool.

"Yes, I've seen him. I was with him this afternoon." I take the stool next to him and accept the glass Beau slides across to me.

"I just left their place."

"And?" I ask.

"Let's just say, the Antarctic is looking pretty fucking appealing for a summer vacation right now." Brad grimaces at me as I down the juice. "What is that shit?"

"Try some," Beau says, pushing a glass toward him. "It'll make you big, strong, and healthy."

"I'm already big, strong, and healthy. And"—he strokes across his stubble—"good-looking too."

Beau rolls her eyes. "You need more in your life than the gym and a strip club."

"Like what?"

"A woman," she says, splitting her attention between Brad and her juice, her eyebrow arched. "Or a long-standing one, at least."

"What the fuck?" Brad murmurs, looking at me. I can only shrug. He returns his attention to Beau, smiling, like she just doesn't get it. "Beau, sweethe—"

"Do not call me sweetheart, Brad. Not if you want to keep your balls."

I laugh into my glass. "That told you."

"Beau," he begins again. "My beautiful, ninja friend." He raises a brow and Beau nods agreeably, going back to her juice. "Why the fuck would I want to do that?" He laughs. "Jesus, we're becoming outnumbered."

"*We're*?" Beau asks, her glass paused at her lips.

"The men," he confirms, as if she needed it. The poor, clueless twat. "We're supposed to be mafia, and soon there will be more women in this mafia family than men. We can't have that."

"No, no, we can't have that," Beau breathes, setting down her glass. "Now, if you don't mind, we were kind of in the middle of something," she says, motioning down her sheet-covered body and to my naked chest.

Brad looks wholly unimpressed as he turns away from Beau to me. "Want a beer?"

I recoil. "Do I want a beer?" I parrot. "Now?" He is one brave man.

"Yes, we need to talk about Danny."

Beau snorts and rounds the island, grabbing Brad by the ear, literally, and dragging him up from his seat. "Out," she demands, switching her hold to his arm and twisting it, getting it up his back in one swift, effective move.

"Arhhhh!"

She ignores him, pushing his helpless body toward the door as I watch on, amused.

"Jesus, fuck, Beau!" Brad bends back awkwardly, trying to lessen the pain. "That fucking hurts."

She shoves him outside and slams the door.

"That's why I won't get a woman," he yells from beyond the wood. "You're all fucking pussy-whipped, you pathetic fuckers."

Beau hauls the door open again, growls, and Brad, quite wisely, backs away. "I can't watch?" He just can't help himself, and I laugh as Beau grabs the nearest thing to her—which happens to be a shoe —and chucks it at his head.

I'm in a full-on laughing fit by the time she's scared Brad off, and, fuck, it feels good to laugh. I wipe at my eyes and find her.

The sheet is pooling her feet.

I look down and watch as my dick stands and tents my boxers.

Magic.

4

BEAU

James brushes his nose across the skin of my stomach as I recover. "We'd better get ready for dinner," he eventually says.

"Rose canceled."

"Danny never mentioned it, so we're going." He rests his chin on my stomach and gazes up at me, his eyes soft as I sink my fingers into his hair. "What are you thinking, Beau?" He's worried about me going back to dark places.

"I'm thinking . . ." I fade off and push some hair from his eyes. "You need a trim." But just a trim. I'm loving his longer hair. And the fact the sun has kissed it, making it lighter and his skin tan.

He peeks up at his mop. "What can I do to make this easier?"

I smirk. "Kill him. Like, *really* kill him." I know James was braced for a total shitstorm amid the other shitstorm. Killing The Bear is a given. Problem is, no one knows how long that'll take.

"And in the meantime?" he asks, sounding as surprised as he looks.

"In the meantime, you worry about me," I answer. It's simple. "Why are we discussing this, when we all know what's going to happen?"

"Are you being smart?"

"Always." I slip down the bed and kiss him. "I accept it. You thought The Bear was Perry Adams and killed him. The Bear wasn't Adams, so now it is back to the drawing board. What else can I do?" The moment I looked at him last night, as he watched me dancing, I knew something had happened. And I feared I knew what. Because, like Rose, I'd silently questioned Perry Adams's capabilities. I didn't know him like Rose did, of course, but he was mayor of Miami. A bit of a dick, to be honest, but The Bear? No.

I've chosen to be with James, and I've been at peace with that decision for a long time. Okay, so sometimes I slip below the surface into the darkness. Some days I don't feel so sure I can look toward the light. Some days, I'm fighting to keep my head above water. But never since finding out who James is, namely, The Enigma, the cold-blooded, silent killer, have I questioned my love for him. Not once. Never have I thought about leaving him. We just take each day as it comes and deal with it as it does. Bottom line, I'm no longer alone. I don't need to fight my darkness in solitary.

I have James.

"I love you, Beau Hayley," he whispers, blinking, his lashes so close I feel them tickle mine.

"Broken, fixed," I murmur. "Happy, sad. I will always remember that."

He smiles mildly and kisses me deeply. "Pregnant, not pregnant," he says, and I pull back in surprise, regarding him. I don't need to ask him what he means by that. I know.

"Are you saying we have to stop trying?" I ask.

"Did you hear those words come out of my mouth?"

"Not exactly."

"I don't want you to be sad if it doesn't happen."

"Are you shooting blanks all of a sudden?"

He rolls his eyes and kisses me chastely. "Are you a comedian all of a sudden?"

"You want to wait, don't you?"

"I want to do what's best for us." He stands and pulls me up, walking me to the bathroom. "Come on, we'll be late."

"I told you, Rose canceled."

"And I told you, Danny hasn't so we're going to Antarctica."

I laugh and let him put me in the shower, standing still while he washes me all over with a soapy sponge. I don't know what's best for us. Less for James to worry about would be best, I suppose, and another life, me having a baby, will be more for him to worry about. But for me?

I look down at my tummy, wondering.

Hoping.

Praying.

We walk down the beach to Danny and Rose's hand in hand, James carrying the wine and my shoes, me carrying my purse. "I haven't seen Goldie today," I say, looking up to the bar where Zinnea sings. It's her night off so the beach and half of St. Lucia are spared the sound of her dulcet tones so she can enjoy dinner with her *family*.

"Me neither," James says, pulling his phone from his pocket and tapping his thumb across the screen before slipping it back in and reclaiming me.

"She didn't say anything last night?" I ask.

"Oh, she said plenty, and none of it suited the dress she was wearing."

I laugh, even if it's misplaced. "I like girlie Goldie."

"I think she's going to be gone for a while." He drops my hand and puts his arm around me, kissing my hair, and I hum my agreement, knowing the news we got last night will likely put Goldie back a few paces on her path to freedom. Brunelli, the man who raped her and turned her into the cold-hearted, emotionless female we all know and love, is dead, and she thought James had exorcised his demons, so a softer, more feminine woman—one who let her guard down, was starting to emerge. One who wore dresses and drank wine. I imagine she'll be feeling quite crestfallen right now. But she won't walk away. Not until she knows James can.

Because when The Bear dies, so does the merciless assassin that James became after his family was murdered. When The Bear dies, so does The Enigma. I'm not deluded enough to believe it stops there entirely, though. Like Danny, you don't make a name for yourself and walk away as if you never tortured and murdered dozens of men, even if they deserved to die. Expect the unexpected. I have to live by that motto if I am to live with James, and I cannot live without him, so that is that.

"There's Otto and Esther," I say, motioning to the path that leads down from Esther's place to the beach. "They're surely not arriving together?" I saw Danny earlier. Today would *not* be a good day to piss him off. I find my pace increasing, wanting to get to them before they make it to Danny and Rose's villa, to warn them about what they're walking into. "Esther!" I yell, waving. "Wait up." I grab James's hand and start jogging through the sand.

"You need to stay out of it, Beau," James mumbles. "Not our problem."

"Do you want Otto to die?"

"Danny won't kill Otto."

I snort. I may not have known Danny Black for long, but I know him well. He's unpredictable. Shoots from the hip. And today, he's in a bad mood. "I'd rather not chance it," I say, reaching them.

"Chance what?" Otto asks, looking between us. "What's going on?"

"Danny."

"What about him?" Esther asks, her voice high and worried. "Did something happen?"

"Yes."

"What?"

"I don't know," I admit. "I went shopping with Rose earlier. She was weirdly cagey, and James said Danny hardly murmured a word while they were out on the jet skis earlier."

"I imagine that's because he drank enough Scotch last night to sink a fucking cruise liner," Otto mumbles. "Understandable, given the circumstances."

"You shouldn't have told us," Esther says, looking between James and Otto accusingly.

James laughs, and Otto rubs at his forehead. I won't join them in openly expressing their thoughts on that, but I have to agree, it's a crazy suggestion. Esther is basically saying we women are gullible. That we don't know our men. That they could disappear for fuck knows how long to find and kill someone and we wouldn't suspect a thing. *For God's sake.*

"I mean it," she affirms, pointing toward Danny and Rose's villa. "If that bloody bear doesn't kill my son, his wife will."

"The Bear won't kill him," Otto says, and I smile at his gruff voice being all soft and pacifying. "I promise you that, Boo."

"Boo?" James blurts, earning a scowl from Otto.

"Say a fucking word . . ."

James's hands come up in defense. "Wouldn't dream of it"—he backs up as Otto stomps off and Esther follows—"Boo," he adds. I smack his arm, and he laughs again, as Otto slows to a stop.

"You clearly want to die too," I sigh, willing Otto to pick up his feet, which he eventually does. I tug James along, watching as Esther catches up to Otto and nudges him with her shoulder. He nudges her right back. But no touching. No handholding. I know Esther's history. I know she deserves happiness and freedom from her guilt. I just question whether Otto—a man renowned for being a frequent visitor of strip clubs—is the man to give her that.

"Do you think they're . . ." I pout. "You know."

"Fucking?"

I flinch on Danny's behalf. "Esther doesn't look like the kind of woman to fuck."

"And that's all Otto does, so if you're asking me if they're going to work out, the answer is no."

Another flinch, but this time for Esther. "Perhaps you should have a bit more faith." I look at him. "I bet a million people would vote against us working out."

His scowl is instant as he looks down at me. "I couldn't give a fuck what a million people think. Only you." He stops us walking, takes my purse, and sets it on the wall with the bottle of wine and my shoes. He turns into me. "So, what do you think, Beau Hayley?" His eyes scan mine as I half smile, his palms cupping my cheeks.

"I think," I say, scanning his glorious face, "I love you."

"You *think*?"

"I know."

He nods, the pad of his thumb dragging across my bottom lip, wiping away the gloss. And he lowers his face to mine slowly, making me wait for his kiss. I inhale, bracing myself, taking hold of his wrists, my eyes closing. I feel when his mouth is level with mine, his breath warming my skin, and I whimper, begging him to indulge me, and yet he makes me wait some more. Makes me burn more. Makes my heart boom more.

And suddenly, the heat dies.

His hands fall away from my cheeks.

I lose my hold of his wrists.

And I stumble forward a fraction from the loss of support before he quickly catches and steadies me.

I open my eyes and find him on his knees. His gaze soft. His mouth straight. His eyes glowing.

His hand held up.

And on his pinky finger, halfway down, sits a diamond ring.

I breathe out and find his eyes. "James," I whisper. "I—"

"I'll always catch you, Beau."

I melt at my very own hard assassin being so romantic and soft, and lower to my knees, joining him. "That's all I need."

"Are you saying no again?"

My eyes pass between James and the ring. "Why do you want to get married?" I ask.

He considers that for a few moments as he regards me closely. "My mother was my father's light," he says quietly, an edge of sadness in his deep voice. "And he always followed the light." His eyes become glazed, and my heart splits. "You are my light, Beau.

And I would follow you to the ends of the earth." He takes my right hand and slips the ring onto my finger. "It can stay there until you see the light," he says, smiling down at my hand.

"Was this your mother's ring, James?" I ask.

He doesn't answer. He just takes my nape and pulls me onto his mouth, kissing me hard and meaningfully. His sentiment is beautiful. Except I don't think darkness is avoidable in our world. And as we've both learned, and how we were both drawn to each other, darkness entices darkness. "Stay in the light with me, Beau," he begs, kissing my lids, my nose, my cheeks, my forehead. "It's all I ask."

I can only try. "We'll be late," I whisper, pulling away and running my fingers through his hair. James nods and stands, pulling me up with him. He gets my purse and hands it to me, and my cell inside starts ringing. I know who it'll be, and I can't avoid him forever, but I've done a good job since that painfully uncomfortable day Dad got caught up in our world. The explosion. His funny turn. His girlfriend, Amber, showing up at the mansion. I'll never forget Rose's face when we walked into the TV room and found her on my father's arm. Or my dad's face when he finally comprehended not only my unwavering decision to be with James, but also the fact that his girlfriend was a gold-digging whore who used to *service* Danny and his men. I flinch on my friend's behalf. And, oddly, my father's.

I answer as James collects my shoes. "Dad," I say on an exhale I'm sure he will detect.

"Beau, it's been weeks."

Weeks. There was a time when months would pass without seeing or hearing from my father. James crouches before me and puts one of my sandals at my feet, and I hold his shoulder as he brushes the sand off before letting me slip my foot in. "How are you?" I ask. I took no pleasure in how embarrassed he was. How foolish he had been. I love my father, but he's hardly God's gift. A little overweight, a lot arrogant, but he's loaded and that appeals to women of a certain variety. He was always going to be a target. A part of me wonders if he regrets betraying Mom. If he wished he'd never been so blinkered and left her for a younger model. I hope he does. I fear my hope is in vain.

"Better than I was," he says. "I'm dating."

Well, that answers my question. "You're dating," I parrot, lifting my other foot for James as he looks up at me on a disbelieving shake of his head. "How lovely." How old is this one? James fastens the small buckle on my sandal and rises, taking the wine off the wall.

"And I'm running for mayor."

"What?" I blurt. "Mayor?" James eyes widen, his mouth falling open.

"I admit, Beau, the competition is pretty stiff. That Monroe Metcalfe is quite popular."

And, oddly, so is my father. But the public don't know him like I know him. They see a businessman, one that gives to charity and serves his community. What the hell do I say to this news? "Good luck," I murmur, hoping and praying he doesn't think he'll be using me as tool in his campaign. I highly doubt it, now he's met James. In fact, he'll be doing everything he can to avoid the public finding out who I'm dating.

"Thank you, darling. Let's do dinner. At my place. I'll cook spaghetti like I did when you were a little girl."

I notice he's not suggesting we go out in public. "Sounds lovely. I'll call you." I hang up.

"He's running for mayor?" James says, stunned.

"Yep. Mayor Hayley. Mayor Hayley with a daughter who's dating an assassin."

"He doesn't know I'm an assassin. And we're more than da—" He frowns. "Can you smell curry?" he asks, just as the waft hits me. Coriander and spices, it's rife.

"And tension," I say quietly, as he leads us up the path. We round the villa and find everyone sitting at the table on the patio by the pool. Everyone except Rose. I spot Goldie first, and as James predicted, her newfound girlie wardrobe is nowhere in sight, the suit back, the cut expression accompanying it. She's the woman I first met. Stoic. Imposing. Business-like.

I find Danny at the head of the table, looking like he's been slapped in the face. It's a definite possibility. "Not drinking?" I ask, pointing at the bottle of water in his hand where a tumbler of amber liquid always sits.

"Not tonight." He rises and offers his cheek.

"What's going on with you two?" I ask quietly, kissing him, but I get no answer, just a shake of his head, telling me to leave it, before he slaps hands with James and drops back into his chair. I look at Esther who shrugs. To Brad who feigns shivering. I round the table and greet everyone with a kiss, finishing with Zinnea. "Where's Rose?"

"In the kitchen," she whispers, as if it's a secret, filling up her glass, obviously deciding only wine will get her through this evening. "You could cut the atmosphere with a damn knife."

I sigh and place my purse on the table where James just took his seat. "Back in a minute."

"Don't offer to help," Esther calls as I leave them to go to Rose and find out what the hell is going on. "She'll bite your head off too."

I enter the kitchen as Rose drops a spatula and sauce splashes up her legs. "Fuck it," she hisses.

"All right?"

She glances up and smiles so bright, I'm surprised the island doesn't short-circuit. "Nearly ready," she sings, dipping to pick up the spoon and tossing it in the sink.

I watch her, wary, as she stirs the bubbling pot of curry, blowing her hair out of her face a few times. "Esther told me not to offer my help," I say, going to the island and popping a spoon in the mango chutney.

She stops stirring and looks up at me. "I've got it."

I nod and unwrap the pappadams. "Do these need frying?"

"Shit, yes, they do." She drops the spoon in the pot and moves on to a pan, where oil is sizzling. She takes the handle. "Fuck!" Drops it and starts shaking her hand.

"For God's sake, Rose," I yell, going to her and flipping on the faucet, shoving her hand underneath. I wince at the glowing red welt across her palm and look at her, seeing tears streaming down her cheeks. Tears from the pain, no doubt, but also tears for something else. "What—"

"Rose?" Danny blurts, falling into the kitchen in a rush and taking in the scene. "Rose, baby, what happened?" He comes to us, taking her arm at the wrist and inspecting the damage. I move back, letting him take over, but Rose's tears dry up in a second, a steely expression falling, and she withdraws from his hold. "I'm fine," she says, sniffing, refusing to look at him. "Beau's got it."

Danny, understandably hurt, looks at me standing awkwardly to the side. There's not one sane man or woman on this planet who would stand in the way of Danny when it comes to his wife, and yet here I am, caught in the middle. "I've got it," I confirm, fearful of the repercussions if I leave them alone together.

He swallows, moving back, stuffing his hands in his pockets. "Rose, I—"

"I'm fine," she snaps, turning away from him. "Just go."

He does, and it rings even more alarm bells. Since when does Danny Black have his tail between his legs? The moment he disappears, I turn to Rose. "We're not leaving this kitchen until you tell me what the hell has happened," I say, shoving her hand back under the faucet.

Her eyes drop, but I still see them welling. "I said no," she whispers. "I said no, and he didn't stop."

"What?" I ask, shocked. She meets my eyes, and the tears begin to trail her cheeks again. "Last night?" I ask. When he was drunk?

"This morning."

Oh fuck. Although Danny was so plastered last night, there's a distinct possibility that he was still drunk this morning. It's not an excuse. I am *not* making excuses. I'm just trying to make sense of this madness. I flip off the faucet. "Where's your first aid box?"

"The last cupboard, top shelf." She points, and I collect it, going to the door and trying to get Zinnea's attention. Esther's standing behind Danny's chair, her hands on his shoulders, her mouth close to his ear, obviously trying to pacify him. Zinnea spots me and sets her wine down, rising and tottering across the patio in her heels.

"Everything all right?" she asks, looking at Rose by the sink weeping.

"We just need some help." I point to the bubbling pot of curry. "Would you mind taking that out? I'll bring the rest in a moment."

She doesn't ask questions, which is exactly why I summoned Zinnea and not Esther. "Of course, my darling." She gets straight to it, collecting a couple of kitchen towels and taking the pot off the stove. "Spoon?"

"In the pot," I say, making her frown down into the curry.

"I'll fish it out." She leaves, and I return to Rose, opening the box and rummaging through for what I need to fix her up.

"What happened?" I ask, dabbing at her hand to dry it.

"I'm trying to think reasonably," she says on a sigh. "He was so completely out of control, and I just felt incapable of sustaining it today."

"So you asked him to stop?" I squeeze some cream onto her palm and rub it in.

"Yes."

"And he didn't?"

"No." Rose looks up at me, and I hate the anguish I see in her dark blue eyes. This will be killing her. Danny's the only man in this world who can hurt her. And right now, she's in agony. I'm not going to stand here and tell my friend I'm sure he didn't mean to do what he did, even though I know Danny's history as well as I know Rose's. I would never play down my friend's distress, not after everything she's been through. Danny's foul mood, Rose's distance, it all makes sense now.

"You need to talk to him."

"And say what?" she asks, exasperated. "Why did you, my husband, take me against my will?"

I notice she refuses to use *that* word. "He looks like a broken man, Rose." I have to point that out, at least. My loyalty lies with Rose, of course, but I feel like I would be doing myself *and* Rose an injustice if I don't raise the obvious, because perhaps during her trauma she's forgotten who she's married to. The Danny Black I know would kill anyone who laid a hand on his wife *with* her permission. Without? It would be slow, messy, and painful. I look back to the garden. I know how he'll be feeling right now. I need to tell James to watch him. "Do you want me to talk to him?" I ask, claiming the bandage and starting to wrap her up.

"No." She snivels and wipes at her nose roughly. "Please don't tell him I've told you."

I smile mildly, fastening the end of her bandage and going to the stove. "I won't." She doesn't want me to think bad of him. She doesn't want Danny to feel any worse than he already does, if that's possible. I don't think it is.

I take one of the pappadams and drop it into the pan, making the oil sizzle once again, the circle expanding rapidly. "Do you want some wine?" she asks.

"No, thanks." I grab some grippers and lift it out, dropping it onto a paper towel to soak up the oil before slipping another into the pan. "You need to wash your face before we go back outside." Who the fuck am I kidding? Nothing goes unnoticed in this group.

Rose goes into her purse on the island and pulls out a little mirror, inspecting herself in it. She studies herself for a while, whilst I watch in between frying. Then she sighs and drops the mirror, looking at me. "It never ends, does it?"

No, it doesn't. As long as we're in this world, extreme stress and helplessness will always feature. "We both knew deep down that eliminating The Bear wouldn't mean they're out." I spoon another pappadam onto the paper towel. "There will always be men out there wanting to be kingpin, and our men have massive bounties on their heads." I'm telling her what she already knows but finds hard to accept. I do too, some days more than others. But when Rose waivers, I have to pick her up. She does the same for me. So long as one of us is strong on any given day, we'll always be okay. "I just spoke to my dad," I say, willing to go there to take Rose's mind off her current anguish. "He's running for mayor." I peek up from the frying pan. She looks like a fish. "Exactly. And he's dating someone."

"Jesus, is she out of college?"

"I didn't ask. I honestly don't want to know."

"Mayor?" Her cheeks blow out. "Well, he has the ego, I suppose."

I hum to myself. "Where's Daniel?" I ask. I'm done with daddy talk. I'm struggling to get my head around how I can feel sorry for someone but at the same time resent them.

"He made a friend," Rose says, loading the chutneys onto a tray. "Barney Benson."

"Cute name."

"His dad's a private banker. Lennox Benson. He's taken the boys out on his private yacht this afternoon."

"With the twins?" I ask over a laugh.

"With the twins," Rose confirms, as if I needed it. Daniel can't even go for a swim in the private pool without Tank and/or Fury following him on an inflatable. "He's single."

I frown at the frying pan. "Who is?"

"The banker," she says quietly. "Lennox Benson."

I stop poking at the pappadam, looking at my friend with a curious eye as she feigns concentrating on stirring the lime pickle. "And you're pregnant," I say quietly. "And married to one of the deadliest men alive."

She peeks up at me on a straight face. "I know."

This is not good. I wouldn't say many relationships are healthy, but I bet there aren't many as toxic as Danny and Rose's. Or, oddly, as passionate and full of love. "I know you want to hurt him right now, Rose," I say quietly, worried, because if Rose breaks out the big guns—namely her flirting—to kick Danny in the balls, Daniel's new friend is going to be an orphan very soon.

"I'm just saying," she muses, lifting the tray, "he's single." And with that, she pivots and leaves. "Nice ring, by the way."

"I still said no," I call, rushing to finish the pappadams, wanting to get back outside before Danny kills Rose or vice versa.

I meet James at the threshold, and he takes the tray from me. "What's she done to her hand?"

"Small accident with the frying pan."

"Right. What's going on?" he asks, circling his spare arm around me and walking me back to the table.

"Lover's quarrel. Something and nothing." I take no pleasure from lying to James, none at all. In fact, I feel guilty, but Danny will be mortified enough, without any of the men knowing what's happened. Not even the not so small matter of James deceiving me about killing my uncle's husband eases my conscience.

"Sure," he says over a laugh. "They look more in love than ever."

"It's pregnancy hormones."

"Can't wait," he whispers, squeezing me before setting the plate on the table and pulling out a chair for me. Was that sarcasm? I honestly don't know. I give him a curious look that he completely ignores. He's expressed his reservations, but he's also not pushed for any birth control. He's also not pulled out of me before he's come. It may not matter, because I might not even be able to carry anymore. *Broken.* I wince that thought away, as well as the fact that I'm due on my period tomorrow, and I look down at the ring that's on the wrong finger. Or is it the right finger?

What about the marriage part? Are we skipping that bit?

"Can't wait for what?" Brad asks, and I shake my head. "Wine?" he goes on, filling up my glass and pushing it toward me, his eyebrows high. "Or am I quitting mafia life?"

I feel James's curious eyes on me, as Brad looks between us. *Broken.* "Not just yet," I say, taking the glass and having a long swig, feeling James's stare rooted to my profile.

I swallow down the liquid and . . . it burns. It burns so much. *Tomorrow.*

"Oh good. One psycho pregnant woman in the family at a time, please." Brad looks at Rose. She's distracting herself from having to face her husband by serving up dinner for everyone.

"It's goat," she says, finishing and lowering to her chair at the opposite end of the table to Danny. "Enjoy."

"What happened to your hand?" he growls, prompting everyone to look at the bandage.

"I wasn't concentrating in the kitchen." Rose reaches for the wine before her, and I still, but Esther swoops in, predicting her daughter-in-law's reckless intention and removes the temptation before Danny, who's twitching at the other end of the table, finally explodes.

"Excuse me?" James says, his hand landing on my knee and squeezing. "Did you change your mind about something pretty fucking monumental and not bother telling me?"

I rest back, the wine in my hand. "You're giving me mixed signals, James." See Doc. Take time to build my strength. But . . . no wine. No protection.

The wine is swiftly removed from my hand and replaced with water. "Let's not turn my mood as dark as Danny's."

I'm so fucking confused. "Are you telling me we're trying?"

"Yes."

Tomorrow. "Don't I get a say?" I ask for the sake of it, surprised by his demeanor.

James turns his eyes onto me, his jaw grinding. "If you were my wife, I may consider giving you a choice."

I balk at him. "You sound like a barbarian."

He growls, losing his straight face and hooking an arm around my neck, hauling me into him, his mouth going to my ear and nibbling the lobe. "I'm going to get a yes out of you eventually, Beau, so let's just cut to the bit when you realize it's the best idea and we crack on with things."

My smile is unstoppable, and it feels so utterly wrong when Rose is across the table in turmoil, although feigning being fine. Smiling. Laughing. It's a bit of an insult, really, to *everyone* here. The temperature is still sub-zero, the atmosphere frosty, as people talk among themselves, pretending they aren't as uncomfortable as each other. Except Danny. He's not pretending to anyone. Seems incapable, actually.

"We'll see," I muse, detaching myself from James and joining everyone, taking a fork. But we're all halted from diving in when Daniel comes racing around the corner on an electric scooter, a friend, Barney, I assume, following.

"Hey," he calls, jumping off like a pro. "Barney's dad has invited me out for dinner with them. Can I go?"

"No," Danny grunts. "Your mum's made curry." He motions around the table. "We have guests."

Daniel rolls his eyes. "I see everyone here every day."

"Of course you can go," Rose counters, standing from the table, completely ignoring, Danny. "Where's Tank and Fury?"

They both round the villa at the same time, as if beckoned, followed by someone else. "Oh no," I murmur.

"What?" James asks, looking at me, not noticing the man behind the two colossal Vikings.

"Barney's dad," I whisper.

"What about him?" James looks thoroughly confused. He wouldn't be if he'd heard the intentions in Rose's tone earlier. Barney's dad passes through the two giants, looking a little bemused by them, and my worries multiply. Because he's hot. Really fucking hot. *Fuck*. This is bad. So bad.

"What the fuck's going on, Beau?" James asks, his eyes passing between me and Lennox Benson.

"Nothing. Nothing's going on." I pray. I pray so hard that Rose sees sense. I've seen her in one of these destructive moods before, and it isn't pretty for the other man involved. Our only saving grace here is Daniel. Danny would never kick off in front of Daniel. And Rose knows it. Which, I conclude quickly, isn't a good thing at all.

"Hi," Barney's dad says, looking around the table, even more bemused by the eclectic mix of people that is our family. "Lennox Benson." The poor man doesn't know who to hold his hand out to, his limb hovering awkwardly in midair.

I close my eyes and inhale when Rose rounds the table, going to him. "I'm Rose Cassidy, Daniel's mom." Oh Jesus, she's holding no prisoners. I flick a nervous look to Danny. His nostrils are flaring as he rises from his chair. Rose *Cassidy*. She places her dainty hand in Lennox's and smiles brightly, and, of course, Lennox Benson is taken aback. Most men are when they meet Rose. Although, wisely and respectfully, trying not to show it.

"Pleasure." He shakes Rose's hand briefly and steps back, out of the range of her magnetic allure. "My apologies, I didn't realize you were eating."

Danny moves in, tall and intimidating. I'm not going to be able to hold my breath for much longer, and as I glance around the table, I can see everyone is with me, the women watchful, the men bracing themselves to pull him back, including James who's tense under my hold of his leg.

"Danny Black." Danny extends a hand, his face deadly straight, his scar looking particularly deep. And, again, Lennox Benson is taken aback . . . as most men are when they meet The Brit. "Daniel's father."

"Good to meet you." He accepts and shakes, and I watch Lennox's face for any sign of discomfort.

Surprisingly, there's none, but then Danny says, "Not a *pleasure*?" and it appears. Uneasiness.

Lennox laughs, nervous, glancing around the table as he takes back his hand. "I'll leave you to eat in peace."

"Join us," Rose sings, motioning to us all at the table. All of us who are silent. Nervous. *Don't do it, Mr. Benson. Run for your life now.*

"Yes, join us." Danny cracks a smile, and Lennox seems to loosen up.

Because Lennox does not know Danny Black, therefore he does not know that the smile currently being splashed around is fake. Deadly.

"No, no." His hands come up as he backs away. "We have reservations at the new restaurant in town. Daniel didn't mention you had . . ." He glances around the table again, and James starts snorting in his chair next to me, laughing. I follow his eyes to Brad, Ringo, and Otto opposite who all have cheesy grins plastered on their faces. For God's sake. If they're trying to appear friendly, it isn't working. "Friends for dinner," Lennox finishes.

"Hey, Mister, can I go?" Daniel asks, kicking the stand of his scooter down and going to Danny, giving him praying hands. "Please?" He knows. He just knows that Danny wears the pants around here, even if Rose is trying them on at the moment. She's wasting her time. The pants definitely don't fit her, and it isn't because she's pregnant.

"Sure you can, kid." Danny dips into his pocket and pulls out a pile of dollar bills.

"Ah, no need," Lennox says, hands up again.

"You don't mind if my men join you?" Danny says, motioning to Tank and Fury as he passes them some cash.

Lennox laughs a little, but he's frowning. "Not at all. What time do you want him"—he eyes the Vikings—"*them* home?"

Rose moves in front of Danny, smiling. "I can pick him up if it helps?"

"She wants to die," James mutters, shaking his head.

I agree. Tank and/or Fury will bring Daniel home. They'll take him now too. That kid goes nowhere without them. Christ knows what Barney's dad is thinking.

Danny smiles darkly at the back of Rose's head. "Yes, we'll collect him." His hand rests on her nape and massages as the Vikings look on, plain confused. "One of the weird pregnancy things Rose has going on at the moment is a craving for pickles around ten at night, so we'll be out picking some up anyway."

"Oh, congratulations," Lennox says, looking at Rose's stomach. "You'd never know."

"But now you do." Danny smiles. "I'll walk you out."

"Sure." Lennox holds up his hand to the table. "Nice meeting you all," he says, getting a collection of murmurs in return.

"I'll come," Rose says.

"No, baby, your ankles are all puffy." Danny turns her by the shoulders back toward the table. "Sit. I insist." His lips move to her ear and kisses it sweetly, and he whispers something before he strolls off to see Lennox Benson out.

"A death threat?" James asks quietly.

"Yep." I take my wine to my mouth, but it doesn't make it there, soon being replaced with water again.

"One domestic is enough for tonight, don't you think?" he says gruffly.

I start stirring my rice into my curry as Rose, looking contemplative, lowers to a chair, but my fork stops halfway to my mouth when I catch Brad's face, and it lowers when he starts coughing, dropping his fork.

"Fuck me," he wheezes, thumping his chest, his eyes darting across the table. "Pass me the fucking water."

Esther is up in a beat, rushing to fill his glass, but Brad doesn't hang around, grabbing the jug from her and virtually tipping it down his throat. His face turns an alarming shade of red, his eyes wide and watery, his brow wet. I look down at the curry on my fork.

"You fucking pussy," Ringo grunts, shoveling a huge forkful into his mouth, and two seconds later, he joins Brad, coughing and spluttering all over the table, wrestling him for the water jug.

I lower my fork to the plate, looking around as everyone starts poking at their untouched curry, all of them probably worrying about upsetting Rose even more. Not Danny, though. He returns to the table, takes a seat, and pushes his plate away. I look at my friend. She's happily working her way through the goat dish, unperturbed and unaffected by the level of heat.

"What the fuck did you put in that thing?" Brad gasps, reclaiming the water from Ringo as Esther disappears into the kitchen to get more.

Rose shrugs, forking at a piece of meat drenched in sauce and chewing through it. "Everything the recipe said to put in it." She taps her phone on the table and brings up a screen, pointing to the list. "I added a couple more Habaneros. One seemed a bit stingy."

"And the seeds?" Ringo asks, flapping a hand in front of his face. "What about the seeds?"

Rose looks down at her fork. "It said the *whole* chili."

"So you put three in?" Brad pushes his plate away, dabbing at his top lip with his napkin. "Fucking hell, I think my tongue's gonna fall off."

"Well," Rose muses, almost happily. "At least no one will ever be able to cut it out."

I peek at Danny, cautious, seeing him shifting in his chair, looking wired. Charged. Ready to snap. And our saving grace, Daniel, has just left the building.

Everyone else? They want to laugh. They want to laugh so hard, but they obviously value their lives more than the need to restrain their untimely amusement.

"I just have to know." Rose pops another forkful of curry into her mouth and chews, absolutely immune to the fact that it's loaded with enough chilies to literally blow someone's head off. Brad and Ringo are proof, their faces glowing and wet. She laughs, and I brace myself for the explosion of Danny, my hand falling to James's leg and squeezing, a silent message to get ready to hold him back. Rose drops her fork and dabs her lips. "What made you think Perry Adams was The Bear?" Her eyes are focused solely on Danny at the other end of the table. No one else. Just him.

"Here we go," Otto sighs, peeking out the corner of his eye to Esther, who's looking nervously at her son.

"I assume you're talking to me?" Danny asks flatly.

"Who else? I think you knew him best out of everyone here, right?" She looks around the table, as if she might get an agreement from someone. "Apart from me, of course."

Fucking hell, Rose. I pinch the bridge of my nose, contemplating getting up and dragging her away.

"It was a tad breezy on the water today," Zinnea practically screeches. "I took the water ferry to Martinique and there was a pod of dolphins that followed me the entire way. I lost my sunhat too."

She laughs. "The breeze took it right off my head! Honestly, I'm surprised it didn't take my wig and lashes too."

I bite my lip and reach for Zinnea's hand, and Goldie smiles across the table at her. My aunt rolls her eyes and sinks some wine.

"Well," Danny says, turning his glass of water slowly, his eyes never leaving Rose as she happily munches through the deadly curry, "we had sufficient reason—"

"I mean"—she laughs—"the prick hardly had the ability to make me come, let alone head up a deadly crime syndicate."

Danny's fists meet the table with such force, everyone's curries leave their plates and splashes the table.

That's it. *Goodbye, my dear friend. I will treasure our friendship forever.*

He stands abruptly, walks the length of the table, pulls Rose's chair out, and takes her elbow. "Excuse us for a moment," he grates, leading her into the villa.

And the moment the door slams behind them, Brad exhales. "Jesus Christ, what the fuck's gotten into those two?" He grabs his Scotch and knocks it back.

"I don't know," Esther breathes, exasperated. "But she sure knows how to rub him up the wrong way. It's not healthy, not for either of them."

"He was pretty fucking smashed," Otto pipes up. "Anyone know what happened? When we left them last night, he was still pissed but back in love with her."

"He's never *out* of love with her," Goldie says. "Just out of patience most of the time."

"I should have gone to work," Zinnea says.

And me? I sit quietly while everyone tries to figure out what the fucking hell is going on, feeling James's accusing stare on me. I peek out the corner of my eye.

"You know," he whispers, just as a deafening bang sounds from inside. "You know what's wrong with them."

"There goes another crystal bowl." Esther slips down her chair, shrinking, and I stand from mine.

But I'm immediately pulled back down by James. "No, Beau," he cautions with so much warning, I'd be a fool to ignore him. So I lower, and the only reason I do is because I know beyond anything I've ever known that Danny would never physically harm his wife. Rose, however, will fight like a cat, pregnant or not. "You are not leaving this table," he warns, his face serious, "until you tell me what the fuck is wrong with those two."

5

DANNY

Too far. Way too fucking far. I keep reminding myself that she's pregnant. I keep reminding myself that I love her. That she's my wife. That I would slaughter anyone who ever laid a finger on her. That includes me, which is why I've spent the best part of the day wanting to slowly kill myself.

I place her roughly on a stool, rest my palms on her knees, get my threatening face up close to hers, and I snarl. "What have I got to do, Rose?" I ask. I have to get us both out of these moods before someone ends up dead. She's hurt, I get it. She wants to punish me like she couldn't punish the others because she knows she can. And I will take it all.

Her eyes are hard, her expression cut as she stares me down, her cheeks pulsing. "I said no," she grates.

I close my eyes, hiding my flinch. "I didn't hear you, Rose." I was crazed, out of my fucking mind. Everything was distorted, and I heard only my mind screaming at me, demanding I kill.

Kill, kill, kill.

How the fuck can I make this right? "I'm sorry," I whisper. "I'm so fucking sorry for not hearing you when you told me to stop. I'm so fucking sorry for making you feel like an object. For failing to end the man who's threatening our happiness." I take her cheek, stroking it softly. "I'm so fucking sorry for being one of them."

She shies away from my touch, and it's the worst kind of pain she could inflict on me. Rejection.

She can't forgive me. And doesn't that make me want to kill harder. Slower.

Lost, I gaze around the kitchen, wondering, what now?

Without her, what? Where am I?

Who am I?

I'm just a killer without a purpose. A man with nothing to fight for.

My eyes land on a small knife, the blade short for precision. "I love you, Rose," I say quietly, taking a step back. "With every dark, dirty, corrupt, illegal, immoral piece of me, I fucking love you." I take the knife, and her eyes widen.

"Danny?"

I pull my T-shirt up over my head and toss it aside. "For not hearing you." I take the blade to my chest and slash it quickly through my flesh on a hiss.

"No!" She lunges for me, but my arm at full length holds her back.

Another slash.

"Stop it!" she yells, her eyes exploding with tears. "Danny!"

"My punishment, Rose."

Another cut.

I bite down on my back teeth, the pain very fucking real. But nothing like how I know it would feel if she walks out on me. I will never lose my mind when I'm taking her again. I will never put either of us in that position. I swear it. Yes, our sex life has always been lewd and frenzied, but never have I lost my senses. Never have I not heard her.

Another cut.

"Danny, please, I beg you," she sobs.

Another cut, this time crossing over the others, my chest

becoming a fucking chessboard, the blood now hitting the kitchen floor in fat, messy drops.

"No," she mumbles, moving back, her eyes darting across my mutilated flesh, but her traumatized face doesn't stop me, my self-hatred fueling me, making me cut more, take more pain, swallow down the grief.

I hold my breath through the fog of agony, seeing Rose move. She grabs something, holds it up, and I blink, trying to clear my vision.

A knife.

And before I can grasp her intentions, she's lifted an arm and dragged it through her flesh.

No.

I drop my blade to the floor, snapped from my own crazy to deal with my wife's. "No!" I lunge forward, knocking the knife from her grasp, and I grab her, hauling her toward me. She's quickly in my chest, hugging me, my blood-drenched skin seeping into the material of her dress.

"I forgive you," she sobs, crying into my neck, feeling at my bare back frantically. "Please, just stop hurting yourself."

I close my eyes and sink into her embrace, my head pounding so hard, my chest throbbing. "I'm sorry," I whisper, constricting my hold. "I'm so sorry." I feel her nod into me, clinging tighter, and I open my eyes when I hear movement by the door. Beau's taking in the scene, the mess of blood, my face, James standing behind her looking a bit *what the fuck?* I'm glad they're here.

"Hospital?" Beau asks, cool and calm, like she knew the outcome of this particular shitstorm.

I shake my head. "First aid box is in the cupboard."

She moves quickly while James wanders in slowly, in no rush at all. His eyes are questioning. He knows. He knows what I did, and I fucking hate the concern I see. I look away, ashamed, knowing he'll be wondering if it's time for me to back away from the frontline before I kill myself, whether that be through drinking too much or cutting myself to shreds. Before I do anything *else* stupid. Either or, my frame of mind is clear.

Fucking crazy.

"Rose, baby," I say quietly, easing her from my chest, sucking back air as her dress peels away from my open wounds. "We need to clean you up." Her hair is sticking to her wet cheeks, her mascara staining her face. I take her arm and inspect the damage, wincing at the deep wound. "You stupid, stupid woman," I breathe as she sniffles and sniffs, motionless before me. "Get Doc."

"He'll be asleep, Danny," James says, looking as disturbed as I feel. "We can deal with this." His look as he stares at my chest tells me he's questioning his own words.

I don't give a shit about me. Doc was only brought here to keep tabs on Rose and do regular scans. No one anticipated he would be wiping up more blood.

"Here," Beau says, setting a bowl of warm water on the counter and tipping some antiseptic solution in with some wipes.

I sit Rose down, sterilize my hands with a few of the wipes, and then start cleaning her up. "Will you go find her a clean dress, please?"

"Danny," Beau says, concerned. "Your ches—"

"Can wait." I hold Rose's arm and dab at the flesh, cleaning away the blood until I'm staring at the open wound. It's not quite deep enough for stitches but too deep for just a plaster. God damn her. "There's some medical glue in there," I say, pushing the two sides together, gauging the work that needs to be done.

James plucks the Dermabond from the first aid box and hands it to me before resting his hand on Rose's shoulder and massaging. "Need any painkillers?"

She shakes her head as I get to work, sealing the cut and wrapping her up, pushing back my anger. After all, I started it. I can't possibly be any madder with her. And yet I am.

Beau appears with a dress and a cardigan. "Thank you," Rose says, and James turns his back as she pulls her blood-drenched dress over her head. Her swollen belly is like a brick to my face, and my eyes drift to her newly bandaged arm. *My fault.*

"Danny?" she says softly, a clear attempt to distract me as she slips the clean dress on with Beau's help.

I take the cardigan from the counter and hold it open for her. "I'm fine," I say, feeling the blood trickling down my torso as she slips her arms into the sleeves. "Will you give us a minute?" I ask, and James and Beau both leave us without a word, although I know they'll only be on the other side of the door. Probably discussing what the fuck to do with me.

I sit Rose down and drop to my knees before her, taking my finger to her chin and lifting so she looks away from my bloody chest to my face. I say nothing, only stare into her eyes as she stares back at me, her lip still quivering. I'm so fucking angry with myself. Not only have I crushed her trust in me and how I handle her body, but I've also made her cut herself again. I made her feel there was no other way. We were past those black, dangerous days when we hurt each other. When we pushed each other's boundaries. But I can't take it back. "Never again."

"You—"

I place my finger over her lips and shake my head. "Never." I'm not demanding anything from her. Not compliance or surrender. Not a promise to never harm herself. "I'm telling you I will never let you down again."

She inhales, her lip trembling more, her eyes filling with new tears. "You didn't let me down."

"I let you down, Rose. I let *us* down. By getting drunk, by losing control, by getting angry and cutting myself. I let us down." I lean in and take her face in my palms. "Never again." I kiss her softly and stand as I do, and she rises with me, letting me apologize some more with my mouth.

"Let me clean you up," she says, but I shake my head, refusing her, not wanting to burden her with the further pain of seeing the mess I've made of myself.

"No." I pull away and wipe her eyes, my nose wrinkling as I lick my lips.

"What?" she asks.

"You taste spicy." I can feel the heat of the chilies. Jesus, Brad wasn't being dramatic at all.

"It could do with a little more of a kick."

"More?" I laugh a little and bend, placing my lips on her tummy as she weaves her fingers through my hair. "Go," I order, rising and turning her around. "Tell James I need him."

"Brad won't like it."

"Brad doesn't know what's gone on between us."

"And James does?" she asks.

"Did you tell Beau?"

"Yes."

Of course she did. And I saw James's face. His worry for me. "Then he knows." I walk her to the door and look outside to see where Brad is and what he's doing because Rose is right. He won't like being in the dark. "He's too busy dying from eating your curry to worry about what James and I are doing." I see him still sucking back water.

A tap on her arse sends Rose on her way with Beau, and I turn to James, feeling his eyes on me. "Don't say a word."

"Wasn't going to." He refills the bowl with fresh water and antiseptic. And there's why James and I get on so well. I go back to the chair and sit down, my back ramrod straight, making my chest as taut as possible, pushing the medical box toward him. "What the fuck are we going to do?"

"Oh, so you're ready to discuss tactics now?" He grabs a chair and swings it around to face me, sitting down and swishing a wipe through the solution.

"Yes," I grate. I'm perfectly aware I've either been too pissed or had my head up my arse the past twenty-four hours.

"We should get the others in first."

"Fine," I mumble, hissing as he wipes me up with a heavy hand. "Anyone ever tell you that your bedside manner is shit?" I ask, making him smile as he continues, ignoring the fact that I'm pushing myself into the back of the chair, trying in vain to shy away from the biting sting of the alcohol on my open wounds.

"You didn't mess around, did you?"

I look down and immediately look away. "I'm a dick, I know."

He hums, concentrating, but doesn't agree. "What did you make of Lennox Benson?"

"Apart from the fact he obviously fancied my pregnant w— Ouch, you fucker!"

"Pussy," he mutters. "Yes, apart from that."

"Take it easy," I grumble, looking down at his working hand. "What's your point?"

"He's a good-looking bloke." James dumps the red-stained cloth in the bowl and rummages through the box.

My shoulders drop. "It wouldn't have mattered if Lennox Benson looked like the back end of a bus. She did what she did because she's a hateful bitch."

"I assume you're talking about your pregnant wife."

"Could I be talking about yours?"

"She's not my wife and she's not pregnant."

I smirk, and he eyes me, knowing I'm about to hit him with some sarcastic wisecrack. So the fucker jabs be in my chest. "Fuck!"

"You were saying?"

"I was saying," I hiss, looking down at my wounds. "You're a cunt."

"Love you too. Are we sticking these cuts together or are you happy with scars wider than they need to be?"

"Whatever. They'll still be quite pathetic compared to yours." Another jab, and I cough over a laugh.

"Seriously," James says. "We need to talk business."

"Yeah, I know." I relent, defeated. "So hurry the fuck up and glue me back together." I glare at him. "Gently, okay?"

"Okay, sweetheart." I continue to hiss in between holding my breath as he sorts me out. "I need to ask you something," he says, not looking at me.

"Sounds ominous."

"I spoke to Chaka earlier about the next shipment."

"And?"

"Did you tell him Rose is pregnant?" He looks up at me, just as I recoil, which gives him his answer. Not that he really needed to ask. "So how does he know?"

"Good fucking question," I muse, falling into thought. *Trust no one.* I've made a few exceptions recently, and one of those exceptions is currently sticking me back together. One of those exceptions is now a solid friend and wingman. I trust James with my life, and not many men have that privilege.

"All fixed," he says, standing and taking the bowl to the sink. "Get a T-shirt on and I'll clear up the mess before I get the men."

I rise from the chair, the unfolding of my body pulling at the skin on my chest. I grit my teeth as I swipe up my T-shirt and grit harder as I pull it on over the bandages he's done a neat job of fixing over the glued wounds. "Meet you in the study," I say, wandering away, wondering why the fuck everything hurts so badly at the moment.

Because... Rose.

And how the fuck does Chaka, my arms supplier who's based in a small settlement in the middle of nowhere in Africa, know my wife is pregnant?

I go to the couch in my office but think better of it. So I consider the chair behind my desk and grimace at the low level of the seat. Finally, I resolve myself to standing, resting my arse on the edge of the cabinet. I scan the various bottles of Scotch. I could do with a drink. *For fuck's sake.*

When I hear the voices of the men, I remove my palm from my chest and try to lengthen my torso. "Motherfucker," I breathe, folding again. I've proper done myself over this time. "Sit down," I say as they all file in, each and every one of them giving me a suspicious or concerned look as they do. I know James won't have murmured a word about the state of my chest and how it came to be mutilated, but I'm not foolish enough to believe that he needs to tell them. They saw Rose. They saw me.

I wait for everyone to get comfortable, noticing for the first time this evening, now the cloud of fury and remorse has thinned, that Goldie is wearing a suit. I frown at her, but she looks straight through me, her eyes telling me to get to business.

"Not joining us?" Brad asks, motioning to the empty chair behind my desk.

I ignore him and push myself off the wood, starting to wander the room as a collection of eyes follow me, waiting for where we might start. Truth be told, I haven't got a fucking clue, and James must sense that because he clears his throat, redirecting all attention to him. "First things first," he says. "Tom Hayley is running for mayor of Miami."

I balk, as does everyone else in the room. "You're kidding, right?" I splutter.

"Nope."

"Fucking hell, I think I preferred Adams." Tom Hayley? Jesus, the man is an egomaniac. And, worse, he hates James and me, so I can only see this going one way. A headache. And we can't kill the fucker because . . . well, he's Beau's father. "Anything else that'll excite me?" I ask.

I can tell by James's face another bombshell is coming. "We need to change the delivery date of the next shipment to the Mexicans."

"Why?" Brad asks, rather than informing James that it isn't an option. Because James wouldn't elect to change anything if it wasn't necessary. You do not alter the terms of a giant arms delivery the day after half the payment is in your possession. It's not good form, and it also provokes mistrust. The last thing we need is the Mexicans on our backs.

"The Coast Guard has an annual training day on the day Chaka was due to deliver. We need to push to the Monday."

"Shit," I breathe. "That's the day the Mexicans want their haul."

"For fuck's sake," Ringo mutters.

"Great," Otto sighs. "So . . . who's talking to the Mexicans?" he asks, pointing to the straws on the drinks cabinet.

"I am *not* drawing straws." Brad laughs. "I'm about as good at drawing straws as Danny is at poker." He gets up and pours two Scotches, bringing one to me. I accept, if only to avoid inciting worry, but I won't be drinking it.

"I'll talk to Luis," I say, looking down at the tumbler in my grasp. "We'll compensate him."

"How?"

"A discount."

"Even more?" Brad looks at my untouched drink, undoubtedly wondering why it remains untouched when I'm clearly in need of it.

"Any other suggestions?"

"So when's the next lot of cash arriving at Hiatus to be cleaned?" he asks, giving me my answer. There is no other way. We need to sweeten the deal, even fucking more than it's already been sweetened. "I need to tell Nolan."

"I'll talk to Luis. We'll rearrange the exchange and I'll let you know." I set the glass down, glad to be rid of the weight. "Now—"

"I have more," James says, pulling my attention his way. What the fuck else could have happened in the last twenty-four hours that I've missed? "An article was released online this morning." He goes to his phone. "By Natalia Potter."

"A journalist, I presume," Ringo grunts as he holds his hand out, taking James's phone. His lip curls more with each word he reads. "The fuck?" His wide eyes find James.

"Yes, the fuck," James says quietly, making everyone in the room go to Ringo and huddle around, trying to find out what's got his shocked attention. I don't join them. One, because I can't bend, and two, because I have a feeling I know what it's about. "She details the story of two men." James looks at me.

"Something tells me they're not law-abiding citizens," I muse, eyeing the Scotch. I know I can drink a good few glasses and not be affected. For fuck's sake, I've been drinking the stuff since I was twelve. But for Rose? Self-control. "What does it say?"

"Exactly?" Ringo asks, and I narrow my eyes. "Okay, and I quote," he goes on, returning his attention to his phone. "'Notorious criminal Danny Black, widely known as The Brit, and the man dubbed The Enigma, who is rumored to have murdered Detective Jaz Hayley, are causing chaos in Miami, and it would appear the police and FBI are powerless to stop them.'" Ringo shifts uncomfortably. "End quote."

"What about me?" Brad grunts, looking as indignant as fuck. "I don't get a mention?"

"Shut up, you girl," Goldie mutters, taking herself back to the other couch, her eyes on James. "You okay?" she asks him.

"Fine." He's thoughtful, his eyes on his feet. Thinking.

"The journalist's source?" I ask.

"Anonymous." James looks at me. "To everyone else."

But to us, this is a plain poke from *him*. A way to smoke us out. Get us back in Miami. The police can't touch either of us, we know that. *He* knows that. This is becoming more about ego than anything else. A game. James can prove he didn't kill Beau's mother, and if the police had anything on me, I'd already be caged. That article is The Bear's way of telling us he's in contact with Potter. "Find out where she is," I say, but Otto is already on his phone. It prompts me to make a call myself.

"Agent Higham," he says in answer, sounding somewhat cautious. I don't know why he declared his name. Perhaps to remind me that he is, in fact, FBI.

"Higham," I say, letting everyone else in the room know who I'm calling. "I'll be back in Miami soon. We should catch up for a coffee."

"An invite to your wedding and now coffee? Anyone would think you're trying to get me in your pocket, Black."

"You wouldn't fit," I retort, and he laughs. "There are a few things we need to discuss."

"Rumor on the street is you've retired."

I smile, looking at the others. All of them have a familiar thirst in their eyes. All except Goldie. She looks plain pissed off because she, more than any of us, wanted to walk away. And now she can't. Or, more to the point, she refuses to. She won't leave James's side. So, yeah, she's pissed. When I thought we'd ended The Bear, I didn't walk away thinking we were done. I walked away knowing we weren't. It's like I said to James one time—if you set the bar, you defend it.

Or you die.

We've set the bar, and I'm damn determined to defend the fucker. The alternative isn't an alternative. The bunker we built at the boatyard wasn't a temporary solution. James can never walk away from The Enigma. I can never walk away from The Brit. With a reputation comes a responsibility—a responsibility to stay alive and keep your loved ones safe. You can't turn your back on this life, and that's a lesson James and I have both learned. We have to continue dealing if we want to stay alive. We *need* to keep control of Miami. The alternative won't just be messy. It'll be the end. That was fact before we found out The Bear's still alive. The Russians are still out there, and that was enough to keep us in the game. Now? Now we finish a job that's annoyingly dragging out. It's simple. But complicated.

So rumors are circulating. Retired? If only it was as simple as hanging up my gun. My knife. Or my letter opener. "Rumors are usually just that," I say, resting my weight on the cabinet again. There are going to be a lot of disappointed people if that's the case, but more fool them for assuming. Nothing should be assumed in this world. "I'm sorry to disappoint."

"I'm not disappointed, Danny."

Oh, we're on first name terms now, are we? Interesting. So is the fact he's *not* disappointed. "That's nice to hear, Harry." I wander over to the chair behind my desk and lower into it gingerly, my curiousness superseding the discomfort. "I was about to offer my condolences."

He laughs lightly. "For what?"

"I expect things are going to kick off in Miami very soon. Hear me when I say, I'm not the man you should be coming after. I'll be in touch." I hang up and look at Brad and James in turn. "Definitely not bent."

"Definitely?" James asks.

"Okay, he's not bent." There's nothing *definite* about our world. "What next?" I ask, my palm resting on my chest.

"Goldie wants to draw us an updated diagram with her ladylike, pretty, neat handwriting," Ringo says, collecting a piece of paper and a pencil and handing it to her. She accepts but growls. And with the appearance of Goldie's suit comes the appearance of Ringo's teasing.

"We don't need a diagram," Brad says, intercepting and removing the tools from Goldie's hand, at the same time giving Ringo a warning look. I'm not the only one treading carefully around our she-warrior. But Ringo is the only one who *isn't*. Hasn't he got the memo?

"Won't everyone stop fucking looking at me like that?" Goldie barks, standing and pulling in her suit jacket, as if to remind everyone that she is, in fact, wearing a suit. Not a dress.

"See," Ringo grunts, looking at us all like we're stupid. "She doesn't like it." He walks over to Goldie, raises a fist, and jabs her in the bicep. And in return, she launches a punch that would take Wladimir Klitschko off his feet, sending Ringo flying across the office like a rag doll. He lands with a thud, holding his massive nose, that's going to be even bigger now. Swollen. Probably a pair of black eyes too. "Fuck me," he moans.

I turn my eyes from Ringo on the floor to Goldie, and I positively hate the glaze in her eyes. "Go," I order, walking over to her, literally taking my life into my own hands by physically turning her away and walking her to the door.

"I'm fine," she argues, rolling her shoulders to remove me. "Get the fuck off me, or I'll—"

"What?" I get up in her face, not aggressively, but a clear sign that I'll take no shit. She wants to be treated like the rest of the men? Fine. I'm here for it. "Control your urges or get the fuck out of this office." I'm a fucking hypocrite, I know. "Clear?"

She nods once, and it's sharp. "Clear."

"Sit the fuck down." I'm not angry. I'm not out of patience. I'm merely giving Goldie what she wants. What she *needs.* Equality. Validation. She resumes position on the couch as Ringo crawls up from the floor, feeling at his nose and checking his hand as he joins her, giving her a curled lip as he lowers to the seat.

Now, where were we? "There aren't many animals left at the zoo," I say, perching on the desk. "We'll assume with the elimination of the Irish, the drugs arm of The Bear's business has ceased."

"For now," James adds.

"For now." There will be men coming up through the ranks, a mad scramble to fill the boots of Vince Roake. "We still don't know where the Polish keep the women they're shipping in." Or, indeed, *how* they're shipping them in.

"Assuming they're not storing them in the vault at the bank Kenny Spittle managed." Otto raises his brows.

"They're women, not fairies, for fuck's sake," Brad mutters. "The drugs and guns are or were being kept at the bank. We have The Shark left batting for the Poles, and The Ox, Sandy, and Volodya winning for the Russians."

Winning.

With the Russian's heading up the guns side of this cozy little setup, they're most certainly winning. We've failed to take out any of the fuckers at the top of *that* tree, and now that we know their puppet master isn't dead? I blow out my cheeks and drag a hand down my face. They must have laughed their way to the bank. Kenny Spittle's bank. I frown, looking at Otto. "There's been no action at the bank?" I ask.

"Nothing. No one going in, no one coming out."

"And Kenny Spittle?"

"He's still in the container, although his scheduled annual leave is almost up. It won't be long before colleagues at the bank start asking questions when he doesn't return to work. Leon's feeding and watering him daily."

"Why?" James asks. "Just kill the fucker."

I smile to myself. "And you tell me *I'm* hasty?"

"The only way Oliver Burrows could have known our old friend Agent Spittle was dead is if his son Kenny told him, since there is no body."

I hum, thoughtful. "And when you left the station after Higham intervened, Burrows didn't follow you, but The Hound did." More fool The Hound, who James quickly blew up. "No activity on his phone?"

"Not a whisper," Otto confirms.

So, no one's apparently active, and there's been no signs of the Russians, not Sandy or that fucker Volodya, who, inconveniently, isn't dead after all. Not dead, but still not showing his face. "I think Luis definitely needs a bit more discount on his order," I muse, looking at James. He nods, hearing me. If the puppet master has demanded quiet on the western front, we'll demand attention, and there's nothing like stiff competition to get me some attention. Or to bring someone out of hiding.

"Do you think the radio silence on the phone is because they know we have Kenny?" Ringo asks.

"Or *think* we *might* have him."

"They'll soon show up at the bank looking for him. Make sure you've got his house covered too. How's the boatyard repairs coming on?"

"Complete," Otto confirms.

"Good." Because we're going to need it. Let's see if we can wake up Miami.

6

ROSE

All eyes were on me as I made my way to the pool and sat on the edge, my naked legs dangling in. No one murmured a word, not for a few minutes, until Brad killed the quiet with another poke at my curry. His attempt to break the atmosphere was appreciated, and I managed a small smile over my shoulder.

A half-hour later, I'm still here, my palm resting over my arm, my remorse thick, as is my headache. I see Beau's reflection in the water and blindly lift my hand. She takes it and joins me, pushing her shoulder into mine. "You're not in this alone," she says quietly, her feet starting to swish through the water. She's not trying to pull my head out of my ass or insinuate that it's not all about me, she's simply reminding me that she's here for me.

I tighten my grip of her hand in answer, and we fall into a comfortable silence for a while. I wonder what she's thinking. I wonder how she appears so stable when the source of her misery has recently declared he's still walking the earth. Still here to taunt us all. But knowing Beau as I do, she hides her grief well. Unlike me. I seem hell-bent on throwing my weight around and making my husband's life even more difficult than it already is. God damn me. God damn the demons that bubble under the surface. Freedom and happiness keep tickling the edges of my life and then retreating, exposing me to the world I thought I'd escaped. God damn *them*.

In our marriage, it has always been me who lashes out. Retaliates. Loses my mind. Just the mere fact that Danny lost all sense of presence and didn't read the signs of my despair when we were having sex speaks volumes for his state of mind. As does the fact he got so drunk. He's not himself. Seems vulnerable, and that isn't my husband. Neither do I want it to be.

"What can I do to help?" Beau breaks the silence.

"Kill the right man next time?" I turn a smile onto her, and she rolls her eyes. "I'm kidding."

"No, you're not."

She's right, I'm not. Beau was like a walking example of serenity in the few short weeks we all thought it was over. I want that for her again. I want that for us all. I look at her, wondering if she's faking that serenity now, because she's still so fucking calm and it's making me feel a bit inferior to be honest. Is she a swan, graceful and together to the world, but paddling like crazy beneath the surface? "How are *you*?" I ask, and she tilts her head, amused. Maybe I should try that meditation she talked about.

"Would it make you feel better if I said I was terrible?"

"Yes."

"Terrible."

I nudge her, and she laughs. Is this us now? The wives of mafia men. Hard-faced, resilient, and scared to death but unable to show it? At least, not to the outside world. My state of mind is obvious to the people I'm closest to. But not to Daniel. Never to Daniel. For that boy, I am the best actress you could find. "Why won't you marry him?" I ask, reaching for the ring on her right hand. It just doesn't make any sense to me. James loves her fiercely, and Beau him.

"I already told you."

There's more to it, there has to be. "Does Lawrence know about Dexter?"

"Jesus, no. He's at peace with the fact Dexter's left him. If he knew James had killed him . . ."

I get it. I look over my shoulder and see the table lacking all men and Goldie. They've been summoned. To plot and scheme and prepare to rain holy hell on Miami.

"It'll be okay," Beau says.

"It has to be." Because who am I if I'm not Danny's Rose? I wince, my hand automatically resting on my tummy, my mind giving me the perfect image of Daniel's face. What the fuck is wrong with me? I'm our children's before I'm anyone else's, including Danny's. He wouldn't have it any other way. But, and it's a painful fact, I'm only who I am now because of Danny, and I'm not sure I can keep that up without him. "Are you going back to Miami with them?" I ask Beau, maybe for the sake of it, because I'm not sure we'll get a choice. Although, admittedly, I'm uncertain which option the men will decide on. Leave us here, away from their watch but also away from the threats. Or take us with them where we're close to their watch but in the thick of the danger.

"I'm going back," Beau says.

"You sound like that decision is yours to make." I laugh, and she tilts her head, eyebrows high, lips pursed.

"Oh, it's mine," she says surely. "You know, Rose, I remember following you into Hiatus one time. Do you remember? When they let us go to the beach that day?"

"Yeah, I remember." I didn't know Beau as well as I do now. I remember watching her standing on the shore looking up at the sun, eyes closed, and wondering if I'd ever seen such a broken woman.

"And I looked at you and thought to myself how together you were. How strong. A force of a woman to be reckoned with."

My smile is ironic. "I'm thinking the same about you now."

"We're both like fucking yo-yos. Strong, weak, determined, defeated. I suppose it's to be expected in a world where our men are who they are and we're dealing with what we're dealing with." Her arm falls around my shoulders, hugging me to her. "But we have each other."

I smile. It's unstoppable. We have each other, and I don't know what I'd do without her. "Love you, Beau."

"You too. And if I'm going back to Miami, so are you."

"Okay," I agree, because amid all this uncertainty, I know one thing beyond doubt. I can't survive this world without my friend available to hug me, comfort me, and pull my head out of my ass when I need it. I just need to convince Danny. Something tells me it'll be a challenge.

Beau starts to stand, encouraging me up. "Come on, we need to check everyone is still alive after eating your curry."

"My curry was amazing. What's wrong with you people?"

"Rose, that thing"—she points at the pot as we walk to the table —"could be classed a lethal weapon."

I lower next to Esther, feeling her eyes lower with me. "Is my son still alive?" she asks, turning her wine glass by the stem.

"Is Otto?" I retort, reminding my mother-in-law that I'm not the only one around here who has pissed off her son. I turn my smile onto her. "Are you ever going to tell me what's going on with you two?"

"No." Esther suddenly isn't interested in me anymore. "Zinnea, are you performing tomorrow night?"

"Yes, darling, I most certainly am. Should I reserve you a table?"

"Why are we talking like we'll be here tomorrow night?" I ask. "Unless you're planning on staying?" I look at Esther, making sure she knows I'm talking to her. There's not a cat in hell's chance she'll remain in St. Lucia if Danny's in Miami. Unless, of course, he demands it.

"I'm not staying," she blurts without thought.

"Oh good, neither am I," I reply.

"You have that choice?"

"I do." I smile brightly. "Do *you*?"

"Oh, I could slap your face sometimes."

My nose wrinkles, and I lean in and kiss her cheek. "Love you too, Mom," I say, and she rolls her eyes as I pull back. I know I exasperate her. I know she really would like to slap my face sometimes. But I also know that she appreciates my apprehension because she feels it too.

"Well," Zinnea coos, pouring more wine, "in case anyone is interested, I will not be returning to Miami."

Beau's face is a picture of shock as she swings her gaze onto her aunt. "What?" I see panic rising in her. I also see her vehemently trying to force it back. "Who will I meditate with?"

"You don't need me, my darling," Zinnea says, her hand finding Beau's on the table. "You have a lovely, gorgeous psychopath to take care of you these days."

A little burst of laughter escapes me and Esther, but Beau's eyes narrow, unimpressed. "James—"

"Not James. I'm talking about Rose," Zinnea quips, and I gape at her while Esther laughs harder and Beau smiles. "Oh don't look so indignant, darling."

Me? "I'll—"

"What? Torture me with more of your cooking?"

Esther's now falling apart, Beau's hardly holding on to her laughter, and I am outraged. "That curry is award worthy," I argue, irritated.

"Oh stop it." Zinnea rolls her eyes in the most overdramatic fashion that only a drag queen would pull off. "Even the devil complained it was too hot."

Tears. There are tears, and even me, insulted as I am, can feel the laughter creeping up on me. And then there are moments like these when I wouldn't change my life for the world. I give in to my desire and fall apart with them, my eyes watering, my tummy aching as Esther squeezes my hand hard. And that's all of us for the next five minutes, laughing uncontrollably, bodies jerking, gasping for air, until I hear movement behind us.

I look over my shoulder, seeing the men filing out of the villa, and all laughing vanishes like it had never been here. I assess each and every one of their faces, and I hate what I see.

Purpose.

Commitment to kill.

I sit up straight and smile weakly when Danny finds me, suddenly terrified that he'll declare his departure back to Miami and leave me here. He couldn't get Daniel and me out of the city fast enough. I can't imagine he'll be so keen to take us back as quickly. And that's another little issue to be dealt with. Our son. It's a miracle we've managed to shield him from the horrors of our lives to this point. Now what? He's not stupid, getting more and more curious each day, and the fact he's got two bearded mountains watching his every move is a huge red flag.

Danny takes his seat at the other end of the table, the farthest away from me, but his eyes regard me carefully, his scar seeming to glisten each time the light catches his face. He takes his water, relaxes back, and continues to watch me. Oddly, I feel vulnerable under the interrogating gaze of my husband. His icy eyes burn. "What?" I mouth, but I get nothing, not even a twitch of his lips. Damn him, what's he thinking?

"I suppose I should go pack, then," Brad declares, not taking his chair but pushing it under the table.

"Me too," Ringo grunts, turning his huge nose up at his plate. "Thanks for dinner."

I look between them, stunned. "Where are you going?" What a ridiculous question. "I mean"—I shake my head—"you're going now?"

"In the morning."

"And what about you?" I ask, looking at Danny. "When are *you* going?"

He sips his water casually, looking all too relaxed. He's the only one, everyone else having tensed, waiting for the fireworks. Then he stands and starts walking to my end of the table and my dread multiplies. He's coming to pacify me. Or hold me down when I go bouncing off around the villa in a temper because he's leaving me here. *Over my dead body.* Which is a definite possibility judging by the veil of steel falling across my husband's face.

I look at Beau, and her expression tells me to be cool.

Be cool, be cool, be cool.

"Time to go," Brad chirps, making a hasty exit, followed by Ringo and Goldie.

"Yes, it's been a lovely evening." Zinnea stands, knocks back the rest of her wine, and scurries off on her heels. But James, Beau, Esther, and Otto remain at the table, defiantly refusing to leave. Probably because they think it's inhumane to let Danny die alone.

I rise from my chair, wanting to have a presence, something my husband seems to find amusing. "Stow away those fists, Rose," he says in warning.

I relax my hands, which I honestly didn't realize were balling. "You're not fucking off to Miami and leaving me here."

He reaches me, rounds me, puts his hands on my shoulders and pushes me back down to the chair. Then he dips and pushes his mouth to my ear. "I know," he says, kissing my lobe. I'm not the only one who relaxes. It seems the whole table does. *Thank God.* He starts massaging into my flesh, and my hands lay over his, my relief making way for contentment. Odd, isn't it, that weeks ago when I was faced with a similar situation, I was pissed off that he was dragging me away from my haven back to a city I hate. But I've learned that my haven, in fact, is Danny.

"That's okay, then," I say, nodding to myself, sounding way surer than I suspect I should. Could there be a catch coming? "And you're not locking me up in the mansion."

"I know."

Oh? "I will happily carry a gun."

"You will."

"And the Vikings?" I ask, flashing a look to Beau. She's smiling mildly, as is James.

"Will be distributed as needed," Danny says, continuing to massage my shoulders. What the fuck is going on? It's as if he's had a personality transplant.

"Am I missing something?"

"Like?"

I look to Esther, who shrugs, as equally perplexed. "You tell me." Am I suddenly bulletproof?

"Happy wife, happy life," he murmurs.

"Okay," I say, standing from my chair, prompting his hands to move from my shoulders. "What's going on?"

"Let's go," James says, collecting Beau and exiting quite speedily.

"What?" Beau asks, appearing to be a slave to James's strength, unable to stop him from leading her away. It's absurd. She'd turn the tables on him with one swing of an arm and a roundhouse kick. So, of course, my worry heightens, especially when Otto declares he and Esther are also leaving.

And then it's just the two of us, Danny and me. His hands find my shoulders and push me back down to the chair, and I wince terribly when he crouches, his jaw tight. His chest. His beautiful, smooth, mutilated chest. A lump in my throat forms, and I damn myself to hell and back as I take his T-shirt and pull it up, as if I need to torture myself some more.

His chest is heavily bandaged, so I can't see the damage. But I see it. I caused that. His maiming. His pain.

Gently taking my hand, he eases it away, and his chest is soon covered again. I move my eyes to his. To this day, I still can't fathom how ice blue can radiate such heat. And yet here it is, hot blue burning through me. This is my husband. Confident and in control. This is the man I was instantly attracted to, the dark creature that reflected a version of me, but, ironically, it was the vulnerable, lost man I saw past the darkness that I fell in love with. The man I saw this morning. I flinch away from that thought, and Danny catches it.

"Never again, Rose," he reiterates, cupping both of my hands in both of his.

I could cry for him. "Stop it," I say. "Just stop it." I need him to be rid of this self-loathing. I must take some of the responsibility. Finding and killing a man isn't a cause for anguish for my husband, but the impact it'll have on me is. I should have supported him in his hopelessness, not kick off and cause him further stress, because his hopelessness was spiked by worry for me. Haven't I learned?

He nods, if mildly, "I have a gift for you."

"You're my gift. I don't need anything else."

He smiles, but it's half-hearted. "I shouldn't have been so careless with you. I shouldn't have zoned-out. I should have been fully aware, and I wasn't."

And I know that will only increase his anger and purpose. God help his enemies.

"If you left me," he goes on, squeezing my hands in his, "I wouldn't blame you. But I'm begging you not to, Rose, because a life without you is not a life I am interested in living."

I remove my hands from his and encourage his crouched body into mine, hugging him carefully so not to put pressure on his wounds. "I'm never leaving you."

"Good. So you'll accept my gift."

"What is it, a slap?" I joke, feeling him smile against my neck.

He pulls away and reaches into his back pocket, pulling something out, holding it up to me.

A ring.

I frown. "Are you proposing, because I'm pretty sure I've already married you twice."

"Oh, how my wife's sense of humor thrills me." His nose wrinkles, and he moves in, slamming a hard kiss on my lips.

"Did you and James go shopping together?" I ask around his mouth, making him pause our kiss and tilt his head, curious. "He asked Beau to marry him again," I say before he can ask. "She said no, but she's wearing the ring."

"No, we did not go shopping together." His lips are back on mine, kissing me with purpose, and, of course, I indulge him until he's had his fix, although, admittedly, and as I have told him endlessly, I could binge on him forever and never feel full. "Now, back to us." He holds up the ring, and I eye it. "It's an eternity ring, in case you're wondering."

Funny, I *was* wondering. "Eternity," I say, leaving the ruby sitting between his finger and thumb. "Does that mean, if I accept, I have to spend forever with you?"

"You already agreed to that when you caved in to my charms and let me take you from the casino floor of the Aria as an insurance policy."

I laugh loudly, my head thrown back. "Oh yes, when you kidnapped me." I let my amusement fade into a chuckle and lower my head. I find him smiling. Such a beautiful smile. He drops a peck on my mouth as he takes my hand and slips the ring onto my finger to join my engagement and wedding rings. He looks down at it. "This is the only red I ever want to see on you," he says quietly as he strokes the ruby, and I inhale subtly as he looks up at me, his scar glowing. "I mean it, Rose." The damage we have both sustained at the hands of others, the damage we have inflicted on *each* other. It stops now.

"That goes for you too."

"Agreed." Our lips come together, and he stands, pulling me up with him and reaching under my thighs to lift me to his body. I wrap every limb around him but loosen my hold when his sucks in air through his teeth. "It's okay."

"It is not—"

His lips hit mine and I lose myself in his mouth's attention as he walks us into the villa and lays me on the bed, his forearms on either side of my head and his knees on either side of my hips, holding him up.

Because . . . the cuts.

Not my round belly. It's because the cuts that are there because of me.

I try my hardest to push those miserable thoughts into a box, but as he kisses me with all the adoration I know he feels, all I can think about is how much stress I cause him. How much worry. How much pain. If I weren't a burden, he'd have simply packed like Ringo and Brad. He'd be fucking his way through whores without care, without concern. My safety wouldn't plague him. There'd be no need to placate the missus before returning to the battlefield. He'd be free.

My head naturally shakes, my body naturally tensing, and Danny instantly pulls away, looking down at me. I smile. It must be lame because his eyes narrow. "Talk," he orders, and I pout. "Now, Rose."

"What do I bring to this relationship?" I blurt out, surprising myself as much as I've clearly surprised my husband. His blue eyes are round and unsure. I sigh. "I make your life even more difficult." I hold up the ring he just put on my finger, and he looks at it, as if he's wary. "Cost you money, time, stress, and what do you get in return?" I have absolutely nothing to offer. No skills. No qualities. God, why am I only considering this now? I'm a total drain. What the fuck does he see in me?

The poor man looks completely lost, his frown deep. Great. So he's wondering the very same thing. What does he get out of me, apart from pain and hassle? Defeated and feeling a heavy sense of failure, I wriggle beneath him, trying to break free, needing to escape the awkward silence. But Danny lowers his body to mine, and his hard, perfectly formed stomach is suddenly pressing into my rounding belly, his maimed chest pushing into my boobs. I still when he hisses in discomfort, and his jaw tight, he stares deeply into my eyes. "You," he says, lowering slowly and pushing his mouth to the corner of mine. "I get *you*."

I could cry. Once upon a time, having *me* equaled having freedom. Not anymore. "That's sweet, but what *exactly* do you get out of me?" I know what I get out of him. Love, safety, freedom, happiness. Although the latter two are sporadic these days. He makes a living, albeit questionably, and he provides. Looks after us. Fucking hell, I'm a complete waste of space. "Tell me."

"You want to kill a few men, because I have every faith you can." He strokes his chin, reminding me of all the times I've socked him in the jaw.

I roll my eyes. "I'm being serious, Danny. Look at Beau."

"What about her?"

"Well, for a start she's a former cop. Trained, qualified. She can decorate, do gymnastics, martial arts, and let's not forget—"

His hand lands over my mouth, shutting me up. "You're my wife. You're my lover. You're my best friend. My be-all and fucking end-all, Rose Lillian Black." Kisses are dotted over every inch of my face. "But most importantly, you are the mother of my children."

His words quickly remind me that I am one thing Beau is not, and once again my heart breaks for her. God, are any of us truly happy with what we've got and who we are? "I want to learn to drive," I say out of nowhere.

Danny looks quite alarmed. It doesn't bode well. "You don't need to drive," he says. "I'll have you driven wherever you want to go."

I knew he'd say that. Some people might think that having every tiny thing done for you is a luxury. Not having to think about anything. "But I want to." I have never learned. There was no point, because I wasn't blessed with the freedom to just get in a car and drive. Not that I ever had the opportunity to actually learn, anyway. But now I do, and I'd like to.

"Why?" he asks, truly perplexed.

"The only skill I possess is the art of seduction."

"Rose," he says slowly, warningly.

"It's true. And I can't even do that anymore, and not only because I'm getting fat."

He looks split between exasperated and plain fucking furious. "You're wrong, you do have another skill, and you're fucking ace at it."

"What?"

"Pissing. Me. Off." Jaw rolling, he lifts his body again, relieving himself of the painful friction of our touching chests. "For fuck's sake, Rose." Getting off me, he sits on the edge of the bed and rests his elbows on his knees, dropping his head into his hands. "Why can't you just be happy?"

I laugh as I push myself up, resting against the headboard. "God, you're a dick sometimes." Our peace was short-lived. *Again.* I could scream. But I don't. Instead, I growl, pushing myself to the edge.

"Rose, wait." My wrist is seized, stopping me from standing, and I look back to see Danny stretching across the bed, virtually lying down to reach me. Pain is etched all over his face. He shakes his head, breathing out heavily. "No more fighting."

"Then stop being a jerk." I shake him off. "I have needs, you know."

"Do I?" he asks, sounding truly surprised. I don't suppose I can blame him. "Because I'm pretty sure you were content. I don't even know what's brought this on."

"Perhaps feeling useless."

"So you want to learn to drive?"

"Yes! I want to be able to take Daniel to school, or soccer practice, or a friend's or . . . or . . . or wherever! And when this baby arrives, I'd like to go to the store if I need to. Or take him to the park. Or have coffee with a friend." What the fuck am I saying? I expect none of those things can happen, but I pray one day they can. Then, when they do, at least I can drive myself around.

"Him?" Danny asks.

"What?" I yell, impatient, scowling at him.

"You said *him*." He gets up, tilting his head. "When you referred to the baby, you said *him*."

I recoil, thinking. "Did I?"

"Yes." On narrowed eyes, he starts stalking slowly toward me. "Do you know something I should know?"

"No."

"You've not asked Doc if he knows the sex?"

"No." I laugh. "I don't want to know. I want it to be a surprise."

I'm seized and thrown on the bed, and he's on me in a shot, pushing my dress up my body to expose my belly. "So, your mother thinks you're a boy." His big palms splay over my bump and stroke, and I exhale, settling again. "This is bad, bad news."

"Why?" I ask.

He bites my hip, and I yelp. "Because I already have an heir for my mafia empire."

I look down at him in horror, seeing him smirking. "That's not funny."

"Neither is your incessant need to rile me." Crawling up my body, he cages me in. "I'll teach you to drive."

"*You'll* teach me?" I ask, looking up at his delighted face. I'm not sure I like the sound of this.

"Yes. It'll give us something else to do together other that fight and fuck." He reaches down to his pants, biting his lip, hesitant. I know what he's thinking.

"Yes," I say, and he breathes out his relief, starting to work his fly. He rolls his hips and he's quickly inside me. I grab his biceps and we both inhale sharply. "Do you think you have the patience to teach me?"

He starts moving, and I follow his rhythm perfectly, relishing the depth he's achieving, loving the look of blinding pleasure on his handsome, scarred face. "You think I don't?" He thrusts suddenly, and I groan.

"I thought you'd be too busy smuggling guns, laundering money, and murdering many enemies to bother yourself with the mundane chore of teaching your wife how to drive." Especially when he doesn't really want to. I know what's happening here. Control.

"I'm never too busy for you, baby." He dips and kisses me while maintaining his dizzying drives, and, of course, I'm a slave to his attentiveness. "We'll start as soon as we're back in Miami." His pace increases, and I moan around his mouth, feeling my veins starting to heat.

"I could just learn with a professional instructor."

"I'm professional."

"At car chases, perhaps. Oh God."

"You coming, baby?"

"Yes!" My head starts to swim with heat, my legs shifting on the bed, stretching, tensing, my mouth ravenous for his as the pressure builds between my legs. Danny's pace increases, urgency overcoming him, and he presses his fists into the mattress, lifting, getting more leverage, his hips moving like pistons. "Danny!"

His head drops back, sweat pours, and he roars to the ceiling, thrusting hard and pushing me over the edge. The explosion between my thighs sends shockwaves through me, and I shake beneath him as he trembles above me, his hips now pulsing, his cock surging, his muscles rippling.

"Fuck." He drops, blanketing me, and our rushed, labored breathing fills the room. "Thank you," he pants. *Thank you for trusting him with my body again.*

He pulls out of me and falls to his back, his face cut, his jaw tight, his jeans halfway down his legs. "God, we fight and fuck like pros," he wheezes, and I laugh as I pull my dress down and get to my knees, removing them the rest of the way for him, taking his boxers with them.

"So you'll teach me?" I ask, my eyes unable to avoid the fact that even though he's naked, he's not naked. His bandages.

"Yes," he breathes. "Is Madam satisfied?"

I push away my guilt and crawl up his body, showing my appreciation—and sorrow—with a long, slow kiss that he accepts and contributes to, but his hands remain useless on the bed. "I need to pee." I get up, smiling at his moan of annoyance. "Back in a m—" A horrific pain bolts through my stomach, and I bend over, grabbing my belly. "Shit," I hiss, immediately short of breath.

"Rose?"

Pain. It radiates through me, making every muscle constrict tightly, an instinctive attempt to curb the unbearable agony. I cry out, dropping to my knees by the bed.

"Rose!" He appears before me, a blur of a man, and I feel his frantic hands grabbing at my arms, my shoulders, my face. "Rose, baby, talk to me, please."

I blink rapidly, trying to turn the blob in front of me into my husband, needing to see his face. "I—" I retch, the pain so intense, it's making my stomach turn.

"Fuck," Danny hisses, and I'm moving, feeling my body being shifted. I recognize the warmth of his body pushed into my back, his hands wrapped around my upper chest, his face in my neck. I sit between his bent legs as he leans back against the side of the bed, and I swallow, struggling to clear my foggy vision, my tummy tight, but . . . the pain subsides a little. It lifts, and I hold my breath in anticipation for its return. Scared. I'm so fucking scared. "Rose, baby, I beg you, please talk to me."

I can't even find the breath I need to speak and tell him I'm okay. Perhaps because I don't know if I am. Am I okay? Is the baby okay? "Danny." I exhale, beginning to panic, the pain still there but nowhere near as excruciating. "Danny, the baby." My eyes dart frantically as I claw at his forearms wrapped around me, like I might find the reassurance I need somewhere in the room.

"Fuck, Rose, I can't leave you." The agony, the conflict in his voice is real. "Can you stand? Do you think you can stand?"

"No." I feel utterly wiped out.

"Fuck it." He maneuvers, and my back is quickly propped up against the bed. He appears before me, still a little blurred, so I fight furiously to win back some clarity. I find his face. The torture. The agony. His scar is wicked and jagged and deep. His eyes haunted. "Are you in labor?" he asks. "Fuck, no, what the hell am I saying? What's happening, Rose?"

"I don't know," I admit. I have no idea what the fuck is happening. I'm certainly not in labor at sixteen weeks.

"I need to get my phone." He gets up. Comes back down. Up. Down. "Fuck!"

"Go," I tell him, starting to take deep, controlled breaths. "I'm okay."

"Fuck's sake." He runs out of the room and is back moments later, his phone at his ear. "She's conscious," he says, falling to his knees before me, feeling my thigh, stroking and squeezing. "In the bedroom. Come straight through." He hangs up and makes another call, and I fear I know to who.

"No," I demand. "Do not call Beau." I can't inflict this on her. It'll bring everything she's trying to forget back. It'll renew her pain, her hurt, her grief.

"You need to come," he says when she answers, standing and grabbing his boxers, pulling them on. "Now."

He doesn't give her a chance to ask why, hanging up and dropping his phone, falling to his ass and shifting in, caging me in with his bent legs. "Does it still hurt?"

"Not as bad." I shift, dropping my head back, trying to concentrate on my breathing. He just came inside of me. Always does, so it's not surprising I can feel the warmth of his cum in between my thighs. But . . . "Danny?"

"What, baby? What do you need?"

"I need you to check." I can hardly get the words out. And I don't need to elaborate. He knows. *This is the only red I ever want to see on you.* I drop my legs out wider, my throat tight, clenching my eyes shut, as Danny lifts my dress to my knees and looks between my legs. I hold my breath, waiting. Praying. Begging.

"There's nothing," he eventually says, his voice thick. "There's no blood."

I exhale and open my eyes. "Okay." I nod, starting to breathe a little easier. "Okay," I whisper, blinking back my tears, trying to keep it together.

No blood.

No more red.

I look down at the ring he's put on my finger, wishing for it in all the ways.

No more blood.

7

JAMES

"What's going on?" I ask from the bed as Beau throws on one of my shirts and yanks some denim shorts up her legs. My naked body is sprawled, my palm resting over my dick, the one that was buried inside her seconds ago ready to detonate. I'm still in pain. I don't know what made her take Danny's call. In fact, I'm quite pissed off she found the strength to answer over the orgasm we were both about to have.

She shoves her feet into some flip-flops. "I don't know. He sounded upset."

I get up and join her in getting dressed, coming to terms with the fact that my pleasure isn't Beau's priority right now. "Angry upset or worried upset?" I ask.

"I don't know," she replies as she runs out of the bedroom. "Both."

I fasten the fly of my jeans and traipse after her, thinking I've had about enough of the drama. Beau swipes up her keys from the table, and I swipe them right out of her hand. "I'll drive you."

She doesn't argue, surprising me, instead hurrying out to her Jeep. She's really worried, which only makes me wonder with increasing worry what the fuck is going on. "What did he say?" I ask as I slide in and pull away. "Put your seatbelt on."

"That I need to go there immediately."

I look across to her. She's beautifully disheveled, but I can't appreciate it past her apprehensive expression. We all know Danny wouldn't hurt Rose, but no one can say with any confidence that Rose isn't capable of something stupid, especially when she's emotional. Her stunt at dinner earlier with the kid's mate's father case in point. She has a very bad habit of pushing Danny's buttons. So could he have finally lost the plot with her? I roll my eyes to myself. Of course not. Those two might behave like they hate each other at times, but they're ridiculously in love. So what the fuck is going on if they've not murdered each other?

When we pull up outside Danny and Rose's villa, I listen for the sound of breaking glass or screams. Nothing. Beau is out in a flash, darting up the path as I follow on her heels. She bursts through the door, and we find Danny pacing the kitchen in his boxers, his expression grave, his blue eyes haunted.

We both slow to a stop, and I watch as Beau looks from him to the bedroom door over and over. She's scared to ask. Can't find her words. "Danny?" I say, moving forward, troubled by the glaze in his eyes.

"There was no blood," he croaks, raking a hand through his hair. "No blood. And then . . ." He looks at the door, pain a blanket on his face. "And then I stood her up and . . ."

Oh fuck.

". . . there was blood," he whispers, dropping heavily to a stool, as if his legs refuse to hold him up any longer. "Doc's in there with her. I couldn't see her like that."

Fucking hell. Painfully, I know exactly what he means. I look at Beau, my throat clogged with warranted worry, with pain that had briefly subsided, and see she's frozen and quiet. Staring at Danny. I can feel square one on the horizon, waiting to claim Beau from me. *Shit.* I pace to the cabinet across the room and pour a Scotch, taking it to Danny and putting it in his hand. He's visibly shaking. "Drink,"

I order, scratching around on the worktop for his cigarettes and lighting one. I exhale and slip it between his lips, turning to Beau. She's still motionless, her eyes now darting across the floor. I go to her, taking the tops of her arms, snapping her out of her trance. She looks up at me. I have not one fucking clue what to say to her. I can't remove her from this situation. I can't take her away from the impending hurt. I can only hope she sees the pain in me as I know she feels it in herself. Together. Always together.

And when she focuses on me, I know she appreciates *my* hurt. She swallows hard, nods, takes my hand and squeezes tightly, then heads for the bedroom, and although I'm desperate to be with her —hold her, support her—I know I must step aside and let her do what she needs to do. Comfort her friend.

I go out onto the patio and get an ashtray, returning and taking a stool next to Danny, helping myself to a Marlboro and lighting up. I should be encouraging Danny from his seat to get him outside before the whole villa in engulfed in smoke, but I don't think an excavator would shift him. And what the fuck should I say? Again, I don't know, so I just sit here watching him pull hard on his cigarette in between sips of his Scotch, his gaze set on the floor, his hands still shaking.

Ten minutes later, he's on his second Marlboro and drink, and he's still not murmured a word. I get up and take two steps toward the bedroom, but just as quickly halt, wondering how I'm going to handle what lies beyond. I've got a girlfriend who's gone from happy to haunted in the space of a phone call, a best mate who looks like he's on the edge of a breakdown, and his wife, my girlfriend's best friend, who is in that room distraught. I can hear her sobbing over Beau's soft hushes.

Fuck.

I resolve myself to getting my arse back on the stool and waiting, my mouth shut until I have something productive to say or useful to do. Right now, it's simply being here.

"Want another?" I blurt, feeling restless and helpless, as Danny turns his glass in circles on the counter.

He shakes his head and looks up at me. "I'm sorry."

"What for?"

"Calling Beau." Shoving his glass away, he sets his elbows on the counter and drops his head into his hands. "Fuck, I wasn't thinking."

"She wouldn't have it any other way." My attention is pulled to the bedroom when I hear the door open. Beau appears, and I breathe in, bracing myself for the imminent meltdown. It won't happen now. Not yet. Not until we're away from Rose and Danny, and she can let down the shield currently helping her keep relatively together.

Danny looks up and stands, and I join him. "The baby's okay," she says with little emotion. Not relief or happiness, not anything. "Doc's monitoring the heartbeat for a while for peace of mind."

"What?" Danny runs past Beau into the bedroom, while I stand, a statue, searching for the calm this news should bring. It's nowhere to be found, and it's not likely to be. While this is the best news for Danny and Rose, and while I know Beau will be happy for them, as I am, I also know this whole situation will set her back again. Bring back memories. Hurt. Heartache.

Losing our baby.

"Okay?" I ask like a total dick.

"She'll need a few days bedrest," Beau says stoically, emotionless. "She needs to calm the hell down, but she'll be all right. The baby will be all right."

"I wasn't talking about Rose."

She blinks, frowning, looking like she's silently asking herself how to respond. "Sure." She forces a smile and passes me. "I'm going to take the beach path home."

I breathe in, my mouth loading and preparing to fire a refusal, but I hold my tongue and let her leave. It's tough and it fucking hurts, but throwing my weight around is not the answer. My own agony right now comes second to Beau's. Let her be.

Except, I can't.

I can't stay away at the best of times. So now, when I know her heart will be aching?

I go to the bedroom and tap lightly on the door, waiting for an okay before popping my head around the wood. Danny is on the bed with Rose, stroking her head as she snoozes, and Doc is adjusting the straps around her tummy.

"Talk tomorrow?" I ask, because there is so fucking much to discuss. Even more now. Our plan to return to Miami in the morning might have to go on ice. At least, for Danny. I, however, must start solving the problem.

Laying a tender kiss on Rose's forehead, he breaks away and gets off the bed, constantly looking back as he makes his way to me. I move, giving him space to step out of the room, pulling the door closed quietly behind him. He casts an eye around the villa.

Looking for Beau.

"Where is she?" he asks.

"Walking home."

His eyes dart to mine, worried. "Fuck," he breathes. "Mate, I'm sorry." His eyes close, his wince harsh. "I . . ."

"I can't shield her from the unexpected." It pains me, but nothing would have prepared us for this. Truly, I don't think anything will begin to heal this particular trauma for us. Her period is due. We don't even know if she can conceive anymore. A bullet in a woman's abdomen is bound to affect her fertility. Right? "I need to go," I say, backing away. "I'm glad Rose and the baby are okay." I turn and leave, pulling the door closed behind me and taking a moment to gather myself. Pull myself together. Calm my building anger.

I fail.

"Fuck." I swing around and bury my fist into the door, and pain radiates through my hand. I rest my forehead on the wood, squeezing my eyes closed. Why the fuck does peace keep eluding us? Giving us a taste and then leaving us hungry for more? Running away, hiding, pretending to not exist feels more appealing than ever before.

It's wishful thinking, I know that.

I push myself away from the door just before it swings open. I don't look at Danny. I don't need to see the concern on his face. Nor the guilt. "I'll call you in the morning." I pace away, praying calm finds me before I find Beau.

I kick my shoes off, toss them in her Jeep as I pass, and take the trail to the beach. The black water sparkles under the moonlight, and I scan the shoreline for her. I don't see any shadows, detect any movement. I make another scan of the length of beach from here to our beach hut. Nothing. I start to trudge through the sand, pulling my phone out as I go and dialing her, my eyes constantly casting back and forth up and down the beach. Her phone goes to voice-mail. "Don't make me worry more, Beau," I warn quietly, trying her again. Voicemail. Again. I hang up on a curse as I reach the water, and the calm rush of the lapping waves does nothing to ease me. I turn on the spot, searching every bit of the beach, my heart starting to beat faster. "God damn you, woman," I whisper, heading in the direction of our place, the water splashing my feet in calm, foamy rushes. "B—" My eyes land on a pile of clothes on the sand before darting out to the ocean. I exhale when I see the silhouette of a body immersed to the waist in the water. "Beau," I breathe, knowing she won't hear me. I would know her shape anywhere. The specific shade of blonde of her hair, even in the restricted light. Her bun has come loose, leaving endless strands of hair splaying her naked back.

My light.

Ever shrouded in darkness.

And as ever, I am drawn to her.

I remove my jeans and boxers, pull off my T-shirt and drop them with my phone to the sand next to Beau's clothes before walking into the sea, making sure she hears me coming. She doesn't look back, doesn't check it's me. She knows. My front meets her back, and I wrap my forearms around her upper body, pulling her back and sinking my face into her hair. I feel her soften against me, her cold skin warming against mine, her hands coming up and wrapping around my forearms, holding on.

"What if it never happens for us again?" she asks the water as my eyes squeeze shut and my heart squeezes in pain. So lost.

"It will happen." I set my lips on her shoulder and kiss her salty skin.

"Do you want it to happen?"

"Of course I do." But I'm worried. Worried about her body's strength. Her mental strength. The journey. "I know I'm a hard man to be with, Beau."

"You're actually very easy to be with." She shifts, and I loosen my hold, allowing her to turn and face me. I look down at her breasts, my hand lifting of its own volition and stroking softly over the cold, solid nipple, before I exhale and tug her into my body, helping her get her legs around my waist, her arms around my neck. I put my mouth on hers as I sink us under the water to our necks, feeling her tense and squeeze me tighter.

"It *will* happen," I say, pushing my tongue into her mouth and swirling slowly, relishing the sound of her sighing happily. Savoring the feeling of calm settling within her. Accepting what I need to do. What I have to give her. My hand slides up her back and encases her nape, securing her to me. "It *will* happen." Because life surely can't be any crueler. Her mouth becomes firmer on mine, her boobs compressed into my chest, her spine lengthening to bring her closer, forcing me to drop my head back to accommodate her.

"I want you now." She locks her arm around my neck, rolls her hips into me, her passion becoming frenzied. Desperate.

"Beau," I say quietly, trying to bring her down a few levels as blood flows into my dick. She doesn't hear or doesn't listen, her purpose getting the better of her. Not to try and get pregnant, but to relocate her serenity. "Beau, baby." I turn my face, and her head drops into the crook of my neck, her hot breath burning my skin. "Easy," I whisper.

I feel her nod, feel her acceptance, as I lift her and reach between us to position myself at her entrance, ignoring the ache of my hand. She slowly sinks onto me and we both suck back air as we join, the feeling fucking beautiful. "Good God," I breathe, fighting the urge to withdraw and thrust hard. "Okay?"

She nods, biting at my shoulder, clawing at my back. "I'm okay."

And I do that. I make her okay.

Kissing my collarbone, she drags her lips across my skin to my jaw, kissing me there too, before pecking her way across my rough cheek and plunging her tongue into my mouth on a broken moan. It's my undoing, and I find my feet, pushing us out of the water with her curled around my body. I need an anchor. Some weight behind me.

Her hands in my hair, gripping, my hands on her waist, holding, I start to move her up and down, struggling to keep our kiss steady as I enter and leave her, plunging, withdrawing, building us up gradually. The friction, the warmth, the mind-blowing kiss, it's all at our usual level on intensity. I feel as consumed as I always do when I am at the mercy of our joining, and yet something is being communicated here, and I'm struggling to find the headspace past the need to work out what.

But as the pace quickens, the desperation increases, and the pleasure climbs, I realize.

She needs me.

My fierce, independent, former cop girlfriend needs me. She's strong but needs my strength. Determined but needs my encouragement. And during those moments of peacefulness, she still needs my peace. We are one. Incomplete without the other.

My lips push harder to hers, my fingers clawing into her hips, my eyes squeezing tighter.

"Look at me," she gasps, making my eyes snap open. Our stares meet, and everything seems to still and become quiet, despite our bodies still moving and our breathing still loud. I've looked at this woman closely endless times. Stared so deeply into her eyes, I've seen a reflection of myself. And yet now, all I can see is hope.

I can't kill that hope.

I end the never-ending kiss and push my forehead to hers,

needing to maintain this vision as we both find our release. I swear, she becomes more beautiful with each second I spend watching her. I thrust on, studying her as she studies me, seeing her teeth sink into her lip, her grip of me becoming harder.

I don't need to ask.

I pull out and thrust hard, my jaw tight, eliciting a cry from Beau, and her head becomes limp, all strength seeming to go to her internal muscles and wring me dry. "Fuck," I cough, my legs shaking, forcing me to my knees, the water reaching my neck again. I kiss her exposed throat, bite it, suck it, shaking as my orgasm tears through me unforgivingly and Beau shudders and moans. I hold on to her for dear life, as we search for the peace past the crazy, our breathing obliterated, the water feeling like a hot bath.

"When are you going back to Miami?" she pants into my shoulder.

"In the morning."

"Am I coming?"

"No," I answer, maintaining our tight cuddle.

She doesn't answer. Doesn't challenge me.

It's a novelty.

My sleep was restless. I know Beau's was too, constantly flipping her body over, huffing, puffing, sighing. She finally gave up subtly expressing her grievance through sounds that didn't involve explicit words at around five, tucking herself into my side and directing my arm around her.

Silly, defiant, magnificent woman.

But while Beau drifted off, I did not. Instead, I spent my time staring at the ceiling as I stroked circles across her thigh, which was lying on my stomach where she'd tossed her leg over me. I wouldn't be surprised if she woke up with a friction burn.

I drop my head to the side and reach for my phone, seeing it's seven, so I drop a kiss on her peaceful face and peel my body from hers. I shower, pack the things I came with, and leave the beach hut.

It doesn't feel good leaving her here. Nothing about this feels good. The Bear is alive, Beau's emotionally vulnerable. My only comfort right now is that she won't be alone. And she's safer here.

I have plenty of time, so I take the beach path toward the airfield where Danny's private hangar is, my bag tossed over my shoulder, breathing in the last bit of St. Lucia I'll have in a while as I call Danny.

"How is she?" I ask when he answers.

"Strict bedrest for a few days. Doc's told her she needs to calm the fuck down." He sounds truly exasperated, and I smile, hearing him drawing on a cigarette. Calm the fuck down. She really does. Unlike Beau, Rose is quite highly strung. "How's yours?" he asks.

"Hovering on the edge of tranquility, as always."

"I didn't help with that. I'm sorry."

"Stop apologizing." I take the right-hand fork in the path, looking out across the ocean. "I'm heading to the airfield."

"Yeah, I'm not."

"I gathered that." Understand that. He wouldn't leave Rose even if she insisted, and I know she won't.

"I'll be in Miami as soon as I know she's okay."

I nod. "I'll keep in touch."

"Make sure you do."

"Oh, Danny?"

"What?"

"I assume I'm good to stay at your place?"

He laughs lightly. "Sure. Every other fucker does." He hangs up as I reach the road and cross over to the airfield, and when I get to the hangar, Danny's private pilot is waiting for me along with a flight attendant. "Sir," he says, tipping his hat. "Everyone is already on board."

"Thanks, Tim," I say, climbing the few steps and dipping to clear the doorway. I see Ringo first, looking as miserable as ever, a definite shadow developing under his left eye from Goldie's right hook. Then Otto, whose eyebrows are as high as me towering over his seated form. "What's up?" I ask as I pass his seat.

"Nothing."

"Nothing," Goldie says too before I have a chance to ask her. What the fuck's going on? I frown, looking back at them.

"Morning," Brad chirps, pulling my attention forward again.

"Morning." My frown deepens. "What are you grinning at?"

"Nothing."

I see Fury, who completely avoids my eyes. What the hell is he doing here? He should be staying with Beau. I drop my bag in the aisle, my patience lost. "What the fu—" My tongue catches in my mouth when I spot her looking all relaxed in one of the chairs at the rear, her hair disheveled and piled high, her face free of makeup, her body in some sweats and a T-shirt, flip-flops on her feet.

Because she didn't have time to fuck about if she was going to beat me here.

"Morning," she says, sounding unsure.

And so she should. I'm at a loss for words. Actually, I'm not, but my language might spark the fuel tank and blow up the jet if I let it loose. What the ever-loving fuck is she playing at? My eyes nailed to her, I blindly kick my bag aside. "What the hell, Beau?" I take the few steps needed to put me before her, my towering, imposing frame shadowing her petite, seated body. Not that she's intimidated.

Her big, dark eyes drop to her lap. She's probably weighing up the merits of talking at all, and she obviously concludes it's probably best to keep her mouth shut because she remains mute. Whatever. She's not staying on this jet. I step forward, dip to scoop her up, taking a hold of her. She doesn't fight me, doesn't tense, she just jiggles her arm and the sound of metal clangs in my ear. *What the fuck?*

I withdraw and see she's handcuffed herself to the seat. "Are you kidding?"

She shrugs. "I thought it was the better of two options."

"What was the other option?"

"Knocking you out."

My blood heats, more so when I hear Brad snickering. "I'll kill you, Brad," I warn.

"Oh fuck off." He chuckles. "You wanted a woman. Now deal with it."

"I'll kill you, Brad," Beau warns, and the fucker gets his amusement under control in an instant, as if purposely riling me more. *For fuck's sake.*

"Get me some bolt croppers." I turn to our audience but am forced to face Beau again when she grabs me by the balls, literally, with her uncuffed hand. "Fuck, Beau," I squeak, my body folding, my stomachache instant.

Her face close to mine, she loosens her grip slightly and kisses me softly. I swallow, unable to resist falling into the slow motions of her mouth's movements on mine.

"You're still not coming," I mumble, feeling her sigh into my mouth. "This isn't up for negoci—"

"I promise to do as I'm told."

I laugh under my breath. "Why do you lie?"

"I need you close, James." She releases my balls and lays her hand across my heart. "Please don't leave me behind."

She's strong but needs my strength. Determined but needs my encouragement. She needs me.

Well . . . fuck.

I swallow, my mind scrambling, as I regard her. I see sadness now. Full force. Her period is due today. Will it come? I don't know. I also don't know if I want it to, but I do know that I need to be around if it doesn't. And, more importantly, if it does.

Jesus.

I nod, kiss her, and turn to take my seat, offering my hand across the aisle. She places hers in mine.

I don't release it for the entire flight.

～

There are three shiny black Mercedes waiting on the runway when we land, each of them intended for different destinations—Beau and Fury back to the house, me to the club with Brad, and the others to the boatyard to check in on the bunker and Liam and Jerry.

I guide Beau down the steps to the tarmac by her elbow and toward the first car. "I'll be back later," I say, opening the door and helping her into the back as Fury puts himself behind the wheel, needing to adjust the seat considerably to fit.

"Where are you going?" she asks, not worried or disgruntled, it's just a simple, curious question.

"Checking in on Nolan at Hiatus," I say, taking her seatbelt and pulling it across her body, leaning into the car to clip it into place. My nose is bombarded by the intoxicating scent of Beau in bed in the morning. One of my favorite smells. Because I'm still all over her skin. Unable to stop myself, I bury my face in her neck and take a long, deep hit to last me until later, then bite down on her flesh.

"I can't come with you?" she asks, pushing into me, grabbing at my shoulders.

"Not now," I say, quickly going on to appease her. "I don't know what we're coming back to."

"And when you do?"

I pull out and stroke across her fair eyebrow. "Can I take a raincheck on answering that?"

She exhales, her body softening. She's not unreasonable. Not all of the time, and I know she knows I won't think twice about carrying her back onto that jet, handcuffing her back to the chair, and sending her back to St. Lucia. "You can."

I nod and drop a chaste kiss on her lips. "See you later." I raise and take the door to close it, but her hand shoots out to stop me.

"Can I at least go visit my mom?"

Her question catches me off guard. *Fuck.* "You don't want to go back to the house to shower and change?"

"Why, do I smell?" She shoves her nose into her armpit and sniffs.

"Yes, you smell of me mixed with a lot of you." Fucking glorious. She smiles. "Then I can wait."

I deflate, tapping the driver's window so that Fury lowers it. "You loaded?" He nods. "Pop the trunk." I round the back of the car and pull out the side panel, collecting the small handgun and checking the magazine as Fury closes it again. "Here." I hand it to Beau, who hardly looks at the damn thing as she too checks it's loaded before lifting her arse from the seat and slipping it into the back of her sweatpants. "Be safe," I order.

She looks up at me with slightly lazy eyes as she reaches for the door, forcing me back. "You be safe," she counters, closing it. Fury wastes no time pulling off, and I watch the car until it turns off the airfield.

"You ready?" Brad asks, shouldering me as he passes and slips into the driver's seat of the last Merc.

"Ready," I say quietly, putting my hand up at the second Merc as it takes Ringo, Goldie, and Otto to the boatyard. I slip into the car and dial Danny, putting him on loudspeaker. "Just landed," I say when he answers. "How's Rose?"

"The worst patient ever."

I smile and Brad chuckles. "Use the time wisely, yeah?" I say, mindful that Brad is sitting next to me and doesn't know the extent of the shit that's gone down between Danny and Rose. This is an unexpected opportunity for Danny to step back and screw his head back on straight. We've got things covered here.

"Yeah," he agrees, but it's reluctant, something both Brad and I detect. I look across the car to him, and he nods, acknowledging the joint observation. We both know his thirst for this particular kill is unrelenting. "You going straight to the club?" Danny asks.

"Brad needs to check in with Nolan and tell him the final payment from the Mexicans will be delayed in light of the late shipment." I flick the aircon on higher, feeling stifled by Miami's humidity already. "I'll call Luis when I get to Hiatus to let him know to hold his money for now."

"Thanks."

"No problem."

"And the discount?" Danny asks, prompting me to look across to Brad again as he hits the main road and puts his foot down.

"I don't know," Brad says, shrugging. "What's the going rate for goodwill discounts on a small arsenal these days? One hundred, two hundred, three hundred grand? Oh, I know. Why don't we just give the Mexican fucker our guns for free?"

I smile and return my attention to Danny on the phone. "I'll deal with it. I'll let you know the new plan once the men report back from the boatyard."

"Sure," he mutters, his voice sharp.

I hang up, leaving Danny festering about that, and rest back in my seat, watching Miami fly by. "Glad to be back?" I ask Brad.

"My dick is," he says, and I smile, knowing he's been deprived in that area while we've been in St. Lucia. "But my inner peace, not so much."

I hum, silently agreeing.

Inner peace.

That fucker is elusive in this life.

I stop on the threshold of the entrance to the club, gazing around. Every light is on, the bar staff restocking, the dancers practicing. Nolan emerges from the office, suited and booted, and the moment he spots Brad and me, a fleeting look of panic flashes across his face before he corrects it and smiles widely.

I tilt my head, curious, as I follow Brad over. "Did you catch that?" I ask Brad's back, my eyes never straying from Nolan.

Brad looks back on a monster frown. "Catch what?"

My eyes narrow. "Nothing."

"Boss," Nolan says. "I wasn't expecting you.'

"Yeah, and ain't that obvious," I say to myself as I pass them, heading straight to the office.

"Let me get you both a drink," Nolan chimes. A drink? It's not even noon. "Mason, get the bosses a drink. Hey, James, you want a drink, don't you?"

"No, I don't," I call back, walking on. "It's the wrong side of noon." What the fuck was he up to in here?

I push through the door.

"Oh," a female yelps, rushing to cover her chest with a cushion from the couch.

"Shit," I curse, swinging back around, just as Nolan lands in front of me. I tilt my head, and he drops his eyes, ashamed. "So when the bosses are away, the kids will play, huh?"

He says nothing, and Brad wanders over, shaking his head. "What have I told you?" he asks, sounding like a reprimanding parent.

"No hooky with the girls," Nolan says, sighing like an admonished child. "Hardly seems fair when Otto—"

"Never mention Otto's previous dabbles with strippers," I warn. Does this mean he's still getting some with the girls? *Not your business.* "Understand?"

"Understand," Nolan mutters, his dark eyes rolling a little.

I shake my head to myself, at the same time trying to reason with myself too. The kid's barely a man, and here he is surrounded by all this temptation. I should cut him some slack. But still, he was told not to go there, and he went there. What else is he doing? "You need to deal with this," I say to Brad. "He's your prodigy." The girl skirts past me, pulling on a denim jacket, and gives Brad beseeching eyes.

"Mr. Black, please, I need this job."

Brad waves her off. "Go," he orders gently, as I turn and step back into the office. Again, I come to a jarring halt when I register what I neglected to register before, when I had a half-naked, panicked employee before me. "The fuck?" I breathe, feeling Brad join me.

"Yes," he says quietly, gazing around. "The fuck, Nolan?" He storms forward and waves a deranged hand around the office. The office that looks like a fucking slum. Okay, granted, it's a show office, a decoy, an illusion, but still, smokescreen or not, it's still a representation of the business.

I shake my head, looking back at Nolan, who looks pretty fucking sheepish, but I don't get a chance to demand an explanation, and, really, it isn't my job. Over to Brad, who swipes up a cushion and tosses it back on the couch where the blankets are strewn. Then walks over to the desk, where there's a toaster, a kettle, a . . . "Is that a fucking smoothie maker?" he barks, poking at the glass jug that's full of some familiar green slop. I pout. I haven't had my morning juice.

"I can explain," Nolan says, hands up, coming at us.

"Please do," Brad yells, wafting his hand out and sending a few kiwis flying across the office. He perches on the edge of the desk and folds his arms over his chest, looking at Nolan with an expectant glare.

"I've got nowhere to go," Nolan says, his shoulders dropping.

"What?" Brad barks.

"He said he's got nowhere to go," I chime in, lifting the glass jug off the base and taking a sniff.

"I fucking heard him fine," Brad mutters, throwing me a scowl then a grimace when I tip the jug to my lips for a taste.

I hum. "This is quite good."

"Thanks." Nolan beams at me.

"What's in it?"

"There's a bit of broccoli, a kiwi, some celery and—"

"Ginger?"

"Yes, ginger."

"For fuck's sake," Brad snaps. "So when I fire your ass, you can get a job at *Joe the Juice.*"

"Oh, come on, Boss." Nolan gives pleading hands, and I take a pew and carry on sipping my way through the juice. "I work my balls off for this club. You know you can trust me."

"Yeah, and I pay you for it. You can't afford rent on an apartment?"

His eyes drop to the carpet. "I will be able to next month," he says quietly. "I had some debts to settle."

I look at Brad, the jug at my lips, and he scowls across at me. "What debts?" he asks. I can see he's thinking what I'm thinking, and I'm thinking there's a hidden office upstairs with millions of dollars of cash being cleaned. We wouldn't miss a few bucks here and there. I set the jug on the desk and stand, making my way to the concealed door.

"I've not stolen from you," Nolan calls, and I stop, looking back. The unmoving embarrassment splattered across his face speaks volumes. "I just needed to get my head down somewhere until my next paycheck."

I look at Brad, assessing his disposition. I believe the kid, and I know Brad will. He's always backed him. Fair dos, he's overstepped the mark, with the woman *and* the accommodation, but employees like him aren't easily found and he runs the club like clockwork. Eager to please. Will only bring us a problem if it's a real problem.

"How much do you owe?" Brad asks.

"Nothing." Nolan picks up a cushion and tosses it on the couch, then approaches the desk, prompting Brad to move. "I made the final payment just last week." He starts tidying up the surface, moving things around.

I can see what's coming a mile off. "For fuck's sake," Brad breathes, heading toward me. "You can stay with me for a while."

"What?" Nolan asks, looking up, stunned. "I'm not fired?"

"No, you're fucking not, but if you so much as breathe on another one of the girls, I'll rape your ass with that blender jug." He disappears through the concealed door toward the upstairs office.

I flinch, as does Nolan, both of us looking at the jug. It's a hefty jug. Thick glass. A few knobbles here and there.

"Now get that office cleaned up." Brad shouts back.

"Or you're grounded," I say, backing away, my face serious. But Nolan still smiles and proceeds to do as he's been told.

I make it upstairs, firing a quick text off to Otto, and wander across to the glass, looking down on the club, while Brad reacquaints himself with the desk. "So, Daddy Brad," I say, feeling his tired eyes on my back. I wander over to the table on the other side of the room and run my eyes over the piles of cash. "What's—" My stare falls onto three sports bags on the other side of the room. "What's that?" I ask, going over and opening one, coming face to face with Abraham Lincoln.

"What is it?" Brad asks, approaching behind.

"Cash."

He swings the door open. "Nolan!" he bellows.

"Yes, Boss?"

"What's this?"

Nolan enters and looks at me crouched by the bags. "Delivered an hour ago," he says. "Final payment of the Mexicans' shipment."

"Fuck!" Brad yells, stomping back to his desk and dropping to the chair.

Indeed, *fuck*. Prompt payment equals prompt delivery, and we can't fucking deliver on time.

"Problem, Boss?" Nolan asks as I collect up the bags and take them to the safe.

"Yes, this should be in the fucking safe," I grumble. "You're really on bad form today, Nolan."

"I was just getting to it, I swear, but then—"

"Your brain fell into your dick." I throw the bags into the safe and slam the door, spinning the dial. "How about I slash your cock off and solve this problem for us all."

His hand falls over his crotch as he steps back. "Easy, James," he says, looking injured.

Fuck me, I can't be angry with him, and that just makes me angrier. "Get the fuck out of here."

Nolan bolts, and I see Brad looking at the endless piles of paperwork on his desk. He scowls. "All this"—he motions to the mess—"is too much for Nolan to handle on his own. The club, the money, the security—"

"The dancers and employees," I muse, taking a seat on the couch.

Brad lifts his eyes but not his head. "The dancers and employees," he agrees. "I need to hire him some help now I'm a little distracted. Someone we can trust."

"Got anyone in mind?"

"Actually, yes."

"Who?"

"B—"

"Forget it."

"Or Rose," he adds.

I'm laughing again. "You think Danny will even entertain the idea? She's pregnant, or did you miss that?"

"It's the perfect solution. He, or you, if you'll give me Beau, will know exactly where they are at all times." He shows the ceiling his palms. "It's a win-win for us all."

I narrow one eye, considering it for a moment. Just a moment. "Absolutely not."

"You can't speak for Danny."

I laugh. "Wanna bet?"

"Fine." Brad gathers up some of the papers and stacks them to the side. "It's a crying shame."

"Why's that?" I ask, feeling my phone vibrate in my pocket. I lift my arse off the seat and pull it out, seeing a text message from . . . I recoil.

"I pay well, and the perks are great."

I look up slowly and tiredly, and he grins like a twat. "No." I get up and start a slow pace of the room, staring down at my phone and the unopened text message from Beth, wondering what she wants. Stupid question. It's been months since I last made her fantasy a reality with her husband. In fact, the last time was the day I met Beau. I need to let them know I'm no longer in the game. Or *that* game, anyway.

"What's up?"

I clear my screen, telling myself I'll deal with her later, and face Brad. "Nothing." My phone rings, and I hold it up.

"The Mexicans?" he asks.

"Yeah."

He cringes, looking across to the safe where I just stored their money, and technically it *is* still theirs and will be for a while longer. Not a great position to be in.

I answer with silence. It's a habit. "You received my money," Luis says, as I click it to loudspeaker so save me the hassle of reiterating the conversation to Brad.

"It's early," I say.

"I need my order sooner. The twentieth."

I shoot my eyes to Brad who closes his in despair. "May I ask why?"

"A private war this side of the border," he says, blasé. "I must ensure we're sufficiently armed."

"That's a Saturday, Luis. A weekend."

"You can do earlier?"

"No, we can't do earlier. We have a Coast Guard training day that's causing issues with our delivery."

"Let me spell it out for you, as I fear you're not sensing my urgency. I have reliable intel that's informed me of an intended attack on my compound. I must act first, therefore I need my order by the twentieth. I'm sure this isn't a problem, is it?"

"Not at all," I say coolly, and Brad's eyes snap open. I shrug. We have to find a way around this or we can add the Mexicans to the Irish, Poles, and Russians, all of which, albeit silent at the moment, want us dead. "I'll be in touch with the plans." I hang up and start to pace, thinking.

"And how are we going to solve this little conundrum?" Brad asks. "Chaka's not delivering until Monday. The order was already going to be late."

"Yes, I know, Brad. I did the math." I drop to the couch, tapping the side of my head with my mobile. "We can sort the guns in a day."

"We won't have any guns to sort."

"We will if Chaka meets the original delivery date."

"How do you propose shipping half a million dollars' worth of firearms through dozens of Coast Guard boats and crew?"

I squint, thinking. "Leave it with me." I punch out a message to Chaka telling him we have to take the guns on the nineteenth and we'll pay him a bonus and not kill him. He answers quickly with a smiley face.

This fucking deal isn't going to be worth doing soon, what with discounts and bonuses. But making money we do not need isn't the purpose of this deal. Smoking the Russians out is the purpose of this deal. And yet the exchange is creeping closer, has been set up for weeks, and there's still been no sight nor sound from them. Of course, the whole criminal web is undoubtedly regrouping and restructuring after the demise of so many significant members, but we know The Ox, Sandy, and Volodya are still breathing. It was the Poles and Irish that bore the brunt of our killing spree, all in the name of finding The Bear. Slimy arsehole. We won't get it wrong next time. Not that Perry Adams didn't deserve to die. Every man who fell victim to us deserved to die, so it's not a total loss. The world is less a few pieces of shit.

But The Bear? He isn't just a piece of shit. He's the king of shits. The puppet master. The man who is the root of Beau's injuries and my baby's death. I blink back the dark spots in my vision. Swallow down the burning anger rising.

Fuck.

I wander over to the drinks cabinet and pour a vodka.

"All right?" Brad asks tentatively as I neck the lot, hoping the liquid will cool the fury brewing. It's been a while since I've felt the rage that used to rule me.

"Yeah." I clear my throat and look down at my mobile when it rings again. "Higham," I say quietly, looking up at Brad.

"What the fuck does that FBI prick want?"

Good fucking question. The last time I saw him, he let me walk free after Beau's ex-boyfriend cop, Oliver Burrows, arrested me for the murder of Agent Frank Spittle. It didn't go down very well with Burrows, and it didn't go down all too well with me to find out I was being followed by The Hound after Higham let me walk free. I smile, remembering that Polish fucker's tattooed face the moment before the grenade I'd bowled under his vehicle blew up. He thought he'd got The Enigma. *Idiot.*

I answer my mobile and hit the loudspeaker icon. "Black's not answering." Higham says, getting straight to the point.

"He's busy."

"So you're back." he muses, and Brad rolls his eyes. News sure does travel fast.

"Danny did warn you we would be."

"You've hardly given me time to prepare for your return."

"How can I help you, Agent Higham?"

He laughs lightly. "You could help me by disappearing off the face of the earth and taking The Brit with you, but we all know that's not going to happen, is it?"

"Nope."

"Thought not. So let's start with why you're back in town."

"We've missed you."

"And why are things going to kick off?"

"Oh, the anticipation must be killing you."

"Don't fuck with me, James. I'm standing here looking at Carlo Black's empty grave."

I recoil, and Brad flies up from his chair. "Excuse me?"

"You heard."

"I think I heard."

There's silence for a few uncomfortable moments, until Higham breaks it. "This wasn't Danny's doing?"

"Danny's not in town. And why the fuck would he dig up his dead father, Higham?"

"To stop some other fucked-up psycho digging him up, I assumed." A car door slams in the background. "Danny's not in Miami?"

"No, he's not in fucking Miami."

"You'd better get over here."

I head to the door, Brad on my tail. "On my way."

"The fuck?" Brad says as I race down the stairs to the club. "Someone could have moved him, right?"

"Like who?" I snap, jogging through the club.

"I don't know. The fucking grave keepers. Fuck me, I am *not* putting that call in."

"One of us has to," I say quietly, breaking out into the sunshine. "We'll draw straws."

"Jesus Christ," Brad breathes, looking a bit pale.

We pull up to the small churchyard on the edge of town, seeing it swimming with cop cars, blue lights on full whack, the peaceful place far from peaceful. Brad's had his mobile in his hand the whole journey, spinning it, tapping it on the wheel, constantly locking and loading his thumb ready to push down on Danny's number but thinking better of it each time.

I seriously do not envy him.

Brad pulls over, and we slowly get out, taking in the scene as we do before meeting at the front of the car, bracing ourselves. We walk side by side over to Higham, passing through a dozen or so cops, all of whom eye us warily or with looks of derision. We ignore them all. I bet their hands are twitching to reach for their cuffs. Even their guns.

With that thought, I stand taller, knowing a slight slump will have the Heckler tucked into the waist of my jeans protruding. I look out the corner of my eye seeing Brad is obviously having the same thoughts I am. Any one of these arseholes could cause us the greatest of inconvenience if they decide they'd like to go on a power trip. And any one of them could be bent. I cast my eye over each and every one. We know for a fact The Bear had men on the inside. Beau's uncle Dexter being one, the two cops that stopped Nathan Butler by the side of the road being two others. Spittle. All now dead. But are there more?

"Gentlemen," Higham says, his arm held out to the empty hole in the ground. His tone is grave. He understands the ramifications of this situation. A very angry Brit on the loose.

"Jesus fucking Christ," Brad breathes on the edge of the grave, looking down at the dirt. I join him, feeling his grief. I didn't know Brad's uncle and Danny's father, he died three years before I dragged Danny from the dead to fight this war with me, but I know Danny loved the barbaric fucker with everything he had. Carlo Black took Danny in off the streets. Raised him as his own. Taught him everything he knows, which is why Danny Black has the deadly reputation he has. This is not going to end well.

I see forensic investigators poking around in the dirt. "Anything?" I ask, circling the grave.

"Nothing."

"Do we know when this happened?"

One of the investigators looks up at me, pulling down her facemask. "The temperature of the unearthed soil indicates very recently. It's still cool, the height of today's sun not yet reaching it. So, yes, within the past twelve hours."

"Cameras anywhere?" Brad asks, and I look at him tiredly. "What?"

"God's the camera, Brad. I'm pretty sure most dead people rely on him to watch over them."

"Well, he's not doing a very good job, is he? You can cremate my ass when I'm gone. Burn me until I'm ash and throw m—"

I flinch, closing my eyes.

"Fuck, man," Brad says quietly. "I'm . . . fuck."

"It's nothing." I shake my head clear, pushing back the memories. The sounds of my family's screams. The sight of the roaring fire.

I find Higham, who's noting a few things down on his pad. "Does Danny know?" he asks.

Brad shows him his mobile. "I'm bracing myself. You should too."

Higham laughs lightly, but it is a laugh of complete despair. "Oh, I am." He holds something up. A ring.

"What?" Brad breathes, taking the gold and emerald piece from Higham.

"Is that a snake?" I ask.

"Yeah, it's a snake." He pockets the ring and wanders off, dialing, and Higham comes to me on the other side of the empty grave. "Any ideas?" he asks, tucking his pad away.

"A few."

"Care to share?"

I look at him seriously. "That would make me an informant."

"You owe me."

"Yeah, you never did explain why you overruled Burrows and let me walk free without question."

"An anonymous tip-off wasn't quite enough on this occasion."

"He was tipped off? Tipped off that I killed Frank Spittle?"

"Yes, like I said, it wasn't enough given the circumstances."

"Circumstances?"

"Well, lack of evidence aside *and* the fact you're dating Burrows's ex-fiancée so it was obviously personal, unbelievably, you and The Brit are the lesser of two evils."

Dating? Fucking *dating*? "Lesser of two evils," I muse. Interesting. "How'd you reach that conclusion?"

Higham motions to the other side of the graveyard, an indication to walk with him, away from the listening ears of the other cops. I catch Brad's eye. He shakes his head and mouths *"not picking up."*

"You have time to change your pants then," I call, earning myself the middle finger. I walk on with Higham. "So, the lesser of two evils." I'm insulted, to be honest.

"Don't misunderstand me, James. Most of the Miami Police Department and FBI know you two foreigners are the most dangerous men in America. I know one of you killed Spittle, we just can't prove who."

I ignore most of his statement. Truth be told, if Danny hadn't decapitated Spittle, I would have. "You telling us to fuck off back to our own country?" I ask.

He laughs. "I know your citizenship is fake."

"Prove it."

He waves a dismissive hand. "I've got bigger fish to fry."

"Like sharks?" I ask, cocking my head, getting another laugh.

"Yes, like sharks. What do you know about sharks?"

"I know sharks don't last long out of water, so if I find one knocking around the streets of Miami, I'll make sure it finds its way back into the ocean." I smile at Higham, and he deflates.

"Let me have The Shark."

"What shark?"

"For fuck's sake," he says on a sigh. "James, you and Danny want The Bear for personal reasons. You're popping off fucking animals left and right. Let's start with the Irish—The Snake, The Eagle, The Crocodile."

"It was The Alligator," I say. "Vince Roake was The Alligator, and he was set to take over the Irish drugs ring. Whoever killed him did you a favor."

His eyebrows are so high he's got a new hairline. "You made a real fucking mess of that club."

"They did?"

"Fuck me," he sighs, losing his patience, but what the fuck does he expect from me? Confessions written in blood? "The Dodo?" he asks. "He was set to take over from Roake but conveniently disappeared."

I look out the corner of my eye. Higham would throw up if he had the gory details of The Dodo's death. "I know nothing about any Dodo," I say casually. "And aren't they supposed to be extinct?" I smile on the inside, seeing all of us laughing our arses off at the boatyard after the poor Dodo's grisly end.

"So who's fronting the Irish now?"

"Your guess is as good as mine. No one's heard anything. In fact, Higham, Miami is scarily quiet."

"Who was in the Escalade that blew up on a side street not long after I let you walk out of custody?"

Oh? So they couldn't identify him? "I don't know what you're talking about."

"Of course you don't."

"Look, Higham," I say, getting tired of the interrogation. "You and I know the best chance the FBI has of getting rid of the scum crawling around Miami is me and Danny."

"Yes, and the problem with that, James, is that you and Danny have collectively killed more people than *all* the inmates of Florida State Prison put together."

"Oh, now, come on, Higham, that's giving us a little bit too much credit."

"Fuck me, you're an arrogant cunt."

"Watch it, Higham," I warn lowly, and he breathes in deeply, nodding to himself, as if coming to terms with what we both know he needs to do.

"You've gotta leave a few for us to put on trial, James."

My lip curls. "The lethal injection isn't slow enough for me, Higham."

"I will stop breathing down your neck. No raids on the club, the boatyard, nothing."

"You planning on raiding?"

"Not me, but you can bet your bottom dollar someone is."

"Are you trying to crawl into my pocket, Higham?" I ask, wanting to hear it.

"I want the war in Miami to stop. We have to get crime rates down, and that's not going to happen with the Russians, Polish, and Irish in town. Or you two, for that matter. You're like a magnet for trouble."

"Let's simplify this, Higham," I say tiredly. "With The Bear gone and us in Miami, your crime rates are gonna drop tenfold, trust me." I pout. "They just might peak beforehand, but it's got to get worse before it gets better, right?"

"Jesus."

"We're not traffickers, Higham. Not drug dealers or rapists or bank robbers. The people dying around you deserve to die." I shrug. "Or so I've heard."

"This really is personal, isn't it?"

"It couldn't get more personal if it tried." I back away, nodding my respect, because, actually, I do have some for Higham. "We need to find Carlo Black's body or there will never be peace in Miami."

His cheeks puff out, and he starts waving his arms above his head, barking orders to his men. I head over to Brad. "Any luck?"

"Still no answer." He looks as concerned as I am starting to feel. The news we have is not the kind of news we should break if Danny's unwell wife has taken a turn.

We start heading toward the car, and just as I drop into the passenger seat, about to call Beau and check in, Brad's mobile rings. He slumps back in his seat and takes a deep breath. I'm not going to lie, I take one too.

"Everything all right?" he says in answer, switching it to the car's Bluetooth.

"Yeah, fine." Danny sounds as cautious as he should. "I'll ask *you* that question. Eight missed calls in ten minutes? What's going on?"

Brad looks across the car to me. I have nothing for him. No advice, no encouragement. It is what it is, and it is going to cause fucking anarchy. Brad takes a hand to his forehead and smooths over his damp brow. "We have an issue," he says, staring out of the windscreen to the swarm of cops around Carlo Black's empty grave.

"What?" Danny's tone says it all. He already knows whatever he's about to learn will send him into orbit.

Brad needs to just spit it out, not try to sugarcoat it. Nothing could water this down. "Your dad's missing." He flinches, and I look at him like the dickhead he is. "His grave. The body."

"Someone's exhumed your father's body," I say in a matter-of-fact tone that earns me a look of disbelief from Brad.

Silence.

"We're at the graveyard," I go on. "Higham's here, a forensics team, cops."

Silence.

"We'll find him, Danny," Brad says, slumping back in his chair. "And when I find out who's done this, I will cut their flesh away with a blade in wafer thin slices."

I truly believe he will. If Danny doesn't get to them first.

Silence.

Brad and I look at each other, all out of words. I can literally feel Danny's bubbling anger dripping through the line. This is a message, like the call from The Bear, like the newspaper article, to entice us back to Miami. He can't end us if he doesn't know where we are. Now he'll definitely know.

He's in for the win. But does he know that moves like this only drive us harder? Stirs the beasts inside? Shakes up the darkness that's dormant?

I can feel it rousing within me, and it's not even my father's grave. My teeth grit. My father couldn't have a grave. There was nothing left of him. Or my mum. Or my sister. My fist clenches, and I wedge it into the door, pushing my weight through it before I put it through the windscreen.

My phone ringing saves the glass, and I try to clear the rage fogging my sight to focus on the screen. And when I see the number, I exhale slowly. "It's him," I say quietly. "Can you keep your mouth shut or does Brad need to hang up on you?"

Danny snarls in answer, and I go ahead and connect the call.

Silence.

We're back to that game, me waiting, him waiting. I've got all the time in the fucking world. He, however, does not. Not if he doesn't want me to trace him.

"James," he says, the distorter making me wince.

"You have the pleasure of us all. Say hello to Danny and Brad."

"Oh, you shouldn't have all come back on my account."

He doesn't need to know that Danny isn't physically here. Something tells me he will be soon, anyway. "I," Danny hisses, "am going to fucking kill you, and it will be the slowest I have ever killed a man, I promise you."

He laughs, and it's like blades across my skin. "We've already established that none of you are very good at killing me."

"Where the fuck is my father's body!" Danny bellows, losing his shit.

The Bear laughs harder, tormenting us all. "Oh, your father's? My apologies. I thought you were looking for someone else's remains." He hangs up, and Brad looks at me, confused.

But I am far from confused.

What. The. Fuck?

"Beau," I say quietly.

"Fucking hell," Brad whispers.

"No," Danny says, and I hear his deep inhale, along with Brad's low curse.

I stare out of the window, my brain on the drag, my body seeming to fail me, nothing working, my mind refusing to give my hands the directions they need to call her.

"James!" Brad yells, and I look at him. "Wake up, man."

I blink down at my mobile. I don't dial Beau. I dial Fury instead, and he answers swiftly. "Where are you. Exactly?"

"Ten paces behind Beau. Walking into the churchyard."

"Stop her," I order, as Brad starts the car and skids off. "I don't care how you do it, force if necessary, but do not let her get any closer."

"Got it."

"Keep her safe, Fury. I'm on my way."

I drop my phone into my lap and scrub down my face.

It couldn't get any more personal.

Famous fucking last words.

8

BEAU

"Roger that," I hear Fury say from behind me, and I turn back as I get to the old, dilapidated gate, my hand on the catch.

"Everything okay?" I ask, seeing his pace increase, like he's hurrying to me.

"I'm sorry," he says, and I frown, wondering what he's got to be sorry for.

"What did you do?"

He doesn't answer but instead dips too stealthily for a giant Viking and flips me onto his shoulder like I'm a feather. "Whoa, Fury!" I yell, my world spinning as he whirls around and marches back toward the car. "What the hell are you doing?"

"Force if necessary," he says, as I bounce up and down in time to his long strides. His answer fills me with dread, because those instructions will have come from James, and James would never tell Fury to use force without good cause. Which means he knew I would fight Fury with either speed or agility. "What's going on?"

"I do as I am ordered, Beau. You know that. I have been told to stop you entering the churchyard, so I'm assuming there's danger in the churchyard."

I wedge my hands into his wide lower back and push into them, looking up to the church, scanning the space, looking for the danger. I don't see a thing. But one thing I have learned, both as a cop and as James's girlfriend, you don't need to see danger for it to be there. I also said I would behave. He will ship me back to St. Lucia faster than I can disarm him if I do not play by his rules. "You can put me down, Fury," I say, wriggling. "I promise I won't go anywhere." He laughs, although I don't hear it, more feel it rumbling through his big body. "If I wanted to get down, I'd pull your gun from your pants and aim it at your ass." Suddenly, a gun appears to my side, Fury waving it to show me where it is. In his hand. I narrow my eyes and reach behind me, slipping my hand under my T-shirt. No gun. "You took my gun?" His other hand appears, and in it is my pistol looking like a toy in Fury's huge, rough spade of a hand.

"I bet you love how I know you so well," he says, grunting each word with each step.

"Thrilled," I murmur, relaxing, residing myself to the fact that I am going nowhere.

When we make it back to the car, Fury doesn't bundle me into the back, but instead rests his ass on the hood, getting comfortable.

"We're not leaving?" I ask.

"No."

"Why?"

"Because I have been told he will be here soon." He locks down his arms more, as if he thinks that news might have me putting up a fight. It won't. I'm just plain confused.

"How long will he be?" I ask, wondering how long I have to wait here draped over Fury's shoulder. Luckily, it's a big shoulder, padded with plenty of muscle and perhaps a little fat too. Fury doesn't answer, telling me he doesn't know. "Great." I sigh, trying to push some loose strands of hair from my face and failing, so I give up, and a good ten minutes of silence passes. Silence and no apparent danger. I can't complain. James is being super vigilant, and I have to accept that.

"Tell me about yourself," I say. Fury's been my shadow for weeks on and off, and all I know is that he's a twin, a tower of a man, with fists like boulders and a beard Santa Claus would be envious of.

"What do you want to know?"

I blow out my cheeks, exasperated. Let's start with something easy. "How old are you?"

"Twenty-nine."

"Who's eldest, you or Tank?"

"Tank. By two minutes."

"And your real names?"

"Tank and Fury."

My shoulders drop. "Come on."

"It's Tank and Fury."

"Fine. Parents?"

"Our father is dead and our mother is in a residential home." He says it with no emotion whatsoever.

"I'm sorry to hear that. May I ask if your mom is okay?"

"She has dementia. Late stages. Some days she recognizes us, others she doesn't."

I wince. "I'm so sorry."

"It's life."

"And your father?" I ask, more curious than I should be.

"Murdered."

I balk at the shiny paintwork of the hood. Again, there was no emotion in there. None at all. "I'm so—"

"Don't say you're sorry," he grunts. "Justice was served."

I press my lips together, knowing that justice did not come from a judge. "By you?" I ask.

"By Tank."

"How?"

He laughs a little, and I roll my eyes. He thinks I'm thirsty for blood. Worryingly, he might be right. "He took off his head with a sword."

"Oh. Prison?"

"Yes. But not for that."

"And you?"

He sighs. "If Tank sleeps, I sleep. If he eats, I eat. If he laughs, I laugh. If he goes to prison, I go to prison."

I smile. "It's cute how close you are."

"We're twins, Beau. We have no choice."

"Stop playing it down. You couldn't live without each other." I poke him in the back. "You don't have to be all macho with me."

"Could say the same for you."

"What do you mean?"

"I mean, stop trying to prove to the world, and more importantly to James, that you're always a-fucking-okay."

I pout. "I *am* okay."

"You're full of shit, Beau," he grunts. "Full of fucking shit."

Recoiling, I wonder if he is right. Of course he's right. Peace is a seesaw. Up and down. Glimmers here and there, threatening to complete me and give me that elusive eternal serenity. I'm a fraud, more to myself than anyone else. Even when I thought the root of my darkness was gone, there was something else to bring me back down to earth. Something else to channel my misery into. *A miscarriage.* "I'm just trying to—"

"Make James feel better? It ain't working, Beau. You're fooling no one but yourself."

"When did this turn into a therapy session?"

"When you tried to make it about me."

I frown. "What do you think Rose is having?" I blurt, the question coming from leftfield. "Could you imagine twins?"

He laughs, jolting me, and then stops abruptly. "No. I think one baby will cause enough stress, don't you?"

"Boy or girl?" I can't explain my curiosity. Part of me wonders is it's something innate that's guiding me. A maternal instinct that's been unearthed and needs sating. Rose is my only outlet. Until, perhaps, she's not. We're nearly twelve hours into today and my period hasn't come. Will it? A weird flutter happens in my stomach, and I smile to myself.

"Boy," Fury says, disturbing my thoughts.

"Do you? Why?"

"I don't know, Beau," he says, exasperated. "I just do." He rises to his full, towering height and turns toward the sound of a car coming down the track. "They're here."

"They?" I ask, pushing my palms into his back and craning my neck, blowing the hair out of my face. "James and who?"

"Brad." He finally bends and lowers me to my feet, and my stomach flips as a result. "Do not move."

"Where will I go?" I ask, helping myself to my gun from his hold and slipping it into the back of my sweatpants. It's disconcerting that he knows me so well. "It was nice getting to know you." I smile sweetly at Fury, and he bumps me lightly in the bicep with one of his boulder fists.

"I'd say the same, but I already knew you."

"Smart-ass," I mutter, going toward the Mercedes that's driving with a bit too much urgency for my liking. What the hell is going on? We've been back in Miami mere hours. What could have happened already?

The car skids to a stop and both Brad and James dive out, both looking at my composed form with a mixture of concern and hesitance. "What?" I ask. "Will someone please tell me what the hell is going on? I just want to visit my mother's gra—" I suck back air, homing in on James's face. I hate his grieved expression. Hate it. Fury stopped me going to my mother's grave. Why?

Panic crawls into my throat and clogs it. I can see James's intention to get to me. To stop me. Can feel Fury behind me moving in, ready to grab me.

No.

I kick my flip-flops off and bolt to my right, the nastiest feeling rooting itself deep in my gut, speaking to me, telling me to get to Mom.

"Beau!" James yells. "For fuck's sake, Beau, stop!" His boots hitting the ground behind me shake the earth, his bellows constant, begging for me to stop. I make it to the gate, and it takes me way too long fiddling with the latch to release it.

"Come on!" I shout, yanking at the stupid old, rusty thing. It doesn't want me to go and farther either. I don't listen. "Open!"

"Beau!"

I look back, seeing James getting closer, his tall, powerful body sprinting, his face straining. I have seconds. Maybe three. I give up on the latch and take hold of the iron gate, getting some leverage and throwing my legs over.

"God damn it, Beau, please!"

I feel his hand brush my arm as I break out into a sprint across the uneven grass, taking the shortcut across the graveyard, right over the graves and mounds, rather than wasting time circling the edge. I can't hear him coming anymore. Can't hear his yells or feel the impact of his boots hitting the ground. But I keep going, trying to focus on the far corner where what remained of Mom rests, but being unable to because of my jumping vision. I look back. James has stopped chasing me. He's just past the gate, and I slow when I register the look of defeat and absolute agony on his face.

Because he can see what my eyes are failing to let me see. Because he's standing still. Steady.

I breathe in and turn toward Mom's grave, breathless, sweating, my muscles aching. Something's different, the shape, the layout, there's something not right. And then I realize.

"No," I breathe, stepping forward, my eyes unable to comprehend what they're looking at. A pile of dirt. A pile of dirt by Mom's grave. I shake my head, refusing to believe it, as I walk forward, my stare unmoving, until I see a hole in the ground. "No." It gets bigger as I get closer, deeper, until I'm standing on the edge looking into a dark, black pit of nothing.

It's exactly how my soul feels now. "No!" I scream, dropping to my knees, my palms slapping the ground hard. Fat teardrops fall, drenching the mud, my hair sticking to my face, my heart cracking. "Why?" I screech, throwing my head back, screaming to the sky. "Why, why, why, why!"

I suddenly can't move, can't breathe, as James seizes me in his arms and hauls me up, and I fight him with all I have. Problem is, I have nothing in this moment. Empty. Broken. Back to square one. My sanctuary has been destroyed. My calm place robbed from me. It was the only thing I had. Mom never wanted to be cremated, so I buried what was left of her. A few ashes and her invisible spirit.

I want to crawl into that hole and die.

I'm carried to the car and James slides onto the back seat with me cradled in his lap, holding me tightly, never letting me go.

I clench his T-shirt in my balled fists, burying my face in his chest, my body wracked with sobs. I can hardly draw breath. Can't swallow. "Why?" I croak, pushing myself deeper into his chest. He says nothing.

He knows why.

Because of him.

9

DANNY

The next morning, I'm onboard my jet on my way back to Miami far sooner than I expected *or* wanted.

With my wife.

On top of the untamable rage simmering, ready to boil over and erupt, is my untamable worry. I can hand on heart say I have never been so stressed. Rose protested, of course she protested, when I told her I was returning to Miami. She saw the monster inside rousing, but she didn't know why. I spat it all out while shaking uncontrollably. Worst thing I could have done. She got out of bed and dressed, then packed *both* our cases. I didn't stop her. Was incapable. She looked as determined to come as I felt determined to kill, and manhandling Rose is out of the question right now. So is arguing with her. I didn't want to bring her. I also didn't want to leave her behind, especially on bad terms. Rose doesn't want to be in Miami. She doesn't want to leave Daniel behind. That fucker The Bear didn't take my father from this life. Beau will be inconsolable. She'll need Rose. And Rose can see the unbridled rage inside me. She's my calm. I'm going to need that. *Fuck.*

I see Ringo on the steps of the mansion as we're crawling down the driveway, his tall, sturdy body static and oozing menace. It reminds me that I am not the only one who loved and respected Carlo Black. Fucking hell, The Bear's move isn't only the lowest of the low, it's the most hard-hitting message that could be delivered, and meant to be.

No move is too low.

I pull to a stop and look up at my rearview mirror to Doc in the back. He looks as impeccable as ever, his tweed suit pristine, his gray beard freshly trimmed. "Take her to our room and get her settled," I say, and he nods, getting out and rounding the car. I can feel Rose's eyes on me.

"Call me anything but my name again, Danny . . ."

I close my eyes, hearing Doc open her door, and she gets out, leaving me behind the wheel once again trying to get my head on straight. It feels like it's constantly spinning on my shoulders.

On a deep breath, I get out and follow Rose into the house, Ringo flanking me. He doesn't speak. I come to a stop at the bottom of the large sweeping staircase, watching her climb the steps. She's wearing jeans and my favorite jumper with the Union Jack emblazoned across the front, her dark hair tied up in a ponytail. I'm momentarily taken back to three years ago, when I watched her walk down these steps before I took her to the boatyard for the first time. To the time she was my prisoner. My bargaining chip. Love fucked me over then. And it's fucking me over now, because I will not make one move without first considering Rose. And that hampers me. She's my Achilles heel. And I love her as passionately as I hate bringing her back to war. I hate that I yelled at her, suggesting she was never happy.

What do I bring to this relationship? I make your life even more diffi-cult. Cost you money, time, stress, and what do you get in return?

I hate that she doubts herself. Doubts how precious she is to me. She brings everything I never thought I'd have to my life. Love. Acceptance. Purpose. How can she not see that?

"Danny?"

I blink and see Rose disappear at the top of the stairs and turn to face Ringo. He's motioning toward my office down the hall. "Talk," I say as we walk side by side.

"James is upstairs with Beau."

"How is she?"

"I don't believe there's an adequate word."

I inhale, knowing that to be true. There's not an adequate word for my anger either. "And James?" He'll be in my camp. Ready to go psycho. All we both fucking want is peace. Calm. Not just for our women, but for us, and every time we think it's ours, the rug is pulled from under us. We both accepted getting out of this world was impossible. That we'll always need to rule it and eliminate all enemies. Easier said than done when you don't know who the enemy is. And on top of that, Tom Hayley is running for mayor and, fuck knows, he hates us and is likely to make our lives as difficult as possible. Or even more so.

"Don't ask," Ringo sighs, opening the door to my office. I stand on the threshold for a few moments, as ever having to brace myself to enter. It still smells of him. Like brandy and cigars are embedded into the walls. Today it smells more intense.

Goldie and Otto are on the couch, and Brad is walking in circles. Our eyes meet, and he shakes his head mildly. "Things are about to get very messy," I say, striding to my desk, laughing to myself. Whenever have things been clean in my world? "If you're not up for messy, you can leave now." I take a seat and cast my eyes across the office to the unmoving bodies of my closest, lacing my fingers and taking them to the back of my head, stretching. It's an impulsive move, as if I'm widening my chest, giving my pounding heart more room to beat. The pain from my slashing mission has lessened, a deeper, more potent pain replacing it. Brad reaches into his pocket and comes to me, setting something on the desk before me. Green eyes stare back at me, dulled by mud.

My throat begins to close as I snatch it up and put it in my top drawer, slamming it shut. "Are we waiting for James?"

"He won't leave Beau," Goldie says, her face a picture of disquiet. She knows what James is capable of. Add Beau's hurt and grief into that mix? Between James and me, we're all in for one hell of a showdown.

"Someone get Higham to the club later," I say, standing, needing to keep moving or risk imploding. Ringo goes straight to his mobile. "How's the boatyard?"

"Ticking over nicely," Otto says. "Liam and Jerry need a raise."

He's right. They do a grand job between them. "Fine," I mutter. "The club?"

"All good," Brad chimes in, and I look at him. Vague, to say the least.

"You sure?"

"I'm sure."

He's not sure at all, but I know Brad better than anyone, and this stance he's taking is familiar. Whatever it is, it's trivial, and he won't bother me with trivial, especially now. And that's fine by me. "The shipment?"

"It's sorted," Brad practically sings.

"What the fuck is going on?" I ask.

"Nothing," he protests, a little high-pitched. "Nothing is going on."

"Talk," I order. "Give me another problem, Brad, because it's taking everything in me not to leave this house with a machine gun in each hand and shoot my way through Miami until I find him."

"We're exchanging earlier with Luis."

I frown, and Otto, Ringo and Goldie all look at Brad like he's lost his mind. "Why?"

"The cash arrived at Hiatus."

"He paid early?"

Brad nods.

The fuckers. No one settles before they get all the goods. They've backed us into a fucking corner.

"James spoke to Chaka," Brad continues. "He's meeting the original delivery date of a week this Friday."

"And then we exchange with the Mexicans the next day?" I ask. "Need I remind anyone that the next day is a Saturday? We generally avoid Saturdays because they fall on a fucking weekend. And correct me if I'm wrong, but I'm pretty certain Chaka said there's a Coast Guard training day that Friday."

Brad shrugs. "James is dealing with it."

I doubt James is capable of dealing with anything right now. I'm mad, yes, but this rage would be so much worse if the casualty of this fucked-up mess was Rose. "So we need James," I say, just as the door opens and the man himself appears.

"You have him." He heads to a chair opposite my desk and drops into it. Everyone's eyes follow him there, everyone silent. So silent, I can hear the burning of the blood in his veins. "Talk," he orders.

I flick my eyes to Otto and Goldie, who look grave. So fucking grave. "The guns," I say with an edge of caution.

"Chaka's delivering as originally planned so we can exchange earlier with the Mexicans."

"Okay," I say slowly. "Wanna give me a bit more than that?"

"Turf war across the border. Luis is running out of time and arms."

"Okay. So we risk our business to save his?"

His eyes turn slowly onto me. "You want the Mexicans on the list of men we need to kill, because I think there's enough on our list at the moment."

I've got to give him that. And now I have been suitably distracted from my anger for a few moments to deal with regular business, I suppose we need to get back to the reason why I'm standing here fighting to control my rage and James is sitting there looking like the devil has been resurrected and is using his body as a carrier.

I've said many times, but I don't think I've ever meant it as sincerely.

God help Miami.

"How is she?" I ask, making him lift his eyes but not his head, as his thumbs circle fast. He's keeping his hands busy.

"Silent. Vacant. Broken once again."

Which means The Enigma is taking over. "And you?"

"How are *you*?" he fires back.

"On the edge."

"I'm with you." He gets up and goes to the cabinet, pouring a vodka. "There wasn't much left of Jaz Hayley," he says, necking his drink. "More than my family, mind you, but still." His back rolls, a sign of him trying to keep his cool. "He hasn't stolen a body, he's stolen a slice of Beau's peace. I need to get her peace back." He pours another vodka and faces me. "So where do we start?"

He wants to get this show on the road, as do I, but first I think we need a little of something else. "Ride on the water?" I ask as he necks his second and sets his glass down, ready to pour another. Fuck knows, we both need to chill the fuck out before we wreak havoc. Alcohol isn't the answer. Getting shitfaced isn't the answer. Especially now we're back in Miami. *Vulnerable.* Look at me being wise. And it occurs to me in this moment, I have never in the time I've known James Kelly, and granted it hasn't been all that long, seen him drunk. Has he ever been drunk? Probably not. He's too controlled. Even when he's raging, he seems in control.

He sets the bottle down, not pouring another, and that's his answer. And I turn to the others and see all hands in the air. We all need a moment.

"Meet you at the boatyard in a few hours," I say, leaving the office, on my way to try and sort something that will undoubtedly make the need for the sea, the air, the thrill, more acute.

"Danny," Otto calls after me, and I stop just shy of the stairs, looking back. "Your mum."

"What about her?" I ask flatly.

"She didn't come with you." He states it as a fact rather than asking it as a question.

"No, she didn't come with me." *And if you question me, I'll fly off the fucking handle.* Mum needed to stay behind with Tank and look after Daniel. It's one less thing for me to worry about.

I take the stairs and walk the corridor to our room, entering and finding it empty. I inhale, gathering patience, stepping back into the corridor and looking toward the endless doors to various rooms, all rooms taken up by various *guests*. "Hotel Casa Black," I mutter, going to the first and swinging the door open. No Rose. The next. No Rose. I barge into James and Beau's room carelessly, my patience gone, along with my memory, it seems. I see Beau curled up in bed, Rose spooning her from behind, cuddling her.

Fuck.

I swallow down my intended bellow of her name and meet her blue eyes, seeing a sadness for her friend so potent, it crushes me. Truly crushes me. I'm plain fucking raging. Beau is plain fucking devastated. Two wildly different emotions. They took my father from his resting place to push me into action. It's low, but taking Beau's mother to push James into action? That's just plain fucking cruel, and they will pay for it.

I enter and close the door quietly, unable to reprimand Rose for not being in our room resting like she should be. Walking over to the bed, I crouch down in front of Beau. Her glassy eyes look straight through me. Wisps of her blonde hair are stuck to her cheeks, her lips dry, her usually peachy cream skin sallow. Empty. Fuck me, hasn't this woman been through enough? Haven't we all?

I reach for her face and stroke across her skin, dropping to my knees and wrapping my big hand around one of Rose's that's clenching onto one of Beau's. "We'll get her back for you, Beau, I swear," I whisper, dipping and kissing her cheek. "Are you hearing me?"

She doesn't even blink. I can't even be sure she's heard my vow. I have my own personal drive, but seeing Beau like this, the hardy former cop, the fierce warrior, so fucking hollow, is driving me harder. I heard of the darkness she was immersed in when she met James. I've seen glimmers of it creeping back into her, but she's always fought it with everything she has. Now? She's a shell.

I hear the door open behind me, and I look back, seeing James on the threshold. I can't comprehend how he's feeling seeing her like this, and I wince at the thought of seeing Rose's eyes so completely dead. We've had our moments over the years, yes, but

Beau truly looks like she has departed from this world, despite still breathing.

I stand as Rose starts to unwrap herself from Beau, climbing up off the bed. I take her hand and lead her out, leaving James and Beau alone.

"Fuck," I breathe as I walk us to our room, running a hand through my hair. I get us inside, close the door, and immediately pick Rose up, ignoring the returned pain on my chest, carrying her to the bed and laying her down. I just need to cuddle her. Be close to her. I can't imagine feeling as helpless as James does right now, and I hope I never do. Loving Rose has made me weak and vulnerable. Something I swore I'd never be.

"I hate you," I whisper, feeling her hands all over my back, stroking me everywhere. "I hate you so fucking much. I don't know what I'd do without you, Rose." I lift my face. She's crying. "Don't cry, baby," I say softly, wiping away her tears. "It doesn't suit you." These tears aren't for her. For us. These are for her friend, but it hurts me no less. "She'll be okay," I say, sure of it. We're all here for her. "We will find her mum, Rose, I promise." I wince to myself. There doesn't sound like there's much to find.

She smiles through her sadness and strokes my rough cheek, and I nuzzle into her touch. "I know you will," she says resolutely. "And your pops."

I nod, swallowing, needing this moment, so I force the rising anger back. "God, how I wish I could be inside you right now." I need it. Need her. Need to stabilize and reconnect. Remind myself of what I have to fight for. But I can't. Take it easy, Doc said. Don't stress out. She didn't have nearly enough bedrest. I bury my face in her neck and lick her, my tongue not getting the message that sex is off the menu for now.

She moans, doing me no favors, and yet I continue licking, biting, sucking at her flesh. Another moan, and I feel blood rushing to where it should not be rushing. But, fuck, can I stop? I lift my hips, giving my growing cock some space, but . . . my jeans.

"Rose," I growl, moving my mouth across her cheek to her lips. "Stop me," I order. "Before I go too far."

Her hands find my hair, gripping, her tongue finds my mouth, twirling. We both need this. And we can't fucking have it. *Fuck.* I rip my mouth from hers, breathing down on her raggedly, as she pants up at me. I slowly start to shake my head, my hard-on throbbing. "We can't." I won't risk it. Never.

"But . . ." she says, taking my hand and guiding it to her jean-covered pussy. "Your mouth here. Gentle. Licking. Kissing. Sucking." She bites her lip, and I'm a goner.

I groan and push myself up, taking her jumper and lifting it over her head, tossing it aside, and then working the fly of her jeans and dragging them down her legs. She kicks her legs, helping me, sitting up and taking the bottom of my T-shirt, pulling it up over my head. I grit my teeth when I stretch the skin on my chest, breathing in deeply, exhaling slowly. My jeans are next, and I roll to my back, lifting my arse, wriggling free of them.

Desperate.

Both of us.

I remove my boxers, pull her knickers down, and ease myself down onto my front, burying my face between her thighs, ravenous. Her yelp of surprised pleasure echoes around the room, as does my groan of satisfaction, my senses getting a hit of her scent, the taste of her, the warmth. "You." *Lick.* "Taste." *Suck.* "So." *Bite.* "Good."

"Fucking hell," she breathes, her legs stiffening, her hands clawing my hair.

"Good?"

"God."

"Yes?"

"God!" she screams, vibrating already, her legs kicking out, forcing me to shift and pin her down. "No!" She bucks, and I immediately pull away, dazed, her essence coating my mouth.

"What?" *Shit.* "Did I hurt you?" Fuck, is she thinking about the other day? When I was crazed? It won't ever happen again, I know it, but how do I convince Rose?

"No, baby," she whispers, pushing into my shoulders, sending me to my back. "I want to see you." She looks down at the bandages on my chest. Swallows. Then takes my hand and guides it to my cock, straddling my thighs, sliding her hand down her swollen tummy to her pussy.

"Oh, fuck," I breathe, circling my girth, holding my breath. Nothing could ever beat being inside her. Nothing. But this? I blow out my cheeks, reaching for her bra and pulling the lace cups down, my eyes passing between her hard nipples. Darker nipples. Rounder, bigger nipples. I drop my dick and sit up, snaking an arm around her back and taking one in my mouth, sucking gently, kissing, then tracing the edge with my tongue as I look up at her. She's getting more beautiful by the day. Tastier. Sassier. I rest my hand over hers as she strokes herself, helping her, continuing my tongues assault on her boob, moving to the other, some attention there, back again.

"Enough." She withdraws and pushes me back down to the bed, and I arch an eyebrow as she reaches for my hand once again and puts it where she wants it.

"You want to watch?" I ask, wrapping my palm around myself.

She bites her lip and brings her fingers to her mouth, licking them. *Fuck. Me.* Then walks them slowly down between her boobs, across her stomach, and into her wetness, her breath hitching. I swallow, take one arm above my head, and start thrusting my hand, my eyes unmoving from the juncture of her thighs, watching her fingers scissor her clit. "Slow down," I order, and she does, whimpering, as I speed up my pace, the throb of my cock sinking into my palm. "Shit, Rose," I breathe, my lungs straining, my thrusts naturally speeding up. I glance down, seeing the crown of my dick glistening. Blood pounding. Veins throbbing. Heart racing. My eyes drag up her body. I find her lips parted. Eyes glistening. Love emblazoned across her face.

My thrusts speed up. Her back arches, pushing her chest out. Her stomach. Fuck, her stomach. "Rose." I choke over her name, grabbing the pillow under my head, yanking at it.

"Oh," she whispers. "Yes," she breathes. "Shit," she hisses, her body convulsing. Blood. Heat. Stars in my vision.

I clench my eyes closed briefly, my body stiff, as the pleasure creeps through me, slowly at first, painfully slowly, but then faster. Faster. Faster. "Fuck!" I bellow, breathing short, fast breaths, releasing the pillow and slamming my fist into the mattress.

"Oh God!" Her body jacks, her chin dropping to her chest, her hand shaking, struggling to remain between her legs, her hips starting to thrust into her touch.

Urgency.

Desperation.

Need.

"I'm going," I hiss. Fuck, am I going.

"Yes!" Her head tosses back violently, wafting her hair through the air, and she yells to the ceiling, going rigid, stilling, whimpering quietly, before her body loosens and she slumps forward, slapping her palm into my stomach to hold herself up.

I just about manage to hold off my release until she opens her eyes. "Look," I order, and she turns her drowsy gaze down at the moment I explode, cum shooting upwards and hitting her stomach, her chest, her boobs, in powerful surges. And with the explosion of my dick comes the deflation of my chest. I exhale, my body rolling, every muscle stiff, aching, painful.

But it's the best kind of agony out there.

Spent.

I peel my grip away, letting my semi-erect cock fall to my stomach, and let my arms rest above my head, closing my eyes as she lowers onto my front, but she doesn't settle on my wounds. So I force her down. And we lie, quiet, peaceful, exhausted, for over an hour, snoozing, holding each other, reconnecting in another way.

"I will never leave you," she whispers, forcing my arms to come down and hold her. She looks up at me, taking a finger to my scar and tracing the length. "Only death will separate us." Her touch moves to the bullet wound by my collarbone.

"Will it?" I ask.

She blinks slowly and settles back on my chest gently, stroking one of my cuts. "No."

Because we cannot exist without each other. It's a hard fact. A frightening fact. Which means I have no choice but to be careful with my life.

"I should get Doc," I say, making to move.

"Why?" She lifts, giving me a look somewhere between tiredness and humor. "Are you going to have him check me over every time you fuck me?"

"I didn't fuck you," I say, pressing a hard kiss on her lips. It's the only hard thing I can do to her right now. "Your fingers fucked you." Holding her around her back, I pull her stomach onto my mouth and kiss her gently there, smiling at her small bump. It's hope when it feels like it's limited. Happiness when it feels like misery prevails. "Rest," I order, getting up and going to the bathroom, flipping the shower on. "I've worn you out."

"You talk yourself up, Danny Black." I only just hear her pathetic insult over the water. "I did all the work."

I smile into the mirror at myself and pluck my toothbrush from the holder. I can't say I like the man staring back at me today. But he's a much better version than he used to be. Still a killer. But a killer with more purpose. More drive. It's a blessing and a curse, because my drive and purpose are what my enemies will now use against me. I load my brush with paste as I stare at my bandaged chest, and I am reminded that my wife can cause me more damage than my enemies ever can.

I scrub my teeth before I get into the shower and do my best not to get my bandages wet. Impossible. I keep my back to the spray and make fast work of washing before getting out and patting myself dry. I peel away the soggy dressing and grab some fresh bandages, refusing to look at the damage as I wrap myself back up, holding my breath, the biting pain back. I walk into the bedroom, and the post orgasm sparkle in Rose's eyes vanishes the moment she sees my fresh bandages. Which is exactly why I refuse to let her redress my wounds. "Where are you going?" she asks from the bed, where she's curled up on her side, the sheets caught up between her legs.

"I'm taking James to the boatyard. He needs to let off some steam." I pull on some jeans and button the fly before slipping my feet into my boots. "Then we're going to the club to sort some business." I go to her and dip, kissing her forehead. "Text me and let me know what Doc says."

"I'm fine."

"Text me and let me know what Doc says."

"Okay." She exhales over the word. "I will text you and tell you what Doc says."

I wrinkle my nose and rub it against hers, then grab a T-shirt and pull it on as I walk to the door.

"Danny," she calls, making me look back over my shoulder. "I still want to find something to do. A hobby, a job. Something."

Absolutely not. "We'll talk about it tomorrow." I leave the room before she can counter my dismissal, pulling the door closed behind me. I find James waiting outside. He shakes his head, telling me not to ask. So I don't. I don't need to.

He gets moving, and I join him. "Ready to race?" I ask.

He doesn't answer.

He doesn't need to.

10

ROSE

I stay on the bed for another half hour, not physically exhausted, but definitely mentally. You'd think by now, after weeks of constant worry and swaying emotions, my body would be used to it. Accustomed to it. And yet I feel as exhausted now as I did the moment James resurrected Danny after being peacefully dead for three years.

A knock on the door pulls my attention there, and I hear Doc calling through the wood. "One minute," I say, scooting to the edge of the bed and reaching for one of Danny's T-shirts on the chair. I slip it on and rummage through the sheets for my panties. "Damn it, where are they?" I mutter. I give up and rush to the closet to find a fresh pair. "Come in." I climb back into bed and pull the sheets up to my waist.

Doc pokes his head around the door and smiles. "Morning, Rose," he chirps, pushing the door open to make way for the scanning machine to be pushed in by Fury.

"Morning, Doc," I reply, catching Fury's eye. Just the fact he's helping Doc speaks volumes. He's without anything to do because Beau is hiding in her darkness. My heart squeezes.

"How is Beau, Doc?" I ask, making Fury look at the old man too, obviously wanting an answer to that question as well.

He starts fiddling with the machine. "I'll never get used to the fact that patient confidentiality doesn't feature in my life anymore." His words prompt me for the first time to wonder about Doc. I know he was retired. I know he ran his own practice for a long time. I know between Danny and James he now earns more than he probably ever has. But something tells me the money isn't what keeps him here. And, oddly, neither is the possibility of death should he refuse to be on standby for our big, fucked-up family. "She's in a state of heightened grief," Doc says quietly, smiling at me as he gets the machine ready. "She's going to need you, Rose."

I nod and settle, and Fury leaves us, letting Doc do his thing or, more to the point, Danny's thing, while I wonder what I could possibly do to help Beau. I come up with nothing, and that just makes me feel like a shitty friend. I know how desperately I want her to find and keep her peace; the blows just keep coming and coming for her, so I can only imagine the level of desperation James must feel. And hopelessness.

"Everything looks just fine," Doc says, bringing my eyes down to my stomach where he's dragging the probe across my abdomen.

"You may as well leave that machine in here," I say, propping myself up on my elbows to look at the screen. "He'll be ordering another scan tomorrow." I smile at the gray, distorted blob, my mind going to bad, bad places. "Doc?" I ask quietly, making his gray bushy eyebrows rise in question. "Can you see the sex?" I spit out the words quickly and press my lips together.

"Oh." He laughs, and then his face is quickly serious. "No, I cannot."

"You're lying," I counter playfully. "You know, don't you? Come on, Doc, I promise I won't tell." I'm suddenly ravenous to know. Desperate. And yet there's still that side of me that doesn't want to spoil the surprise.

"No." He wipes the probe and slips it back in the holder. "I have paused the screen so that your husband may have a peek at his . . ."

He fades off, looking out the corner of his eye at me. ". . . baby, if he should like."

"Spoilsport," I mutter.

"You and Mr. Black come to me together and make such a request, I will more than happily oblige."

"It's my body."

Doc laughs, pushing the machine to the side of the room. "I don't think Mr. Black will agree. Now, remember what I've told you?"

"Yes, I must take it easy and not stress out." Landing a tried look on him, I sigh. "Did you miss who I'm married to, Doc?"

"I did not, which is why I am passionate about you taking care of yourself and the baby." He presents me with a little bottle. "Lavender oil. Put it in your bath, on your pillow, in your purse if you must. It's soothing, physically and mentally." He sets it on the nightstand.

"Thank you." I fall to my back. "Can I ask you something?"

"No," he says flatly, and I pout.

"You don't know what I'm going to ask."

"Exactly. I have always lived by the rule that if someone asks you if they may ask you something, you either won't like the question or they won't like the answer."

"Oh." I consider his logic for a moment, and I soon think better of asking my question. I can't, however, decide whether Doc would not like me asking him why he's here, or whether I would not like the answer.

"How is your palm?" He cranes his head as he packs his bag, and I turn it over to show him the mild red blemish from my frying pan incident.

"It doesn't hurt."

"And your arm?"

I look at yet another injury on my body. It's nothing compared to Danny's chest. "It's fine."

"And Danny's changing his dressings regularly?"

"Yes," I sigh, knowing why he won't let me do it. "Just now before you got here."

"I'll leave some more waterproof dressings and fresh bandages here." He pops some on the nightstand and collects his bag. "Perhaps you could pop in to see Beau now. I believe Mr. Kelly has left the house with Mr. Black."

I nod and sit up. "Any advice?" I ask.

"Patience." He smiles as he backs out of the door. "Lots of love and patience." He disappears, and I get up, taking a shower and throwing on a loose blush-pink sundress and some flip-flops. I coil my hair into a bun, then I call Esther.

"How's Daniel?" I ask, letting myself out onto the terrace. I cast my eyes around the expansive area, rewinding to three years ago. Three years ago when a missile took the old terrace out with me on it. I flinch, hearing Danny bellowing my name, scrambling to reach me as I dangled precariously off the edge. Scared to let go. But even more scared not to. Because I had fallen in love with the monster who'd taken me, and the repercussions of that were terrifying.

"He's out with Barney and his father again," Esther says, sounding a little flat and short, bringing me back to the present. "They collected him when his tutor left after lunch."

"I'll try his cell," I reply, lowering to a sun lounger and looking across to the tennis courts. "Lawrence?"

"Working."

"Does he know about what's happened? About Beau's mom?"

"Well, I haven't told him," she says, as the sound of crockery clatters in the background. "It's not my place."

"And you? Are you okay?"

"I'm fine."

My head tilts. She doesn't sound fine. "Are you sure?"

"Yes."

"Right," I say slowly. I won't push it. There's little point. I expect it has something to do with Otto being here and Esther being there but, again, I'm not pushing it. "I appreciate you taking care of

Daniel." Esther takes care of everyone. It's second nature to her, but I would hate for her to feel unappreciated.

"He's settled. Best not disrupt him." She's saying out loud what she's told herself endlessly. That this was her decision. We all know better, including Otto, and I can't imagine it went down well with him. "I had better scoot. I have a pie in the oven. I need both hands to get it out."

Or she could switch me to loudspeaker. "Okay. I'll call you tomorrow." I hang up and consider my cell for a few moments. She doesn't want to be in St. Lucia because Otto is no longer in St. Lucia. I never appreciated that Danny was being tactical when he asked Esther to remain behind to look after Daniel so that his studies weren't affected. For me, it was more about safety. My husband, as always, is one step ahead.

I dial Daniel, and it rings and rings and rings and then goes to voicemail. I don't bother leaving one as he won't listen to it, so I text him instead, requesting a call back at his earliest convenience. A small part of me, selfishly, is sad he's too busy with his friend to take my call. A bigger part is relieved he's distracted from the cruel world we live in. God, I miss that boy, even though he doesn't exactly give me much these days. A brief hug. A quick "love ya, Mom" as he dashes out the door. He's smart, and we would be stupid to underestimate him. It's only a matter of time before he figures out what Danny does. Who his family is.

I leave the room, finding it so ridiculous that I take deep breaths between my room and Beau's, bracing myself, nervous to see her. I knock and get no invite to enter, of course, so I let myself in. I find the room shrouded in darkness, the curtains pulled, the lights all off. "Beau?" I call quietly, squinting to try and see her on the bed, the light from the corridor helping. She's curled up on her side, facing away from me, and even though I can't see her face, I can feel her anguish. My heart constricts and I close the door, walking in a straight line to the curtains and tweaking them just a fraction so that a slither of light takes the room from pitch-black to hazy.

I go to the bed and climb in with her, lying opposite, mirroring her pose, my praying hands under my cheek. Her eyes remain closed. Her body still. "I think Otto's pissed off with Esther," I say quietly. "For letting Danny dictate what she would be doing." I get no acknowledgement, and I didn't expect one. "Daniel's out with Barney and his hot father again. He's probably not even noticed I've gone. What do you think about me getting a job?" I ask. "Something part-time. Not too strenuous. Do you think I'll be allowed?"

Her eyelids flicker, and I hold my breath, praying she can bring herself to open them and face me. Face the world. I smile when she eventually reveals glassy blue eyes. "No," she says on a croak, and I pout.

"Do you miss working?"

"All the time," she whispers. "If I was working now, I would be hunting the cunts who have taken my mother. Instead, I have to stand back and let the men around here solve my problems. Problems I wouldn't have if I wasn't here." Her eyes close again, and I flinch, mainly for James, but a little for me too. Our lives aren't conventional. They're tough, draining, emotional. But better than empty, hollow, and dark.

"You sound like you're considering walking away," I say tentatively, certain she would never, but not certain enough. After all, everyone has a breaking point, and as I look at my friend now, my beautiful, resilient, strong former cop friend, I wonder if this is hers.

"I am," she says flatly.

"Beau," I breathe, releasing my hands from under my head and taking one of hers. "Things will be right again."

"Will they?" she asks, looking at me. "Will they really, Rose? Because every time I think I'm in a place of acceptance and semi peace, someone launches a missile that seems to hit one of us in the gut and we're back to square one. Constantly chasing tranquility. Always hoping for calm. Quiet."

This isn't my friend. This . . . negativity. I don't like it on her. We never both seem to be in the same headspace, one of us always holding up the other. "I don't like this version of you," I say without thought.

"This version of me is who I am, Rose. It's who I've been since Mom died. I thought, *hoped*, James was what changed that. I was wrong."

I want to yell at her for being so beaten, but I cannot. I have been there myself many times, but I am certain I have not sounded as resolute as Beau sounds now. I'm worried. This cannot be the end for them. She cannot let them take all hope from inside of her. No. I refuse to allow it. I want to slap the strength back into her. But brute force isn't going to work. I need to be tactical. And perhaps a little sneaky.

God forgive me for this.

"I'll be back, Doc needs to scan me." I get up and go to the door, opening it, finding Fury on the other side. "Will you fetch Doc?" I whisper, making him frown but nod, as I pull the door closed behind me. I go back to our room and push the machine over to the bed, kick my flip-flops off, then climb in, pulling my sundress up to my chest.

Doc walks in with a mighty frown, Fury following. "Pretend to scan me," I order.

"What?"

"Just hold the stick on my tummy." I point to the screen. "Baby, whatever sex it may be, is still on the screen. That'll do."

"I expect there is a method to your madness." He approaches and settles on the edge of the bed, taking the probe to my stomach and resting it there.

"Go tell Beau I need her," I say to Fury, who inhales, seeing where I'm going with this.

"Oh, crafty," Doc says, smiling up at me.

Actually, I'm desperate. I rest my head back on the pillow, breathe in, and only three seconds pass before Beau is at the door, her clothes as crumpled as her hair is messy, her sleepy eyes scanning me, her tear-stained face being roughly wiped with the back of her hand. "What's happened?" she croaks, her voice rough.

I lift a hand and reach for her, silently beckoning her to me, and she comes, of course she comes, carrying her desolate body over and sitting on the bed. She takes my hand and squeezes, looking at Doc as he plays the game with me.

"Just a few more twinges," I say, hating myself for being so manipulative, for using my unborn child as bait, but I reassure myself it's for a good cause.

"Doc?" Beau asks, sniffling and wiping her nose as he concentrates on doing absolutely nothing of any importance. "Is everything okay? Do I need to call Danny?"

"No, no," he says quickly, pressing a button. "It's okay. We're okay. Baby is absolutely fine."

I see Beau physically relax, her hand tightening around mine. I knew she wouldn't let me down. I wish she could be as strong for herself and James as she always seems to be for me.

"Is that a penis?" she asks out of nowhere, leaning into the machine.

"What?" I sit up quickly, making Doc lose his grip on the probe and therefore its place on my stomach. *Shit*. I quickly lie back down and he rushes to replace it before Beau figures out we're big fat frauds. "A penis?" I ask, straining to see the frozen image of my baby.

"Yeah, there." She takes a pointed finger to the screen. "See?"

"No, that's the umbilical cord," Doc says over a laugh. "A bit long for a penis on a sixteen-week pregnancy."

"I don't know why you're laughing," I say. "You've not seen his father's bits."

Doc chokes on nothing, and Beau shoots her eyes to me, shocked. I shrug. And it happens. Her lips twitch, and it is *life*.

"You're terrible," Doc sighs.

"Terribly loose," I mutter, and Beau chuckles. "To be expected, I suppose. This kid is going to fall out of me."

"Rose!" Beau shrieks, falling to the bed beside me. I look at Doc, and he smiles, nodding, telling me it's a job well done, but I'm quickly frowning, and Beau shoots up. "Wait," she says. "Are you saying there is no penis at all?"

My eyebrow lifts, curious for Doc's answer.

"No, Beau, I said it was the umbilical cord, not a penis."

"So there *is* a penis?"

"I . . . it's . . ." He blows out his cheeks.

"You do know what's in there," she says, pointing to the screen.

I love how curious she is. "Tell Beau," I demand, making them both swing stunned looks my way.

"What?" she asks. "No, Rose, you've always said you like the element of surprise."

"I don't want to know," I confirm. "But I want *you* to know."

"You do?"

"Yes, I do."

She bites her lip. "And you don't want me to tell you?"

"Can you manage that?"

"I used to be a cop, Rose," she says, placing her hands over both of my ears and blocking my view to Doc, so that when he tells her if I'm having a boy or a girl, I can't lip-read him. She soon frees my ears, looking at me, her smile wide. I'm not even going to ask. All I care about is that smile on her face. I know it's temporary. This is a brief distraction. But it gives me hope. She's not all out.

"Happy?" I ask.

"Thrilled."

"Good. Now you can teach me how to drive." I pull my dress down and get up.

"What? Where?"

"Around here," I say as Beau's phone starts ringing in the distance. She looks toward the door, and I notice Fury is still on the threshold.

He holds up her cell. "Mr. Hayley."

"I'll call him back."

I'm certain her father has heard what's happened to Beau's mother's remains. She won't want to discuss it, least of all with him, and I don't force it. Because, honestly, I'm relieved. She's up and about. Okay, looking like hell, but at least she's responsive. "Thought you could teach me in Dolly," I say, my steadfast determination never wavering. I know that old, rusty, banging thing brings her peace. Closer to her mother. But she cannot drive it. At least, not outside the grounds of the mansion. No one said anything about inside the grounds. I link arms with her and lead us to her room. "Perhaps wash your face first."

"That bad?" she asks, reaching for her cheeks and wiping.

"Like death on a bad day."

She laughs lightly, coming in closer to me. "I love you, Rose."

And perhaps, I hope, on top of her undying love for James, our friendship is another reason for Beau to stick this out. "I love you too," I whisper.

I chew on the inside of my lip as Beau fiddles under the hood of Dolly, trying to get her started. Her denim shorts are riding up her ass, her long, smooth legs glimmering in the sun. "If I were a man, I'd be wolf-whistling at you right now."

"I think the battery is dead," she says over a laugh, coming up for air, oil smeared across her cheek. She wipes it and considers the engine for a few moments. "Are any of the cars here?"

"There's one out front."

"Wait here," she orders, jogging off. I check my phone, as if I wouldn't hear it if it rang in my hand. Damn that kid. Just a call, that's all I ask. A check in. *Anything.* I exhale and start a slow wander down the pathway, eventually reaching the stream that leads to the pool. I look down into the water at my reflection staring back. My hair falls forward, covering my face. It needs cutting. Maybe I'll book Beau and myself in for a pamper day. I smile at the thought of Fury having a pedicure alongside us. It drops when I consider the fact that despite being unreasonably gorgeous, Beau is also the least girlie girl I know. Not that I know many girls. Still, it isn't about being girlie. It's about rest and relaxation.

Calm.

I shake my head to myself as I pull my hair back and fasten it with a tie. I'm not sure any amount of pampering could rest or relax us. Stress is inbuilt now. We just condition ourselves to handle it.

Soak it up. Or not so, as Doc kindly pointed out. But I must, or the alternative will be Danny caging me.

I hear a car and turn, seeing Beau pulling up with Otto. "What are you doing here?" I ask as I approach and Otto goes to the trunk of Dolly. I thought *all* the men were out on business.

"I needed to pick up something." He appears a few seconds later with some leads of some kind.

"What?" I ask, watching as he flips the hood of the Mercedes and squeezes some metal claw things.

"A few grenades and a harpoon." He bends over the engine, and I roll my eyes as Beau collects the other ends of the leads.

"Then you're in the wrong place. I believe all weapons are now stored in the swanky new bunker buried underground at the boatyard."

He exhales and unbends his body, looking at me tiredly, and I smile sweetly.

"I just spoke to Esther."

His face becomes thunderous, and he goes straight back under the hood.

"Have *you* spoken to her?" I ask.

"Little point, isn't there?"

"Why?" I press. "I thought you two were getting along nicely." Too nicely for Danny.

On an impatient grunt, Otto straightens again. And smacks his head on the underside of the hood. "Fuck!"

I flinch, and Beau flies around, still armed with the claw clips on the cables. "What happened?" she asks.

"Fuck!" Otto yells again.

"Shit!" I rush over as he rubs his head. "Is it bleeding?" I take his hand and check, seeing his palm smeared with blood. "Ouch." I look beneath the hood and spot a catch on the underside. "Of all the places you could hit your head, you hit it on the only spot with a metal catch."

"Rose," he hisses, looking at his bloody palm. "Oh fuck."

"What?" I ask, assessing him. "Shit, Otto, you're pasty white."

Beau drops the cables and hurries over. "Otto?"

"I think I need to sit down," he mumbles, his speech becoming slurred, his eyes starting to roll.

"Oh my God," I cry, as he starts to sway. "He's going to pass out!"

Beau hooks an arm through his on one side, and I take the other, just as Otto becomes a dead weight between us. "Fucking hell," Beau gasps, as we both crumple to the floor under the strain, unable to hold Otto up, not surprising really, since he's probably double our size. "Get Doc," she orders urgently, having me making a mad dash for the house, yelling as I go.

"Doc!" I shriek when I make it into the hallway, out of breath, my throat scratchy. "Doc, where are you?" I run into the kitchen, the TV room. "Doc!" *God damn it.* I pull my phone out and dial Danny, and he answers in just one ring. "Is Doc with you?" I ask urgently.

"No. Why would Doc be with me? I left him at the house to scan you."

"He did scan me, and now—"

"What's wrong? Are you okay? The baby?"

"I'm fine. We're fine, but Otto isn't."

"What?"

"He hit his head and lost consciousness."

"How the fuck did he hit his head?"

"He misjudged how much head height he had." I'm being very sketchy with the truth, but Danny doesn't need details, this is an emergency, and I don't want my plans to learn to drive ended before they've begun.

"Rose?"

I turn around and find Doc at the top of the stairs. "Never mind, I've found him." I hang up and wave my hands frantically. "Otto's hurt," I tell him. "You need your bag."

"My God." He turns to go back to his room. "No rest for the wicked," he grumbles. Never has a statement rang truer.

While Doc is gone, Danny calls me back. I answer and pace. "Never, and I mean never, hang up on me," he warns.

Doc appears, hurrying down the stairs as fast as his old body will allow. "I'm here, I'm coming, I'm armed," he sings.

"I'm sorry." I flank Doc as we rush back out to the gardens. "I've got to go."

"There are so many questions I want answered."

"They'll have to wait." I take my chances and hang up again, needing to brief Doc on what's happened. "He hit his head on the metal catch on the hood of Dolly."

"What?" He looks at me in utter confusion.

"Beau's car. Dolly. Then he passed out."

"I see."

We make it to them, and I'm surprised to see Otto sitting up, his scowl epic. "You came around," I say, as Beau gives me a look that tells me to tread carefully.

"I'm fine," he grunts, trying to get to his feet, wobbling.

"Let us not be smart," Doc says, moving in as Otto gives up and drops like a rock to the ground. He checks Otto's head. "Superficial," he murmurs.

"Superficial?" I blurt. "I saw the blood. Not even any stiches?"

"No." He squeezes a tube of liquid onto Otto's head and starts wiping.

"I don't like blood," Otto grunts, making both Beau and I balk. He's a killer, and he doesn't like blood? "My own blood," he adds quietly, looking up at us moodily. I'm forced to press my lips together, as is Beau, but I quickly look away from her.

Laughing could get us both killed. My cheeks balloon. I snort through my nose. It's no good. I catch Beau's eye and burst into fits of giggles, clenching my belly, my eyes streaming, my breathing ragged. "I'm sorry!" I blurt, hearing Beau snickering too. "I'm so sorry."

Otto mumbles and grunts, shooing Doc's dabbing hand away and forcing himself up to his feet, still a bit wobbly, and stomps off as best as his unstable body will allow. Oh no. "But we need help getting Dolly started," I call, getting a dismissive wave of his hand in return.

"We don't need him," Beau says, chuckling over a few words as she dips and collects the cables, taking them and fixing them to something under the hood of Dolly so both cars are connected by the cables. Then she starts the Mercedes and gets behind the wheel of Dolly. "He'll be back soon, anyway."

"Why?" I ask. He looked about done with us.

"He forgot his car," she says, just as Dolly roars to life and something under the hood of the Mercedes sparks. "Shit," Beau yelps, flying back in her seat.

"What happened?"

She gets out of Dolly and into the Mercedes. "I think I blew the electrics." She looks around the inside of the car. "Nothing's working." She tries to start the engine. Completely dead.

"Well," I chime. "At least Dolly's alive."

"An eye for an eye," Beau says, grinning as she hops out and joins me. "I remember Reg telling me once that you should never jump start an old car with a new, flashy car."

"Who's Reg?"

"An old boy with five teeth who used to rescue me whenever Dolly quit. Reg the Rescue Truck."

Otto stomps back around the corner, his face like thunder, and we both wisely keep our mouths shut and our laughter under control as he yanks the cables out from the Mercedes, tosses them aside, slams the hood down, and throws himself into the driver's seat.

"Does James know you're driving that death trap again?" he asks, a definite curl to his lip.

"I'm not driving it, Otto," Beau retorts, eyebrows high. "Because where the fuck will I go?"

"He's not driving anything either," I whisper, and Beau snorts as Otto flashes another snarl. "God, he's a miserable bastard today." Beau knows as well as I do that James won't give a fuck if she's driving Dolly again. He'll just be glad she's out of bed.

Otto tries to start the Mercedes. Obviously, nothing happens. "God damn it!" He smacks the wheel.

"I think Dolly killed it." Beau rests a delicate hand on Dolly's rusty paintwork, and I'm forced to turn away to hide my tears of laughter. I hear a door slam and the unmistakable pound of Otto's boots stomping away as he yells for Bud at the gate.

"Get in," Beau calls, shuffling across to the passenger seat. A wicked shiver courses through me. Excitement? I bite my lip and hurry over, putting myself behind the wheel, casting my eye over the buttons and switches. Dolly looks far more complicated than any of the Mercedes I've been in.

Bang!

"Shit!" I yelp, jumping in my seat. "What the hell was that?" I look across the car to Beau. She's smiling.

"That, Rose, is Dolly." She reaches for her seatbelt and pulls it on, prompting me to do the same. "Let's go."

Yes, let's go. Not far, granted, but let's go. I take the lever by the wheel, pull it, and put my foot on a pedal.

And jerk forward, bunny-hopping my way up the driveway at the side of the house. "She's not very smooth, is she?"

Beau chuckles, stroking across Dolly's center console with a palm delicate enough to stroke a butterfly. "Easy on the gas, Rose."

"I'm being easy," I insist, picking up speed gradually, feeling relatively calm.

"You need to shift gears."

"It has gears?" I ask, looking around the wheel. "None of the cars the boys drive have ge—"

"Watch Cindy!" Beau yells, just as a black and tan blob flies across my path.

"Shit!"

"And Barbie! Shit, Rose, hit the brake."

"Which one's the brake?" I yank the steering wheel to the left, adrenaline charging through me fast.

And plough straight into a bush.

11

DANNY

I'm merciless on the throttle, flying across the water like a bullet, out of my seat, James flanking me. The salt spray hits my face, making my skin tight, the roar of the engine and pound of the water filling my ears, drowning out the voices telling me to go on a killing spree. But I'm still strung. Still tense. Still edgy.

As the corner of the cove comes closer, I slow so I can loop without being thrown off. I'd love to yank on the handlebars. Being rag-dolled across the water might distract some of my muscles from being infinitely tight. I slow until I'm barely moving and look down at my wetsuit, considering the bandages and Dermabond beneath.

"Not wise," James says as he chugs over, circling me.

"I know." Freefalling will offer only a momentary sense of lightness. Is there anything in the world that can alleviate the pressure completely? Yes, there is, but I can't spend all of my spare time fucking my wife. "I think I'll take the coastline back," I say. An hour racing across the water at breakneck speed has done nothing to lessen the stress. Maybe a leisurely chug back will.

James nods and turns his jet ski. "Don't be too long."

I leave him and head toward the rocky coastline on the east side of the bay, where commercial buildings stand over the water, some still midway through development. Ruined. They're destroying this private bay. I slow to a stop and bob on the water when I reach the small cove where Winstable Boatyard once stood. The boatyard Pops built. The place where I learned to ski, to swim, and how to hide firearms. I smile. Fond memories.

Cranes still loom over the site, diggers rumbling across the muddy ground, but there's one building complete, and it looks nothing like the educational facility I was told it would be. It looks more like a hangar. If I didn't now have Byron's Reach, a far better site, I might hold it against the developer. I can't blame the old boy I rented the place from, nor his son who sold it from under my nose. I wonder how his knee is after I blew it out? Naturally, I don't give a fuck. Just wondering.

I continue slowly along the coastline. The area is so much bigger than I remember, or perhaps that's because most of it is now flattened, each side of the piece of land nearly touching the nearest developments on either side. I turn to face the other side of the bay, seeing Byron's Reach in the distance, a dot on the horizon. And the big fucking problems awaiting me. Problems that aren't going to be fixed while I bob out here on the ocean.

I rev the engine and pick up speed, concluding a slower, safer pace isn't helping. Every time my mind goes back to Pops, to The Bear, to the fucking zoo he keeps, I burn hotter. Breath heavier. Shake more violently.

By the time I make it back to shore, I'm no less calm. James is coming out of the yellow container. "Is he still alive?" I ask as I trudge toward the cabin, knowing James would rather Kenny Spittle was not breathing.

"And kicking." He slams the door and bolts it before securing the padlock.

"And is he still insisting he didn't tell Agent Burrows we killed his father?"

"Yes, he is. Apparently Burrows got a tip off that I murdered Spittle. Anonymous."

"How the fuck do you know that?"

"Higham."

"And you didn't think to tell me?"

James's eyes shine with something quite ugly, and I hold my hands up in surrender. "It slipped my mind," he grates. "Besides, it's bollocks. For one thing, *you* killed Spittle, not me. Plus, there's no fucking body to prove anyone killed Spittle at all."

I curl my lip at the container where Spittle's son is being held. "His phone?"

"Silent."

"And the bank?"

"Still nothing according to Otto."

"Fuck it!" I yell, kicking the dirt, walking in circles, my breath short. Even if his phone wasn't silent, answering it would be pointless, because the accent on the other end would be Russian, Irish, or Polish, and that tells us nothing more than we already fucking know. But it'll tell *them* we have Kenny Spittle. "How much damage have you done?" I ask, looking at James.

"No damage."

"What?"

"I've not touched him."

"You sure?" I reach behind me and pull down my zip, wriggling out of my wetsuit and pushing it down to my waist.

"Pretty sure. And if you're wondering why I've not mutilated the fucker, it's because I reached the same conclusion you did while out on the water. How was your trip back alone, by the way?"

"Reminiscent. What conclusion?"

"We need to release him and maybe buy him a few minutes at a tanning salon so that when he gets back to work at the bank, everyone will believe he's been on vacation."

"Get Otto to track him."

"Your bandages are wet. You need to replace them before the Dermabond dissolves." James motions to my chest, and I look down, scowling at the damp material. "Why the fuck didn't you wrap up in waterproofs?"

"Distracted." I march over to the container as I unravel my bandage and toss it aside, then fight to get the padlock undone, swinging open the door. And cough. "Jesus," I breathe, holding my fist to my mouth. The smell is musky. Fucking putrid. Totally unbearable. And the sight of him isn't much better. Kenny Spittle looks up, squinting with the bombardment of light attacking his eyes. I push the door closed.

"D-Boss!" Liam sings, appearing at the top of the steps to the cabin. His hair is longer. Wilder. And I'm quite sure his board shorts haven't been washed since the last time I saw him some weeks ago. His eyes fall to my chest and nearly fall out of his head, and I look down, confused. Then not when I see the mess I've made of myself. *Fuck me.*

"Where the fuck have you been?" I snap, trudging toward him. "We had to get our own fucking jet skis ready because Jerry was dealing with clients and the girls in the café were busy serving."

"I don't think you had a long enough vacation," he murmurs as I storm past.

"You'd be right."

"Get our skis in," James says, pulling his wetsuit down too. "Then come join us."

"Sure, J-Boss."

I laugh sardonically. "Your back, my front. It's a fucking horror show around here." I help myself to a water from the fridge and cast my eyes around the busy café as I swig. My stare lands on a man in the corner, who is watching us both standing by the fridge. My stomach turns and questions run amok through my mind. Has he found Pops? Beau's mum?

"Come," James says, encouraging me toward Higham. "And keep your fucking cool, okay?"

Keep my cool. I look around the café again, wishing everyone gone so I don't have to bother keeping my cool. "Everyone's looking at us."

"My back, your front," James says. "And since when do you care?"

"I don't."

"Then shut the fuck up."

Higham's eyes are nailed to my chest as I approach, and one look warns him not to ask. Pulling out a chair, I lower to the seat, setting my water on the table as James gets comfortable beside me, folding his arms over his impressive chest. I don't fold mine. Can't. *For fuck's sake.*

Higham takes a sip of his coffee and pulls his jacket in, resting back in his seat. "I'm sorry about your father," he says flatly. "And your girlfriend's mother. Jaz Hayley was a respected agent."

"I don't want your condolences," James says quietly, a lethal edge to his tone.

"What do you want from me then?"

"Nothing." he replies. That's not true. "Or maybe a pardon when I find out who it was and butcher the fucker."

"Let us have this one," Higham says, coming in closer.

"You don't know who *this one* is," James points out.

"No, but I know two pretty fucking determined men who can find out." He looks between us, and I raise my eyebrows. "This is personal for us now too," he goes on. "Like I said, Jaz was a respected agent."

James laughs, scrubbing his hands down his face. "Higham," he says lowly, getting closer. "If I go home and tell Beau that the bureau suddenly cares enough about her dead mother to find what was left of her after she was blown to smithereens, she will, and I am not joking you when I tell you this, tear every last FBI agent limb from limb."

"Beau is a former cop."

"Who knew her mother's death was not an accident but wasn't allowed to prove it, despite the evidence." James sits back, and I take over. He's going to blow. The simmering anger seems to be alternating between the two of us.

"There are so many bent cops on the force and bureau, Higham," I say, taking more water. "I don't even know if I want to be talking to you right now."

"I'm not bent."

"That's what they all say. Any news on my father's missing body?"

"We all know you and your friend The Enigma have more chance of finding your father's body than the FBI."

"So that's why you're here? For our help?"

"Would you rather me be here to arrest you?"

I sigh, falling back in my chair heavily to demonstrate just how fucking tired I am of his egotistical shit. "Higham, if you could arrest either of us, we'd already be in cuffs."

"You'd be a big catch for me."

"Are we back talking about sharks again, Higham?" James asks, making me frown.

"What about sharks?" I ask.

"Higham likes to fry big fish."

"You don't get much bigger than us." I smile at an exasperated Agent Higham.

"Indeed you don't, but as I have explained to James before you arrived back in Miami, as much as I know you two have more murders to your names than the inmates of Florida State Prison put together, there are either no bodies or no evidence."

"Oh, I see." I look at James. "Do you see?"

"I see."

"We see," I confirm, facing Higham, who looks like he's about ready to bash our heads together. I chuckle to myself, peeking out the corner of my eye to James. His face is dead straight, but I can see he's getting a bit of light relief with me. "So, for the avoidance of doubt," I go on. "Are you saying that in order to cuff us, you need some dead bodies or evidence to prove James and I may or may not have killed a few men?"

"Yes."

"And while we're pretty big fucking fish, probably the biggest, you accept you will never get us in those cuffs?"

"Yes."

"And you accept that our *supposed* crimes—because they *are* supposed, Higham, let's be clear on that—are a direct result of the other scum roaming the streets of Miami trying to rule it, and if they were not around, you accept the crime rates would, as everyone wants, including us, drop significantly?"

"Yes."

"And the FBI and MPD will ease the squeeze around our necks if we intercept a few supposed murders and hand the culprit over to you to prosecute?"

"I suppose that is indeed what I am saying."

I slap the table with my palm, smiling. "Why didn't you just say so?" I fall back in my chair. "I feel like we've been around the houses a bit, Higham."

Exasperated, he stands, picking up his coffee as he does and finishing it. "If there was ever an award for most sarcastic crime lord, Danny, you'd get it."

"I'd rather win the award for most dangerous, actually."

"Fight you for it," James practically growls beside me. "And I'll win."

"We'll see," I reply, smiling at Higham. "I'll let you know how this pans out."

"And my offer?"

"We'll think about it."

"Maybe this will sway you." He pushes a picture across the table, and James and I both lean in to look. "We believe this may be The Chameleon."

I frown. "The Chameleon? I've never heard of The fucking Chameleon."

"Now you have. Polish. Replaced The Hound, who I now suspect was in the vehicle that blew up after James was released from custody after being wrongly arrested for Frank Spittle's death. The Chameleon works under The Shark." Higham pushes another picture toward us. "And this here, we believe, is The Leprechaun."

"Don't tell me." James places a fingertip on the picture and drags it forward. "Irish."

"Good guess," I mutter.

"Replaced The Alligator, Roake, who replaced The Snake."

James looks up at Higham. "Where did you get this information?"

"Well, while you two were slacking on vacation, I used the time productively."

"But you didn't find The Bear and you don't know who dug up my dead father?" I say.

Higham doesn't look impressed. "I'll keep the Feds and MPD out of Hiatus until you've had a chat between yourselves about where our relationship goes next." He smiles smugly and it's all I can do not to roll my eyes. Everything about Hiatus is legit . . . until you get to the glass office, and they won't find that. They won't find anything, except a few naked women. I pout to myself. Bless Higham's cotton socks. Thirty feet beneath him is an underground gun store bigger than this café. Granted, not fully stocked right now, but still.

"Very kind of you," I say, my eyes following him as he struts away, his walk screaming *cop*.

"Oh." He stops just shy of the door, his index finger pointing skyward, as if he's just had a lightbulb moment. That award he's talking about? If there was one for cops . . . "I nearly forgot," he muses, turning back to face us. Liar. He didn't nearly forget at all. This will simply be another little nudge. Higham needs to know I don't like nudges. "Heard of a man named Kenny Spittle?"

"Nope."

"Thought not." A sarcastic smile, and he's gone.

"*Still* don't like him," I mutter, turning to James. "What are you thinking?" Ironically, Higham gave us these two pictures as a sweet-ener. He's happy for us to kill these men, because he knows their deaths will lead to a bigger catch. Problem is, he wants The Bear, and so do we.

"I'm thinking he's trying to make the same arrangement with me as Beau's mother did." James stares at the pictures on the table, his eyes narrowed to slits, his lip getting a punishing chew. "I killed them before she got them in front of a judge."

If James and I were women, I'd be giving his hand a reassuring rub about now. "Difference is," I say, thoughtful. "Higham knows who we are. Jaz Hayley—"

"Knew who I was," James reminds me, also reminding me that Beau's mother also knew who The Bear was. Jesus, this story, the connections, the mysteries.

"I can't die until we figure this out," I say, swiping up my cigarettes and lighting one, offering them to James. He takes one. I knew he would. I draw and exhale thoughtfully. What I really meant is, I can't *live* until we figure this out.

None of us can.

Which means we need to do what it takes to figure this shit out. "Are we putting Kenny back in the bank?"

"I'll have Goldie arrange his sunbeds," James says, relaxing back too, looking out at the cove. "I'm not interested in helping Higham hit government targets." He takes us back to business and away from Beau. Fair enough.

"Me neither, but I *am* interested in making our lives as easy as possible." I stub my barely-smoked cigarette out. "Ready to head to Hiatus?" I ask, looking at his phone on the table when it rings. "Beth? Who's Beth?"

James makes a pretty speedy job of rejecting the call. "No one." Standing, he strides back to the changing room, and I follow, my eyes lasers on his brutalized back. He yanks his locker open and pulls his clothes out, stripping out of his wetsuit. James is never particularly light and breezy, it's not in his DNA, but he's especially deadly looking right now, as he wrenches and pulls at his clothes. Even when he's quite funny, there's still an edge of deadliness laced through his words.

No one.

Interesting.

.   .   .

By the time we get to Hiatus, the place is booming, the bar packed, and the stage is adorned with five sets of boobs, all different shapes and sizes.

"Don't ever let it be said that Hiatus doesn't cater for all tastes," Brad says, motioning to the office, obviously knowing what I'm thinking. "Somewhere quieter?"

Yes, my head's fucking ringing. I wander across the club, acutely aware of the hushed whispers, people staring but trying not to stare. The Brit is back. A-fucking-gain. And this time, he really isn't going anywhere. I walk through the staged office, open the bookcase, and look back to make sure everyone's in the holding room before punching in the code on the wall mounted panel that releases the iron door on the other side of the room. It creeps open, I pass through, climb the stairs, and find Otto, Ringo, and Goldie huddled around a laptop. "Something going on?" I ask.

"Just checking The Chameleon and The Leprechaun against facial recognition," Otto says, not looking up. He's wearing a baseball cap. *Otto hit his head.* How?

"Who?" Brad asks, closing the door behind him.

"How do you know about The Chameleon and The Leprechaun?"

"Who's The Chameleon and The Leprechaun?" Brad pours himself a drink.

"James sent me the images." Otto remains devoted to the screen of his laptop.

"What images?" Brad asks.

"Very prompt of him," I mutter, giving James the eye as I help myself to a Scotch too. "Vodka?"

He shakes his head. "And you've found nothing," James says, joining them and taking a peek.

"Actually . . ." Otto fades off, his eyes narrowing thoughtfully.

"Actually what?"

"Where's the original image?" he asks, looking between me and James. I point my drink to James, who dips into his back pocket and pulls out the pictures, handing them to Otto, who's accepts while stroking his beard with his other hand, concentrating.

"Who the fuck is The Chameleon and The Leprechaun?" Brad yells.

"Two new members of The Bear's zoo," I answer. "Polish and Irish. Replacing Roake and The Hound."

"Great. What the fuck is this, a breeding program?" Brad swigs his drink and refills, while I return my attention to Otto, wondering what the fuck he's looking at in that picture with such interest.

"Are you going to enlighten us?" I ask, impatient.

"I see it," James takes the picture from Otto and unbends his body.

For fuck's sake. "Well?" I press.

"There's a reflection on his shades." James squints and looks closer. "Part of a neon bar sign."

"Which one?" I ask.

"Irish."

Everyone, including me, crowds James, trying to get in on the picture. I see the glimmer of pink lighting, squinting too. "Don't tell me the FBI missed that." Ringo grunts, his fat nose wrinkling. "It's obviously the Pink Flamingo Lounge Bar Downtown."

"They didn't miss it." I move away and sip my drink, going to the window and looking down on the busy club. "These two men are a gift."

"What?" Brad asks, confused.

"Higham wants The Bear. He knows we're the best way to achieve that, whether he uses us as bait or our skills as hunters." I pout at the window. "Drive everyone else out of town so there is only us, and we bob along quite nicely on our own, don't we?" I face the room. "I can't deny it, it would be quite peaceful with only us."

Brad laughs. "Are you joking? We're like magnets for the rookie crime lords. And the non-rookie ones, for that matter. Russians, Polish, and Irish case in point. And is everyone forgetting Beau's dad is running for mayor? That prick is not going to make our lives easy as long as *he*"—he points a finger at James—"is dating his precious daughter."

"Precious?" James coughs, on the verge of knocking Brad out. "She wasn't so precious when he left her in a hospital."

I step in before all hell breaks loose. Or, at least, I delay it. "Who's running against him?" I ask.

"Monroe Metcalfe," Otto answers. How the fuck does he have the answer to everything? And what the fuck is with that baseball cap? It doesn't suit him. "Lawyer.," he continues. "Moved in from Boston in 2020. Wife, two daughters, and a shining reputation. Charity work, upstanding citizen, pro-bono work."

"He's definitely bent," I say, making James look up at me. "No one that glowing is that straight. Dig deeper. See if he'd be open to discussions."

"You want to talk?" Ringo asks. "What about?"

"Whether I need to threaten him or if he'll play nice and take a bribe." It looks like I'm going back into politics. "People will be more reluctant to step foot in Miami once we're shot of The Bear and his zoo. Anyone steps in, Higham gets them. And we get to live happily ever after."

Every single person in the room snorts their thoughts on that. We'll never live in complete peace. But it's the closest we'll ever get, and they all know it.

"Are you saying we're giving Higham The Bear?" James asks, his tone unimpressed.

"Yeah, I'm saying that. Got a better idea?" I ask, raising my brows.

He doesn't get to answer, his phone ringing and interrupting. Beth again? And who the fuck *is* Beth? "I've got to take this," he mutters but, surprisingly, he doesn't leave the room, instead pacing in front of the glass.

"So what are we doing with this?" Goldie asks, picking up the picture and inspecting it. "Paying a visit to The Pink Flamingo?"

"You craving some girlie cocktails?" Ringo asks, earning a death glare. "Sex on the Beach?"

"How about a Screwdriver?" Goldie counters, her lip curled. "Plunged into your eye."

Ringo's face drops like lead. "I was playing."

"I don't play," she mutters, slamming her body down on the couch and raking a stressed hand through her hair. She's pissed. I get it. Freedom was a whisper away and now due to loyalty, she's going nowhere. As soon as we've dealt with this shit, she'll be gone, and she will go with James's and my blessing.

"You want some time out?" I ask her, earning myself a death glare too.

"Why the fuck would I want time out? I want to get on with this shit and get the job done."

I nod. I like her attitude. Sometimes.

"The lobby bar. Half an hour." James hangs up and faces the room, therefore my curious face. Which he ignores. "Are we done?" he asks.

"No, I want—" My phone rings, and as soon as I see who's calling, I hold it up to James before answering. "Chaka," I say, telling everyone else in the room who it is as I click to loudspeaker. "How's my favorite king of Africa?"

"Black," he says over what I know is a small laugh. "You woo me."

"You're not calling with a problem, are you, Chaka?"

"No problem. Just checking the finer details for the delivery."

"Details to come," I say dismissively. "Now, let me ask you something, Chaka, my friend." I perch on the edge of Brad's desk and cross one ankle over the other, hearing the building threat in my own voice. "And only the truth will do here, or that peaceful community of yours in that beautiful village far, far away from civilization might be blessed with a firework display very soon."

"I thought we were friends, Black."

"We are, which is why it pains me to threaten you."

"You're in pain?"

"Agony. Now, tell me," I go on, bracing myself for the imminent exploding of *myself*, the anger brewing dangerously. I swear, whoever's been shouting their mouth off, I will cut them up. Slowly. With a blunt knife. "How the fuck do you know my wife is pregnant?"

"Because you told me."

I jerk. Frown. Cast my eyes around the room. "What?"

His laugh is deep and rumbling. And really fucking irritating. "When you called me a few nights ago from St. Lucia as drunk as I've ever heard a man."

"Oh."

Brad starts laughing, as does Ringo and Otto, and Goldie rolls her eyes, blowing her cheeks out in despair. And James. He's expressionless. Deadpan. Seriously unimpressed.

"I guess I told you I was in St. Lucia too, huh?" Fuck my life. Fuck my stupidity. Fuck everything.

"Sure did. Now, are we done?"

"We're done." I am not living this down.

"Back to business," Chaka says.

"I said I'd send you the details."

He's laughing again. "I'm talking about the other shipment."

"What other shipment?" I ask, feeling all attention on me.

"The one you ordered that night after telling me you'd slice off my black balls and feed them to the hyenas if I didn't fulfil it."

"Oh," I murmur again, as James shakes his head at me and the rest of the gang look at me like they feel sorry for me. They should. I'm feeling quite sorry for myself too. "*That* order." I have no fucking idea what he's talking about. "Don't suppose I can cancel it?"

"Oh, Black, can I suggest a vacation?"

"I'll be in touch." I hang up and uncross my legs, standing. *Fuck it.* "We have a second shipment coming."

"No shit," Ringo grunts.

I have a weird moment, a flashback, my mind taking me back to that night on the beach after we found out we hadn't killed The Bear and my wife lost her shit, basically throwing me out. I see myself, slumped on the sand, a bottle in my hand, my mobile at my ear. And I hear part of the conversation.

I want to double the order. You can deliver, can't you, Chaka?

Otto coughs, knocking me from my thoughts. "And do we know how we're taking this delivery yet?"

I glare at him, silently telling him to fuck off before I fuck him up.

James heads for the door. "I need to be somewhere."

"You look like you're in a rush."

"I am."

"We have the delivery to coordinate," I call. "It was you who had this bright idea to keep the delivery to a Friday when the Coast Guard is training."

"Just trying to keep all the criminals happy while staying alive," James mutters, not stopping.

"Where are you going?" I yell.

"None of your business."

I recoil, throwing a curious look to Otto, who shrugs, and to Goldie, who is still scowling. Am I the only one wondering what the fuck he's up to?

12

ROSE

"Fuck it all to hell!" I mutter, staring at the bush that now has a hole in it the shape of Dolly's hood. "Beau, I'm so sorry." I turn to my friend, praying for forgiveness—fuck the bush. This car is sentimental. A hunk of junk but so sentimental.

Beau's just staring at the car, and my heart sinks, as I reluctantly turn my eyes onto the paintwork to look at the damage. *Oh God.* Scratches. Everywhere. "I'll pay for it to be fixed," I tell her, ignoring the little part of my brain that's asking me how the hell I'm going to do that without having to ask my husband for some cash. And I have a horrible realization in this moment. Awful! I have no money, not of my own. Everything has been signed over to me, yes, but I can't get at it. I didn't earn any of it. Work for it. God damn it, I'm still a prisoner. He controls me. All of me.

I feel a lump forming in my throat, and I hate myself for it when my best friend is staring at her most precious possession—something her mother gave her—that I have just crashed. I was supposed to be distracting her. I'm so fucking dumb. Beau turns her eyes onto me, and my lip wobbles, my mouth loading with a million apologies to pour. She jerks a little, as if snapping out of a daydream. "I'm so s—"

"Jesus, Rose, are you okay?" Beau dashes over to me and places both hands on my little bump, and I withdraw, taken aback.

"I'm fine," I say. I hardly moved in my seat, felt no pressure on my tummy. "But Dolly isn't."

"Dolly's fine. Are you sure you're okay? The baby, does she feel okay?"

I still in front of her, my mouth falling open.

"Can you feel her moving?"

"It's too early to feel movement," I say quietly.

"It is?" Beau rubs circles on my tummy, as if trying to stimulate movement. And in answer, a mild flutter of bubbles pop as if telling me she's okay. As if she knows my friend needs that reassurance.

"Oh my God, I felt her. She's moving," I say, laying my hand over Beau's. She inhales, eyes full of wonder staring at me. She doesn't even realize what she's said in her panic. "*She* is fine."

"Thank God," Beau breathes smiling mildly. Then it drops, as do her hands from my stomach, and she steps back. "Oh shit." Her hand slaps over her mouth, and I laugh. It's too late for that.

"I'm having a girl?"

"No." She shakes her head. "Nope, nay, noh, nein."

"I'm having a girl!"

"God damn it!"

"I'm having a girl," I say, bracing my hands on my knees to hold me up, starting to laugh hysterically. "My God, he's going to have a fucking fit." Another girl to worry about? He'll be sectioned.

"You can't tell him I told you," Beau says, as I lower myself to the ground, feeling weak, and very worried I could pee my panties at any moment. "Rose, for Christ's sake, will you promise me you won't tell him?"

"I promise." I chuckle, on my back, looking up at the clouds.

"I'm so stupid," Beau moans, joining me on the ground, lying next to me and taking my hand. I turn my face to hers, wiping my eyes, my body still sporadically jolting with the aftermath of my laughing fit. And Beau smiles. It's a true smile, the kind of smile that lights her face and dampens the darkness that shrouds her life. "I don't know what I'd do without you," she whispers, her voice ragged.

I exhale and settle. She wouldn't know what to do without James either, but that goes without saying. And I guess girls need girls sometimes when men just do not know what to do. "They'll fix this," I say.

"I know they will. I just wish more stuff for them to fix would stop turning up. And I wish more that I could maintain a consistent, calm, accepting aura."

I smile, wishing the same for myself too. But we should cut ourselves some slack. "You're allowed to wobble, Beau. So am I."

"You're pregnant, you have a valid excuse for your unreasonable behavior."

I can't even challenge her. I know I'm unreasonable. Danny knows it. Everyone knows it. God, I hope she will be pregnant one day too. A glimmer of light to grow and chase away the demons forever. James needs that too. "It's not unreasonable, really. Not when you consider who we're married to."

She swallows and nods, looking up at the sky. "He thinks I hate him," she whispers. "I don't. I love him more fiercely than I've ever hated anyone. Even the man who ordered my mother's death."

"I know you do." I squeeze her hand. "Maybe he needs to hear that."

She nods. "My period was due yesterday. It didn't come."

I inhale subtly. "Do you think . . ."

"I don't know. But James definitely needs to hear that I love him." Looking at me, she flashes a small, unsure smile. "Where are they?"

"At Hiatus. I'll call and check."

"Okay." Jumping up, she looks down her body. "I'm going to wear a dress."

I accept her hands when she offers them, and she pulls me to my feet. Beau in a dress is as rare as James smiling. "Have you ever worn a dress?" I ask, as we walk back to the house. "Except for my bachelorette party?" Which was an epic fail. I shudder, remembering Danny smashing an admiring man's face into the table just before he ordered me down off the stage in Hiatus in the calmest, deadliest voice. "Oh, and at dinner in St. Lucia. My cream dress."

"Yeah, one time when James took me to the opera to assassinate a judge." She says it so casually, so coolly, and I look at her, not surprised. I've heard the story before, and even if I hadn't? Well, our world. "James had a dress delivered to Lawrence and Dexter's," she goes on, smiling, although it's sad. I've not heard this part. "Before we knew it was Dexter who killed my mother under order." I squeeze her hand, and she laughs lightly. "The thought of going to the opera filled me with dread, but at the same time I really wanted to." She shrugs. "It was when I was particularly bad at being in crowded places." Beau isn't all too great now, but I know of the panic attacks that ruled her back then. "I went to Walmart on a Saturday afternoon to try and prepare."

"Why would anyone go to Walmart on a Saturday?"

"Exactly." She laughs. "Anyway, it didn't work out too well and I was on the cusp of falling apart when guess who shows up?" She looks at me, and I smile. I don't need to answer that. He'd been following her for some time, trying to find the man we all know as The Bear, the man who ordered the deaths of both James's family and Beau's mother. James knew he would go after Beau too if she didn't give up her relentless need to prove her mother's death wasn't an accident. James just didn't expect to fall in love with her. And I must admit, neither did I expect to fall for her. To be honest, when James dragged Danny from the dead, I hated Beau before I had met her. Then the four of us had dinner and after a spikey start, I was soon head over heels.

And here we are.

A pair of molls.

"He helped me do my shopping and picked me up later. He wore a black suit," she says over a sigh. "And he looked so fucking handsome."

"And the dress he bought you?" I ask.

"He said I looked out of this world."

Truth is, Beau looks out of this world in ripped jeans and a tank. She's naturally stunning—casual or glam. "We've never gotten ready together," I point out. "Like girls do."

"We should do it. Get ready together." She turns a smile onto me, and I love the sparkle I see in her eyes. "I'll take a shower and head over to your place." She releases me and jogs off, and I laugh. My place is down the corridor from her place.

I head to the kitchen to get some water and make the first of a few calls to Esther. "Before you ask, he's not here," she says when she answers. "He and Barney have become quite pally. He's back and forth between here and there like a yo-yo."

I can't be anything but pleased about that. He's got a friend, and it's so important he has those, especially in this life. This life that's so different from his previous life with Hilary and Derek, even if we're trying to keep it relatively normal. We're deluded. I know Esther's also been on his back to keep in contact with Hilary. She had every day with Daniel since he was a baby, so I can only imagine how hard this change has been for her. "He's keeping up with his studies though, right?"

She laughs. "Yes, powering through them, getting top grades in everything, making extra effort so he can dash out the door to see Barney."

"I'll call Barney's dad," I say, taking the stairs. "And you? Are you okay?"

"How's Danny?' she asks, swerving my question, which basically gives me my answer.

"He's fine. Esther, how are *you*?" This isn't sitting right with me. Danny can't dictate how his mother lives her life, and neither can I. I should never have allowed Danny to call the shots. I need to be with my husband, of course. But I also need to be with my son.

Danny brought me here, and he wouldn't if he truly thought I was at risk. So why can't I have my boy with me? "I want to come back," I blurt. It's probably best for everyone.

"No," she snaps, adamant. "Without you around to stabilize him, Christ knows where Danny will be."

I let myself into my room and drop to the bed, my head in my hands. "I don't think I stabilize him, Esther. If anything, I'm tipping him further over the edge."

"That's nonsense."

"I miss Daniel."

She laughs. "Why? If you were here, you would hardly see him anyway. Now, I've got to go. My pasta's boiling over. I'll text you Barney's dad's number so you can reach Daniel." She hangs up, and I stare at my cell, waiting for the number to drop. Barney's dad didn't ask for this. He must feel like he's got two kids given Daniel's spending so much time there.

My phone pings, I save the number, and then I call Barney's dad's. "Mr. Benson?" I say when a deep, gruff voice answers. "It's Rose, Daniel's mom. I hope you don't mind, Esther gave me your number."

"Oh, Rose, I don't mind at all. How are you?"

"I'm good, thank you. And you?"

"Very well. Daniel's grandmother said you're on vacation with his dad."

I smile tightly as I look around our luxurious suite at Danny's Miami mansion. "That's right. I was just checking in. Esther said Daniel's with you *again*."

"Oh? Is that a problem?"

"Not at all," I rush to explain. "I just wondered if it's too much. It doesn't sound like you get much of a break from him."

He laughs lightly. "Honestly, it's fine. It's nice for Barney to have the distraction."

"Oh?" I can't contain the curiosity in my voice.

"Well, I'm working most of the time, from home, of course, and his mother has gone back to Sri Lanka."

"Oh, he misses her?" I open the French doors and step out onto the terrace, pouting to myself. He misses his mother. How sweet. *Miss me, Daniel! And answer your damn cell or at least my messages.*

"No, we're going through a messy divorce. She left the country to be with her new boyfriend. Barney wanted to stay with me."

My eyes widen. Shit. What the fuck do I say to that? "I'm sorry." I sound as awkward as I feel.

"Everyone is," he says over a laugh. "Anyway, Daniel is fine, Barney is fine, the big unit following them around is fine, and in case you're now worried about me, I am fine too."

How cute. "Well, I'm glad everyone is fine." I smile like an idiot. "You have my number now, so just call if you need me. I mean, need anything Daniel related."

"I'll call you, Rose," he says, laughter in his tone. "Enjoy the rest of your vacation."

I hang up and look across the grounds of the mansion. "I will," I say to myself. Oh, please. Lennox saw us all sitting around the table. He met my *friendly* husband. He's got a seven-foot Viking trailing Daniel and Barney. He knows we're not on vacation. I wish we were.

"All right?"

I look toward Beau's voice and find her on the terrace of their room. "Yeah, I'm good. You?"

"I have no dresses."

"Then you'd better get that sweet, slim ass over to my place." I go back inside and a few seconds later, Beau's next to me by the closet rummaging through my clothes. "Take your pick," I mutter, looking at all the dresses solemnly. "None of them fit me anymore."

She pulls out a white dress, looking it up and down. "This is the dress you wore the night we met."

"And this is the one you wore," I say, reaching for the cream piece I also wore the night Danny took me to a lovely Italian place and murdered two men.

"I think I need to go shopping," Beau says quietly.

"Yes!" I hang the dresses back up. "I'm getting fatter by the day, and you need some dresses. I'll plan a shopping trip." *Somehow.*

"And until then?" she asks, looking across the rails of dresses.

"You should wear this one," I say, pulling out a lovely Boho chic tiered piece that falls just below the knee. "I've not worn it yet, which means no one has died in the presence of this dress."

She laughs and takes it from me. "You sure?"

"Yes, I'm sure. It suits your free spirit better, anyway." I start looking for something to wear myself. Something stretchy.

Beau's cell rings, and every inch of her tenses, telling me exactly who is trying to reach her. "Miami's next mayor?" I ask as I pull out a gold slinky dress that's got some give.

"What the hell am I going to say to him?" She toys with her phone, torn between answering and ignoring. "Actually, I'm more worried about what he might say to me." She takes a deep breath and connects the call. "Dad." She starts pacing, her eyes low, the dress in her hold, and I pray this call won't have her returning to her room and bed. "I'm sure they're doing everything they can," she says, looking at me, shaking her head. "I don't know, Dad." She lays the dress on the bed and starts walking again, watching her feet. "Tonight? I'm sorry, I have arrangements with a friend." She's cringing. But I also sense her conflict. She feels sorry for him too. So do I, the old fool, being hoodwinked by a gold digger, but I still don't like him. I also don't care if he lost every penny he has, but I do because that's Beau's inheritance, and I can think of no one I'd rather have Beau's egomaniac's father's money less than Amber. I shudder. Amber who was the in-house whore when I arrived at Casa Black. Amber who Danny has fucked. And suddenly, I can hear them, her screams, the bangs on the wall. Because he wanted me to hear, right after I'd practically offered myself on a plate and he rejected me.

Stop!

"They're my friends, Dad," Beau goes on, bringing me back to the present. "I know you're running for mayor." The heel of her palm meets her forehead. "Then I won't come on campaigns with you. Simple." She pulls the phone away from her ear and covers the speaker. "I can't even deal with him right now," she whispers to me.

"He's at a hotel downtown. Wants me to meet him for dinner in the lobby bar. Is it bad I'd rather eat razor blades?"

I shake my head.

"I've got to go, Dad. I'm late. We'll do dinner next week, okay?" She hangs up, ties her hair, and pulls her robe in. "Where's your makeup?"

13

JAMES

I walk out of the lobby bar of the hotel and immediately slip a cigarette between my lips, my body tense. I frown at the flame of the lighter as I hold it on the end. It's not only flickering, it's shaking, and I move my eyes down to my hand. My *trembling* hand. "What the fuck?" I mutter, inhaling and slipping the lighter into my back pocket, looking up and down the street as I cross the road, forcing my body into relaxing and failing miserably, struggling to understand this extreme reaction. I slip into my Range Rover and let the window down to let the smoke out, taking a moment to calm my pounding heart. Unshakable.

I'm stumped.

I don't know why the fuck I'm shaking. I've done the right thing. I only pray Beau thinks so too. *When* she starts talking to me again.

I start the engine and pull off, having one last pull on my cigarette before flicking it out of the window, heading back to Hiatus. I turn on the stereo. Music. Music will calm me. Pulling up at a red, I smile at the irony when Paradise Circle joins me, and signal to turn right.

But I don't turn right.

I look over the crossroad, seeing a pink neon light glowing my way. Enticing me. Tempting me. Telling me more relief can be found through those doors. I turn off the signal and put my foot down, passing the club. The chances of him being there? Slim. But it doesn't hurt to check. I park around the back and go to the trunk, pulling the base up and collecting a Glock, tucking it into the back of my jeans with its friend before taking the rucksack. Then I google The Pink Flamingo to check who owns the place. Elsa Dove. I nod to myself, checking her out, finding an uptight looking middle-aged blonde in a trouser suit. Divorced. Previous socialite. Wealthy parents. Then I check out who manages the place. Des Stanton. Single. History of drugs. Parents dead. It tells me all I need to know.

My strides are long and purposeful as I walk to the front, getting eyed by the men on the door. They both look me up and down, then to each other. "We gotta search ya, man," one says, the brave one.

"You don't gotta search me," I assure them, turning and lifting my T-shirt. "I just want to see if there's someone in there, then I'll be gone."

They throw each other wary glances. "And if that someone is in there?"

"I'll remove him, because I'm pretty sure the owner won't want him frequenting her establishment, even if the man running the place for her does."

"Yeah, okay, cool, man," the other says, hands up. "We're not paid enough to deal with this kinda trouble, man."

Wise men. I brush past them, then push my way through the double doors, scoping the joint from one side to the other. The shit music. The tacky décor. The cheap furniture. I have to squint to protect my eyes from the glare of the sickly pink neon lighting assaulting the place.

I drop the rucksack by the door and start a slow circuit, eyeing every table, every patron, the staff, the people on the dance floor. There's not one camera in the place. It speaks volumes. I come to a slow stop when I see a VIP area in the corner, a crowd of young women swarming the edge. Desperate young women. Desperate young women wanting attention, money, drugs, a sugar daddy. All disingenuous, but all blameless.

I wander over, a head and shoulders above them, and see him. A bottle of champagne in one hand, a woman in the other. An innocent woman. He has the same shades on as he does in the photograph Higham handed us. Who fucking hires these imbeciles? Jesus Christ, his nose is powered with white stuff, his body visibly buzzing, and I bet if I could see his eyes, they'd be like fucking saucers.

I feel my guns against my back, begging me to put an end to one more obstacle. Except . . .

I can't.

Not only because he's surrounded by ignorant idiots who don't deserve to die. We need information.

I push my way through the crowd of youngsters crowding the VIP space and step over the red rope holding them back. My presence gets the other guy in the area, who also has a woman on his lap and cocaine dressing his nose.

And suddenly, the woman isn't on his lap, being shoved aside for something else. His gun. I pull both of mine at lightning speed, before he's even figured out where the fuck his trousers are, and have one aimed at each of their heads. Two pairs of hands rise into the air, and screams overpower the music. "Pleasure," I say, gesturing with my guns. The music stops, so very conveniently. "And if anyone moves a muscle, that bag by the door will take this club and everyone in it into the next galaxy." All eyes fall to the rucksack by the door. "Let's go."

"Feck, you're The Enigma," he breathes, lifting his glasses, confirming what I thought. Pupils the size of fucking Mars. Fuck me, they're really scraping the barrel to build this fucking web again.

"And guess who I'm taking you to see?" I whisper, cocking my head.

"The Brit and The Enigma?" his mate says, full of dread. "Fuck 'dat."

I see it coming a mile away, and just as he bolts, making it approximately two feet, I turn my gun and put a bullet in his back. More screams. "Your chances of survival are stronger if you cooperate."

The Leprechaun, hands still up, stares at his drugged-up mate now bleeding out on the floor as he edges out of the space and walks to the door. "Aye, I'll cooperate."

I collect my bag, give the doormen a polite nod, and lead him to my car with my gun pushed into his lower back.

"I've always admired ya, you know," he says, stumbling along.

"Shut the fuck up." I pop the boot and present him with a tennis ball.

"I'll tell ya every-tin you wanna know, I swear it."

I shove it in his gob and hold up a cable tie on a tilt of my head, and his wrists are held out in a second. I bind them and shove him back, taking care of his ankles before putting some tape around his mouth and a bag over his head.

I close the trunk, get in the driver's seat, and head back to Hiatus.

I'm still tense after my meeting at the hotel bar, and I'm fucking pissed I can't shake it off. That Irish fucker's lucky I need information more than I need his blood.

I get the biggest fucking scowl from Danny when I find him at the bar. "Where the fuck have you been?" he yells over the music, turning to face me.

I ignore him and order a vodka, perching on a stool. The music is so loud, I can't hear myself fucking think. It might be a good thing.

"And who the fuck is Beth?"

My vodka lands on the bar and I neck it, slamming my empty down. The bartender, Mason, a younger version of Otto but with extra piercings and added tattoos, immediately pours another. I take the glass, looking over to the DJ booth, seeing the resident DJ, his name escapes me, holding one side of his headphones while working the decks with the other. David Guetta gets the crowd pumped with *Love is Gone*, the bass brutal, the endless speakers pulsing.

Beau.

I should go home to Beau. Try and coax her back to the land of the living. My face screws up, my hand reaching for my temple. Why so fucking loud? I look at Danny seeing his mouth moving, but not hearing a fucking word. Necking my second, I slam the glass down, growl, and stand, marching to the booth and taking the six steps up to it in two strides. I don't bother speaking, he won't fucking hear me, so I shove him aside, my ears ringing, and start turning all the dials I can see, until the volume comes down to a more bearable level and my mind no longer feels so chaotic. I exhale and turn, finding the DJ behind me looking absolutely petrified. "That's your max," I grunt, passing him and going back to the bar, Danny's eyes following me the whole way until I'm sitting back on the stool.

"Better?" he asks, as Brad pulls a stool over and joins us.

I don't answer. At least we can talk without yelling. "Where have you been?" Brad asks, waving to Mason for a drink.

"Why is everyone so concerned by where I've been?" I snap. "I had something to deal with. It's dealt with."

Danny's eyebrows arch dramatically, and he peeks out the corner of his eye to Brad, who peeks out the corner of his eye to Danny. "Someone's touchy," Brad says.

"Standard," Danny grunts.

What the fuck do they expect? My girlfriend is currently zombi-fied, The Bear is back in pole position, and an FBI agent is trying to make bitches out of us. My recent meeting has only made my mood fouler. "What the fuck are you playing at, anyway?" I bark, going on the attack. "Two shipments?"

Danny shrinks on his stool and looks at the glass in his hand, turning his nose up at it and placing it on the bar. "We're not all fucking perfect, are we?" He looks around the club. "Where the fuck is Nolan?"

"Yeah, where the fuck is Nolan?" I parrot, pointing my attention to Brad along with Danny, both of us happy to divert the subject elsewhere. I forgot about that matter.

Brad all but snarls at me. Couldn't give a fuck. "He's at my place."

"Why?" I press before Danny can, cocking my head.

Narrowed eyes join his snarl. "You fucking know why." Brad's hand clenches the bottle of beer Mason just pushed toward him.

"What do you know, how do you know, and why the fuck don't *I* know?" Danny asks, looking between us.

"Nolan's got nowhere to stay," Brad grunts, filling his mouth with the bottle and swigging. "He was crashing in the office while we were in St. Lucia."

"And smashing into one of the girls," I add.

"The fuck?" Danny breathes. "So Hiatus is a hotel now too?"

"He was paying off some debts," Brad explains, making Danny jump to the exact same conclusion we did. "He's not taken a nickel."

"How'd you know? There're millions up there. You count every dollar?"

"He's not taken any cash." I back Brad up, feeling charitable. "The kid worked his way out of his debt. I had Otto check out his accounts. He drew cash on every payday, meaning his rent bounced so he got evicted. If he was stealing from us, he would have paid his rent."

Brad blinks, surprised, and Danny settles, happy we're not being fleeced. "Still," he growls, "the girls are off limits."

"I've had a word," Brad assures him as Otto and Ringo join us.

"What's with the baseball cap?" Danny snaps, but Otto bypasses the question and shows us his phone.

A green dot blinks on the screen. "Spittle's phone. He's gone home. I expect he'll go to work tomorrow," Otto says. "My guess is, though, whoever stored with him will have moved on. They won't risk it. He's been away from the bank for too long. They've made alternative arrangements, I guarantee it."

"Maybe they're storing the drugs and guns wherever they were storing the women they're shipping in," Danny muses, staring into space, thinking.

"Wouldn't surprise me." Ringo stands. "They're one big happy fucking family, after all." He looks past us, and we all turn to see Goldie coming out of the ladies'. She looks tired. I hate it. If Ringo makes some wisecrack now, I might slam a screwdriver in his eye myself. "I'm taking her for something to eat," he says, clearing his throat, as we all swing stunned looks to him. He scowls. "She needs some energy. And a timeout from this fucking circus."

He's going to start treating her like a lady now? Does he have a death wish? "Ringo," I say quietly, checking Goldie isn't close enough to hear. "She doesn't want a timeout. She wants to find The Bear and crack on with her life."

"She needs energy to do that, doesn't she?" he practically growls at me, and I back off because . . . well, Goldie.

"Bon appetite," I say, and he marches off, grunting something at Goldie as he passes her, to which she snarls at his back.

Then follows him out.

"I've got shit to do," Brad says, slipping down off the stool. "Catch you motherfuckers later."

"Don't be too late getting home," Danny calls. "You need to tuck the kids up in bed."

Brad's middle finger appears over his back, and Danny chuckles, turning back toward the bar. "All right, back to—" He looks past me, his face interested. "Ooh. So who's this, then?"

I crane my neck to look over my shoulder. And balk. "Oh fuck," I breathe, facing Danny again. How the hell did she find me here?

"Well?"

I lift my eyes and find raging curiosity staring back at me. "I used to fuck her." I wave a hand dismissively because my statement deserves that kind of detachment. "While her husband watched."

Danny barely flinches. Because, of course, thanks to Beau and

Rose sharing *everything*, he knows more about me than I'm probably comfortable with. But I know a shit load about him too, so we're on equal ground. "Cozy," he says, looking past me again. "Which one?"

"The blonde one. Beth. I don't know who the brunette is."

"Oh, *Beth*. I don't see a husband."

Danny's observation doesn't bode well. Why has Beth been calling me?

"So this is the woman Beau walked in on you fucking?"

"Yes." And, worse, I knew she was watching, but that was before I knew what Beau would become to me. Life. Freedom. Love. I inhale when I feel a hand land on my forearm, and look down at the long, painted nails. Nothing like Beau's short, bare nails. I look at the suit Beth's wearing, probably designer. Nothing like the ripped jeans and baggy shirts Beau's sports most days. Then up at her perfectly styled and sprayed blowout. Nothing like Beau's wild blonde waves. And finally to her polished, makeup covered face. Nothing like Beau's natural, makeup-free skin. Why the fuck am I comparing? One woman means nothing to me. The other means the fucking world. Hell, heaven, and everything in between.

"James," she purrs, her voice as delighted as her eyes. "It's been too long."

I beg to differ. I can feel Danny's interested stare jumping between us, his body comfortable, settling in for the show. "What are you doing here?" I ask.

"Girls' night out."

"At a strip club?"

"Actually, my friend's sister works here. We're picking her up." She smiles. That's mighty convenient. But also very possible. "How have you been?"

I move my arm from her reach and resist asking Mason for an antibac wipe, but when I catch his eye, polishing a glass looking on with interest, I wonder if he might offer one without prompt.

How have I been?

Glorious. Dire.

Elated. Miserable.

Stable. Crazy.

"What can I do for you, Beth?" I ask, deciding nothing but directness will work here, and I know Beth is accustomed to boldness. Just not the kind I'm adopting now.

"Just seeing how you've been," she says, easy-breezy.

"Is that why you called him too?" Danny pipes up, pulling my attention his way, as well as Beth's and her friend's, who I notice now is eyeing Danny. Thank fuck the girls aren't here. It would be a bloodbath. Or would it? I know Rose wouldn't react too kindly to another woman all over her husband, even if it's just her eyes on him, but what about Beau? Is she even capable of caring? Does she have the capacity? Would she even really fucking care? I jerk away from that thought before it sends my mood lower.

"Danny," he says, as way of introduction, without offering his hand. "A friend of James."

"I'm Violet," the brunette replies, thrusting her hand toward Danny. "Pleased to meet you."

Danny doesn't look at her, but looks at her hand briefly, leaving it hanging, then returns his eyes to Beth, and the brunette, Violet, awkwardly withdraws her offering.

"I don't remember you," Beth says.

"James and I have only recently reconnected." He smiles, and it makes me laugh on the inside. He's being protective. Not of me, but of Beau. Is it wasted? "Through our better halves," he adds, taking a drink casually after coolly dropping that information.

"Oh?" Beth breathes.

"I understand you're married," he goes on, ignoring her reaction. *I'm* now settling in for the show. Beth's not exactly unbearable, but not exactly tolerable either, unless she's gagged, of course.

"Was." She looks at me. "I *was* married. We separated recently." Her back straightens, her chest pushing out, an air of superiority coming across.

"Shame," Danny grunts, making her inhale, as if gathering patience.

She turns toward him and smiles. It isn't sincere. "Would you mind giving us a moment?"

Naturally, Danny looks at me, his drink at his lips, and I nod, just wanting to get this done with and get Beth out of here. Danny leaves, the brunette following, biting at his heels, and Beth takes his stool, calling for a wine. I don't know why; this will be over before Mason pours it. "Again, what can I do for you, Beth?"

She smiles coyly, and it gets under my skin. Pray do tell me she doesn't think there was anything more in our meetings than raw, carnal fucking. Scratching an itch. She served a purpose for me, and I thought I did for her and her husband. But now she doesn't have a husband. I'm not even curious as to why. How she came to be here, however? A friend who works here? "You've not taken any of my calls."

"Because I don't want to speak to you."

"I thought, well, maybe—"

"Didn't you hear my friend? I'm with someone."

She laughs, and it's like blades across my skin. She doesn't think I'm capable of anything but fucking? "You?"

"Yes, me." I look past her, seeing Danny watching, the brunette getting dangerously close to him. She must have zero social awareness, because Danny's fuck-off vibes are reaching me all the way over here. "This friend of yours who works here, who is it?"

The awkwardness staring back at me tells me she's bullshitting. What the fuck is she playing at, and how the fuck did she know I would be here?

"So who is the lucky girl?" she asks, bypassing my question.

I don't bother telling her it's the blonde I found in my apartment the last time I was seeing Beth and her husband out. Why the fuck am I even entertaining this shit? "That is none of your business, so if we're done?" I go to stand, but both her hands land on my thighs, and I drop back to the stool. She gets to her feet, moves in closer, pushes her mouth to my ear. My skin crawls, every muscle tenses.

"I want you to bind me," she whispers, licking the shell of my ear, "gag me, and fuck me black and blue."

I clench my eyes closed and grit my teeth to deal with the unbearable closeness as I push my mouth to her ear. "Fuck," I whisper, "Off." Taking her forearms, I push her firmly but gently away. The indignation staring back at me amps up my anger. That anyone thinks I would even consider betraying Beau, whether they know her or not, riles me. "Goodbye." I turn on my stool, away from her, facing the bar, and only breathe easy when I feel her move away. I look out the corner of my eye and find Danny wandering back over, looking toward the entrance, watching Beth and her friend leave.

"She was a bold one," he says, perching on the stool. "Good job she's gone, because Beau's on her way."

"What?"

"Rose just called. She's managed to get Beau out of bed and they're coming here. I agreed, since I assume you want to encourage her leaving the house."

"She's coming here?"

"Yes."

My phone pings, and I look down at the screen, inhaling, taken aback by the woman staring back at me. It's my wild, free-spirited, baggy-jeaned girl, but today she's in a dress, cowboy boots, and a denim jacket. Little makeup, hair piled messily up. She looks out of this world, smiling but clearly nervous, looking almost shy. Will she understand why I've done what I've done? Will she accept it? I don't know, so I won't be telling her. Not until I'm sure.

Rose put her up to this picture. I need to thank her.

For helping her out of her darkness too.

14

BEAU

"He'll love it," Rose says from beside me in the back seat.

A man of many words, I think, as I look down at my cell, waiting for a reply. He's clearly speechless, and I can't blame him. From zombie to party girl in a few hours flat. I look across to Rose and smile, taking her hand and holding it. She looks gorgeous in a gold long-sleeved body-con dress. "You look amazing," I say, my eyes resting on her little bump.

"Not just fat?" She wriggles in the seat, pulling at the fabric around her waist.

"Shut up." Fury pulls up at the front of the club. The line outside is long, clients, mostly males, waiting to be granted entry by the two mountains on the door. "Ready?"

"Ready."

Neither of us get out, not until Fury opens one of the doors after no doubt running a quick check and probably calling for extra men to assist. Rose steps out first, and I shift along the seat, stepping out too, just as two more suited men exit the club. I want to say it's unnecessary. I can't.

We stand and wait for them to sort their positions, Rose reapplying her lipstick, me . . . not. Instead, I look at the line of dozens of people and wonder just how many there are inside. My heartbeats increase as a result, and I start the same old routine, practicing controlled breathing. I will not be pushed back in that element of my life. This I *can* control.

"You okay?" Rose says, placing a hand on my arm.

"It's busy." My thoughts tumble from my mouth without instruction, telling Rose where I'm at, so I rush to reassure her. To play down my threatening panic attack. *James is in there. I just need to make it to Ja—* "Oh," I yelp, being knocked a few steps back.

"Shit, I'm sorry," a woman says, her purse falling to the sidewalk, her things scattering. She crouches, and Fury moves in, prompting me to put my hand up.

"I've got it," I say as I lower to help, collecting a lipstick and a pack of condoms.

"Here." I look up, just as she glances up at me too.

"Thanks." Her smile falters, her head tilting as she takes her things, stuffing everything back in her purse.

"You look familiar," I say, taking her in, wracking my brain for where I might know her from.

"Beau," Rose says, helping me to stand as the woman rises with us.

I hear Fury calling me, and I let Rose pull me on, looking back at the woman on the sidewalk, still wondering where I know her from, as she clearly does the same with me. I don't have the mental capacity right now, so I give up, returning my attention forward.

Naturally, there are a few grumbles from the waiting patrons when we bypass the line and we're escorted in.

"Who was that?" Rose asks, as we follow the two mountains, Fury tailing us.

"I don't know. I know her face, though." My cell chimes, and I look down at the screen, the name slowing me to a stop.

"Beau?" Rose says, as Fury's front meets my back.

"Okay?" he asks, whistling for the two men up front to stop.

I stare down at my cell, my heart that was racing with anxiety now racing with dread. I honestly thought he'd got the message. I'm in love with a deadly assassin and nothing is going to change that.

"Beau?" Rose presses.

"It's Ollie," I say, looking at her, for what I don't know. "A message from Ollie."

Her face twists. "He's got some seriously thick skin. Can't you block him?"

I might have to, because if James finds out he's still trying to reach me or turn me against him, Ollie will be dead, and while he's been a dick, I don't wish him dead. I nod and open the message, ready to click on his name to get his contact details to block him, telling myself not to read his words. But they're not words. He's sent me a picture. A picture of James.

James with a woman hanging off his front, his mouth at her ear. "What?" I whisper, recognizing the trouser suit. And where I know her from hits me like a brick in my face. I exhale and swing around, searching the sidewalk outside for her. I don't have to search far. She's not moved.

Staring back at me, I see the recognition on her face. She's realized where she knows me from too. She smiles mildly, and it's knowing, small but interested.

On top of the image of her hanging off my man's body, it's too much, my stomach feeling like it's been sucker punched. My veins heat, anger consuming me. Blinding me. I feel Rose take my cell from my hand. I hear her quiet curse. I see her move toward the woman before me, ready to do God knows what, but she doesn't make it.

Fury swoops in, lifting her from her feet and removing her. "You are not in any fit state to cat fight," he grumbles, looping his spare arm around my waist too and lifting me, carrying us both away from the woman into the club.

He places us down and looks at me. "I'm sure there's a reasonable explanation."

"And what would that be?" I ask. "Tell me, Fury, because I am oh so fucking curious why my boyfriend would have his tongue in another woman's ear."

His bearded jaw rolls, his nostrils flaring, and I can absolutely appreciate that it's because he's mad with James too. "I don't know," he grates.

"Then let's find out," I say, pivoting and walking into the club. I collide with James just inside the entrance, and I conclude he was obviously coming to meet me. Or the other woman. *Beth*. That's her name. Beth. Or maybe he was checking that Beth had left the building before I arrived.

I feel so fucking stupid. All dressed up like this, so unlike me, sending coy pictures. No wonder he didn't reply. He was busy.

"Hey," he says softly, holding on to my upper arms. "You're here."

The anger swirls in my gut, burns my blood, gaining momentum unstoppably. The pressure in my head is beginning to hurt. "Get the hell off me," I yell, yanking myself out of his hold, squaring him with a look I'm sure could kill.

His frown only heightens my anger. "Beau?"

"Where the fuck is her husband?" I seethe, seeing Danny approaching behind James, his face a picture of concern, which makes me wonder how crazy I must look. As crazy as I feel? I'm certain it's not possible. "Masturbating in the corner somewhere?"

James steps back, hands up, as if handling a ticking time bomb. "What?" he says warily. He knows. He absolutely knows what, but I absolutely do not mind telling him.

"This." I thrust my cell in his face, and he is forced to seize my wrist and hold it still so the screen stops shaking long enough for him to see the image. "Tired of dealing with the shit you're creating?" I ask. "Not getting enough out of this relationship anymore so moving back to old habits?"

His jaw rolls. It's a fucking insult. "Stand down, Beau," he orders in a deadly tone I should probably pay attention to. And yet I don't. My rage is ruling me. My body trembling, a red mist fogging my vision. I feel like control is slipping away rapidly. I need to let go of this pressure. I need to explode.

"I will not fucking stand down!" I yell. "How fucking dare you? *You* stand down!" I shove him out of my way and march to the bar, not ordering a drink, but swiping up a glass of red that's already there, not bothering to check whose it is or if they mind. I'm pretty sure they won't challenge me.

I down it, praying the liquid cools my temper, and gasp, slamming it back on the bar and motioning for another. I can feel many eyes on me, but the music still plays—Swedish House Mafia *One (Your Name)* right now—and the dancers still dance. I order a second wine before turning around and leaning against the bar, raking a hand through my hair to pull the loose strands off my hot face. I see Danny pull Rose away. I see her grave face. I see Fury looking torn between attempting to remove me from what's fueling me—James—or leaving me to . . . detonate.

I cast my eyes across them all again. The music seems to get louder by the second, like it's building to a crescendo along with my temper. Then I look at James. I look at him with all the contempt I feel on a curled lip. I just want to lash out. Hit things. Be rid of this unbridled anger. Release the pressure.

Standing there, his stance wide, his fists balled by his thighs, his jaw ticking, he looks like a deadly mix of power and control. I hate both on him in this moment when I'm straining not to lose my shit. I drink down my second wine and blindly push the glass on the bar behind me. *Hurt him. Hurt him. Hurt him.* My eyes glued to his, I walk to him, lifting my chin, my whole body rolling with the effort to breathe. I see the veins in his throat pulse. His Adam's apple sinks and protrudes. His lips twitch. The hollows of his cheeks pulse under his stubble. I find his blue eyes. Eyes that are flames right now. "We're done," I say emotionlessly, backing away.

"We're never done, Beau." He speaks calmly but looks anything but, his powerful, muscled frame shaking from the strain of keeping his cool.

I turn and walk away.

"We're never done, Beau Hayley!" he roars. "Broken, fixed, happy, sad, we're never fucking done!"

I turn calmly and come nose to chest with Fury. "I'm not his anymore, so you do not need to tail me." I look up at him and get a hint of his mood. Furious. "Back off," I order, but he says nothing, just moves aside, not because he's backing off, but because he's giving James access to me. "No," I yell, my hands coming up and blocking James from seizing me. "Keep your fucking hands off me." I turn to leave again, or I try to, but an arm snakes around my waist and lifts me from the floor. "Get off me," I scream, my arms and legs flailing, throwing my head back, but he anticipates my move—the only move I have in this position—and gets his nose out of the way of my thrashing head.

"Stand fucking down," he bellows, fighting to hold down my flailing arms. He carries me out of the club, and the looks coming at us are, expectedly, shocked.

I kick, I scream, I fight his hold with everything I have, my anger driving me. I can't stop. I need this pressure to leave me. I need to be exhausted. But no matter how much I fight, I can still breathe easy.

I need to stop breathing easy.

Stop breathing altogether.

I'm carried across the road, and I hear the sound of brakes screeching, driver's yelling for us to get out of their way. I think a missile could hit James now and he wouldn't budge an inch. He stalks down an alleyway to where his car is parked and the headlights blink, the doors opening. He is *not* putting me in that car. "I said we are done," I yell.

"Shut the fuck up, Beau."

I am out of my fucking mind. Untamable. Uninhibited. And as if to prove it, I twist my arm and reach behind James's back, pulling his gun from the waistband of his jeans, disengaging the safety. He stops just shy of his car, his body still but his chest pulsing wildly into my back. I turn the gun around and point it at both of us. "Put me down," I say calmly, and he does because he knows. He knows I am fucking crazy, and he's sent me further that way.

I turn the gun around in my hand and face him, and I look straight into his eyes. "We are done," I assure him. He shakes his head, his expression incensed. "Yes," I counter.

"No." He moves fast, reaching for his back and before I can blink, I have a gun aimed at me. "As long as I live and breathe, Beau Hayley, we will never be done."

"Then I guess you won't be breathing for very long."

"You're the one who doesn't want to marry me, so stop being all insecure. It doesn't suit you."

My free hand lashes out of its own volition, cracking him around the face, and my palm bursts into flames, his head snapping to the side where he holds it, his lip curling. "Been taking pointers from your best friend?" he hisses.

"Fuck you."

"Wouldn't that be nice?"

The pressure in my head bursts, and I scream like an unhinged mad woman, squeezing the trigger. I jolt, flying around and slamming into something. The back of my head collides with a wall, the rough bricks pulling at my dress. The gun is gone from my hand, and James is armed with both. He heaves and pants in front of me, and then he roars to the black sky and fires both guns, one after the other, over and over, the sound of bullets leaving the chamber piercing, echoing off the bricks of the dank alley.

Then ... quiet.

Except for the last shell casing hitting the ground with a pretty ping.

"Would I like to let off some steam?" he asks, breathless. "Yes, fuck, I need that." He comes closer and breathes down on me. "Will I take it elsewhere? No." I hear the sound of the two guns hitting the concrete, then his hands are in my hair fisting it harshly. "I know only your pussy now, Beau."

"This pussy doesn't want you."

"Taste only your lips. Ram my cock only into your cunt. Suck only your nipples." He dips and licks the shell of my ear. "I will only ever restrain *you*. Fuck *your* arse." Pulling away, he looks at me with wide, wild eyes, his hold of my hair unmoving. "My mind knows only you. My body knows only yours." Slamming his mouth onto mine, he kisses me brutally, forcing me up onto my tiptoes. "My damn fucking black heart can only ever love you, Beau Hayley, so get your fucking head on straight and show me that all this anger and stress is worth it, because if you really mean it when you say we're done, I'll slip back into the shadows and pick up my life where I left off the day you walked into my apartment and watched me fuck that woman."

Stunned, I stare at him. My anger hasn't subsided from his words. It's multiplied. This fucking world. Our fucking lives. Why? *Why, why, why?* When will the blows stop coming? To James, I am nothing but stress and helplessness. I don't even let him fuck me how I know he likes to fuck anymore.

He turns his face away from me. "We're fine," he says, letting whoever's come to check on us know that we're still alive. And the second he's facing me again, I let my anger out in another way. I'm on him like a starving wolf, kissing him like I might not ever again, gripping his hair harshly. And he accepts.

I climb his body, wrap my legs around his waist, pull him as close as I can get him, my hands fisting his hair, my mouth relentless on his. My tongue circles and whips, frenzied and fast, an unbearable throb hitting me between my legs.

"Are you hard?" I gasp over my words, releasing one hand and feeling around his crotch, hearing his moan as I stroke over his erection. "I want you to fuck me. Hard. Tie me up and fuck me." I need that. Him. All over me. I need to be taken back to the beginning and reminded.

He pushes me into the wall, his tongue merciless in my mouth. "Everything was in my apartment."

His apartment that was blown up. And he hasn't replaced anything, because he's either been too busy, out of the country, or he thinks dirty, filthy, debased fucking shouldn't feature in our relationship anymore.

Well, I need it. Clearly. I need that sense of freedom, to be taken away from this life. "Fix it," I order, and he nods as our kiss continues, not slowing, not softening. "I can't wait."

He breaks away and heaves in my face as he walks to the car, puts me down, and opens the passenger door of his Range Rover. He turns me around, bends me over the seat, and yanks up my dress, my panties aside, and I yelp, my fingers clawing into the leather seats. Two fingers sink into me on a groan from him and a moan from me.

"Drenched," he growls, removing them, leveling up, and ramming into me.

"Shit!" The fullness sates me immediately. Calms the animal inside. Lightens the darkness. Cools the burn in my veins. I sigh and settle against the seat, eyes open, staring at the back of the chair. I already know this is going to be a ruthless fuck. Angry. I'm here for it.

I close my eyes, breath in deeply, relax further, and sink into myself, letting him pound into me like a man possessed, yelling, frantic, chaotic.

And me?

I'm at peace. Calm. I needed this more than I knew. Needed James. I am taken away from the world I'm struggling in, into a place I thrive.

Being James's. Possessed by him. Owned by him. Cured by him. He was right. We'll never be done. I cannot live without this. *Us.*

He strikes harder, grabbing my hair and pulling it. The pain travels through my body and hits me hard between my legs. "I'm going to come," I say calmly but loud enough for him to hear, and he bellows, pounding harder, yanking harder, breathing harder.

"Fuck!" He withdraws, circles, and pounds into me one last time, grinding on a moan, and I come, so hard but so serene, the pleasure rolling through me, dowsing the anger that ruled me only a few moments ago. I feel his heat flood me. His grip releases, and he massages my scalp as he circles his hips. "Are you okay?" he asks, wheezing.

I don't answer, pushing my hands into the leather and standing, inhaling when he slips out of me. I feel him trickle down my leg, and I wonder . . . did any stay inside of me? Enough? And would my body accept it?

I feel him pull my panties into place and my dress down, before turning me to face him. His jeans hang open, and I help fix him while he watches me intently. He eventually lifts my chin with a finger so I'm looking at him. "I told you once never to question my love for you. Today you questioned it. Who sent you that picture?"

And just like that, my serenity is lost, and I am back in a world I can't cope with today. "You know who sent me that picture."

The hollows of his cheeks pulse. "I told you to block his number."

"And I ignored you." I move away, out of his reach. "Why was that woman all over you?"

He closes his eyes, gathering patience. "She's been calling me. I assumed she and Darren wanted to play. I ignored her. She showed up tonight. It's rather convenient that Burrows was here too, don't you think?"

"So it's his fault you had another woman hanging off you?" Is he saying Ollie set him up?

"I've handled it."

"You sure did," I breathe, laughing under my breath.

"What the fuck is that supposed to mean?"

"I'm going home." I pull at my dress to straighten it. "Fury can take me."

"Are you saying I *can't* take you?"

"I'm saying I can't be around you right now."

"I was just inside you, Beau. Fucking you. And *now* you can't be around me?"

"Yes," I yell, obviously all over the place and feeling it too.

"For fuck's sake." James swoops up his guns and tosses them in the footwell of his Range Rover. "So what was that? Scratching my itch in case I was tempted to take Beth up on her offer?"

I stare at him, wanting to slap him again. "If you want to take her up on her offer, don't let me stop you." I don't know what I'm saying, and the flash of hurt that flickers across his bristly face spikes a twinge of guilt. To think I could lose him to another woman? To think I might be without him? To go back to the dark places I frequented before James, hollow and lonely?

"You're destructive," he says quietly. "You know me, Beau. Do you think I'm capable of betraying you?"

I don't answer, looking away, ashamed. And he knows it.

"Fucking answer me."

I look at him. Stare at him.

"You can be angry at me," he whispers. "Hit me, punch me, fucking shoot me. None of it hurts as much as you not trusting me." And again, I look away, unable to face the gray, damaging storm swirling in his eyes. "If you think I would hurt you, we may as well add me to the list of men I'm going to kill."

"Stop it."

"No."

"It—" I hear my cell ring, and I search the ground for my purse. I find it by the rear tire of James's car and dip to collect it. I don't recognize the number. I also don't get a chance to answer. James plucks it from my hand and takes the call for me. "What the hell?"

"Stand the fuck down," he growls, connecting and answering with silence, his eyes narrowing. "Speak," he eventually demands, getting edgier the longer the caller remains silent, and as a consequence, I do too. But then his scowl turns into a frown, and he looks at me. "Who?"

Just the fact he's asking that means I can safely say it's not my ex. "Who is it?" I ask, impatient.

"Frazer Cartwright," James replies.

"What?" I question, reaching for my phone but getting nowhere near, because James moves back. "The journalist?"

"Yes, the journalist."

What could he want? Jesus, if my father has set this up, I can't say I won't lose my shit again. He wants me to play the doting daughter to the respected businessman who's running for mayor? Absolutely not. And James should not be talking to him either. I reach for my cell again, and this time I get a growl. "Give me it, James."

"No."

I drop my purse, lift the skirt of my dress, jump and spin, kicking my cell away from his ear. It hits the wall with force and drops to the ground, and I scoop it up. The screen is cracked, but the call is still in progress. "This is Beau Hayley speaking," I say, my eyes on James's fuming form. His nostrils are flaring. His jaw pulsing. I ignore it all and walk away before he blows me back when he explodes.

"Miss Hayley," Cartwright says. "My name—"

"I know your name and who you are. What do you want?"

"Your father—"

"What about him?"

"He's dead."

I cough, stilling, my stomach feeling like it's just fallen to the ground at my feet. "What?" I whisper, turning my eyes onto James. I know they must be wide because his irritation dissipates in a second and he's in front of me, his expression questioning. I don't know what to do. What to say. How to react. I feel . . . empty. And despite emptiness being a constant threat in my life, this feeling is new. My cell falls away from my ear, my arm limp, my eyes searching around me as I turn on the spot, as if I might see my father here and now and confirm I didn't just hear right.

"Beau?"

I blink, running back over the conversation I just had.

"Beau?"

He's dead?

"Beau, for fuck's sake." James takes the tops of my arms and shakes me, dipping and getting in my field of vision. He recoils when I look at him, then feels down to my hand, taking my cell. He looks at the screen. Cartwright has disconnected, and I blink rapidly, seeming to come back into my body at the sight of James's concern. I reclaim my phone and dial the only person who comes to mind, putting aside my grievance with him, and James will have to too.

"Ollie?"

"Beau," he breathes in answer, and the second I hear his voice, I know. I just know.

"Don't tell me you were just going to call me," I beg anyway, praying for an explanation. "Please don't tell me that."

"I was just going to call you."

"No," I whisper.

"How do you know?" he asks.

"Cartwright called me."

"Fuck. I'm on my way there now, Beau."

"Where is there?"

"A hotel downtown."

"No." God damn it, I should have met Dad for dinner. His heart. I knew there was something wrong. But Doc checked him over. I look at James, and the moment he catches my expression, he withdraws, standing down, his ego wilting. I can't find the words to tell him what's wrong, and he sees my struggle.

He takes my cell and puts it to his ear. "It's James," he says shortly, holding on to my shoulder. "What's going on?" He inhales in an obvious attempt to gather patience. "Now's not the time to throw your ego around, Burrows. Whatever you were doing at Hiatus this evening, I couldn't give a fuck. Whatever you hoped to achieve sending Beau that picture, I couldn't give a fuck. What the fuck's going on?"

Dead. He's dead. He's dead and Ollie, an FBI agent, is on his way there. A journalist has called me. It wasn't a heart attack? A seizure? A stroke? I startle, and it's the oddest feeling, like a switch just flipped inside of me. Like I'm going into business mode, except I am not a cop anymore, and my father isn't any old victim. I grab my phone from James, and this time he lets me take it. "Why are you going there, Ollie?" I ask. "And why the hell are journalists calling me?"

"Witnesses are claiming to have heard a gunshot."

"A single gunshot?" I ask robotically.

"A single gunshot," he confirms. "I'm just relaying what I've been told. There's no sign of a struggle. Nothing taken from his person."

"So it's someone he knows?"

"He knows a lot of people, Beau."

"I know," I say, starting to pace. *Thinking, thinking, thinking.* "The gun?"

"Missing."

"Shell casing?"

"No shell casing." He doesn't hold back at all, telling me things he really shouldn't be telling me. Because I'm no longer a cop. "I'm so sorry, Beau," Ollie says, his voice soft. "I know you and Tom had a love-hate relationship, but he was still your dad."

I swallow, nodding. "I'm on my way. What's the name of the hotel?"

"Beau, you know that can't happen."

"I—"

"I'll call you later, I promise."

I take a deep breath and reason with myself. I need to play ball. Keep Ollie on side. "Okay," I say reluctantly. "As soon as you have more information."

"You got it." He hangs up, and I take my cell to my mouth and nibble the corner as James moves in, his arms reaching for me. I step away, not looking at him.

"I'll take you home," he says.

"No." I face him. "I don't want to go home. Why would I want to go home?"

He frowns, looking confused, a limp hand lifting to point at my cell. "Well, unless I'm missing something, I'm pretty sure you just took a call from your ex-*fiancé* who advised you that your father's been murdered."

"Why such emphasis on fiancé?" I snap. "What's your fucking problem?" *What's his problem?* Why would I ask such a ridiculous question? Ollie was here, still trying to turn me against James.

That's his fucking problem. I am losing my mind fast. Pressing buttons I shouldn't be pressing. Saying things I shouldn't be saying. The walls. They're suddenly getting higher around me again, brick by brick.

I can see James is fighting to keep calm. "Your father is dead, Beau. You're allowed to be sad. You're allowed to be vulnerable."

"My father was a narcissistic prick who left my mother for a brainless gold digger. My father put me in a psychiatric ward and left me to rot. My father hid me from the world to save his sparkling reputation. My father was a hollow, heartless asshole who worried more about his public image than his daughter's welfare." I walk past James. "I don't want to go home," I yell back, knowing I've left behind one very perplexed man. A man who saved me from drowning in the darkness of everything I just listed to him.

The man who might not be able to save me again.

15

DANNY

"Who the hell was that woman?" Rose is up in my face, and it's all I can do not to growl back in hers. I'm not wasting my words when she's going to be getting all the juicy details from Beau the moment they're together again.

"Are you getting spiky with me?" I ask seriously, walking into her, making her back up. To everyone around us, my move would appear threatening. Borderline intimidating.

It is.

And my wife in all her glory will have none of it. "Fuck you, Black," she spits, making me recoil, walking forward, turning the tables, having *me* back up. "What's been going on while your little women have been tucked away safety in your mansion?"

My mansion? I laugh on the inside. It's not been *my* mansion for some time. More like a hotel for fucking reprobates. But back to the matter at hand. She wants to know what's been going on? "What the fuck do you think's been going on?" I ask, incensed. "Personal lap dances? Or something a little more"—I push my face up in hers —"physical? A good fuck with a willing whore? Is that what you're asking?"

She flicks her long dark hair over her shoulder, giving me a run for my money in the snarling department. "You wouldn't dare."

She's right, I wouldn't, but I'm not about to admit it. Besides, I wouldn't fucking want to. This is fucking ridiculous. How the fuck did James and Beau's disagreement become ours? "Carry on like a psycho loony bitch, I might." And there it is, her palm locking, loading, and firing. My hand shoots up and catches her wrist, and she quickly yanks it free.

"Carry on like an asshole, I might too." She shoves me aside, the argument now done, and I laugh like an idiot as she stomps to the bar, her ever curvier arse jumping beautifully. That gold dress looks fucking perfect on her perfectly pregnant curves. I suppress a growl and discreetly adjust myself, following her, aware of the eyes on us. She's made it onto a stool by the time I make it to her, and I push into her back with my chest, vehemently ignoring the biting pain the pressure brings, my hard-on wedging into her arse. She gasps and sits up straight, her hand splaying the countertop.

I push my face into her hair at her ear. "Get upstairs."

"Fuck you."

"No, I want to fuck *you*." I physically lift her off the stool and place her facing the right direction. "Move." I rest one hand on her nape, squeeze a little, the other I slide onto her tummy, stroking softly, and I walk her through the throngs of people toward the office.

"You gonna listen to me if I say no this time?"

Oh, how she tests me. "Yes," I grate, because of course I'll fucking listen. Jesus Christ, she'll never let me forget that, the spiteful bitch. She knows I'm beating myself up about it constantly. I don't need her help, although she'll undoubtedly stick the knife in further when she feels like it.

"No," she snaps, and I stop dead in my tracks, loosening my hold of her neck.

I breath in deeply. Calmly. "Why do you want to hurt me?" I ask. It's a perfectly reasonable question. Every damn fucking time she's got the hump, she kicks me in the balls. I know I've always said she can take everything out on me, but there's only so much a man can stand. Yet at the same time, the twisted fuck in me loves being the one person who gives her the chance to fight back, even if she's out of line. Like now.

She flexes her neck and faces me, her hand resting on her tummy where mine was a moment ago. "I don't want to hurt you, baby." She smiles, and I hate it. My eyes narrow, waiting for the blow, and she steps toward me, looking up as she slips a finger past my lips and circles it around my tongue. She pouts, licking her lips, and my wilting arousal springs back to life. She comes closer. Strokes my lips from side to side, watching, concentrating. I realize I'm heading for a fall here, and yet I cannot find the will to remove myself from the reach of her vindictiveness. "I want to pain you," she whispers, stroking down my front and cupping my dick. I swallow a grunt and close my eyes.

So she's going to deprive me? Jesus. Deprive me, knowing I won't ever force myself on her. She's done this before, of course. It's her weapon, her ace card that she flaunts when she's feeling particularly cruel. Or, actually, helpless. But whereas before I could convince her in my own way, I cannot now. Not after my fuck-up in St. Lucia. "I fucking hate you," I wheeze in my darkness.

She pushes her lips to mine and kisses me gently, and I naturally fall into it, but my hands remain dangling lifelessly at my sides, scared to hold her. "If you think you're leaving me at home while you sit in a strip joint having girls drooling all over you, you'd better think again, Black." She drops me. "And I want Esther and my son back here with us."

I snort. Not a chance in hell. But I don't say that; I don't want to escalate things further. Rose passes me, and I turn, my trousers tight, seeing Beau walking back into the club, and a few feet behind, James, looking as murderous as I've ever known him to look.

Beau puts herself on a stool at the bar and signals Mason, and Rose joins her, not signaling Mason.

"Fucking hell." I scrub a hand down my face and go to them.

Beau's face. It's grim, and an uncharacteristic urge comes over me to help my mate out and explain. "Beau, let—"

"Don't, Danny," she warns, in a tone so deadly I listen. It's rare to see Beau the cop. But she's here now, firm in her stance, looking pretty fucking gritty, and I'm quickly very worried for that Beth woman.

"Go take a seat in one of the booths," I say. "I'll get Mason to bring some . . ." I falter, looking at James. He doesn't look like he wants Beau drinking anymore. I don't think I want her drinking anymore either.

"Wine," Beau says, not looking at me. "And we'll be staying here." She remains on her stool and Rose doesn't question it. I've just about had enough of insolent women for today. I wave Mason over. "Water for that one," I say, pointing at Rose, who is quick to swing around and give me daggers. I push out my bottom lip. "Did that hurt, baby? Me talking about you like you're an object, did that hurt?" I'm so fucking childish. Her fault. "And a bottle of Scotch and vodka for the table over there, since it looks like we've been banished."

I join James. "If it's any consolation, I'm in the doghouse with you," I say, sliding into the round booth seating, reaching under the table and pushing into my semi-erect dick, willing it to behave. Two bottles and two glasses land on the table, and I nod my thanks to Mason. I'm pretty sure he's had more tattoos. His neck? The bloke is covered, head to toe. I pour us both a drink and push James's across the table, taking my own and sipping while I watch him stare at it. "Yo, bud?"

"Tom Hayley is dead," he says to the glass, flat and emotionlessly.

I still, my drink hanging in midair. "What?"

"He's dead."

I look across to the bar and see Rose with her hands over her mouth, looking at a very still and quiet Beau facing the bar nursing a bottle of red. And Fury's face says it all too, as he looks at me, as if to check he's heard right. What? How? When? Who? *Why?* I shake my head, trying to straighten out my thoughts. "He's dead?"

"I don't have many details. Frazer Cartwright called Beau."

"The journalist?"

"Yes, the journalist."

"He's a man in the know, isn't he?" I quip. "Perhaps we need to talk to him."

"Agreed."

"And it's confirmed?"

"Agent Burrows confirmed it." James looks at me through hollow eyes. "He was on his way to the scene."

"Fuck. All this transpired just now?"

"Yes, while Beau and I were"—he cricks his neck, his hand wrapping around his tumbler—"ironing out a few differences."

"Well, you're a shit ironer if that shiner on your cheek is anything to go by." I toast the red mark as James feels at it, then have another sensible sip of my Scotch, wanting to, or needing to, down the lot and get a solid hit of alcohol. But I can't do that. I can never do that. In fact, I shouldn't be fucking drinking at all. And yet . . . I take another sip. "Dead?"

"Gunshot reported."

I nod, thinking. If I'm brutally honest, the world won't be so hard done by with no Tom Hayley in it and, being even more brutally honest, it's one less thing for James and me to worry about, because that man was gunning for us. But . . . Beau. I look at the girls at the bar again, seeing Rose now rubbing Beau's back, her stool closer, but Beau hasn't moved. "Who sent her that picture of you with Beth?" I ask, going back to the initial problem.

James looks up at me as he plays with his glass. "Burrows."

"But he was on his way to the scene. From here? And why the fuck would he come here, anyway? To make peace?" I laugh. I doubt it. Or . . . I frown and look up at James. "Or he's got someone in our club." I glance around the expansive space, up the stairs to the mezzanine floor. Staff? A client? It could be anyone.

"I think it's simpler than that, but I'm gonna have Nolan look into it to be sure." He goes to his phone and taps out a message.

"Wise." Now, back to the matter at hand. "Do you think this will knock Beau back more?" I ask, topping up James's drink. She wasn't exactly head over heels in love with her father. "Her mum, now this?"

"No," James says. "I think it'll be worse than that." He turns his glass slowly on the table, oblivious to my questioning expression.

"What could be worse than her returning full tilt to that darkness?" I ask, and James looks up at me. I hate the answer before he's even spoken it, his face so impassive. It's truly worrying.

"Taking me with her," he whispers, turning his eyes to Beau at the bar.

Fuck, yes, that would be pretty fucking horrific. There's no denying James is on the upper end of the fucked-up spectrum, even now, but at least he's got a purpose beyond revenge. "How do we stop that?"

"I'd have to let her do what she's planning on doing."

"What is she planning on doing?"

"Becoming a cop again."

I shoot back in my chair like I've been shot. "What the fuck?"

"I saw it," he says quietly, still turning the glass, as if clinging to it to keep himself rooted. To stop himself going on a killing spree here and now. "She loved her father but hated him. Her thoughts of him mirrored ours. Narcissistic prick. But the orphan in her will feel guilt, and the only way to ease that guilt would be to end their relationship by serving his honor."

She can't find her mother's killer, so perhaps she can find her father's. "Shit," I hiss, taking more than a sip of my drink. So what James is saying, basically, is either way, he'll lose her. *Fuck*. I know Beau's relationship with her father was strained to say the least, but if there's anyone in this world who can relate to being orphaned, it's me. Before Carlo Black found me, filthy and hungry in a London alley, I often felt alone. My mother was terrified of my stepfather, unable to protect me.

There's nothing better to build some resilience like needing to be vulnerable but not being able to be. By being forced into being strong. I forgave Esther for abandoning me. It brought me some peace. Beau thinks she'll find peace if she does this. Never. There's always something to fuck that up for us. She let her defenses down when she met James. She became vulnerable, and so did he. Not dissimilar to Rose and me, really, but still so very different. Now? Now the world that brought them together, the darkness that they shared is pushing them apart. Because if Beau picks up her badge, she's no longer a part of this family.

I have no fucking clue what to say. "What are you going to do?" I ask, feeling as stumped as James. *Fuck Tom Hayley for fucking dying.*

His smile is inappropriate. He's amused by his thoughts. "She's going nowhere near Oliver Burrows or a badge."

I blow out my cheeks. "And the darkness?"

"I'll fight to keep her in the light." He throws his drink back and slides the glass into the middle of the table, an instruction for me to fill again. "Kill whoever I need to kill. I'll do whatever it takes, Danny."

"Yeah, do, but promise me one thing."

"What?"

"Do not go back there yourself." What a fucking mess. As if there's not enough shit to deal with. But no. It keeps coming and coming and coming. "We need to talk to Higham," I say, keeping James flush in vodka. "Maybe while he's helping us out finding the fucker who dug up our dead parents he can find the fucker who popped off Tom Hayley." I feel at my creased forehead. "Something tells me it could be one of many people." Because I'm sure as shit, along with me and James, there are plenty of other criminals, businessmen and politicians in Miami who thought Tom Hayley was a prick. But enough to kill him? I laugh to myself. He would only need to say the wrong thing to the wrong person, because, let's face it, he said plenty of wrong things to us, and if he wasn't Beau's father, I would have ended the fucker. I know James feels the same.

"Can I get you two anything?"

I glance up and find Nolan at the table looking smart in a three-piece. "Put your dick in any one of the girls again, I'll have Cindy or Barbie bite it off," I say, as James slowly rotates his glass on the table and Nolan places a palm over his groin.

"Roger that." He looks over his shoulder, prompting me to crane my head past his body to look. I see one of the girls looking this way. Or Nolan's way.

"That's not going to be a problem, is it?"

"Not at all." Nolan pulls his jacket in. "Where's—"

"Daddy's upstairs," I say, making James smile a fraction and Nolan roll his eyes as he leaves us.

A long silence falls, both of us out of words, just sitting here, mulling things over, drinking. I'm about to stand and declare my intention to take my willful wife home when there's a distinct change in the atmosphere. I frown and turn toward the door, seeing the units Brad has guarding the door, Drake and Des, two black men built like rhinos, scanning the club. I slide out of the booth, showing them where I am, tilting my head in question. One approaches, the other remains by the door. Securing it? Who the fuck is out there?

"What is it?" I ask, my eyes unmoving from the door.

"Someone wants to see you."

"Who?"

"Some Russian dude."

I step back and James, obviously overhearing, is next to me in a heartbeat. "Outside?"

"Says to tell you he comes in peace."

I laugh out loud, and it is so fucking psychotic. Peace? What the fuck is peace? "How many?"

"Four. All unarmed."

"Is that what they told you?"

"I patted them."

I raise my eyebrows, impressed. "Did you ask them if they want sugar in their tea?"

Looking unsure, he flicks his eyes between us. "He's fucking with you," James says, sighing.

"I'm fucking with you," I confirm, making his big shoulders drop. And trying to buy myself some fucking time. I look at James. "Am I walking out there and shooting the cheeky fuckers?" I ask, as he stares at the door, lost in thought. It makes me pause for thought, and I hate my thoughts. *Oh fucking hell.* "You're curious, aren't you?"

"We're never gonna find him if we kill everyone linked to him before we interrogate them."

"Fuck . . . me," I grouse, passing Drake and heading for the office. "Anyone would think you like torturing people. Weren't you ever taught that curiosity killed the—"

"Crime lord?"

"Fuck you," I snap, pushing my way into the office and going to the bookcase, just as Brad comes out with Nolan.

"What's going on?"

"Russians outside. Apparently want to talk." I jog up the stairs and head for the locked cabinet in the corner.

"What's going on?" Otto asks from the couch, his laptop on his lap, his phone at his ear.

I grab a machine gun and a belt of bullets, attaching it as I head back out, Otto now on my tail. "I've got to go, Boo. Call you later."

Boo? I swing around, now armed, and Otto backs up, hands up, his phone held high.

Facing me.

My mother's name on the screen.

"Be cool, Danny," he says.

"Be cool, Danny," Brad parrots, their pleas having the opposite effect, my blood beginning to boil. A difficult, callous wife, cheeky fucking Russians, missing dead parents, and now this fucker is trying to get my mother into bed? I step forward. "Stay the fuck away from my mum."

He has the nerve to look pissed off.

"And how the fuck did you hit your head?"

Otto frowns and reaches for his baseball cap. "How—"

"Forget it, I don't give a shit." I point my machine gun at him. "Stay away from her." I leave him with that warning and throw Brad a shotgun before hurrying back downstairs. "And get more guns," I yell back, entering the club again, seeing James still with Drake.

I pass the girls at the bar. "Danny, what's going on?" Rose calls. "Danny!"

"You move from that stool, Rose, I swear to God . . ." I stop and show her my incensed eyes, and she wilts, knowing now is not one of the times she should push me. Thank God. I toss the belt over my shoulder and load, ignorant to the attention of those who have noticed The Brit striding through the club armed with a fully automatic AR15.

I make it onto the street where Des is alone, guarding the entrance, a Heckler outnumbering the unarmed Russians.

None of which I recognize.

Not Volodya. Not Sandy. So . . .

"The Ox," I say, taking in the guy up front in a badly fitted gray suit.

"The Brit," he purrs, smiling. "Is this how you greet all your guests?"

"Ones I want to kill, yes." I smile and hold up the gun, dipping into my pocket and pulling out my Marlboros. I grip one with my teeth, slide it out, and light it, never taking my eyes off him. "You deal in guns, and yet you turn up here unarmed," I say.

"I told your Black friend here, I come in peace."

"There is no peace in my world, never will be, so what the fuck do you want from me, except certain death?"

"I am a fair man, Black. I want to do business and exist in peace here in your fine country. You returning to Miami has upset my balance."

"Perhaps some yoga will fix that." I pout, exhaling smoke, hearing the other men join me, all now armed.

"You're supplying the Mexicans," he says.

"Correct. Are we done?"

"You're undercutting me. Practically giving away the guns for free. Go back to wherever you were."

"Well, you see, Mr. Ox, I would love to, but some fucker dug up my pops from his resting place. You know anything about that?" I lift the gun a fraction more.

Hands up in surrender, he takes a step back. "I think I can help you there."

"You have information on my father?"

"Yes."

I nod, lowering my gun, pulling on my cigarette and inhaling the nicotine deeply. "Why don't you step into my office?" I ask, gesturing with the gun and moving aside, smiling my welcome.

Looking wary, as he absolutely should, he casts his eyes over me, James, and Otto, then indicates for his men to follow. I look across to the girls as I wander through, seeing both looking uncomfortably . . . comfortable. Like this is normal. Everyday life.

As I pass the DJ stand, I look up at the DJ, nodding my approval to the current track. Adamski *Killer*. "Can I get you a drink?" I ask. "Vodka? That's what you Russians like, isn't it? Or is that the Polish?" I look back at James, and he shakes his head in dismay, exasperated, but if I don't adopt this style, I'm likely to make a mess of Hiatus.

"I prefer rum," he grunts, as I let him in the office. All three of his men pass, all silent, not one having murmured a word yet. They can't speak English.

Then my men follow, giving me questioning eyes as they step inside and I turn, closing the door. Just before the wood meets the frame, I see the DJ, his hand poised on the volume dial. I shut the door and face the room. "I'm assuming whoever dug up my father wouldn't want to drag a dead body far," I muse, almost thoughtful, holding up my cigarette and looking at the stick as it hisses, burning, glowing. "So I'm guessing we should be looking in the eastern area, because that's where the cathedral is and *that* is where he's buried." I look up at The Ox. "Or *was* buried."

"Correct."

I nod, inhale, breathing out deeply. I see James, Otto, Brad, and Nolan in the edge of my vision move aside and hear the music in the club crank up. I slip my cigarette back between my lips. I'm done with his bullshit, outraged that he thought he could turn up here unannounced and tell me what I can and cannot do, where I can and cannot be and, worse, tempt me with knowledge of my father's whereabouts.

I give no warning, no hint through my expression.

I turn and open fire, spreading the bullets between all four of the fuckers. Their arms lift and shake, like they're fucking break-dancing, and I don't stop until my belt is empty and my gun is click-ing. I pull on my cigarette and breathe out, long and happily. I needed that. One less spider in the web. Or fucking animal in the god damn zoo. Whatever. But fuck . . . "What a fucking mess."

"And still," James says, looking across the carnage. "Nowhere near as messy as when Nolan lived in here."

I look at him, bemused. "Seriously?"

"Mate, there was shit growing on shit."

"True story," Brad sighs, slapping the man himself on the shoulder.

Nolan shows the ceiling his palms. "Should I get this cleared up?"

"You should," I grumble, dropping the gun. "And now I'm taking my wife home." I open the door. "Don't ask me if I'm going to fuck her or kill her, because I haven't made my mind up."

"Jesus," I hear Brad breathe. "I guess I'm going too, in case he opts for option two." He faces Nolan, pointing at him. "Be-fucking-have."

I stop outside the office and have another drag, finding Rose at the bar, still facing this way, waiting. I point my cigarette to the door, and she gets up quickly, kissing Beau's cheek and heading out of the club. Brad passes me to accompany her, and I make my way over to Beau. "The way I see it," I say, prompting her to look up at me. "You've got two choices."

"And what are they, Danny?"

"Live or die," I answer, raising my brows. "I know which one *I* want you to take."

"Are you saying you'll kill me if I don't stand down?"

"No, Beau, I'm saying *you* will kill you if you don't stand down. And you'll kill James too, because he and I share the same ethos when it comes to living." Her head tilts in question. "We can't do it without our hearts, as black and damaged and fucked up as they fucking are." She knows I'm not talking about our internal organs. "Get some sleep," I order. "You look like fucking shit." Exhausted. Drained. Angry.

"Thanks," she mutters as I walk away.

"That's what friends are for," I call back. "And for the record, I'm sorry about your father."

I find Rose by the doors, and she launches the moment she has me within reach. "What happened?" she asks, scanning me up and down, looking for signs of damage.

"So *now* you're talking to me?" I take her elbow and lead her to the car, putting her in the back as Brad slips into the front, aware of Tank's absence.

"I'm not talking to you. I just want to know what happened."

"What happened?" What happened today is I learned *never* to think that things can't get any worse *or* more personal. What a fucking day.

16

ROSE

He went straight to his office when we arrived home. Alone. An hour later, he came to our room, undressed in silence, and showered alone, and he didn't give me the opportunity to reject him in bed, turning over and going to sleep in minutes, obviously exhausted. Me? I laid awake in an unbearable state of insomnia, staring at the bandages covering Danny's chest, begging my mind to shut down and rest. It was having none of it. Neither was the baby, who seemed hell-bent on making me feel her presence, either with heartburn or nausea. In a sense, it was reassuring, but with the relief came worry and guilt. Is my restlessness affecting her? My recklessness?

As soon as dawn breaks, I leave Danny in bed, slip on a robe, and go down to the kitchen, and the moment I enter, it feels so empty. No Esther puttering around, baking, cooking, making tea.

Tea. I need a cup of English tea.

I make myself one and take a seat on a stool at the island, taking my first sip. My nose wrinkles. It's drinkable, but certainly not in Esther's league. I miss her. Not just her tea, but her ability to reason with me. With *everyone*. What would she tell me right now? Other than threaten to slap my face, she would remind me of who I'm married to and why I am married to him. It's so easy to forget, to lose sight of forever and happiness, when I am immersed in the violence and trials that being with The Brit brings.

For over an hour, I tussle and argue with myself, often looking down at my tummy, coming back to the same conclusion.

I shouldn't be here.

I serve no purpose but to rile him daily. I am incapable of handling my emotions, even more so now, but more than anything, I should go for all our safeties. Danny can focus, I can be with Daniel, and the baby and I will be out of harm's way. Or, more like out of Danny's way. Neither of us can do right for doing wrong, so it's for the best.

I nod to myself and turn on my stool when I hear dainty footsteps coming down the marble steps. With Esther still in St. Lucia, it can be only one person.

I get up and go to the door, seeing Beau nearing the bottom, her slight, toned body adorned in gym clothes, her hands in her hair tying it. She looks like she got about as much sleep as I did, dark circles around her eyes. I don't need to ask how she and James are. The fact she's up at six o'clock heading for the gym tells me. This tragedy definitely hasn't brought them together, and after listening to Beau last night and watching her monitor her cell like a hawk, waiting for a call from her ex-fiancé—God help us—I know it's not likely to either. She wants to get out there and get all the details. She wants to find out what happened, the circumstances, the perpetrator. She wants to be the cop she once was, and that's going to go down as well as a missile hitting the mansion.

I see a raging fire. Heat. Damage.

I flinch, shaking those thoughts away. Or I try to.

Beau hits the bottom of the stairs and looks up, finding me by the kitchen. "Okay?" I ask, a stupid question I know, but what else can I say? In the space of a day, her murdered mother's remains have been stolen and her father shot dead.

"Have you spoken to Lawrence yet?"

"No, I'm building myself up to that."

"Did you hear from Ollie?"

She reaches behind her and pulls her cell from the back of her gym pants, looking at the screen. I'm taking that as a no. "I'm going for a workout."

"Do you want a tea?"

She shakes her head, swallowing, so obviously holding back her emotions. "My period came."

Oh God. "Beau—"

Her hand comes up. "Please, Rose, do not give me sympathy."

"I'm your friend. What do you expect me to do?"

"I don't expect anything, but I hope you'll hear me when I say I can't. I just . . . can't." She backs away from me, sadness a veil all over her, and there are endless reasons for it.

Oh, Lord, have mercy on this woman and give her a fucking break.

"Beau," I blurt, sounding urgent, stopping her halfway to turning. "I'm going back to St. Lucia." This makes her blink in surprise. "I think it's for the best." My hand falls to my stomach, and so do her eyes. It's not the first time my heart breaks for her, and it won't be the last. "Danny and I are at each other's throats constantly, the pressure to be fine is just way too much, and in my condition—" I wince at my own stupid words. "I mean—"

"I understand." She comes to me and hugs me, and still, even with her heartfelt embrace, I'm injured. I hoped she'd beg me not to go, because I'm certain *I* would if she declared she was leaving. I couldn't be without her. I deflate in her arms, my eyes stinging. She's too focused on her loss. Or her newfound mission. Jesus, trying to find her mother's killer nearly broke her. If she does this, she might not come out the other side. And starting her period will only make her more determined to distract herself. "Come with me," I blurt, feeling panic setting in. I push out of her hold and take the tops of her arms, and she looks at me with a heavy forehead.

"Me and you, back to St. Lucia. I know you and James are struggling too."

"You mean since my ex sent me a picture of him all over another woman?"

Okay, it didn't look good, I admit that, but . . . "Haven't you wondered why Ollie was there?" She looks away, telling me she has. But she's choosing to ignore that logic. "And that Beth woman. How did she know James would be at Hiatus, because I'm sure as shit she doesn't look like the kind of woman who pops into a strip club for a drink?"

She won't ask herself those questions because she's too busy thinking about how her ex can help her rather than how he can ruin her relationship.

Beau looks at the screen of her phone again. "I don't have the bandwidth, the capacity, or the energy to fix this right now, Rose."

"Because you're too focused on finding your father's killer?" I ask quietly. "But what if he wasn't shot? What if . . . what if there's an explanation? A heart attack? A stroke? What if there's no killer to find?"

She smiles softly and rubs my arm. "I'll be in the gym," she says, walking away, taking her phone to her ear as she does. Calling her ex. How many times has she done that since last night? And why isn't he answering? The asshole. He better hope he doesn't find himself in a room alone with me. I look down at my tummy. Roll my eyes.

I go back to the kitchen and jump out of my skin when I find someone in there. James. He's making himself a coffee, shirtless, fiddling with the machine. I frown. How did he get in here without me seeing? "Morning," I say to his scared back as I go to the stool.

"Morning," he replies, not looking at me. "I saw you talking to Beau and took an alternative route." He obviously read my mind. I look at the French doors onto the garden. They're ajar. They also would have been locked, but that wouldn't be a problem for The Enigma, and clearly it wasn't. "Coffee?" he asks, giving me his attention as the machine spits one out.

"No, thanks." I hold up my mug. "Tea."

He nods and takes his cup, joining me at the island, and I find myself sitting back, withdrawing. Damn it, he's going to pick my brain. "How are you feeling?" he asks, nodding at my tummy that's concealed beneath the countertop.

"Fat."

He laughs under his breath and necks his caffeine in one hit. "The only thing big about you, Rose, is your willful streak."

If he's about to lecture me for causing Danny unnecessary grief, I'm not game. I lecture myself enough without anyone else's help. "Are you tired of fighting?"

He looks at his empty cup as he places it down, then peeks up at me. "You?"

I breathe out, exasperated. "How does this keep spinning back onto me?" I think I'd rather him pick my brain about Beau. I lean forward. "With respect, when it comes to relationship issues, you and Beau are definitely out in front." And I wonder . . . does he know her period started? Will he be relieved? Disappointed?

James looks back down at his cup, and something tells me he's considering getting more caffeine. Or perhaps some vodka. "What do I do, Rose?" he asks quietly, spinning his cup. My heart splits straight down the middle, and suddenly my own problems don't feel so heavy anymore. Danny must know I am not going anywhere. Maybe to St. Lucia, but I'm never leaving him. He's confident of that, I'm sure of it. James, though? He doesn't look like he's confident of much right now. "A few days ago, she was practically begging me to try for a baby," he murmurs. "Today, she doesn't even see me."

"Her father just died."

He winces, his jaw tightening. "She didn't even like him."

"None of us liked him." I reach for his hand and pull it toward me, resting my elbows on the counter to lean in. "But he was her dad, James, and no matter what we think, she's going to feel guilty. Maybe like she should have made amends before he died."

He sighs, long and heavy. "I know that."

"She's going to wish she'd met him last night."

James withdraws, eyes wide. "What?"

"Before we left for Hiatus. Tom called her, said that he was at some hotel downtown for a meeting. He wanted Beau to join him for dinner."

James looks away, his expression between a scowl and a frown.

"If she'd have gone, this might not have happened," I say. "That's what she'll be thinking."

He turns his eyes onto me. I see the darkness there, the demons he fights back every day. "He didn't deserve her."

"She didn't deserve to see you with another woman all over you either," I say, my lips pursed. "Are you going to tell me what the hell was with that?"

"She's from my past." James breaks our connected hand, pulling away, looking defensive. "I'm sure Beau's told you all about how we met."

"Of course she has." Both Danny and James know there's not much, if anything, that Beau and I don't know about each other. "But what the heck was she doing at Hiatus? Has this got something to do with her ex?" I ask. If Beau won't admit it, at least James will confirm it.

Exasperated, which is a cheek, James stands, exhaling loudly. "Otto got into Beth's phone records. She's in contact with Burrows."

My mouth falls open, even though I suspected.

James laughs with zero humor. "Looks like he will do anything to turn her against me."

"I thought he'd given up."

"I'd hoped," he says. "Because I seriously don't want to kill him."

Oh Jesus, what a mess. "You're not telling Beau?"

"Don't know if you noticed, but she's not talking to me right now, Rose," he says, swilling his mug under the faucet and resting it on the side.

I narrow my eyes on him as he faces me. "Have you told Danny?" I ask.

"Yes, because he's talking to me."

"Don't try me, James. One murdering asshole is enough for any woman to deal with."

He comes to me and dips, kissing my cheek. "Thank you for getting Beau out yesterday."

"For what it was worth."

"Make friends with him."

"Or else?"

"Don't try me," he grunts, walking away. "One disobedient female is enough for any man to deal with."

"Where are you going?" I call after him.

"*Not* to the gym."

"Thank God," I murmur, lowering back to the stool. And for another hour, I sit, mentally planning the conversation I need to have with Danny and how to approach it. I still haven't figured that out by seven o'clock when he walks into the kitchen, his hair wet, his tall, hard body wrapped up in a gray suit. My heart sinks.

Business.

Didn't he deal with enough business last night?

He passes me, silent, and slips a cup under the spout of the coffee machine, keeping his back to me while it pours—or drips— his hands braced on the edge of the countertop, his fingers drumming. Then, when it eventually finishes dispensing his coffee, he takes the small handle on the cup and turns, resting his ass against the marble and looking down into his drink while he sips, as slowly as the damn thing dripped out of the machine.

I'm too tired for this childish game of who will break first. Good for him, he's got a good night's sleep and is ready to go great guns. I am not. "I'm going back to St. Lucia," I say, my voice strong.

He stops with his annoying sipping, holding the cup at his lips, seemingly thinking for a few moments, before he leisurely places it down and heads for one of the French doors, pulling out his cigarettes as he goes.

And he just leaves? "I said I'm going back to St. Lucia!" I yell to his back.

He stops on the threshold of the patio, lighting his cigarette and exhaling calmly. Then he looks back at me, and I see it in his blue eyes.

The monster that lingers beneath the surface. The devil that's waiting, ready to show himself. "You're not going back to St. Lucia, baby," he says calmly, his face deadpan, his voice even. Then he leaves, and I drop my gaze to the counter, uncertainty plaguing me. Unpredictable Danny. Volatile Danny. The man who appears calm on the outside, unless you know the signs. I know the signs. His scar was glowing.

"I'm going," I say to myself, glancing at the door, twiddling my fingers, feeling . . . lonely. Lonely and unsure. Everyone is so distant, and my pining for Daniel multiplies in this moment. It's not as if I was with him constantly when we were in the same country, but the mother within me feels like I need to be near someone who really does need me, even if his social life is more important than his mom right now.

I pick up my cell and dial him, and my heart sinks further when he doesn't answer, although my reasonable side reminds me it's not long past seven and no thirteen-year-old is up at this time if they don't need to be. I sigh and start to tap out a message to Esther, but Danny appears at the door.

And he looks furious. Obviously, he's run dry of the energy required to contain his temper. "Why the fuck is Beau's car wedged in a bush around the side of the house?"

Oh.

Shit, shit, shit. "How would I know?"

Otto appears next to Danny, his eyebrows high, and I scowl at him. *Snitch.* I hope his head is banging. "Nice cap," I grate, making his eyebrows lower, his eyes narrowing.

"Rose," Danny says, his voice tight along with his face. "Answer me."

"Beau took me for a lesson."

"And it went swimmingly, I see," Otto mutters, before leaving me to face the wrath of my husband alone.

"I told you *I* would teach you to drive." Danny flicks his cigarette into a nearby plant pot and steps into the kitchen. "Why the fuck can't you listen to me for once?"

"You were too busy on a killing spree to see to your family's needs," I snipe. "And to be clear, I *am* going back to St. Lucia."

He laughs. It's evil. The kind of laugh reserved only for the men he's about to kill. Then it stops abruptly, and he comes close, heaving, sweating fucking fury. And because I'm me and he is my husband, I stand from my stool and square up to him. He pushes his forehead to mine, hard, and I put up some resistance, pushing back, not backing down. "No," he hisses.

"Yes," I counter. Can't he see it's for the best? At least until this shitstorm has passed.

"I'll die first."

My cell rings, and Danny pulls away, looking for where it is. He finds it in my hand and snatches it, looking at the screen. His nostrils flare, his jaw ticking like crazy, and he turns it to face me. Lennox Benson's name glows at me. *Oh shit.*

"How the fuck does he have your number?"

Is he for real? I swipe it from his hand. "Our son is staying with him most of the fucking time, Danny, and like I said, you're too busy killing the fucking world to have time to deal with your wife and child." I shove him aside, and he goes with ease, still heaving like a beast, mind you. I answer, not only because *fuck Danny*, but because it's early and there must be a reason Lennox is calling. "Hello," I answer tentatively, pacing up and down.

"Before you start worrying, don't worry," he says quickly, and I exhale. "I heard Daniel's cell ringing and he's crashed out, so I thought I'd ring you back to let you know all is okay."

My palm meets my forehead. "Thank you. I woke up and missed him more this morning for some reason." I feel Danny twitching behind me, probably locking down every muscle to not intercept this call. "How are you?" And there I just signed my death warrant.

"Yeah, good," Lennox replies. "Just about to go for a run down the beach, then I'll wake the boys up. Maybe do some surfing later. The wind's good today."

"Sounds amazing," I breathe, and then flinch, nervously

peeking back. Jesus Christ, he's going to erupt. *Be wise, Rose.* And then something occurs to me . . .

I turn away from my twitching husband. Is this why he won't permit me to go back to St. Lucia? Because he's jealous? Paranoid? "Have a great day. And thanks for calling," I say, now keen to end the conversation. "I'll call again later if that's okay?"

"Sure."

"Thank you." I hang up. Okay, I may have, in a stupid, pathetic fit of idiocy while in a mood with my husband, purposely poked him, but does he really think I'm capable of betrayal? And while I'm fucking pregnant? I swing around, immune to the warning signs flashing before me. "If you think you're keeping me away from my son and safety because you"—I point my cell at him—"are a paranoid asshole, think again, Black."

"I saw the way he looked at you."

"And I saw the way that woman last night looked at you!"

He explodes, picking up a mug off the counter and launching it across the kitchen, and it smashes against the wall, sending shards of porcelain spraying. I startle as the echo of the collision and Danny's bellow combine and bounce around the room, and look at him, shocked, my eyes wide. He doesn't back down. "You are not leaving me!"

Leaving *him.* That is how he sees it. I don't know when he went from demanding I stay away to demanding I stay close, but we're here, and it is an insight into his frame of mind. Insecure. Uncertain. Even more fucking crazy. *Deadlier.*

"Sort your fucking shit out, Danny," I hiss, feeling emotion creeping up on me. But I will not allow him to see it. No. This pull between anger and distress is overwhelming. I leave him to cool off and walk aimlessly, brushing at my eyes as I go.

"Rose?" Goldie says, coming down the stairs, seeing me marching across the lobby.

"I'm fine," I snap, seeing Brad coming out of the office up ahead, stretching. His arms freeze in midair above his head when he spots me. "I'm fine," I say, passing him and entering the office, closing the door behind me, needing a quiet room. Alone. Away from the house and the people in it.

I rest against the door and breathe in and out a few times, calming myself, mindful of Doc's words. Relax. Jesus fucking Christ. That's never going to happen here. This baby deserves more than this madness. Deserves more than parents like us.

My lip wobbles. How easy it is to forget the good times. The passion. The love.

I eye Danny's desk and pad over, dropping into the big chair, exhausted by the day already. I've been in here many times. And never sat in this chair. I gaze across the surface, then pull the drawer open. A pretty gold letter opener lays across some writing paper. I pick it up and run my fingertip down the edge to the tip, pushing into the pad of my finger until it pierces my skin. I hiss and suck the blood away, looking down into the drawer. Danny's father's name is printed across the top of the paper. I smile a little, pulling out a sheet, and as I do, I reveal a photograph of him. I pick it up and gaze at the image of a well-built man with happy blue eyes. His cream suit looks expensive. A brandy is in his hand, a cigar resting between his fingers. He was as formidable as he was handsome. Just like his son.

I swallow and place the picture back in the drawer, seeing something glimmer in the corner. My breath hitches, my hand automatically reaching into the drawer. I pick up the ring and hold it up in front of me, staring into the emerald eyes. I want desperately to sneer at it. Laugh. I can't.

Silly girl, Rose.

She's bleeding everywhere, for fuck's sake.

She's hemorrhaging. She'll need a transfusion.

Is it alive?

Smack!

A baby's scream.

The feel of him latching onto my breast.

My hands begin to shake, and I drop the ring. It hits the wooden top of the desk and clangs as I push the chair away, but no matter the distance, the emerald eyes of the snake shine at me, as if coming to life. A sign of those terrible days coming back to claim me. Imprisoning me again. I look down at my stomach. "Oh God," I breathe, feeling sweaty but cold, heart palpitations taking my breath away, making it harder and harder to find air. "No, no, no," I gasp, standing, but I immediately sit down again when my legs give, grabbing the edge of the desk. I close my eyes and try to breathe steadily. I try so hard.

Will she be able to carry again?

Unlikely.

The moment he was ripped from my arms flashes through my mind.

Please!

You can't take care of him, Rose.

Gone.

"No!" I yell, my hands grappling at the wood of the desk, searching for an anchor. *Breathe. Just breathe.*

The door flies open, and I see Danny vibrating on the threshold of his office. But he's hazy. I can't see his face. Can't focus. Can't see the man who won't let the evil get me again. "You are not fucking going!" he bellows.

I can't.

I can't go back.

I can't.

Air. I need air.

I stand.

I think.

And then there's just . . .

Darkness.

"Rose? Jesus, Rose, can you hear me? Rose, answer me. Come on, baby, open your eyes. Please, please, open." His voice is broken with emotion. Ragged and strained. "I'm sorry. I'm so fucking sorry."

"Rose, can you hear me?" Doc asks softly.

"What the hell happened?" James.

"Rose?" Beau's here. "Oh my God, is she okay?"

I open my eyes and immediately slam them shut again, wincing at the harsh glare from the ceiling lights. "My head," I murmur, my brain feeling like it's bouncing around in my skull. I blindly reach up, but a hand claims my wrist and lowers it back down.

"Can you open your eyes, baby?" Danny asks, soft and begging. "Please, let me see you."

I slowly peel them open and focus, finding his face above mine, upside down. He's sitting on the floor, my shoulders in his lap, and his face is fraught, his damp hair falling in his face. "I'm not talking to you," I croak, and he exhales, dipping and kissing my face anywhere he can reach.

"Are you in pain, Rose?" Doc asks. I shake my head, hearing him hum and feeling him pressing into various parts of me. "She fainted."

"Why?" Danny demands.

"Distress, maybe," Doc says, his tone knowing. "I heard you both yelling."

Danny lifts his face, and I see Doc on his knees beside me, and James and Beau by my feet. Doc tilts his head, looking between us both with disapproval. "If the body can't cope, it shuts down. Simple. I have told you both endless times, Rose needs to calm down. Chill out, as you young people say."

I peek up at Danny and see the guilt take hold. I start to sit myself up slowly with Danny's help. It was a panic attack. I blacked out because I couldn't breathe. I look at Beau, and for the first time I can truly appreciate how debilitated she has been so many times. God, that was horrific. Struggling to reason with yourself, fighting for air, pushing back flashbacks.

Danny gets to his feet and lifts me into his arms, carrying me out of the office silently, up the stairs to our room. He lays me on the bed, removes my robe, and tucks me in. Then lies down beside me on top of the sheets, fully clothed. His hand goes on my tummy.

His head on my chest. I slip my hand into his damp, dark waves and massage his scalp.

"I'm sorry," he mumbles.

"I didn't pass out because we fought."

He lifts his head and looks at me. "What?"

"I found a picture of your pops in the drawer of your desk. And the ring . . ." I shake my head mildly, not wanting to go there again but needing Danny to be rid of the guilt grabbing him. I know the ring I was looking at was Carlo Black's, not Ernie's, his brother, the man who took Daniel away from me when he was only minutes old. But those evil, emerald eyes. They got me.

"Fuck," he whispers. "They found the ring by Pops's grave. I didn't think—"

I put my hand over his mouth. "Stop it." I wriggle, forcing Danny to move, and I shuffle up the bed, resting my back against the headboard. "Come." I offer my hands, and he takes them, letting me pull him closer. He straddles my thighs, resting his ass on his calves, and I smile down at his suit pants stretching across his thick thighs. "I'm glad I saw it," I say, looking up at him.

He balks at me. "Rose, baby, what the fuck?"

Okay, so my initial reaction wasn't all too great, but now? "That green ring is a reminder of how far we've truly come. How many obstacles we've overcome. And have still to overcome. We are stronger together." That's a fact. "Sometimes, we both just need a little reminder of that." I guide his hand to my stomach, and he looks down. "I hate you."

He exhales on a quiet curse and wedges his fist into the mattress, leaning forward and kissing me. "I fucking hate you more."

And the universe aligns again, the rollercoaster slowing to a more manageable pace. I hook my arms over his shoulders and fall into the slow, calm motions of his kiss. It's the longest kiss, neither of us willing to break it. He slips one arm under my lower back, and then falls to the bed, bringing me to rest on top of him. "Your cuts."

He kisses me harder.

"You'll be all creased," I say around his mouth, my naked body squishing into his suit. Creased to kill.

He hums, moans, pulls me in closer, and my body comes alive, need taking over. I sit myself astride his stomach, never breaking our kiss, and lace my fingers through his hair. I hear his phone ringing from his pocket. And then I feel it. "Oh," I yelp, lifting my ass from his body to escape the hard vibration. He laughs into my mouth, forcing me to withdraw, just so I can get a glimpse of my chuckling god. It's good to see him. I smile, feeling into his inside pocket for his cell and pulling it out.

"Throw it away," he orders, and just as I'm about to do just that, he stills. "Wait." His cell is suddenly gone from my hand, as is my chuckling god. It was a brief appearance. He stares at the screen.

"Who is it?" I ask, as he kisses my forehead and helps me to my back, laying me down.

"I don't know." Another kiss on my cheek before he answers with silence.

I hate the instant tension his body radiates.

17

JAMES

After Danny took Rose upstairs, I followed Beau into the kitchen. She poured herself water, downed it, then left, not looking at me once. So I followed her to the gym. She *will* talk to me. She's already been in here for over an hour this morning. Clearly, she's not sweated enough. She places her phone on the bench and starts pulling on some boxing gloves, ignoring me standing by the door. The punching bag is about to get hammered.

I wander over to the corner and pick up the pads, slipping my arms through the bands and going to Beau, standing before her, forcing her to look at me. I widen my stance. Raise the pads. "Come on then, Beau," I say quietly. It's me she wants to hurt. Well, here I am. "Let's get this out of your system."

Her lithe body engages, and I bend slightly, bracing myself, seeing the intentions in her eyes. Her first roundhouse kick connects beautifully, knocking me back a few paces. I step back into position. "Again," I order, cricking my neck, loosening my muscles.

She comes at me, launching a round of punches, one after the other, right hooks, jabs, and uppercuts. The pads absorb them all, every blow, and I start to move around the mat, encouraging her movements too. "Again," I demand, thrusting the pads forward, and she yells, delivering another combination of kicks that have me staggering back until my back hits the wall. She backs off, wiping her sweaty brow with the back of her gloved hand, letting me reset. "Again," I whisper, dipping, my eyes on hers, goading, part of me wondering what the fuck I'm doing, encouraging this kind of training when I know she's on the verge of walking out on me and taking up her past as a cop. But the other part is relishing this. Knowing she's getting what she needs, knowing she'll be revisiting our past, seeing us in the kitchen of my apartment when she first took me off my feet, both physically and mentally. The first time we had sex. The moment we both succumbed.

On that thought, I throw the pads aside and give her me in my entirety, unprotected. Unarmed. Exposed. Always exposed with Beau. She looks at me, her face painfully expressionless. This is the woman she was. The one she tried to forget existed but now wants back. The woman with power and unbridled strength. I've always needed Beau to be this version of herself. Away from the darkness. But always with me. If she goes back, if she steps into her cop boots again, she won't be with me. *Can't* be with me. "I see the woman you were," I murmur, and she swallows, knowing what's coming. "The woman you're trying to forget existed." *Mine.* She's trying to forget she's mine. It's the only way forward for her. If she's going back, she needs to forget she was ever in my world. I won't let her. Never. She's feeling helpless, guilty, like she needs to be free of the ropes tying her down. I can make that happen without her picking her badge back up, because, frankly, if she does go back, I'm worried about what she might discover. "I want you to find that woman. The woman you were. I need you to find her, Beau." I step forward. "And give her back to me," I whisper, seeing the tears in her eyes building. And then she yells, coming at me. I block each punch, deflect every kick, my body unmoving, absorbing her attack, hit after hit, kick after kick, until she's out of steam and falls into my chest on a whimper of defeat, her gloved hands bunched in front of her face as she weeps into them.

And I hold her.

Tightly.

My chin resting on top of her head.

Calm. She's giving herself back to me. But I'm under no illusion that she'll stand down, and I have finally concluded that *that* is something I need to accept. Like she has accepted I kill. I know she can never truly go back, not with her history since she met me, and perhaps that is part of her problem. Resentment. I can't change that. Just like I can't change the inbuilt instincts in her that made her a formidable cop. The instincts she inherited from her mother. The instincts that help her survive being mine.

"My period came," she breathes.

I clench my eyes closed, not knowing if I should be relieved or disappointed. Not knowing how she feels either. It's a total fuck-up. I breathe into her hair, my arms locked around her neck, as her body jerks gently against me. I don't know how the fuck I balance this. She wants to try for a baby. Then she wants to go all Lara Croft around Miami on a manhunt. I was unsure about the former. I'm dead set against the latter. Which makes the former a lot fucking more appealing. But her period came. Fucking hell, what am I thinking?

I'm thinking about pretty much trapping her. Fucked up.

But that's what we are.

I reach between us with both hands and take the gloves, easing them apart to expose her face, my chin on my chest as I look down at her. "Show her to me," I order, and she looks up, her face a mess of tears but still so fucking beautiful. I wipe under each eye as she watches me, sniveling. "I love you," I say softly, stroking through her hair, and she nods, a few fresh tears rolling. "I love you so fucking much, Beau. Broken, not broken. Happy, sad. Pregnant, not pregnant. I will do anything for your peace. Kill *anyone*. We need to figure this out before it kills *us*."

On a whimper, she launches herself into my arms and hugs me, sobbing into my neck. I love it when she's vulnerable. When she needs me. I also loathe it.

"My love for you walks hand in hand with my hate for the world," she whispers, and I clench my eyes closed, hearing her point. Hearing myself.

They are equals. Passion fueled. Your love and your hate are what makes you, Beau, and mine is what makes me. I will treasure your love, and I'll nurture your hate. Because without your hate, you're not the woman I love.

Jesus. Hate. It's consuming us.

"Ollie sent Beth to the club, Beau," I say, tense, bracing myself for her reaction.

She pulls away. "How do you know that for sure?"

"Otto got into Beth's phone records. She and her husband split and . . ."

"She has feelings for you."

I shrug like a chump. "Like Ollie does for you."

"We were engaged."

"Don't remind me." I sigh, wiping under her eyes. "Look, I don't know what the fuck is going through Beth's head, but she's very deluded if she thinks there was ever anything more than fucking." Painfully, I realize Ollie had way more than fucking with Beau. I honestly think he's obsessed, but with Beau or with me? Beau, because he loves her, me because he has an axe to grind. Either or, I can never kill him. "I love you, Beau. And it hurts so bad when you pull away." I lift her up and carry her to the horse, sitting her on it and stepping between her legs. I take her gloved hands in turn and start unfastening the ties, pulling them off. She flexes her fingers, and I lift her tank, dipping and kissing her scar. Then I devote some time to her arm, kissing down the length of scar tissue to her hand. I find the ring on her right hand and spin it slowly on her finger, the diamond sparking up at me.

Light.

I see it on my mother's finger. I see it in the ruins of our country estate surrounded by ashes. I swallow, and Beau's other hand is suddenly before me. She removes the ring, and my heart stops beating, waiting for her to hand it to me. She's done. Can't sustain this anymore, can't fight through the darkness with me to find our light.

But she doesn't give it to me. She puts it on the index finger of her left hand.

I shoot my eyes up to hers, my hands splaying her thighs. Her face is breathtakingly impassive. But her eyes speak to me, and she lowers her face toward me, her hands slide through my hair and grips, and she pushes her lips to mine. "Yes," she whispers into my mouth, and the word finds its way into my chest and fuses to my heart.

Lightness entices lightness.

And I feel like I'm floating right now. "Yes?" I ask, needing, *wanting,* to hear it again. I pull her off the horse, her legs around my waist, and stand, indulging in our kiss, moaning my contentment. Bliss.

"Yes," she says around my lips, tightening every muscle around me. A sign. She'll never let me go. "Yes." She bites my lip. "Yes." Swirls her tongue through my mouth. "Yes." Dots kisses all over my face.

I groan and pull back, looking at her. Taking in every exquisite piece of her. "I might not show it on the outside, Beau Hayley, but you make me an extremely happy—"

"Assassin?"

I smile, kissing her again. "We will be okay."

"I—"

The gym door flies open and Brad appears, looking a little ruffled. "Jesus, do you two ever put each other down?" He waves a hand at us, exasperated. "I'm glad you've made up. We have a development. Danny's office now." He turns and leaves, and I feel Beau stiffen in my arms. And here we have our first challenge.

"Development on what?" she calls after him. I place her down and look at her seriously. "We're yet to discuss boundaries," she says, kind of nervous, kind of cocky. "And part of the crazy I'm feeling is not knowing what the hell is going on."

Of course, because her craving information, scratching around for the truth, is what made her an incredible cop. It's as essential as breathing to Beau . . . and I've denied her that. *Fuck*. "And there I was thinking you putting that ring on the correct finger was a sign."

She looks at me like I'm stupid, because, obviously, I am. "You know who I am, James." She tucks herself into my side and lets me walk her out of the gym. "As I know who you are."

A cop.

A criminal.

I don't release her when we reach the lobby. I don't order her away or send her to our room. No. She'll always be by my side. Even when I'm walking into fucking battle. Fuck my life, I lead her into Danny's office, and when every eye in the house turns our way, I silently dare any of them to challenge me.

Of course, Danny doesn't heed the warning. "Are you fucking joking?" he asks from his chair behind his desk.

I don't answer. He knows as well as me that we need to flex, so here I am, flexing. I release Beau, and she goes to the couch and lowers in between Goldie and Ringo, her lips pressed together.

Shaking his head, Danny stands and rounds his desk, approaching her.

She looks up at him, not speaking a word, but I know she's got plenty to say. Yet in this moment, Beau knows what's good for her, and showing willingness is what's good for her. Like putting that ring on the correct finger. A ploy?

Danny's eyes narrow, and I stand back, letting this play out. "This isn't a place for a wom—"

"Don't do it," Ringo warns, as Goldie's body visibly straightens on the couch. "Please, Danny, I beg you, do *not* do it."

Danny turns his eyes onto Goldie, while Beau fights her smirk. "If you smile, I will kill you," Danny hisses, making Beau get her lips quickly in check. But not mine. Or Brad's and Ringo's and Otto's and Goldie's. We're all fighting smiles. Except Danny. He takes a patience-gathering breath. "I'm letting this slide for now."

I look at Beau, whose face tells a different story.

"I've had a call from The Shark," Danny goes on.

All amusement leaves us.

"The fuck?" Brad blurts. "Do people google 'The Brit' now and find your height, wealth, and fucking cell phone number?"

"Interesting after The Ox showed up at the club last night," I muse. *What the fuck's going on?*

Danny looks at me, his face as thoughtful as I guess mine is.

"Wait, The Ox was at the club?" Goldie asks, throwing a frown around the office. "When?"

"When Ringo took you for dinner," Danny mutters, eyes never leaving mine.

"He didn't take me for fucking dinner. He took me for food. So The Ox showed up and—"

"I killed him," Danny says, blasé, still looking thoughtful. "After he politely requested we stopped supplying the Mexicans."

"And what did The Shark want?" I ask.

"Guns," Danny says quietly, his fingers forming a steeple, resting against his top lip, thoughtful.

"Are you really considering arming our enemies?" Brad asks, looking as concerned as everyone else in the room.

"Yes," I answer for Danny. "Sounds like the Polish and the Russians are no longer working in harmony," I muse, perching on the edge of Danny's desk. "Looks like word is getting round that The Brit is offering a cracking discount on weaponry."

"And what about The Bear?" Brad asks. "I don't want it to be taken as gospel, but I'm pretty fucking sure he wouldn't want his minions doing business with The Brit and The Enigma, since both want his identity so they can fucking kill him."

"Perhaps he doesn't know," Goldie pipes up, getting a grunt of agreement from Ringo.

I nod, looking across to Beau, who's being surprisingly quiet. What's she making of all this? I tilt my head, and she shrugs, nonchalant. Who the fuck is she trying to kid? "Talk," I order, making everyone in the room look my way.

She scowls at me. But she talks. "It's falling apart," she says, all eyes turning onto her. "He thought he had you both at the boatyard the night Perry Adams died. You proved him wrong. Made him look like a dick, even if you looked like dicks yourselves for killing the wrong man."

I hear Danny cough under his breath, probably in disbelief. She's fucking pushing it. "You killed him, Beau," I remind her.

"My point is—"

"She has a point?" Danny asks. "Oh good. I thought she was just here to piss me off."

Beau smiles, and Danny mutters something about preferring her as his wife's friend.

"I can see me being here is a problem for you macho men." Beau stands. "So I'll take my conclusions elsewhere." She takes three steps, and Danny swoops in, lifting her from her feet gently and taking her back to the couch. I smile. He knows she's got skills. He's objecting simply because it's Beau. My girl. His wife's best friend. His friend, too. And...a woman. He needs to get over that.

"Sit," he orders, frowning, glancing at me. I raise my brows and he shakes his head. "Please," he exhales.

Lowering, Beau breathes in. "The Bear didn't expect Perry Adams to die that night," she says. "So despite all of you feeling cheated by finding out Adams *isn't* in fact The Bear, he'll be feeling even more cheated. More than half his army has been taken out, he's being forced to rebuild, but he can't do that quicker than you can kill. So . . ." She shrugs. "I'm thinking many are deciding that it's safer to go it alone because remaining under The Bear's control is likely to get them killed by any one of you fine gentlemen." She looks at Goldie and smiles. "Or gentlewoman. But the real question is, what was keeping them under The Bear's control all this time that they're prepared to walk away from now?"

We all look at each other. "Secrets," I answer. "He was black-mailing Derek Green. Spittle."

"You think he's blackmailing all these criminals?" Brad blurts. "What the fuck do they care if anyone finds out if they perhaps like to jerk off over pictures of cats, or like inserting interesting objects up their asses?" We all look at him. "What?" He laughs. "These people are animal obsessed. Makes sense they'd want to fuck them." He shudders. "Don't ever give me a nickname, and definitely don't make it an animal."

"Your mind though, Brad," Beau breathes. "He's always had someone on the inside. Dexter"—she turns a look onto me— "before my boyfriend murdered him."

"Fiancé," I correct her, earning semi-shocked but more interesting expressions from our audience. But no one says a word. I like to think it's because everyone knew it was a given.

Beau's face remains eternally blank. "Then there's Spittle and the two guys who stopped me and Nath. My guess is, The Bear has no one else on the inside, so he can no longer fulfil his word of immunity or protect all the criminals under him from prosecution should they find themselves in cuffs."

Danny pouts, thoughtful. "He has no one on the inside."

"He could be resourcing, but you can't just advertise for a bent cop. It's just a thought," Beau says, shrugging, nonchalant, but she knows her thoughts are valid. "Worth considering."

"I'm considering," Danny murmurs, pacing. "Why hasn't he been in touch since Tuesday? He had our dead parents dug up and then . . . nothing. He can't have been abandoned by everyone, unless he got a shovel and dug them up himself."

"A lot can happen in a few days," I say, hearing grunts of agreement. "And all the signs point to his animals going freelance. The Ox wanted you to back off, The Shark wants guns."

"Speaking of guns," Danny says, taking his chair and motioning me into the other. "The delivery."

The fucking delivery. "I've been distracted."

He laughs, looking across to Beau. Then he scowls at her. "You know, if you really wanted to help, you could stop distracting your fiancé."

Brad shakes his head, looking at Danny like he's crazy. Brave. Stupid.

"Enough," I say lowly, making Danny sneer at me across the desk.

"So how do you propose we get our guns across the bay to the yard while dodging the Coast Guard out on their training day?" Danny asks.

My eyes burn into his, angry, frustrated. Truth is, I don't fucking know. I would have devoted a lot more time to figuring that shit out if every minute of the past two days hadn't been a never-ending ball-ache. "I'm working on it."

"Well work fucking faster. Chaka's turning up a week this Friday with our guns."

"Do you want to change your tone?"

"No."

I stand, wedging my fists into the desk, leaning in. "I highly recommend you do."

"Oh fuck," Otto moans from the couch as Danny mirrors my pose on the other side of the desk.

"Or else?"

I move fast, grabbing his jacket and fisting the material, pulling him closer, and he does the same, pulling me in so we're snarling in each other's faces. I do not need his ego or his frustration aimed this way. "I said I would deal with it."

"Then fucking deal with it."

"I'll do it," Beau says quietly from beyond.

I frown. Danny frowns. We both look out the corner of our eyes toward the couch. Beau is now standing, and everyone's eyes are on her. "Do what?" Danny asks.

"Take the delivery." She looks at me, appearing confident, but I can see her nerves. She thinks I'll refuse to even entertain listening to whatever nonsense she's thinking. She's right.

I shove Danny away. "Time for you to go," I say, claiming Beau by the elbow and walking her to the door.

"What? No, James, I—"

"It was good while it lasted," Danny calls, forcing me to turn a dark look back at him. Why does he have to goad her? He yanks his suit jacket into place, his eyes narrowed, the scar that decorates his face deep and bright. Then, quite suddenly, Danny's blue eyes widen and a collection of inhales sound.

And something connects with my ankles, taking my legs from under me. I land on my back with a lung-draining thwack. "Fuck," I cough, looking up at the ceiling.

Then, sniggers. They all clearly want to die.

Enraged, I lift my head and find Beau in the chair I was sitting in not a moment ago.

"Well, that told you," Danny muses, hands braced on the top of his desk, stretching to look at me on the floor. "Need a hand?"

Don't lose it. Don't lose it.

I slowly get to my feet and visibly draw some long deep breaths, wanting Beau to know it's taking everything in me not to fly off the handle. "Talk," I order, willing to listen, if only to appease her in this moment. Whatever she has to say, whatever bright idea she's got, it's a no.

"I'll meet Chaka and accept the delivery," she says, nibbling on her bottom lip.

God love her. "That simple?"

"Nothing about being with you is simple, James," she says, taking the atmosphere in the room one step closer to thick. Multiple sets of eyes swing back and forth between us.

"So what do you propose?" I ask. Let's hear it. Because, actually, I'm really fucking curious.

Beau pulls her hair over one shoulder and combs through with her fingers. She looks so feminine doing that. So . . . lovely. "We tow empty jet skis across the bay, fill them with guns, and tow them back."

I blink, withdrawing, and feel all eyes land on me, like, *what do you think of that, James?* "What?" is all that comes, and the peanut gallery all turn their attention back to Beau.

"There's nothing odd about moving jet skis from storage."

And back to me. "Absolutely not."

Back to Beau. "Why?"

Heads swing, facing me again. "Because I said so." *The end.* "Now it's time to go." I take one step and stop when Danny clears his throat. *Oh no. Don't do it, Danny.* I glare at him, for what it's worth.

"It's not a bad shout," he says quietly.

Is he hell-bent on getting his nose broken today? "Come again?"

"A couple of young surfer sorts on the ocean pulling a load of skis behind them? Nothing unusual about that," Brad adds. I turn my deadly glare slowly onto him.

"And who do you propose those surfer sorts are?" I ask like a prick. Every fucker in here knows the answer to that.

"Leon and—"

"Me," Beau pipes in.

"No." I laugh. Brad's suggestion to have Beau working at Hiatus suddenly seems very fucking appealing.

Beau regards me, almost disappointed. "Jame—"

The door swings open and Rose appears, and the moment she finds Beau at the desk, her mouth falls open. "What are you doing in here?" she asks, indignant.

"Oh fuck," Danny breathes.

"Busted." Brad laughs. "I'm out of here. Let me know if we're doing business with the The Shark and his Polish army anytime soon."

Not likely. The Polish traffic women, but they aren't my priority right now. So her period starts and all of a sudden she's spouting off crazy ideas that either have her running around Miami chasing killers or gunrunning. What kind of fucked-up crazy am I in?

A mobile starts ringing, and everyone looks at each other as Beau stands. She glances down at the screen and does a fine fucking job of being cool. "Excuse me," she says, avoiding my eyes as she leaves.

All attention is on me when the door closes. I can't stand it. *Fuck!* "I'll be in the gym," I say, leaving pronto, my focus forward, ignoring my mind's demands to find her, take her phone, and tie her up. I make it to the gym and kneel on a mat, taking some stretched, deep breaths, before laying my forearms down, engaging my stomach muscles, and pulling my body up. The rush of blood to my head is welcome, and I close my eyes and focus.

I focus so fucking hard.

Focus on fighting the urge to find Oliver Burrows and kill him. I already owe him for arresting me and texting Beau a photo of Beth groping me. Now Tom Hayley is dead? That fucker just got a pardon from Beau for trying to interfere in our relationship again, because she knows her ex is the path to answers. Burrows will be harnessing that to his advantage, enticing Beau in, manipulating his position, and using her loss and need to his advantage.

And here I am restraining that instinct in her. Holding her back.

Denying her.

Fuck.

18

BEAU

I felt his eyes like daggers in my back as I left Danny's office. I also felt my guilt as strongly. Despite knowing it would be frowned upon, he took me into Danny's office. And despite The Brit's immediate aversion, he kept me in there because he knows I have value beyond freedom and love for James. I may have appeared hard-faced and steadfast in my determination, but remaining in that office had nothing to do with my grit and everything to do with the men's acquiescence. Until I spoke my thoughts and, absurdly apparently, suggested a solution to their problem. James's dismissal was an insult.

And now Ollie has called, and because I wasted time removing myself from James's space, I missed him. And now he's not picking up.

"Damn it," I mutter, pacing around in circles on the terrace. "Answer."

"Maybe he's busy gathering more shit to throw at James."

I look up and see Danny on his terrace, his shoulder leaning against the door. He takes a drag of his cigarette and wanders across to the railings that separate this terrace from theirs, his stride casual. It's the kind of walk he walks when he's calm but raging. "Maybe," he muses, "Burrows hopes the shit will stick this time."

My shoulders drop. "Whatever you want to say, just say it, Danny. I'm busy."

"Busy trying to get in touch with your ex?" He raises his eyebrows as he stops in front of me, only the metal separating us. He reaches across and brushes gently across my cheek. "You have a hair across your eye."

"Thanks." I brush at it too, even though he's already removed it.

"Can you see better now?" he asks, making me exhale tiredly. "He's your ex, Beau." He slides his palm onto my nape and holds me by my neck, as if he's worried I'll pull away. "Try and see this from James's perspective. He's your ex, and he just sent you pictures of another woman all over James, to which, I don't mind reminding you"—he squeezes a little, dipping to ensure he has my eyes—"you didn't take too kindly to."

"We've talked about it," I grate. "And we're fine."

"Come on, Beau. Your snake of an ex is going to make the most of this situation. He had James arrested. Be wise with your trust."

"I need to know what happened." God damn me, I can feel my lip wobbling, and Danny moves in and hugs me over the divider between the terraces. The mild smell of nicotine fills my nose. "How's your chest?" I ask, mindful that I'm pressed against it.

"It's nothing," he murmurs.

"Sure."

"Ollie isn't the only way, Beau."

Maybe not, but he's the easiest way, and God save my soul, I know he will share a lot more about Dad's death than anyone else. He's not the only one who can manipulate. But is it worth the friction between James and me? "Would you ever try to change Rose?" I ask, feeling Danny still, as if breathing is suddenly an effort and he needs to concentrate.

"I feel like this is a loaded question."

I exhale into his chest. He knows where I'm going—I don't need to say it. My suggestion for their delivery problem is the perfect solution. Everyone knows it. But because I am who I am and belong to who I belong to, everyone keeps forgetting the not-so-small detail that I used to be a cop. And while I was making myself pretty for James last night, my father was dying. I snivel and break away, wiping at my face. "I should have met him at the hotel," I say quietly. God damn me, why didn't I meet him?

"What?"

I look up and find Danny frowning. "Dad called me last night. He was at a hotel Downtown. Business. He wanted me to meet him there and have dinner. I made my excuses."

He looks past me as he pulls on his cigarette, the air around him a light smog. "Don't blame yourself."

I shake my head, sighing. "Where's he gone?"

"Gym."

To stand on his head. My guilt becomes unbearable seeing James in my mind's eye vertical, his eyes closed, his body solid and straight. Trying to find his calm.

My cell rings, and I inhale as I drop my eyes to the screen. I shouldn't take it. Danny's right, Ollie isn't the only way. But the pull, the promise of distraction, the long-lost instinct being tempted out of hiding? I need to resist it. I look up at Danny, finding him observing me closely. I reject the call, looking past him when Rose appears.

"You look better," I say, assessing my friend more closely.

"You *don't*," she counters, wandering over. Danny tucks her into his side the moment she's close enough. "Have you spoken to him?"

"No."

"So is anyone going to tell me why you were in on a meeting?" She looks up at Danny with narrowed eyes, while he rolls his.

"It doesn't matter." I turn my cell in my hand. "It was apparently a waste of everyone's time and won't be happening again."

"We're going out," Danny says to Rose, taking one last puff of his smoke and dropping it into an ashtray.

"We are? Where?" she asks, as he drops a kiss on her forehead and wanders back into their room.

"To visit Pops," he calls back. "Or the empty fucking hole where he once was. Oh, and Beau?" He comes back to the door. "For the record, I think your way is the only way if we're going to meet the Mexican's deadline."

He leaves and Rose faces me. "What is he talking about?"

I bring my hands to my face and press into my eye sockets, so fucking tired. "I offered to help with the gun delivery."

"Help how?"

"Tow a line of loaded jet skis through Coast Guard infested waters."

She laughs and then stops abruptly. "Your ring," she blurts, seizing my hand and staring down at it.

"I changed my mind."

"Why?"

"I—" I don't know how to answer that. Maybe to appease James. Show him I do love him. *It can stay there until you see the light.* Maybe because it's simply the right thing to do—be his constant light. Except . . . I'm not. "How are you feeling?" I ask instead, stumped. "You'll be lucky if Danny doesn't glue you to a bed made of cotton wool."

"I'm fine. Are you going to talk to Ollie?"

"What do you think?"

"I think you know you shouldn't, but you won't be able to help yourself." Leaning over, she kisses my cheek. "Just try to see things from James's perspective. I'll see you later." That's exactly what Danny said. They're either in sync or it's the universe telling me I need to consider their words. Taking my hand, she squeezes and backs away, letting our joined hands stretch out between us until she's too far away and I lose my grip.

I go back to my room, slipping out of my gym wear and putting on some denim shorts and a shirt before I track down James. Reassure him. Tell him I'm sorry. For making him doubt my love, for stupidly doubting his. For holding it against him for needing to keep me safe. *Try to see things from James's perspective.* Danny and Rose are right. I can't do this to him, not even for my father. James has been a rock, determined to drag me from the darkness. Dad seemed determined to send me further into it.

I tie my hair up, grab my cell, go to the door, and freeze when it rings in my hand, my eyes on the wood before me, not wanting to look down. *Fucking hell.* I pull open the door, finding Fury on the other side. He looks down at my ringing cell.

"Are you gonna take that?" he asks.

I don't answer, my face screwing up, and I reverse my steps, shutting the door on Fury, the temptation too much. "Ollie," I answer, clipped and short, starting to walk circles around our room.

"Beau. How are you?"

"My dad's dead. My mom's remains have been taken." Civilities out of the way. He's lucky I'm not ripping into him about setting Beth on James. "What happened?"

"We should meet."

I stop still, staring at my bare feet on the plush carpet. "Meet?" I parrot like a fool.

"I can't talk over the phone."

I frown, taking the few steps needed to get me to the bed and dropping to my ass on the edge. "What's going on, Ollie?"

"Meet me, Beau."

My imagination has gone into overdrive, my cop senses buzzing. But I don't press more. I know how this works. "Fine, okay, I'll meet you." I have not one fucking clue how I'm going to manage that when James practically has me tracked twenty-four/seven. "When?"

"I'll be in touch. In the meantime, you're going to get a call from a Detective Collins."

"A detective? I thought you took the case?"

Silence.

"Ollie?" The line goes dead. "Shit," I yell, slamming my cell down on the mattress. As if I needed luring anymore. My guilt multiplies, and it's fast superseding my misery. I haven't even found the man responsible for my mother's death. I am still without peace there, and now I'm dealing with the death of another parent, again, by all accounts, under suspicious circumstances. What the hell was Dad doing at that hotel? Who was he meeting?

The tussle between standing down and stepping up is becoming unbearable. But one thing I am certain of? I can't argue with James. I get up and leave the room, and Fury falls into stride behind me, reminding me that escaping and meeting Ollie is about as likely as Danny allowing me to give Rose another driving lesson. *Poor Dolly.* "I'm going to the gym," I call back.

"That's lovely."

I look over my shoulder, giving Fury a tired look. "Missing Tank?"

One of his eyes narrows, his huge shoulders rocking as he walks. "I don't like the look in your eyes."

"What look?" *Fuck, am I that transparent?* I return my attention forward and wait for his answer. But he says nothing. And not because he's doubting what he's seeing. What he knows.

I make it to the gym and face Fury. "Take a break," I say quietly, grasping the handle behind me and pushing my way inside.

"You never mentioned *that* bit," Danny hisses, and I come to a sharp stop, seeing James sitting on a bench rubbing his hair with a towel, looking insultingly bored, and Danny standing in front of him looking pissed off. And then Danny sees me and looks plain awkward, and James quickly becomes the angry one. Because of me. Because he knows I've been talking to Ollie. "Rose is waiting for me," Danny says, stomping away, and I follow his path across the gym with my eyes. He slams the door behind him.

Never mentioned *what* bit? "Everything okay?" I ask, and James laughs sardonically.

"Fucking dandy, Beau."

I face him on the bench. He's still dabbing at his hair with the towel, slowly, purposely, watching me. He looks fucking furious. What can I say to him? That I don't love Ollie? That my contact with him means nothing? That he's being jealous and it's ridiculous?

After my performance when I saw him with Beth?

Show him.

My hands start working on autopilot, and I reach for the fly of my denim shorts, unbuttoning them and pushing them down my legs. His eyes don't move from mine, but the towel slowly lowers. I'm nervous. I can't let him see me nervous. I step out of my shorts and unfasten the buttons of my shirt as I pad toward him, hoping, praying his craving for me outweighs his annoyance.

The towel drops to the floor.

His thighs spread a fraction more.

I breathe in, my nerves vanishing and desire appearing, hot and potent.

The moment I'm within reach, his arm extends, snaking around my lower back, and he tugs me into him, pulling my shirt apart and kissing my stomach, his huge hands on my hips, holding me, mine resting on his shoulders. I exhale raggedly, looking down at the back of his head, sliding my fingers to his nape and playing with the fine hair there. It's fairer than when I first met him.

Because he's spending more time in the light. More time in sunshine.

His fingers slip into the sides of my panties and pulls them down, and he looks up at me, his eyes clouded and desperate. I stroke across his stubble and lower my mouth to his, kissing him softly. "She's here," I whisper. "She's here and she's yours."

He groans and stands, lifting me and settling me on the bench, yanking my legs apart as he falls to his knees before me. "My period," I gasp, my back straightening, my hands not knowing whether to hold on to James or the bench. But then he growls, slams his mouth between my thighs, and my decision is made for me, my hands grabbing onto his hair.

He bites at my thighs, kisses, sucks my flesh, and despite him avoiding entering me, I start to shake violently, yanking at his hair, making his head jar and jerk. And just when the pressure is about to release, he pulls away and stands, and I moan my loss. He dips and pushes my shirt from my shoulders, pulling it off each wrist and tossing it aside, then yanks the cups of my bra down. With the absence of his hot mouth, the air between my thighs suddenly feels cooler, and it is welcome. I watch, awed, as he pulls his T-shirt off, his chest undulating as he does, and then his shorts are gone and he is gloriously naked and impressive before me, his cock ready and dripping. I swallow and reach for it, hungry, eager, and circle him at the root, opening my mouth and moving in, looking up as I do, seeing him watch me. I lick. A groan. I bite. A jerk. I suck. Vibrations.

The feeling of his vein throbbing against my tongue encourages me to take it all, and he hits the back of my throat hard. It takes everything in me not to gag.

"Fuck," he grates, quickly pulling himself out and taking me under my arms, lifting me from the bench. He holds me against his body and turns, sitting down and lifting me a fraction. "We shouldn't," I say for the sake of it, knowing he won't stop. Can't stop. I don't want him to stop. I drop my forehead to his and reach between us, removing my tampon as I close my eyes. I need him inside me. I need this, for me, for him, for us. I falter for a moment.

"My towel," he whispers, and I look around, seeing it on the floor. James bends, lowering me, and I swipe it up, quickly ridding myself of what stands between us in this moment. Then I take what I need, guiding him to my entrance and sinking down slowly, both of us exhaling.

God, that feels incredible, him filling me so completely. Pulsing. Close. I place a hand on each of his shoulders and link my ankles around his back, pulling away so I can see his face, his chest, his thick biceps, his abs rolling. It's all magnificent, but his face . . .

It's straight now, not a hint of his pleasure showing as he watches me move on top of him, letting me do all the work. "Do you want me to kiss you?" I ask, and he shakes his head. "Do you want me to move faster?" Another shake of his head. "Stay like this?"

A nod, a palm slipping up my body from my hip and sliding onto my exposed breast. He strokes and molds, and still his eyes never leave mine as I circle my hips, thrust slowly, leisurely building our pleasure.

The way he's studying me.

Absorbed.

He takes in every piece of me, his eyes moving slowly across my face, my wounds, my body, his lips slightly parted, his breaths short and strained. I swallow, feeling the rush of my climax taking hold, giving me no warning. James nods, reclaiming my hips, guiding me, and every muscle I can see hardens before my eyes. I gasp and slap my palms into his pecs, bracing my arms, my pace increasing. He shakes his head, stilling, and I cry out, my head falling back as my orgasm retreats. "Fuck," I breathe, starting slowly again, working both of us back up, being sure not to go faster than he wants, as I bring my eyes back down to his face. It's all I need to get me to the edge again.

It tickles, teases, temps me to grab it and claim the pleasure, begs me to move faster.

I don't.

James groans, it's suppressed, and his thighs harden beneath me. Then he nods, and it seizes us both, snapping our spines straight, forcing our chests together, as well as our mouths, and I am kissed into oblivion as he spills himself inside me, his strong arms wrapped around my waist, holding me tightly as we shake and kiss and moan.

I puff and pant into his mouth, sliding my face away and burying it in the crook of his neck. "Okay?" I whisper, not liking his silence.

He nods, feeling out my finger and turning the ring.

To remind me it's there.

"I love you," I murmur.

And he nods.

James moves around the kitchen silently, the shadows between his shoulder blades growing and shrinking each time he reaches into a cupboard or opens a door or drawer. He slides a plate across the island to me. "Eat," he says, clipped.

"I'm not—"

"I can't remember the last time I saw you eat, Beau." He picks up a piece of toast and thrusts it toward me. "So eat."

I accept and he goes to the fridge, pulling out an array of green fruit and vegetables, placing them all onto the counter before collecting a chopping board and a blender. I nibble the corner of my toast as I watch him move quietly and efficiently around the kitchen, peeling and cutting and loading into the blender. "I've been thinking."

"Be careful," I quip, getting a brief warning look thrown my way as I chew.

"You can take the delivery."

I swallow slowly, still on my stool. I'm surprised, but I fight not to show it. "What's changed?" I realize that's a stupid question. Ollie's phone call is what's changed. Or has standing on his head leveled out his reasonable side? Or . . . did Danny just speak to him? Reason with him? Convince him they haven't got a lot of choice? That I'm capable.

"Nothing's changed." He tips a glug of apple juice into the blender. "I still don't want you to do it."

"So why are you agreeing?"

Pausing with his juice making task, he considers the jug for a while, as if waiting for it to offer up the best way to give it to me. "Because, Beau, if I don't control my instinct, I will be suppressing yours." He looks at me. "I can't lose you."

I relax on my stool, softening. This immense, powerful killer looking so uncertain carves out a piece of my heart. "You're not going to lose me."

A sharp nod as he goes back to juicing. "So what did he say?" he asks, not looking up at me.

I pause mid chew, wiping a few crumbs from the corner of my mouth. "I will get a call from—" My cell jumps across the marble, an unknown caller lighting the screen. James's finger stills on the blender button, his eyes on my cell too. "From a detective," I finish, placing my toast down and brushing off my hands before taking my cell to my ear rather than putting it on loudspeaker for James to hear. "Beau Hayley," I say, as James abandons his green juice and collects a dish towel, wiping his hands as he observes. I want to leave the kitchen. But I can't do that.

"Miss Hayley, Detective Clarissa Collins, MPD. Is now a good time?"

Is there ever a good time to have these kinds of discussions? There absolutely is. Preferably when my boyfriend isn't in the room. And then it occurs to me . . . should I know about Dad? Ollie didn't mention anything other than he couldn't talk on the phone, which tells me he didn't feel safe. *Private.* "How can I help you, Detective?" I ask, feeling so fucking uncomfortable under James's watchful gaze. He's questioning why I haven't opened up the conversation to him.

"I wondered if I could trouble you for some time."

"Sure. Now?"

"I was hoping to see you in person, but I stopped by the address we have on file for you and the house is empty."

She wants to see me? "I don't live there anymore."

"With your uncles?" she presses, making me frown, her answer telling me she probably knows a lot more about me than I would like, especially if she's been digging around in the police files. I look at James. Does she know I'm now engaged to marry a mass murderer? *Jesus fucking Christ.*

"Yes. They separated," I say, trying to sound willing with the information. Cagey will get me nowhere. "My uncle Lawrence is away on vacation." I make a point not to say where. "And . . . well, his husband—" I look at James. Won't he stop with the concentrated, annoyed stare? "He left and we haven't heard from him since."

"You mean Dexter Haynes? MPD?"

"That's right."

"But a missing person's report hasn't been filed?"

She knows why that is. It must be common knowledge in the force that Dexter was bent. "Have you called me to talk about my uncle, Detective Collins?" The moment I utter her name, James has his cell phone out of his pocket, undoubtedly to message Otto and have her checked out.

"No. No, I wasn't," she says, her voice softening. Softening ready to hit me with the grim news that my father is dead. "Can I take your address? I can be there in half hour."

I look around the kitchen of The Brit's Miami mansion. "I'm afraid that's not possible." And she'll know why that is too. "Whatever it is you need to talk about, we can do over the phone."

"I don't th—"

"We can do it over the phone," I reiterate, getting agitated.

"It's your father," she says, as I stare at the board full of chopped fruit. "I'm so sorry, Miss Hayley."

"What happened?" I ask, trying not to sound robotic but being unable to help myself.

"Wrong place, wrong time," she replies, making me blink my surprise and look up at James. His brows are heavier than usual, his expression questioning without being questioning. I click my cell to loudspeaker and set it down, if only because I need someone to hear the bullshit I know I'm about to be insulted with so that when I go on a rampage, he will understand why.

"Wrong place, wrong time?" I mimic.

"There was an incident at a local hotel. We haven't got the finer details just yet, and I am limited on what I can divulge, but it appears there was a dispute between two local gangs that spilled into the hotel. I believe your father had a meeting there. He got caught in the crossfire."

"Excuse me?"

"I'm very sorry, Miss Hayley."

I look at James, hoping to see some semblance of surprise, but instead I find only an impassiveness that confuses me more. Caught in the crossfire? My God, are they honestly going to try and convince me *again* that I've lost another parent by sheer bad luck? "Thank you for the call."

"One more thing," she says, stilling my fingertip just shy of the red icon on the screen. "There's a journalist. He's already leaked information and pictures. I didn't want you to be surprised when you see it on the local news."

James goes straight to his phone again, and I thank Detective Collins once more before hanging up. "We need to find Frazer Cartwright," I say immediately, getting down off my stool. "I can't believe they're doing this to me again." I sink my fingers into my hair and clench. "Caught in the crossfire?" I say over a laugh, feeling tears pinching my eyes. And then . . . I gasp, dropping my hands from my head, staring at the floor. "Is he dead because of me?"

"What?" James barks, sounding angry? "What the fucking hell are you talking about?" He grabs me and spins me around to face him, getting up in my face, furious. "If you'd have met him for dinner, you could be dead too, Beau."

"I don't mean that. I mean Tom Hayley, my father, was running for mayor, and his daughter is me." I jab a finger into my chest. "And I am with *you*."

James flinches and backs up. "You think he was the target?" he asks.

"It makes sense."

"Wait, Beau." His palm rest on his forehead, his eyes closing. "Why would anyone want your father dead?"

"Because his daughter is me," I yell, guilt overwhelming me. "Miami can't have a mayor with a daughter who's involved with the biggest crime family this side of the Atlantic." Then something else occurs to me. "Or maybe his competitor had him murdered," I say, pacing to the window and back again, thinking.

"Monroe Metcalfe?" James laughs over his name. "Beau, Monroe Metcalfe has a résumé that glows brighter than the sun at the height of summer."

He shouldn't sound so disbelieving. Look at Perry Adams. He had everyone fooled. I laugh to myself, facing James. "I—" His hand lands over my mouth, silencing me, and he holds it there, his spare on my nape.

"Shhhh," he whispers quietly. "Calm the fuck down."

"I'm calm," I mumble into his hand, reaching up and carefully pulling it away.

"Damn you for being a cop." He sighs and lets his mouth drop onto my forehead. "I will find Cartwright," he says. "I promise. I've already got Otto on it."

"Why?"

"He seems to know a lot about a lot and we want to know how." He leans back and gets me in his sights. The hard-faced, impassive killer is gone, and my soft, expressive fiancé is back, and right now he's looking at me like he might love me more than life itself. Soothed. Calmed. "I've neglected you," he whispers, scanning my face, dragging his thumb across my lip. "I'm taking you out for dinner tonight."

"You are?"

"I am." He turns me by my shoulders and sends me on my way with a smack to my ass. He's trying to introduce some normal. It's gallant, if wasted. We're not in St. Lucia now, and no number of romantic dinners will make me feel normal. "And, Beau?"

I look back.

"You should call Lawrence," he says gently, and I nod.

I didn't call Lawrence. I did everything, *except* call Lawrence. How do I even begin to explain what's happened? Mom? Dad? I'll call him tomorrow. I did call Ollie though. Repeatedly. He didn't answer. It feels like Nath all over again. I'm worried for Ollie, but more worried for myself, because returning to those places I went to after losing Mom feels scarily close.

I take the steps down to the foyer to find James after he left me in the bedroom an hour ago to make a few calls. He spent the rest of the day at the boatyard with Otto, Goldie, and Ringo. Probably to tell them he's bowed and agreed to me helping. I bet he's also taken the opportunity to fill them in on Detective Collins's call to me. *Wrong place, wrong time.* I'm not being crazy. This all just feels . . . off. And while I can't claim to be consistently settled, this persistent edgy feeling, like I'm constantly on the verge of a panic attack, is how I existed before James.

Consistently settled. There are times. They're always brief but blissful. The times when James takes me away. He's mastered the art of calming me. Problem is, he can't devote every minute of the day to doing that. Not here in Miami, at least. He makes a damn good try in St. Lucia, though.

I reach the bottom of the stairs and smell him before I see him, the creamy, manly scent with an edge of spice. Heaven. Then I see him, and I feel my heart race and settle at the same time. Gray trousers, open-collared blue shirt that makes his eyes shine, a light tan belt to match his shoes. Stubble. Sleeves rolled up. He's smart casual. So damn handsome. Looking at him now, even when his face is unreadable, it's hard to imagine him as The Enigma.

"Special occasion?" I ask, making his lip quirk.

"I don't know, is it?" He comes to me, motioning down my black tiered dress that I borrowed from Rose's closet, of course. I know she won't mind. I really should go shopping.

James seizes me, takes in my loose, wild blonde hair, smiles, and then kisses me deeply, leaning into me, forcing me to lean back.

"Must be," I counter, pecking at his lips. "To take a night off from work."

His nose wrinkles, he rubs it with mine, and then takes my hand, ignoring my quip. "You look out of this world," he says, leading me out to a Mercedes. "We'll have to take Danny's car." He opens the passenger door. "I was blocking him in earlier when he went out with Rose, so he took mine."

I slip into the seat and pull my seatbelt on, watching James round the front, admiring him. Dinner. A normal, regular dinner, like a normal regular couple. He opens the door, but he doesn't make it into the car. The gates up ahead open and James's Range Rover appears. "Oh, they're home," I say, releasing myself from the car to say hello to Rose before we leave. I step out and watch Danny drive toward us, and the second he stops, he's out, looking pretty fucking murderous. *Oh shit*. What's happened now? Naturally, I look at Rose. She looks apprehensive.

I tilt my head. She shakes hers.

"The fuck?" Danny yells, marching toward James. "Have you lost your fucking mind?"

Now I know this isn't about me taking the delivery because Danny told me he thought my idea was a good idea. So, again, what the hell has happened now? I look between the men, worried they might get up in each other's faces again, take out their frustrations on each other. "What's going on?" I ask Rose, joining her.

"Oh, you'll see," she says, opening the back door and dragging out piles of bags. "We had a lovely shopping trip, just me and my husband." She smiles. It's fake.

"Why are you lying?"

"I'm not. It was wonderful. Then we were driving home and—"

"You're fucking insane," Danny shouts, wrestling his way out of his jacket and slamming it on the ground. Then he obviously remembers he needs something in the pocket and snatches it back up, rummaging through.

"What the hell are you banging on about?" James mutters, obviously tired of watching Danny tearing away at his jacket because he claims it and goes straight to the pocket, pulling out his Marlboros and passing them over with his zippo.

Danny lights one, inhales deeply, then puffs out the smoke, pointing at the Range Rover with his cigarette. "Join me." He smiles, the kind of smile none of us want to see, and paces to the back of James car, releasing the trunk with the key fob. James follows, and, of course, Rose and I too. The trunk lifts slowly, taking forever, as we all stand and wait for whatever is going to be revealed, and when it is, James is the first to speak.

"Ah, fuck," he grunts, as I stare at a motionless body that's bound and gagged.

"Ah, fuck?" Danny says, laughing. "That's what you've got to say? Ah, *fuck?* Who the fuck is it and how long has he been in your car? Because it fucking stinks."

I step forward and sniff, as does Rose, and immediately slam a palm over my mouth. "Ewww." Stale urine. "You are *not* taking me for dinner in that," I blurt.

"Oh, you're going for dinner?" Rose sings, facing me, her shopping bag whirling with her.

"We *were*," I say, as James steps forward and prods the body. "Now I have a feeling we'll be getting rid of a body."

"He's still alive," James says. "He's only been in here since last night."

"I know he's still a-fucking-live," Danny yells, pulling on his cigarette urgently, like it's the only thing keeping him on the ground. "Because he yelped when I threw my wife's shopping in the trunk."

"Threw?" Rose says, outraged. "There's a Jo Malone Candle in there, Black." She starts rummaging through the dozens of bags, looking for her candle.

"I know." Danny laughs. "It hit him on the head."

I look between Danny and Rose, then to James, absolutely . . . amused. I'm amused. And unable to push it back, it pours out of me, forcing me to drop my purse and use my hands to hold on to James. I catch Rose's eye as she looks up from her bags, abandoning her check of the candle, and she falls apart too, obviously realizing how crazy this is.

And the men?

They smoke, and they watch, letting us hang on to them while we get it out of our systems. I think I've gone mad. Definitely, actually.

"So," James says when I've straightened and composed myself, although I can still hear Rose's random chuckles, the aftermath of her laughing fit dragging out longer than mine. "Are we going for dinner or not?" he asks.

"Yes, dinner," I reply, sniffling and wiping my nose. Lord knows, I need some wine, and while this is all so inappropriate, it is respite from dealing with . . . everything. "What about him?" I ask, pointing to the trunk.

Danny pushes the button on the underside to close it and flicks his cigarette butt away. "He can wait." He scowls, looking at James. "Wait, who is it?"

"The Leprechaun."

"Irish by any chance?" I ask, dipping and collecting my purse, prompting another chuckle from Rose, but this time through her nose, making the most unattractive sound.

Her laughter stops abruptly, and she slaps her hand over her mouth. "Oh my God, I just snorted." She looks absolutely horrified, looking at me with wide eyes, and I'm off again, laughing like a hyena, my makeup ruined by tears.

James moves in and holds me up. "He was at the Pink Flamingo last night," he says to Danny.

"That's great, I'm happy for you, but in future, would you mind letting me know if you do a lucky dip on a bar and score?"

"I was a little distracted," James retorts, looking out the corner of his eye at me, prompting everyone else to too. My face straightens. *Kill the mood, why don't you?*

"I drove home like Miss Daisy," Danny grumbles. "Saw a thousand cop cars and sweated a million *oh shits*."

"He really did," Rose pipes up, walking toward the house.

"Where are you going?" Danny calls after her, making her lift the bags in her hands as if to show him, like he could have missed half the mall she's carrying.

"I'm taking these to our room."

"Watch the candle," he yells, lighting another cigarette. "You two don't mind if we join you?"

I smile, not minding at all. We'll get our alone time when we're home. It's nice for us all to be together again, *and* all talking. "I don't mind."

"Good. There's a lovely little Italian place I know."

"Oh, where we'll have murder for our main course?" I head for the car and slip into the back, but before I can pull the door closed, Danny's there, leaning in.

"You two talk too much."

"Stressful day?" I ask, nodding to the cigarette between his lips.

"A few unexpected surprises, yes." He looks over the car. To James? And then I remember in the gym earlier. *You never mentioned that bit.*

Said with such emphasis on *that.*

What were they talking about?

"So you're joining the ranks, eh?" Danny says, blowing smoke in my face, forcing me to waft it away.

"You need to quit."

He laughs hysterically. "Beau, sweeth—" He thinks for a second. "Beau, if I don't smoke, I'll kill."

"Maybe you need to learn to control your impulses," I retort casually, brushing the creases out of my dress as Danny bares his teeth. I roll my eyes. "You don't scare me, Black." I reach for the door and pull it shut, nearly taking his nose off as Rose slips in beside me, dumping her cell and purse on the seat between us as she buckles up.

"Ready," she breathes, joining our hands and resting them on the leather. Her phone dings, and I instinctively look down.

"Esther's coming to Miami?" I ask, seeing a short preview of her message. "You're not going back to St. Lucia now?"

Rose looks at me, putting her finger to her lips for me to hush.

Oh God.

I lean in closer. "He doesn't know, does he?"

She peeks out the corner of her eye at me, that look saying it all. "I can't go to Daniel without Danny, so Daniel must come to me. As my husband keeps pointing out when I'm feeling misplaced, I am a mother. That's my job," she whispers. "A hard job to do when one kid is in another country and the other's not even born yet."

"He's going to go mad."

"I'll give him one last opportunity to stop being a stubborn dick. If not, I'll take the matter into my own hands. He'll get over it. We all know Otto is part of the reason Esther's not here, and I'm not in St. Lucia with my son because—"

"You were worried about Danny."

"True. But worrying is stressful, and as everyone keeps saying, I need to chill the fuck out. Besides, I thought I'd be gone a few days. Not weeks. And now Danny's got a bee in his bonnet about Barney's dad and *that* is why he won't let me go back to St. Lucia without him."

"I'll look forward to the fireworks." There's no way Danny's agreeing to Daniel coming here or Rose going there. The doors open and the men slide in, and, of course, we both shut up, prompting both of them to turn around in their seats and eye us.

I remain mute.

As does Rose.

I just want to enjoy a nice dinner in relative calm.

19

DANNY

A week of silence. Oddly, silence in Miami makes me feel more uneasy than constantly dodging bombs and bullets. I watch the water rippling around my bare feet, feel the sun on my bare chest. It feels good after being wrapped up for so long, the Dermabond dissolved, the cuts red but no longer raw. I listen to the roars of engines on the ocean. Smell the salt. The sand.

My wife.

"I'm giving you one last opportunity to be reasonable and get them on a plane to Miami."

Or else?

My shades slide down the bridge of my nose, sweat assisting, so I push them back, facing Rose. She's always a pleasing sight, but today especially so, with her ever increasingly curvy body adorned in a gold bikini, her boobs bulging against the material, her hair bundled up high.

I feel myself twitching against my wetsuit as I reach for her and pull her close, pushing a wave behind her ear as I kiss the corner of her mouth. "You've caught the sun," I whisper, pulling back and slipping a finger past the taut material of her bikini top and easing it down a fraction, revealing a tan line just north of her nipple.

She peeks down too, but not for as long as me. "Don't change the subject." She pushes my hand away and slips her fingers into my hair, holding my dark waves in her clenched fists threateningly. "Are you really that passionate about keeping Otto away from your mom?"

For fuck's sake. She doesn't say it, but I know she's mentally considering the fact that I'm also keeping her away from that Benson bloke. "This has nothing to do with Otto and everything to do with Daniel's stability and education."

"Stability? He's there, and I'm here. And he can have a private tutor in Miami. Are we going back to St. Lucia?"

Won't she stop? I groan and swoop in for another kiss. And get blocked with a dick-slicing glare. I roll my eyes—though Rose can't appreciate my silent mocking with my shades hiding it.

She reaches for my glasses and lifts them, revealing my eyes. "Don't roll your eyes at me."

"I didn't," I say, stealing a kiss before she can shove me away. Her rejection is probably a good thing. My tight wetsuit might become tighter. I'm not arguing with her. We've done enough of that recently. So . . . "You're staying here, and Daniel is staying there." I'll tell her instead. Another stolen kiss as I pass her, heading for the cabin. She's soon chasing my heels, protesting. "You're being unreasonable."

"I know," I say over my shoulder, not denying it.

"What?"

I stop, exhale loudly, and face her frown. "If you think for a moment I'm letting you go back to St. Lucia without me—"

"In case I'm swept off my feet by a single, handsome banker?"

I seize her face, squeezing her cheeks until she has duck lips. Why must she rile me? "There will be no sweeping, there'll only be mopping." *Blood.* "Remember that if you're ever tempted to be swept." I slam my lips on hers, kissing away her scowl. "Are we clear?"

"Fuck off."

Smiling darkly, I watch her wrench herself away, but my amusement loses its darkness and gains some true light when my focus lands on her arse as she stomps away, the two curvy peaks jiggling beautifully, her bikini bottoms cutting high across each one. I groan on an exhale and push my shades up into my hair, fixated as I blindly pick up my cigarettes off a nearby wall and light one, never taking my eyes off my wife.

She stomps up the steps to the cabin as James exits with Brad, and they both part to let her through, following her path with raised, knowing brows. She tosses both arms in the air, and the wind carries her muttered insult to my ears. She hates me. I'm an arsehole. "Same story, different day," I say to myself as the boys look my way. They're both freshly showered after a few hours out on the water with me. I've been distracted by the ocean and a willful wife during the time it's taken them to change. I make my way to them and up the steps, puffing my way through my cigarette.

"All right?" Brad asks as I pass through the middle of them and take a right into the café.

"Brilliant," I mutter, grabbing a water from the fridge and holding it up for the young girl who's serving to see, prompting her to run it through the system and add it to my tab. "Where are the others?"

"Out on the balcony," James says, taking a beer instead of a water. I look at it in his hand as he screws the cap off. He's drinking more lately, a result, no doubt, of stressing over where Beau is every second of every day or, more to the point, who she's with. That woman would give Houdini a run for his money. "I just checked in with Leon on the delivery for Friday."

"Where's Beau?" I ask, prompting James to point his bottle to the decking and me to look through the open concertina doors and past the dozens of occupied tables. I spy her at the very end of the wharf, reclined in a chair, her feet kicked up onto the railing, her face pointed upward. Toward the sun. "Still nothing from Burrows?" I ask, chugging down some water.

A veil of menace drops at the mention of the arsehole. "Not that she's said."

"She's here," Brad says, passing us and heading outside. "And we all know she wouldn't be if she'd heard from Burrows." He's right. She'd be off playing detective, and that would be the perfect opportunity for Burrows to try and worm his way back into her affections. So where the fuck is he?

James and I follow Brad out into the sunshine. "Rose hasn't mentioned anything?" James asks.

"All Rose has done this past week is be difficult." I look at him. "In what fucking world do we depend on the girls for enlightenment?"

"This fucking world," he mutters. "I've got Otto keeping tabs on Beau's phone."

I laugh. "Does she know?"

"What do you think?"

"I think you haven't told her, but she knows."

"Of course she fucking knows." He looks out toward Beau, and I follow his line of sight, seeing Rose tugging some denim shorts up her legs with heavy hands. She leaves them undone, and I smile. She can't get the buttons fastened anymore. "Good girl," James says as Rose picks up a bottle of sunblock and squirts some in her hands, rubbing it into Beau's arm while she obviously slags me off. We make it to the other men and pull up chairs; as Otto taps away on his laptop, Ringo chomps his way through some chips, and Goldie sips tea, very ladylike as I draw on my Marlboro.

"What?" she asks, the cup at her lips. "What are you looking at?"

"You had a haircut?" I ask.

Her spare hand goes straight to her hair and smooths it behind one ear, then the other. It's shorter, probably as short as it could be without losing the convenience of being able to tie it back. "A trim," she says on a scowl, hating me for noticing she's done something so girlie like have a visit to a salon.

"Looks nice," I say honestly, feeling James watching me, probably waiting for me to crack a joke. I have no intention. I'm being genuine.

"Thanks," she grunts, taking some tea. "You could do with a cut yourself."

I feel at my hair. It's been weeks, but my wife claims to love the longer look on me, and hair is something I *can* give her, so I'll carry on poking up with the tickle on my nape. "Rose likes it like this," I say, running a hand through it and knocking my shades off my head. James dips and picks them up.

"You too," Goldie says, nodding to James, who freezes in his half-bent position, looking at everyone as everyone looks at his longer-than-average hair.

"Letting yourselves go," Otto grunts, not looking up from his laptop but feeling at his neat, well-groomed beard. He's lost the cap, the egg on his head having gone.

"Did we meet for coffee and girlie chit-chat about hair and beauty, or did we meet for beers and a briefing on what the fuck is going on and where the fuck The Bear has disappeared to?" James asks. It's been over a week since he called James and advised him that our parents had been dug up. Since then, we've had The Ox ask us to back off with our deal with the Mexicans, which he paid for dearly, and The Shark called soon after asking for guns.

I smile and take another hit of nicotine before stubbing it out in the ashtray. "Over to Otto," I say, blowing my smoke his way. His lip curls, but he doesn't look at me.

"The detective who got in touch with Beau over her father's death..."

"Collins," James says, reminding everyone. "What about her?"

"Hungry," Otto replies. "Very fucking hungry."

"Something to prove," I say, resting back in my chair and kicking an ankle up onto my knee. "Why? Apart from being a woman in a man's world?" I look out the corner of my eye to Goldie when I feel a pissed-off glower pointing my way. "Did you have highlights too?" I ask, making her swipe up a bottle of water, unscrew the cap, and throw it in my face. I laugh, wiping at my eyes.

"You asked for that," James says, looking at me with a shake of his head.

"I'm playing." I stand and round the back of Goldie's chair, taking her shoulders, feeling her tense beneath my hands. I dip and kiss her cheek. "I'm sorry."

"Get the fuck off me before I—"

"Before you *what*?" I ask, interested and sounding a little bit ominous. Something tells me I might regret it.

"You sure you want to have this conversation?" she asks.

"You started it," I snap like a child.

"I'm giving you an opportunity to back down."

I laugh. "Never."

"Fine. Before I tell your wife that you told your mother that your wife *wants* Daniel to stay in St. Lucia."

What the fuck? I stare at Goldie as she tucks her freshly high-lighted, freshly cut hair behind her ear again. She didn't need to. It was already perfectly tucked; she was merely making a point. *How the fuck does she know that?*

She must see the question in my stunned eyes. "Esther called me," she goes on. "Told me she understands why Rose would want that and, actually, Rose should be here if only to stop you from self-destructing. Or getting locked up. Or killed."

Fuck. We all know Goldie wouldn't dare tell Rose that, but what Goldie has succeeded in doing is reminding me that Rose will go nuclear on me if she finds out that I'm playing her and Mum against each other.

Brad snorts as I get back in my cage, visibly shrinking before everyone's eyes. But I do give one last look at Otto, who is blatantly occupying himself on his laptop to avoid my threatening stare. There's only one reason my mum would want to come back to Miami, and I'm staring at the fucker, so intently, I hope he bursts into flames and turns to ashes. Otto is causing me a headache I do not need.

I look at James like he can help me, and he looks at me like, what do I expect? What do I want for my mother? I don't know, but it isn't Otto. "Back to Collins?" he asks, tilting his head.

"Back to Collins," I mutter, slumping down in my chair, moody. "So she's hungry. Hungry for a bit of British meat or hungry for some Polish, Russian, or Irish animals?"

"Yet to be determined," Otto says, infinitely poised over his laptop. "But I'm gonna use my initiative and say she'll take whatever she can get. She's smart. Graduated from Yale with a law degree before she followed in her mother's footsteps and joined the LAPD. She moved to the East Coast a few months ago. Higham confirmed she's causing a stir."

Followed in her mum's footsteps? I look at James. He's blank. Probably thinking what I'm thinking. Jaz Hayley. Beau Hayley. Beau was definitely following in her mother's footsteps . . . before The Bear blew her mother up. "Who is her mother?"

"Sharon Collins. FBI. San Francisco."

"And causing a stir for them or us?" I ask.

"For everyone."

"And she was pressing Beau on Dexter," I muse. "Building a picture?"

"Oh, for sure." Otto laughs. "She's been checking out files from the archives left and right."

"How'd you know th—"

"Higham," he grunts, tapping away at the keys. "And I have a name on The Shark." Otto sits back, twirling the ring in his lip, comfortable, whereas everyone else at the table sits forward, intrigued. He remains mute as we all wait. I look at James, exasperated, after seconds of no enlightenment.

"Well?" Brad asks, just before I'm about to. Otto takes his laptop and turns it to face us, revealing a face. His nose is absolutely colossal, his forehead larger than my desk, his eyes close together, his ears, I'm sure, making it impossible for him to pass through a door without brushing them on the frame. His buzzcut only reveals how fucking huge his head is. "Fuck me, he's even uglier than you, Ringo," Brad says on a laugh as we all take in the man dominating the screen. Or less of a man, more of a fat head. Goldie chuckles, it's girlie, and she appreciates that because she soon clears her throat in time to apologize to Ringo when he turns a curled lip her way.

"Who is he?" Brad asks what we all want to know.

"Former polish military," Otto says. "Marek Zielińska. And since you told him where to swivel for his guns last week, he's been on a little spending spree around Florida with a fake gun license."

"Oh?" I say, impressed. "And what's Marek Zielińska, AKA Mr. Shark buying?"

"Everything from grenades to M249s from any store he can find."

"So he's desperate if he's stretching to buying with the commoners," I muse out loud.

"And what of Beau's thoughts?" Ringo asks, making us all look toward the end of the wharf. Rose now has her cropped T-shirt on, and Fury is holding out her bag to her. Beau is still face up to the sun.

"I think she might be on the right track," I say, as James nods. "They're all jumping ship and scrambling to protect themselves."

"So where is The Bear?" Goldie asks, looking agitated. She knows if he's disappeared off the face of the earth, the chances of us finding him are slim, which means James and Beau's peace will elude them, which also means Goldie's freedom will elude *her*. "His last move was ordering the exhumation of Danny's father and Beau's mother. No one's heard anything from him since?"

"Not a peep," James says quietly, sinking farther into his chair, thoughtful. "And Frazer Cartwright?"

"There's a camera opposite his apartment. He's not there, nor has he been there. Not since he called Beau. He seems to have disappeared along with The Bear. It's Tom Hayley's funeral tomorrow. He might be there."

"He might not," I say quietly.

James looks at me. Just me. "Tom's funeral can't be anything but a funeral."

"Understood. The delivery on Friday."

"Beau understands the assignment."

"I can't believe we've agreed to this," I mutter. "I definitely can't believe *you* have." But I get it. If James doesn't keep Beau close, keep her mind as occupied as possible, she'll be gone.

"You got any other suggestions?"

I blow out my cheeks in answer as Otto's laptop pings, and all attention is soon rediverted from me to the screen. I join the masses, looking at the small pop-up that's appeared in the bottom right-hand corner. It's not small enough. My mum's name glows at me.

There are a few *oh fucks* as Otto speedily drags his laptop back and turns it. "You," I say, pushing my hands into the table and rising.

"Danny," James warns.

"You . . . you . . . you . . ."

"Calm the fuck down."

"Fucker," I hiss, my temperature going through the roof.

"I think a lot of your mother, Danny," Otto says, standing. "A *lot*." Everyone else at the table shrinks into their chairs, while I twitch like I've been tasered. *A lot?* What does that mean? Love? Sex? I inhale. Has he got her into bed? "You won't control her anymore." Otto goes on, obviously not done. "You won't hold her to ransom and use her past against her."

What? I do no such thing. "What the fuck are you talking about?" I only want what's best for her, and a man with a history of fucking and indulging in strippers isn't it.

"I'm talking about her well-being being in *my* hands, not yours," Otto goes on. "And I'm not about to stand by and watch you throw your toys out your pram. Get fucking used to it."

"Fucking hell," Brad breathes.

"Sit, Danny," James says, grabbing my arm and fighting to pull me down. I'm unmoving.

"You've brainwashed her," I seethe. "Shown her a bit of attention and taken advantage of her naivety."

Otto laughs. It's the worst thing he could do. I'm across that table like a bullet, rugby tackling him to the floor and delivering a brutal right hook, sending blood from his nose spraying. "You keep your filthy hands to yourself," I yell, falling to my back when Otto shoves me off him.

"I'm nothing but respectful around your mother. You're lucky you're her son or you'd be dead," he growls, wiping his nose of blood as I scramble up, ready to charge. But someone's between us before I'm out of the docks.

"Move, Rose," I order.

"Fuck off." She takes my arm and manhandles me outside, and I don't fight because . . .

Rose.

"What the hell are you playing at?" She shoves me down the steps, gaining the attention of many. "You're a fucking child."

And because she's right, I retaliate. And maybe because I've concluded that I'm already in her bad books so I may as well spill a few secrets. "Esther's not coming back to Miami," I snarl.

"Wrong." She smiles, and it's one hundred percent smug. "And Daniel's coming too."

"What?"

"Lennox has business in Montenegro to see to before he brings Barney to Miami to see his parents, so he can no longer babysit while my husband shoots his way through the city and holds me against my will because he's worried I'll have my head turned by a dashing, single banker."

Good Lord, save me before I kill her. I have no words. Am incapable of talking. She's one step ahead. Seems like everyone is. "I . . . it's . . . why the—" I throw my arm out toward the cabin. "He said he thinks *a lot* of my mother."

"Good." She pokes me in my naked shoulder. "You will stay out of it."

I snort. Never. "Get your arse home," I snap, barging past her, set on going to finish what I started with Otto. I get precisely two paces before something connects with the back of my head with force, immediately putting stars in my vision. "Fuck!" I hit the deck, my head instantly throbbing, and roll on to my back, dazed.

Rose appears standing over me. "I'm going shopping," she says. "So I can make my son and his grandmother something nice for dinner when they arrive."

"They're really coming?"

"Yes." She sneers. "*Your* dinner will be in the dogs." She pulls her hair free of the band, shakes it out, flicks it over her shoulder, and saunters off. "I'm taking Fury," she yells back. "And I've text you your mom's flight details so you can pick them up from the airport when you've seen to business for the day."

I lift my head, watching her go, her arse cheeks very nearly poking out the bottom of her denim shorts. "Those shorts are too short!"

Two middle fingers appear and, sick fuck that I am, I smile, rubbing at my head as I stand.

"She's a handful," someone says.

"Higham." I don't look his way just in case he's looking Rose's way—to those peachy cheeks poking out—and I'm forced to kill him. But I do look to the cabin, seeing everyone on the steps. I throw the traitors a dirty look and trudge to the shore where it's quieter, Higham following, along with everyone else. "What do you want?"

"Peace, Danny. You know that. I trust my intel was of use to you."

"You mean the identities of The Leprechaun and The Chameleon?" I ask, seeing Jerry coming out of the container where The Leprechaun is being held. A week he's been in there. For a week James has had his fun with him, and he's not spat one word of any use, only pleas for mercy. He's either very loyal or he really doesn't know a thing about The Bear. I expect it's the latter. Just a jumped-up kid who's been offered a scrap of power and brandished it. Or tried to, until The Enigma found him. "It was fuck-all use to us," I say, facing Higham, just catching his frown. "And we skipped The Chameleon and hit straight in on The Ox."

"What?"

"We've also just discovered the identity of The Shark, so tell me, Higham,"—I tilt my head—"we need you, why?"

James wanders casually over, standing just shy of the shore now he's fully dressed. "I'd ask if there's any news on the whereabouts of Jaz Hayley and Carlo Black, but I expect that would be a wasted question."

"Probably," Higham mutters. "We all know you're not finding those remains." A hand rakes through his hair. "Believe it or not, I am sorry about that."

"And Agent Burrows?" James presses, piquing my interest too. "Heard from him?"

"He took annual leave." Higham looks between us. "He *has* taken annual leave, right?"

I feel James look out the corner of his eye to me, wary. "Your guess is as good as ours," I say. Has James killed him and not told me?

"No," he says, reading my mind.

I've had enough of today. "Are we done?" I ask as Brad, Ringo, Goldie, and Otto join us, circling, imposing.

"It's getting harder to deflect attention from you, Danny," Higham says. "Collins is like a dog with a bone and she's expressing a real interest in The Brit and The Enigma."

Oh, for fuck's sake. "She wants the ultimate trophies?" I ask, feeling James's mood dip further.

"She wants recognition."

"Put her on a fucking leash," I say, getting up in his face. "You want peace in this city, you need to stand down and let me run it. If you want crime figures down, you need to let me eliminate the fuckers that are shipping in women and drugs and hiring the down-and-outs to do their dirty work."

"I need them alive, Danny," Higham hisses. "Otherwise, you make the figures fucking worse."

"With no bodies, there's no evidence. The population merely drops. I make sure there are no bodies."

He inhales, closing his eyes. "Collins has a woman in custody," he says on an exhale. "She was found at a rest stop on the freeway. Disorientated, dirty, foreign."

"And?" James asks, moving in closer, risking getting his boots wet.

"She was taken from her home in Serbia. Trafficked. She escaped." He opens his eyes. "She talked about where she was held, the languages being spoken by the men, what they looked like."

"Polish?" James asks.

"Yes."

"And where was she held?"

"It sounds like an airport. A factory or hangar." Higham looks at me. "I'm just saying, Danny." He casts his eyes over to James and the others. "If Collins brings in the Polish or the Russians, she plans on making a deal with them."

"A deal?" Goldie says.

"Yes, a deal. Their—"

"Freedom in exchange for us," James finishes. "She wants them to lead her to us."

"She knows where to find us," I say. "Every fucking copper in Florida state knows where to find us."

"But they don't have the evidence they need to put us in cuffs." James laughs under his breath.

"She thinks they can help her get that evidence." Higham looks embarrassed. He should.

"Who is this fucking woman? She swans into Miami, reads a few files, and thinks she has the answer to eternal peace in the city?" I'm fucking fuming. "Does she fucking know who she's dealing w—" I cast my eyes across the bay, my mind going into overdrive. "A hangar."

"What?" Brad asks, dipping his toes in the water to join me.

"Higham, you said the woman in custody mentioned she was held in a hangar."

"Yes."

I inhale, facing the others. *Fuck!* "Otto, I want every detail you can find on the purchase of Winstable Boatyard three years ago."

Without a word, he goes back to the cabin, and I follow, our recent brawl forgotten. "Leon!" I yell, and a second later he appears from one of the containers. "Get the skis ready."

"Sure thing, D-Boss."

I look at him, nodding, holding up one finger, and he acknowledges me, running off toward the container that houses a few loaded jet skis.

"What the fuck's going on?" Brad asks as James overtakes me, pulling his T-shirt up over his head, revealing his mammoth scar. The sight still makes me flinch.

"I know where the Polish are holding the women." *Fuck, how did I miss this?*

"Where?"

I can hardly say it without wanting to throw up. "The boatyard Pops built."

"No." Brad wants to laugh but worry is stopping him. "That was sold to be developed as an educational facility for disadvantaged kids."

It's been over three years since I stepped aside to let that happen. Of course, I wasn't willing to at first. Was prepared to break a few legs to keep the land. Then the disadvantaged kids' card was brandished. It's as if whoever needed Winstable knew I'd soften to that. *Fuckers!* "Do you see an educational facility over there?"

Brad looks across the water, not that Winstable is visible. Just a dot in the distance. "Jesus."

"Yeah." I take the steps fast as I pull my wetsuit up and when I enter the changing room, James is ready to get back on the water. "I want you two and Otto to take the road," I say to Goldie and Ringo. "We'll go in from the water. Distract them. Get them all out front."

"And do what?" Ringo says. "Ask for directions? For fuck's sake, Danny. Think about this. They'll know our faces."

"I can help."

We all whirl around and find Higham in the doorway. His face is serious. His stance unmoving. "A routine stop by. A few questions about a local robbery. Ain't nothing as distracting as the Feds at your door."

We all look at each other, none of us willing to admit it's the solution we need.

"You don't kill anyone," Higham goes on. "Not on my watch. But you scope the place, find out what you need to find out, and go back at nightfall when I am not there."

"Deal," I say, and James looks at me incredulously.

"You want to discuss that with me?"

"Nope. The others can use the boat." I leave the changing room, on a mission, trying not to think about Rose. Trying not to remember where she came from. Who she was before I took her.

A slave.

I suppress a growl, marching on and wading into the water, climbing on my ski. Brad is beside me, getting on his. "You need to take a few breaths, Danny." He frowns when Leon tugs around a loaded ski and ties it to the back of the boat as Ringo, Otto, and Goldie get onboard. "Higham said—"

"You want to go in unarmed?" I ask, feeling the top of my head for my shades. No shades. And then Leon appears, holding them out to me. I accept and slip them on.

"Fuck me," Brad breathes, looking across to James. Then we all look back to Higham driving off.

"Let's go," I say, chugging out. "We go in from the left, close to the cove. There's a concealed, dilapidated jetty a quarter mile from the shore," I go on, more for James's benefit, since he isn't familiar with our old base. "We'll go on foot from there."

I get no acknowledgment, everyone silent and taking a moment, before I put pressure on the throttle and stand from my seat, picking up speed, but not so much that Ringo can't keep up.

We stick close to the outskirts of the bay, and as soon as I have Winstable in my sights, I don't take my eyes off it, doing everything I can not to let my anger rule me. The place my father built when I was fifteen, my childhood haven, now being used to hold abducted women? Lord, have mercy on my soul, I will butcher them all, and when I find out who bought it? Who fooled me into standing down? My teeth clench.

Calm.

I shut off the engine when I'm a few feet offshore and let the current carry me onto the pebbles next to the jetty. "Fucking hell," Ringo mutters, eyeing the disintegrating wood. "If the current picks up and pulls the boat, this thing is collapsing and going under." He gingerly steps onto the wood and leaves some extra rope before winding it around a stray post, the sturdiest he can find, which still isn't too sturdy.

"Will it hold?" I ask, stepping onto the shore. My boots land a few feet away, courtesy of Goldie, followed by James's and Brad's too.

"Pray," he grunts, and I do, stepping on board to help Otto drag the loaded ski closer.

"What's inside?" he asks, steadying it as I reach for the catch at the back and release it.

"I don't know." I let the hydraulic levers slowly hiss their way up.

"So it's like a Pick N Mix for criminals?" he asks, and I chuckle, but quickly stop when I remember . . .

"Fuck off," I snap.

"Easy, son," Otto mutters, pulling out a harpoon.

Son? My nostrils flare, and I grab an AK47, pointing it his way. It's not loaded, but he'll get the gist.

"Boys!" Goldie hisses, smacking my gun away, followed by Otto's harpoon. "I'll kill you both myself."

I snarl, as does Otto, and we get back to business, passing back all the weapons and loading up. "Higham's five minutes away," Ringo says, holding his phone between his teeth while he slips bullets into a magazine.

I start jogging along the shoreline, getting more charged the closer I get to Winstable. A few times, I lose my focus and cast my eyes out onto the ocean, seeing me, a young lad, recklessly riding across the water. Then I see me, a grown man, kissing a woman. Then being blown up. *Fuck*. I realign my focus.

We make it to the shore, and I spend a moment taking in the drastic change in the landscape close-up. It's derelict. Tidy, sparse, the land clear, except for the hangar, which makes hiding impossible from this side. The dense bushes and trees remain on the entrance side, hiding the hangar from the road. I hear Ringo's phone chime quietly and look at him. He nods. Everyone locks and loads and moves in.

Then James holds his hand up and we all stop. A man appears, lighting a cigarette. He looks up, spots us, and just as I'm about to fire, James moves in, forcing me to lower my gun. In one swift, stealth move, he grabs the man, applies pressure to his neck, and he's soon crumpling to the ground, unconscious. We all crowd around his lifeless body. "Don't ever do that to me," I say, hearing Brad chuckle. "Wait, I know that face."

"The Chameleon." James looks down at him, his face expressionless but deadly. "So your hunch was right. They're operating from here."

I blow out my cheeks, an icy chill tickling its way down my spine as I kneel and pat down his body. I pull out a VP9. The fuckers. I was right. *I was fucking right!* I'd love nothing more than to put a bullet between his eyes, but for the sake of keeping our presence undetected, I resist the urge.

We move forward again, James now leading, and I'm fine with that. The bloke spent years in the shadows, unseen, unheard, and I'm not arrogant enough to admit I could learn a thing or two from The Enigma. And that move back there? He's showing me how it's done. It could come in handy when my wife won't heel.

"Right," Otto says flatly from behind me, and James is suddenly moving again, stealth as fuck, somehow making it behind a tall, lanky fucker before he has a chance to raise his gun. He drops like a sack of shit and his Glock lands in James's waiting hand before it hits the concrete.

"Good catch," I say quietly, moving forward, poised, wondering what the fuck Higham is playing at. "Wasn't he supposed to distract them?" I ask.

"Left," Goldie mutters, making James turn quickly, sweeping his leg out, taking another man off his feet. He hits the deck on his back with a thwack, and everyone winces at the sound.

"I'm changing his name from Rambo," Brad says. "Meet Bruce."

"Wayne?" I ask, accepting the Glock James hands me and dipping, throwing a brutal punch, knocking out James's latest victim and taking his gun too.

"Wayne?" Brad asks. "No, Bruce Lee." He claims the second Glock. "Who the fuck wants to be a rodent?"

I shrug, just as Otto raises his gun at me. "Are you for real?" I ask, standing taller, raising both of my guns too.

He steps a fraction to the side and fires, and I flinch, the whoosh of his silencer short and sharp. I look to my right, seeing a pool of blood growing near my feet. "This does not mean you can date my mother."

"I don't want to date her, you moron," he grunts, pushing past me.

"Oh, right, so what? You want to love her?"

He stops, his whole body twitching. "Doesn't she deserve that?"

"Yes, she deserves that, but from someone worthy," I hiss.

"And who would that be?" he asks, facing me. "In your world, Danny, who the fuck do you expect to swoop in and take care of her? A school teacher? An accountant? Need I fucking remind you who you are?"

I snarl, raise my gun . . . and get tackled from the side by Ringo. I stagger a few paces but remain on my feet. "Calm the fuck down and save it for later." He gets up in my face, furious. "I wouldn't mind leaving here intact."

"Fine." I push past him, my attention shooting to Goldie when I hear her sharp inhale. She's opened a door, and whatever is on the other side has stunned her. "What is it?" I rush over, everyone else on my tail, and cautiously peek through the small gap. "The fuck?" I breathe, seeing two rows of beds, perhaps ten in each row, many with women on the dirty, bare mattresses. All with lines into their arms. "Jesus." I stand, stock-still, and all I see is my wife. My wife as a young girl, and my mum.

I'm consumed, ruled by the anger rising. "Get them out," I say on impulse, counting the occupied beds. Ten.

"Danny, how?" Goldie asks, sounding so fucking torn and disturbed. It's a fair question. There are too many. Most completely spaced out, drugged up to their eyeballs. They'll need carrying, and there's not enough of us.

"Fuck," I hiss, moving deeper into the room, feeling everyone at my back, armed, poised, ready to fire, whereas my gun is limp by my side, shock keeping it there.

"We can come back," she says, an attempt to pacify me.

"We can't come back." James steps forward, assessing the lines of beds. "There's two unconscious men and a dead body out there."

I look to my left when I hear a murmur and see a young woman writhing on a bed, distressed. I stalk over and remove the line from her arm, bending over her body. Her eyes open and widen, disturbed when she sees me. "No," she mumbles. "No, please." Her accent is thick, but I can't place it.

I hush her, trying to settle her down. "You're going to be okay."

"We have to let the police take them in," Otto says.

"Agreed." James moves in. "But in not so long, we're going to be discovered and all these young girls will get caught in the crossfire."

"So, what?"

"We take them," I say, starting to work my way through the young women, gently pulling the lines from their arms one by one, being left no choice but to leave each of their punctures exposed and hope they don't bleed too much. "Call Doc. Have him ready at the house. We'll deal with the police when I've cleared my head."

"Fucking hell," Brad whispers, joining me, helping remove the lines. "We'll have to do two trips. Ten extra bodies, Danny."

"We've got three jet skis. Otto and Goldie can hop on with two of us. Ringo can take the boat. It'll be a squeeze, but we can do it.

We don't have time to wait." I look up at James, who nods. He gets it. "Goldie, call Leon and have him close down the boatyard."

"And Higham?" Ringo asks.

"Tell him we need more time." I pull up the eyelids of the girl in the final bed on the first row and look into her comatose eyes. Blue eyes that look black from the sheer level of dilation. I see a million flashbacks in the dark, lifeless pits. "At least half an hour." I need to pull my head out of my arse and get this done before I grab my gun and shoot to kill.

"Done," Ringo joins us, assessing each girl. "Can any walk?"

"If you'd been pumped full of sedatives for fuck knows how long, would you be able to walk?" I ask, dipping and picking up the girl and getting her onto my shoulder, placing one arm over her thighs and keeping my other free. Armed. "Goldie stays here to keep an eye. One of us stays at the other end when we get there. That leaves four of us to get ten girls out of here. We've got some working out to do. Get moving."

"Fucking hell," Ringo sighs, claiming a girl, as do the others. Never before have I been so grateful that I work out.

After the first drop, Otto, the oldest and most indignant about it, stays behind to watch the girls while James, Brad, Ringo and I file back like ants, all of us blowing out of our arses already, to collect the remaining girls. I'm not clockwatching, but I know we're close to the wire.

"Time," I call back to Ringo as I jog along the ragged cove back to the hangar.

"He's lost their attention. They're all filing back in."

"Fuck!" I yell, my pace naturally picking up. I reach the back of the hangar, just as Goldie flies out of the door.

"Time's up."

"I'm not leaving without all of them."

"You'll get us all killed, Danny."

I hold up my gun, looking at her, and I see the moment she realizes I'm unmoving. She blinks slowly, inhales, and matches my pose. She could go. Tell me to go fuck myself. What the fuck does

she care about those women? Her life, James's life, all of our lives
are precious. But, and it's a small mercy, we're not animals. Inhumane. *Rapists.* "There's two doors fifty feet from the beds. One's
bolted, the other ajar. They'll come through there."

"How many?"

"Fifteen, at least."

"Go," I order, and she runs back inside, covering the door, while
we go to the final bed. James heaves a blonde onto his shoulder,
Ringo a brunette, and Brad moves in on a black-haired girl, and all I
can think is that they're clearly trying to cater for every taste. I look
down at the pasty, washed-out face of the blonde before me, and
her eyes flutter open. The glassy pools are blank.

"Brace," Goldie says lowly, prompting me to get moving, lifting
her floppy body onto my shoulder and turning to face the door,
holding up my gun. I hear laughter from the other side, rough
foreign voices. I sneer, willing them through the door so I can blow
out their sick minds.

"We have one more," Brad hisses, going to the final bed. "Fuck!"

"I can't carry *and* cover." Goldie looks between us and the door.

"She's awake." Brad dips. "Can you walk for me?" he asks. "I'll
help you."

She nods, it's strained, and she starts to push herself up, losing
her balance constantly, her arms lifting to steady herself. I wince
and look away when her ragged tank slips down her arms, revealing
breasts tinged purple and yellow. *Fuck me.* I swallow, blinking away
the vision of the bruises decorating Rose's back when I met her.
Brad helps the redhead, easing her top up to save her dignity, all the
while holding the other woman on his shoulder, leaving him
unarmed.

"Let's go," James grunts, leading the way out, looking back at
Goldie. She's closed the door and pushed a nearby bed up against
it, buying us some time. "Goldie, move it."

"I'm coming." She jogs across the open space, the thuds of her
boots echoing around the vast space, and just as she reaches us, the

sound of metal scrapping concrete sounds along with a collection of rushed, foreign words.

Curses.

Then, gunfire.

Then, screams.

I spin, raising my gun, having a split-second check that everyone is behind me before I squeeze the trigger and send bullets raining as I walk backward. It's our only option with no cover. Nothing to shield us. I roar, the muscles in my arm burning from holding my position, my shoulder aching from holding the woman.

"Back up," James yells, appearing beside me, his shoulder bare. A quick glance to Goldie tells me he's handed her the woman he was carrying. He has two machine guns. Two belts. Endless bullets, and he sprays them, the guns drifting effortlessly from side to side, ensuring he covers every inch of space. Men drop like flies before me as they run through the doorway, too eager to be a hero, insufficiently armed.

The yells and screams persist, chaos at every turn. It's all happening in slow motion but at lightning speed. I make it outside and drop my gun, using both hands to hold the woman as I jerk my shoulder, getting her slipping body back into place. I look back and see Brad helping the stumbling, dazed, redhead along while struggling to keep another unconscious woman on his shoulder.

"Get moving, Danny," Ringo barks as he jogs past, the woman on his shoulder now awake, alert, and crying.

James appears out of the hangar, slamming the door and pushing his back up against it while he reloads. "There's five more," he pants, knackered. "I can hold them."

"Fuck that," I say over a labored laugh. "Get your Rambo arse in gear now."

He turns a snarl onto me. "I work better alone, now fuck off and let me deal with this." His eyes meet mine, and I try so fucking hard to push friendship aside and remember who James is. *The Enigma.*

"Fuck!" I bark. "Brad, you good?" I go back to him, taking over with the redhead so he can get a better hold of the woman he's carrying.

"We need to up our game in the gym," he pants, shifting, reclaiming the woman from me and breaking out in a steady jog, taking the lead. He looks down at her bare feet. At the rocks and uneven ground we're treading.

"Blank it out," he says, and she looks at him. "You can do it."

She frowns, and it occurs to me that she probably can't even understand him. But her pace increases, so perhaps she does. I look back, seeing James still against the metal door, his body jerking with every jar from the other side. He looks up at me, just as I round a corner, losing sight of him.

And then, gunfire.

I exhale, grit my teeth, and focus on getting the women to safety. We make it to the boat and skis, and Otto is literally hanging on to the rocky cove by his fingertips, the jetty in pieces of rotten wood floating around the boat. He says what I knew he would the moment he sees me.

"Where is he?" he growls, looking past me as Brad helps the redhead into the boat before we both lay the women on our shoulders down. I see many of the others are coming around, looking absolutely terrified. "Where the fuck is he, Danny?"

I take a fresh pistol from the loaded ski, the only one left, and check the magazine. "You go," I say to no one but everyone.

"What?" Brad grunts, standing tall, rolling his shoulder. "No."

I turn sober eyes onto him. "Go," I demand, and everyone looks between each other, waiting for another protest. "Take James's ski."

Ringo, reluctant, gets on and starts the engine, looking to Goldie in instruction to get moving, then to Otto, who releases the rock he's clinging to, allowing the tide to carry the boat out. He starts the engine and gives me a look that tells me I'm dead if I don't bring James back.

I believe it.

"I'll see you in a minute," Brad says, and for a moment I think he's talking to me, but then he appears by my side, checking the chamber of a rifle. "Say one word," he pants. "I'll fucking shoot you."

Again, I believe it.

And I haven't got time to waste trying to reason with him.

I nod and get on my jet ski, Brad jumping on his, and as soon as the current has turned me, I slam down on the throttle and head around the cove toward James. It takes only a few seconds to make it to him, and I find him still with his back to the door. "I'm out," he yells, tossing his guns aside and forcing farther back into the metal door. I turn my ski and keep just enough pressure on the throttle to counteract the current and remain stationary. I look back at James, nodding.

"So we're stuntmen now, are we?" Brad asks, locking and loading.

"Hey, Rambo Junior," James bellows, easing off the door a little, revealing endless bumps from endless bullets. "Don't miss."

Brad laughs. It's sardonic. "Ready when you are."

James nods, and there's no countdown. No bracing. He releases the door and runs at me full pelt as gunfire rings out and sparks light up the dusky sky. "Hit the throttle!" he yells, diving off the nearest rock and sailing through the air. Fuck me, a little too much, he's missing. Too little, he's overshooting the ski.

Jesus!

I mentally calculate the distance and speed his big body's traveling and hit the throttle a little harder."

"Fuck!"

I went too much. He smacks the water, his hands catching the tail of my jet ski. "Go!"

I flinch when a bullet hits the handlebar.

"Fuck, go, Danny!" Brad yells.

I look across to him, seeing him standing, guns poised, firing, his face as psychotic as I know he is beneath his dry wit. I regain my focus and hit the throttle, praying James can hold on, and zoom across the water, looking back constantly to check I can still see his tanned hands holding on amid the foam and Brad's ski following.

The roar of the engines is loud, but I still hear the bullets firing. My heart pounds, as I will the approaching curve in the bay to come sooner. "Come on, come on," I breathe, releasing the throttle the moment I round it. I turn and wait for the churned-up water to settle, and when it does . . .

No James.

"Fuck!" I bellow, looking back through the stream of white water, searching for him. Brad rounds the corner and slows, and as soon as he sees my face, his turns grave. "We go back," I order, taking my seat again and turning my ski . . . just as a head pops up and a string of explicit language rings out.

"Motherfucker!" James says on an exhale, coughing, choking, shaking his head. I swear, every muscle in me turns to mush, and I flop forward over the handlebars, suddenly out of breath. "Were you worried about me?" he pants.

I don't look up, too exhausted. "Fuck you."

And then laughter.

Brad breaks out, James too, and I look up, seeing them in pieces. Relief. It has to be, because I'm suddenly laughing like a twat with them. "Get the fuck on," I say, labored, chugging over to him to save him the swim.

He takes my offered hand and climbs on the back, wrapping an arm around my waist, looking to Brad. "How many are left?" he asks.

"I saw three drop."

"So two?" I ask. "Assuming the hits were fatal." Brad nods, and I swear I see him wince. "You okay?"

"Dandy," he grunts, taking the handlebars. "But I really need a fucking drink."

"Me too," I mutter. And a Marlboro or twenty.

"Me three," James adds. "Take me home, mate." He smacks my shoulder and then massages into it a little. "And thanks."

Has anyone ever saved The Enigma's life? Apart from Otto and Goldie, of course.

I smile to myself. Beau saves his life every day.

. . .

It's like the homecoming of Christ when we make it back to shore. The relief on all their faces is palpable. I feel it. One look at Ringo in question and he jerks his head toward the cabin, telling me the women are all inside being fed and watered. "Len's bringing another car and Doc."

I nod as James gets off the jet ski and pulls his wetsuit down his chest as he wades out of the water. Beau is waiting for him on the shore, her arms crossed, her eyes scanning every square inch of his body as he approaches her. "Are you okay?" she asks as he lifts an arm, silently ordering her into his side.

He kisses the top of her head when she settles there, seeming to breathe her into him. "I'm okay," he assures her.

"Fuck."

I turn and see Brad easing himself off the ski, his face pained. "What's up?" I ask, watching as he yanks down the zip of his wetsuit and wriggles out of the sleeves on plenty of hisses. "Shit," I whisper. Blood. Lots of it. My curse pulls James to a stop, makes Ringo throw a few fucks too, and has Otto dashing toward Brad with me, seeing his eyes rolling. "He's going," I yell, as he hits the water face first, passing clean out. I splash my way back into the water and turn him over, dragging him to the shore.

"Blood loss," Otto grunts, assessing the bullet wound in Brad's shoulder. He lifts him, turning him slightly to see his back. "Straight through."

I look up when I hear tires, seeing Higham's car skidding across the gravel. He gets out and paces over, looking as stressed as he should be. But not as stressed as I am. "I said no fucking kills! What the fuck happened back there?"

I'm up in his face like a rabid dog, snarling, probably foaming at the mouth too. "Ten drugged-up, battered, and raped young women, that's what fucking happened."

His eyes widen and he wisely backs up, clocking Brad on the ground behind me. "Fuck."

"Yeah, fuck. Now are you done, 'cause I'm kinda busy?"

"Fuck!" he bellows, kicking the gravel. "Fuck, fuck, fuck!"

I leave Higham having a fit over the unexpected turn of events and go back to Brad, kneeling beside him with Otto. "Will he be okay?" I ask, assessing his pasty face.

"I'm no Doc." Otto remains, applying pressure to Brad's shoulder. "He's lost a lot of blood."

I hear a car speeding across gravel and see a Mercedes joining the fleet of vehicles already here. Len jumps out, and I'm relieved to see Doc struggling out of the passenger seat with his brown leather bag. "Here," I yell, waving him our way. I very nearly go to the old boy, pick him up, and carry him the rest of the way.

Doc creaks down to his knees and starts doing all the things, humming, mumbling, poking, prodding, assessing. "The bullet?" he asks.

"Exited," Otto says.

"Good. Very good." Doc slips a line into Brad's arm and hold up a bag of fluids. "Where was he shot?"

I look at him like he's stupid. Where the fuck does he think he was shot? His arse? "His shoulder."

"No," Doc mutters. "I can see very well he's been shot in his shoulder, Danny. I'm asking *where*? Here? Can I work on him, or are we in danger?"

"We're safe."

"And how long ago? So I may ascertain what I'm dealing with. Fast blood loss, slow?"

"Oh." I frown, trying to get my brain working.

"About twenty minutes ago, at a guess," James says, joining me on the ground. I see Beau lower by Brad's head and stroke his wet hair out of his eyes, true concern splattered across her face. "It was a hairy escape."

"Adrenaline," Doc concludes. "It's quite a fuel when the body needs it." He stands with effort, holding the bag of fluids, and wags a finger at all of us. "Let's move him into the car so I may take him back to the house and get some blood in him."

"You have blood?" I ask, taking Brad's feet as James gets him under his arms.

"I have everything, Danny," Doc says, walking alongside us to the car, never taking his eyes off Brad. "Conditioning myself to expect the unexpected has been quite a godsend since I became the private doctor for the world's most wanted."

"That's not official," James grunts. "We're not even on the list."

"And I pray you never are, because I can save you from bullets, burns, and broken bones, but not when you're behind bars."

James catches my eye, and he raises his brows, as do I, silently amused.

And quite sobered by Doc's statement.

We place Brad into the back of one of the Mercs, and Beau tries her hardest to get him comfortable, huffing and puffing, not happy with his position. "I'm going with him," she declares, slipping into the seat and lifting Brad's head onto her lap. It's an endearing sight. Seeing her worry. Seeing her care. Sadness and appreciation in equal measure wash over me. Appreciation for our women. And sadness that Brad hasn't got his own to fret over him. He has ours, though. Always.

Beau looks at James and me in turn. "And someone needs to give Rose the heads-up on the guests we're expecting."

Fuck it.

I need to be the one to do that. I'm terrified this whole messy situation will trigger something in her. Like the ring did. "Be vague," I say, looking as awkward as I feel when Beau shows her incredulity.

"Ten women are about to arrive and check into Casa Black, Danny. What do you want me to say? That you and James became the Pied Pipers for women in Miami?"

"Ha ... ha," I drone.

She sighs. Beau knows what this could mean. "I'll do what I can." Doc passes her the bag of liquid, she pulls the door closed, and Len pulls off once Doc is in the car.

"What a fucking day," I breathe.

"And it's not over yet," James says, holding his hand out. Leon places my Marlboros in them and he's quick to light one, handing it to me before lighting one for himself.

We both turn in unison on deep inhales and long exhales, creating a sizable cloud of nicotine that conceals us from Higham, and when it clears, his face is a picture I'll never forget as Ringo, Goldie, Otto, and Jerry lead out ten women from the cabin and put them in the cars.

"My God," he says, shaking his head, waving a limp hand at the cars as they drive off. "All sedated?"

"Yes."

"And what carnage is there to mop up?"

"About fifteen dead Polish fuckers." I smile. "You. Are. Welcome."

He breathes in, looks to the sky, and breathes out. "I'll be in touch."

"I'm busy for a few days," I call, thinking the last thing we need is FBI, whether friendly or not, hanging around while we're taking a delivery. Or burying Beau's dad. "So only call me if you have news on my father."

He throws a hand up, dismissing me, and gets in his car, wheel-spinning away. I look at James, who nods, catching my drift. We both head into the cabin, help ourselves to a beer, and drop into a chair, slurping and smoking in silence, staring into space. Just taking a moment. *He'll be okay*, I think, over and over.

"He'll be okay," James says out loud, as if hearing my silent worry.

"I kn—" I'm interrupted by my mobile ringing, and I frown, searching it out. Leon holds it up. "Who is it?" I ask, making him look at the screen.

"Private number."

James and I glance at each other, and I hold my hand out. As soon as Leon places my mobile in my hand, I answer and take it slowly to my ear. Silence. And then a voice. But a voice I *definitely* wasn't expecting.

"Danny?"

My eyes must widen because James leans in, frowning. "Amber?" I say, telling him what he wants to know. Surprise is rare on James Kelly. Only Beau can usually ever spike it, so his perplexed expression right now is quite a picture.

"I need to see you," she says, naturally having me wonder why the fuck my ex-in-house whore from over three years ago, and most recently Beau's father's bit of arse, could possibly want with me.

"And I quite like my balls, so I'm afraid it's a no." I hang up and fall into thought again, staring at nothing, as does James as we take another needed few minutes to reflect, try to wind down, and wonder . . . *what the fuck just happened?*

"Not curious?" he eventually asks.

"Not enough to risk my wife turning psycho bitch on me. Amber's probably in up to her neck again. Needs protection, money, who the fuck knows. She's a waste of fucking space and she pulled a gun on my wife and mother." So it's definitely not wise for me to see Amber. And suddenly, I'm angry. So fucking angry. It's one thing after another, problem after fucking problem. I get up, slip my cigarette between my teeth, and go to the changing room, pulling out a gun from my locker.

I march down the steps to one of the containers, take a long-arse time unbolting the thing, swing it open, and fire one shot before throwing it closed again. I pass Leon my gun as I head for the car, and James follows my path with his eyes, casually leaning on the wooden handrail, smoking.

"Better?" he asks.

"Much. He was the most useless of all your catches." I get in the passenger side of his Range Rover and wait for James to get in. And wait. And wait. It's probably only a few seconds but it feels like hours. Exasperated, I press the ignition button and let the window down. "Are you taking me home or not?" I yell, and he smiles, trudging down the steps and scooping up a bag.

"Yes, princess," he coos, as Leon scurries along beside him, opening the driver's door for him.

"Ooh, smells yum in there," Leon says. "Jasmine?"

"Who the fuck knows, but it's better than stale piss."

James slips in, grimacing, lifting his arse out of the leather seat when it squelches. He tosses the bag on my lap, and I grunt.

"What is this?" I ask, looking inside, seeing stacks and stacks of soaking wet cash. "The fuck?" I blurt, looking at James. "In the midst of all that, you managed to get this out?"

He shrugs. "We've got ten new mouths to feed, dear."

"Hey D-boss," Leon says, leaning in through my window. "I was thinking we need a few more water sports on the cove. Paddle-boarding, scuba diving, that kind of thing."

James and I both let out a bark of laughter. Scuba diving? Jesus, it must be like a mass graveyard on the seabed of this cove. "No," I say shortly, dipping my hand into the bag and pulling out a handful of bundles, maybe a hundred grand. "Share this between you and Jerry," I say, stuffing it into his chest. "And lose this in the accounts." I toss the rest of the cash at his feet and cluck his cheek. "Good work today." I face the windscreen as my mobile rings. "Nolan." I answer and get straight to the point. "Brad's been shot."

"What?"

"Shot, Nolan. He's been shot."

"Oh my God, I'm on my way. Where? Where am I going?"

"Nowhere. He's fine. Doc's seeing to him back at the house. We need you to keep things ticking over there. I'll keep you updated."

"Yeah, okay." He sounds completely bewildered.

"He'll be okay, kid." I say, softening, before hanging up and letting my body go heavy in the seat. "Now get me the fuck home."

James smiles at the wheel and pulls off, and I relax back, bracing myself for the next shitstorm.

20

ROSE

I follow Fury toward the kitchen, mentally estimating how much weight he has hanging from his arms in the form of groceries. A whole cartful. "Are we feeding five thousand?" he asks as he heaves them upward and places them on the island.

"Every time I come home it feels like someone new has moved in." I drop my purse on a stool and start sorting through the bags. "I miss Esther."

He drops to a stool and flexes his hands. "I've missed the boy."

My working hands falter, my heart squeezing. Soon. He'll be here soon. "Me too." I smile and pull out a bottle of orange juice, holding it up. Fury nods, so I fetch a glass and pour him some. "And you must miss Tank." I push the glass toward him, and he drinks it all before answering.

"Not as much as you," Fury says with a hint of a smile. "You have me until you get him back." He looks at his watch, as I roll my eyes. "What time do they land?"

I glance at the clock on the stove as I pull out a huge bag of pasta. "About now." Excitement flutters in my tummy. "You want to slice some zucchini?" I take one of Esther's aprons and slip it on.

"Suits you."

I raise a brow and he opens his arms, welcoming my offer to join me in my domestic . . . bliss.

"You got an axe?"

I laugh and fetch a knife and chopping board, placing a bag of vegetables in front of one of our resident Vikings. "Here you go. Nice and thin, please."

Fury gets to work while I unpack the rest of the shopping and start preparing a feast. I try not to look at the wine longingly as I set it on the middle of the island. I catch Fury with a half-smile behind his wild beard, eyeing me in between slicing. "Stop grinning," I mutter, collecting a pan and filling it with water, setting it on the stove. "I've been meaning to ask you." I sound casual, as intended, though he still peeks up at me cautiously. "What are your names?"

"Tank and Fury."

I turn, armed with my bag of pasta. "Your real names."

"Tank and Fury."

"Come on."

"It's Tank and Fury." He doesn't look up from his slicing.

"Right." I sigh and give up, getting back to cooking, and the next hour passes by in a comfortable quiet, Fury chopping, me cooking. Or trying to. Damn, I really do miss Esther. I push the dish into the oven to bake for a half hour and turn back toward the kitchen.

And cringe.

"You cook like a man," Fury says, laughing, casting his eye over the mess with me. I hear a car in the driveway.

"Shit." Suddenly, the mess looks . . . messier. "You get the dishwasher, I'll start clearing." I push everything cluttering the island toward the dishwasher so Fury can load, and dash around like a madwoman, wiping down the countertops. In only a couple of minutes, we're in far better shape. I dust off my hands.

"Want a clean one?" Fury asks, motioning down my front. There's not a thread of material on the apron not splattered with oil, tomato, or grease. The state of me defies the now semi-gleaming kitchen. I quickly untie it and run to the laundry room, shoving it in the washer, and as I'm returning to the kitchen, I hear . . . Doc?

My heart naturally picks up pace and Fury is up out of his seat in a second, stalking to the entrance hall.

"Some help, please," the old man yells, spotting Fury and gesturing him urgently to join him outside.

"What's happened?" I ask, following them. I see Len opening the back door, and I see Beau on the back seat with Brad's head on her lap. My hands cover my mouth. "Oh my God."

"He's taken a bullet to the shoulder," Beau calls, inching her way out, holding Brad's head as Fury stomps over, his face grave, and helps Len ease Brad out of the car. I catch sight of his shoulder. Blood.

Beau comes to me and instantly starts trying to reassure me, which only worries me more. "The men found where the Polish hold the women they ship in," she says, looking so fucking sympathetic.

"Where?"

"Danny's old boatyard."

"What? Winstable?" My God. "He sold it to developers," I say, watching Fury carrying Brad into the house, Doc following. "They were building a facility for underprivileged kids." Danny will be seething. He'd only relinquished it for a noble cause. To know he was deceived? As if my husband needs any more excuses to go on a rampage. This will tip him over the edge.

Beau takes my hand and leads my stunned form back toward the house. "The men went in and got the women out."

My body is instantly cold. "How many?" I ask quietly, trying not to allow any flashbacks to take hold.

"Ten," she says, leading me up the stairs behind Fury, who's carrying Brad like he's a small child. Effortlessly. "They were all drugged."

I swallow, walking on numb legs, my hand naturally falling on my belly, thinking how different my life could have been if I was never taken. No. I wouldn't have Daniel. Danny wouldn't have found me. I have to believe that every bit of hell I endured was worth the distress, heartache, and pain.

Focus on Brad.

I nod and disconnect my hand from Beau's, picking up my pace and entering the bedroom Fury's taken Brad into. "Can I help?" I ask Doc, who gets straight to work, hooking the half-empty bag of fluids onto the headboard.

"I need my IV stand," Doc says. "In my room. In the fridge you'll find various bags of blood. I need the one marked O positive."

"What?" I blurt. He keeps blood? I look at Beau, who looks equally surprised by this. "You know all of our blood types, don't you?" I recall now, Doc requesting Daniel's a few weeks ago in St. Lucia, and I thought it a bit random. I didn't have the foggiest idea what blood type my son is and thought no more of it. I make a mental note to make that a priority.

"Indeed, I do," Doc replies, injecting something into Brad's line. "Nice and quick, please."

"I'll go," Fury says, leaving the room to fetch Doc's requests.

"Will he be okay?" I ask, crouching beside Brad, looking over his pasty skin, his hollow cheeks.

"Just as soon as we've topped up his veins."

I nod and look back when Beau touches my shoulder. "We should prepare for the arrivals."

I'm blank. Then— "They're bringing the women here?" I stand, stunned, and Beau nods, just as I hear more wheels across the gravel. "Oh God," I whisper, feeling wholly unstable. Thinking about ten women drugged and mistreated is one thing. Seeing them is another.

"You've got this," Beau says, leading me out of the room. And there she is, doing what we both do best. Reassuring each other, talking sense, but struggling to do that for ourselves.

We approach Fury, who's holding a bag of blood at arm's length while dragging along a metal stand. "Coming through," he says, as we move to the side of the corridor, letting him pass. My eyes follow him all the way to the door and through it.

"Where are James and Danny?" I ask Beau without looking at her.

"Come on," she says gently, not answering me, coaxing me away. "What can I smell?"

"You won't want to eat it."

"Smells good."

"Well, it looks atrocious. Have you heard from Ollie yet?" I ask, diverting from my own trauma, if only briefly.

"Nothing. I've reached out a few times, but he's not answering. And it's not like I'm being given any space to visit him, is it?"

We both know Beau could break away if she wanted to, which tells me she's nervous to do that, and not because of her safety. It's because she's scared of what she'll find out. "And the detective?"

She shakes her head. "I already dislike her, and I hate myself for it."

"Why?"

"Because she's doing what I would do in her situation." She turns a small smile my way. "Funny how my instincts have changed, huh?"

"No." I laugh a little. The cop's still in there. It's just mixed up with a bit of crime these days, making it a weirdly immoral moral cocktail. "But you're okay, aren't you?" And here's me ready to hold her up when I'm collapsing over my own traumas.

"They've asked if I want to see him."

I'm confused, and I can't hide it.

"My father," she goes on. "They've asked me if I want to see him before I lay him to rest."

I'm the worst friend. "Will you?"

"I think . . ." She nibbles her lip, unsure. "Something tells me I should. I couldn't with Mom because, well . . ."

Because there was nothing left that Beau would want to see. I slip an arm around her shoulder. "Do you want me to come? If you decide to go, of course."

"I think James will want to do that." She gives me a sardonic look. "He needs me to need him at the moment. I'll think about it. I

don't even know if I want to. The funeral will be hard enough and"
—she looks unsure for a moment—"I have absolutely nothing to
wear. What should I wear?"

I won't ask her what she wore for her mother's funeral. Something tells me she wouldn't remember. "Then we'll go shopping."
We keep saying it, and it never happens. I need to make it happen.

"Shopping? To buy something for me to wear to my father's
funeral? Great. I hate shopping at the best of times."

Of course. Absolute *worst* friend. "Or . . ."

Beau smiles softly. "Actually, no, we should. I need to keep up
my momentum when it comes to busy spaces."

There it is. She so desperately doesn't want to go back, and I'll
do my best not to let her. I take her hand and hold it up, flashing
her ring. "So when can we start planning the wedding? I need some
joy in my life."

She looks at my belly, and I cringe. As a friend, I'm on fire today.

"Stop it," Beau snaps firmly. "Stop watching every little thing
you say about babies or pregnancies or bumps or joy or death.
Everything happens for a reason."

Is that what she's telling herself these days? I smile lamely as we
take the stairs, and when the front door swings open and Goldie
steams in with a woman across her arms—a woman with long dark
hair—I freeze, losing my breath, seeing . . . me. Not being rescued,
but unconscious. Helpless. "Oh God," I whisper, taking hold of the
gold handrail as Goldie stares up at me. Why? Why is she looking
at me?

"Where?" she asks shortly, and I blink, shaking my head, as
more women come through the door, all disheveled, all with ripped
clothes, all looking lost, bewildered, and terrified.

"Rose, where?" Goldie asks, firm but also gently.

"The TV room," I blurt, looking around me, as if seeking
approval from someone that it was the right answer to give. "I . . .
we . . . they . . . I need to check the bedrooms." I finally convince
my legs to take me down the rest of the stairs, thanking everything
that Esther will be back in Miami imminently. My mother-in-law

is a pro at taking care of houses and people. She'll know what to do.

Goldie leads the line of women into the room, and I follow her there, clearing the enormous couches of scatter cushions to make room. "Doc's busy with Brad."

"How is he?" Otto asks, the last to enter after all the women and Ringo.

"Still unconscious. Blood loss."

He nods, and when one of the young women looks at him, he tries his hardest to give her a friendly smile. If the whole situation wasn't so tragic, it would be hilarious. He looks so awkward, as does Ringo, and Goldie doesn't look all too comfortable either.

"There's a pasta bake in the oven," I say, ushering them out, looking at Beau, telling her she's staying. "Tell Doc to come straight here when he's done. Order some pizzas or something. And get some water."

Otto stops at the door and looks back at me. "Esther here yet?" he asks.

"Very soon." I force my brows not to raise and shut the door, facing the women. They still look utterly terrified, and in a moment of lucidity, I wonder if they think we've kidnapped them.

"Oh shit," Beau says, joining my side. "They think we've kidnapped them."

"English?" I ask, casting an eye across them all. "Anyone speak English?"

A few hands raise—I count three—and someone speaks up. A redhead. "I'm English," she says, tucking her vibrant bobbed hair behind her ear. "From London."

London? Beau and I look at each other in shock. Not many are taken from countries like England or the States, but then again . . . me.

"My name's Pearl," she goes on, looking around the group of women. But as I too look again, I think *girls* is more apt. *So* young. "Melitza and Jana are from Serbia. Zala is Slovenian. Maria and Inessa are from Russia. I don't know the other's names. Their

English is non-existent." She points to the unconscious girl. "And Anya is from Romania."

I nod and go to Anya, feeling her pulse, if only because . . . isn't that what you're supposed to do? It's strong. Her chest is moving up and down.

Goldie knocks and pokes her head around the door. "Water." She enters with a tray resting on one hand and places it on the coffee table in the middle of the sofas before silently leaving. I start pouring, and Beau starts giving out glasses to accepting-but-wary hands.

"How old are you, Pearl?" I ask, perching on the coffee table before her.

She sips, looking over her glass at me with suspicion that I just can't stand. I need her to know she's safe now—I need everyone here to know they're safe.

"I'm Rose," I say quickly before motioning to Beau behind me. "This is Beau. She used to be a police officer."

"Rose," Beau breathes in disbelief, and I look back at her, as if to ask her what the hell she thinks I should tell them. That our respective others are criminals? My husband, The Brit, a renowned mafia crime lord and her fiancé, The Enigma, the silent, deadly assassin extraordinaire? I show the ceiling my palms, and Beau shakes her head, joining me on the table, nudging into me so I scoot along.

Pearl looks between us, like we're a pair of crazy people. Worryingly, she might be right. "I did used to be a police officer, but now I'm not."

"Why?" she asks, lowering her glass.

"I chose love over duty." Beau smiles mildly, and I'm compelled to reach for her hand and squeeze, because when she says love, she means her mother. But I have no doubt she'd choose James over duty if it came to it. In fact, she already has. Although Pearl doesn't know this so, of course, her next question makes sense.

"You're married?" she asks, looking at Beau's finger, prompting Beau to reach for her ring and spin it.

"Engaged to be."

"I'm married," I blurt. "This is my husband's house. My house. *Our* house." And was once my prison. *Good lord.*

Pearl gazes around. "What does he do?"

Fuck. "Umm, he . . . yes . . . umm." This is harder than I thought it would be.

Pearl's shoulders drop a little, displaying exasperation. "Forgive me," she says, tucking her short hair behind her ear again. "I don't know which one was your husband, but they were all carrying guns." She makes a point of having a good look around the plush, substantial TV room that has a screen big enough to play ping-pong on. "They stormed the place we were being kept. It was all a bit of a blur, but they looked like they knew what they were doing when they fired those guns."

Beau and I both shrink.

"You don't have to tell me anything," she goes on. "In fact, I don't want to know. But . . ." Looking between us, she chews her lip, and I notice a little hole in the right corner. An old piercing? "Are you good people or are we"—she motions to the other girls—"about to leave one level of hell and drop to another?"

"God, no," I say, desperate to reassure her. "We're good people." I can feel Beau's skeptical eyes on me. I ignore her. I know to many we're not, but to these girls we're definitely good, and I'm taking comfort in that. "My husband saved me from a life of sex slavery."

"He did?"

Beau squeezes my hand. "He did."

"Who is he?"

Fuck it all. "His name's Danny."

She nods, looking at Beau in question, and I discreetly exhale my relief that she hasn't pressed for more. She wants to know Beau's situation. "Mine's called James," is all Beau says.

Pearl nods, accepting, and then smiles. "Danny Black and James Kelly."

Beau and I jerk like we've been hit by a bullet. "What?" Beau says, dropping my hand, moving forward. "You know them?"

"I heard some of the men saying their names." She frowns. "It was the only English I heard, along with The Brit and The Enigma." Pearl looks at me. "Your husband is The Brit." She looks at Beau. "Yours is The Enigma."

"I'm not married," Beau breathes quietly, moving back, looking at me. I don't know why. I have nothing to say.

"How old are you?" Beau asks.

"I'm twenty-one," Pearl replies quietly. Then she frowns. "I think."

"You think?"

"I don't know what month it is."

"It's May," Beau says, glancing at me, wondering, no doubt, how long Pearl has been away from home.

"Then I'm twenty-one," she says, almost sadly. "In April. The fifth."

Twenty-one. Such an important birthday. I remember mine. I was on a yacht in the Adriatic Sea. Sounds luxurious. Lavish. Dreamy. It wasn't. I was fucked and beaten black and blue every day for weeks by a corrupt diplomat until I'd gotten Nox the information he needed. And then I was beaten black and blue again because it took me longer than he'd liked.

I lose my breath for a moment and fight to get it back, looking around the TV room if only to remind me of where I am. "Clothes," I choke out, getting up to check on the unconscious girl, her pulse, her chest, before hurrying toward the door, just as Doc pushes his way through.

"Next," he says with a hint of humor, scanning the crowd of potential patients.

"How's Brad?" I ask.

"He'll be fine." He's quite dismissive, but I can't blame him. He's run off his feet today.

"You should start with the unconscious one," I say like an idiot, making Beau roll her eyes.

"They all need checkups." Beau takes over, looking back at Pearl. "This is Doc." She smiles as she comes over and rubs the old

man on the shoulder. "He's the best." Then she moves into Doc's
ear. "They're nervous."

"Understandable," he says, looking solemnly at the girls. "I'll
start with the unconscious one"—he looks over his spectacles to
me, and I feel myself turning a fetching shade of embarrassed—
"before I check the others over. I think perhaps I should like you
girls to assist. As Beau said, they'll be nervous and, well, I'm a man,
if a little decrepit."

"I'll send Goldie in," Beau assures him. "We need to raid Rose's
closet." Linking arms with me, she walks us on. "The unconscious
one?" she whispers in disbelief.

I can only shake my head at myself.

"Oh, Beau," Doc calls.

"Will you get Goldie?" She unhooks her arm and goes to Doc,
not giving me a chance to answer.

I frown my way to the kitchen and tell rather than ask Goldie to
go to the TV room, and she does without question. By the time I'm
back at the stairs, Beau's back on my arm. "Okay?" I ask.

"Yeah, fine, I was taking Brad's pulse in the car. Doc needed the
numbers."

"Oh," I murmur. Something else she's useful for.

"Did you notice the small hole in the corner of Pearl's lip?" she
asks.

"Old piercing," I say. "They would have removed it." I flinch. "To
make her—" Fuck, I can't believe I'm saying this. "More universal."
No piercings, no tattoos, no deformities.

"Are you okay with this?" Beau asks, pushing her way into our
room.

I nod, taking a deep breath, having a stern word with myself.
Those girls have been rescued before they've endured the same
unimaginable level of hell that I did. Rescued before they were sold.
That's a blessing, although none of them could possibly think that
in this moment. And suddenly, I feel energized. Full of purpose.
They can have a life.

"I want everything you haven't worn in six months," Beau declares.

"Can't we say everything I *won't* wear for the next six months, because that'll be easier?"

She laughs and swings open the doors of my closet. And exhales her exasperation.

Twenty minutes later, Beau has arms full of clothes that don't fit me, and I can't even be miserable about it. "We should bring them up to change," she says, kicking material away at her feet, removing the tripping hazard as she walks to the bed and dumps the clothes there. "Maybe shower."

I nod.

"Which rooms?"

"Umm . . ." This is a twenty-bedroom mansion, and I can't be sure there are any spare rooms.

"Rose?"

"Wait," I say, tapping the side of my head, mentally figuring out who's in what room and which room is free, if at all there is one. "There's one down the hall, but Brad's in there. Danny's father's room," I say quietly. "It's the only other one I know is definitely vacant." And it's totally out of the question. Damn it, if Esther was here, she'd know immediately.

Beau sighs. "You check on Brad. There must be another *somewhere*. I'll go investigate." We leave together and while Beau starts working her way up and down the corridor, I go to Brad, knocking before entering. The bag of blood is what I see first, half empty, and then Fury sitting guard by the bed.

"I'm awake," Brad grunts, opening one eye. "Where's Danny and James?"

"They're not back yet."

He shifts on the bed, hissing, before he settles exactly where he was. "Why?"

"I don't know."

And suddenly I'm worried. I look at Fury, who shrugs, looking at Brad, as if he might answer his own question. "Why aren't they back yet?" I ask.

Brad squints, straining to think. "I don't fucking know. All I can see is red."

Blood. What happened after Beau left the yard with Brad? I'm out of the room like a rocket, flying down the stairs. I rush into the kitchen and find Ringo staring at my pasta bake dubiously with Otto and Len.

" Danny and James. Where are they?" I demand, making them all look at each other. But no answer.

I growl my frustration and go to my purse on the stool, rummaging through and finding my cell. I see a few missed calls from Esther but ignore them in favor of calling Danny. He doesn't answer. Neither does James, not the first time I try, or the second or third. "God damn them!" I yell, just as my phone rings in my hand. My heart lunges. And drops when I see Esther calling me, not Danny or James. I place a hand on my forehead, closing my eyes and breathing easy, trying to sound as calm as possible. "Hey,"

"Hi," she says, sounding chirpy. Because she's back. "Where is he?"

"Danny?" I look at the others, who, again, toss looks between each other, starting to get worried too, all going to their phones.

"Yes. You said he was picking me up from the airport."

"Oh God," I murmur, giving Ringo pleading eyes. I can't take this anymore. The constant worry. Stress. My blood pressure sky-high.

"What's happened?" Esther says, not sounding all too easy breezy now. "Rose?"

The cell is suddenly gone from my hand and Otto is guiding me to a stool to sit me down, taking my phone to his ear. "I'm leaving to get you now," he says, not releasing my arm. I'm becoming breathless. Pathetic! I should be used to this torture by now. Not knowing. Fretting.

"Someone get Doc," Ringo yells.

"No." I wave a hand. "He's busy."

"Rose, every drop of color has drained from your face."

Is it any wonder? "I'm fine." *Breathe, breathe, breathe.* I cannot fall apart. I must not fall apart. I know my husband. It would take a nuclear bomb to kill him. Oh God. Why am I talking such shit? He's human, like me, like everyone. One bullet in the right place—instant death. *I'm really not fine.* I throw my head between my legs and pant.

"Rose?" His voice drifts into my hearing, and for a moment I wonder if I'm imagining it. But then I hear James asking where Beau is, and I fling my head up and find my husband in the kitchen, his wetsuit pulled down to his waist, his hair a matted mess of salt and wind.

"What's up?" he asks, peeking nervously around at the crowd all watching him.

"Esther's waiting for you to pick her up," Otto says, and Danny frowns down at his cell.

"I haven't even opened that message."

"I'm going to get her," Otto tells him—*tells* him—a look of pure daring on his face as he passes. *Go on,* it says. *Tell me not to go.*

Danny heeds the warning. "Where's Brad?" he asks.

"In his room," Ringo pipes up quietly. "He's okay."

He nods and I, with a lack of anything else to do but lose my shit—and I'm so tired of doing that—get off my stool and drag the oven dish toward me, starting to spoon out the pasta and slap it on plates. I pass some to Ringo and Len, who both take it gingerly, and put the rest back in the oven to keep warm for the others. Then I head for the TV room to help Goldie and Beau.

Danny's body turns with me as I pass him. "I've had a really shit day at work, baby. I'm starving."

"Yours is in the dog," I spit as I leave the kitchen.

"That's probably a blessing."

I stop, outraged, and stare ahead, weighing up my options. Punch him.

Or . . .

Punch him.

I turn.

And find him grinning, his scar deep, his blue eyes gleaming. *Asshole.* I look at Ringo and Len, who both quickly shove forks full of pasta into their mouths to stop them laughing. *Fuckers.*

I'm at a loss, my relief making way for anger. And if the pasta doesn't get it, Danny will. I go to the oven, yank it open, pull out the dish, and pile two plates high with pasta before I go to the French doors and open them. "Cindy, Barbie," I call. They soon come running and sit at my feet like good little girls, their stumpy tails wagging. I tip the plates, sending the pasta to the ground with a splat, and they gulp it down in a few greedy mouthfuls, licking their lips. I smile and pat their heads. "Away," I say, sending them off before pivoting and breezing back into a silent kitchen.

He's still fucking smirking. "Why the hell are you laughing?"

"Because, my beautiful wife," he says, lighting up a cigarette, "seeing, hearing, and being the brunt of your rage is a fuck load better than seeing and hearing your distress." He moves in, seizes me, and drapes me back across his arm, exhaling a plume of smoke above my head. The smell is comforting.

And just like that, I soften. He knew bringing those girls here would risk triggering me. I've fought it so hard. He'll know that too. "I was worried. Why didn't you answer my calls?" The second I utter the word, his phone starts dinging, and he looks down at it, turning the screen to show me the notifications that have just this minute come through. Missed calls. From me.

"I must have dropped service for a few minutes."

"Well don't," I snap.

"Where are the women?"

"Girls," I say. "They're girls, Danny. One is barely twenty-one, and she looks like one of the eldest."

He flinches and returns me to vertical, taking another pull of his smoke.

"They're in the TV room," I go on. "Doc's checking them over and then Beau's taking them upstairs to shower and change. Goldie's ordered pizza."

He kisses me, bombarding me with his comforting mild smell of nicotine, and starts walking me out of the kitchen. We find James in the entrance hall with Beau's arms and legs wrapped around every part of him. James looks up from his place in her neck, but Beau remains exactly where she is. Buried. The doors to the TV room are open, and Doc is handing out pills. Meds for pain. Not meds that'll help these poor women forget their trauma.

"Beau mentioned one of the girls is British," James says to Danny. "She knew who we were."

Danny's eyebrows jump up, and he cranes his neck to see through the double doors into the TV room. "The redhead," I say, pointing to her on the couch. "She's bright. Well-spoken. Her name's Pearl. She's twenty-one."

Danny breathes out, long and stressed. "I guess we should call the police."

"What?" I blurt, looking up at him. "The police? Why?"

"What else can we do, Rose?"

"There's ten of them," James says, backing Danny up.

"They'll be deported," I say, my tone shaky. "And fall straight back into the hands of corruption. You can't do that to them." I stand back, pointing at myself. "*I* can't do that. I can't let them be taken away and not know what's happened to them."

"Their families," Danny says quietly, hesitantly. "They'll have families waiting for them to be found."

"What if they don't?" I feel James and Beau watching on, respectfully quiet. "I didn't," I say, then point at James. "He didn't." Then I point at Danny. "And if you were given the option to be returned to your stepfather, would you have gone?"

His jaw visibly clenches. I'm certain I've made my point, but just in case . . . "Where would you be now if Carlo Black had not taken you off the streets?"

"I get it," he grates.

"Good." We're all fucking orphans in one sense or another.

"So what do we do?" James asks, looking back into the TV room, as if to remind himself how many lives are currently in our hands.

"Those with families, we arrange reuniting them." My husband has a private jet. That simplifies things no end. "Those who have no families, we give them options."

"What options?"

"They go into police custody or they don't."

"And if they don't?" Beau asks, knowing where I'm heading.

"We help them," I say, leaving them all in the entrance hall to absorb the facts. I retrieve my cell from the kitchen and download a translation app as I head back to the TV room and cast my eyes around the space, to the faces of the girls, to the eyes full of fear and uncertainty. All I want to do ease them. Reassure them. I look over my shoulder when I feel Danny behind me. He's leaning against the door jamb, watching me, his face straight.

I go to my cell, type into the app YOU ARE SAFE, and slowly work my way around the room, translating it into Russian, Serbian, Slovenian and Romanian. Each girl I show my screen to either trembles, cries, or hugs me, and the lump in my throat grows by the second until I'm at Pearl. I don't show her my screen, but she sees my face with perfect clarity.

"What happened to you?" she whispers, pulling her tank strap up her shoulder.

I can't tell her that I likely faced worse than she has. I can't devalue her trauma. But the truth is, I did. These girls have been saved before they were conditioned for the life I endured. I swallow and sit next to Pearl, as Goldie leaves and Beau enters. I don't tell Pearl what happened to me. No one needs to hear that, especially not a young woman who was on the cusp of becoming what I was. A sex slave. A punching bag. An empty vessel of a human. Plus, Danny is in the room, and I can't send him over the edge. He stares at me for a few moments, then he gives me a small nod and backs out. Today, I have to be the strong one. Today, I protect and shield *him*. I've got this because I know he cannot handle anymore.

"Who was that?" Pearl asks.

"That was The Brit."

"Your husband?"

"Yes, my husband."

"Another man was trying to carry Anya." She points to the unconscious girl, who has now come around and is sipping water. "I was trying to keep up but was struggling. He helped me too. My legs were dead. But he didn't leave me."

"Brad," I say without thought. "Brad was helping you. He was shot."

Pearl swings alarmed eyes onto me, her hand covering her mouth.

"He's okay," I say, settling her, admiring her beautiful, vibrant hair. It's the only thing on her that isn't dull today.

"Can I see him? Say thank you?"

I nod, smiling mildly. *All I can see is red.* Brad wasn't talking about blood. Pearl is a beautiful young woman. *Young* being the operative word. "I'll take you later. First, we figure out what happens next."

"What do you mean?"

"I mean, we reunite everyone with their families." I know better than anyone that deportation is risky. "The last thing I want is for any of you to fall into the wrong hands again, so we'll manage that."

"I have no family." Pearl clears her throat and levels a sure look on me.

"No one?"

She shakes her head. "I left London to backpack across Europe. I met a man at a hostel in Albania. He asked about my family, my friends."

Jesus. "And he took you."

"When he established I wouldn't be missed."

My God, what is this world we're living in? "Your parents?"

"Murdered. Burglary gone wrong. The man was arrested on the scene. Druggy just looking for his next hit."

Jesus Christ. "I'm so sorry." I take her hand, for what good it is, like a gentle squeeze might make everything okay. And weirdly, it might. "Will you help me communicate with the girls?" I ask. "I've forgotten names already. Where they're from."

Pearl nods on a snivel.

"I speak a little Romanian," I say without thought.

"You do? Where did you learn Romanian?"

I blink, checking the room, worried Danny might have heard me. "In a previous life," I say quietly, forcing a smile at Pearl.

And I accept in this moment that she isn't going anywhere.

A few hours later, everyone is showered, changed, watered, and I think Beau and I need therapy, a ridiculous thing to claim. But, Jesus. We know all the girls' stories. Eight came from good families which, when we called, were out of their minds with worry. Missing people's cases had been opened, and police in various countries involved.

Reunited.

But Pearl and Anya? They remain at the mansion and will do for the foreseeable future. The eight other girls have gone to stay at a hotel by the airfield overnight and will be flown home tomorrow, where loved ones await their return.

Insane.

Insane but real.

After settling Pearl and Anya into a spare bedroom together, Beau and I plod down the stairs, exhausted but energized at the same time. I get a glass of water and Beau drops onto a stool. And then she's up again fast on a gasp. I watch, alarmed, my water at my mouth, as she zooms across the kitchen.

Into the waiting arms of her eccentric Aunt Zinnea. "You're here," she sobs, clinging to her like she could go under if she lets go.

"My darling, I'm here. Always here," she breathes, eyes closed, hugging her niece tightly. "Why didn't you call me? I would have come straight away."

Beau sniffles and breaks away, wiping at her nose. "So much has happened, and . . ." She steps back. "Wait, do—"

"James called me."

Her shoulders drop. It's relief. "He did?"

"Of course he did." She takes Beau's hand and leads her to the island, sitting her down. "I know your father and I didn't see eye to eye, but he's still my brother. *Was* my brother. Oh, how terrible!"

"They said he was in the wrong place at the wrong time," Beau says, and Zinnea visibly recoils. She should. If Beau pursues this, it could be a disaster. "I think they're lying to me, Lawrence. And now Ollie's missing, and a new cop's shown up asking questions."

He doesn't even correct her for using his birth name while he's his alter ego. That's how worried Lawrence is by Beau's splurge of words. He just looks at her in sympathy.

"Did you actually travel in that?" I ask, motioning to her canary-yellow fishtail dress, needing to give Zinnea a moment, time to think about how she might approach this.

She looks down her front, as if she might have forgotten she's wearing the blinding monstrosity. "This old thing?"

"You bought it last Easter," Beau pipes in. "It's barely a year old."

"Oh, did I?" Zinnea, rests a hand on her chest, feigning thinking, and I laugh in disbelief, going to her, welcoming her back with a kiss.

"Good luck," I whisper in her ear, feeling her squeeze my hip in reply, then I go in search of my boy, finding him in his room on his bed, his phone, as ever, glued to his hand. I'm blessed with his attention when I walk in, and it is all I can do not to throw myself at him and hug the life out of him. Today has been a constant, cruel, consistently painful reminder of a past life I'm slowly accepting I will never be allowed to forget. But I also feel so . . . accomplished. Lucky. The shit aside, I feel like I've done something worthwhile. Not be a wife or a mom or a friend. But something for someone else. I feel like I've done something that might change the world in a tiny way.

"Hey, Mom," Daniel says, tossing his cell aside and getting up. His dark hair is wildly overgrown, and adorable on him. My lip wobbles, and I quickly get it under control.

"Hey, baby." My arms lift of their own volition, beckoning him to me, and it's as if he appreciates in his selfish, teenager head that I need a moment. Just a moment. He comes to me and hugs me and, God, he's gotten even taller in the time I've not seen him. A week. That's all. But after all the years I missed out on, a week feels like so much longer.

"You okay?" I stick my nose in his hair and smell St. Lucia. The sea, the air, the salt and sand. I miss being there. But more so, I've missed this boy. I hate that the only connection we've had is via technology that he barely uses for me. But I get it. I just miss him.

"What's going on?" he asks. "Who were all those women?"

I freeze, my smile falling. I'm so glad he can't see my face because it's currently twisted. "Just a few friends who needed help."

"Oh, please, Mom." He breaks away and looks at me with eyes too knowing and earnest for a thirteen-year-old kid. And now he can see my face, and since my son isn't blind or stupid, he can see the sheer shock and awkwardness I'm feeling. I knew I wouldn't be able to hide this life from him forever, but I was banking on a few more years and a little more maturity so that when I give him my story—*our* story, Daniel's and mine from the moment he was born—he might comprehend that this life we're in, Danny's job, our family, is a blessing, and how me meeting Danny was what saved me. Saved me and reunited me with my son. "I know what Mister does," he goes on in a matter-of-fact, almost nonchalant tone.

Shit. I am not prepared for this. It's been an emotionally draining day at best. "You mean jet skis." *Please say yes.*

"He's mafia, Mom. Everyone knows it."

"Everyone?" I squeak, rather than laughing at the absurdity of his suggestion, or even denying it.

"Yes, everyone. Even Barney's dad knows."

"Oh." *Someone help me.*

Daniel rolls his eyes at me and goes back to the bed, collecting his phone and showing me the screen. An article about James and Danny fills it. "Who showed you that?" I ask, swiping it from his hand.

"Barney."

I suddenly don't like Barney. "Well, just so you know, this journalist is a bad, bad person."

"Has this got anything to do with Mom and Da—I mean Hilary and Derek separating?"

My God. "How do you know about that?" I practically screech.

"She called me. Said she'd moved out of town. But Derek is still in Miami."

What the hell do I tell him? That the people he knew as his parents for ten years bought him on the black market? That because of that, Derek got caught up in a whole other fucking mess trying to get Danny killed? "I don't know anything about that."

Daniel rolls his eyes and claims back his cell. "Next you'll be telling me Tank and Fury are my nannies."

"When did you get such a smart mouth?" I ask as he drops to his back and resumes whatever he was doing before I arrived. I don't care what, so long as he avoids stories about mafia crime lords. How do I assure that? *How? Oh Rose. You get your husband to kill the journalist who dared pen the article.* Perfectly reasonable.

"Where is Tank, anyway?" I ask, with a lack of anything else to say. I need to regroup. And talk to Danny.

"Having Pizza with Fury. Then we're catching up on COD."

"What's COD?"

He drops his head to the side, looking at me tiredly.

"Never mind," I say. "Have you eaten?"

"Pizza."

"Is Esther in the kitchen?"

"Yes."

Back in her element, I expect. "Where's your luggage?"

His hand drops and points to the corner. So we're back to one-word answers or no answers at all? Right now, I'm thankful. I take his luggage and open the case, pulling out his dirty laundry and dropping everything else on the chair in the corner. "And tidy your room," I say, carrying it out.

"Yes, Mom," he drones.

I start to pull the door closed but stop when I hear him call me. I push my way back in, bracing myself for more deflecting. "What?"

"I think Otto's in love with Grandma."

I press my lips together, restraining my amusement. I know I should have given my son a bit more credit. I can't say I've underestimated his intelligence, but perhaps hoped he was too caught up in video games, jet skis, and soccer to notice the stark reality of the world around him. A world that's too close. "Do *not* tell Mister."

He smirks and returns to his phone, and I make my way downstairs on constant groans to drop his dirty clothes off in the laundry room. When I make it to the kitchen, everyone is crowded around the island, and Esther is in full swing. It's a sight to behold, as is watching Otto watching her.

"Here she is," Esther sings, looking up from wiping crumbs from the countertop. "My favorite daughter-in-law."

"I'm your *only* daughter-in-law, so I have to be your favorite." I go to her, falling into her warm, welcoming embrace. "Daniel knows."

"He's not stupid, Rose."

Agreed. I'm the stupid one. "I'm so happy you're here," I say, exposing my vulnerability. It would be stupid to try and hide it from Esther.

"What on earth has been going on? We had young ears in the car from the airport, so we had to talk about the weather and soccer."

"I would love to talk about the weather and soccer," I say, releasing her.

"Then I get home to a house full of strange women."

"Most are gone now," I say. "We only have two extra mouths to feed."

"What are we going to do with them?" she asks gently.

"I don't know," I admit. "All I know is that Anya looked plain terrified when we asked if she had anyone we could contact in her homeland, and Pearl, the British girl, has no one." I take a seat next to Tank and lean into his side. "Missed you," I say sincerely, getting a grunt and an awkward arm around my shoulder, hugging me close very briefly before he lets go and takes another slice of pizza. "Thanks for watching Daniel." Another grunt. "Where's Danny?"

"Office," Otto says, getting up and leaving, giving Esther a peculiar look as he does.

I look between them, seeing Esther shying away from it. She catches me watching and smiles brightly. "I'll check on the two girls, make sure they have everything they need, then I think I'll get myself an early night." She raises her arms in the air, imitating a poor yawn. "Anyone need anything?"

"Maybe you should ask Otto?" I say, casually playing with the salt pot on the island. Hastily, Goldie, Tank, Ringo, and Fury all get up and leave, and I watch them all go. Good. I turn to Esther. "What was that look?"

"What look?" she asks, making her getaway, avoiding my eyes.

"Esther, come on," I say, laughing. "You and Otto are the worst-kept secret around here. Even Daniel's figured it out."

Shoulders dropping, she faces me. Her clear skin is glowing, and it isn't from being kissed by the sun. "I don't know what to do," she admits, coming back to me and sitting. "Danny is so adverse, and I don't want to be the cause of added stress."

"So what was your excuse when we were in St. Lucia and Danny had no stress?"

She peeks at me. "What do you know about Otto?"

I'm taken aback by the question. The truth is, not a lot. "I know he was James's father's righthand man when he was alive. I know they were close." I imagine like Danny and Brad are. "And I know he's loyal." I move in a little closer. "You're unsure because of how little you know?"

"A little, I suppose. I overheard Goldie making a comment about him." She grimaces. "Well, you know."

"A player?"

"Plenty of women. And all young, by the sounds of things."

What is wrong with her? She has a banging body and youthful face for a woman her age. "You're beautiful," I say. "The best example of a woman I know, Esther, and if Otto can't see that, *and your beauty*—then he needs his eyes looked at."

"It's not just that." Her gaze drops to her lap, her thumbs making rushed circles where her hands are joined. "The last time I —" She shakes her head and looks at me, and I positively hate the anguish I see in her blue eyes. "Sex has only ever been a horrible experience for me. Painful. Danny's stepfather, then the endless men that came to the dirty bedsit where I was held after Carlo's cousin took me from the pub."

"Oh, Esther," I whisper, choked up. My heart breaks for her. I know the type of desperate vulnerable state she speaks of.

Sex has only ever been a horrible experience for me.

An unstoppable question has popped into my mind. What about Danny's biological father? I know about his stepfather, the monster, but what about his real father?

"I was a zombie as I lay on that filthy mattress, Rose," Esther goes on. I store the question. I can't add what I know will be another layer of grief. Her hand grabs mine and constricts so hard, holding on, as if she's scared she could be taken away again. "My body was useless, I couldn't fight, but I saw, felt, and heard everything."

I flinch, my mind suddenly crowded with a million flashbacks that I've done so well to box away at the back of my mind these past few years. But more recently they're starting to plague me. They're creeping out and haunting me. But this now isn't about me. "Does Otto know your story?" I ask.

"I haven't told him, if that's what you mean. Why on earth would I?"

To make him understand you! But Danny talks to Brad and James. James is close to Otto. I'm thinking he *has* to know. "Do you like Otto?" I ask, and she looks at me. Of course she does. I've only ever seen him be patient and gentle around her. "Daniel thinks he's in love with you." I smile when she lets out a bark of laughter.

"Don't be ridiculous." Her hand instinctively goes to her hair and fixes it. "Danny's probably right. He's likely after one thing."

I outwardly express my annoyance. "Is that what you're telling yourself?"

Esther withdraws, putting some distance between us.

"Esther." I sigh. "Hiatus is full of young, willing women that Otto has access to. He's been a total grouch since he's been here."

She peeks out the corner of her eye. "He was annoyed I stayed in St. Lucia. He was annoyed Danny insisted, but I understood Danny wanted to reassure you, and you wanted me to stay with Daniel there."

Oh? The crafty little fucker. "He told you . . ." I fade off. There's no point burdening Esther with her son's conniving stunt. Just wait until I find him. "You need to talk to Danny. Tell him how you feel. Tell him to stand down."

"Danny? We're talking about the same man?"

"Yes. You're letting your guilt rule your life. Enough." I stand and she looks up at me, alarmed. "He cannot tell you who to be or who to see. You can be his mom and be a woman too. You've paid your dues. Now it should be about you." I dip and kiss her cheek. "Life is too short to stroke egos, Mom. He'll have to get used to it. Look on the bright side. At least you know Otto can take care of himself. Imagine if you fell in love with a wimp?"

I leave the kitchen and Esther behind chuckling. "Wait!" she yells. "In love? I'm not in love with him."

I roll my eyes, but I melt too. They've not even been intimate, and the feelings are obviously strong. My husband needs to back the hell off.

I make my way to Danny's office, walking in without knocking. It's empty. So I go to the TV room. No Danny. I go to the gym. No Danny. But James is standing on his head and Beau is lying on the mat before him, her chin resting on her palms as she watches him. "Have you seen Danny?" I whisper.

She shakes her head.

"I saw him heading upstairs." James doesn't open his eyes. I throw a little wave to Beau, backing out, leaving them to their . . . workout?

I hurry upstairs, down the corridor, and push my way into our bedroom.

He's face first on the bed, sprawled out, fully dressed.

Snoring.

I sigh and pad over, climbing on next to him and stroking his hair from his face. He murmurs. Grunts a few times. I rest my head on the pillow next to him and watch him sleeping. It's the only time he looks peaceful these days.

"Sleep well," I whisper, kissing his head.

It's not long before I'm gone too.

His pained groan wakes me, his body squirming lethargically next to me. "Fuck me, that hurts," he complains, groaning more, making tiny movements and stopping, slumping, moving, stopping, moaning.

"What hurts?"

"Shoulders," he hisses. "Arms. Chest." His head lifts and then drops back down heavily. "Everything. Everything aches."

I prop myself up on my elbow and stroke his back. He's not moved position since I found him last night. "You know I hate you," I mumble.

"Yep, and I hate you more," he says easily, and I smile. I can't help it. God, I love this man.

I'm sure he'd rather be more awake for this conversation, but, honestly, who knows when we'll get another minute to ourselves? "You used me, you shit."

"For what?"

"To keep your mom in St. Lucia away from Otto." I won't mention Lennox Benson. Not now. We have enough grievances, and the man is inconsequential, really.

"Yeah, I did that," he says, sighing, obviously without the energy to deny it. "But she's back so you can stow away the sass."

Never. The conversation I had with Esther last night is playing on my mind. Perhaps now is the time to convince Danny to back off, since he looks quite immobile. "She's a wom—"

"I'm in pain, Rose," he mumbles into the pillow. "Moody. Don't make it worse."

I narrow my eyes on the back of his head. Fine, but we *will* be talking about it. Onto my next issue. "Daniel knows what you do."

"Jet skis?"

"No, not jet skis. He saw an article in the paper about you and James." What I can see of his jaw tenses.

"Right." He goes to get up, like *who have I got to kill?* Then drops back down on a howl of pain. "Jesus fucking Christ."

I wince, reaching to touch him but not wanting to touch where he might be tender. "What happened? Wait . . ." They were all drugged. Incapable of walking. "Did you carry them out?"

"Yes. About a quarter mile down the coastline. Twice."

Dodging bullets. God, he's a hero. And to think I once thought he was a monster. I'm sure many still do, and sometimes he is, but . . . he's *my* monster. "Anything I can do?"

"Massage." He lifts his head with effort and looks at me with a cheeky smirk, his overgrown hair in his face.

"Massage what?"

"My dick. It's the only part of me not hurting right now." I smack his arm and he laughs, then winces. "No, seriously, baby, I'm in agony here. I can't move." His face plummets into the pillow. Another groan. "You've got to rub some life into me. Ouch. Fuck, ouch, oh you motherfucking cunt!"

I scan up and down his body, getting to my knees. "Where should I start?"

"Shoulders."

"I need something to rub in." I get up off the bed and go to the bathroom, searching the vanity for any kind of oil. I find the lavender oil Doc gave me and take it back to Danny. His phone rings.

"You'll have to get that." He peeks up, flinching. "Who is it?"

"James." I click it to loudspeaker and hold it close to him.

"What's up?" Danny asks, his words delivered on a croaky exhale.

"How much pain are you in?" James asks.

Danny's eyes snap open. Hopeful. As if he's excited to not be in his painful misery alone. "You too?"

"Jesus Christ, I can't fucking move, mate."

"Yes! Ouch. Fuck!"

"Keep still then," I order, restraining my laughter, just as the door flings open and Beau appears in her panties and a tank.

"Do you have any oil?" she breathes urgently. "I can't find any."

I lose my battle to hold on to my laughter and fall apart on the bed, hearing Beau breaking down too.

"Fuck you," Danny mumbles, useless. "Where's my mum?"

His gripes only increase my laughter, as does the sight of Beau holding on to the doorframe, tears streaming down her cheeks. I fall to my back, not judging the available space all too well in my hysteria, and bang Danny's back with my forearm.

"Arhhhhh!" he yells, throwing his head up, jerking another stiff muscle. "Fuck!"

My cheeks blow out, and Beau slides down the wood, crumpling to the floor, her face wet and hair sticking to her cheeks. I can't breathe. My stomach aches.

"What's going on?"

I look up and see Brad behind Beau in the corridor, his hand wrapped around the metal pole of a metal stand, the empty bag of blood dangling by his ear. The sight of him, hardly holding himself up, snaps me out of my laughing fit and has me rushing over.

"What the hell are you doing?" I ask, taking his arm and leading him to the closest bed. Ours. The dressing on his shoulder looks damp and stained. "Lie down."

He drops down on a grunt and Danny lifts his head a fraction. "You're a dickhead," he grumbles. "I fucking told you to go with the girls."

"Fuck off." Brad lets his head settle on the pillow and looks at Danny. "What's up?"

I snort, as does Beau. "He's aching," I say, placing the lavender oil on the nightstand.

"This isn't aching," Danny snaps. "I don't know what the fuck it is, but it's more than aching."

I think I might be killed with a look if a laugh anymore, so I make a point of avoiding Beau's eyes, trying to hold on to my amusement, as Beau comes over, assessing Brad. "How's it feeling?" she asks.

"Like nothing you could believe." He blinks, and his face falls as I look at him incredulously. I can't believe he just said that to a woman who was shot. "Shit."

"You dick," Danny mutters.

"Don't sweat it," Beau breathes.

"Sorry." Brad pouts and relaxes, and a few bangs and curses sound from the hallway, forcing all our stares that way. James appears, holding on to the wall, his face a picture of discomfort, and I'm off again, rolling around on the end of the bed, Beau joining me, every muscle and bodily function failing me.

Thump!

"Ouch!" I yelp, landing on my ass with force.

"Shit, Rose." Beau crawls over to me.

"Rose?" Danny yells. "Rose?"

"I'm fine." I chuckle, grimacing, my butt numb. "I'm fine." I crawl up the end of the bed onto my knees, poking my head up. Brad's chin is on his chest, and Danny's trying with everything he has to crane his neck back and see me. "I'm fine."

"Good," he grunts, slumping down. "Now fix me, woman." I snarl and poke him in his calf. "Fuck!"

"Mind your manners, Black," I warn. "I'm your only hope."

"Not true," he mumbles sulkily with an edge of smugness too. "Mum will help me."

"Don't count on it." I get to my feet.

"What's that supposed to mean?"

"Shut up, you're annoying me."

His head flies up, his eyes, or what I can see of them, enraged. "Rose," he growls. "I'm warning you."

"What are you gonna do?" I ask, sauntering around the bed to his side and getting my face up in his? "Chase me?"

Brad titters next to him, as does Beau at the end of the bed.

"Fuck!" James curses, pulling all attention his way again. He's taking tentative steps toward us, and each time he places a foot down, he curses.

"Fuck"

Step.

"Fucker."

Step.

"Fuck me."

Step.

"Fucking hell."

Step.

"Fuck it!"

Step.

Until he's at the end of the bed and gingerly crawling on, flopping to his front at Danny's and Brad's feet on a grunt and one more *fuck* for good measure.

I look at Beau, just as she looks at me, and quickly look away. But, in all seriousness . . . "Should I get Doc?" I ask.

"No, just rub me," Danny sighs, settling.

"Beau," James groans. "Please."

"You two are pathetic," Brad mutters.

"Aren't you aching?" James asks, looking up at him at the top of the bed.

"Well, I don't fucking know, do I?" Brad snaps, lifting his head from the pillow and directing a lethal glare down the bed to James. "I could be, but I can't tell through the pain of being fucking *shot*."

"Pussy," James mutters. "You'll be fine in a few days."

My eyes fall to the scars dominating every inch of his back. I grimace at the ugly sight and immediately feel terrible for it.

I look at Danny. The cuts on his arms. The scar that stretches from his lip to his eye. The bullet wound I can't see on his collarbone and the healing slashes on his chest. Then I turn my eyes to Beau. Her scarred arm that's uncovered, but only because she's jumped out of bed and mindlessly dashed here. And to her stomach.

And finally to my own arms. The evidence of my darker days. In this room there are nightmares galore. We're all fucked up. Disfigured. And somehow, that's a comfort.

I take the oil and climb onto Danny's back, resting down gently and dripping the lavender oil onto his skin before handing it to Beau as she straddles James's thighs.

"What's going on?" Brad asks, looking between us. "Did someone arrange an orgy and not tell me?"

I chuckle as I start to rub. "Oh God," Danny mumbles, his shoulder blades pulling in as I work into the muscles. "Oh yes. Oh yeah. Oh fuck. Ohhhh . . ."

"Oh, yes," James groans. "Fuck, yeah. Yes, Beau. Harder, Beau." He grunts, and Beau chuckles. "Yes, just like that, baby."

"Well, this is fucking weird," Brad muses, resting back, getting comfortable. "You two swapping?"

"Brad," Danny and James growl in unison.

He pouts. "No rubs for me?"

Danny's hand suddenly and quite quickly lifts and prods him close to his dressing.

"Fuck!"

"Shut the fuck up or get the fuck out."

"I can't fucking move," he mutters. "It took everything in me to make it here."

"Then shut the fu—ohhhh God." Danny's head lifts, his neck stretching, and I smile as he lets out an almighty groan, rolling his shoulders. "You're a goddess."

"Yeah," James whispers. "A total goddess."

"And what do we have here, then?" Zinnea appears in the doorway, her false lashes so dramatic they practically reach the hairline of her wig.

"Want to help?" I ask, hearing Beau sniggering next to me. "Brad needs a foot rub."

"Oh, I'm here for it," she sings, wafting her tiger print kimono as she walks as if on a runway to Brad's side of the bed. Poor Brad. He looks in a frozen state of shock.

"I . . . I . . . I . . ." He looks at me, then Beau, while James and Danny chuckle and hiss at the same time, their amusement and pain combining. "Oh fuck it," Brad says, offering Zinnea his feet. "Help yourself."

Zinnea's long, rainbow-striped talons move in, and the moment she touches one of Brad's feet, he giggles. She withdraws. "Sorry." Brad looks down at her. "I'm ticklish. You need to be firm."

"Just lie back and think of England," she purrs, getting to work, checking Beau and me and blowing us both a kiss. She just makes the place . . . lighter. Brighter. Not so serious, and we all need that from time to time, especially in this world.

My hands begin to ache, my fingers sore, but I don't stop rubbing his muscles back to life, because, frighteningly, if Danny and James are out of action like Brad, we're all in fucking trouble.

After the chaos and drama of yesterday, it was nice to have a day at home with Danny, just . . . being. Vegging. Kicking around the house, eating, *massaging*. He's showered, taken Advil, and is in a lot better shape than he was when he woke up. After dinner, I spend some time with Daniel while he yells at the TV screen, feed the dogs, check in on Pearl and Anya, who both have some color back in their cheeks, and then go find Danny. He's in his office, alone, quiet, nursing a glass of Scotch.

"Do you want to talk about it?" I ask, disturbing him from his thoughts.

He looks up. Smiles mildly. "Do *you*?"

"I'm really fine, Danny," I lower to the couch, not liking the torment in his eyes. "In fact, it felt good to help them. All but two had families worried about them or thinking they'd run away from home."

He nods, clearly struggling with the memories being raked up. "You know, all I saw in that place was you." He opens the drawer and picks up the gold letter opener, turning it in his hand, staring at the blade. He's imagining killing Nox and Ernie all over again — or any man who has ever touched me. He shifts in the chair, as if uncomfortable, his now-working muscles flexing.

"What do you know about your father?" I blurt out of nowhere, the question I thought I'd filed, obviously not being filed well enough.

Danny stills, turning his icy blue eyes my way. "What?"

I look down, wondering what the hell I've done. But I've asked now. No going back, and at least he's not heaving like an angry gorilla over my past anymore. "Your biological father," I say. "I've never heard you or Esther talk about him." Perhaps because they simply don't talk about anything from their pasts.

He frowns, and suddenly my husband turns from my master-piece killer into a lost little boy. "I've never asked." I expect getting his head around Esther was tough enough, and I also know he only ever saw Carlo as his father. "Why are you asking?"

I shrug lamely. "I don't know." My hand goes to my stomach, and that tells him everything. And perhaps subconsciously I am wondering, since I have no parents.

He smiles, standing and coming to me, kneeling before me and resting his hands on my thighs. "This family not big enough for you?"

"Of course, it's just—"

"Carlo Black is my father. Carlo Black is Daniel's grandfather and our baby's grandfather."

I purse my lips. Understood. But I don't say that. Instead, I smile and feel at his face. "We need to talk about the girls that are here. Pearl and Anya."

"Can we do that later?" he asks.

"Sure." I relent easily. I just want to make his life easier for a while. "Coffee?"

"Thought you'd never ask." He stands and stretches, making a noise about it too.

"I'm going shopping with Beau tomorrow to buy something for her to wear at her father's funeral."

"Oh?"

"Do not try to stop us."

"Would I?"

I snort and head for the door as Danny's phone rings and he mumbles something about there being no rest for the wicked. I look back as I get to the door, seeing him gazing down at his cell on the desk with a dirty look. And I'm reminded that I can try all I like to make his life easier, but I will never fully be able to take him away from this life.

Danny answers in silence as I take the handle, and just as the door meets the frame, I hear him say, "What do you want, Sandy?"

And I walk away wondering who the hell Sandy is.

21

JAMES

"What the fuck is wrong with you? You've been a grouchy fuck since we came back from St. Lucia." I stir my coffee, eyes on Otto, as he moodily taps away on his laptop at the island in the kitchen. Esther's back. I was banking on that putting a smile on his face, but Esther was here all day yesterday faffing around the house and everyone in it, and Otto was nowhere to be seen.

"Winstable was bought by someone called John Theodore Little," he says shortly. Okay, so he wants to talk shop.

"And who is John Theodore Little?" I ask, humoring him.

"Don't know. I can't find anything on him."

"That's strange, isn't it?"

"Very. I'll keep digging. Still nothing on Cartwright and I've got Len following Natalia Potter."

"And Burrows?" I ask, wondering what his fucking game is and *where* he is.

Otto looks out the corner of his eye at me, then back over his shoulder, checking the coast is clear. "Beau's tried calling him. He's not answering." He turns his screen toward me, showing me Beau's phone records, and I sink deeper onto my stool. It could be in shame. It's not that I don't trust her, it's not that Burrows is her ex. The last time they spoke he wanted to meet her, and now nothing? He's not at work. Annual leave. Escaping? Hiding?

"What are you thinking?" Otto asks.

"I'm thinking Beau is right. Maybe The Bear doesn't have anyone on the inside anymore, which is why everyone appears to be jumping ship." I look at Otto. "Which means my conclusion on Burrows is wrong."

"You don't think he's bent?"

"I don't know," I muse. It would fucking suck if he's not, because it would remove one solid good reason from my list of solid good reasons to kill him. Aside from that, how would The Hound know where and when to find me the day I was arrested for Spittle's murder if Oliver Burrows didn't tell him?

"Or maybe they all simply want independence again," Otto says. "Besides, I'm afraid the Burrows situation is not dissimilar to the Dexter situation. Even if he is/was bent, Beau isn't going to let you touch him. Torture him. Keep him against his will."

"If she knows," I say quietly.

"You're a dick if you think you'd get away with that." He's right. And once again I'm damning my girl for being a former cop.

"Not that it matters because no one knows where the fucker is." I clench my fists and push them into the worktop. *Just give me The Bear.* The thought of him disappearing without a trace fucking pains me. *Justice. Vengeance.* It might never be ours.

"Has anyone spoken to the girls?"

"You mean Pearl and Anya?" I ask, and he nods. "Rose and Beau have been with them. And Esther. It's a *gently does it* situation." We can't go steaming in demanding every detail they can tell us. Well, we could, but Rose would have something to say about it. I would have guessed she'd be the one most deeply affected by Monday's events. Turns out she's found fuel in the situation. It's Danny who has struggled.

"Let me know." Otto snaps the lid of his laptop closed and gets up. "I'm going for a workout."

Workout. Just the word makes my muscles hurt again, and I stretch my arms high, relishing the pull. "Where's Danny?"

"His office. I'm passing by so will let him know about the buyer of the boatyard."

"Don't kill each other, will you?" I return to my coffee, mulling things over. I didn't think the plot could thicken more, but here I am chewing it over like a piece of fat that refuses to break down.

I pick up my phone and look down at the screen. At the email I received this morning—the one I was expecting but not prepared for. Not prepared at all, which means Beau definitely won't be.

"Morning."

I quickly clear the screen and turn on my stool, finding a sweaty Beau behind me. "You were up early," I say, following her path to the fridge, pouting, my eyes fixed to her firm, peachy arse.

"I didn't think you'd be game for a workout." She takes some orange juice and drinks straight out of the carton, leaning back on the countertop. She has a long-sleeved running top on that covers her scar.

I get up and wander casually over, and she pulls the carton away from her mouth a fraction, swallowing, eyes on me. Yesterday I was good for nothing except moaning and hurting. The day off was welcome. Beau seemed present, only marginally distracted. I'd like to put that solely down to her father's funeral tomorrow and the delivery the next day. Unfortunately, I can't. Burrows is missing and Beau's had her suspicions piqued by him, Cartwright, and now Detective Collins. The chances of them all fucking off isn't likely. So is the chance of Beau letting it go. Accepting her father really was in the wrong place at the wrong time. What a shitter this is. I need her focused. Focused on me, focused on what she desperately wants. Which leads me back to my day off yesterday. It felt totally wasted not being able to spend it buried in Beau.

But I'm feeling a *lot* better today. Still a little sore, but I'm not feeling quite as debilitated as I did. "Not *that* kind of workout," I say quietly, reaching her, standing toe to toe but keeping my hands to myself as I look down at her.

Go on. Shine for me. Do it.

Blinding white sparkles pop in the depths of her dark eyes, and my heart pops with love. I take the carton from her limp hand and put it on the counter behind her, and then dip and sink my face into her neck, breathing out long and slowly when she wraps her arms around my shoulders and hugs me. Bliss. I lift her from the ground and squeeze her to my body, wanting her as close as I can get her, and she reciprocates, humming her happiness. The signs are good, and I'm quickly hatching a plan to get her back in bed and make up for lost time. But first . . .

"How are you feeling about tomorrow?" I ask, grabbing under her thighs and placing her on the counter.

"How are your muscles?"

Translated, she doesn't want to talk about her father's funeral. Okay. "How are you feeling about the delivery?"

She smiles as she watches her fingertip draw a line across my bottom lip. "Fine."

"You sure?"

"I'm sure I can manage towing a line of jet skis from point A to point B and play a dumb female should the Coast Guard stop us."

"Play?"

She gasps, punching my bicep, and I hiss. I hate that she's way more at ease with this than I am, but that's just Beau. And I am me —totally besotted and maybe a little protective—so I need to be at ease too. "I think I need another massage."

"Oh, you do, do you?"

"Oh, I do." I swoop in and claim her mouth, pushing my tongue deep and rolling wide, forcing my chest to hers.

Someone clears their throat, and I pull away quickly, my attempted seduction interrupted. *Fuck it.* Beau smirks and claims her juice, looking past me. "Morning," she chirps as I glance back, releasing her. Esther goes straight to the dishwasher and starts emptying it.

"Morning, you two."

"Otto's in the gym," Beau says nonchalantly, making her freeze in her bended position, armed with handfuls of knives and forks. She lifts her eyes. I raise my brows. Beau presses her lips into a straight line.

"Good for him." She goes about her business, and Beau and I peek at each other, me warning her to leave it there. In all the years I've known Otto, I've never known him to be committed to one woman. I hate doubting that he has it in him, but I'm being a realist. We have a nice balance here, everyone gets along, and any fornicating could rock the boat. Danny and Otto are already at each other's throats. This will end only one way. Blood. Because the chances of Otto settling down, and it would be settling down because Esther wants and deserves that and her son wouldn't have it any other way, is about as likely as Beau becoming consistently submissive.

Of course, Beau doesn't heed my warning. "Glad to be back?" She slips down off the counter and has another swig of the orange juice.

"Yes, I am, th—" Esther puts a pile of plates down, looking disgusted, and marches over to Beau, swiping the carton from her hands. "How many times do I need to tell you, don't drink straight from the carton."

"You've never told me that." Beau laughs, claiming the plates and putting them away.

"I haven't?"

"You definitely haven't."

"So many people in this damn house." Esther tips the remaining juice into a jug and puts it in the fridge. "I need to call a family meeting. Remind a few people of the house rules." She returns to faffing around the kitchen, and I jerk my head at Beau, telling her silently to move her arse.

She tilts her head. I tilt mine. She drops her eyes to my groin. I pout as she glances back up. I see hunger. Another jerk of my head. I need her in the best mood today, the most amenable mood. This is a good start.

Goldie walks in, stops, looks between us. "What's up with you two?" she asks.

"Nothing."

"Nothing."

Dubious, she goes to the fridge and pulls out the jug of orange juice, tipping it to her lips, still watching us. Beau snorts, I smile, and Esther yells, "Goldie!"

She jumps, sending the juice everywhere, mostly up her nose. "How many times have I got to tell you?"

"Tell me what?" Goldie asks, between coughing and spluttering.

"My God." Esther swipes the jug from her hand and wipes around the rim. "Use a damn glass!" she yells at the top of her voice, obviously hoping the whole house will hear.

Goldie looks thoroughly scorned, shrinking in her suit on the spot. It's quite a sight. "Sorry."

"Never mind," Esther breathes, exasperated. "Eggs?"

"Please." Goldie settles on the stool, peeking at us in question, to which we both deny any knowledge of Esther's short mood. "Where's Otto?" she asks.

Beau chuckles, exiting the kitchen sharply, and I'm soon going after her, eyeing her sweaty form as she takes the stairs, mentally ripping her sticky gym gear from her wet body as I tail her.

I reach for her wrist as we near the top and seize her. "Finally," I whisper, hauling her around and up my body, taking her mouth. She wraps her limbs around me and devours my mouth as I walk us back to our room. Distract her with work, distract her with sex. That is my mission, and I choose to accept it.

"There you are." Rose's voice has Beau pulling away, and I groan my protest, looking up to see her pulling the door of their room closed. She looks like she means business, adorned in a cream silk floaty summer dress and enough gold bangles to stretch her arms to the floor. "Why aren't you ready?" she asks as Beau slides down my front, rubbing me in places I shouldn't be rubbed unless we're alone.

"For fuck's sake," I mutter. "Ready for what?" Where on earth do they think they're going?

"Shopping," Rose says confidently, too confidently, fastening her purse as she comes to us, looking at Beau in disapproval.

"Shopping?" I snort. "I don't think so." But Beau and Rose leaving the mansion isn't my main issue here. I have somewhere I need us to be.

"I have nothing to wear tomorrow," Beau says quietly, losing all lightness.

Fuck. Tomorrow. And quickly, I'm reminded that distraction isn't an easy feat when we are us and we're in this fucking world. How do I play this? I tussle over that question for far too long, wasting all our times, because there is only one answer. Be reasonable. I *have* to be reasonable. I turn to Rose. "How long will shopping take?"

She looks at me like I'm stupid. "How long is a piece of string?"

I show the ceiling my eyes, exasperated. Rose and I both know Beau hates shopping, so I expect it'll be done far quicker than Rose is expecting. Or hoping. "Tank and Fury go with you," I say, just as the men themselves emerge from rooms down the corridor, looking like they're about ready to burst with excitement, which tells me they already know what today entails for them, which means Danny knows too. "Didn't anyone think to tell me?"

"I forgot," Beau says, sounding apologetic. Forgot? She had all day yesterday to tell me this. All day! I can feel myself getting worked up, trying to mentally reason with myself. It's hard when so much is uncertain. *Where the fuck is Burrows?*

"Call me when you're done," I order, my vocal cords straining to keep my voice gentle. I slide my hand onto her neck and peck her lips. "I'll pick you up."

"Why?"

"I have a surprise." I leave her with Rose and make my way down the corridor, passing the big guys. "Have fun," I quip, getting grunts from them both.

I pass through the entrance hall, just as the front door opens and Zinnea struts in on sky-high platforms wearing a silver sequin embellished pair of trousers and a bustier covered in feathers. Could be me, but since she heard about her brother, she seems to have become a more extreme version of herself, and Zinnea was pretty fucking extreme already. "Morning," I say, passing her, forcing her to look up from rummaging through her purse. Her blonde wig is a little wonky. I smile.

"What are you grinning at?" she asks.

I raise my hand to my head. "You're a little"—I jiggle my finger—"skew-whiff."

She quickly totters across to the wall-hung mirror to straighten herself out. "I was throwing the ball for the dogs."

"Dressed like that?"

She looks back, her hand pausing on her head. "Dressed like what, exactly, James?"

"Fabulously, of course." I smile, and she sniffs.

"How's Beau doing?" She goes back to her bag and pulls out a tissue, dabbing at her top lip.

I glance up the stairs, thoughtful. "She's okay." I frown. "I think."

"You think?"

"She's still trying to get hold of Burrows."

"She never could let things go." She breathes in and looks up the stairs too. "I'm hoping a bit of shopping today will distract her."

"For her father's funeral?" I ask on an unamused laugh. And distract? I'm beginning to wonder if it's possible to distract Beau Hayley, and that's a massive disadvantage for me.

Zinnea stands tall, obviously pushing back her own warped grief for her egotistical brother. "Zinnea makes anything fun, darling." She struts past me and stops, pouting her over-glossed pink lips and making her eyes sultry so her fake fans of lashes flutter. "Which is why I'm being Lawrence less and less," she says in her natural, masculine, deep voice. "Arrivederci, darling!" she sings, high again, as she walks like a catwalk model into the kitchen and shrieks a *good morning* to Esther.

When I get to Danny's office, I find him at his desk turning the gold letter opener over in his hand. He looks up, acknowledges me with a cold stare for a few seconds, then returns to deliberately spinning the weapon in his hand. Because that letter open has definitely killed more men than it's opened letters. I take a seat and let him have his thoughts, while I wonder who's on the end of that letter opener next.

"John Theodore Little," he muses, his blue eyes narrowing to slits. This will be driving him wild. Irritating him. Angering him. He was fooled, and Danny Black is no fool.

"Otto has nothing, but he will have."

Danny places the letter opener down and gets up, wandering to the drinks cabinet, looks it over, probably realizes what the time is, then wanders back. "How are your muscles?" he asks, rolling his shoulders.

"Better."

"Yeah, mine too." He pouts. "The delivery Fri—"

"You know I'm not happy about it."

He hums, walking to the window. "I know. You want to call it off?" He looks back, and I can tell that if I demanded it, he would support it. Fuck the Mexicans, we'd deal with the repercussions. But it's not the Mexicans I'm worried about.

"I have to let her have this." It fucking pains me, but if I call a halt on this shit, Beau will retreat and I can't have her retreating. Not with this afternoon's appointment and the funeral tomorrow and the fact that her ex is waiting in the wings to . . . what? Make her fall back in love with him? Turn her against me? He's tried it all already. Failed. And, again, where the fuck is he, anyway? Does it matter? Beau will do what Beau will do . . . if I let her. Which I won't. Can't. *Fuck*. But I've long accepted she's not an average woman. *Lara Croft*. But if she was pregnant . . .

I shake my head to myself. "And to be clear, this wouldn't be happening if it were an exchange." Dealing with Chaka and the Coast Guard is one thing. Dealing with the Mexicans is another.

Danny laughs under his breath. "You're a better man than I am."

"Our women have different needs," I point out. "Rose needed to help those women. You bowed when she insisted on Pearl and Anya remaining in our care."

"True." He settles back in his chair. "Sandy called me last night."

I balk. "And you're telling me this now?" I look at my watch. "Twelve hours later?"

"I was enjoying my day off." He tosses the letter opener into the middle of the desk and focuses on it. I don't challenge him. I was enjoying a day off too. "He heard about the Poles. Told me we left two alive. A prize for guessing who one was."

"The Shark," I muse.

"And guess what?"

"Don't tell me Sandy offered you a name?" How many people are going to claim to know who The Bear is? If I hadn't spoken to the elusive fucker personally, I would think he's a figment of all our imaginations. A nightmare that haunts our dreams, but not reality.

"You're so clever." Danny turns his eyes up to me. "But that's not all he offered."

I raise my brows, thinking. It doesn't take me long. "Volodya," I breathe. "Sandy's offered you Volodya too." So there really is unrest in the camp, because not so long ago, Sandy and Volodya were playing nicely together under The Ox. Now he's dead too, the Russians and Poles are offering each other up left and right. Of course Sandy would offer Volodya to Danny; he knows that's a prime piece of meat for The Brit after he turned on him at the Winstable massacre. But is the not so tiny detail of Sandy organizing a hit on Beau when she lay in the hospital with a gunshot wound being forgotten? Surely not. It's the whole fucking point I ended up resurrecting The Brit after he faked his death.

"I assume you declined."

"Not exactly."

"Don't piss me off, Danny," I warn, shifting in my chair. "He had a—"

He holds up a hand. "I know. But let us not forget, Volodya shot me of his own accord. Sandy was ordered by a higher power to kill

Beau because she was uncomfortably close to exposing *him*, like her mother was."

I settle in my chair, but I'm far from comfortable with where this is heading. "He still acted, whether ordered or not. Rose doesn't have a target on her head. Beau has been a target since she started digging around into her mother's death."

"We're past that," Danny says, appearing as frustrated as me. "The FBI and MPD buried that case for a reason, and since you were implicated in the evidence that was destroyed by Dexter and it wasn't only The Bear's name in that safety deposit box, we should be grateful. This is personal now, James. Beau doesn't want justice like she used to want justice. She wants justice like *you* want justice. With death. Blood."

"Pretty fucking impossible when the man we want dead has disappeared off the face of the fucking earth." The Bear vanishing pains me more than him terrorizing us. "He called us in St. Lucia. Took the greatest of pleasure in informing us he's still alive, that we got the wrong man. We come back to Miami to deal with it. He calls us the day we arrive to tell us he dug up your pops and Beau's mother, and over a week down the line, nothing. Not a fucking peep."

"I think Beau's right. He's lost their confidence."

Whoever he is. *Who the fuck is he?* Facing the idea that we may never know is torture. There was a time when no one knew who he was. Now, apparently, every fucker does if the amount of offers of a name is a measure.

"About tomorrow," Danny goes on, swiftly changing the subject. "The funeral." He eyes me curiously.

"What about it?"

"I'll ask you again. Did you kill Beau's father?"

"I've told you repeatedly, no, I didn't fucking kill her father." Wanted to. God, did I want to.

"Then what the fuck were you doing at the hotel?"

I breathe out, defeated. It's time to share since Beau will find out later anyway. I pull out my phone, find the details, and slide it across the desk. "I wasn't at the same hotel as Tom Hayley."

Danny frowns as he picks it up and starts scrolling through the images. "What's this?" he asks, splitting his attention between my uncomfortable form and my phone.

"I've bought us a place," I tell him, a bit unsure, because, honestly, I'm still feeling it, and I can't put my finger on exactly why. Would Beau like it? Hate it? "I was meeting the realtor at the lobby bar to finalize some paperwork."

"Why didn't you tell me?"

"Because you'd tell Rose and Rose would tell Beau." This needs a gentle approach too. "I need her in the best frame of mind. Stable. Positive."

"Is it an apartment, or is it a glass box?" Danny looks up at me. "It's very . . . exposed."

"And?"

"And nothing. I'm just saying, it's very . . . glassy."

"Very observant."

"So why haven't you told Beau?"

I reclaim my phone. "I'm trying to minimize stress. She's got a lot on her mind at the moment."

"You're worried she'll say no to moving in together."

"We live here together."

"Minimize stress," Danny muses, his forehead creasing, his brows heavy. What's taking so much of his brain space at the moment? "It's her father's funeral tomorrow."

"Again, very observant. Brad's rubbing off on you."

"I don't think it's a good idea," he says, and I recoil, surprised.

"The funeral?" I say. "It's kind of necessary. They happen when people die."

He looks at me tiredly. "No, not the fucking funeral. The apartment, and I'm not speaking completely selfishly. Beau needs Rose as much as Rose needs her. Plus, you'd have to move Fury in there. Is there even enough room for him because it looks kinda small?"

"I hope we get to a point when I don't need Fury stuck to Beau constantly. We need our own space."

Danny gets up, appearing agitated, pacing. "Not if you're fucking dead," he says gravely, stopping with his circling of the room.

I'm recoiling again. "She needs some normal."

"This is about as normal as our life gets, mate. Cleaning cash, gunrunning, and fighting off the daredevils who try to move in."

"I know that."

"Then why?"

My teeth grit. "I have to give her hope that we can be . . ." I pause, thinking, trying in vain not to get worked up. "I don't fucking know. Something other than dark. Some normality. Or something close."

"For you or her?" he fires back.

"Her," I murmur unconvincingly, shrinking into my chair. "Everything is for her." I'm not lying. "She wants a baby. She's said she'll marry me. Why wouldn't she want our own place?"

"Are you prepared to give her a baby?"

I scowl. "Anything."

"You've changed your tune," he muses, looking at me like he knows. He just . . . knows. "She's with you, James. She accepted when she held Burrows at gunpoint and shot Perry Adams that normal would not feature in her life anymore. She chose you."

"What if she's regretting it?"

"That's bollocks." He dismisses me easily. "You've got to stop thinking you can bring her to heel."

"That's rich coming from you."

He smiles, and it's fond. "I know when to let Rose have her way. As you pointed out, I wasn't comfortable having those two girls in my house, but Rose needed that. I'm not all too fond of the fact that she cracks me one on the nose every now and then, but she needs that too. Your Beau is like a champion racehorse being forced not to run. It doesn't work. They'll always end up bucking. Do you actually want a baby, or do you just want a reason to keep her close?"

"The fuck?" I blurt.

"It's a serious question."

"It's a stupid fucking question." I push back in my chair, standing abruptly, my fists clenching, and Danny takes a wary step back. I manage amid my instant anger to ask myself why his question has triggered me. It's easy. Because he's bang on the money. Our baby was a healing balm on both of our wounds. All of them. And we have a lot of fucking wounds. Mental, emotional, and physical. Why wouldn't Beau want that again? And me. Not just for all of that, but because she would have no choice but to tame the Lara in her. I'm such a dick. An apartment won't solve my problems. Marriage might not either. But a little piece of her and a little piece of me in one little person to call ours?

"Calm down," Danny murmurs, and, weirdly, I do, taking a few deep breaths and lowering back to my chair. But then something else comes to me.

"You should have run it by me before you agreed to let them go shopping," I snap. "And why the fuck do they need to go shopping for anyway? They can get everything they need online. Beau hates shopping."

"Because a shopping trip is one tiny bit of normal we *can* offer."

He's right, of course, but I'm obviously not feeling very reasonable today. "You should have fucking asked."

"I'm sorry, okay?" Danny wanders over to the drinks cabinet and takes a couple bottles of water, bringing one to me. "Drink. You look parched."

"I'm fine," I mutter, swiping the bottle from his hand. Fuck. He doesn't think our own apartment is a good idea? I've been so focused on trying to give Beau what I think will fix us, I've forgotten what she might actually *want*. Problem is, I'm not certain what it is she actually wants. A baby? A badge? Our own place? This house is as fucked up as a house can get. And yet . . . it works. And, really, having so many friends and family close by is a comfort. Support. Respite in a world where there is little relief. "So you're telling me I might have just wasted five million dollars?"

He smiles. "Plenty more where that came from, mate."

The door knocks behind me, and I look back when Danny calls an okay to enter. Goldie walks in first, followed by Otto and Ringo. All have a quick scope of the room before settling on the couch in a line. "All right?" Ringo grunts, looking down his colossal nose at us.

"Fine," Danny says.

"Fine," I mutter moodily, firing off a quick email to the realtor telling him I can't make our meeting today.

"In other news," Danny says, his eyes on my silently uneasy form. "Sandy's been in touch."

"And what gifts has he offered to bring to the party?" Goldie asks. "Wait, don't tell me—"|

"No, no," Ringo chirps. "I know the answer to this. Is it a cuddly toy?"

"And a Russian," Danny confirms, eyeing me, waiting for me to react. How's he being so fucking calm?

"A Russian?" Otto asks, looking between me and Danny, as does Goldie. I don't need to answer.

"Sandy's offered Volodya?" Goldie balks. "No. Kill Sandy. Kill the fucker or I will." She stands, practically cracking her knuckles.

Danny's hands rise in a pacifying way I'm not feeling, and Ringo reaches for Goldie's arm, gently easing her back to the couch. "We're taking a moment to decide how best to approach this."

I know how. A machine gun and a few belts of bullets. Fuck, why did I think the apartment was a good idea?

"A meeting without me?" The door pushes open, and Brad stands on the threshold in his boxers looking sulky, his hair all over the place, his shoulder bandaged. Danny and I are both up from our chairs quickly, helping him across the office.

"What the fuck are you playing at?" I mutter.

"I'm bored."

"You're shot." I point out like a chump.

"Get off," he grumbles, rolling his shoulders and hissing in pain as a result. "I'm fine."

Danny looks across at me, jerks his head in signal, and we both link our arms behind him, making a little seat for him to perch on. "I said I'm fine!" he snaps.

"Sit the fuck down or I'll drag you back to your room," Danny retorts as everyone gets up, making space, Goldie perching on one arm, Ringo on the other, and Otto setting his laptop on Danny's desk and taking one of the chairs.

"I'm not a fucking invalid," Brad grumbles, relenting and lowering to the makeshift chair.

"You are an invalid, you dick," Goldie says, plumping a pillow at her end as we carry him over. We lay him down, getting him comfy, and he gives each of us a filthy look.

"This is the worst. What's going on?"

"Nothing important." Ringo holds up his phone. "Want me to order you a coffee?"

"Oohhh, yeah."

"I hope that order isn't landing with my mother." Danny's face is pure and utter disgust as he makes his way back to his desk.

Ringo doesn't entertain him—he knows better—and puts in a call, ordering a round of coffees from Starbucks to be delivered.

"So." Brad snuggles down, hissing and spitting as he tries to get comfortable. "What's the latest?"

"Sandy's throwing us treats and James is about to blow a gasket."

"Normal day then," he says. "What kind of treats?"

"Russian and bear-flavored treats." Danny raises his brow to match Brad's. "Hungry?"

"Starving. Volodya?" We both nod. "So they *are* turning on each other." We both nod. "And Sandy must know what'll happen if he makes false promises." We both nod. "So he knows who The Bear is?" We both shrug. "I'd love to stick a corkscrew in Volodya's eye." Only Danny nods. "And I bet you'd love to chop up Sandy into a million bite-sized pieces." Brad looks at me, and this time only I nod. He really can't help stating the obvious. "So where does that leave us?"

"We're still deciding," Danny says, glancing at me. He doesn't need me to tell him that if Sandy comes within a foot of me, I'll skin the fucker alive. I know he feels the same about Volodya, so we're at a stalemate.

Brad blows out his cheeks. "What to do, what to do," he muses to himself. I hear Goldie breathe out her exasperation, and I look at Danny, smiling as he rolls his eyes at yet another Brad moment. "And why are you blowing a gasket?"

"Stressed," I grunt, throwing off vibes that warns Danny not to murmur a word and the others not to press. I'm seriously re-evaluating my bright idea to move us out of the mansion, if only now because I don't want Beau to think it's a sign of relaxed rules. Quite honestly, I'm wondering what the hell I was thinking. In time, perhaps, but now?

A small tap on the door sounds, so light we almost miss it. So light, everyone looks at each other as if searching for confirmation that there was, indeed, a tap. Another tap answers our question. Esther. Only Esther would knock so delicately.

Naturally, my eyes go to Otto when she enters. As does everyone else's, and they all shrink like dying flowers when they see Otto giving her an encouraging nod. "Ohhhh," I breathe quietly, turning my attention to Danny. He's the only one who doesn't look uncomfortable, which means he's the only one who hasn't yet grasped why his mother is here. Is he in denial? Or is this plain ignorance?

"I wondered if I might have a word," Esther says, straightening her shoulders, standing tall, trying with everything she has to appear steadfast and confident.

"Sure." Danny frowns, but is that because he's suddenly sensed the atmosphere of Esther's unusually bold disposition. "We'll be done in just a moment."

Esther once again peeks at Otto, who gives her another small, reassuring nod.

"Oh boy," Brad whispers, pushing his hands into the couch on either side of him, as if trying to get himself up, sucking back air, sustaining the pain.

"Actually"—Esther steps forward, standing even taller—"I have grocery shopping to do, so now works better for me."

"Someone want to help me?" Brad calls, looking to everyone in the room. We all ignore him. "Okay. Looks like I'm staying." He slumps back down. "I can't watch." He takes the pillow from behind his head and covers his face.

Tilting his head, Danny's eyes pass over all of our awkward forms, his face straight, but his eyes blazing with realization tell me he's grasped what's about to go down. "And you have to leave this moment?" he asks.

"I do."

"You can't wait five minutes for me to finish?" He's being difficult now. Plain difficult, because he's worried. I might join Brad under that pillow.

"Like I said," Esther says. "I have things to do, and I would like to get on and do them."

Danny looks at Otto briefly. Briefly but with enough of a sneer for me to be concerned. "I never appreciated your schedule was so regimented, Mum."

"Oh, for fuck's sake," Otto mutters, rising from his chair, prompting Ringo, Goldie, and me to jump up sharpish and announce our departure.

"Take me!" Brad sings, flinging the pillow on the floor.

"Sit down," Danny barks, rising and slamming his fist on the table.

"Yes, sit down!" Esther yells, and Danny flinches like he's been shot.

We all lower, except Danny and Otto, who remain poised and growling at each other over the desk.

Esther looks a little red in the face, like she could be holding on to her temper. I will her to let it go, release the pressure and let Danny have it. I might not be sure about Otto and Esther, but they're fucking grown-ups. This is not Danny's call.

Breathing heavy, fists clenched and white where they're wedged into the wood of his desk, Danny shakes. Whether that be with anger or restraint, I don't know. It takes everything in me not to fall apart when I see Brad stretching for the pillow, grappling at thin air, unable to reach it.

"Sit down!" Esther snaps again, and Danny drops to his chair with eyes like saucers and his mouth slightly agape. I'd laugh if I knew he wouldn't shoot me. I peek at Goldie and Ringo. Both of them look red in the face from holding their breath and their amusement in check.

"Right." Esther plants her hands on her hips, meaning business. "Let us get this out in the open, shall we?"

"No," Danny grunts.

"Please, no," Brad says quietly.

"Shut the fuck up, Brad," Esther, Otto, and Danny all yell in unison, and he retreats quickly, covering his face with his hands. He should watch, because The Brit is about to be put in his place, and it's going to be entertaining.

"I'm seeing someone," she declares.

I smile, brushing the side of my index finger across my mouth to try and hide it.

"No, you're not," Danny grates.

"Yes, she is." Otto pipes up. "Me." As if he needed to say it. Goldie is now sucking her cheeks in, Ringo looks more worried than amused at this point, and Brad is shaking his head in his darkness.

"I beg to differ."

"Come on, Danny," I say gently.

He points at me. "Shut the fuck up."

I'm letting that slide, but only because he's emotional.

"No, Mum. No. You're better than-than-than"—his pointed finger turns to Otto—"*that.*"

I've known Otto for many years. He has the patience of a saint. It's about to snap and I'd rather not be here for it. *What the fuck, Danny? Back the fuck down.* "Are you saying you're a better man than I am, Black?" Otto rumbles, his chest seeming to expand, his breathing deepening.

"I'm saying nothing about me."

"Boys!" Esther cries.

"You're saying you deserve Rose?" Otto muses menacingly. "But I don't deserve a woman like your mother?"

Jesus, if Danny's nostrils flare anymore, Otto's fists will disappear up them when he punches him. I glance at my oldest friend, silently urging him to look at me so I can will him to take a few deep, calming breaths and not do anything stupid. It's the whole fucking point Esther is here, to try and appeal to Danny's reasonable side, since no one else can. And she's one of the only people in this world who Black wouldn't hurt. *Fucking hell.* But Otto doesn't look at me, his bearded, pierced face becoming more menacing by the second.

"Well?" he prompts.

"Leave my wife out of it." Danny stands again, and I reluctantly accept that shit is about to go down, and no one can stop it, not even Danny's mother. I doubt Rose could either, if she was here. It's just a matter of who launches first.

"Is it safe to come out yet?" Brad asks, peeking out from under his arm, just as Danny flies across his desk and takes Otto off his feet.

"That's a no, then." Brad retreats back into his darkness, and Goldie gets up, looking at me, palms up, asking what the fuck we should do. Honestly, I don't know.

"Leave them," Ringo says, holding an arm out in front of Goldie, as if holding her back. I take his stance. I'm not getting in between them either.

"Oh God," Esther says, as Otto rolls them, getting the upper hand, straddling Danny. He launches a fist right into his face, and everyone winces at the sound. Blood sprays, Esther puts her face in her hands, and Danny roars, flying up, blood spread over every inch of his scarred face. He looks like a fucking psycho. An absolute, raving, psycho, his teeth bared, his cold eyes wild. Otto's got a few years on Danny, he's sturdier, heavier, but I'm worried for him.

I step back when they come toward me, Danny throwing Otto

on the desk and returning the favor, making a mess of his nose too. More blood. And Otto, the crazy fuck, laughs dementedly. It's the worst thing he could do. And all of a sudden, both men are a blur of swinging fists, deafening bellows and downright craziness.

Punch after punch, kick after kick, yell after yell, they go at each other like rabid cavemen, smacking into walls, knocking the glasses over on the drinks cabinet, knocking fucking pictures off walls. This has been brewing for weeks. The small altercation in St. Lucia and at the boatyard didn't cut the mustard. They need to get this out of their system. Again.

We all move out of their way, me pulling Esther from the path of their wild, flying limbs more than once, but there is nothing I can do for Brad, who's a sitting duck on the couch, hiding from the ugly.

"I'll fucking kill you!" Danny yells.

"Fucking try it," Otto roars. "You fucking brat."

Then they land on Brad and his scream is ear-piercing, his face draining of blood in an instant. Danny and Otto snap out of their fits immediately, scrambling up, and look at Brad, who is in absolute agony on the couch, holding his shoulder. "Fuck!" he shrieks, as I hurry over, barging the two idiot kids out of my way to get to him. His dressing is drenched in blood, the wound open beneath. "Fuck, fuck, fuck!"

"Someone get Doc," I order, pushing Brad's knees down, stopping him from curling into a protective ball so I can get to his wound.

"Fuck!"

"You're good," I say, peeling the dressing away and pulling my T-shirt off, pressing it into the wound.

"Doesn't fucking feel it."

"Stiches have popped." I can hear Danny and Otto sniffing and heaving behind me, and I look back, livid, just as Esther moves between them and gives Danny a stinger of a slap, followed by Otto. Both men blink in surprise, and Danny reaches up to his face, feeling it.

"Mum?" he questions, looking like a lost little boy.

"No more," she says firmly, her jaw tight as she turns to Otto. "And if you ever lay a hand on my boy again, we're done." She comes to Brad and crouches, assessing him. "I'll get you some tea," she says, stroking his hair. "Sugar?"

He nods. "Please, Mom," he murmurs, clenching his eyes closed. Esther gets up and leaves, not giving Danny or Otto a second look, and Doc enters, bag in hand.

"Open stitches," I say, moving to give him space.

"Oh dear. How did that happen?" All eyes turn to Danny and Otto, who both look pretty sheepish. "And what happened to you two?" Doc asks.

"Misunderstanding," Otto mumbles, swiftly leaving, no doubt to go after Esther and try to apologize.

To my surprise, Danny stays in the room. "Fuck it," he hisses, wiping his nose with the back of his hand. "Brad, mate, I'm sorry."

"Fuck off," he hisses. "You're being a fucking child. Take me to my room."

I press my lips together and look at Doc, who nods his acceptance. Ringo comes to help, and we carefully help him up. "Can you walk?"

"Yeah, I can fucking walk." Brad puts his good arm around me as Ringo moves into his other side, ready to be leant on, and Goldie runs ahead to makes sure our path is clear. It's probably just as well—Danny needs a moment alone to calm the fuck down. "We should check in on Hiatus later," I say shortly, reminding The Brit that while he's behaving like a child and throwing a hissy fit over who his mother, a grown woman, chooses to see, we still have shit to deal with. "Nolan's holding the place up on his own."

He nods and drops to his chair, looking at his phone when it rings and flicking it away on a dismissive snort.

Our progress to Brad's room is slow, taking a good few minutes to make it to the staircase. "You should have stayed in bed as instructed," Doc says as Daniel dances down the stairs, slowing down when he sees the state of Brad between us. "Uncle Brad?" he questions, the concern in his voice and on his face a good indication of how terrible Brad looks. "Is that a bullet wound?"

Fuck it. "Uncle Brad's feeling a bit under the weather, kid," I explain as we carry him past.

"I would too if I'd been shot," Daniel says, chasing our heels. "You're not gonna die, are you, Uncle Brad?"

"I feel like it, kid," he murmurs.

"What happened?"

I look across to Ringo, who shrugs, lost too. I need to call Rose. Give her the heads-up.

"Is this mafia business?" he asks.

"The fuck?" Brad blurts, stopping from dragging his feet, forcing me and Ringo to stop too. "No, this is red paint."

"I know you're all mafia." Daniel rolls his eyes. "Everyone knows."

We all stand like plums, none of us knowing what the hell to say. "Mafia?" I laugh like a dick. "What movies have you been watching?"

"Daniel?" Esther appears at the end of the corridor, a tea towel in her hand. She's obviously not entertaining Otto right now, because he's nowhere in sight. Retreated? Cleaning up his wounds? "What are you doing?" she calls, eyes darting between Daniel and Brad.

"Brad's been shot." He says it too nonchalantly, like it's normal. He's not my kid, but I'm really not cool with this. Yet how the fuck do you shield him when he lives under the same roof as *this*?

"I've not been shot," Brad argues. "Mister and I were . . . paintballing. He's a shit shot."

"He's shit at poker too. Did you know that?"

"Watch your language!" Goldie snaps.

Daniel rolls his eyes. "Where is he, anyway?"

"Mister? Umm," I stutter, seeing the bloodbath that was Danny's face and his psycho eyes as I left. "He's—" The office door flings open behind us and Danny steps out, his face smeared in blood. I close my eyes and exhale. Rose is going to hit the fucking roof.

"Mister?" Daniel says, anxious, moving forward. "What happened?"

Danny waves it off like it's nothing. "Otto and I had a disagreement. I'm fine."

"Is it because he's in love with Grandma?"

Goldie snorts, I cringe, and Doc orders us onward.

"Come on, Daniel," Esther says, a little high-pitched. "I need some help in the kitchen."

His shoulders drop. "Mom said I could go out on the water when I've finished my studies, but the Vikings have gone shopping with them."

"I'll take him," Goldie volunteers without hesitation, clearly needing a break from us idiot men.

"I'll come too," Esther says, lifting her nose. "I could do with some air and adult company."

Ouch.

"Mum," Danny murmurs, sounding sorry.

"I'll be ready in a minute." Dismissing him, Esther leaves, and the door behind us slams.

"Go get ready," Goldie orders Daniel. "Meet me at the car in five."

He nods, looking back at the office door, concerned. "He's okay, kid," I say, carrying on with Brad. "Go get ready."

"And you, Uncle Brad? Are you okay?"

"I'm fine, kid," he groans. "Just a graze." Then he curses under his breath. "If you're lucky, I'll whoop your ass at COD later."

Daniel snorts, reaching Esther. "I'm unbeatable."

We make it to Brad's room and get him on the bed, and Doc cleans him up while I take care of a few emails. "Just a graze," Doc says, peeking over the top of his glasses, making me raise my eyes from my mobile on a small smile. "All back together again." He nods at his own handiwork and sniffs. "This time, when I say strict bedrest, I mean strict bedrest."

"Yes, sir."

"Don't mock me." Doc snaps his bag shut. "Remember who

supplies the pain meds around here." He slips two pills on the nightstand.

Brad sighs, settling into the mattress and closing his eyes, and Doc wanders to the door.

I watch the old boy go. "Hey, Doc," I call, pulling him to a stop. He looks back. "Thank you."

He nods, short and sharp, and leaves, and I stare at the wood for a while, remembering the first time I set eyes on Doc in a hotel after I'd removed Beau from hospital. I know nothing about him, other than he came out of retirement to help me when Beau had been shot. Now, though? Now I'm wondering where he's been, who he is, what he's done. I return to my phone and pull up Google, typing in Doctor . . . "Fuck," I breathe, laughing to myself. I don't even know his name.

"What are you laughing at?" Brad asks, opening one eye to look at me.

"Do you know Doc's name?"

"Yeah," he says, patting down the covers with his good arm.

"What is it?" I go back to Google, poised, ready to type.

"Doc."

"You dick," I mutter, and he smiles. "Feeling better?"

"Peachy." He wriggles his head on the pillow. "Bet you're reconsidering letting me hire Beau now, huh?"

"Do you honestly think Beau would be fulfilled doing the club's accounts?" I ask on a laugh. "She was nicknamed Lara Croft, Brad. Pen-pushing isn't in her."

He pouts. "Accepted."

"Good, now shut the fuck up about it."

Knock, knock.

"Come in," I call. "That'll be your coffee. Or your tea." A few seconds later, the door opens. It's not a Starbucks, and it's not one of Esther's good old English cups of tea. An explosion of red appears. "Pearl?" I say, getting up from my chair, thinking she's probably lost. Looking for the TV room. The kitchen. The—

"Hi." Her accent is local to London. Surrey, at a guess. She looks better, brighter, more awake and less sallow.

"You okay?" I tilt my head, curious, seeing her look past me.

"Just checking on . . . Brad?"

"Yeah," I murmur, looking back, seeing the man himself as stiff as a board on the bed. "That's Brad." His eyes are fixed on Pearl. The atmosphere is thick. I feel like an imposter.

Should I leave?

She's nibbling her lip, awkward as fuck, and Brad is doing nothing to make her feel comfortable. "I'm just gonna use the—"

"What can I do for you?" Brad asks, sounding cold and curt. Intended?

"I just wanted to thank you."

"For what?"

"Well"—Pearl glances at me, taking the hem of her shirt, definitely one of Beau's, and twists it in her grasp—"for rescuing me."

"This ain't no fairy tale," he grunts, scowling at himself, resting a palm over his wound. "I'm no white knight."

"I never said you were." She stands taller. "I just wanted to thank you."

"Thank him too, then." Brad points at me, and Pearl smiles awkwardly. What the fuck is he doing, other than making himself look like a total wanker?

"Thanks."

I wave it off. "Good to see you looking better."

She backs out of the room, looking uncomfortable, and as soon as the wood comes between us, I turn to Brad. "What the fuck was that?"

He huffs and looks away.

"You didn't have to be such a dick."

"What does she want from me?"

"Nothing. Maybe an appreciation of her appreciation."

"She's deluded. She thinks because I helped her out of there I'm some sort of hero."

"She's twenty-one. Of course you're her hero, you knob."

He darts stunned eyes my way. "Twenty-one?"

"Yes, twenty-one."

"How do you know she's twenty-one?"

"Because Beau told me she's twenty-one."

"Twenty-one," he murmurs, settling, staring down at the blankets. "That's—"

"Twenty-one," I say, confirming it, as if I need to.

"Quite young."

"Thirteen years younger than you. Nearly fourteen."

"Doesn't sound so bad when you put it like that."

Oh fuck. "Brad," I say slowly. "What the fuck?"

"What the fuck, what?"

"Oh shit."

"Where's my damn tea with sugar?"

"I'll let you ask Esther in that exact tone."

"Yeah . . ." He scowls, and it's fucking fierce. "No."

I settle in my chair, watching him falling into thought. I'm no woman, but I'm so fucking curious what those thoughts are. I pull out my mobile and send a text to the girls, asking them what they know about Pearl, and, as I should have expected, I get a one-word answer from both of them.

Why?

Why? Yes, why? Why can't women ever just answer a question without a fucking question?

"Who are you texting?" Brad asks.

"No one." My thumb darts across the screen, explaining why I'm asking.

"Then what are you doing?"

"Shut up. You're like a woman sometimes."

"Fuck y—"

The door flies open, and Otto fills the doorway with his laptop resting on a palm. I don't like the look in his eyes. The glimmer of threat tells me he's just discovered something I'm not going to like. "Cartwright's turned up."

"Where?"

"At the beach."

I'll ask, but I know I don't need to. "And what was he doing at the beach?"

"Being dead."

I slam my phone into the arm of the chair. "Fuck!" This is going to add fuel to Beau's fire, and the flames will be justified. Something very fucking dodgy is going on.

Otto paces toward me and crouches down, showing me the screen of my laptop. "Bud just sent me this."

I stare at a picture of a washed-up dead body. "Well, it's a nice day for sunbathing," I muse, just as Ringo strolls through the door with a Starbucks in one hand and a cup of Esther's tea in the other.

"That's not all." Otto delights me with another image that makes me laugh under my breath. "Yeah," he says, studying it as well, turning the ring in his slightly swollen, very purple lip. "Natalia Potter sure does have some interesting friends."

"Hello," Brad calls, having us both look up. Otto turns the screen and he recoils. "Think I'll take a Scotch instead."

"What's going on?" Ringo asks.

"Cartwright is dead and Agent Higham's lunching with Natalia Potter."

He sneers. "The journalist who wrote the—"

"Are you about to state the obvious?" Brad asks, claiming the cup of tea on a flinch.

"No, I'm asking a question to confirm where I think this is leading." Ringo looks at me, and I nod. It's leading to Beau going full force into cop mode.

"No one breathes a word of this to Beau," I say, hating the disgusted look on Brad's face. Couldn't give a fuck. I'm protecting her.

My phone rings in my hand, and everything inside sinks when I look at the screen. The tension I'm suddenly feeling must be palpable, because when I look up, everyone is staring at my phone. I know I don't want to take this call. I *know* it. Cartwright turning up dead doesn't only mean Beau's about to get the extra shove she doesn't need, it also means that small part of me that hoped The Bear had disappeared will be disappointed.

I inhale, push my fingertip into the screen, then click it straight to speaker, swallowing down the anger crawling up my throat.

Silence.

And with each second that passes, my heart booms that little bit harder.

"Did you miss me?" he finally asks. The sound of his voice, the distorter, makes me close my eyes and force my breathing to steady before I explode.

"As it happens, yes," I say quietly. "I thought I'd been robbed of the opportunity to tear you apart."

"So you're pleased to hear from me?"

"Thrilled."

"Good. Then I'll make my next move." The line goes dead, and the tension in the room goes through the roof, everyone still, quiet, looking at each other.

Waiting.

For what? An explosion? A bullet? A fire? A missile through the fucking window?

Fuck!

"Someone get Danny up here," I say as I dial Fury, going to the window and looking out onto the grounds. For what, I don't fucking know. "Now!" I yell. Fury answers. "Get the girls home now," I order.

"Boss," he confirms, hanging up, getting straight on it.

"Call Goldie. Get them back from the boatyard." I pace, cursing under my breath. "Get Leon on the phone. Tell him to clear the cabin."

"The club," Brad says from the bed. "Nolan, the girls. Someone pass me my phone." I take it off charge on the nightstand and hand it to him, and he strains to sit up, dialing and taking it to his ear.

Otto has the CCTV stream for the club up on his screen before I have the chance to ask, and I watch the shot of the front of the building, holding my breath, as if waiting for it to blow up there on the screen.

"He's not answering," Brad says, frustrated, immediately dialing again.

"Can you activate the fire alarm from the system?" I ask Otto.

He lifts a finger and pushes it down meticulously. "Done." Everyone on the screen seems to still for a moment—bartenders pausing cleaning, dancers pausing mid-practice—before the place clears and we all wait, watching, Ringo with Leon on the other line.

I can hear the beats of everyone's hearts, and the silence is only broken when Danny steams through the door at one hundred miles an hour, his face a dried bloody mess. "What's going on?" he asks, taking in the scene and wandering over, looking at the screen of Otto's laptop.

I can't tell him that we're waiting for something or someone to blow up. "Call Sandy," I say. "Tell him you'll meet him." Just because we now know The Bear is still in the game doesn't mean he still has control of the Russians, or anyone. I can get past the fact Sandy tried to kill Beau if it means I get The Bear.

"Why?" Danny asks.

"Just do it."

"So you can kill him?"

I look at him, and I don't answer because I can't promise I won't. "An old friend just called."

"Fuck," Danny breathes, raking a hand through his hair. "The girls? Mum? The kid?"

"All being brought back." I've got to face Beau. Tell her the man she desperately needs to talk to in relation to her father's death is dead. Another blow. Another setback amid the endless fucking setbacks.

Danny nods, his eyes dropping to the carpet. "I don't know whether to be relieved or stressed." I think he's speaking for us all.

"He's definitely been lying low. Waiting for something."

"But what?"

"I don't know." I look out of the window, returning my eyes to the outside world, scanning, watching. *Come on, what's your next move?*

"Pick up, Nolan," Brad hisses, his lips pursing, part impatience, part pain. "Fuck it." He dials again. "Someone call Mason."

Danny pulls his T-shirt up and wipes the drying blood on his face as he dials him. "Tell Nolan to check his phone," he orders shortly. Then he frowns, looking at Brad. "Nolan's not there."

"What?"

"Called earlier and said he'd be in at lunchtime."

Brad curses, continuously dialing, trying to reach Nolan. "Little fucker."

"Is everyone out of the club?" I ask.

Danny nods, going back to Mason. "Just taking precautions. I'm sending Otto over to check." He scowls. "You're asking too many questions, Mason. Just keep everyone out the back and tell Nolan to fucking call when he shows up."

That kid's getting a slap when I catch up with him, because I'm sure as shit Brad won't give him one. I bet he's living the dream in Brad's swanky loft apartment while he's laid up here recovering. In fact, I bet he's late to the club because he's cleaning up the mess from last night's afterparty back at Brad's.

"What the fuck took you so long?" Brad barks down the line when Nolan finally answers. Then he frowns. "What are you doing there?" A pause, and his frown turns into a scowl. "Fine, whatever. The club's been evacuated. Just a precaution. Otto's on his way over to check. I need you to come to Danny's. I've got some things I need to go over with you." He hangs up, muttering under his breath, and settles down. "He's at my place, just getting in the shower." he says calmly. "Heading over in a bit."

I nod, still looking out of the window, dread gripping on unrelentingly. "Fucking with us?" Danny asks, joining me.

"I don't know."

Brad's phone starts ringing, and both Danny and I turn back to face the room. It takes every effort for him to lift it to see the screen.

"Who is it?" Danny asks, seeing what I'm seeing in Brad's expression. A bit of confusion.

"Unknown number."

Looks start getting shot around the room again, everyone still and quiet as Brad answers with silence, his eyes darting across the sheets covering his waist. He's exhales, relieved. Peeks up. "It's my neighbor."

I roll my eyes, along with everyone else in the room. "Probably complaining about the noise," I mutter, but then Brad pales and his phone slides from his hand and hits the bed.

"What?" Danny asks urgently. "Brad, what is it?"

He swallows hard, his gaze jumping across his lap, and I step forward, every inch of me tense. "My . . ." He turns haunted eyes our way. "My apartment just blew up."

22

BEAU

Everyone was silent as we were driven home by Tank and Fury, with no explanation as to why our shopping trip ended so abruptly. I know we're all wondering what the hell has happened now. Of course, the moment I saw Fury's face when he answered his cell, I put the pants I was considering back on the rack and calmly walked out of the store, calling to Zinnea and Rose as I did. They too left without fuss.

When we pull up at the mansion, I see a few cars missing. So a few men have been deployed. For what?

"Home Sweet Home," Zinnea says sardonically as the three of us walk up the steps to the house. "Brace yourself, girls."

"Always," I murmur, looking across to Rose. Her lips are straight, her eyes fixed on the door. I can see it's taking everything in her not to barge into the house and scream her frustration. "Remember what Doc said," I say, as Zinnea rests a pacifying hand on her arm.

"I remember." She visibly takes a few deep breathes. "I live for the day when I'll wake up and not wonder who will try to kill my husband today."

"Well, that'll never happen," Zinnea quips, trying to lighten the mood. "Because not a day can pass without a wife wanting to kill her husband for one thing or another. It's basic marriage semantics, darling."

Rose manages a smile and, surprisingly, it's not forced, as I spin my ring on my finger. Esther answers the door before we can let ourselves in and gives us a look I'm sure we all hate. "Upstairs," she says, letting us all file in. "Brad's room."

I'm off up the stairs like a bullet, worried, and as I jog down the corridor, I see Pearl up ahead looking a little misplaced and worried. "What's going on?" I ask, slowing.

"I don't know. He was brought up a while ago. In a lot of pain. Doc came by his room, and he seemed okay when I went in to thank him. Grumpy but okay. James was in there with him."

"And now?" I ask, looking at the door, plagued by uncertainty.

"Now *everyone* is in there with him."

Everyone? "Right," I say quietly, taking the handle, scared to enter.

"Will you let me know if he's okay?" Pearl asks, and I look back over my shoulder, seeing her hands fiddling, her eyes worried.

"Of course." I push my way in, and the tension slaps me in the face. Everyone is standing, except Brad who's on the bed, but I can't see his face because Danny's blocking him. I probably don't *want* to see his face. A bedside vigil? My heart drops. Danny looks back, sees me, then looks past me. "She's coming," I say, hearing Rose behind me. "What's happened?" My eyes won't move from Brad's legs.

"Is that Beau?" Brad's voice throws me, and I quickly round Danny and find his eyes open.

All air drains from my lungs, my palm meeting my chest. "I thought you were dead," I say, relief getting the better of me.

He shakes his head, looking absolutely shell-shocked. "I should be," he says quietly, staring at the sheets around his waist.

"What happened?"

"We got a call from The Bear," James says, pulling my attention to him. I don't want to believe it. Part of me hoped he'd disappeared. Gone. I could imagine a million gruesome ways in which he died. It was the only way.

"And?" I ask, looking to Danny as Rose puts herself in his side, looking up at him. I take this moment, while I'm waiting for James to answer, to assess everyone's faces. All grave. All stressed. All grief-stricken.

"And he blew up Brad's apartment."

"Oh my God," Rose whispers behind me.

All I can think is *Thank* God. Thank God Brad was here. But something tells me I'm getting ahead of myself, and as I scan the room, mentally doing a headcount, I realize . . . "Nolan," I say quietly, dropping to my ass on the mattress and taking Brad's hand. *Oh God no. No!* Brad liked that kid. We *all* did. The right amount of cheek and charm with rough and ready. He'll be blaming himself. "Brad, you can't bl—"

"Don't say it, Beau." He pulls his hand free of mine and rubs into his eye sockets harshly. Pushing back the tears. Refusing to cry because he's Brad Black. "Leave me alone," he whispers, his nostrils flaring, anger taking over. "Everyone," he roars, exploding. "Get the fuck out!"

I stand and turn, leaving, indicating to everyone that they should do the same, and they do, giving Brad space. Letting him have a private moment to let those tears out. The anger out. I pull the door closed behind me and rest back against it.

"Is he okay?"

I drop my head and find Pearl looking anxious and out of place. "He needs a moment."

"What happened?" she asks, as everyone leaves, disbursing to various parts of the house. "Am I allowed to know?"

I swallow down the lump in my throat. "You probably don't want to."

Anya rounds the corner up ahead. She looks a hundred times better, her hair shiny, her complexion glowing. Spotting me, she smiles widely, but it drops when she sees how busy it is outside

Brad's room. I nod to Esther to take over, and she moves in, coaxing Pearl away from Brad's room and collecting Anya. I hate the curiosity on their faces. Hate it even more that being here in this house, in this world, was a better option than returning to their home countries.

I feel James's eyes on me, and as I face him, I just catch Danny's short, sharp nod as he walks Rose away and she fusses over him, rubbing gently at the blood on his face while shaking her head, biting her lip, tears in her eyes. "What the hell happened to your face?" she asks.

"It doesn't matter," Danny answers shortly, dismissing her.

"We need to talk," James says, but I don't face him. Something tells me I won't like what I'll see. "Beau?"

"I don't want to talk." I turn to him and walk into him, crawling up his body and clinging on. I just want to be for a moment. Be quiet and lost. He holds me under my ass and carries me into our room, and once he's placed me down, I make slow work of stripping him down, feeling him watching me as I do, his stance solid, his hands lifeless by his side, his tired eyes studying me. He doesn't help. Doesn't even try to rid me of my clothes. So I do it myself and push him onto the bed. Then I climb on top of him, lock eyes with his, hold his arousal upright, and sink slowly onto him on an exhale that shakes me, each inch taming the unrest within. His hands move to my hips, his lips part, his eyes become hooded, as I start to circle him slowly, my palms braced on his chest.

"Did you find anything to wear tomorrow?" He strains the words on a hoarse voice, and I smile serenely. He's trying to make normal conversation during quite abnormal sex.

"Shut up, James," I order, dropping my chest to his and kissing him hard, my hands delving into his hair and fisting.

I have the upper hand for only a few seconds before I'm flipped onto my back. He pants down at me as his hips gradually push forward and he fills me again, watching me as he does. I suck in air and his eyes smoke. "That good, Beau?"

I shove my hips up, taking him all the way, and he hisses

through his teeth. "I don't know, is it?" I swivel a few more times, working him up, and then shoot up, sending James to his back again, but this time we land on the floor with a thud. I take his dick again and guide him to me, slipping down onto him.

He groans, his back arching, his hands taking my breasts and feeling, pinching, pulling. "Fine," he relents, moving one hand to my arm and stroking down my scar before taking it to my stomach and circling my bullet wound.

"Want me to help you escape?" I ask. He darts his eyes to mine, surprised, and I grind onto him firmly, swallowing back my whimper at the deep invasion, closing my eyes for a few moments. I see me. Standing before James in his glass box, begging him to take me away. And he did. I don't know what he wants to talk about, but I know I won't like it. I see the anguish on his tired face. The suffering. The need to have this done with. I open my eyes. "Give me your hands," I whisper, and he does, holding them up. Unlike him, I won't restrain him. Tie him up. Make him helpless. I thread my fingers through his and hold them, moving lazily, watching our hands grip, flex.

Fused.

"I love you," he whispers.

"I think you're talking too much."

He smiles mildly, flexing his fingers more. "Are you going to gag me?" He bites down on his bottom lip. He's close.

"I don't think we have time." I take our joined hands down to his stomach and hold them there, gaining memento, thrusting more. He holds his breath. My skin burns. "Go on, James. Let it bend you. Let it break you." I'm jolted when he jerks violently, throwing his head back, his spine arching harshly, and while watching him bend and break, I come calmly on a mild tremble, my pleasure intense but calm, and mostly coming from watching James fight his way through until his body goes limp and sweat trickles down his temples, wetting his hair. He breathes heavily. Taking a moment in his darkness while I watch him. Feeling his hot essence warm my insides.

I swallow and rest my cheek on his chest, feeling his hand come to my back and hold me. I close my eyes, knowing what James is thinking in his darkness as he strokes me softly between my shoulder blades, slowly throbbing inside me, unsheathed, dripping his seed. Wondering if my body has accepted it. My guilt flames.

"What did you need to talk about?" I ask, cowardly trying to distract myself from my dishonesty.

"It can wait."

I don't argue. I just need to be here, quiet, still, and calm for a while.

When I wake up, I'm in bed and James isn't, which means he's got us off the floor at some point and put me in here. I didn't even stir. Slightly disorientated, I sit up, glancing around our light bedroom before I get up and stretch my way to the bathroom, putting myself in front of the mirror. I tie my hair back and open the drawer of the vanity, rummaging to the bottom. I pull out the pack of pills from a cosmetic bag and pop one, pushing back the stupid guilt. Stupid because James didn't want to try. And now, neither do I. I hide them in the drawer and leave the bathroom, pausing in the middle of the room, looking around me, my brain now more awake. My heart starts a relentless beat. Dad's funeral.

"Shit!" I search for my phone in the bedsheets, on the night-stand, growling when I don't find it. I throw on James's T-shirt, pull on his sweats, and pull the door open. I nearly charge into Zinnea who's on the other side, fist poised ready to knock. I look down her front, blinking back the blinding sparkle of her outfit. I'm surprised she's chosen to go all out as Zinnea for Dad's funeral, to be honest. But then again, it's the best way to give a final *fuck you* to her bigoted brother, one he can't retaliate to, since he's dead.

"I'll be ready in just a minute," I say, looking back at the room. "Fuck!" I won't because I don't have anything to wear. I go to the closet and swing it open, rummaging through my endless pairs of jeans and shirts.

"Ready for what?" Zinnea asks from the door. I pause sliding hangers across the rail and face her, noticing, now my brain is a little more awake, that she's wearing the same clothes as yesterday.

"What day is it?" I ask.

"The same day it was a few hours ago when we got back from our brief, rather unproductive shopping trip."

"Oh." My shoulders drop, and I laugh a little. "I thought today was . . ." I rub at my forehead. I must have been in a deep, deep sleep.

"Have you eaten today?" she asks, concerned.

I shake my head, my stomach rumbling in response too. "I'm starving," I admit.

"Esther's got a big pot on the stove." She holds her hand out to me, and I take it, letting her lead me to the good stuff. The smell hits me as soon as I get to the top of the stairs, and the sounds from the kitchen confirm it's as good as always. I walk in and find everyone around the table, and James drops his spoon, standing. "I didn't want to wake you," he says.

"Have you seen my cell?"

He holds it up. "I didn't want to wake you," he reiterates, pulling out the chair next to him. I go over, lowering next to Brad.

"You should be in bed," I say softly, and he smiles, equally as softly, but he remains quiet, not like Brad at all.

I tuck in, catching Rose's eye at the other end of the table as she butters some bread for Daniel and places it on his side plate. "Okay?" she mouths, and I nod, observing the subdued mood around the table. Everyone is quiet. Talking between themselves.

Grieving the loss of one of our own.

"Need any help?" I ask as Brad struggles to rip some bread off to dip.

"No."

"Stop being stubborn." I tear some off and turn into him, dipping it in his dish. "Open," I say quietly. He scowls but humors me, opening his mouth and taking the bread. "If this isn't a sign that you need a woman in your life—"

"I'd rather be shot again."

"So dramatic."

He falls quiet once again, stirring his stew, his sadness palpable. I don't know if any of us can convince him that this isn't his fault. I wish we could. He peeks up, but quickly looks back down again, his stirring becoming a bit heavy-handed, making his gravy splash up the side of his bowl. I look down the table and see Pearl and Anya talking to Esther, and I hum to myself, thoughtful.

I can't ask him if he's okay because that's a dumb fucking question. He's getting more worked up the longer he's sitting here, looking like he's having a mental row with himself. Blaming himself.

"Brad," I say, unable to watch him slowly spiraling again. "You—"

"I have to go," he says, standing up abruptly, grabbing the side of the table on a pained growl. The table falls silent, or even more silent, everyone's attention on Brad.

"Are you okay?" I ask, and it's impulsive. I drop my spoon and rise, moving into him.

"I have to go," he says again, keeping his eyes and face low as he turns and leaves the kitchen, everyone's apprehensive stares following him. I glance at Doc for guidance, ready to go after him. He must read my intention because he holds up a palm, making me lower slowly to the chair.

"He'll be okay," James says.

"I'm not so sure." I reclaim my spoon, but when the sound of tires screeching fills the room, I drop it, worried, and watch as Danny gets up and goes to window that looks out onto the front of the house. I stand to see, looking on as Brad drives recklessly down the driveway to the gates. He's got the use of one arm, for God's sake. "He's probably going to the club."

"He shouldn't be going anywhere," Danny says coldly. "And not because he's injured." He pinches the bridge of his nose, taking a few calming breaths, and Rose fills his wine glass and taps Daniel's hand, a signal that he may leave the table, before nodding to Tank and Fury, who both stand and follow him out. She thinks Danny's going to lose his temper.

I look at James as he slowly chews and swallows, setting his spoon down and wiping his mouth, ready to pin Danny down when he explodes. But he doesn't. He turns slowly and calmly walks back to the table, taking a seat and looking at James, who nods his acknowledgement. They will all be going to Hiatus after dinner to sort Brad out.

Everyone gets back to eating. Small talk. Then once again silence falls when the front door opens and closes. I look at James, James looks at Danny, Danny looks at Ringo, Ringo looks at Goldie, Goldie looks at Otto, like a Mexican wave of curious looks.

"He forgot his toothbrush," Danny muses, picking up his wine and pointing his attention back at the entrance into the kitchen, ready to welcome Brad home, as everyone around the table chuckles lightly, as relieved as Danny that Brad's pulled his head out of his ass long enough to realize that leaving was a bad idea, if only because he's not at full strength at the moment.

I settle back in my chair and collect the wine Brad left at his place and sip around my smile. And nearly spit it out when someone—not Brad—walks into the kitchen, cool as can be, casual, even a fucking smile on his face. And all eyes follow him from the door to the seat that Brad just vacated. So close to me, I can smell him. Clean. Fresh.

Not dead.

"Hmmm, looks yum," Nolan says, diving into the stew Brad left a moment ago as we all stare, mouths hanging open.

"What the fuck?" Danny eventually says, slowly lowering his wine to the table.

Nolan pauses, hunched over the table, just about to take another mouthful of stew, and looks up and down at the peanut gallery all looking like . . . well, like they've seen a fucking ghost. "What?" he asks, head swaying back and forth as gravy drips off his spoon. "What did I do?"

"What did you do?" Danny seethes, standing up from his chair slowly, his fists clenching. "What did you fucking do?"

Poor Nolan is as still as an ice sculpture, and probably feeling as cold too.

"You fucking died, you moron!"

"I did?" Nolan looks down his front, dismayed, as if checking he's actually here. "When?"

"Fuck me," James breathes next to me, rubbing at the lines on his forehead as Danny marches around the table and gets Nolan by his ear, literally, and drags him off out of the kitchen. Naturally, James is up in a beat.

"Not too much of that," he says, tapping the rim of my wine glass, making me shrink in my chair. He leaves the kitchen, probably to make sure Danny doesn't do the job he thought had been done—kill Nolan—and Otto, Ringo, and Goldie get up and follow.

"Just a regular family dinner," Esther says wistfully, starting to clear some plates. "Ice cream anyone?"

"Would love some," Rose says, going to the freezer and pulling out a huge tub, presenting it to the room. "Anyone else?"

"Please," Pearl calls, starting to help Esther.

"Please," Anya replies, polishing off her stew and sighing. "You are expert chef," she says to Esther. "Like my mama."

My bottom lip pushes out as I watch Anya smiling sadly. I've often felt alone, even though I've always had people around me. But to actually be alone? "You know," Zinnea says. "I was going to call myself Anya. Anya Dolly Daydream."

"Yes?" Anya replies, her eyes lighting up. "You know what it means? Anya?"

"Tell me," Zinnea orders, getting her wine and flicking her hair over her shoulder.

"It means grace."

"Oh?"

I laugh as Rose joins us back at the table with the tub of ice cream and a jar of something. "Zinnea suits you better." She pops off the lid and starts digging into the tub. "And Anya definitely suits you," she says, smiling at Anya. "And Pearl suits you. Unusual, like your ridiculously bright red hair."

Pearl reaches for her hair, tucking it behind her ears. "I always hated having red hair and green eyes."

"Why?" Rose blurts, outraged. "Oh my God, women would kill for that combination. Do you know how rare you are?"

Pearl smiles, and Rose falters in her enthusiasm. Rare. Which is exactly why she was probably taken. Like Anya, with her unique look, heart-shaped face, almond-shaped eyes, thick brows, the fullest lips, chestnut, poker-straight hair and almost gold eyes. Rare.

Not knowing what to say, Rose holds up the tub and they both nod. "I see it went well with Danny," she says with a heavy dose of sarcasm, and Esther snorts.

"You were the one who told me to put him in his place."

I catch Pearl and Anya looking curious, so I help them out and explain. This is something I *can* tell them. "Otto, that's the big hairy one with piercings, he's got a soft spot for Esther, who is Danny's Mom."

"And Danny's Rose's husband," Pearl says.

"Correct." Rose smiles across the table at her as she spoons ice cream into a few bowls. "And he's not very happy about his mom"—she points the spoon to Esther—"dating . . . well, anyone. Especially not one of *the* men."

"He's a little protective," Esther says, almost with a proud edge. She means it. Really, Danny couldn't do much wrong in her books. Murder, kidnap, gunrunning. But fighting with Otto?

"What about Brad?" Pearl asks, making Rose, Esther, and me all freeze in our chairs.

"What about him?" I ask, looking at Rose, who's looking at Pearl as curious about this as I am, as she passes a bowl across the table to her.

She picks up her spoon and starts stirring, all casual. "I just wondered if he's . . . taken." She quickly pops some ice cream in her mouth and smiles through pursed lips.

Oh dear.

"Yes," Rose blurts.

"No," I say at the same time.

"I think what the girls are trying to say," Esther says gently, "is that Brad's probably . . . umm, I think he's . . ." She looks to me for help. I have nothing.

"He's a total dick," Rose says, handing out the rest of the bowls. "You'll hate him."

Pearl smiles and Rose grabs the jar and proceeds to tip out the contents all over her ice cream.

"And he tells terrible jokes," I say, frowning at Rose's bowl.

"So, so bad," Rose confirms.

I look at Esther. She's also frowning at Rose's bowl. And Zinnea. And Anya and Pearl. And Rose is oblivious, stirring her spoon through the ice cream, mixing the pickles in with it, humming happily before getting a big spoonful and opening wide, taking it all and closing her eyes in bliss. It's fucking bliss.

"What the hell, Rose?"

Her eyes pop open and she swallows, looking down at her bowl. "I know," she cries. "It's so gross." She grits her teeth, gripping the spoon in her fist. "I can't stop it," she grates, angry with herself and this new disgusting craving. "Yesterday, I sprinkled sugar on my Mexican food." She drops her spoon and puts her head in her hands.

I see my phone at James's place and collect it, laughing at her as I stand and walk to her end. "I still love you," I say, rubbing her shoulder. "I'm going to see if they've killed Nolan yet."

Her hands fall. "I want every detail," she says.

Naturally, I think, leaving the kitchen. "Thanks for dinner."

"You should be in here helping us clean up, not in the office with the men," Esther calls, making me roll my eyes.

"I'm sure the men agree," I say, heading across the house to Danny's office and pushing my way in without knocking. The first person I see is Goldie, reminding me that they're not all men. Very good.

I close the door behind me, ignoring Danny's exasperated look, and regard Nolan on the couch, looking a bit shaken up as I stand to the side, out of the way, quiet and watchful. I'm giving no one any reason to see me out, and when I catch James's eye, I see he's caught my move, his eyebrows high. I look away.

"So if you weren't at Brad's like you said," James asks, "where the fuck were you?"

"My last installment," he says. "I was paying off my last install-ment with the loan shark."

A loan shark? Not good news. I look at James. He's scowling. "You told us you paid off the final installment *just last week.*"

"I lied. I didn't want you to think I wasn't good for the money. And Brad would have paid it for me. I'm not comfortable with that." Nolan looks around the office. "Where is he, anyway? He said he had business to discuss."

"We don't know," Danny says quietly, lowering to his chair.

"What do you mean, you don't know?" Nolan stands, his eyes wide and worried.

"He's probably gone to the club."

"He's not here?"

"No." Danny's lips twist. "He stormed out. Don't know whether you noticed, but for some strange reason, he's quite attached to you." I smile on the inside when I see Nolan's worry lift a fraction to make way for happiness. "He was quite cut up when we thought you'd gone up with his apartment," Danny goes on, getting up and wandering over to Nolan, getting up in his face. "So what lesson have you learned today, boy?"

"Not to lie."

"Be straight with us, you hear me?" He pokes him in the shoul-der. The Brit is capable of so much more but, even if Danny's not saying it, he's quite attached to Nolan too. We all are. "Now sit down."

"He's injured." Nolan looks between us. "Doc said he should be resting."

"I told you to sit the fuck down," Danny barks, frustrated.

Nolan moves a few paces and squeezes between Ringo and Otto, forcing them to shift and yank their jackets out from under Nolan's ass.

"Now." Danny sits back at his desk. "Someone call Brad and tell him his pet's alive and well."

"He's not taken his phone," Otto replies.

"What?" James is across the room in the second, looking at Otto's screen, which I expect shows Brad's phone's location. Here. "Why the fuck would he do that?"

Danny goes straight to his cell. "Is Brad there?" he asks. Then he curses, giving us all the answer. "Where the fuck has he gone?"

Nolan stands, panicked, and James approaches behind him, pushing into his shoulders, forcing him back down. "We'll find him," he says robotically, his face straight, looking at Danny, who looks plain furious.

I feel like a fly on the wall, observing our men in their natural habitats. Being The Brit and The Enigma.

My head is ping-ponging back and forth, watching, listening. Fascinated.

James gets his cell out of his pocket and starts pacing, his attention on the screen, and Danny shakes his head to himself, still angry, but I know he'll be more worried. "I haven't got fucking time to go on a wild goose chase. Get me Len's location. I want to know what the fuck happened to Fra—" His phone pings, and he growls, swiping it up, his eyes traveling across the screen. Then he looks at James. Thinks. And calmly puts his cell down and stands. "Find Brad," he snaps, stomping out of the office, my eyes following his pent-up form. That's it?

"Come," James says, ushering me out, and I go, despite being suspicious. Danny wasn't finished with business.

And then suddenly, he was.

What the fuck's going on?

23

JAMES

"That was weird," Beau says, looking up at me as I walk us down the corridor with absolutely no idea of where I'm taking her. Just away. From Danny. From the men. Anyone who might accidently blurt the latest news about Frazer Cartwright's death. I need to think about this. Beau will be off around Miami trying to solve this mystery before I've had a chance to jump-start my brain. "Danny seemed like he wanted to say something and then didn't."

I keep my attention forward. "He did?" Lame. So fucking lame. Everyone in the room sensed what Beau sensed, but I had no choice. I could see Danny was about to launch into one of his little recaps on all the shit going down, and that recap would have included the fact that Frazer Cartwright's dead. So I sent him a quick text telling him to shut the fuck up. Luckily, he got my message before his mouth caused us more problems.

"Yeah, he did." Beau stops us walking and turns into me. *Fuck.* "What's going on?"

I laugh, and it's natural. "What's going on?" Where the fuck would I start? "You know what's going on. You're making a point of knowing what's going on."

Her eyes narrow accusingly. I don't shy away. "And what happened to my surprise?"

Fuck.

"It—"

Her phone saves me, and Beau huffs, looking at me like a woman looks at a man when she's communicating silently that she's not done. "Hello," she answers, sounding irritated. Then her face drops, and our previous discussion is forgotten. "Oh," she breathes, making me cock my head in question. She inhales, as if bracing herself, and nods. "I'm sorry. Is it too late?" She covers her mobile with a hand and moves it away from her ear. "Can you take me somewhere?"

"Anywhere," I answer quickly, slightly surprised.

She nods and goes back to her mobile. "I can be there in an hour." A swallow. "Yes." Her eyes close briefly. "Thank you." Then she hangs up, and I stand before her waiting. Looking patient but not feeling it.

"Where am I taking you, Beau?" I ask, after a long few seconds of silence.

"To see my dad," she finally says, shuddering, like ice could have just glided down her spine. "I want to see him before the funeral tomorrow."

I withdraw, taken aback. I can't hide my surprise.

"I was never able to see Mom." She frowns as she toys with her phone.

"Are you sure?" I ask, placing a hand on her shoulder, rubbing into it gently.

She smiles. It's weak. "No," she admits, and I nod, understanding. "But I know I'll regret it if I don't." Moving into me, she wraps her arms around my waist and . . . hides.

I can hear her mental war as I drive her to the funeral home. Guilt is driving her. Nothing but guilt. She's spinning her ring on her finger, checking the GPS constantly to see how far away we are.

When I park, I turn in my seat to face her. No typical words will suffice here. I can't ask her if she's sure she wants to do this. I can't question whether she would prefer to remember her father as he was. Alive. Beau's memories of him aren't exactly fond. So instead, I say, "Okay?" and I feel like a useless sack of shit for it.

On a nod, Beau unclips her seatbelt, takes a visible inhale, and gets out of the car, looking up at the front of the building as she does. I join her on the sidewalk. "Do you want me to come in?" I ask. She nods, so I hold my hand out for her to take and lead the way, hating this uncertainty on her. The door opens before we get there, an old fella who's suited greeting us with a sympathetic smile.

"You must be Miss Hayley," he says, his voice loud, like he hopes to raise the dead in his care. He opens the way, allowing us to step into the reception area. It's cozy in a sickly way. Full of florals—the paper, the prints, the carpet. But it reeks of death. "I'm Arnie Gluttenhiem."

"Thank you for keeping open so late," Beau says, gazing around, moving into my side and clinging on to my arm.

"What, dear?" he yells, leaning in.

"I said—"

"What was that?"

"I was going to say—"

"Damn hearing aid has broken again." He taps his ear, where a wire hangs just below his lobe.

"Thank you!" Beau yells, making me wince.

He waves off her appreciation. "Death isn't a nine-to-five job," he shouts, sweeping an arm out toward the back of the room where three doors are. "The one on the right. Your father's ready for you."

Beau stares at the door, frozen, breathing heavily.

Torn.

"Take your time," I say quietly. "Do you want to sit down for a moment?"

She shakes her head, stepping forward. And again. And again. I follow her lead, until we're at the door. She takes the handle. Stills.

"Do you mind if I go in alone?" she asks, looking up at me, almost in apology. "I have some things I want to say to him."

"You do what you have to do." I detach her from my side and drop a kiss onto her forehead. "I'll be here."

I take a seat on one of the floral chairs and watch as she starts again to build the strength she needs to go inside and confront her father. Because that's what she'll do. Confront him. Have it all out. Tell him how he made her feel, how much she needed him. That he wasn't there.

Closure.

I mentally will her on, encourage her, push her, my body tense in the seat. She takes the doorknob. Her shoulders raise with a confidence-hitting inhale.

Then she drops her hold and moves back, exhaling. "I can't," she says to the door, forcing me to my feet. "I can't do it." She swings around, her eyes flooded with tears ready to fall, her head shaking, dislodging them, making them tumble down her pink cheeks.

I don't get the chance to go to her. She comes to me, crushing her body into mine, holding on. Needing me. And I fucking hate it. I envelop her in my arms. Safe. "I don't want you to regret it," I say, my nose in her hair, feeling her tears soaking through my T-shirt and finding my skin.

Then she's out of her hiding place again, roughly wiping at her cheeks, looking back at the door, the internal battle ongoing. "Okay," she says to herself, going to the door again. I hate this. How she feels. Her inner turmoil. Because there is fuck all I can do to fix it. She takes the knob, turns it, pushes the door open a fraction, takes another deep breath.

I'm watching her so closely, my eyes fixed, my mind focused, that I startle when my phone rings. Beau swings around to face me, watching me rummage through my pocket. I pull it out. Roll my eyes at the screen. "It's just Goldie," I say, letting it ring off, returning my attention to Beau. And so now we will begin the whole torturous, painstaking task of building the strength to enter again. "Go," I say, soft but firm, nodding to the ajar door. She looks over her shoulder, contemplating the wood.

My phone dings. Goldie. And what her message says sends chills down my spine.

Incoming!

I look over my shoulder to the door as I draw my gun, seeing shadows of men approaching through the frosted glass. "Fuck," I hiss, scanning the reception area, noting the old boy at the desk lost in paperwork, the cameras, all the doors. Beau's attention is back on me when I find her, eyes questioning but knowing. She starts scanning the place too, and she's off across the carpet fast, heading for a door in the corner. I go after her, looking back, seeing the shadows closer, motionless on the other side of the door. Checking their weapons.

Beau pushes into the door and I follow her through, closing it quietly behind me, taking a moment to reassess where we are. The metal drainage channels on the floor tell me before I have a chance to look up and see the dead body on the slab. Ice-cold air radiates from the corpse, making me shudder, and Beau stares at the old woman, as still as her.

"Beau," I say, taking her arm and pushing her toward a door on the other side of the room with an illuminated EMERGENCY EXIT sign above it. I believe this might be an emergency. I push into the metal handle and break out into a yard. The metal gate on the other side is chained and padlocked. "Fuck it," I mutter, grabbing one of the many industrial trashcans and pushing it up against the wall as something flies past me. I freeze and look up, seeing Beau on top of the wall. She looks down at me halfway to positioning the trash can to use as a lift.

"Take your time," she says casually, turning and falling to the ground on the other side.

"Beau," I hiss, livid, as I haul my big body up the wall on a few grunts, my muscles yelling for a break. She didn't even check if the fucking coast is clear.

I drop down the other side. "Don't ev—"

"The coast was clear," she says tiredly, motioning to the empty alleyway, just as a thud sounds behind us. She looks back, and I just know what she's thinking. "The old man."

"We can't be sentimental, Beau." We're running for our fucking lives.

"But—"

I move onward, my gun in one hand, Beau in the other, practically manhandling her. "He'll be fine." I don't know that at all.

"What if—"

"Beau, I haven't got time for this," I hiss, poking my head around the corner, seeing my Range Rover up the street. A BMW is directly outside the funeral home, a driver at the wheel. Where the fuck is Goldie?"

And like she's heard me, she appears at the back of the BMW, armed, and walks down the side of the car. The whooshing of a bullet leaving a chamber sounds and blood splatters the screen.

Goldie looks at the door to the funeral home, and I whistle to get her attention, just as a thud sounds behind us, accompanied by a rush of foreign words. Polish.

I release Beau, giving her a look to suggest that if she moves, she'll be getting it, and she holds her hand out. I'm not a stupid man. I give her my gun and arm myself with the other in the back of my jeans as I lift a trash can and gently place it down by the wall, stepping up and plastering my back to the bricks. I'm about to tell Beau to get in position by the gates, but she's already there, poised, ready. I hate the sense of unstoppable pride I feel. Hate that she knows what she's doing.

A head appears over the wall, and before he has a chance to spot me, I grab his jacket and haul him over. He hits the floor with a splat and Beau has a bullet in him before I've even aimed.

"Three more," Goldie says, joining us.

Bang!

"Two." Beau moves back against the wall and looks at me. There's no amusement on her face. No smugness. She's just doing what needs to be done, and I fucking detest that she does it so fucking well.

"Concentrate," I order, peeking up as another head appears. I reach back, straining, gritting my teeth through the pull of my muscles, and yank the fucker over. His gun fires while he's sailing through the air, and I see Beau lean back, her eyes widening. "Beau," I yell, a million unwanted memories flooding back as I jump down off the trash can and run to her.

More bullets fire, one after the other, pinging off the metal rods of the gate. I flinch and duck, feeling one graze the back of my arm. I make it to Beau, slightly confused when I find her still standing, dread squeezing every one of my internal organs.

She looks at me, lifting her arm. I see a hole in the sleeve of her shirt and flat-out panic, yanking it up her scarred arm. Nothing. I turn her arm over, checking every inch of it. No holes. No blood. "Jesus," I whisper, pushing her against the wall with my body, effectively hiding her. Being a human shield.

"One more," Goldie says, standing above the motionless body of my latest victim and pulling the trigger.

"Where's the girl?" a thick Polish accent says.

I inhale, feeling Beau moving ever so slightly, her eyes pointing downward, like she's gaging something. She is. Fuck me, I need to stop underestimating her. Worry is natural. She lines her legs up with mine and stills, slowly lifting her head and looking up at me. Her eyes tell me what to do. I follow the sound of the voice, looking behind me, seeing a gun aimed at Goldie, another at me.

Goldie immediately drops her weapon, and I follow suit, keeping my arms by my side, making myself as wide as possible as I return my attention to the wall. And to Beau. "One o'clock," I mouth.

If I wasn't body to body against her, I wouldn't know she'd moved.

Bang.

"Fuck me!" Goldie yelps, as I fly around, seeing The Shark hit the deck, his eyes open, a bullet hole placed precisely in between his eyes. Beau's soon pushing her way past me, going to the body and standing over it. She considers him for a few moments, then pokes his thigh with the toe of her converse, like she needs to check he's really dead.

I look at Goldie. She's staring at Beau, somewhere between awe and shock. *Jesus fucking Christ.*

I go to her, taking the gun. "Stay," I order seriously, before going to the gates and peering through. A bin labelled INCINERATOR is by the door. "Bolt croppers?" I look back at Goldie, who nods sharply and jogs off, returning a few seconds later. She takes care of the thick chain raveled around the gate with ease, the metal pinging loose with one cut, and I pull the huge trash can out onto the alleyway and flip the lid open. Beau takes the initiative to hold it, stopping it from rolling away, while Goldie and I start collecting up the bodies and dumping them inside one by one, my muscles getting another punishing. We leave the biggest for last, Goldie and I considering The Shark for a moment, also taking a quick breather, before moving in. I take his arms, she takes his legs.

"Jesus," she grunts, going a little blue on the face. "They should have called him Megalodon."

I have to agree. The guy is a ton weight. "Ready," I heave, bracing myself to hoist him up.

"Yep."

We both strain under the weight of him and slowly but surely ease him up to the trash can, getting him on the edge and nudging him in on top of his men. Beau flips the lid and frowns when she tries to push it back into the yard of the funeral home.

I give her a hand, ignoring her indignant look when I push it along with relative ease. "Don't even think about lifting more weights," I warn, knowing she would, just to prove a point. I love her petite, athletic frame.

"Arnie," she says, taking off around the front.

"God damn it, Beau," I breathe, going after her.

"She's a constant flight risk," Goldie moans, following. "Why can't she be like all the other women at home?"

"Because then she wouldn't be Beau," I say to myself as Beau pushes her way through the door, coming to an abrupt halt. I make it to her and look past her, to the old boy who's just coming out of the room where Beau's dad is laid. The confusion he's sporting is quite endearing. Then he spots us and that confusion multiplies. He looks back to the door, then to us again.

"I think I need a vacation."

I look around the place. Nothing is touched. There's no blood, no evidence that anyone was here. Gentle, calming music plays, and I wonder what the fucking point is. Old Arnie here can't possibly hear it. "Are you okay?" Beau asks.

"What's that, dear?" he yells.

My God, his lack of hearing may have saved his life. "I said, are you okay?" Beau shouts.

"No need to shout, dear." He thumbs to the door behind him. "I have to close sometime this evening."

"Yes, of course." She steps forward. Then stops abruptly and reverses, her back meeting my chest. "I'm good," she says, forcing her body into me so I walk back too.

"You don't want to?"

"No." She shakes her head vehemently. "I've seen enough dead bodies for today. Thank you, Mr. Gluttenhiem," she calls, but of course the old man just puts a hand up, not hearing. "Let's go."

"Wait." I stop her, taking the tops of her arms and hunkering down. "Are you sure?"

She nods, swallows, and that's all I need. I put an arm around her and lead her back to the car. "You were following us," I say to Goldie, who completely ignores me. "Did you know they'd be tailing me?"

"No, but I wasn't taking any chances after Brad's place was blown up."

I put a quiet Beau in the car and close the door, facing Goldie. "Thank you."

"Shut the fuck up and finish this shit." She stomps off.

"Goldie?" I call.

"What?"

"Ever leave the house alone again, I'll kill you."

"I'm beginning to think death is the more appealing option to life right now." She gets in her car, slams the door, and screeches off, and the stench of burning rubber fills my nose.

"Never," I say quietly, climbing into my Range. I look across to Beau, the words I need to say ready to fall out of my mouth. *Tell her! Tell her Cartwright's dead!*

Except I can't. I know she'll already be wondering why the fuck The Shark came after me at the funeral home where her father is being kept. Wondering if he had anything to do with Tom's death. Adding the dead journalist to the mix will guarantee me a headache of epic proportions. I feel like we're inching closer to some fucking answers, so the last thing I need is Beau performing one of her disappearing acts.

24

BEAU

Voicing my suspicions won't do me any favors. It'll just make James lock down his already secure hold of me. The Polish turning up at the funeral home where Dad is was easy to explain. They followed us. Simple. But followed us from where? The mansion? I doubt it. That place is overrun with cameras. A pussy cat on the street would be considered suspicious and would be brought to Danny's or James's attention if it hung around long enough. So a BMW full of overweight Polish men? Not likely. That alone makes me question what the fuck is going on. Add in the small matter of Danny so obviously catching his tongue in his office before he said something in my presence, my ever-present cop senses are going into overdrive.

When we got back to the house, I left James to go fill in Danny and the rest of them on what went down, taking myself off to our room. I tried Ollie again, my worry increasing. I can't call the police —they won't talk to me. I no longer have contact details for his parents either. At desperation point, I searched social media for them, knowing I was searching in vain. Ollie's parents are in their seventies and could never fathom anyone's interest in living their lives online.

I gave up and dropped off to sleep, wishing the next day here sooner so I can get it out of the way.

And deal with the other avalanche of shit sliding our way.

I step out onto the driveway, smoothing down the black pencil dress that Rose pulled out of her closet for me. My hair is in a loose bun, my face free from makeup, my toes pinching in shoes that are too high. I can hear the hushed whispers coming from the lobby behind me. People arguing but not wanting to burden me with the politics of my father's funeral. I expect the talks seeped into the night, the men trying to figure out how they will handle today after the incident at the funeral home and Brad's apartment blowing up.

I hear steps approaching behind me. "Don't tell me I can't go," I warn, slipping my cell into my purse.

"I'm not comfortable with this, Beau."

"And I'm not comfortable not going, so we have a problem, don't we?" I look at James, all suited and booted, ready to pay respects he doesn't want to pay. Ready for a funeral he doesn't even want us to go to. Which tells me he knows he's losing this one. "I'll be late." I take the steps down and slide into the passenger seat of his Range Rover. Rose is at the door before I close it, her face solemn. "It's fine," I assure her. "I knew it was coming. Besides, no one liked him. Not even me."

"We wouldn't be going for him. I should be there. Everyone should be there for you." She holds my hand.

"But you can't be there." I reach for her head and pull her sunglasses off. "Mind if I borrow these?"

"Sure." She looks down my bare arm, contemplative. If she asks why I have my scar on full display today, I would never be able to tell her. "Have you put sunscreen on?"

"Yes, Mom."

"Good." Leaning in, she kisses my cheek. "Heads-up," she whispers. "He's going to put you in a bulletproof vest."

"What?" I blurt, looking down the lovely chic pencil dress. I want to say he's being ridiculous. I can't.

"I've put a light trench coat on the back seat. You're gonna need it."

I don't express my exasperation because, really, it's a wise move on James's part. "Has anyone heard from Brad?"

"Not that I know of." Rose looks up over the roof of the car. "Here comes Zinnea."

I slip the shades on to protect me from the unfathomable glare of her rainbow-striped sequin suit. "I should be there," she gripes. "He was my brother."

"He was horrible to you," I point out.

"'Tis true." She pouts her pink glossed lips. "Be safe."

James gets in beside me and starts the car, tense and annoyed, and I say a silent goodbye to Zinnea before she pushes my door closed. But James doesn't pull off, he just sits stationary on the driveway, drumming the steering wheel with his fingers. I glance at the clock. "We'll be late."

The back door opens, and someone gets in. I look over my shoulder. Danny's eyebrows are sky high, daring me to question him. But, of course, I do. "You're coming?" He doesn't answer, just stares at me with icy-blue unhappy eyes as he wedges his elbow into the door, getting comfortable. I return my attention forward. "Can we all agree that my father's funeral doesn't turn into a massacre?" It's a possibility that Ollie will be there, as well as Frazer Cartwright, and perhaps a few police officers too.

I get no answer.

But Danny passes something forward to me.

The coat Rose put in the car.

And a vest.

· · ·

I've felt eyes on me constantly. Had people approach me and offer their condolences. I've remained silent, accepting their words with a small, tight smile. I'm overwhelmed. There are so many people at the crematorium, many are having to stand. It's like a concert, as many bodies squished into the space as possible. This, of course, means James and Danny are twitchier. It also means it's impossible to see Ollie or Cartwright. If at all they are here. The number of mourners paying their respects says much about my father. Esteemed, generous businessman, who gave both time and money to various charitable causes. These people are mourning the loss of a pillar in their community. But is that what they're doing? Paying their respects? Mourning? Or are they here for the same reason I am? Selfishness. So that I may walk away and know I've at least made silent peace.

It's bullshit.

I'll never be at peace.

In fact, being here is making me feel worse, and that's on top of the anxiety rising within me from just being in a crowded space. All these individuals here for a man who let me down so many times. A man who wasn't there for me. A man who left me to slowly wither in a psychiatric hospital. How can he be so valued to all of these people? I want to stand up and yell at them. Tell them how much and how often he let me down. Can I? Will it make me feel better? Cure me? I'm chewing that over for most of the service, and I have my answer by the time the funeral celebrant requests we all pray. I might feel better for a few moments. Enjoy the release of pressure of simply shouting. And then I will return to wondering if he ever truly felt guilty. If he had any regrets. Because now, I *cannot* ask him. I can't ask him why he let me down. Why he kept his distance. Why he wasn't the dad I needed him to be.

I will never know!

Everyone around me stands on instruction and bows their heads. I follow, pulling the tie at the waist of my coat, tightening it, worried it will fall open and reveal what I'm wearing underneath. I don't bow my head. I don't pray. I look back to all of the people in the room, all of their faces down. My urge to yell becomes too much.

I swing back around, feeling James peek up at me, curious. "What is it?" he asks, stepping into me, prompting me to push into Danny who's on my other side. He too looks up at me.

"Nothing."

"Amen," the congregation murmurs, all lifting their heads as Dad is blessed and somber music begins to play, the curtains slowly drawing around his coffin.

Cremation.

It feels like one last kick in the gut from my father. Why would he ever wish to be scorched? Why would he make me stand here and watch his body be drawn into a raging inferno? My arm starts to tingle, and I try to blink away the black dots springing into my vision.

Burn.

My breathing diminishes.

The heat.

My heartbeats become erratic and sharp.

The unbearable, blinding heat.

Panic. It's coming.

I look up at James, finding him watching me closely. "I'm not okay," I whisper.

He's moving fast, pulling me out of the aisle and down the center of the seats, through people, all who look terribly sorry for me. *Poor girl*, they're thinking. Can't bear to say goodbye to her daddy.

Get me out!

I feel Danny close behind me, but the exit door seems to be getting farther and farther away, the room becoming smaller and smaller, the people multiplying.

I stagger along on wobbly legs, hot, dizzy, sweating, and as soon as James pushes out of the door and daylight hits me, I drag in the fresh air ravenously, releasing James's hand and resting against the wall outside. "Why would he do that?" I ask them, breathless. "Burn himself. Why?"

Of course, no one has the answer to my question, probably not even my father. I curse out loud and walk on, James and Danny as close as they can be without touching me, watchful, listening, and when we reach the end of the graveled pathway, I find myself at the foot of a wall covered in plaques, and in the center, in shiny, glimmering gold, is my father's memorial.

THOMAS JOHN HAYLEY
1964-2022
BELOVED HUSBAND AND FATHER
TAKEN TOO SOON

I stare at it. Just stare. Committing himself to an inferno wasn't his last blow at all. How can he with only four words crush me so completely? Beloved? He betrayed her! He let me down. Endlessly! Beloved? I laugh out loud.

"Beau," James says quietly.

"Did I tell you he arranged everything himself?" I say, lifting a limp arm and pointing at the plaque. "The place, how, this?"

"Let's go." Danny slips an arm around my shoulder, but I shrug it off. "If you're so sure my father's death wasn't suspicious, why do you have me in a bulletproof vest?" I ask. "And Ringo, Goldie, and Otto in position?" I look across the grounds, seeing various men in various areas.

"Brad's apartment was blown up, Beau," James says softly. "We're sitting ducks here while you say goodbye to your father."

"That's not it," I argue. "There's something more." I face them both, giving each of them a moment of my eyes, finishing on Danny. "Yesterday in your office, you were about to tell the others something." I look at James. "Then you had your cell out, and suddenly Danny was getting a message." I'm back with Danny, who's straight face gives nothing away. *Practiced.* "Then suddenly you shut up? You suddenly had nothing to say?" I look between their quiet, still forms, waiting for an explanation. I get nothing. Of course I get nothing.

"Miss Hayley?"

I look past the two unmoving towers of muscle before me to the voice and find a clean-cut looking man with short hair and an immaculately pressed blue suit.

"Monroe Metcalfe," he says, prompting James and Danny to look too, but their bodies remain facing me. Blocking me. Or blocking the world. Metcalfe gives each of their sharp faces a dubious look. "I'm terribly sorry for your loss." He smiles awkwardly, and all I can think is . . . *no, you're not sorry. You're elated, because now you have a clear path to the position of mayor.* I remain quiet before him, and Metcalfe becomes more and more uncomfortable. "He spoke of you fondly. Was very proud of you."

"What?"

James coughs, and Danny shifts, uncomfortable, and Monroe Metcalfe steps back. "Well, I should be going." He bows his head, throwing one more look at James and Danny, then backs away, buttoning his jacket as he goes.

I look around, seeing everyone filing out of the building and walking the path toward us. "Fucking hell," Danny mutters. "Higham."

My eyes dart to where they're looking, seeing a plain-clothed cop standing by the wall. Then across the way, a woman, another cop without a doubt, watching me. I know who she is. Collins.

The wise thing for me to do would be to leave. Go. Walk away. I'm not feeling very wise right now. Only reckless. Full of hatred and disappointment. I push past the men and head toward Collins.

"Whoa," James says over a non-humorous laugh, pulling me back. "That's not a good idea."

"Yes, terrible." Danny blocks the way between me and Collins, and I look between them, interested.

"How do you two know who that is?" I ask.

"How do *you*?" James counters.

"Educated guess," I retort. "Once a cop, always a cop."

"Don't I fucking know it," he mutters, taking my arm. "We're leaving."

"No." I yank myself free. "How do you know that's Collins?"

He gets up in my face, snarling. "Educated guess. Once a criminal, always a criminal."

I recoil, wounded by his cruel reminder of who he is. He's telling me without telling me there's more. "The slaps in the face just keep on coming today, don't they?" I say quietly. "Why don't you ju—"

"Oh, for fuck's sake," Danny says, pulling both of our attentions his way. His face is pure disgust with a little bit of despair too. "Burrows. I thought this was a funeral, not a fucking reunion."

My heart jumps twenty beats and James growls as I push past him. Ollie's familiar eyes speak to me, tell me to play the game, and when he gives the same look to James, I pray he reads it. Keeping his eyes on my fiancé, Ollie comes at me, lifting his arms slowly, like he's approaching with caution. He is. I remain still and unwilling as I'm taken in a hug that feels as wrong as being at my father's funeral. "Collins is asking too many questions about you, Beau," he whispers. "She's digging. Be careful."

"Get your fucking hands off her before I rip them off," James hisses ominously, making me tense everywhere in Ollie's embrace.

I gently break away and move back. "Where have you been?" I ask him. "You said you needed to speak to me and then nothing."

"I took some leave." Ollie obviously feels uncomfortable talking in front of James and Danny, his eyes constantly shooting to them, as if he thinks there's a risk of them drawing and firing at any second. "Collins is watching me like a hawk. She thinks I'm on the inside for your boyfriend and his buddy." Ollie looks at Danny and James, and Danny starts laughing in clear disbelief.

"She thinks you're working for your ex-fiancée's fiancé?" Danny's eyes move to the woman watching us from not too far away as Ollie's eyes shoot to me, and then my hand, which I find I naturally cover, much to my own annoyance, and definitely James's.

Maybe I subconsciously hoped to limit feelings from being hurt. Instead, I've poked an already coiled rattlesnake.

"No," Ollie replies, his jaw ticking slightly. "She thinks I'm being blackmailed."

"Is that why you've taken annual leave?" I ask, locking eyes with Collins. Her face suits her voice. Superior. An attractive lady, but with quite pointed features and eyes that are constantly narrowed. Suspicious. All of the time. Of everything. I know better than anyone that constant, natural suspicion doesn't necessarily make you a good cop. But it definitely makes you a less than liked one.

"I needed to step back," Ollie goes on. "Not be around when shit goes down."

"Love the way you look at us when you say that." Danny's jaw rolls. "And doesn't your absence look a bit dodgy?"

"Every step I have taken in the past week can be checked and verified," Ollie replies, making Danny laugh again.

"*Every* step?"

"Every. Single. Step."

"Even from your bed to the pisser?"

Ollie nods, looking out the corner of his eye at me. "The woman I'm seeing can vouch for every step taken in my apartment."

I feel my heart tighten in my chest, and I have no idea why. The woman he's seeing? His apartment. The apartment we shared together.

"She's an attorney," Ollie continues, as I drop my eyes to my purse and pointlessly rummage through it. Danny and James are both watching me. Looking for my reaction. I pray I'm not giving them one. I expect it's no accident that Ollie's dating a lawyer. An upstanding member of the community. Someone who would never dream of lying in a court of law.

Dating. She's staying at our place. *His* place. "What did you want to meet me for?" I ask him, forcing myself to look at him. Forcing myself not to appear hurt. I'm deplorable. I don't love Ollie anymore. Not like that. And yet . . . it still stings. Maybe it's just because I'm feeling particularly tender today. Maybe it's because

James and I are more and more at odds these days. I don't know. I want Ollie to be happy. Truly, I do. And now, as I look at him, I see the burning resentment that's been in his gaze in recent times is gone. So maybe it stings because, right now, he seems happy, content, and I am not.

Ollie clears his throat. "I wanted to tell you before you heard it from someone else."

I blink and lean back. "What?"

"About Jolene and me."

"You wanted to see me to tell me you're seeing someone?" I've spent all this time stressing out, thinking he had news on my father, and all the time he just wanted to tell me he's moved on?

"Like I said, I thought it was better to come from me."

"And the photo you sent me? Of James and his ex-fuck. If you're so happy in your new relationship, why?"

"I still care about you, Beau."

I cannot believe what I'm hearing. But . . . am I more disappointed that he's seeing someone, or that he hasn't got any information on my father? *No more hate.* This has to be a good thing. Ollie will back off, and James and Danny won't kill him. Because despite everything, I still fucking care about him too. *Pull it together, Beau.* "I'm happy for you." I force a smile and reach for his arm, giving it a brief, caring rub. "Truly. Take care, okay?"

"You too." He looks at me, almost vacant. It's weird. "Goodbye, Beau."

"Goodbye," I whisper.

Ollie gives James a look of pure hatred before he leaves, and I watch him go, my forehead heavy, something . . . off.

"Beau, we should go," James says, surprisingly softly, pulling me back to the present.

Go. Yes. I pick up my feet and get precisely two paces before I'm intercepted by a short, round man with a moustache.

"Miss Hayley, I'm Walter Foster," he says, looking quite stressed. "Your father's attorney. I have been trying to reach you at . . ."—he frowns and looks down at a piece of paper—". . . 4563 Hillcre—"

"I no longer live there. Haven't for some time."

"Ah, well, that would explain it." He lifts a knee and rests his briefcase on it, opening it while hopping around a few times, trying to keep his balance. I look at James, my eyebrows high.

He moves in and holds the man's arm. "Here, let me help you."

"Oh, very kind." He pulls out a card, puts it between his teeth, and closes his briefcase, returning to two feet.

"You know," Danny says, motioning to the card as Mr. Foster removes it from his mouth, "there's this great little device on the market that holds business cards in a handy pocket-sized contraption that you can actually keep in your pocket." He plasters on an amazed expression. "Maybe put it on your Christmas list and if you've been a good boy, Santa Claus might leave one under the tree for you."

James pinches the bridge of his nose, his eyes closed, and I turn my back on Danny, in no mood for his threatening, backward jokes.

Neither is Mr. Foster, who semi scowls before getting back to business. "I was charged with your father's financial affairs. He named me executor."

"You?"

"Yes, me. As I understand it, your parents were divorced, and my client and yourself were estranged."

"Depends when he wrote his will," I mutter, looking up to the sky for strength.

"Can we make an appointment for the reading of the will? Perhaps you could let me know when you are available." He passes me the business card.

"Now," I say, leaving the card between his fingers. "I'm available now."

"Oh, well." He pulls the sleeve of his jacket up and peers at his watch. "I have a commitment in Little Havana shortly."

"I don't think you heard the lady, Mr. Foster." Danny, hands in his pockets all casual, steps forward, and I look at him in disbelief.

"The *lady* can handle this," I say through a tight jaw, making James give Danny a *sorry* look and Danny give me an indignant one.

I return my attention to Mr. Foster. "I'm available now." I reach for the card that's in his now limp grip by his side and read the address.

"Very well." He clears his throat. "After the wake?"

"I'm not attending the wake." I walk away with James and Danny quickly on my heels, and I tell myself that the day couldn't get any worse. Then I tell myself off for telling myself that, because . . . haven't I learned? And then, like a fucking omen, something catches my eye on the other side of the parking lot, someone loitering, and I slow to a stop, trying to focus. "That's Amber," I say, not taking my eyes off her as she puts some sunglasses on and pulls a hood up over her head, slipping away, obviously because she's been spotted.

"I saw," Danny says, stepping in front of me. "What the fuck is she doing here?"

"Good question," I say quietly, overtaking Danny and running as fast as my heels with carry me toward her disappearing form.

"Beau!" James yells after me.

"For fuck's sake," Danny shouts, just as my wrist is seized and I'm pulled to a stop. I damn the heels; he would never have caught me if I were in my sneakers.

"She's gone," James breathes, the sound of screeching tires filling the air. "What the hell are you playing at?"

"If she was a gold digger, why would she be at Dad's funeral?" I ask. Danny scowls at me. I ignore him and give James my attention. "Well?"

"I don't fucking know, Beau," he admits. "I don't fucking know a lot."

"We should go," Danny says, pulling our attention his way. Collins is standing on the edge of the parking lot, observing. "Come on." He leads the way, and James claims me, marching me back to the Range Rover. "I don't like her," Danny says as we pass and her beady eyes follow the three of us.

I think he speaks for all of us.

· · ·

It's not the kind of office I would expect the attorney of my father to operate from. It's poky. Drab. Unassuming and unimpressive. I'm sitting in an uncomfortable chair opposite Mr. Foster, flanked by two men who hardly fit in their chairs, their big bodies shifting constantly to try and get comfortable. "Can I take your coats?" Foster asks.

The vest beneath my trench coat becomes heavier, and James and Danny both lift their asses in unison and pull their coats in a little more. "No, thank you," I say, swallowing, just wanting him to get on with it.

"Very well." He starts fiddling with papers on his desk, leaving the room to fall silent.

"You could have waited outside," I say quietly to Danny, as his cell rings. He reaches into the inside pocket of his coat and pulls it out. I see Rose's name on his screen. She'll be worried.

"You know, I think I will." He stands and connects the call, striding out. "Baby," he says softly, closing the door behind him.

I feel James's hand take mine where it's resting on my knee, and I look down at it, then up to him. I hate the torture in his expression. The helplessness. And yet I am without the capacity to reassure him. How can I when I'm struggling to calm myself? And how can I when I know I'm being kept in the dark? It's disheartening when we have both fought so hard to be free of darkness. How willing he is to leave me there.

Mr. Foster twiddles with the end of his moustache as he looks over the papers on a poorly concealed frown, like he could be struggling to utter the words before him, so after a few painful minutes, I take the lead. "Mr. Foster, let me make this easy. I would like everything from my father's estate to be donated to the World Society for Burn Victims." He would probably turn in his grave . . . had he not chosen cremation.

When I feel James's eyes turn onto me, I shrug. I don't need my father's money. Don't *want* it. My hand is squeezed in support as Mr. Foster looks between us with a bewildered expression.

"Oh, well, that's very kind of you, Miss Hayley." He takes a pen and scribbles down a few notes. "I'm afraid I cannot do that on your behalf. You would need to sell the car and send the proceeds from that to the charity in question."

"Car?" I blurt out.

"Yes." He's back to scanning the paper. "A BMW M4 Convertible. Color, red. Year, 2020." He hits the perfectly tidy pile of papers onto the desk, and I laugh to myself. He bought me that car for my birthday. I didn't accept it.

And he delivers yet another kick to my gut.

I absolutely *hate* that I have to ask this, and as I lean forward, closing the space between me and Mr. Foster, I lower my voice. "He left me a car? *Just* a car?"

"A very nice car, Miss Hayley."

My God, he thinks I'm ungrateful. I'm not. I'm fucking confused. I look back at James and, thank God, his forehead is a mess of wrinkles, telling me he's puzzled too. I show the ceiling my palms, asking James what the fuck I'm supposed to do with this. He takes my arm and pulls me back into my seat, leaning forward himself. "Mr. Foster, Beau's father was a very wealthy man."

"Indeed, he was."

"His first wife passed away, his only child is Beau, and he was singl . . ." James fades off and looks at me, the same thought falling into his head at the same time it falls into mine. "Single," he breathes, the wrinkles on his forehead back. "Until recently."

When Amber was exposed as the gold-digging whore she is. I nod, dreading what I'm about to hear. He'd been dating someone else. Just dating, though. "Mr. Foster, who else is named as a beneficiary of my father's will?" I ask.

"Miss Amber Kendrick. Unfortunately, I am unable to locate her."

"Oh Jesus." James rubs at the lines on his head. "Everything?"

"Except the car, of course."

I stand abruptly, and the tie of my coat unravels, revealing the vest beneath. Mr. Foster stares at it, alarmed. "Thank you, Mr.

Foster." I turn and leave, retying the belt as I go, swinging the door open and bowling through, nearly crashing into a waiting Danny.

"Beau," James calls.

Danny's cell is still at his ear, and he takes in the scene, James coming after me, before going back to his call. "Baby, everything is okay, but I need to call you back in a minute." He cuts the call with a slow press of his thumb on the screen, continuing to look between us, waiting. "Anyone want to tell me what the fuck's going on?"

I look back at James and start to pace the small reception room. I know he won't want to share. Danny hates Amber, as does Rose. Not surprising when the stupid woman threatened to kill her in a ridiculous crime of love to win Danny. But it can't be avoided. I want her dead. And yet I can't utter the words.

"Tom Hayley left everything he had to Amber Kendrick," James says, his voice low, closing the door to Foster's office behind him.

"Excuse me?" Danny coughs over his words, tilting his ear forward, as if he's improving the chances of hearing right when James repeats himself.

"Except a car," I add.

"What?"

"She did it." I slap the ball of my hand into my head. "How did I not see it?"

"See what?"

"Killed him!" I say over a laugh. "Before he could change his will back. She fooled him into making her the sole heir, or as good as, was then exposed for being a gold digger, so she killed him before he had the opportunity to amend his will."

"Beau, hold up," James says, sounding nervous, his hand rising in a pacifying way I do not like at all. "Let's not get ahead of ourselves."

"She's capable!" I screech. "She had a gun aimed at Rose when Danny kicked her out of the mansion." I look at Danny, desperate for him to confirm I'm right. To justify my ramblings. "Tell him, Danny!"

"I know that, Beau," James says, while Danny stands

awkwardly silent, not wanting to make matters worse by confirming. "But aiming a gun and firing are two entirely different things."

"Fine," I say, pulling out my cell and calling Ollie. He answers immediately, and I'm completely thrown after weeks of being ignored. But he doesn't have to avoid me now. I know about his new woman.

"Beau?"

I start to pace again, watchful of any hands coming my way ready to grab my cell. "I think Frazer Cartwright knew what happened to my dad." Of course he did. He was a close friend of my father, wrote endless shining reports about him and his businesses and charity work. He must have spent time with Amber. He must have seen *something*. "I need to find him."

James is suddenly before me, reaching for my cell. I dip stealthily out of his way.

"I need your help, Ollie."

"Beau!" James yells.

"Frazer Cartwright is dead, Beau." Ollie's words hit me like a brick to my face, and I swing around, my mouth lax, finding James and Danny looking as guilty as sin before me. They know what Ollie's just said. I don't need to tell them.

"Dead?" I ask, needing confirmation. "Frazer Cartwright is dead?"

"Yes. Washed up on the beach."

I cut the call, my mind a mess. "You knew," I whisper. They both knew. That's why Danny shut up in his office. That's why James took my cell to the kitchen with him while I was sleeping. He was worried Ollie would call me. Tell me. "Why would you keep this from me?"

Danny swallows and steps back, giving the stage to James. He looks so lost. It's a massive insult. "I can't lose you, Beau," he says simply, like that fear in him makes everything he does, all the secrets he keeps, acceptable. I immediately shy away from my conscience that's reminding me I'm no angel when it comes to secrets. What I'm doing now. That I haven't told him something so important. But I can't.

I step back, seeing James's body getting taller, his muscles engaging, ready to seize me before I run. I reach into my purse and pull out my gun.

"Fuck's sake, Beau," Danny yells, making James lift his hand to quieten him, like he's got this. Like he's a pro at how to handle me. How to deal with me. That alone infuriates me. I know what's about to happen. I'll be disarmed before I can blink and be taken back to the mansion, maybe even locked in our room to ensure I can't escape. One of them I could handle. Two? And not just any two, but The Brit and The Enigma.

I have one chance.

I turn the gun onto James and pull the trigger, then straight onto Danny. His face is a picture as James flies back and hits the wall. "Beau—"

Bang!

Danny joins James against the wall with a thud, and both men look utterly disorientated as they feel down their jackets. I turn and leave before James has a chance to collect himself, draw his gun, and immobilize me, because I know in this moment, he absolutely would.

25

DANNY

The door to Foster's office swings open, the drip of an attorney taking in the sight of two mean-looking motherfuckers on their arses propped up against the wall. "Go back to work," I gasp, and the door is quickly shut. "I can't believe she just did that," I wheeze, thoroughly winded, my chest feeling like it's been hit with a hammer by the Incredible fucking Hulk.

"I can." James inhales, struggling to his feet, wobbling, practically crawling up the wall. He takes a moment, head back, his face pained. Not only because his chest probably hurts like a bitch too. She shot us. It doesn't matter that she knew we were vested up. It doesn't matter that she knew we'd be on our feet again in a few seconds. She fucking shot us.

I try to get up too, hissing and spitting my way to my feet, the healing wounds on my chest stinging like a bitch. "Your woman wins today, mate." I say, wanting to laugh but knowing I'll be putting my life on the line if I do. "She's fucking crazy."

"I shouldn't have kept it from her." James takes a few steps and stops, breathing in deeply, blinking slowly. Then his eyes clear and a rage like no other consumes them. "Fuck!"

"Do you think Amber killed Tom Hayley?" I ask.

"No, I think emotions are getting the better of Beau and she's telling herself fantastical stories to make her father the hero she always wanted him to be."

I blink a few times, taken aback, "Ever thought of being a therapist?"

"Fuck off, Danny." James strides out into the sunshine and scans the carpark. Beau's long gone, and when he puts his mobile to his ear and then curses, I know she's also turned off her phone. Jesus, I don't envy him. What the fuck is she playing at?

Otto pulls up with Fury, then Ringo and Goldie swing into a parking space, all of them getting out. "Where's Beau?" Fury asks, his bearded face screwed up in worry.

"You didn't see her?" James says, scanning the carpark again.

"See her when?"

"Just now." He motions to the door we've just fallen out of. "She left."

Goldie looks at Ringo and Fury, all of them looking as concerned as I'm feeling. She's emotional. Irrational. Un-fucking-safe out there. "We were across the road," Goldie says, her voice unusually quiet. "Haven't taken our eyes off the door. She didn't leave."

"Oh fuck." Fury rubs at his forehead, and I exhale fast and swing around as James flies back into the building like a charging rhino. She didn't leave. *The little fucker.* I run on behind, hearing the others coming too, and follow James into the women's restroom. He proceeds to push every door of every stall open, and each one slams against the wall behind on a deafening bang that's accompanied by a thunderous curse when he finds each one empty. "Beau!" he roars, kicking the last one open with brute force.

Because he knows she's not in there.

But there's a window.

And it's open.

"Fuck!" His bellow ricochets of the tile, echoing loudly, the sound going on and on.

I look at Ringo, Otto, and Goldie behind me, their faces all grave as James proceeds to punch the wall over and over. "Fuck, fuck, fuck, fuck!"

"James." He can't hear me. "For fuck's sake," I hiss, grabbing his shoulder and hauling him back before he punches his way out. "Calm the fuck down." I don't see it coming. His fist. He swings around, crazed, and lands me a corker on my cheekbone, sending me flying into the sink unit behind me. My head connects with the mirror, shattering the fucker, my brain feeling like it's exploded. "What the fuck?" I breathe, dizzy, double vision getting me. "Are you fucking serious?" I go at him haphazardly, charging and hoping I connect, tackling him at the waist. We both crash into the wall on grunts and hit the deck.

"Cut it out!" Goldie yells, bravely putting her body between our sprawled-out forms.

"You're a fucking cunt," I seethe, dragging myself up, everything fucking hurting. "Don't ever ask for my—"

"I'm sorry," James mutters, sucking air through his teeth as he stands, his palm on his chest. Winded. Both of us. Twice in as many fucking minutes. "I'm sorry," he says more quietly, defeated, turning into the wall and resting his forehead there.

Fucking hell. "We'll find her."

He lets out a sardonic, exhausted burst of laughter, just as the sound of an engine drifts in from the open window. James freezes, as do I, listening, then we both face Ringo and Otto, who we find are patting down their pockets. Both pull out their keys and hold them up, but I don't feel any relief. I move my stare onto James as he inhales sharply and goes to his pocket, feeling around. "No," he whispers, his eyes darting to the window, the sound of a car pulling away at some speed filling our ears. A car that sounded scarily similar to James's Range Rover.

"She's not seriously dipped your fucking pockets?" I ask. "When the fuck did she do that?" I would never say that I have ever underestimated Beau Hayley. Until now.

James is gone again, darting out of the door, everyone following, but we all slow to a stop when he breaks out into the carpark and his run turns into a sprint. I have no fucking clue where he's got the fuel from. My face contorts in pain, my head pounding, and the vest that's done a fine fucking job of keeping me alive today, from my wife's fucking best friend, suddenly feels tighter. I shrug my coat off and remove it from my body, opening my shirt and wincing at the tidy bullet hole-shaped bruise nestled amid the healing slashes. "Motherfucker," I breathe, looking up to James's body getting smaller and smaller. Adrenaline. He's like the fucking Terminator.

But then his Range Rover screeches around the corner onto the main street, and his pace slows until he's standing motionless in the middle of the road.

"Who the hell shot you?" Goldie asks, coming to me, inspecting my wound.

"Beau." I rebutton my shirt and pull my coat back on, leaving the now useless vest on the ground.

"Beau shot you?" Ringo asks, once again looking at the others, checking to see if they heard the same as him.

"Oh, I'm not taking it personally." I laugh, throwing my head back, feeling slightly demented. "She didn't just shoot me; she shot her fiancé too." I kick the vest away and pull out my smokes, lighting one and dragging in the nicotine, praying it'll calm me. "Her dad left everything to his ex-girlfriend."

"Amber?" Ringo asks, stunned.

Another puff as I nod. "Yes. She was seen nearby at the funeral. Looked like she was trying to conceal herself."

"Why would she be there?"

Good fucking question. And why the fuck has she been calling me? *I need to see you.* "Higham was at the funeral too." I go on. Another drag of my Marlboro. "Didn't speak, but perhaps that's because he's worried we're onto him and his little coffee dates with that journalist Natalia Potter. We also had a debut appearance from Collins. Weird-looking woman. The kind with a face you instantly want to punch."

"Can you actually say that about a woman?" Fury asks.

God bless my soul. "Yes, I fucking can." Especially when the woman in question is a fucking cop on our backs. "Along with Amber, Higham, and Collins, we also had Burrows." Another long drag. I blow out the smoke to the sky. "He's got a new woman. One that happens to be an attorney." I wave my cigarette, thinking, thinking, thinking. "Jolene something. She knows every step he's taken since he's been off work."

"That's handy," Otto grunts, getting his laptop out of the car and placing it on the roof of the Mercedes, starting to tap at the keys. "She's turned the fucking tracker off on the Range Rover." He slams the lid shut and rests his head on the roof. "That fucking woman."

"Beau knows Cartwright's dead," I go on, "and now thinks Amber killed her dad for the inheritance and possibly Cartwright too." I finish on a megawatt smile. "Oh, and we still don't know WHO THE FUCKING BEAR IS!" I launch my fist into the window of the Mercedes, and the fucker resists, making it bounce back off. "Fuck!" The sound of my phone ringing saves the window from another attempt, and I shake my bastard fist as I slip my Marlboro between my lips and answer. "Hey, baby."

"What's happened?" Rose asks, as calm as could be.

"Nothing's happened, my darling. I'll be home for dinner. And I'll need a hot soak in the bath." I bravely hang up. I'll be paying for it. But . . . *fuck me.*

"I suggest someone finds Amber before Beau does," James says, out of breath as he stalks past us to Otto, holding his hand out for the keys to his car. "Or pray I find Beau first."

"She killed the tracker."

James laughs. It's as demented as I feel. "Of course she fucking did!" He gets in, starts the engine, and pulls off fast before Otto's put one foot in front of the other to join him. The car screeches off, and Otto's laptop leaves the roof and flies across the carpark, smashing into a few million pieces when it hits the concrete. And Otto just stares at it. Stares and breathes deeply for a few minutes while we all watch him fighting to keep his cool. I have to hand it to him, he's doing a far better job of that than me or James.

Eventually, he collects up just one piece from the scattered remains of his laptop—the motherboard, no doubt—and faces us. "I need a lift home."

"I'll drop you at the gates." Because if I step foot on the grounds of our house, Rose will be on me like a wolf and leaving again will likely cause World War III. I go to the remaining car and get behind the wheel.

"Where are you going?" Ringo asks, his crabby old face screwed up as if I've already answered that question and he doesn't approve.

"To find any number of people who need to be found." I start the car. "Brad, Amber, The Bear. Take your pick."

"I'm coming with you," Goldie declares as they all pile in the back.

"And me," Ringo mutters.

"Can we stop off at Best Buy?" Otto asks as he slips onto the passenger seat, looking at me for an answer. He's serious. He's fucking serious.

"No, we can't fucking stop at fucking Best Buy," I yell, starting the car and slamming it into drive, screeching off.

I drum my fingers on the steering wheel as I wait in the carpark outside Best Buy, my thoughts twisted, my brain hurting, and not because it's had a belter of a whack. There's just so fucking much to unravel, the web thick, dense, and fucking massive. Yet all that remains of The Bear's network is Sandy and Volodya. Two Russians, one of which wants to work with us. I pout at the windscreen, my eyes narrowing. If Burrows was taking leave from work to eliminate the risk of Collins thinking he's working for us, he could also be taking leave because *we* suspect him of being The Bear's inside man. He could be out of the game. Or trying to be. Washing his hands of The Bear. Hence, the animals, or what's left of them, scattering. But if he did that, surely he would be dead by now because not in any criminal lord's world would they let their mole crawl away. Perhaps that's why he's been in hiding. *Fuck me.* I text James my contemplations, not that I expect them to sink into his brain right now. My conclusions also won't improve his mood but, let's face it, it couldn't get any fucking worse.

I'm typing away but lose my screen when Rose tries calling me. "Forgive me," I murmur, rejecting her call and carrying on with my message. She calls again. "Not now, Rose," I say quietly, hitting the red, *forbidden* button and continuing with my message. It rings again. "I'll call you back, I promise," I say, rejecting her once again and getting back to my message to James.

Ring!

"For fuck's sake!" I answer. "I'm trying to write a long-arse fucking message, Rose, and you keep interrupting me." I hang up, my thumbs working at an epic speed to get done before she calls me again. Because she will. I finish, click send, and exhale, relaxing back in my seat, exhausted, feeling like I've just run a grueling army assault course. I dial Rose. "Baby," I say when she answers.

"Baby to you too," she replies sweetly, definitely through gritted teeth. "A little tip if you wish to remain married."

"What's that, sweetheart?"

"Answer my fucking calls."

"I was dealing with something important." I cringe the moment the words fall out of my mouth and catch Ringo, Fury, and Goldie in the rearview mirror shaking their heads at their phones. If the situation wasn't so dire, the sight of them would be laughable, their bodies wedged in the back, their shoulders all up by their ears. "I didn't mean more important than you." *Fucking hell.* "Rose, baby, you won't believe the day I've had."

"What's happened?" she asks, her voice softening.

"Beau's dad's attorney showed up at the funeral, along with many other friendly faces."

"Like who?"

"Her ex. He's moved a new woman in."

"Into their apartment? That's a bit insensitive."

"Is it?"

"Yes. She shared that place with Ollie. Imagine if you and I split up and I kept the house. How would you feel if I moved another man in?"

I look at the roof of the car. Why? Why does she say shit like that? I bite my tongue because it won't do me any favors biting her head off. "It's not Beau's apartment anymore. She has an apartment with James." *Oh fuck.* My eyes widen at the mirror and the three sets in the back shoot to me.

"What?" Rose asks.

"Or they had an apartment before it was blown up." I cringe.

"No, James had an apartment. It wasn't Beau's. She wanted to buy an apartment on her own and James showed up at the viewing and basically told her it wasn't happening."

Why doesn't that surprise me? "Any—"

"That's not all he did either," she continues. I can hear the smile in her voice. "So are you telling me James has bought an apartment?"

Fuck it. "No, stop putting words in my mouth." My sore head bangs harder. "The lawyer told Beau her dad left everything to Amber."

"What?" Rose screeches.

"Everything except a car."

"A BMW?"

"Yeah."

"The asshole. He only left her the car he bought for her birthday? She didn't want it back then!" I won't ask how she knows about the car. Or the apartment Beau was looking at. Or what happened when James showed up at the viewing. "And he left *everything* else to that gold-digging whore?"

I hum my confirmation.

"Well, one out of two isn't bad, is it?" she asks with light humor.

"What?"

"Amber. When she didn't get anything out of you, she moved on quite quickly and got her claws into another man."

Is she comparing me to a middle-aged, overweight, graying, egotistical prick? "I'm sorry, I don't follow." *Do not kill her.*

She laughs. "Oh, baby, did you think Amber was with you for love?"

Yes, actually. Because she was, among other things, of course. *Don't kill her, Danny.* "Rose, I—" It lands in my brain like a bomb. Why Amber's been calling me. What she wants. *Fuck!* Okay, I considered love, but she knows that ship's sailed. I considered money, but that boat's gone now too, loaded with fucking cash from her inheritance from Beau's father. Amber would have known she was set to cop it all. So why the fuck has she been persistently calling me?

"Danny?" Rose says. "Are you there?"

"Fuck me," I breathe, looking at the rearview mirror to everyone in the back. "I'll call you back," I say, hearing Rose tell me I won't as I hang up.

Goldie, Fury, and Ringo wait patiently for me to unravel the words and speak them, and Otto gets back into the car, placing a laptop box on his thighs. He slaps it and turns a smile my way. It falls when he finds my blank face. Then he turns in his seat and looks at the others in the back. "What?" he asks. "I've only been in there for five fucking minutes. What's happened now?"

"Good question," Ringo grunts.

"We're waiting for Miss Marple here to enlighten us on her enlightenment." Goldie nods toward me.

"Protection," I say. "She's scared. Amber was looking for protection, and not from her ex-lover's disgruntled daughter when she found out her inheritance went to Amber."

"If not for that, why would Amber want protection?" Otto asks, starting to spin the ring in his lip. "And why was she at the funeral if she's scared?"

"Me. She was hoping to see me. And she did, but I was surrounded by cops so she couldn't approach me. Plus Beau made a run for at her." Why didn't I consider this before? "She knows something." I go to my phone but smack the steering wheel when I remember Amber's calls to me recently have been from a withheld number. Another red flag. Shit, I don't have a number for her.

Keeping the contact details of an in-house whore was something I would never do. "Fuck it."

"What could she know?" Goldie asks. "And about who? From my understanding, she got about a bit." She raises her brows. "I'm thinking there were a few men in between your fine self and Mr. Hayley all, I'm sure, with gleaming personalities or even shinier criminal records."

My lip curls naturally. "If you weren't a woman, I'd punch you daily," I grate, knowing the simple fact that I'm being a sexist pig will hurt our fair lady as much as actually punching her in the face.

She mirrors my lip and I'm pretty sure she growls too, but my phone saves me from a face-off with Goldie. No number. Amber. I answer quickly, but I don't get her annoyingly purring voice. No. Instead, I get a rough, Russian, grainy voice.

"Black," he grunts.

"What do you want, Volodya?" I haven't got time for this ridiculous game of *Who Knows the Bear.*

"Guns."

I burst out laughing, hanging up and dropping my mobile into my lap, holding onto the steering wheel, arms braced, my body convulsing. *What the ever-lovin' fuck?* Anyone else want our guns? "Jesus." I chuckle, my eyes leaking as I roughly wipe at them, then at my coarse cheeks, then run a hand through my overgrown hair, my body making random jumps as I try to recover from my laughing fit. I find all eyes on me when I'm done. "Volodya," I say, digging between my thighs to find my mobile. "He wants some guns."

"Tell him to join the fucking queue," Ringo mutters, uninterested, going back to his phone as mine rings once again. "It's busy today," he adds, his voice flat.

"Tell me about it." I raise it to my ear. "Yes?"

"Mr. Black, I don't know if you'll remember me—"

"Try me," I say over a laugh. "You'd be surprised. I've got ghosts cropping up left and right at the moment."

"Jeeves?" he says, and I frown.

"Who?"

"Jeeves, sir. The concierge from The Four Seasons."

Jeeves? Well, shit. I never showed it, of course, but I really liked this guy. He can find you anything, anytime, for a fee, of course. He's never failed. "What can I do for you, Jeeves?"

"I hope you don't mind me calling. You see, I held your number from when you used to stay here regularly a few years ago." Over three years ago. Before I met Rose. "We have a situation."

"What's that?"

Jeeves launches into a detailed report of the situation, and I listen, not quite believing what I'm hearing. "Mr. Black, you're the only man who can help me."

He's right. and I can't refuse him the help he's pretty much begging me for. He's a good guy, and I owe him. Plus, I really need an outlet right now. "I'm on my way, Jeeves." I hang up and send a quick text. Fuck me, I'm going to enjoy ripping the *situation* limb from limb.

I stroll into The Four Seasons with the other's forming a wall behind me, and the bustling lobby falls utterly silent as we walk across the perfectly polished cream marble tiles, the only sound a mix of our collective footsteps and the staff behind the reception desk tapping away at their keyboards.

Until they look up.

I can't tell if their looks are that of dread or relief. Maybe a bit of both. "Mr. Black." Jeeves rushes out from behind the concierge desk, coming at me with his hand held out, his face one of gratitude. "Thank you. Thank you for coming."

"Anything for an old friend," I say, discreetly placing a bundle of hundred-dollar bills into his hand. It's not often there are rooms available at The Four Seasons, and Jeeves always found one for me when I was single and looking for somewhere other than our busy house, somewhere private, to fuck. I'm married now sure, but I can guarantee that one day, my wonderful, glorious wife will boot me out. I need to keep Jeeves sweet in case I need a bed for the night, since all the spare rooms at my house are fucking full.

He looks down at the cash with utter confusion, probably wondering why I'm thanking him when I'm here to help him, before he quickly tucks it away. "Let me show you." Jeeves motions toward the elevator. "Please, I beg you, can we keep it clean?"

"I can't promise that, Jeeves," I say to myself, though I know he hears because he breathes out his despair.

As we ride up, Jeeves's concern only grows as he takes in my gang of misfits, and when I pull my gun from the back of my trousers, he pushes his back against the elevator wall, his despair real, as I check the magazine. The doors open and Jeeves remains inside where it's safe. "We can take it from here," I say, taking the key card from his grasp. "Thanks, Jeeves." The elevator doors close, and I face the corridor. "Just when I thought today couldn't give any more." I pace toward the room, armed with my key card and my Glock, making sure my steps are light, unheard, and when I'm before the wood, I ensure I don't stand in front of the door viewer, keeping my back against the wall, checking the others are ready. They all nod, hands on their backs as I slip the card into the slot. The light flashes green, and I gently push the door open.

The smell hits me like a brick to the face.

Alcohol, nicotine, and sex.

I walk quietly through the suite, taking in the empty bottles on the table, a few stray lines of cocaine, cigarette butts overflowing in a few tumblers. And then grunts. Grunts and pathetic screams. Lame screams from a woman who's pretending to enjoy herself.

I push the door open with the end of my gun and find the woman in question straddling a waist, riding hard. Releasing the safety, I aim and clear my throat, breaking through the sounds of her embellished pleasure, and she flies round, her long black hair fanning the radius of the bed. The moment she spots me filling the doorway, she screams.

"Now, *that's* a proper scream," I say as she jumps up, terrified, her massive tits bouncing all over the place.

"Please don't kill me," she begs, her hands moving to hide various parts of her as I walk to a chair and pull off a towel, throwing it at her. "Notice where my gun is pointing," I say, jiggling it. "Now get out."

She's gone like a rocket, and I return my attention to the bed.

Just as Brad lifts his head.

"Evening," I say, walking over, pushing the gun into his temple. "How's your shoulder?"

"Sore."

"How's your dick?"

"Sore."

I drag my eyes down his torso to his waist, where his semi-erect cock twitches, mourning the loss of its most recent pussy. I'm sure she wasn't the first. "I'm feeling all reminiscent," I muse.

"Fuck off." He slams his head on the pillow. "Are you going to fucking shoot me or bottle it like your pops did?"

Oh, he didn't. I move my gun an inch and pull the trigger, putting a bullet in the pillow beneath his head, around about an inch away from his temple, sending goose feathers billowing up into the room and Brad shooting up from the bed on a pained cry.

He clenches his shoulder, his face a map of agony. "What the fuck, Danny?"

"Shame. I expect it was a top-quality pillow." I ram the gun in his forehead, my patience lost. "What the fucking hell are you playing at?"

Brad smacks the gun away and drops back to the bed. "I needed a timeout."

"Nolan's alive."

His startled face swings my way as the man himself bowls through the door into the bedroom of Brad's suite. "Brad?" Nolan gasps.

Brad looks at him like he's seen a ghost. "You're not dead?"

"He wasn't at your place when you called," I explain. "But that's a story for another day." I take a seat in the cozy chair in the corner and cross one leg over the other, resting my gun on my knee. "What a lovely reunion."

Brad's face. It's an awkward mix of pain, relief, and plain fucking fury. He gets up, stalks over to Nolan and swings at him, delivering a punch that knocks the poor kid back a few paces. But he takes it on the chin. Literally. The alternative is me shooting the fucker for causing all this unnecessary stress.

Brad yelps, Nolan rubs his chin, and then pouts. "Sorry," he murmurs, and Brad hauls him into his chest and hugs him. I smile on the inside. Not on the out.

"Now." I stand, waving my gun around the room that looks like a load of frat boys have had a cocaine and alcohol fueled orgy. "You've upset Jeeves and some other guests with all the noise you've been making."

"Well, they should have put me in the Presidential Suite. Do you know this suite is eight grand a night?"

I sniff my surprise, looking around at the one-bedroom space. "Really?" The Presidential is only another two grand? And considerably larger.

"Yeah, really. And who the fuck's complaining about the noise?"

"The people in the Presidential Suite," I say, walking to the door.

Brad snorts his revulsion. I can literally hear him cracking his knuckles, ready to march over there and put whoever's in the Presidential Suite in their place. "Who the fuck's in the Presidential Suite?"

I turn at the door, my eyebrows high. "The president."

"Oh."

Nolan sniggers.

"Shut the fuck up," Brad warns.

"Get dressed. I'm taking you home." I carry on my way, tucking my gun away as I pass the others, who are all looking around in disgust at the mess Brad's made with fuck knows how many women.

"I haven't got a fucking home," he yells. "Some fucker blew it up."

"Then it looks like you and your pet are staying with me," I shout over my shoulder. "Why the fuck not?" I murmur to myself. "Everyone else is."

"I can't," Brad calls, more quietly, making me turn at the door, my expression questioning. "I just . . . can't."

"Why?"

He scowls. "I like my own space."

"You don't have a choice." I get on my way. "Sort your shit out, Brad, or I'll sort it out for you."

When we pull up at the house, I see the car James took to go find Beau is parked haphazardly in front of the steps. But there's no Range Rover, and when I get into the lobby and find Mum waiting, her face pensive, I know he's not in a good way. "How bad?" I ask. "On a scale of one to Incredible Hulk?"

"He's even greener than that," Mum says quietly. "He went straight to your office after he grilled Rose."

"Bet that went down well," I muse, looking toward my office. "Where is she?"

"Running her palm under the cold tap."

"Oh, fucking hell," I breathe, heading to the kitchen. I find my wife looking fucking livid. "Hey, baby."

Glancing up, her lips twist more. "He deserved it."

I have no doubt. I can only imagine James trying to squeeze Rose for information. "We found Brad." I see her small exhale of relief.

"Where was he?"

I swerve that question. "So has she?" I ask, going to her. "Been in touch?"

"No, she hasn't, and even if she had, I wouldn't tell *him*."

I take her hand and check her palm. It's pink. Ouch. That's a stinger. "He's worried."

"I know, but I don't appreciate being grilled. He was fucking relentless. Following me from the sink to the cooker to the fridge, around and around, question after question. He was frenzied. I had to snap him out of it."

I flinch for James. Of course, I know Rose slapping him would never have been because he laid a finger on her. He wouldn't dare, and not just because of me. He loves Rose.

"Where the hell has she gone, Danny?" she asks, truly worried.

"You really don't know?" I ask, shocked. She's not giving us lip service? "You've not spoken to her?"

"No," she mutters, indignant. "Her cell's off."

I take a towel and dab her hand dry, wincing at the red mark. It was just a slap, and Rose has delivered plenty of those and come off without injury, but her palm still hadn't fully recovered from being burned by the damn pan in St. Lucia. "You couldn't have used your other hand?" I ask, lifting it to my mouth and kissing it.

"If I had taken a moment to think about it, yes. It hurts like hell."

Mum comes in and gets a pot out of the cupboard, placing it on the stove. "They're in your office," she tells me. "Rose, Daniel wants you upstairs."

"Why, what's wrong with him?" I ask.

"Something about Barney."

Barney? My nose wrinkles. "If that kid's spewed any more—"

"Lies?" Rose cocks her head and leaves the kitchen. "I'm certain Lennox will never allow Barney to see our son again."

"Good," I grunt, but immediately feel shitty about it. Daniel didn't ask for this kind of childhood. I know he loves us, loves everyone, but he's restrained here in Miami. "What do you think about sending Daniel to school?" I ask Mum out of the blue as she slaps a few spuds on the counter.

"I'm sorry, what?" she asks, not looking at me.

I frown. "School. What do you think? For Daniel."

"I think," she says on an exhale, not stopping what she's doing, "before I give you any opinions on anything, I would like an apology."

Otto. *The fucker.* My anger for that particular grievance is renewed. Unfortunately, I have other priorities. "I'm sorry," I grunt. "But—"

Her knife comes up fast, pointing at me. "No buts, Danny. I am a grown woman, and I am your mother. Do you hear me? Your mother. I take care of you, take care of everyone around here, so you will back the hell off."

"You deserve more tha—"

"A murdering criminal?"

I scowl. "This isn't ab—"

"Do I deserve more than that in a son too?" she asks. "Because if anyone asked me to swap you for a more moral version, I'd tell them to fuck off." She catches a breath, and I step back, alarmed. "Because I love you just the way you are, Danny, and everything you are is because you're a fucking survivor."

I recoil.

Fuck.

Me.

Received loud and clear. "I'm sorry," I say, my tail between my legs.

"Good."

"So what do you think?"

"About what?" she snaps, impatient, and still slightly breathless from her rant.

"School for Daniel."

She sighs, her body loosening. "I think it's a very good idea if we can find the right one, of course."

A safe one. "Me too."

"Do you want me to look into it?"

I nod. "But let me speak to Rose first." Just as soon as I've dealt with the other shit. "I'll be in my office." I go to my mum, standing before her like I'm asking permission. I suppose I am. She lets a small smile free and gives me her cheek, not surrendering her potato or knife, and I drop a kiss there before leaving her, telling myself I need to shut the fuck up where her love life is concerned. But, I swear, if he hurts her, I won't hold back.

I pass Pearl and Anya in the hallway, both girls in gym kit, both a little sweaty. "Good workout?" I ask as I pass.

"Oh, you're back." Pearl looks straight toward my office. "Any news on Brad?"

Oh? My feet slow to a stop, my body turning toward them. Anya has a nearly undetectable smile on her face as she looks at Pearl out the corner of her eye. What's this then? "He's back," I say, watching her closely.

Her face. It's shocked, pleased, nervous. *Oh fuck.* "He is?" she squeaks. "How is he?"

"Grumpy."

"Standard," she says over a laugh. "So where's he been?"

Now . . . do I tell her? This girl is twenty-one. Brad is thirty-four. He was twenty-one when Pops dragged him out of a hotel and gave him a lesson in acceptable levels of indulgence. Pearl was eight when Brad was twenty-one. *Jesus.* So, yes, I do tell her. She's young. Delusional. The best thing Pearl could do is hate Brad, so let's make that happen. "He locked himself in a suite at The Four Seasons and fucked his way through hooker after hooker."

Her face. Disappointment, hurt, sadness. I take no pleasure from it. But . . . I also know Brad. He values women about as much as the devil values confession. "Esther needs some help in the kitchen." I get on my way and enter my office to find everyone still and silent. James has his back to me, quietly seething in the chair, Brad's on the couch, looking a fucking wreck, Otto's setting up his shiny new laptop, and Ringo and Goldie are on their phones. "Glad to see the party didn't start without me." I close the door and go to my desk, assessing James. He really is green. Probably sick with worry. "Where's Nolan?"

"Gone back to Hiatus," Brad says. "I'm here for the lowdown, then I'm going." Escaping. Running away. *Because of Pearl.* Fucking hell, he can't stay here because of her. Is she coming onto him? Does he find the redhead attractive? Doesn't he trust himself?

All questions for another day.

"So, a recap?" I ask the room.

"Sure, why not." Ringo sets his phone aside, ready for a rundown on the day's events, and fuck, it's been quite a day.

Understatement. "We have Luis, Sandy, Volodya, and before Beau killed him, The Shark, all wanting our guns."

"It's a good job you drunk ordered more then, huh?" Otto says without looking up from his laptop. He's pushing it. I hope Mum made him feel as shitty as she made me feel. And I hope that fat lip he's sporting means it hurts like a bitch if he kisses her. *Have they kissed?*

"Volodya?" James questions, distracting me from socking Otto one in the face.

"Yes. He called earlier."

"When are we meeting Sandy?" he asks.

"I don't know."

"I told you to arrange something."

He *told* me? "I'm sorry, I've been kinda busy trying to *not* fucking die." I stand and shrug off the coat I've been wearing all fucking day. "And maybe now, in light of Volodya calling, I might not be agreeable to meeting Sandy."

"Does Volodya know anything?" James asks. "Did he promise anything?"

I laugh. "You think Sandy knows who The Bear is? Oh, come on." *For fuck's sake.* "No one knows a fucking thing! The Bear's had everyone under him, tore through Miami with guns and bombs, and now he's got *no one* under him and he's doing the fucking same!"

"Okay then, who are we calling?" Brad pipes in, happy to poke us both. "Sandy or Volodya, because both of you have a beef with both of them, so who's winning this one?" He smiles. "Draw straws?"

I should have moved that gun an inch to the left. "Fuck off to Hiatus."

"Not until I know what the fuck's going on."

"Good luck with that." Ringo sneers at nothing. "None of us know what the fuck is going on. We might not need Sandy or

Volodya if Amber Kendrick really does have information. Wouldn't that be nice?"

"Glorious," I say quietly. *What the fuck does she know?* I look at my mobile, willing it to ring. "We need to talk about the delivery we're expecting tomorrow." Beau was supposed to be tugging those jet skis with Leon because, simply, Beau and Leon are the least criminal-looking members of this fucked-up family, aside from my wife, mother, and kid, of course. "So who's towing the skis back now?"

"You and me," James says, his attention still on his phone. He's dialing Beau. Repeatedly. He looks back at Otto who shakes his head at the screen of his new laptop, and James curses, going back to his mobile.

"Are you sure?" I ask, thinking, James's head is not in the right space for playing it cool while we smuggle endless weapons through endless Coast Guards.

"Sure."

I won't argue with him. "Collins is watching Hiatus," Otto says out of nowhere, pointing at his screen as if all of us in the room can see it.

"Lovely. Invite her in for a drink when you get there," I say to Brad. Speaking of drink. I get up and help myself, pouring James a vodka as I do.

"And Higham? What do we make of his little rendezvous with Natalia Potter?"

"Dodgy as fuck."

I hum, rolling it all over, placing a tumbler on the desk before James. Higham. Definitely bent.

"Can we hurry this along?" Brad scowls at me, the irritable fucker. He should have fucked a few more whores and laid off the Florida Snow. And speaking of Florida Snow. "Where the fuck did you get that shit from?"

Brad opens his mouth and snaps it shut again, his lips pursing, as if it's just occurred to him that he should have wondered this before. He was probably too drunk on both alcohol and lust.

"Jeeves," he says slowly, a frown creasing his brow. I don't need to ask anymore. Brad's also wondering where Jeeves would have got it from, now that we've taken the Irish out. I make a mental note to find out but, again, not a priority.

"What about Potter?" I ask.

"Nothing," Otto confirms. "But she did report that Metcalfe is set to take the title of mayor."

I laugh. Of course he fucking is. He has no competition now. Then I pout, falling into thought.

No competition.

I lower to my chair and sip my drink, considering that. No competition. He's going to walk straight into the Mayor's office. Maybe he needs some competition.

"Danny!"

I startle, looking for the source of the voice. Otto's frowning at me, wondering what I was thinking so intently about. I won't share. I'm quite sure he already thinks I've lost the plot. "What?"

"I can't find Amber Kendrick anywhere."

"Typical," I say on a laugh, closing my eyes and resting my head back. *Breathe. Just breathe.* She has to show up sooner or later. I just hope she's not dead.

I open my eyes.

James has got his arm extended over my desk, his fist balled, and in the middle . . .

Two straws.

26

ROSE

I lay nestled between his thighs with my back on his chest. The water falls just shy of my nipples, leaving them exposed to the cooler air. Hard. Dark. Danny's big, capable hands are splayed across my tummy, my legs touching the inside of his from thigh to ankle, and with every deep inhale he takes, a little bit more of my boobs are exposed. It's quiet and still, just the calm sound of water rippling keeping us company.

Neither of us could sleep. I'm so worried about Beau, spent all night listening to see if I could hear her coming home, and Danny knew it. By the time the sun was rising, I gave up chasing sleep and ran a bath. He silently wandered in and joined me, abandoning our bed too. He dozed off within a few minutes of submerging himself in the water and positioning me on top of him, his heart beating into my back sending me off too.

Now, I don't know what time it is, but the water is tepid. Only our touching skin is keeping the chills away. "Are you awake?" I ask, and he hums, starting to circle his palms across my stomach. "She didn't come home."

His arms move up to my shoulders and circle, hugging me, and

I cling to them, but he says nothing. We're all worried. God damn her. I peel Danny's arms away and stand, water pouring from my body, goosebumps finding every inch of my skin, my wet hair sticking to my back. "Wait," he says, reaching for my wrist. I turn in the bath as he gets to his knees and pulls me down to mine, slipping his hand onto my nape and pulling my mouth onto his. The scorching hot heat contrasting with the chills of my skin is divine, and when my breasts press into his chest, the chills vanish immediately.

"Your cuts." I hold on to his wrists, clench hard, ready to pull away.

"Are fine," he replies, hypnotizing me with the swirls of his tongue, his nibbles, the sucks, while he holds my neck firmly. "Just kiss me." The roughness of his voice added to the already intoxicating ingredients takes me to the next level of pleasure, a need overcoming me to just . . . kiss. I tilt my head, open wider, swirl softly, suck gently. It's the slowest kiss we've ever shared. The softest. "Beautiful," he whispers again, pushing his body closer, urging me on, his hands slipping up onto my head, his thumbs on my cheeks.

I'm so lost. So hot. So consumed. Moving my hands to his hair, I stroke through the length to his nape, locking my arm around his neck to pull me in closer, humming my happiness, swallowing down every sound of indulgence he makes. This kiss is bingeing. It's greedy and powerful and dizzying. Neither of us want to progress it, just enjoy it.

It goes on and on.

The perpetual kiss. My head turns one way, then the other, my free hand moves across his body, his face, his hair, my nipples grazing his chest. "Are you wet?" he asks, slipping a finger between my legs. I pant in answer, nipping his tongue. So wet. Burning. Needing. I kiss him harder, urgency now taking the lead. "I'm so fucking hard for you." He takes my hand and places it on his cock, and I immediately start working him as he massages my clit.

I thought I was happy with a kiss.

Now, I just need to detonate and hope it takes some stress with it. I know he feels the same. I kiss him harder still, biting at his lip, stabbing my tongue into his mouth, thrusting my fisted hand up and down his shaft as my body folds forward with the pleasure he's delivering. I whimper, my lips leaving his, my head going limp as every muscle I possess starts to harden and the pleasure charges forward. I feel his finger slip under my chin and force my face up. I can hardly keep my eyes open.

"Look," he demands, his icy eyes blazing. "Will you come hard for me, baby?" he asks. "Come all over my hand."

I whimper, my hand action getting a bit chaotic, forcing Danny to take over working himself and me at the same time. I place a hand on each shoulder and look down at the sight of him pleasuring both of us. Unreal. His fist is tight, working steadily, the crown of his cock glistening, and his pleasure-coated fingers thrust into me in time, his thumb working my clit in between. My cheeks inflate with the strain not to scream as the pleasure grips me, slithering through my veins, all heading to one place. I bite down on my lip and look up. His wet, parted lips past his dark stubble, the slight swell of his nose from his bust up with Otto, his burning, drowsy eyes, his scar.

I lean in and lick the length, from below his eye to his lip, then across to the other side. He tenses. I slide my hand down his chest to between his thighs and stroke softly across his balls. He convulses. Loses his rhythm on me for a moment. It's a moment I need to pull myself back and get in line with Danny. I kiss him briefly and go back to watching him work us, splitting my attention between his hands and his face. His eyes drop to my boobs.

My hands find them immediately, and his head drops back, his stare rooted there, his mouth falling open more, his blues becoming drowsier.

Deadly handsome.

Deadly sexy.

Just fucking deadly in every manner of the word, and I love him. Would die for him. I abandon a boob and stroke down to my belly, holding it, feeling the urge to bend over and suppress the impending explosion between my legs. His eyes move to my tummy. His hands start working faster.

Coming.

Coming.

Coming.

I swallow, my body jerks, and it rushes through me without mercy, forcing me to grab on to Danny's shoulder. I look down just as he twitches, murmurs, and the head of his dick swells and surges, shooting his cum all over my stomach as he gasps for breath and grabs the side of the tub, the water splashing. "Shit," he hisses, pushing deeper into me and stilling, letting me wrap every internal muscle around his thick fingers and cling on. I circle my hand across my stomach and spread him all over me, clawing my nails into his bicep, unable to keep my eyes off his beautiful cock still erupting, his essence now hitting my arm. I reach for his hand and slowly pull his fingers free from inside me and lower my ass to my heels, taking a few breaths.

He looks otherworldly there before me recovering from his high, his wet hair falling into his eyes, his body jacked, every muscle pulsing. "Okay?" I ask, splashing water onto my tummy to wash it. Danny says nothing. He sucks his fingers clean, kisses my cheek, and stands, looking like Poseidon rising from the sea. He steps out, takes a towel and dries. "What are you doing today?"

Danny looks at me as he leaves, which basically tells me if he speaks, it will be a lie, so he won't speak, and then he can't be accused of lying. "I love you," he calls back, putting a small smile on my face, even though I have just served as his in-house whore. A stress reliever. But he would never kiss an in-house whore like that. Neither would he tell them he loves them. And they most certainly wouldn't be carrying his child.

"Have a good day, dear," I say quietly, getting out and drying off, at the same time praying for Beau's safe return and an end to this never-ending nightmare.

I should know by now that God doesn't hear sinners' prayers.

· · ·

I throw on my Union Jack sweater and some stretchy pants before heading downstairs to see what the mood is like in the camp. I know it'll be low, but how low? I find Daniel at the island shoveling Lucky Charms into his mouth while Pearl and Anya look on, astonished, eating their muffins with a little more grace. "Morning," I say, joining them and pouring some juice.

"Any news on Beau?" Anya asks.

Daniel's spoon hits his bowl with a loud clang, and Esther stops wiping the countertop behind me. "What's wrong with Beau?" he asks, looking at me for an answer. "Did she get shot again?"

Anya's hand goes straight over her mouth, her apologies spilling through her fingers. "I'm so sorry."

I can't be upset with her. I offer Anya a small, reassuring smile before turning to Daniel. "Beau's fine." I think. "She's got her cop head on, is all."

"Once a cop, always a cop," he sings, returning to his breakfast, and I laugh lightly.

"Where did you hear that?"

"Beau. No, wait, it was James. Hold up, no, it was Mister." He frowns. "Or did I see it on CSI?"

"You shouldn't be watching CSI," Esther says from across the kitchen.

No, because there's enough dubious stuff happening around here to keep his curious mind busy. God damn it. How I wish he could go to a regular school and be a regular kid while he's there. He needs friends.

"Hey, Grandma, does Mister know yet that you and Otto are in love?"

I press my lips together and peek at Esther, who's face is beetroot red. "What are you talking about?"

"Does this mean he'll be my grandpa?"

"No, it doesn't." Otto appears at the door, and Daniel laughs, shoving his spoon in his mouth, milk dribbling down his chin. I will him to keep quiet.

"You're alive," Daniel quips. "That means Mister doesn't know."

"Know what?" Danny appears at the door, and I virtually hear Esther's despair in the form of clanging pots and dishes as her fussing ramps up a few levels.

Daniel shrinks into his chair and gets back to his Lucky Charms. It's a wise move. Those Lucky Charms aren't lucky enough to save him from Danny's wrath if he doesn't pipe down.

"Nothing." I assess my husband, every towering inch of him. He's suited. Dressed to kill. "Coffee?" I ask, but Esther's already taken care of it, pouring one from the jug and sliding it on the counter for him. Then she gives one to Otto. It's a tactical move, and Otto doesn't appreciate it, his eyes annoyed slits on Danny while he sips, and Danny knows it, which is undoubtedly why he showers Esther with affection, putting an arm around her while he drinks his coffee.

"Hadn't you ought to be getting to the boatyard?" he asks Otto. I mentally put my head in my hands as Anya and Pearl ping-pong looks between them, each with a cup at their lips, trying to look absorbed in their drinks. Daniel's our saving grace here. But then the sound of ceramic scraping across the marble counter pierces the air and he's up and gone, declaring he wants to get his assignment done and submitted before he goes out on the water.

"Not today, kid," Danny calls after him, making him screech to halt at the doorway.

"What? Why?" he whines, his whole body deflating, making him look like a little boy again.

"Yes, why?" I ask.

"Because I said so." Danny releases Esther. No flex whatsoever? That means only one thing. There's a delivery or an exchange or . . . I quietly inhale. The delivery is today. I look at my husband. He's suited. Is something happening before the delivery? And wasn't Beau supposed to be helping with that?

Daniel stomps off, sulking, and my heart hurts for him. He just wants to go out on his jet ski. I'm pretty sure if he did that every day, he'd be happy. But he can't because it's the freight terminal for all illegal weaponry coming into the country for his gun-running stepdad. I growl under my breath, as annoyed as my son. I know that Danny can provide an amazing life for our children, but it's also a life of constraints, and there is fuck all I can do about it, and that just makes me feel like a shitty mom.

I down my juice, scowling at Danny's back as he and Otto leave the kitchen. "Don't say it," Esther warns, obviously reading me as she always does. "Not today."

"What's today?" Pearl asks, too curious.

"Nothing," Esther and I snap in unison, making her startle. I smile awkwardly and get back to my juice. If we can't hide things from a not-so curious son, I haven't a hope of hiding it from a *very* curious twenty-one-year-old who is also asking too many questions about Brad.

Nolan swaggers into the kitchen, buttoning his suit jacket, looking very suave, his hair pristine, his tie knot faultless. He looks handsome. And he's early twenties. My eyes shoot to Pearl. Now *this* would be a healthy attraction. A more well-suited object for her attentions. But she's not given him a second glance, her attention on the coffee cup she's slowly spinning on the counter. *Fuck.* I catch Anya's eye, and she shrugs, smiling through pressed lips.

Esther pours Nolan a coffee and adds some sugar. "There you are," she says, moving on to another task, baking if the ingredients she's pulling down are a clue.

Nolan's attention falls onto me. "Brad mentioned you might be coming to work at the club."

I blink, surprised, double checking who Nolan's talking to. "Me?"

"Yeah, something about bookkeeping?"

"Me?" I repeat, my finger pointing at my chest. Working at Hiatus? A small smile starts to form. I'd have my own job? Get paid? Have my own money?

"Brad has a club?" Pearl asks, interested.

"It's strip joint," I clarify. And a place for laundering money.

"Figures," she says over a small laugh, and I recoil, surprised, making Pearl wave a hand dismissively, getting up and refilling her coffee.

"Does Danny know?" I ask Nolan.

"Know what?"

I turn and find my husband at the door again, his legs wide, his hands in his trouser pockets, relaxed. "Will you stop doing that?" I say, swiveling on my stool and facing him. "You never mentioned Brad said I could work at the club."

The dark look Danny throws Nolan's way is lethal. It tells him he better leave or he'll die. Not surprisingly, Nolan abandons his coffee and makes a hasty exit. I fold my arms over my chest. I mean business. "Well?"

Danny walks slowly over to me, hands still sunk into his pockets, and stops before me, bending to get his face close to mine. I peek out the corner of my eye and see Pearl back at the island with a fresh coffee. She and Anya are smiling behind their cups. I don't know why. This isn't going to be funny. Infuriating, perhaps, but not funny. I give my husband my attention. His hair needs trimming. His stubble too. "I didn't mention it," he says, giving me a kiss that I don't reciprocate. "Because it will never happen."

I huff, not at all surprised, and turn my face away, getting off the stool and going to the fridge. I pull out a jar and unscrew the lid, pulling out a chili. "Maybe Anya and Pearl could learn the ropes on the bar." The poor things must be bored out of their minds, and since they're apparently not going anywhere, we should at least find something for them to do so they can earn some money.

Danny looks across to the girls, who are looking very interested in my suggestion. His eyebrows are high. "It's Brad's club, not mine." He shrugs, and I laugh under my breath. It's Danny's club too, for Christ's sake.

The room falls silent when James walks in, his focus set forward, the atmosphere thick, as well as the tension radiating off him. He goes to the fridge, stands there just looking inside. "I chopped some for you," Esther says, reaching past him and pulling out a glass of green stuff.

James looks at her, blank. "Thanks."

"Welcome." She puts the glass in his grip and leaves him by the fridge studying it. "Kiwi, blueberries, banana, broccoli, and mango."

He visibly swallows, staring at the glass. "Mango," he says, looking at me, and my heart breaks, not only because he reveals the side of his face that I slapped and the evidence is there, but because mango is one of Beau's favorites. I have to look away, unable to see the utter hopelessness on him. It's shameful of me, cowardly. I hear the glass meet the counter and look up. He's not touched it.

"James," I call as he walks out, but he doesn't stop. I glance at Danny and see the same despair as I feel. I jump up and grab the green juice and go after him. "James, please. Stop." I catch him at the bottom of the stairs and grab his arm, stopping him. Of course, he could shrug me off if he wanted to, but he doesn't, and I'm grateful. He doesn't face me, so I round his big body and take one step up, putting myself in front of him. And because of the height difference, I see his face. The pain etched across it. The deep stress lines making him look older than he is. Seeing him like this makes me unreasonably mad with Beau. I know why she's doing this. I feel her despair as much as I do James's. It also has me making a silent vow to never run out on Danny and leave him wondering and worrying if I'm alive.

"I'm sorry I slapped you," I say quietly, resting the guilty still-stinging palm on his forearm. "I really haven't heard from her, I swear it." I don't want him to believe I would be cruel enough to leave him in this desolation if I could remove him from it. But I haven't heard from her so I can't.

He swallows and lifts his head a fraction, and my heart splinters more when I see his eyes are glazed with tears he's fighting to hold back. "I need to find her, Rose. Before someone else does." He clears his throat and roughly wipes at his cheeks on a sniff, and I hold out the glass.

"Drink," I order, hoping the concoction reloads him with some strength that's been kicked out of him.

James smiles mildly and humors me, knocking it back and putting the empty back in my hand. "Thanks."

"No sweat." I catch him off guard and sling my arms over his wide shoulders, hugging him hard, hoping he feels my love for him. He is literally the only person in this world who can fix Beau. I know it. Danny knows it. Zinnea knows it. Even Beau knows it deep down. He can't cave. He can't be anything less than The Enigma right now.

James returns my embrace, dipping a little to accommodate me, holding on to me as tightly as I'm holding him. It takes everything in me not to cry on him.

"I have to go," he whispers, not breaking away, but instead waiting for me to.

I nod and release him. "Find her, okay?"

He nods and strides off. "Tell Danny I'll meet him at Hiatus." The door closes behind him, and a few moments later, Otto appears from the corridor to the office, cursing as he goes after James.

"I told him not to fucking leave without me." He swings the door open and slams it behind him, just as Goldie stomps out too, also hauling the door open and slamming it behind her. It makes me feel significantly better knowing James isn't out there alone.

But Beau is.

I am going to seriously kick her ass when she gets home. *If* she gets home. I flinch and throw a prayer skyward, to a god I don't believe in, and head back to the kitchen. I walk in to find Esther and Danny on the far side, alone, close, talking in hushed whispers. They both see me and shut up. And doesn't that piss me off? What am I being kept in the dark about now? I look between them, my expression fierce. "What's going on?" I ask, not confident I'll be told but wanting them to know I'm not stupid. Or happy.

Esther looks at Danny and nods, and he steps forward, looking a little awkward. "Mum's found a school for Daniel," he says. I look straight to Esther in my shock, as if I need confirmation that I'm not hearing things. She nods. *What?* I've hoped for it, many times, but I thought regular schooling was out of the question. "I don't want you to get too excited." Danny comes to me, taking both of my hands. "But it's looking promising."

My heart leaps with joy. "Where?" I ask. "How many kids go there? What's the name? Is it mixed sex? Because it's important for him to be with boys *and* girls."

"Whoa." Danny laughs. "The principal can answer all the questions we have when we visit."

"We're visiting?" I cry, excited. "Like regular parents visit regular schools to see if they want their regular kid to go there?" I inhale, something coming to me. "Wait, what did you tell the principal you do?"

"Well, obviously I didn't tell him that the chances of me falling onto America's Most Wanted List any day is rather high."

"That's good," I say, looking into thin air, thinking of all the things Daniel will need. Bags, books, pens, sports equipment. We'll need to go shopping. "When are we going?"

Danny smiles at my enthusiasm and drops a peck on my nose. "I've some business to clear up first."

"We shouldn't mention it to Daniel until it's definite," I say. He'd be broken if I gave him this and then took it away. Danny smiles as he goes, reading my thoughts and fears. If the principal does find out Danny's who he is, Daniel won't be getting into that school. Simple. I will do everything in my power to make sure the principal thinks Danny shits rainbows and goes to church every Sunday. Will they check that? If he goes to church? I need to speak to Father McMahon.

"Come with me a minute," Danny says quietly, taking my wrist and pulling me out into the hallway. He has a quick check around before he speaks. "What do you know about Pearl?" he asks.

"What?" I ask, my forehead bunching.

"She's been asking after Brad."

"Ohh," I breathe. "You too, huh?" I look past him to the kitchen. "James was asking too."

"I think that's one of the reasons he fucked off to the hotel and fucked his way through fuck knows how many women."

I look at Danny, disgusted. "He did what?"

He shrugs, like it's standard. *Standard.* "Wait, did you tell Pearl?"

"Yes, I fucking told Pearl. We need to nip that in the bud."

Is he for real? "What, like you're trying to nip Otto and Esther in the bud?" I ask. "Because that's going well."

He blinks, surprised.

"What are you?" I rant on. "The love police?"

His surprise morphs into irritation, and I roll my eyes dramatically, not doing myself any favors, but . . . screw him. "Rose, we hardly know her."

I laugh hysterically. "You didn't know me."

"She's twenty-one."

"Don't forget the small matter that she's a foreigner."

"She's British," he says, confused.

"Precisely." I poke him in the chest and immediately apologize for it when he withdraws, grunting with pain. Damn it. "I'm sorry."

"Forgiven."

"Anyway, your little plan to put her off Brad may have worked," I tell him. "She looked appalled when I told her Hiatus is a strip joint." Innocently, of course.

"Good."

I suppose Danny's right. Brad's not a one-woman kind of guy. Pearl's young, naïve. Brad will only hurt her. I sigh. I would say Pearl should be kept away from this world, but she's already exposed to it. Already in it. "You'd better go." I reach up on my tippy-toes and kiss his scarred cheek. "James said he'd meet you at Hiatus." I turn and head back to the kitchen, but he grabs my sweater and hauls me back to him, draping me over his arm. I let out a surprised yelp and find his eyes.

"You know the best thing about having a fiery marriage?" he asks, and I smile, despite myself. I love making up with him. I sickly love sparring with him. Bickering. Arguing. Fighting. It's the reasons why we fight that I hate. I grab his cheeks and land a big kiss on his lips, and Danny quickly takes it deeper, introducing his tongue. I lap it up on a contented hum and swallow every magical sound of pleasure he makes until he returns me to my feet, turns me by my shoulders, and sends me away. I hear the front door close and go to the window in the kitchen that looks out onto the front, seeing him sliding into the passenger seat of one of the Mercedes. Ringo's at the wheel.

"This kitchen gets busier and busier," Esther says as Brad strolls in with a face like a slapped ass. He's suited, but the sling supporting his shoulder takes it from classy to creased.

"Morning," I say, casual, going to the chopping board and picking up half a lemon.

He grunts, looking at the girls at the table as he passes them, not uttering even a hello. Pearl looks down at her coffee, and Anya looks at me, her thick, beautiful, naturally shaped eyebrows high.

"I think Pearl and Anya should come work at the club," I say, nibbling the corner of the lemon.

Brad freezes, looking at me in horror. "I don't need any staff."

"Umm, actually, I recall Mason saying he'd lost a few girls."

His eyes widen, and warning comes at me. What's his problem? He doesn't even deal with the bar staff. That's Nolan's job. It could be mine if my husband would relax a little. Besides, Pearl's clearly gone off Brad. "It's a no."

I look at him in disbelief. "They need something to do."

"I said no," he bellows, swinging around and knocking his shoulder on a cupboard. We all recoil in shock at his outburst. "Fuck!" he yelps, dropping his coffee cup. It shatters across the floor, Brad curses some more, and then stalks out of the kitchen, leaving behind a gallery of speechless spectators.

"Oh, I say," Esther breathes, going to the cupboard and digging out the dustpan and brush before snatching a towel off the counter. "Whatever has gotten into him?"

I look at Pearl.

She looks away.

This house right now is like a box of tension. A pressure cooker waiting to explode. I have to get out. I leave the kitchen and take the stairs fast, running down the corridor to Daniel's bedroom. I swing open the door and find it empty. TV room. I backtrack, taking myself back downstairs, finding Daniel on the couch with Tank. Neither of them look up at who's entered, their serious attention on the screen.

"You're not needed today?" I ask.

"You're here," Tank says, his thumbs working hard on the console in his hand. "And so is the little man. I'd be out with Fury looking for Beau if I could."

"We're going out for pizza," I say. Those simple words. Simple but so strange. So strange, in fact, both Daniel and Tank stop playing and look at me like I need checking in at an asylum. "We are," I assure them, pulling out my cell.

"I'm going nowhere unless I get it from the boss's mouth."

"Mom's the boss," Daniel says, making me smile. That's not quite true, but I'll take it.

I pull some confidence from nowhere and dial Danny, taking my cell to my ear. "Miss me?" he asks in answer as I start to pace in front of the fireplace.

"It's painful."

He laughs softly. "What do you want, baby?"

"To take Daniel out for pizza." I hold my breath, turning away from Tank and Daniel so they can't see my screwed-up face.

"Okay."

My face drops. "What?"

"I said, okay."

Okay? Just like that? I click my cell to loudspeaker and turn to Tank. "Can you repeat that, please?"

"You can take Daniel for pizza."

"Cool!" Daniel chucks his controller aside and turns off the TV.

"Thank you." I smile sweetly and disconnect the call. "Not that I needed his permission," I add, leaving a laughing Tank and Daniel behind. "Be ready at one." How ridiculous that I'm this excited to take Daniel out for plain old pizza? Crazy!

I take the stairs two at a time, dialing Beau, begging her to turn her cell on and pick up. She doesn't. I pass Zinnea's room and slow, reversing my steps and knocking on the door. "Come in," a voice calls, and I push my way in. I'm not faced with the vivacious alter ego Zinnea Dolly Daydream. Lawrence is sitting in the chair by the window in an unusually plain red kimono, his natural hair damp from a recent shower—no lashes, no makeup, nothing. I pout when he looks at me sadly.

"Come for pizza," I say, giving him begging eyes.

"Where the bloody hell is she?" he asks, sounding as ordinary as I have ever heard Lawrence sound. Frankly, it doesn't suit him. "I should have stayed in St. Lucia. I can't stand this worry."

"She'll be home." I go over and take his hands, pulling him up. "Come on. The boss has given me permission to leave our prison. I'm not going without you."

"Fine, fine," he sighs, waving me off. "What time are we leaving?"

"One."

He looks at the clock on the nightstand that shows it's just gone ten. "Good Lord, I better get a move on." He scuttles off to the bathroom and shuts the door, and I go to my room, dialing Beau yet again. I get her voicemail *again*, but this time I leave a message.

I beg her to call me. The wobble in my voice is not fake.

I'm so fucking worried about her.

In those three hours from ten until one, Lawrence didn't find it in himself to transform into Zinnea. Instead, he pulled on some Bermuda shorts, a Hawaiian short-sleeved shirt, some black and white checked Vans, a tie-dyed baseball cap that he has on backward, and has some thick-rimmed round spectacles covering his puffy eyes. But he's here.

"Daniel, it's not growing legs and running off your plate," I say, astonished, as Tank chuckles around his slice and Lawrence rubs his hair. I have never seen anyone eat pizza like it. I hate to think he's making the most of his freedom, eating as much as he can as fast as he can. We can order pizza anytime, but it's not the same as eating out.

My cell rings, and I blindly reach for it as I toss Daniel some napkins, answering. "Hello."

I expect to hear Danny's voice. Checking in. I don't. I shoot up from the table. "Beau?" I blurt, and everyone pauses chewing and looks at me, eliminating any chance I have of keeping this from James. Not that I would or could. The man is a broken, lost mess.

"I'm fine," she says, as I step away from the table, getting a warning look from Tank. I don't go far, wandering in front of the bar area.

"Where are you?" I ask.

"I need answers."

"That's not what I asked," I retort. "Where are you? You didn't come home, Beau. I can't believe how stupid you're being." I love her, understand her, but I cannot accept this level of recklessness. "James is so worried."

"I know." She sounds quiet. Defeated. "I don't want him to worry."

"Are you joking?" I stop with my pacing and look at the top shelf in disbelief. "You don't want him to worry?" She really is acting stupid right now. "Beau, after killing, that is what our men do best. They worry about us. We've discussed this before."

"I know."

"Come home," I beg. "Please."

"Where are you?" she asks, obviously registering the hustle and bustle.

"At a pizza place in town."

"With?"

"Tank, Daniel, Esther, and Lawrence." I hope she also registers the fact I've mentioned her uncle, not her aunt.

"Lawrence is there?"

"Ye—"

The phone is snatched from my hand and Lawrence is soon yelling down it. "Beau Hayley, you will get your ass home this minute, do you hear me?" His mouth falls open and he looks at the screen. "She hung up on me!"

Burying her head. Being a coward and not facing the hurt and worry she's causing. I put an arm around Lawrence and lead him back to the table. I want to point out the quite important fact that her call at least tells us she's alive, but I don't. I lower, get a knee rub from Esther and more questions from Daniel. "Why won't she come home?"

I shamefully push the pizza toward him to shut him up. Of course, he doesn't, looking at me tiredly as he talks over his food. "I'm fourteen soon, Mom."

"I know," I mutter, thinking talk of school would do the trick, distract him, excite him, but no. I'm not tempting fate. If the principal of this school finds out who we are, Daniel won't be going anywhere near his school. Also, Danny could change his mind. Anything could happen. He might not be satisfied with the security. It might be too far away. Too . . . anything.

I take a chili from a pizza and pop it in my mouth, noticing Tank's on his cell. He's silent. And his face pales. Oh God. I chew and swallow as he hangs up and looks down at the table blankly. What the hell? I wave for a waitress to box up the rest of our pizza to take home and wait for Tank to declare our immediate departure. But the waitress comes, she goes, returns again with the boxed pizza, and he still hasn't spoken. The rest of us all look at each other in question, and then Daniel puts a hand on Tank's big arm and wins his attention.

"Are you all right, Tank?" he asks.

"That was the nurse." Tank winces, reaching for his head and rubbing a hand across the back. "It's my mom."

"What about your mom?"

"They said it won't be long." He gets up, sits down, gets back up again, clearly in a muddle.

Oh no. "You must go." I stand too, collecting my bag and the pizza boxes, putting some cash on the table.

"I can't," he says, motioning to Daniel, then me.

"That's why we're going with you." I make it clear it isn't up for discussion, looking to Esther and Lawrence to get moving. I don't know what Danny will say. I don't actually care. He won't hold it against Tank, I'll make sure of it. "You should call Fury too." I take Daniel's arm and lead him out of the restaurant. "Perhaps someone else should drive." Tank looks shaken up, completely lost.

Daniel looks up at me as we walk down the sidewalk to the car, Tank close behind. "I feel bad for him, Mom."

"Me too, darling."

"He and Fury really love their mom."

I nod, keeping myself together, trying not to think about all the lost years we've had. "Do you hate me?" I blurt out of nowhere, my fears spilling out of my mouth.

"Why would I hate you? You're my mom."

I exhale, exasperated with myself, and stop us just before the car. Lawrence and Esther are catching up, and Tank gets straight behind the wheel. "I wish I could give you more." Good grief, I don't even have to look down at him anymore.

He doesn't say anything, his poor thirteen-year-old brain probably doesn't know *what* to say. But he does hug me. And it's the best thing he could do.

I so need it.

27

JAMES

It was fifty-fifty. Part of me hoped it would be Volodya sitting here so I wouldn't currently be aching with the effort it's taking me to remain in my chair, but the practical side of me knew Sandy was our best option.

So it's a good thing I drew the shortest straw.

"John Theodore Little," Sandy says, looking between Danny and me. "That's the name of the man who bought Winstable?"

"That's what I said," Danny replies quietly, as I watch the men standing behind Sandy, who's sitting comfortably on the couch in the office at Hiatus, much to my displeasure. "You told us you had information."

Sandy nods slowly. Dragging it out. Milking this situation for everything it's worth. The Brit and The Enigma wanting something from him. Or, more significantly, needing it. "Let me ask you this," Sandy says, his accent not as thick as Volodya's, as he crosses one leg over the other, spreading his arms across the back of the couch. "You English, what is the name Theodore . . . how do you say it? Reduced to?"

"Shortened?" Danny tilts his head.

"Yes, shortened. Theodore shortened."

Danny and I toss frowns at each other, and Brad sighs from his chair. "Ted—" He pauses, darting wide eyes Danny's way as ice glides through my veins. "Jesus."

"Teddy," Danny whispers, looking shook.

"And John Little," Sandy goes on as it all falls into painful place in my mind.

"Was a bear," Brad says, hitting his desk with a balled fist.

I exhale on a disbelieving, unamused burst of laughter. I don't believe this. How the fuck did we need this Russian prick to help us figure *that* out?

Sandy nods, and Danny starts pacing the office, the stress and anger radiating from him on a whole new level. "Fuck!" he roars, punching a filing cabinet.

"It's a penname," Sandy goes on, unperturbed by The Brit's temper.

"An alias," I correct him quietly.

"Potatoes, tomato."

Danny stares at Sandy like he's a fire-breathing dragon, and Otto goes straight to his laptop, tapping away frantically.

"He had men on the inside," Sandy continues.

Had. "He doesn't anymore?" Danny asks, his chest rising and falling slowly, a result of him trying so fucking hard to contain his rage.

"I say no." Sandy's rugged face takes on an edge of disgust. "I was being watched by entry police."

"Immigration."

"That stopped as soon as I accepted The Bear's offer to join him. Just yesterday, my bank accounts were frozen. I expect they'll catch up with me again soon. These are legitimate accounts for a legitimate business. That speaks to me that he has lost whoever he had on the inside. I also had a call from a Detective Collins. She said if I give her details on some things, she will ensure my accounts were thawed."

"Unfrozen."

"My English—"

"Will do." I look at Danny, shaking my head. Details on us. Collins wants details on us. Higham told us this. But is he covering his arse? In too deep? Naturally, we don't mention Higham.

"I'm not interested in being a mouse." Sandy gives each of us a moment of his eyes. "I want to remain here and run my business. I want Volodya gone."

I laugh under my breath. That'll please Danny. "What's the deal with you two?" I ask, helping myself to another vodka. Just one more before I go out there and search the streets. Again. Up and down, up and down, hoping, calling her repeatedly.

"He cannot be trusted."

Danny laughs loudly and holds his glass out for me to refill. I'm barely done and he's necking it. He won't be getting another. We've got a long afternoon ahead. The last thing we both need is to be stopped for riding jet skis under the influence while smuggling in our guns. Fucking hell, now more than ever I wish the delivery wasn't today.

"He's ex KGB," Sandy continues.

I finally feel like we're getting somewhere, and it's bittersweet with Beau missing. I need to get to the bottom of this today so I can call her and get her back. Problem is, even if we get answers, I can't fucking get hold of her to share. And this man in front of me, who could potentially end this for us, still tried to kill Beau. A flashback of her lifeless body on the bed after Dexter shot her invades every corner of my mind. The bullet wound on her tummy.

Where our baby was once growing.

Was.

The Russian nurse who tried to inject her. Kill her.

I see red and am up in Sandy's face before I can think better of it. "You tried to kill my girlfriend."

"You killed half my men, including my little brother," he hisses back, not backing down.

"Easy," Danny says, pulling me away, giving me a look to suggest he'll kill me himself if I fuck this up. "Easy," he says again, patting my arm and guiding my tumbler to my mouth. Turning to Sandy, he holds out his hand, and when Sandy takes it, Danny shakes it like a gentleman rather than squeezes threateningly. It's a strong message to Sandy.

"What now?" he asks.

"Now," Danny says thoughtfully, "you tell me if you find out anything else, and I will return the favor."

"And business?"

"We'll talk about that once we've dealt with this little issue. In the meantime, I assure you, you have one less man vying for your blood."

Sandy looks at me, waiting. "I can see you will be harder to convince."

I stare.

"Perhaps," he goes on, not shying away from the threat in my eyes, "if I told you a close contact of mine reported a sighting of your automobile in a parking lot of a hotel downtown? Would that help?"

"What?"

"You're here, so I am wondering what your automobile is doing there?"

"What hotel?" I get up in his face again. "Tell me."

"The Hilton."

I can't bring myself to thank the fucker. I fly out of the office, pulling up The Hilton hotel on Google Maps.

There's no easy or cheap way to do this, and I haven't got the time or patience to fuck about. "Just remember," Otto says as we walk through the lobby. "A smile gets you everywhere in this world."

I flash the man on reception a peek of my gun, not a smile, and slide a bundle of notes across the counter. "Simeon," I say, taking his name from his badge as I show him a picture of Beau on my screen. He quickly takes the cash and studies the photo.

"May I?" he asks, taking my mobile when I nod. He rounds the desk and wanders over to the concierge, showing him my phone. He shakes his head.

"The waitstaff?" I ask in vain, knowing I'm clutching at straws now, rather than drawing them. Either way, I'm about as lucky with straws as Danny is with poker. If Beau doesn't want to be found, she won't be found.

"I will ask housekeeping too," Simeon says, walking off. Naturally, we follow, and he looks back, uncertain.

"You have my mobile," I point out. "And probably one on you to call the police if you choose, which I wouldn't recommend."

"Definitely wouldn't recommend." Otto's bushy eyebrows rise as I motion for Simeon to continue, and he leads me into the bar, proceeding to show the staff my phone. All of them shake their heads. All of them eye me warily. None of them have seen my girl. "The rooms," I say.

"Sir, we have over one hundred rooms."

"And cameras," Otto says, looking around, thoughtful as he spins the ring in his lip and casually pulls his jacket back as a subtle reminder. What the fuck happened to smiling? "Where's the control room?"

Poor Simeon. His forehead becoming shiny from his stressed sweat, he clicks his fingers and tells the staff member to take Otto to the control room. Then he produces a key card and invites me to accompany him to the elevators.

"May I ask who she is to you?" Simeon asks, making small talk as we ride up to the top floor.

"No."

An hour later, I have entered every room in that fucking hotel and she wasn't in one of them. Our search and endless invasions of people's privacy has cost Simeon hundreds in complimentary drinks. For that alone, I hand him another wedge of cash and tell him to put my number in his phone. "Call me if you see her."

Simeon nods and gives me directions to the car park, where I find Otto looking over my Range Rover.

"Engine's cold," he says, feeling at the bonnet. "And cameras show nothing in the hotel. This space here falls into a blind spot. She knew what she was doing."

"You can't just park in any old hotel car park. You have to be a guest."

"Maybe she doesn't plan on collecting your car." Otto rounds my Range and gets up close and personal with the back window. "There's a train station down the street. Goes straight into MIA."

My stomach turns. "She won't get answers if she leaves Miami." I try the handle on the passenger side for the sake of it. "Did you see her pull in?"

"Yes, at eleven last night."

"But she didn't go into the hotel?"

Otto shakes his head and checks his watch, reminding me that we have somewhere we need to be. She won't come back while I'm here. I know that.

I nod and leave the car park, constantly looking back to my motor as Otto slips a tracking device under the wheel arch.

Where are you, Beau?

28

BEAU

I pull the hotel room door closed behind me and wander down the corridor to the elevators, feeling exhausted in every sense. I didn't get any sleep, just lay there battling the anger, the frustration, the unknown.

The grief.

Losing my focus on Mom's murder and redirecting it to Dad's is playing havoc with my conscience. Mom didn't deserve to die. Dad didn't either. But Dad's selfish choices mapped his path. Mom's self-lessness mapped hers.

I step in the cart and move to the back when a few more guests join me, turning on my cell and wincing at the endless missed calls from everyone I know.

And love.

And who love me.

The elevator dings, the doors open, and I walk to the reception desk armed with my key card, sliding it onto the counter. "Ah, Beau." Quinton leans over the counter and takes my cheeks, air-kissing each one. "I'll have the valet collect your vehicle from across the road." His beautifully plucked and dyed eyebrows lift as he looks over his rimless glasses at me. "Care to enlighten me as to why you needed parking away from the premises?"

"No."

"It's not stolen, is it?"

I laugh as he checks me out. "You think I've gone from cop to car thief?" *God, it's so much worse than that.*

"Well, it's all very strange, and coming from me, a man of the world who works in a bustling hotel, strange requests are part of the job." He staples a few sheets of paper together and folds them precisely. "How's Zinnea? God, I miss working the circuit."

"She's good," I say, suffering another pang of guilt.

"And Dexter?" he asks, curious. It was common knowledge Quinton always had a soft spot for Zinnea. "How is he?"

Dead. I smile tightly. "He left."

"What?"

My fiancé murdered him. "They split up."

"Oh. Oh, my. May I ask why?"

Because he was a crooked cop. "I'll tell her you said hi."

Quinton withdraws, removing his glasses and cleaning them, watching me too closely. Then he puts them back on and slips a card across to me. "I would love to see her. It's been too long." Another air kiss. "And there's always a Cosmopolitan waiting for him."

I take the card and wave it, backing away. "Good to see you, Quinton. And thank you."

He waves off my gratitude. "The valet will bring your car round."

I make it outside onto the sidewalk and keep close to the wall, scrolling through my contacts, not for the first time. As if a new name might appear. An old colleague who would be willing to help. It makes me miss Nath, not because he was my sounding board, but because he made me feel close to Mom. I have no one to turn to. No one who can help me.

"Beau?"

I look to my left. *Oh Jesus.* "Dr. Fletcher." My old therapist approaches, every limb she possesses as perfect as I remember, long and slender, smooth and soft. She smiles, it's hesitant, and adjusts her purse on her shoulder. I find myself doing the same.

"It's good to see you."

Alive. That's what she's thinking. It's good to see me alive. *Have you ever thought about ending your life, Beau?* I smile, and it's unstoppable. Smiling suggests someone is amused. "Good to see you too." I back away before I can get drawn into a conversation I don't want to have. I went to therapy for one reason and one reason alone. Because it was a better option than a hospital, and that's where I would have been sent by my father.

"Beau?" she calls, stepping forward, her arm rising. "You stopped coming." She's wondering why, since I clearly wasn't cured. I swallow and nod, and Dr. Fletcher smiles. "You look well, Beau. I hope this means you've finally found something to save you."

I stop in my retreat, her words hitting me like a sledgehammer. The truth is, I have way more demons now than I had when I was seeing Dr. Fletcher.

Something to save me. Have I found it? Or have I found something that will ruin me forever? Not a something, but a some*one*.

I turn and walk away, asking myself the question on repeat.

JAMES

We stopped by Tom Hayley's place on the way to the boatyard. Also Amber Kendrick's. Both empty. Both cold. No signs of life. Danny's right. Amber must know something. She'll get what she wanted—Tom's money—and now she's skipped town?

I pull up and see Danny with his wetsuit around his waist, his arms around Rose, hugging her. I give him a questioning look as I approach, and he gives me one to suggest he needs a moment, so I head inside and get into my wetsuit. A locker closes behind me, and I look back to see the kid in his gear. "Hey, kid," I say, placing my phone on the bench and standing. He looks proper forlorn. "What's up?"

Daniel looks at me, his eyes falling to my shoulder where my scars creep onto my front. He's seen it plenty. Never asked. I think that might change now. Something about the kid seems ... different today. "How—"

"I got caught up in an explosion," I say. "Trying to save someone."

"Who?" His eyes widen and his mouth falls open, his hand

reaching for his arm. He's thinking about Beau's scars. "Is she back?"

I shake my head, unable to tell him she will be. All I can think about is the trainline near to where we found my car. She could be long gone already. Perhaps she's done chasing the truth. Maybe she wants to escape.

Escape me?

"So are you going to tell me what's up?" I ask, jerking my head for him to come. I slip my arm around his shoulder as we walk out of the changing rooms.

"Tank and Fury's mom died."

I look down at him. "When?"

"We were out for pizza. Tank got a call and we had to go with him and Fury to the nursing home where their mom lives. She has dementia. Or . . . *had*. She died a minute before we arrived. Just a minute, and now I feel so bad because I hugged Mom by the car and she dropped the pizza box and it took two whole minutes to pick it up. That means they would have been at the nursing home one whole minute before she died. They would have been able to say goodbye." He throws his arms up and lets them drops heavily. "So it's all my fault."

"Ah, kid." I pull him into my side. "You can't blame yourself. There are a million things that happened today that steered the course of history, and you hugging your mum is only one of them. Is that why she's upset?"

"Yeah. Mister had us picked up so Tank and Fury could stay for a while. Grandma and Lawrence are in the café having tea."

"Bet it's not as good as your grandma's."

He chuckles and stops, forcing me to stop to. "Do you think we'll ever go back to St. Lucia?"

"Who knows, kid."

"Do you think I'll ever be allowed to go to a regular school?"

Fuck. "Maybe."

"Do you think I'll be able to go to college?"

That pizza's gone to the kid's head. "I'm not Mister, kid. Do you want to ask me a question I can answer?"

He smiles sadly and walks off, kicking the floor as he goes, head down.

"Hey, kid," I call, and he looks back. "Ask me if you're loved. If you have a family. A massive one, full of people who'll do anything for you. A family you can go out on the water with and race." *While they take delivery of their guns.*

Daniel's mouth lifts at the corner, and he nods as I join him, walking him back out. "You any closer to beating Mister yet?"

"Today's the day," he assures me, racing off to help Leon get his jet ski on the water as Otto jogs over.

"She turned her phone on briefly."

What? "And?"

"And she was across the road from the hotel."

Again, what? "The car?"

"Moved fifty yards and has been stationary since."

We both look up when the sound of tires crunching across gravel sounds and see my Range Rover pulling into the boatyard. My heart leaps. It fucking leaps. And then she gets out and it's an effort to stand steady. Relief. It's making me wobbly. Beau walks over, and the sight of her is like a salve to my cracked soul.

"What the fuck?" Otto grumbles, going back to his phone, obviously to check the tracker.

Beau holds up said tracker, clicks it on, and places it in Otto's hand. His phone starts beeping immediately. "I'm here," she says, looking at me, her dark, dark eyes a storybook of hopelessness.

"Where have you been?" I ask.

Her beautiful face is impassive. Emotionless. "I needed space."

She needed space? From me? It's a kick in the fucking teeth when all I've ever tried to do is protect her from the world. Keep her in the light. I've been tortured all night because she needed space? My relief is short-lived. Hello, irritation. "You didn't think to let me know you were okay? Alive?"

"You didn't think to tell me Cartwright had showed up dead?"

So it'll be like this? Tit for tat? "You fucking shot me."

"I was mad."

"So you shot me?" I ask, my voice rising in pitch. Otto slowly slinks away, leaving us to it. "You can't go off around town on your own playing detective, Beau," I yell.

"Beau!" Daniel cries, coming at us, his face significantly happier than a few moments ago.

"Not now, kid," I warn, holding up a hand to stop him. She is hearing this. "I've told you that repeatedly," I go on as Daniel joins Otto, moving cautiously away. "I need you to trust me. When the fuck are you going to lis—" I stop talking as Beau picks up her feet and walks past me, heading for the cabin as she shrugs off her trench coat. "Where the fuck are you going now?" My God, can't she stay still for just a minute?

"I didn't come back to argue." She doesn't look back.

"So I've just got accept that you'll up and leave whenever the fuck you like?" Am I getting this right, because that seems really *fucking* unreasonable? "Beau!" I'm off across the stones on my bare feet after her, feeling the eyes of many following my fuming form. "I didn't sleep a wink last night." I stalk up the steps behind her. "I've been calling you repeatedly." She disappears into the female changing rooms, and I'm right there with her. The three women in there, thankfully, are fully dressed, and all leave hastily, giving my looming frame a wide berth. Beau goes to her locker and pulls out her wetsuit. "I've been worried sick, Beau." She strips down to her underwear, completely ignoring me, and my eyes fall to her arm. Where it all began. My own scars tingle in response. "Running around town looking for you." Then she starts tying her hair in a high ponytail rather than covering herself, which I'd be really grateful for in this moment. I've missed her. Want to hug her, kiss her, spill my love all over her. But I'm mad at her too.

I rip my eyes away from her incredible, beautiful, war-beaten body and find her face. She won't look at me. Won't face me. Is she even hearing me?

She slams her locker door closed and sits on the bench, getting her feet into the suit, carrying on as if I'm not here. "Haven't you got anything to say?" Standing, she pulls her suit up her body and slips one arm in, and then the other before reaching for the zip and dragging it up her back. She looks at me, and I wait, bracing myself, pensive.

She inhales, like she's ready to speak.

But she doesn't.

She walks right on out, leaving me standing like a cunt in the middle of the women's changing room, wondering what the fuck I need to do to penetrate her. Her walls are up, her defenses high. She won't let me in.

Ever again?

I yell and punch the nearest locker, then stalk out, sweating frustration. We are *not* done. I don't give a fuck where we are. Who's here. What needs to be done. She does *not* get to come and fucking go as she pleases and expect me to hang around like a fucking puppy begging for any scraps of affection or sense she might throw my way. No.

I yank the door open, charge out, and meet the full force of Danny's body. He grunts, I grunt, both of us ricocheting off each other. "Get the fuck out of my way."

"Intervention it is," he says, putting up resistance, not letting me leave the changing room. "Now is *not* the time."

"Now's the perfect time." I strain against him, my shoulder pressing into him, each of us putting our full weight and more behind us. "Move, Danny."

"There's a delivery to collect."

"And we'll collect it." Just as soon as I've dealt with my Houdini fiancée.

Wait.

I still.

Think.

Why's Beau in a wetsuit? Where's she going now? "Fuck." The delivery. I relax, making Danny stagger forward. "She's getting the delivery with Leon," I murmur.

"That's what we agreed."

"I agreed. I never said I liked it. And part of my reasoning was to give her a little of what she wants, to get what I want. Clearly it hasn't worked, since I've been scouring the fucking city searching for her for the past twenty-four hours." It's give-and-take. She wants to be included, I want her to trust me. "I've changed my mind." Fuck this shit. I was going against every instinct I have letting Beau be involved in the delivery from Chaka. But I agreed. I agreed and hoped it would help her. I failed. She's more distant than ever.

"You know it's for the best." Danny holds a hand up, as if readying himself for my imminent charge. "She's come back. Beau knows if you or I go out there on the water while it's swarming with Coast Guards, we'll be pulled."

I'm incapable of reasoning with myself. Powerless to stop my hurt. She came back, but only to collect the delivery? What about me? What about us? I just have to sit here and wait for her to return whenever she disappears? Alive? In cuffs? *Fuck!* For the first time, I get a small glimpse of how Beau feels every time I leave her. I'm fucking livid, but her hurt, her utter frustration at how much control she has lost in her life hits me. In protecting her, I've been taking away even more control. She was a fucking amazing cop, her life on a trajectory to achieve much and do good. And now? Now she's relegated to the side-line against her will. But it's to protect her. To love her. To keep her safe.

I hold my hand out and Danny's Marlboros land in my palm. I quickly light one and drag in the nicotine. "This is a no-smoking area."

"Fuck off." I exhale my smoke all over him and fall back against the wall. "Leon ready?"

"Yep."

"Jet skis on the water?"

"Yep."

"Beau's on mine, right? She prefers mine." It's slightly bigger. More comfortable.

"She's on The Enigma."

I nod and take more nicotine. "Good."

Danny wanders over to the bench and lowers, lighting up too. "So, John Theodore Little."

"Your old boatyard was another sweetener for the scumbags," I say what we've both been considering. The Bear properly screwed Danny over on that front. Bought himself the perfect storage facility in the perfect location to entice the criminal fuckers who are now all abandoning him.

"Yeah," he says calmly, though I know he won't be feeling it. It's just another reason for us all to want the bastard. The question is, who gets the honors when we find him? "You should know," he goes on, "Tank and Fury lost their mother this afternoon. I've given them some time off."

I join him, thankful for the distraction. "The kid told me. You should know, he's struggling."

"I know," he says quietly. "I'm trying to fix that."

"How?"

"School. We're looking at one next week. Popular with security-conscious parents, if you know what I mean."

"Criminals?"

"Celebrities."

I laugh under my breath and look at the door, smoking my way through my cigarette. Is she out on the water now? Does she know what she's doing? Where to head? The signals? "Ringo's out there, right?"

"Shark fishing."

"And Goldie?"

"Paddleboarding."

"I didn't know she could paddleboard."

"She can't," Danny says over a laugh, but I don't join him, too stressed. Worried. I knew this wasn't going to be an easy wait, but the fact we're not on talking terms is making it worse. "Hey." Danny nudges my knee with his, knocking my attention away from the door. "The challenges we're facing now won't be around forever." Something tells me he's not just talking about business. "Work, family, wives, kids." Danny pulls on his cigarette and pouts, looking up at the ceiling and exhaling. "This is the rising, mate." He blows smoke up into the air, and it rolls and swirls above us. "There's only one thing that will stop us from staying on top once we've killed all the fuckers in our way." He drops his eyes but not his head. "Hell hath no fury like my wife." He smiles, and it's sick. "She terrifies me more than anyone. Including you and Beau."

"Beau terrifies you?" I ask over a laugh. I get it. She petrifies me. My laughter fades off, and Danny nods.

"If we didn't have them, we wouldn't need to be doing this. But we can't play dead. And we can't live a normal life."

"And we can't be without them," I finish.

"Precisely." He stands, pointing at me with his cigarette. "So let's get the fuck on with rising and make sure we never fall, because that, my friend, is the closest we're ever getting to normal."

I get up and head to the door.

"She'll be fine, James."

"I know," I say to myself. We both know Beau's trained and capable in keeping her cool in the face of danger. We both also know she's incapable of keeping emotion out of it since her mother died. She's pissed off with me. She may not be showing it, but she's hating on me—for constantly treating her like she's glass. It's in my nature where she's concerned, and I can't promise I will ever change, so we need to compromise. She's more delicate than she allows the world to see, but I know her now. To her core, I know her.

She needs me.

And I sure as shit need her.

If not for each other, why the fuck are we going through this hell?

30

BEAU

I'm pretty sure Leon is stoned, because he won't shut the hell up, rabbiting on at a guy who's dressed in traditional tribal garb, popping question after question—where's he from, does he like Caribbean food, has he been to Zambia, Congo, the Sahara?

Eventually, he lifts his shades, revealing eyes as black as his skin, and Leon pipes down. "Friendly," he mutters as the guns are transferred from the boat to the empty skis.

"They're not here to be friendly." I wade toward the first ski, pull down the handlebars and press into the padded seat, putting my weight behind it until I hear the catch click into place. I take the rope that connects the first dummy jet ski to James's jet ski and feel my way to the next. "A bit of help?"

Leon flashes the friendly black guy a smile and comes over to assist helping me to get all the skis closed again. The water is busy, boats crisscrossing constantly, but Chaka's catamaran is concealing us from the open water while we move the goods. I can't lie, my heart is going crazy in my chest, my eyes constantly scanning the space, both water and land.

"Are we done?" Leon asks as the final catch on the final ski at the end of the rope attached to his clicks into place.

"Done." I face the five guys on the small speed boat. "Thanks." I inwardly frown, wondering how I went from upcoming FBI agent to gun smuggler. The Enigma. That's how. Him and a whole heap of corruption.

Mr. Friendly moves his shades back over his eyes. "Tell Black the next shipment will be ready next week."

Great. We don't have enough guns? "Aye, aye, captain," I say quietly, retying my hair as I head back to my ski and Leon gets on his.

"Take it easy, okay?" he says, squeezing the throttle in demonstration. "Don't jerk. We have a bit more weight going back."

I nod and follow his instructions, my heartbeats starting to gain momentum as we chug farther out onto the water. "Have you had a joint today?" I ask.

"Yes, I've had a fucking joint today." He reaches for his bandana and pushes it back into his wild hair. "Not just because I'm nervous as fucking shit, man."

"Why else?" I ask. Keep talking. We look more casual if we're chatting.

"Because, Beau, babe, if we get pulled by the Coast Guard, they're smelling my weed before they're seeing the guns."

"Are you saying you'd go to prison to save Danny and James?"

He laughs hysterically, looking back at me. "I wouldn't be saving the bosses. I'd be saving myself, because I'm a dead man if we don't make it back to the boatyard with these guns." He takes one hand off the handlebars, relaxed. Good for him. I should have asked him for a puff of his joint. "It's all right for you," he says. "They won't kill you, will they?"

Don't be so sure. "They won't kill you either. They like you."

"They do?"

"They only have people they like work for them." We stick to the coastline, moving at a reasonable speed. I can see the curve in the cove that'll take us back into the bay. As soon as we're around it, we'll be able to see the boatyard. My heart slows for the first time, my muscles softening, and I sink into the padded seat of James's ski. The water twinkles at me, the sun seeping through the rubber of my suit, warming me. It's peaceful out here, despite the busy water today. But the Coast Guard seems to be keeping their distance, getting on with their training, because no one in their right mind would smuggle a small arsenal into the country in plain sight.

Not for the first time, I wonder why I'm doing this. And not for the first time, I can't say with my hand on my heart that I'm not trying to prove to James that I'm not made of glass.

Beep, beep!

I startle and look back, seeing a boat tailing us. A Coast Guard boat. "Fuck," Leon hisses, reaching into his suit and pulling out a small bag.

"What are you doing?" My galloping heart is back.

"I told you." He pulls out a joint and a lighter.

"Leon, no!" I look back at the boat, waving an arm in the air, acknowledging them. "Hey!" I call, easy-breezy, my mind racing, trying to think of another way out of this. I will not let him go down for possession. "Can I help you?"

"You mind telling me what you're doing, ma'am?"

I look at Leon. "I'm warning you," I say through gritted teeth. "I'll kill you myself if you light that joint."

"What the hell else do you suggest?" He looks back, worried.

"Just give me a minute." I stand in the seat, shading my eyes with my hand as I turn my shoulders and look back. "Just towing the new skis from storage for the boss, sir."

He rests his palms on the metal railing along the side of the boat, looking up and down the skis. "Were you aware we're training out on the water today? If people want to use the water, they've been asked to keep within the boundaries."

"Oh?" I frown, playing dumb. It physically hurts. "I'm sorry, sir, we're just doing what our boss asked." And now I'm going to give him some crocodile tears and pray for the fucking best. I look at

Leon, hoping he realizes this isn't only for Danny and James. "Are we in trouble, sir?" I ask, forcing tears into my eyes.

His lips straighten, but I can see he's thinking he hasn't got time for this. "Make it back around the cove quickly before someone else stops you." He takes off his cap and waves it, like *run along now*.

"Fuck, fuck, fuck," Leon whispers, eyes wide as he returns them forward, tucking his stock away. "Beau, babe, you just saved my life."

"Stop calling me babe." I start moving, slowly but surely, my heart not relenting. I make sure I keep my stare forward, not looking back, because I was always suspicious of anyone who looked back at me after I'd let them walk when I was a cop. Always.

But then I hear the building sound of an engine getting closer, and I look around instinctively, searching for the source. Nothing.

Then...something.

The loudest roar penetrates the air, and a jet ski comes from nowhere, zooming across the front of us, so fast, it's a blur. "Shit!" I yell, frightened out of my skin, the spray hitting me, forcing my arm up in defense. I follow the white, foamy trail with my eyes, my ski rolling atop the waves that have been created, and stand in my seat, looking back, seeing the jet ski circle the Coast Guard, performing a few donuts, kicking up enough water to making it impossible to see the rider.

"Hey!" the guard yells, running to the other side of the boat, signaling to his colleagues.

Anger finds my veins and starts to burn them as I catch sight of the scroll down the side of the ski. But I'm not stupid enough to think it's Danny on it. James couldn't use his own because *I'm* on it.

He circles, switching direction abruptly, maintaining the constant roar and spray, before thrashing the throttle and speeding off across the open water, away from the shore. Away from me. Away from the boatyard.

And the Coast Guard is soon in pursuit.

"Beau, come on," Leon yells, as I watch James get farther away, lowering into my seat.

I squeeze down on the throttle and head back to the boatyard, and I am seething the entire way, hoping to cool down.

Danny is in the water when we arrive, and he directs us to the shore rather than the jetty, where Jerry's got the trailer waiting, attached to the jeep. The moment he looks at me, I make sure he knows I'm not happy. I get off and help get each ski wedged into the seabed on the shore, holding my tongue.

For now.

Jerry starts getting the skis on the trailer as Ringo returns with Goldie and a paddleboard onboard his boat. "Beau," Rose calls, coming down the steps of the cabin. I look up and shake my head, warning her away. I don't want my friend to get caught up in the shrapnel that's about to fly.

I take myself fifty yards down the beach and start pacing up and down in the water, my hands on my hips, my face pointing toward the sun, my eyes closed, praying for calm. *Bring me calm before you bring me James!*

My prayers aren't answered. I look out to the ocean when I hear the distant roar of a jet ski hitting the waves and see him. I hold my breath, waiting for the Coast Guard to follow him. No boats appear. It's just James coming at us at full speed, standing in the seat.

He slows as he gets to the shore and the moment he can, he jumps off, landing in the water up to his waist and wading through. "Jerry, get this in the bunker," he yells, pushing it into the bed and running a hand through his hair before yanking down his zip and struggling out of the top half of his wetsuit. An angry bruise on his pec has me looking away from his chest to his face.

James's eyes find mine, and he turns his body to face me, inviting me to give him all I have because he's fully expecting it. "What the hell were you doing?" I yell. There's no build up to a shout. No warmup. I'm right in there, exploding, giving him my all.

"The Coast Guard was on you, Beau."

"I handled it!" I throw my arms up into the air. "What are you, a white knight, saving me when I didn't need fucking saving?"

He breathes out on a small laugh, turning away from me. "Of

course. Beau Hayley doesn't need saving, does she? Because she's Lara fucking Croft. Former cop. Upcoming, talented FBI agent." He swings around, his face red. "Except she's fucking broken and as fucked-up as this fucked-up white murdering fucking knight."

I recoil, injured, and James's lip curls, his disgust a slap in the face that I probably deserve.

"I'm done with this shit, Beau. I don't know what you want. What you don't want." He stalks off, throwing an arm up. "You're clearly hell-bent on doing what the fuck you please, and I'm fucking exhausted trying to stop you. I don't understand you anymore."

I stand on the shore watching him walk away, his brutalized back a beacon of ruin. He's never walked away from me before. Never. I look around me, circling on the spot, finding many eyes on me. Sympathetic eyes. "I . . ." What am I going to say to them? Try to make them understand my grievance? Will they? "Fuck!" I hiss, spinning around and walking down the shore, my hands in my hair, gripping tightly, punishing myself. I see James's scared back. My scared arm. His gunshot wound, mine too. I look to the sky and yell, deranged, and walk on, breathing heavily, my heart thundering.

I hope this means you've finally found what's saving you.

I need to stop trying to prove that I'm not glass. Because I *am* glass. I have shattered time and again, and James hasn't fixed me. He's broken with me, and sometimes having someone who understands you is all you need. Someone to take you away. Someone to escape with. *I don't understand you anymore.* Those words hurt. I drop to my ass on the sand and look out at the ocean through my teary eyes, feeling so fucking lost, and my mind wanders to months ago. To his glass apartment. To the time we both folded under the pressure to stay away.

The pleasure. The pain. The complete and utter exhilaration.

I was numb to a world that had tortured me for years. And my senses were heightened to a man who would be a constant in my life. "God damn it," I whisper, propping my elbows on my knees and burying my face in my hands. It's true. I do have more demons now than I did when I saw Dr. Fletcher. But I don't feel any worse. In fact, I feel more stable than ever. Low every now and then, maybe even depressed, completely mad sometimes, but the panic attacks are few and far between, the dark thoughts gone, and I am no longer a zombie, staggering aimlessly through the darkness, trying to find my way out. I no longer consider death better than living.

James.

He is my therapy.

My cure.

My peace amid the chaos.

And I keep pushing him away. Keep allowing the ghosts to take me.

Why am I living for ghosts when I have James?

I hear the door of his Range Rover slam shut and shortly after wheels spinning on the stones. I look back and see the rear end fishtailing, kicking up a thick smog of dust, and everyone is watching. And once James is out of sight, they all turn their attention to me sitting on the shore.

Rose comes and lowers beside me, motioning down the wetsuit she's sporting. "Sexy, huh?"

I smile. "He let you out on the water?"

"No. I was watching Daniel close to the bay with Danny."

While I collected their guns. A silence falls between us, and I focus on the soft slap of the water around my feet.

"Okay?" Rose asks.

"No," I answer honestly.

"He's right, you know, Beau." She leans into me, attempting to lighten her hard truths. "You can't do as you please to that extent. It's not fair." I can feel her eyes on me, and like the coward I am, I don't look at her, keeping my welling eyes on the calm, crystal waters. They're a stark contrast to the murky chaos of my mind.

"When Amber held a gun at you," I say, hating myself for having to ask but needing to ask, nonetheless. It's playing on my mind. "Did you think she'd pull the trigger?" I look at my friend and see despair. Despair for me, for James, for everyone who's involved. "Truthfully."

"Yes." Rose places her hands in the sand and fists. "If Esther hadn't showed up, I think she could have in that moment, yes."

I nod and go back to gazing at the ocean.

"You honestly think she did it?" she asks.

"I think Cartwright knew something that would incriminate Amber. He spent a lot of time writing about my father." I give her an ironic look that's way out of place. "Dad was probably paying him."

"He was a bit of a megalomaniac, wasn't he?"

I laugh. That's out of place too. "A bit."

"So do you think Amber killed Cartwright too?"

"I don't know. You know her better than I do. Do you think she's capable of that?" I know what I'm doing and I'm doing it unashamedly. No, I don't know Amber, but I know what Rose has told me. And I know my dad, a sensible, shrewd businessman, left her every penny. Whether he did that as one last kick while I was down or because he loved Amber, I don't know. But I saw his face when Amber was exposed as a gold digger. He was mortified. Hurt. And I also know how he treated me. So actually, I'll never have an answer for why he did it. But I may get closure on his death.

Rose's expression says it all. Amber is perfectly capable. And why would she run from me when I saw her loitering in the parking lot? "It's dog eat dog in this world," Rose says quietly, looking off at the horizon. A pang of guilt stabs me. She's thinking about when she had to survive in this world. When she didn't have Danny. I've no doubt Rose would have killed if she needed to. "So what are you going to do?"

Good question. It seems I can't keep James happy *and* try to prove this. "I'm going to try and salvage what's left of my relationship." I push my way to my feet and offer my hands to Rose. "I know I can't be a cop and be James's. Your husband has reminded me of that."

Rose takes my hands and lets me pull her up. "Very kind of him," she says. "So which will you be? A cop or James's?"

I link arms with her and walk us back to the cabin. "I need a beer," I say, ignoring her question. I can't promise to stand down, and I won't. I have to get justice for at least one of my dead parents. I have to figure out how I do that without ruining James and me. "Where's Fury?" I ask, scanning the place.

Rose sighs and then stops dead in her tracks on a slight hitch of breath. "Wait. Shit, you don't know."

"Know what?"

She faces me. "The Vikings. Their mom died."

I step back, my sadness immediate. "No."

She nods. "Danny let me take Daniel for pizza. Tank got the call while we were there. He called Fury, but they didn't make it to her in time. Danny gave them some time off."

I pull out my cell and dial Fury, needing to check if my bullet-proof bodyguard is okay. He doesn't answer. "You went for pizza?" I ask as we continue to the cabin.

"I know. We're also looking at a school for Daniel."

"What's going on?"

"I hope the end is going on. You should go inside and see Lawrence before you leave."

There are only a few occasions when Lawrence makes an appearance. When he's hungover, when he's exhausted, or when he's worried.

I don't make it inside. He appears at the top of the steps of the cabin in all his mismatched glory, his face disappointed. I don't need it. Not now. "I need a beer." I ask as I approach.

"And a scold." His eyes behind giant spectacles follow me as I pass. "You fix this, Beau Hayley, do you hear me?"

I turn, inhale, and take a few breaths. "I hear you."

"I'm going back to St. Lucia. I can't stand the constant despair and worry being in this city brings."

I nod, not surprised, not hurt. "Okay." I fetch a beer from the fridge and flip off the cap as Leon comes at me, nearly knocking my teeth out when he hugs me.

"You're a goddess."

"Watch it," I snap, pushing him away, the stench of marijuana invading my nose. "You stink."

"I'm celebrating. Where's J-Boss?"

Lawrence folds his arms over his chest and rests his weight on one hip, tilting his head. *Jesus.* I go to the changing rooms with my uncle hot on my heels. "It was reckless and selfish."

"I know." I pull my locker door open and something falls to the floor at my feet. I dip and pick up the card. Oh, yes. This is just what I need right now. "Do you remember Quinton?"

"Oh, the cute Cuban?"

"Yes." I hand Lawrence the card. "He said hello. Mentioned that it would be nice to see you."

"He did?" A blush crawls its way onto his cheek as he plucks the card from my fingers and reads it.

I smile and get changed.

Get ready to fix the mess I've made.

I ride back with Otto and Goldie, who are definitely giving me the silent treatment. So, basically, everyone is against me. I'm not being a victim. I'm accepting that I'm a headache. For everyone.

I walk into the lobby of Danny's mansion—my *home*—and Goldie and Otto head to the kitchen, where I can hear people chatting. I don't go there. I go straight to our room.

But it's empty.

I dislike the sudden thrum of my pulse immensely. My shortness of breath. The panicked heat rising inside. "James?" I call, going to the bathroom. No life. The shower's not been used recently. The sink has no water splashes in the bowl. I go to the terrace. No one.

The gym.

He'll be balancing. Trying to calm down and find his center.

I race down the corridor and the stairs two at a time, and jog to the gym, pushing my way in.

Empty.

"Shit," I curse, fighting back the rising panic, relaying every awful thing he yelled at me. *I don't understand you anymore.* He told me one time that my hate walks hand in hand with my love for him. I swallow. Hate has lost a grip on love. I hardly understand myself anymore.

I back out and go to the kitchen. Everyone is in there, at the table, the island, helping Esther, talking. And it falls silent when they all spot me at the door. "Where is he?" My voice cracks over my question, the worst dread coming over me. That dread only multiplies when people start looking at each other in question, clearly waiting for the person who knows where James is to speak up. No one says a word.

I'm done with this shit, Beau. I don't know what you want.

You're clearly hell-bent on doing what the fuck you please, and I'm fucking exhausted trying to stop you.

Otto goes to his phone. Danny's relaxed face turns tense. And it occurs to me . . . "His car." I run to the window that looks out onto the front, not remembering seeing it. "It's not there." I face the room, my body starting to convulse with the strain I'm inflicting on myself just trying to force steady breaths rather than gasp. I realize I have no right to feel like this after what I've put James through in the past twenty-four hours. But . . . it's unstoppable. The panic. The fear. The worry. He didn't come home? "Where is he?" I yell, feeling my way to the closest drawer and yanking it open. "The paper bags. Where are the bags?" I slam it shut and yank open another, searching for them. "Dexter always kept the bags in the drawer." I don't understand. I haven't had a flashback. I'm not in a busy, chaotic space. Why is this happening?

A burst of activity breaks out around me, and Rose is quickly in my sights. "Beau, calm down." She tugs me across to a chair and pushes me down onto the seat, and Doc holds a glass of water at my lips. I sip it, never taking my eyes of my friend, willing this episode to fuck off.

"We'll find him," Lawrence says, with absolutely no conviction in his voice, looking at Danny for guidance.

He's punishing me. This is how James felt when I was missing. My head bats back and forth between everyone around me, waiting for one of them to talk. Tell me where he is. Pull me free from the claws of panic. I've pushed him away.

"He's in the office."

Everyone looks toward the door as Brad walks in, his arm still in a sling. "What?" I breathe.

"The office."

I get up and hurry to the office, music coming from beyond, getting louder and louder the nearer I get. I burst in unannounced. The music is deafening.

Labrinth.

"Oh Jesus," I whisper, my hand on the knob as *Still Don't Know Your Name* blares. I take in the sight of him. My panic leaves me in an instant and guilt swoops on in and takes its place.

He's drunk.

So drunk, he hasn't even registered someone's in the room. Staggering around, waving a drink in the air, tossing the liquid left and right before refilling and doing the exact same. Still in his wetsuit. It's like . . . like he's having an argument with someone who's not here.

Me.

Except, I *am* here. I've never seen him like this. I close the door and look around for where and how to turn off the music, my ears ringing. I could scream and he wouldn't hear me. I resort to covering my ears and going to him, trying to get his attention. I put myself in front of him. He stops, stills, looks down at me.

Sees straight through me.

I'm not here.

Pain slices me clean in half as my hands drop and he pushes

past me, going to the couch and dropping heavily onto it, letting his head fall back, his eyes closing. He can't look at me.

Danny appears in the doorway, his icy eyes taking in the scene. James plastered. Me standing like a useless fool in the middle of the room. He pulls his phone out, presses the screen, and the music dies. "Fix it," he orders, throwing a disappointed look to James, pulling the door closed. But he was telling *me*. Not James.

Fix it. How? Anything I say won't be remembered in the morning.

I go to him and lower to the couch beside him, reaching for the empty glass in his grasp. He doesn't give it up, fighting with me. He wins. Of course he wins. His eyes open, revealing . . . nothing. The expressiveness they've gained since we met has gone and the soulless, cold pits are back. "I can't be around you," he says, fighting to get his big body up from the couch. "I'm supposed to be enough, Beau."

I wince, not asking if I'm enough for him. I know I am. "Can't I have justice for at least one of my dead parents?"

He spins so fast, his big body is a blur, and I back up, wary. "Not if it means I fucking lose you!" He throws his glass, and it hits the frame of the Picasso on the wall, shattering, making me flinch and cower. "Finding *him* isn't about revenge for me anymore. It's about me and you!" His words are clear. There's no slurring. But his body continues to sway and stagger in between his bellows. It's as if alcohol has hit his body but not yet his brain. He sounds lucid but looks trashed. "It's about us having a life together. Happiness. Fucking *health*." He smacks his temple with the ball of his hand, making it clear that health doesn't just mean physically. "Do you want the same? Am I enough?" He walks on heavy legs to the drinks cabinet and takes a bottle of vodka, swigging more than a glass full, his naked, scared back glaring at me. "Or will this innate instinct in you always win?" He faces me, his eyes tortured. "I can't take part in a fight I can't win, Beau."

"You can win," I say, my vocal cords straining, my voice shaky, wanting to go to him, but I'm too scared. Not of his physical presence. But of rejection.

"Can I?" He comes to me, his eyes never leaving mine. I find it hard to maintain our eye contact. "Because everything tells me otherwise. You. Your actions." He swallows, and it's lumpy. "My gut."

"No." I step forward, my emotion choking me, and James steps back.

Rejection.

"And these." He holds up something, and my watery eyes try to focus. My birth control pills. *Oh God, no.* "You wanted a baby," he whispers

I feel all breath leave me, my eyes low, the cruel claws on panic creeping up my back again.

"You told me, Beau. In every way, you told me."

"And you didn't want it," I say feebly, going to the couch and lowering, my eyes down, unable to face the mess I've made of him. He said I wasn't ready for a baby.

He throws the pack of pills on the couch. "It had nothing to do with me not wanting it." His voice is starting to rise again, his temper flaring. "I was worried about you! Fuck, Beau! What is it?" I look up at him, my mind not helping me. Not telling me how to explain. "You don't want a baby anymore? You don't want *me*? Do you want to be a cop again? Oliver Burrow's fiancée again?" Another swing of vodka, his hand shaking violently as he takes it to his mouth.

"You can win," I say over a sob. "You can."

"It's bullshit!" he roars. "Don't tell me I can win when you won't fucking let me." This time, he throws the bottle, and I jump on a cry of shock as glass pours down like rain, the building tears starting to fall as James's body vibrates, rolls, burns before my eyes.

"James," I choke, getting up to go to him.

"No." His hand comes up, halting my advance, and he looks at me. It's a look I'll never forget. One of contempt. Pain. Hopelessness.

"I'm not okay," he says on a whisper, swiping another bottle off the cabinet and leaving.

The door slams, and my eyes explode with tears, my ass hitting the couch, my face hiding in my hands.

Please don't leave me. Please still love me. Want to keep me.

"Please," I sob. "Please, please, please."

Don't tell me I can win when you won't fucking let me.

I cry. I cry so fucking hard, my sobs ragged and broken.

Tattered.

Like my heart.

31

JAMES

This is exactly why I don't drink in fucking excess. My body won't cooperate, and my mind? It's unbearably clear. Not nearly as foggy as I need it to be. I focus hard on placing my hand on the polished gold rail and then one foot in front of the other as I climb the stairs, having a break for a swig every five steps or so. I don't know how long it takes me to get to the top. Maybe half a bottle.

I hear the front door open and turn very slowly and carefully to look down the stairs. Fury and Tank enter, both suited. Danny comes from the kitchen and looks up the stairs to me. I'm sure I see his head shake in disapproval. He can go fuck himself.

"What are you doing here?" he asks, looking between them.

"Reporting for duty," Tank says sardonically.

"No. You need time off and, with respect, I need men with their heads in the game."

The twins cast looks at each other, both unsure. It's Fury who speaks up. "Our heads are perfectly in the game, Danny, I assure you. And, *with respect*, now's not the time for you to be down two men."

My eyebrows rise, though slowly. *Alcohol.* Fury's right, but I can't seem to make my mouth work to tell Danny to listen to him. Good. The alcohol is finally going to my head.

Beau comes from the corridor that leads to Danny's office, her eyes puffy, and spots the boys, and Fury is immediately on her, questioning. "I'm fine," she assures him, offering comfort when she needs it herself, reaching over his huge shoulders and hugging him.

I turn and go to our room, swigging as I go. I can't look at her. Can't bear to hear her pathetic excuses, whatever they may be. It's bad enough she disappeared for twenty-four hours straight because she *needed space.* To tell me she wants a baby and then do something that pretty much guarantees she won't have one? I don't get it. Waiting to see if she comes on her period was torturous. Was she going to leave me to go through that each month? The worry, the disappointment. Wondering how she'd take it. How she'd react? Bracing myself for the backlash. Feeling so fucking helpless. Worried.

I snort, disgusted, and push into our room, slamming the vodka down and dropping to the bed, peeling my wetsuit off and tossing it in the corner. I reclaim my alcohol and take myself outside, laying on a lounger and staring at the sky.

She doesn't want a baby. Fine. She's proven today she's definitely not ready for it. *Irresponsible. Reckless.*

More vodka.

The clouds begin to travel faster through the sky. They circle, roll, tumble. "Fucking hell." I grunt and struggle up, blinking back the spin as I stagger to the bathroom, my body telling me it's had enough—to stop pouring alcohol into it at a stupid rate. My head, however, is still too lucid.

I sup back more liquid, feeling my way across the wall. My body will have to soak it up.

I feel so betrayed.

Really? Because I'm certain you had a fleeting thought to get her pregnant and trap her.

I stop in my tracks and look around, confused. "What?"

Yes. To make it impossible for her to go off around town playing Lara Croft with her ex-fiancé.

I recoil, stunned, turning on the spot, looking for the source of the voice. "I didn't tell anyone that."

You told me.

I lose my footing and fall into the nearby wall. I try in vain to save myself, but my drunken body isn't responding to my slowing brain nearly fast enough, and I land with a thwack, smacking my head on the toilet. "Shit," I mumble, my words slurring now too, as I fight my way back to standing, somehow managing to still have the bottle in my grasp. Chuffed with myself, I finish my vodka, tilting back on my heels, my face pointing at the ceiling to make sure I get every last drop. It's now official. I've never been so drunk.

Finally. May the numbness commence.

I gasp, release the bottle, and raise my foot to break its fall, catching it on the bridge. I remain on one foot, and it's a fucking miracle given the state of me. I see Beau. On a ladder under the spotlights of my office. I see her carrying endless equipment. Bumping into me. Dropping it all.

"You know, I'll get this finished much faster if you give me some space."

"Space," I replied quietly. "I was just trying to help."

"I don't need your help."

She never did finish decorating my office. Because Beau finally decided whether she hated me or wanted to fuck me.

She took the latter.

Is she regretting it?

I gasp and reach for the wall when I wobble, placing my foot down.

Do *I* regret it?

I look down my chest, my hand coming up, my fingertip moving in on the bruise on my pec from where the love of my life, my blood, my fucking heartbeat, fucking shot me. I miss it by a few inches and am forced to close one eye to turn ten bruises back into one. "Fuck me," I breathe, letting my hand drop heavily. I go to the mirror, bracing my palms on the edge of the sink, leaning in, so close I'm practically kissing the glass. I take in my hair that's fairer these days. Lighter.

From being in the sun.

From being in the light.

"But you're not enough," I slur, watching my mouth move slowly, my eyes blink slowly, my body sway slowly. Even in my drunken state, I can appreciate how impossible Beau and I were. How . . . toxic. Harmful to ourselves but more harmful to each other.

I've failed to keep us in the light.

I curl my lip at the letdown staring back at me, closing my eyes, unable to face him. I pull my head away, inhale, and send it crashing back into the mirror.

When I open my eyes again, what I see matches how I feel.

Shattered.

I shy away and turn, feeling my legs failing me completely now. I make it two staggered paces and fall into the tub on a grunt and a clatter. I roll to my back, close my eyes and sigh. The cool enamel on my disgusting skin feels good. Better than the reason for those scars. Trying to save a woman who didn't want saving. Still doesn't.

Failure.

"I bought an apartment for us." I laugh out loud, thinking how ridiculous it was to ever believe we could be normal. So fucking absurd. Danny was right.

"If we didn't have them, we wouldn't need to be doing this. But we can't play dead. And we can't live a normal life."

"And we can't be without them," I'd answered. Like a fool, because I may not get that choice.

"So let's get the fuck on with rising and make sure we never fall, because that, my friend, is the closest we're ever getting to normal."

Failure.

I settle and doze off, the bathroom spinning like an out-of-control merry-go-round, slowing every so often, not enough to get off, but just enough and for long enough to give me a complimentary memory. All Beau. She's dominated my thoughts since I met her, and slowly over that time, my tortured past has been replaced with another kind of torture.

Loving Beau Hayley.

32

BEAU

It's agony seeing him like this. Knowing I'm the cause. James told me once about the aftermath of his parents' deaths. How he coped. Basically, he didn't. He lost himself in drink and when Otto finally pulled James out of his self-destructive mode, all hell broke loose. Many people died and are still dying. I wonder now if that's why he doesn't drink himself into oblivion anymore. Because it takes him to places he wants to forget. Hopelessness.

I've taken him back to those times. Those feelings.

I approach him quietly, watching his face, lines still cutting his features in his sleep. His long, hard body spans the tub and then some, his shoulders slightly bunched to his ears, his face turned in. I lower to my knees and reach for his forehead, seeing a crisscross of tiny cuts in the center. "What did you do?" I ask, brushing his hair off to get a better look. It looks like someone's pushed gravel into his flesh. And he has a tidy bump near his temple. "You are enough," I whisper, scanning his exquisite, tormented, damaged face.

His eyes pop open, and my hand freezes on his forehead. And we stare. We stare for so long, I have stored every silver fleck in his blue eyes to memory. Every line on his face. Every bit of his stubbled jaw. I take comfort in the fact he appears to be doing the same, although his eyes are drowsy and travel more slowly across my face.

He reaches up to my wrist and circles it, then pulls me into the tub with him. He shuffles up, opens his thighs, and positions me in between, easing me back to his chest. A bath with no water. But endless fire.

"Can you hear me?" I ask quietly.

"I'm drunk, not deaf."

I smile, though it's small, as I find the courage I need to try and explain my logic. To explain my betrayal. "Waiting for my period is a pain I can mask," I say, swallowing, digging deeper for the strength I need to do this. To make him understand. "Each time I bleed, I wonder if that part of me is broken too." I swallow. "If I take the pills, I will never wait with bated breath to bleed. I know it will happen. I will never have a baby, but at least I am in control."

James remains silent behind me, but as if wanting me to know he's hearing me, he starts stroking my scarred arm.

"I do love you," I say, spreading my palms on his thick thighs, stroking across the hair. "Don't ever question that."

"I follow your light, Beau," he says, his voice husky with alcohol and sleepiness. "But you're fading fast and I'm losing you."

"And I'm terrified of losing yet another person in my life. Especially you. But also another baby." *I'm not equipped to cope with more loss.*

"I can't lose again either, baby," he whispers.

Yes, the bath is empty.

But I could cry enough tears to fill it.

33

DANNY

There's always one of us less stressed than the other. It's usually because of the women. It's easy for the other to pass judgment, throw out advice. Only James walks in his shoes, only I walk in mine. We face different challenges when it comes to our relationships, but in business, we're both on the same page.

I smash out another twenty reps and lower the bar, using it to pull myself up on the bench. My face still creases with discomfort, though, despite relieving my stomach and chest of the strain. I look down at the mess of my torso on a sigh. Ironic that all my current injuries are a result of a woman, and not just my own. Pops would turn in his grave.

If he was in his fucking grave.

I quickly shake that maddening thought away before it distracts me from my day and get up, grabbing a towel to wipe my wet brow before laying it around my neck. I fill a cup and down the water, looking at the door when it opens. I lower the cup. "What are you doing in here?" I ask Brad, looking up and down his half naked body, shorts and a sling the only things he's wearing.

"Working out."

I follow his path to the Peloton. "You look like shit." Probably still hungover from his marathon binge on everything forbidden.

He gets on the bike and sits up straight, keeping his hands off the handlebars. "You don't exactly look as fresh as a daisy yourself." Nodding at my torso, he starts pedaling and tapping at the screen.

I refill my cup and neck some more water. "My injuries, both physical and mental, are a result of a love interest." Rose would slice my dick off if she heard me refer to her like that. "I know what caused your physical injury. Care to enlightened me on why you're a tetchy fucker lately?" Something tells me it's nothing to do with his overindulgences.

"What the fuck are you talking about?"

"Pearl." I get straight to the point. I've got things to do.

The fleeting recoil I catch before Brad manages to get his facial expression in check worries me. "Who's Pearl?"

"Oh, for fuck's sake." I toss my cup in the bin and go to the bike, standing in front, hand on the bars, eyes on Brad. "How long have I known you?"

"Too fucking long."

"Agreed." I watch his shoulder jolt as he pedals. "Engage your core," I order. "And sit up straight." He does both with a scowl. "She's twenty-one," I point out. "You're thirty-four."

"Is this going somewhere?"

"Have you fucked her?"

His mouth falls open and his pedaling slows. His reaction alone tells me no. "No, I've not fucking fucked her."

"Do you want to?"

Brad's face. Fuming is putting it lightly. Honestly, I'm not sure how to interpret it. "No. She's twenty-one, for fuck's sake, Danny. Practically a child. Whatever fantastical idea she has about this world, I'm not interested in feeding it."

"So why are you mean to her?"

"What?" he snaps, impatient.

"You're mean to her. Impatient. You give her filthy looks." I raise my brows as Brad visibly scrambles for a reason. "I'm not the only one who's noticed. It's causing an atmosphere."

"*I'm* causing an atmosphere?"

"Yeah, by being grumpy. People aren't used to it."

"Then I'll apologize."

"Probably best you just stay out of her way. She thinks you're a dick."

He flinches. "Why?"

"Well, because you fuck hookers and own a strip club."

"How does she know that?"

"Because I told her." I'm certain I can hear his teeth grinding. "Rose thinks she finds you repulsive."

"Is everyone talking about this?"

I shrug, amused, taking this light relief while I can get it.

"Good," Brad snaps. "I'm glad she finds me repulsive."

I nod, not convinced, "So why the fuck are you a miserable fuck lately?"

"Has everyone around here amid the drama their women are creating—which, I will add at this moment in the aftermath of your interrogation, is the very fucking reason I will never take myself a woman—missed the fact I've been fucking shot? And my fucking apartment was fucking blown the fuck up, Danny. I don't have a home." He starts pedaling again, his top half jerking all over the place.

"I think it's you who's missed the fact you've been fucking shot. Doc will string you up if he sees you on that thing."

"I'm stressed."

I laugh. "You're a dick." He totally wants to fuck Pearl. It's a good job she hates him now because that would only end in tears. Hers. And Brad's when Rose and Beau beat him black and blue. "I'm going to get a shower."

"Hey, your cell," Brad calls as it starts ringing from the mat in the corner where I was stretching. I wander over and crouch, swiping it up and turning it over. I look back at Brad. His pedaling slows. "Amber?"

I connect the call and rise, walking to Brad, waiting for whoever's on the end of the line to speak.

"Danny?"

Brad's eyes shoot to mine, and I exhale. I've never been so glad to hear her voice. "Amber." Tread carefully, but not too delicately. This woman has only ever known brutality and coldness from me. "What do you want?"

"I'm in trouble, Danny. Serious trouble."

I figured. The gym door opens, and with the lightest of breeze comes the most incredibly pungent stench of stale alcohol. I look over my shoulder and grimace. He looks like death warmed up. And what the fuck's happened to his head? "The kind of trouble you get in when you take the inheritance that rightly belongs to someone else?" I ask, trying to clue a comatose looking James into what he's walked in on.

"I had no idea about the money."

James walks over, interested, as I laugh. "Come on, Amber."

"Danny, I swear. Tom and I split up. He called me and said he missed me. Wanted to have dinner at his place. I went and we rekindled."

So was Amber who Tom had been dating? "You loved him? Didn't just want his money?" We all huddle in, waiting, listening. I can't say Amber is transparent, because I'm pretty sure she loved me, despite the fact I showed her no love, fucked her regularly, and shared her. My money and power were a bonus. But, and forgive me for bashing a dead man, I'm a fuck load better looking and a few decades younger than Tom Hayley.

"I did what I needed to do to survive after you threw me out."

"Oh boy," Brad murmurs, pulling back from the phone, his worried eyes on me.

"What can you tell us about Tom's death?" I ask, knowing James is going to be jumping in any moment if I don't get this moving.

"I need something in return."

"What?"

"Well it ain't money, is it?" Brad says on a sardonic laugh, earning dark looks from me and James. "Hi, Amber," he adds.

"Brad." She strains his name, no love lost there. Yeah, I shared Amber, but never with Brad. He despised her. Prefers to take his women as strangers, mostly in hotels. There's never any backlash for him. No whore biting at his ankles wanting money or safety.

James nudges me, pushing me on. He looks green, like he could throw up at any moment. "Well," I push.

"Protection."

"My protection is expensive. It depends what I get in return for protection."

"You get a teddy bear."

The room becomes still and quiet, all our bodies straightening. Somehow, this offer feels more serious than any other. What I'm thinking though, is how the fuck does the lover of Beau's father have information about The Bear? "I can give you protection."

"How?"

"I have a place abroad. Secluded, solitary, no one knows about it." I am saying and thinking so many things lately that could get me a divorce. "What do you know about The Bear?"

She's quiet, for so long I wonder if she's hung up, but a quick glance at the screen tells me she's still there. "Not on the phone," she eventually says.

We all sag. *Fuck.* "Where?"

"Where's safe?"

I immediately look around the gym that's in my sage home but quickly dismiss it. That wouldn't end in divorce, that would end in death. Whether at the hands of Rose or Beau, I couldn't say, but it is not a risk worth taking. But . . . where else? *Fuck it.* "Come to the house," I tell her, looking at Brad who shakes his head. "Three o'clock. Call me when you're at the gates." I hang up.

"I don't like this," Brads says, now motionless on the bike.

"Here is safest." We all know it. I get another strong waft of stale alcohol and move away from James. "Mate, get a shower, I beg you."

Brad's nose wrinkles too and he slips down off the Peloton after a pointless workout. "My question now is, how are you two going to distract the girls while we deal with this?"

I look at James. He doesn't look capable of dealing with anything. "Are you and Beau okay?" I need him on the ball today. It's a ridiculous statement when he's drunk enough vodka to sink an island, but whether he and Beau are all right will tell me if we're at risk of an AWOL woman again and if that might steal his time chasing around town looking for her.

James lowers to a bench and sinks his face into his palms on a groan. "I know nothing."

"Are you saying she's a flight risk?"

"Who the fuck knows?" He scrubs down his face. "She wants a baby, she doesn't; she thinks her dad wasn't murdered, she does; she wants to be married, she doesn't; she wants to be a cop, she—"

"We get it," Brad says. "We can't depend on Beau to behave. What about Rose?"

I laugh. "If she sees Amber in her house, she'll attack."

James raises his hand, a message that even if we contain Beau and stop her disappearing, we have to then stop her attacking Amber too.

"Do we put her in a cage?"

James's head slowly lifts, his mouth a twisted shade of murder, and I purse my lips, thankful on Brad's behalf that he's not on form today, or I'm pretty sure Brad would be embedded in the wall right now. "Why don't you ask her?" James growls.

"No, thanks." Brad takes a seat next to him. "So if we can't cage both of your pets, what do we do with them?"

"You've got a death wish, Brad." I start pacing, chewing the edge of my phone, thinking about what we can do with the women that won't have them suspicious. The boatyard, nope. Fuck knows what might go down. And Hiatus isn't an option when we're not there. What does Rose want? A school for Daniel. I'm working on it.

Driving lessons. When I have time. Another baby. Check. Do regular shit with the kid. I sent them for pizza yesterday. "Independence," I blurt, slowing to a stop.

"What?" they both say in unison, impatient.

"Rose wants independence. A job." I face their frowns. I'm a fucking genius. "She's going on about jobs and freedom constantly, not just for her but for Pearl and Anya too." I get on my phone and pluck out the first one I find, dialing, then lowering to the bench beside them.

"Good afternoon, Red's Salon and Spa, this is Petal speaking, how many I help you?"

"Hello, Petal," I say in my most friendly voice, very thankful Petal won't be meeting me in person. "I would like to book your spa facilities for a private party." Brad laughs under his breath, and James puts his head back in his palms.

It wasn't possible for me to privately hire Red's today. Something about existing appointments. So I gave them a reason to make it possible. One hundred thousand reasons. A bargain, if you ask me.

The one thing I didn't consider, and it's quite an important thing, is Daniel. I'm not sure a mani or pedi is going to get the kid excited, so I've sold my soul to the fucking devil. A good-looking devil who happens to be a single dad and a private banker. Rose mentioned they were visiting his parents. Great. So after talking very nicely to Mr. Benson, he agreed to let Barney go shark diving for the day with Daniel and Tank. Tank looked traumatized. Fury laughed his big Viking nuts off.

Until I told him he was going for a pamper day. Whether Benson agreed through fear or not, I couldn't give a fuck.

Now, to handle my wife . . .

I push the door of our bedroom open and poke my head round, hearing the shower. Perfect. She's more amenable when she's naked. When I'm naked. When we're *both* naked.

I push my shorts down my legs and go to her. She's facing the spray, face up, her hair wet, stuck to her back, skimming her arse. I groan and look down my body, watching my dick wake up and slowly rise, pointing the way. I lay a palm over it, taming the fucker, as I step into the stall. She stills, her hands in her hair, pausing running the conditioner through it.

She peeks back. It's like rocket fuel to my cock. I give up trying to talk it down and let it protrude, skimming her lower back. Silently, I take her wrists and direct them to the tile, lowering my mouth to her shoulder. Flames. A moan. Raised shoulders, her head tilting. I release her wrists. I don't need to tell her to keep them there. I slide my hands up her arms while I kiss every hot piece of her neck, licking the water away, working my palms onto her breasts, her stomach, her hips. Head falling back, she moans, vibrating against my lips on her throat, her arse pushing back against me.

I bend my knees and swivel up, sliding inside of her, breathing in and holding it. Rose's hands ball into fists on the tile. The water becomes hotter. I slowly start to pump, holding her waist. "I have a surprise for you," I say calmly, watching her head roll on her shoulders.

"What?"

I grind, taking my mouth to her nape and kissing.

She moans, then brings one hand back and slips her fingers through my wet hair. "Show me."

"In good time, baby." I bite down. "I think you're going to love it." I am on dangerous ground, but I will deal with that later. Today feels like it could be the end. Anything is possible. I have to make sure the girls are out of harm's way. I jolt, and Rose moans harder, making me pause, trying to rein myself in, close already. I sit my chin on her shoulder. She looks at me. That alone has my dick twitching, and she feels it, smiling, rolling back, ending my attempt to save myself. I slam my mouth over hers and kiss her, and start driving in and out, firm but slowly, my cock buzzing. I know she's coming because she tugs my hair and bites my lip, so I let it claim me, rolling through my release on a moan into her mouth and a squeeze of her hips as Rose constricts and drains me, her wet body twitching against me. I bite her lip in return and pull back, wiping her face of water and moving us out of the spray, withdrawing and turning her. I push her into the cold wall and crowd her, kissing her softly, finding my planned words again as we both come down.

I don't find them soon enough for Rose. She ends our kiss and cups my cheeks, pulling my face to hers. "What?"

"You want some freedom," I say, taking her wrists and pulling them away, relishing her intrigue.

"I do . . ." she says slowly.

"I booked you a pamper day." She should get a pamper year for how much I paid.

Rose leans back as far as she can, which isn't far with the wall behind her. "Pardon me?"

I smile. This is the wedding all over again. A tactic on my part. "I've booked out a salon spa thing for the day. For you. And the other girls." I'm relying on Rose to make this happen too. I need everyone gone from the house.

"Why?"

"To pamper. Get your hair done. Have a manicure."

"Right . . ." Her suspicion is warranted, of course, so manipulation has to come in here, and I will be shameless. "What's going on?"

I make sure I appear offended. "What do you mean?"

"I mean, all of a sudden, Daniel can go to school, I can take him for pizza, and now I'm going off on a pamper day at a spa. So I'll ask you again, my lovely, gorgeous angel-faced assassin, what's going on?"

I scowl. Why the reminder of who I am? Stupid question. Fine. Here comes the manipulation. I pull away, solemn, and leave the shower. "I was only trying to do something nice for you." I grab a towel and yank it down. "I know it's not easy being married to me, Rose." I throw it over my shoulders and tug it from side to side. "I'm trying here." I finish drying and go to my closet, avoiding my suits, because they're dead giveaway if I'm dealing with business, and instead pull on some gray joggers and grab a sweater, grumbling away to myself. I still, my arms in the sleeves, ready to pull it over my head when I hear her behind me. I wait, looking out the corner of my eye, ready to accept her apology and her gratitude.

"Fuck off, Black, what are you up to?"

My head drops back. Why? Why, God, did you give me such an arduous fucking woman?

Because you need that.

On to Plan B. I pull my sweater on and down as I turn. She's still naked. Wet. Pregnant. Her arms crossed over her chest, nestled between her boobs and her rounding tummy. I look at her tiredly, waving a hand at her magnificent figure, like, *come on!*

She just tilts her head and raises her brows. I roll my eyes and go to her. Plan B better work, because Plan C is the truth, and *that* means our shower just now will have been the last time I fucked my wife. I take her arm and tug her to the bed, sitting her on the end and kneeling before her. And because I'm a cunt, I pull her legs apart and drop my mouth into her pussy, sucking on her clit on a salacious smile when she drops to the bed.

I work efficiently, slipping my fingers inside of her, hooking them up, making sure I get her sweet spot as I massage, bite, kiss, lick her nub of nerves, flicking my tongue quickly when her back arches and she gathers the sheets in her fists.

Okay. So this wasn't part of Plan B but I'm not the kind of man to pass up these kinds of opportunities.

She comes all over my face on a high-pitched, broken moan, and goes lax beneath me. I crawl up her body and trap her beneath me, kissing her, sharing her release. "You need a wax," I say, smiling when she snorts over a laugh. "It's a bit prickly down there."

Her head shoots back, her laughter addictive. I take the opportunity and pay some attention to her throat, her jaw, until I'm plunging my tongue into her mouth again. "Why would I want to go to a spa when I get all the pampering I need right here at home?" she asks.

"Can you trust me?"

She groans, and I know I have her. "Danny, please." She holds my head and looks at me, and I hate the fear I see in her eyes. "Every time you ask me to trust you, epic shit goes down."

"Yes, but we always come out the other side, baby," I remind her, praying she hears me. I can't tell her anything about Amber. She will lose all reason. "Today's just meetings, I promise. James and Beau aren't great. If she pulls one of her disappearing stunts again, it could fuck everything up, Rose. We're getting somewhere here. Not only is she in danger every time she galivants off around town, but James is also distracted. I need his head on straight today."

She loses all fight before my eyes and deflates. "You actually think Beau will accept my offer to be pampered all day? Have you ever met such an ungirly woman in your life?"

"True. But I have every faith in you." I slam a kiss on her lips. "Make it work," I say, nipping her lips.

"Yeah, yeah. What about Daniel?"

"He's out for the day with Tank and Barney."

She laughs. "Fucking hell, you really are desperate."

"Rose," I warn.

"Wait. Lennox agreed to let Barney hang out with Daniel? Even after the newspaper article?" Her eyes narrow. "What did you do to convince him, Danny?"

I smile on the inside. "I was as nice as pie."

She snorts. "A British flavored pie?"

I don't want to talk about Lennox Benson. I saw the way he looked at my wife. So I get up, ignoring her, and look down my front. My cock is jutting out. Gluttonous. I peek up at Rose, my eyebrow high.

"I have a spa day to get ready for and a few friends to convince to come with me." She gets up and saunters off, leaving me with a raging erection. She stops when she gets to the door, looking back. Her playfulness has vanished.

"I'll be careful," I say before she can demand it.

A nod, a swallow, and she disappears into the bathroom.

By the time Brad, James, and I make it Hiatus, it's past noon, a good thing because I could do with a drink. We enter from the back, and I wave to Mason who has a Scotch on the bar for me where Goldie, Otto, Nolan, and Ringo are lined up.

Mason doesn't only have a Scotch for me, he has one for Brad too. And a vodka for James, who physically heaves and turns away from it. I smile as I take a sip. I should have sent him to the spa with the girls, because he doesn't look like he'll be of much use to us.

I take a stool and drag it away from the bar so I'm in front of the others. "What's up?" I ask, detecting a bit of tension.

"Tell them," Ringo says, his big, suited arms folded over his chest, his eyes on Nolan.

I look at Nolan.

"A cop staking out over the road," he tells me. "She was there when I left last night and here this morning at seven when I took a delivery."

Collins. James leaves us and walks to the entrance of the club, disappearing for a few moments before coming back, shaking his head. "The cameras?" he asks Otto.

"She left at ten."

"She probably needed her morning poo," Ringo mutters, and we all turn half amused half questioning looks onto him. "What?" he asks. "Women are like clockwork, aren't they? Same time every morning?"

"And men aren't?" Goldie looks at Ringo like he's another species. I'm beginning to think he is.

"No, men shit in the evening."

I laugh, looking at the others, hoping I'm not alone. They're all looking at Ringo with expressions that basically say *what the fuck?* "You shit in the evening?" Otto asks him.

"Yeah, I shit in the evening. Don't you?"

"No, I shit in the morning."

"I shit every three days," Nolan says, thoughtful. "Could be morning or evening. It's a bit inconvenient, to be honest." He looks at Goldie. "When do you shit?"

She gets up and walks away, increasing my laughter. She only wants to be a part of the gang when it suits her.

"Well shit," Ringo sighs. "I always thought it was a man-woman thing."

"What the fuck made you think that?" Brad asks him.

"When I was a kid, all my mates had a shit when they got home from school. Stanley, my best pal, he had a sister, and he told me she shat in the mornings, as did all her friends. So, yeah, men shit in the evenings, and women shit in the mornings. It's because women are organized, you see. They think ahead. It starts when they're girls. They don't want to be shitting in the school toilets because they're fucking grim. Boys don't have that foresight. We would dash home from school to shit. Obviously, there were the odd few who got caught short and were forced to shit in the school toilets, hence they were grim."

I look at Ringo, my mouth hanging open, as he shows the ceiling his palms. "You've thought way too much about shitting, Ringo."

"That may be so, but apparently it's been a waste." He looks at Nolan. "Are you sure you only shit every three days?"

"Yeah."

"You know what that means, don't you?" I say, toasting Nolan's shitting habits.

He looks worried. "What does it mean?"

"It means that more often than not, you're full of shit."

Everyone laughs, including James and Brad, which an achievement on my part. "Anything on John Theodore Little?" I ask Otto, getting a shake of his head. "What about Higham?"

"Len's bringing him here."

I nod. Good. Let's hear what he has to say about his coffee dates with the journalist. "I've heard from Amber."

Not surprisingly, Ringo's and Otto's ear prick up, and I'm sure Goldie's have too. I can't see her to know. "Does she want to get back together?" Ringo asks.

I smile. Rose wouldn't. She'd kill. "She mentioned a teddy bear."

"Oh really?" Otto twiddles his beard, and Ringo's lips straighten into a grim line.

"Really. I'm meeting her at the house at three."

"Is that wise?"

Probably not. "All the girls are out for a pamper day."

"Not true," Ringo nods to Goldie, who gets herself back on the stool next to him, her lip curled in disgust. "Since you find me so repulsive," he goes on, "why don't you join the girls for a pamper day?"

"Why don't you," she retorts, looking down at her watch, "have a colonic, since you're so full of shit too. It's nearly time to evacuate."

"Enough," I say, smiling around the rim of my glass.

"I've got something," Nolan says, raising his hand. "I need to replace one of the girls."

Oh? I lower my glass, not liking his shifty persona.

"Which one?" Brad asks.

Nolan looks away, muttering something. "The one we found in the office with him," James says, and Brad curses.

"Oh dear." I give Brad a look that says, *you hired him, you deal with it.* "Did she get a bit of a handful?"

Nolan breathes out, his cheeks ballooning. "She's got a bit attached, yes."

I laugh. "And what lesson have we learned today, students?"

Nolan rolls his eyes and trudges off, and I ignore the looks of utter disbelief coming at me from everyone else. They can fuck off. Rose is different. Nolan stops and looks back. "Hey, what about those two girls you picked up?" He clicks his fingers constantly, thinking, and my eyes naturally fall to Brad, interested. "Pearl and Anya."

My eyes automatically go to Brad, my lips pressed together around the rim of my glass. He seems to have frozen in place. Did he hear? I can't be sure; he looks a bit vacant. So just in case . . . "He said—"

"I fucking heard." Brad stalks off, holding his shoulder. "Do what the fuck you like," he growls. "But if you fuck another member of staff, I'll fuck you with a hammer drill."

"It'd be way less comfortable than the blender," James says under his breath, making Nolan snort his laughter. I'm obviously not in on this private joke, but I give the kid a look to suggest he best rein himself in before Brad, the moody fucker, goes crazy on his arse.

"Higham's here," Otto pipes up, turning the screen to us. I lean in and see him getting out of his beamer, taking a long-arse time straightening his cheap suit jacket. Bracing himself?

"We'll stay in the bar," I look back at the stage. "What time are the girls due to start practice?"

"An hour," Nolan calls.

I look at James. "Enough time to torture the truth out of the fucker?"

The blackness I both love and hate washes over his face, giving his pasty, hungover skin a little color. "I need ten minutes."

"Ooh, feeling feisty, huh?"

He doesn't find my joke funny, lowering his arse to a stool, pretty much cracking his knuckles. I'm blaming it on his hangover. I lean forward and hold my glass out, prompting Goldie to take it and pass it back to Mason to refill. "This needs a gentle approach," I say to James. "No flying off the handle. He's—" My mobile interrupts me. Mum. *Fuck.* I don't dream of ignoring her, knowing she wouldn't call me unless it's necessary. "Mum?" I answer, edgy. "Everything okay?"

"What's going on?" She hits me with her demand fast and abruptly, not answering my question, and that gets my back up. But the days when I spoke to my mother with little respect and even less love are over.

I reach up and pinch the bridge of my nose. "Do you want to elaborate?" I ask calmly. If she mentions anything about Otto, my mood will slide. That would be a shame, since I'm feeling almost chirpy today, which is more than I can say for Brad and James. Things are coming together. It feels good.

"You're buying Rose a spa?"

My hand drops from my face. "Say what?"

"A spa. You're buying her a spa."

"Am I?"

"Well, according to your wife, yes. So again, what's going on?"

I feel my nostrils flare. My mood takes a nosedive. Trust my wife. I hang up and smash my thumb across the screen, walking away from the bar to reduce the risk of the top shelf of liquor shattering when my booming voice hits it.

"Hello, dear," she says happily.

"Don't *dear* me. What the fuck, Rose?" I ask, relatively calmly, all things considered. I can see what's coming, and I seriously do not like it.

"You told me to *make it work*. So I'm making it work."

Yes, she's making it work. For herself. The conniving bitch. "And how much is *making it work* going to cost me?"

"I'm in negotiations," she declares, a strongness to her voice that doesn't bode well. It's cocky. "But I've assured the proprietor that money isn't an issue, is it, darling?"

No, it's not, but her having an interest other than me is. "Rose?"

"Yes, darling."

"You're pregnant."

"Am I?" she cries, sounding surprised. "Shit, I wondered what the fuck was going on with my body."

I look up at the ceiling. God, please, make her stop before I do something I regret. Like kill her. "You're blackmailing me."

"I'm harnessing my power."

I laugh. "Oh, baby, you sure do have power." And she exerts it unapologetically. I can't fucking blame her. She never had power before she had me.

"Danny," she says, sounding way too matter of fact. "You told me to make it work. Did you honestly think Beau was buying some horseshit about me wanting to bond over a facial and a bikini wax?"

"No, but she might have bought some horseshit about you wanting to slag your husband off over a facial and a bikini wax."

"Oh, that wouldn't have been horseshit. I've been bad-mouthing you all day."

"I hope not, since I'm about to part with hundreds of thousands of my money for you."

"It's mine."

"What?"

"Your money. It's mine. You left it to me three years ago when you drowned at sea. And the asking price is five million."

My eyes nearly pop out of my head. "What?"

"Don't worry. I think I can get her down to four."

"God, I fucking hate you."

"I'll get over it. Have a lovely day, dear." She hangs up, and I yell a few times, punching thin air before me.

"Love," someone says from behind me. I swing around. Higham. Is he for real? He's going to come in here and brandish his fucking sarcasm? I look at the others, maybe searching for a sign that my thoughts are reasonable, because I seriously want to kill him.

"Danny," James says quietly. "Don't do it."

I steam forward and take the prick off his feet, deciding today I get to do the torturing. He grunts when he lands, and I straddle him, sit up, and start launching my fists into his face one at a time, over and over.

Bang, bang, bang, bang.

"Danny, for fuck's sake!"

Bang, bang, bang, bang.

Blood comes like rain hitting a lake and splashing up into my face, but still I don't stop, the outlet exactly what I need.

"Danny!"

A pair of hands grab my shoulders and hauls me back, and I land on my arse a few feet away, my fists covered in blood, my face and suit splattered. Higham starts rolling around on the floor, his face a broken, bloodied mess, groaning. "Fucking hell, Black," he chokes. "You fucking madman."

I snort, wiping my face with the sleeve of my jacket, and push myself to my feet, putting my boot in his stomach with force, making him cough. I drop to a knee, fist his jacket, and haul him up. "Why the fuck are you having coffee with Natalia Potter?"

His face drops, and doesn't that speak volumes?

"Love his gentle approach," James says, retreating, leaving me to my own devices. Good. Today I want to kill, and I don't feel like doing it slowly. So much for my good mood.

"Talk!"

"I'm seeing her." Higham strains the words, his face pained, and not because he's in fucking agony.

"What?"

"I'm having a fucking affair, okay?" He pushes my hands away and sniffles, roughly wiping his bleeding nose with the back of his hand.

"With the woman who wrote a report about me and James?"

"Yes," he yells, distressed. "Fucking hell, yes. I told her she was on dangerous ground. She wouldn't fucking listen, would she? She's young. Hungry."

I peek up at Otto. He said that. "So you didn't feed her information on us?"

"God no, I value my life."

"Then . . . who did?"

"She wouldn't say."

"Oh, come on, Higham."

"I swear, she wouldn't say."

"So, we need to have a little chat with your girlfriend?"

His eyes widen, worried. I can't figure out if he's concerned for her or himself. "Danny, come on."

Yeah, maybe he's sticking his dick in another woman, but how did they get to know each other in the first place? It's all rather convenient if you ask me. I get my face up in his, fisting his jacket again. "I don't believe you."

"Oh, how cozy is this?" a female voice asks. One I can't claim to recognize.

Higham's bloodied face drops, and I hear a few quiet curses behind me. I look back, still with Higham in my grasp. Collins is standing in the club. Her smile salacious. "Oh, we finally get to chat," I say, smiling. It's as salacious as hers.

She pouts, looking at Higham in my grasp. "Assaulting an FBI agent? I've only been here five seconds, and I already have a reason to arrest you." She pulls out her cuffs and dangles them. Fuck me, I've met some cocky cops in my time, but this female is taking the fucking cake.

"It's fine, Collins," Higham says. "This is FBI business, not MPD. I'm handling it."

"Your face suggests otherwise. Have you asked them about the explosion at Brad Black's address?"

"Gas leak," I say flatly.

"Yeah," she purrs. "Do we believe them, Agent Higham?"

Fuck, I want to punch her. This woman does not give two fucks about who she upsets on her path to success and recognition. She wanders over, and James steps into her path, looking down threatening. She's not fazed, or if she is, she's doing a really fucking good job of hiding it. "Oh." She looks him up and down. "You must be the one they call The Enigma."

"You can call me James."

"How's Beau?"

Historically, such a simple question asked has ended in tears. So how's he going to handle this? "Well, she's not a cop anymore, so I think we can safely say she's good."

Collins laughs. "Perhaps not so good when I arrest her for the murder of Marek Zielińska. I believe you all know him as The Shark."

My eyes shoot to James. *Oh fuck.*

"Very interesting CCTV footage has come to light," she goes on, wandering up and down, thoughtful, like Poirot used to do when he was detailing to an audience how he came to figure out who the murderer was. It's fucking annoying. "Very interesting indeed."

"You're lying."

"Am I?" She stops pacing and rests all her weight on a hip. Cocky. "Then explain how I know you dumped the bodies in the incinerator bin. Explain how I know that you were hiding your girlfriend from The Shark with your body pressed to hers against the wall? Did it turn you on?" She grins. "Your girlfriend killing someone for you? Did your dick get hard?"

Jesus. She needs to stop.

James steps into Collins, breathing down on her. "I think it's time for you to leave."

"Is that a threat?"

"Yes, that's definitely a threat," I say, getting up, leaving Higham to shuffle to his arse and prop himself up against a nearby booth.

"Then I'll take you both." She produces another set of cuffs. "I'm doing well today, aren't I?"

"Blinding," I retort, joining James. Intimidating much? She asked for it. "I present my wrists to her, as does James. "Which one of us are you taking first?" I ask.

"I think I'll call for backup. I sense a bit a friction, if you know what I mean." She pulls out her mobile and steps back, taking her phone to her ear.

"Where's your partner?" I ask.

"What?"

"You sorts. You usually travel in pairs, don't you?" I tilt my head in question and laugh. "Oh, I know. No one can work with you, can they? Because, like us, they end up just wanting to smash your fucking face in." I look at Higham. "Am I right, or am I right?"

He looks away.

"I think you're right," James says, his eyes lasers on Collins.

"I like my own company." She goes back to her phone.

"Or don't like sharing the credit."

She shrugs. "I'm competitive."

"Be careful, Collins. That competitiveness might be the death of you."

She smirks. "Another threat?"

"Yep," James says.

"You clearly like living on the edge. How's your girlfriend. After she was shot?"

Fuck.

Another cop is about to be squashed, and it won't be me firing the punches this time.

"I heard she and Burrows have been getting friendly again." Collins raises the phone to her ear, and I ask myself with true wonder if she realizes who she is poking? What he's truly capable of? Or does she really think she's above us because she's holding a badge? This one isn't fitting in our pockets, that's for sure.

"Incoming!"

The guys at the bar all dive off their stools, and James rugby tackles me from the side, taking me off my feet. I look up, stunned, dazed, fucking confused. *Fuck!* Volodya and a gang of heavies are forming a line that spans half the space, and they are all armed with machine guns that start spraying the club.

"Move," James hisses, crawling combat style to a nearby booth and getting himself behind the wood, sitting up and pulling his gun.

"That looks rather insufficient." I join him, arming myself, and peek out, popping off one of the brutes. I have a quick scan. A very alive Collins has found her way to the end of the bar, her gun poised, ready to take a shot. It's a crying fucking shame. Volodya could have done us a favor.

"Danny!"

I look toward the other end of the bar and see Mason. He holds up an AK47 and then slides it across the floor to me, followed in quick succession by another. I don't know where the fuck they've come from, and in this moment, I don't care. I toss one to James, load, and lean out, firing on the fuckers on a roar. I watch three drop and the others scatter like ants, and I retreat to reload, just as James takes my place and starts popping bullets.

There's a brief pause in noise, and I hear a door open. I look up and see Brad. His shoulder still strapped, his good hand holding a harpoon. A fucking harpoon. "Get back in there," I warn.

"Fuck off." He fires, and I follow the arrow's path until it ploughs straight through one of the Russian's eye sockets, pinning him to the wall behind him. *Jesus Christ.* Brad retreats behind the door and James gets up on his knees, resting the tip of his gun on the top of the booth seating.

"Where are the others?" I ask, joining him, scanning the place. Ten men walked in. There are only six lying on the club floor, and none of them are Volodya. "Pray do tell me they've not left, because I need that fucker dead *now*."

My phone dings in my hand, and a message from Otto appears. A link to a live stream. I click and see the club fill my screen. "They're in the round booth nearest the door."

"Give me a cigarette," James orders.

Good idea. I fish them out of my pocket and light one for him, putting it between his lips before sorting myself out. I breath in the nicotine. Breathe it out. "Ready?"

"Yep," he exhales, moving out, creeping across the club, heading for the round booth by the door. I follow, my eyes split between the screen of my phone and where we're heading. They're reloading. James looks back at me and jerk his head, sending me to the other end. We crouch behind the booth. Then he holds up two fingers. Drops one. Then another.

I nod, we stand, and point our guns over the top. "Hi." I smile, my cigarette between my teeth, and we start raining bullets down on them, watching through the plumes of smoke before my eyes as their bodies jerk and jump and pieces of foam from the plush padded seats pop up into the air with beads of blood and chunks of flesh.

I don't ease off the trigger until it starts clicking, pulling on my cigarette and breathing out, relaxing. "I promised my wife today was just meetings." I sneer, pulling my pistol and putting a bullet straight between Volodya's open eyes. "That's for making me break a promise to my wife." I pop him again. "That's for turning me over three years ago." *Bang!* "And that's for good fucking luck."

"I think he's dead," James says, setting his gun on the table of the booth, gazing around the club. "Everyone good?"

Three heads pop up from behind the bar, followed by Mason.

"Do you get asked for an AK with a dirty martini often?" I ask.

He shrugs, assessing the state of his bar. All things considered, it isn't too bad. "I might need a hand sorting this if you want us to open tonight."

I wander over to the bar and check the others, finding them all brushing glass shards gingerly from their clothes. Goldie has a few nicks on her face. I don't address them. She won't appreciate it.

I walk to the end of the bar and find Collins still on her arse, still armed. I bet the fucking chamber is still full too. She didn't want the Russians dead. "I'd say that was an unprovoked attack."

She gets to her feet, her eyes assessing the club, the bodies, the mess. "I'd say you've just given me"—she nods around the club, counting the bodies—"ten more reasons to arrest you."

"Really?" I ask tiredly. I should let James at her. But killing a cop is a whole different ballgame to killing ten Russians. We can lose the Russians and they won't be missed. It's trickier to lose a fucking cop. More of a headache. So, we need to think hard about how we handle this since, technically, we really have just given the cocky bitch ten reasons to arrest us. We're in the state of Florida. If I'm going to die, I'd rather it not be by lethal injection.

I look back at James as I take a final drag of my cigarette, asking him silently if he has any suggestions. His mild head shake tells me no. A few grand isn't going to cut this. But a few million could. I drop my cigarette butt in a nearby empty glass and—

Bang!

I jump and swing around, just as Collins starts plummeting toward me. Confused as fuck, I hold out my arms, catching her. "What the fuck?" I ask, scanning the space behind her. I see Nolan at the door that leads to the offices, his gun still poised. "What the fucking hell?"

He frowns. Lowers his gun. "Who is she?"

I blink, recoil, and let Collins's body drop to the floor. She lands on her back, eyes open, staring up. "She's a dead cop," I say, looking up at Brad, who's just followed Nolan out.

"A cop?" Nolan comes over, standing over Collins body. "I thought she was with them." He looks up at me. "Fuck!"

I lose my shit and swing at him, cracking him on a jaw and sending him sailing through the air. He lands on his back with a thud, and I march over to his startled, splayed form. "You," I say, pointing a finger, "are a *fucking* liability."

"She's a cop?"

"Was, Nolan. She *was* a fucking cop, and now you have given me the biggest fucking headache!" He's lucky I'm out of bullets or I'd shoot the fucker. Then I remember . . . I reach for his gun and snatch it, turning it on him.

"Danny, I'm sorry!" His hands come up, his body curling into a protective ball. "I thought I was helping."

"Whoa," Brad intercepts me, disarming me. "He fucked up."

"Yeah, he fucked up." I look down at the dead cop in our club. Anger. "We're fucked!"

"Not necessarily."

I scowl in the direction of the voice and find the bloodied result of my handiwork before Volodya showed up. Higham struggles to his feet. "What are you saying?" I ask.

"I'm saying you clearly don't trust me. And I'm saying I can solve this."

"How?"

"We get her across town. I'll have someone call in a burglary. Make sure Collins's radio answers the callout."

"And what do you want in return?" I ask. Never have I thought I'd get Higham onside. Then again, I don't suppose I've left him much choice after the shootout at Winstable with the Poles.

"You leave Natalia alone."

"Oh fuck," I breathe. "You really are in love with her."

He looks away. "I'll find out where she got the information from to print the article."

"You do that. And while you're at it, you can get rid of the footage Collins was talking about that shows Beau shooting The Shark."

He nods. "I'm feeling a little worn out, Danny."

I laugh. "You cops all say that around this point in your careers."

"What, then they reach fifty-ish?"

"No, Higham." I drop my gun and leave. "When they meet me."

Three o'clock comes and goes. Four o'clock. Five o-fucking-clock. "Where the fuck is she?" I yell, calling Bud on the gate once again.

"Nothing," he confirms.

"Check the street. Any cars knocking around? Cops?" *Anything* that's going to have her running?

"Quiet."

"Fuck it!" I hang up and look at James. He shrugs. "Fat lot of fucking help you are." I look at my watch. They'll be coming back from the spa soon, and if Amber shows up late when the girls are here, there will be nothing I can do to save her. My phone rings, and I practically dive across my office to my desk. And curse some more when I see it's Luis calling. And I remember . . .

I glance at James. Is he thinking what I'm thinking? He knocks back a vodka, the earlier shootout having chased away his hangover. Funny how a minor dabble with death does that. "Cancel," he says. He *is* thinking what I'm thinking. We haven't got time for an exchange right now. The club's a graveyard, currently being cleaned up, Amber's nowhere to be seen, and we have a dead cop on our hands.

I answer, not giving Luis a chance to ask. "I'm afraid we need to rearrange," I say, working my way to the middle of the room and putting my phone on loudspeaker so everyone can hear just how pissed Luis will be.

"No, Black, you obviously didn't hear me before. I need the guns and I need them now."

"And you hear me *now*, Luis. I haven't got time to deliver them. I'll have your cash returned." I cut the call and wait for the verdict.

"Well, someone had to take Volodya's place on our shit list," Brad chirps.

"Agree." I laugh to myself. Where's the fun in having *no* enemies at all? Now, where the fuck is Amber?

34

ROSE

I peek over the top of my magazine to Beau. She looks as comfortable as I expected as she messes with her cell—not comfortable at all—her attention elsewhere. As it has been since we arrived. A distracted Beau makes me uneasy. I can only imagine how it makes James feel.

Today is just meetings. That's what Danny said. I don't believe him, and now I've somehow gone from trying to keep Beau busy to buying a beauty spa. I'm rolling with the fates.

If she pulls one of her disappearing stunts again, it could fuck everything up, Rose. We're getting somewhere here.

Getting somewhere. Does this mean this nightmare will soon be over? And . . . does Beau know?

I slam the magazine shut with more force than I planned, silencing the room. Esther and Lawrence look back over their shoulders, their nails half painted, and Pearl and Anya lift their heads from the massage chairs. Beau, though? She doesn't look up from her cell next to me where her toes are under a UV lamp. I wait for everyone to get back to whatever treatments they're having and reach over, poking her. She looks up at me, vacant.

"What color did you go for?" I ask.

She blinks and peeks down at her feet, reminding herself. "Nude." But of course. "You?"

I don't look down. "Red." But I do look at the ruby on my finger. *This is the only red I want to see on you.* I frown, seeing the red, slutty dress I was wearing the night Danny took me. The slutty red lipstick he rubbed off my lips when I wore it simply to piss him off. "Excuse me," I say to the therapist working on my toes. "I've changed my mind. I'd like pink, please. Or maybe coral."

Beau goes back to her cell, and I make sure she hears my exasperation. "What?" she says, dropping it in to her lap heavily.

"You've not spoken a word since we arrived. This is supposed to be a girlie pamper day."

"Oh, please. You are my best friend. You know me, and this"— she points at her toes and then around the lovely spa—"is not my bag."

"I know," I grate.

"So why am I here?"

I feel like she's goading me, pushing me into a corner, pressuring me to confess. "I already told you, I'm buying it."

She laughs, prompting Esther to look back at us. She knows shit's going down too. In fact, we're all here doing a terrible job of pretending we're blissfully unaware that our men are murderers who are quite possibly murdering someone right now. *Just meetings.* I snort to myself.

I turn to Beau. "What's going on?" I ask. She's not mentioned a word since her meltdown in the kitchen when she thought James had left. Nothing.

Her attention remains on her cell, and it's beginning to piss me off, like I'm not worthy of an explanation. "Rose—"

"And last night? Danny said James was trashed. He never gets drunk, Beau. *Ever.*" She's disappeared before. They've argued before. It's a constant challenge not to become a bag of nerves in this life. Beau's an integral part of what keeps me sane, and I know I am for her too. But she's distancing herself. It's not helping with my nerves. "Are you and Ja—"

"He found my birth control pills."

I shoot back in my chair like I've been hit with an arrow, and Beau closes her eyes, hiding from my reaction.

"What?" is all I can muster. "I thought you—"

"I don't." She won't look at me. Face me. Face the truth.

Self-preservation. She's trying to control what she can't control, and she doesn't even know if it needs controlling. "So that's it?"

"Yes, that's it."

"You're a dick." I sit back in my chair and open my magazine, roughly turning the pages, not reading the words, but staring at the pages briefly. Then I slam it shut and face her startled face again. "Is this why you're playing cop again?"

"What?"

"Running off around town telling yourself your dad's been murdered so you have something to do? A mystery to solve? Something to focus on instead of you and James and the..."

Her lip quivers. "Amber's inherited it all. You don't think that's suspicious? And Dad's friend, Cartwright. He washed up on the beach. Not suspicious?"

Okay, very suspicious. But . . . "You're not a cop anymore, Beau."

She withdraws, looking stung. "I know, Rose. Everyone keeps reminding me." She removes her toes from the lamp and gets up, walking off toward the changing rooms, and I look down at the young girl who's tapping my toenail to check it's dry.

"You have a massage," I call, desperate, jumping up and going after her, feeling everyone watching us. I push into the changing rooms and find Beau getting her Converses on. "Beau, come on," I beg, not because I've been told to keep her busy, but because I hate this. Us fighting. I hate it.

"I'm okay," she assures me, swinging a shirt on over her tank and fastening one button.

"You are not okay," I say through my teeth as she bends and

turns up the bottom of her frayed jeans. She can't leave. I'll never forgive myself if something happens. "Beau." I grab her arm as she tries to pass me, and she freezes. "You'll never know if you can have a baby if you don't allow your body to tell you."

Biting her lip, she stares at the floor, the silence roaring. Short of tackling her and tying her up, I'm fucked. "James doesn't want one, so this is a pointless conversation."

"He doesn't?"

She looks back. "No, he doesn't, so actually this is all for the best, right?"

I laugh. Anyone who has to end a confident statement with a *right?* is either not confident at all, or totally full of shit. Beau is both. "Right." I cannot believe what I'm hearing. "You're maddening." I retie my robe, with a lack of anything else to do with my hands other than strangle my best friend, and I can't do that because I fucking love her. Everyone in this family knows James was mad for a baby. Everyone knows it broke him. Everyone knows he'd do anything to help Beau stay in the light. He was simply worried about her. "So fucking maddening," I mutter, wrenching on the tie. I suddenly don't feel like being pampered anymore. "So where are you going now?" I ask, my voice strong. She knows I can't stop her. "To chase around in circles some more? Put yourself in danger? Leave us all here worrying about whether we might see you alive again?" I disregard the wideness of her eyes. The hurt on her face. Or I try. Goddammit, guilt flares within, and I quickly leave the changing rooms before Beau detects it. She needs to be told.

I close the door and growl, catching Esther's questioning eye. I shake my head and have a quiet, stern word with myself. I walked into this place filled with excitement. A girlie day. It didn't matter that my husband engineered it to help his cause. It was something normal in a world where we can't do normal. I knew I wasn't getting Beau here for a pedicure or massage unless I made my cause believable. So I told her Danny was buying me a business and I needed help on the interior design. It escalated from there. I listened to Pearl tell me how she studied hairdressing at college. And Anya, apparently, is a super talented nail artist. It was like the fates were talking to me. Hope. I had hope. It's probably going to cost my husband a few million, but . . . we need *something*.

I let my head rest back on the door, half expecting it to swing open at any moment. But a few minutes later, I'm still standing here, and Beau hasn't appeared. Naturally, I scan my mind for whether I saw any means of escape in there. "Shit." I push my way back in.

Beau's on the bench in the center of the room.

Sobbing.

That guilt? It flares.

I hurry over and sit beside her, pulling her in for a hug. "I'm sorry," I whisper.

"Don't be. You're so right." She snivels and wipes at her face. "I can't bear the waiting game, Rose. Every month, holding my breath, waiting to see if I'm broken there too."

My eyes instinctively drop to my tummy. More guilt. I hug her tighter.

"Having to face James." She looks at me. "I never knew I needed it. I was so stunned when I found out I was pregnant." She laughs quietly, looking down at her feet. "And then I looked at James and saw what he saw. Hope. He saw hope for both of us. One more reason to love and not hate. Constant light to chase away the darkness."

I can hardly breathe through the ball of grief wedged in my throat. "You have to believe it can be yours again."

She looks at me, her dark eyes welling. "What if it can't be?"

And it occurs to me. "Are you worried James wouldn't want you anymore?"

"Maybe." She looks away.

"He loves you."

"I know. But I can see him giving up."

"That's because you're hiding, Beau. You're hiding from facing this, telling yourself you want to be a cop again when you should be asking yourself something else."

"What?"

"Ask yourself if you can exist without James."

Her bottom lip wobbles. I don't know why we're going the long way round to the point when, really, that's the crux. They are now one, and without each other, merely empty vessels with a heartbeat.

"Let's go home," I say, done with pampering for today. Beau nods, making me breathe a little easier, and I call Danny to let him know. "Hey," I say, hoping he's calmer than when we spoke before.

"Hey," he breathes, sounding exhausted. "Good day?"

Small talk. I'm not game. "We're leaving now."

"What?" he blurts, making me still, pausing for thought. "Already? Aren't you having fun?"

Fun? Fun pretending to relax and have fun? No, I can't say I am. "We've been here for—"

"Did you negotiate? Get her down to four?"

"What's going on?"

"Nothing."

I look at Beau, who's looking too interested for my liking. And probably James's and Danny's. "Where are you?" I ask.

"The club. Why don't you go home? We'll meet you there."

"Okay," I say quietly, thoughtfully, hanging up. "They're at the club."

"And?"

"And that's where we're going." I pivot and take myself back out to the spa floor, finding Fury. "Danny said to take us to the club." *Please don't call and check.*

"Fine." He goes back to the copy of *Hello!* that he's been reading since we arrived.

What the hell is going on?

. . .

Fury drives like Miss Daisy from the spa to the club. "Anytime today," I quip, getting a tired look in the rearview mirror.

When we pull up, I see Ringo up ahead hopping out of a Mercedes and running across the road. I slip out and walk into the club, gazing around. Could be me, but the atmosphere feels a bit . . . tense. Mason is stacking the top shelf, and a few other staff are sweeping the floor and mopping. "Where are they?" I ask, making Mason look over his shoulder.

"Oh, Rose, Beau, ladies, what a surprise."

"Yeah, I bet," I say, heading for the office as the others go to the bar. I wander in without knocking and find Ringo looking out of breath. I eye him. He looks away.

"Where's Beau?" James says, standing.

"At the bar." He settles, but the worry and stress etched all over his face doesn't lift.

"Hey, baby." Danny smiles. "I thought you were heading home."

Fucking dickhead. I should slap him for treating me like I'm stupid. "Well, I thought I would surprise you." This is ridiculous. I go to my husband, hand him a card with the details of the spa owner, and reach up to kiss his cheek. "When is Daniel home?"

"I spoke to Tank an hour ago. They're bowling."

"Oh, lovely."

"Mum here?" he asks.

"Having a glass of wine with the girls."

"Oh, lovely."

"Isn't it?"

I give him another kiss. "I've had the best day, thank you."

He smiles and seizes me, indulging me. "You're welcome, baby. You can thank me properly when we get home."

I smile coyly, detach myself from my conniving husband, and saunter out, my alarm bells going wild. I close the door.

"You dick, Ringo," Danny hisses.

"I thought you told Fury to hold back?"

"I did."

"Well," Ringo pants, "he clearly didn't hold back enough. I'm fucking sweating here."

I stand on the outside of the office staring at the wood, my eyes narrowed. "What are—"

I swing around and hush Beau.

"You're eavesdropping?"

"Yes, I am." I go back to the door, and the next minute, Beau is pushed up next to me. "Did you see Ringo arrive?" I ask Beau, making sure I'm not completely losing my mind.

"Yes, I saw."

We both listen hard.

"Well, I couldn't very well have them go back to the fucking mansion," Danny whispers. "If I had told them to come to the club, she would have gone home. If I told her to go home, she'd come here. I know how my wife thinks."

I balk at the door incredulously. He wanted me to come here? Why?

"What if Amber shows up there?" Danny rants on.

I still. Shocked. Amber?

"So instead," Ringo snaps, "you had them come to the club where a few hours ago it looked like Hannibal Lecter got jaw ache and opted for the more humane approach to killing his prey."

"It was a stupid idea telling Amber to go to the house," Brad chimes in. "Really fucking stupid."

"She's got information on The Bear," Danny growls, and Beau steps back, her eyes going back to the wood. *Oh no.* "Not that it matters because she's missing in fucking action."

"Beau," I say, stepping toward her. "Beau, please." She shakes her head, turns, and heads for the ladies'. "Beau!" I whisper shout, swinging my head back and forth between my fleeing friend and the door to the office. "Fuck it." I turn the other way and go back to the club, finding Fury. "Would you take us home in an hour? Esther's finishing her wine."

"Sure."

"Thanks." I smile and brush past him, going to the others at the bar, looking back to see Fury going to the office. To check with the boss if he can indeed take me home in an hour.

"Everything okay?" Lawrence asks.

"Everything's fine." So, so fine. I smile and place my purse on the stool next to Pearl, pulling my cell out and slipping it into my back pocket. "Will someone order me a lemonade, please? I'm just going to the restroom." I leave my purse on the stool and walk away calmly, and as soon as I round the corner, I break into a jog, cursing Beau to hell and back for putting my neck on the line like this. But I will be damned if I am letting her disappear on her own again. I will check in with the men. I will let them know we're okay. They must appreciate that.

I burst through the door and work my way down the cubicles until I find Beau's petite body squirming to get through the small window above the fourth toilet. She grunts as her body dislodges, and her legs disappear through the small gap. "Well, if she struggled, I'm fucked," I scoff, getting up on the toilet seat.

I peek out and see Beau jogging down the alleyway and curse her to hell again as I pull myself up and clamber through. But I completely misjudge the drop to the ground, which looks farther away now that I'm hanging out of the window. "Beau!" I whisper yell, clinging to the frame. "Fuck." I turn my head and see her stop and look back.

"What are you doing?" she shouts, running back to save me, reaching to help.

"I'm coming with you."

"Oh, no, you're not." She retracts her helping hands, just as I lose my grip. "Shit!" She catches me, breaking my fall.

"For fuck's sake, Rose."

I get to my feet. "For fuck's sake, *Beau*." I retort. She has nothing to say to that. "And how are you getting to Amber's anyway?" I ask.

"I'll get a cab."

I reach into my pocket and pull out Fury's keys. "Okay. You get a cab, I'll drive."

The keys are quickly swiped from my hand and Beau is

heading to the side of the club to collect Fury's car. "That's a sure-fire way to kill us both," she says, and I gasp, outraged, going after her.

"I'm not *that* bad at driving."

"Get in," she snaps, slipping in behind the wheel.

I do as I'm told and get my seatbelt on. "We are both going to die when the boys find out we're not in the club, so who drives is a moot fucking point."

Beau ignores me and pulls off rather calmly, though I see the storm in her eyes. "What are you going to do, Beau?" I ask.

"I'm going to get some answers."

"Great," I say, settling in for the ride. "And good luck." Not just finding the answers that nobody seems to be able to find, but good luck when James gets hold of her. We're both dead.

Beau gives me an impatient look. I give her a begging one.

Please don't get us killed.

I keep quiet as Beau drives us around town, drumming my lovely pink-polished nails on my thigh, watching the screen of my cell like a hawk, just waiting for the call. Waiting for the signal that will suggest all hell breaking loose. The moment they realize we're gone. It's been twenty minutes. We're doing well, although God only knows what Esther and the others think I'm doing in the restrooms.

"She's not at his place, or hers," Beau suddenly says out of the blue, pulling my eyes from my cell.

"What?"

"Amber. She's not at Dad's place, and she's not at her apartment."

"So where is she?"

"I don't know," Beau muses, taking a right, heading toward Miami Beach. A small inhale of breath tells me she may have just had an idea. "The penthouse." The car is abruptly going significantly faster, her lightbulb moment injecting some urgency into her. "Dad told me he would give me the penthouse of the new development he was investing in."

"You think she's there?"

"I'm out of other ideas." She looks across to me. "I'm really mad you're here."

"You won't be the only one," I mutter. "If he calls, I'm answering."

"I know," she says, holding up her phone. It's on. Therefore, trackable. It still won't lessen the wrath we're about to face, though. But it offers me a mild comfort that Beau doesn't see this latest mission of hers as long-term. James will fly off the handle when he knows she's missing again. Then he'll wonder what the hell is going on when Otto can track her. And as if they've heard us discussing how mad they will be and how they might handle us, my phone starts ringing on my lap.

"Oh God," I whisper, pushing my back into the seat, trying to escape it. "Even the rings sound angry." I gingerly pick it up, cringing as I answer. I don't even have the opportunity to talk before he's yelling down the line at me.

"Where the fuck are you?"

I look across to Beau, whose cell is flashing in her hand. James. "Track Beau's phone," I say, hanging up and then texting him a million apologies and kisses. This is both our faults. Mine and Danny's. I shouldn't have eavesdropped. Beau wouldn't have heard, and I wouldn't currently be riding shotgun on a vigilante hunt for Danny's and Beau's dad's ex-lover. My lip curls just thinking about her. Granted, Beau's got more to hate, but . . . ughhhh I hate her. "Answer," I say to Beau, seeing she's thinking twice about it. "You can't avoid him forever, Beau."

"We made love this morning." She looks at me. "I'm not avoiding him." She answers and drops her phone into her lap, and her shoulders lift, defying her stone façade. "Amber knows something about The Bear," she says with a strong voice.

"How do you know that?" James asks, sounding cooler than I expected.

"I heard Danny in the office."

I silently thank her for not dropping me in the shit as my phone rings again. I reject the call and text him.

> We're okay.

His reply is quick.

> You won't be.

I reach for my forehead and rub away the wrinkles. I'm in now. And I'm not leaving Beau, so we will face their wrath together.

"Where are you going, Beau?" James asks.

"To find Amber. As always, if you'd just let me in where you feel I don't belong, we might be out of this mess a lot faster." She hangs up and takes the wheel with both hands, dipping and looking up to an apartment block in the distance.

She looks so determined.

And my nerves go through the roof.

The silence is screaming by the time we pull into the parking garage. I have a dozen missed calls from Danny and as many texts, all quite angry, which means I'm definitely not answering his calls. Beau's cell, however, hasn't rung once. Beeped once. Lit up once. James will be tracking her. My husband knows that. He just wants me to know how pissed he is.

Someone needs to tell him I know. I really, really know.

Beau parks and we both get out. She wanders around the back of the car and opens the trunk, pulling up the lining, revealing a pistol and a vest. Beau takes the pistol and hands over the vest, her jaw tight, waiting for me to argue. I don't. I *can't*. I accept and slip it on. "I left my purse on the stool." Why would I be so stupid? Remember my phone but forget my gun?

"Here." She pulls hers from the back of her jeans and hands it over. "Be careful."

I look down at my hand holding the pistol, not knowing what to do with it, I have no purse. So I tuck it into the back of my pants as we wander to the elevators on the other side of the garage. There are three. Two serve all floors. One serves only the penthouse. I look at the keypad and then to Beau as she goes to a door to the stairwell and tugs. It doesn't budge. "What are you thinking?"

"I'm thinking the stairs would be painful anyway." She steps toward the elevator and punches in six digits into the panel. A red light flashes and Beau curses. "I thought it would be his birthday." She punches in six more. Another flashing red light. "Damn it." She proceeds to enter various combinations, and all refuse her entry.

"Beau, you don't even know if your dad bought this place." We could be trying to break into a perfect stranger's home.

Her shoulders drop and she exhales, turning to head back to the car. *Thank God.* She's seen sense. But she stops and stills for a moment before looking at it again. "What?" I ask, my eyes batting back and forth between Beau and the keypad. "What is it?"

She approaches and bends, looking at it from every angle before getting her phone out and shining the torch on the shiny metal buttons. "I don't believe it." She stands and stares, so hard she might burn a hole through the metal plate. I don't ask what she doesn't believe because I know I won't get an answer, so I wait for her to make her move. Reaching forward, she slowly pushes one button after the other.

A green light blinks and the elevator starts moving. "Oh my God," I blurt, jumping when Beau releases the safety on her gun. "Oh my God, Beau!" My hands find my head and she moves to the side of the elevator, looking at me like I should do the same, so I do, my heart racing. The doors slide open, and Beau checks if it's empty.

"Put your phone on silent," she orders, stepping inside the cart. "In fact, why don't you just wait in the car for me?"

I laugh and hurry in with her and, of course, she doesn't fight me. I want to think this arming herself business is all unnecessary. I can't. I've been on the receiving end of Amber's resentment. That woman has no scruples or boundaries. "What was the code?" I ask.

"The date of my mom's memorial."

I swing a stunned expression her way. "What?"

"Fucked up, eh?" She stares forward, a million flecks of hate in her eyes. Just when I didn't think her dad could not be more of an asshole.

The doors close and we both look up at the dial above the door, watching as it ticks up through the floors at an epically slow rate. And when it dings to announce our arrival to the penthouse, we both inhale and step to the side. I stare into Beau's dark eyes as the doors slide open, waiting, tense and shaky. It's quiet, only the drone of electrical appliances breaking the silence. The soft glow of the apartment is a stark contrast to the artificial, blinding lights of the elevator.

Beau swallows and edges to the front and pulls her phone out, getting the camera screen up and turning the image as if she's about to take a selfie. Then she angles it out, checking the space. She looks like she knows exactly what she's doing. I hate that she does. I hate that she used to be a cop. But I also appreciate it.

"Nothing," she finally says, moving out but keeping her gun poised. I follow on a held breath, taking in the uber-modern penthouse as Beau scopes the place.

"Anything?" I whisper, putting my vibrating phone into my back pocket.

She opens a door and looks inside, where a bank of screens displays live footage of the parking garage and the stairwell. "Was your dad security conscious?" I ask.

"I hardly knew my father," she replies, leaving the door open and wandering deeper into the open space. A kitchen spans the back, and a staircase sweeps up to a mezzanine floor where I can see the top of a headboard.

And then I hear it. A voice.

"I'm here," it says.

I look at Beau, just as she aims her gun to the stairs, and she starts moving toward them, quietly but efficiently. I inhale when I see a figure at the top, and Beau pauses from taking the first step, her foot hovering in mid-air. "Beau?" Amber sounds shocked, coming out of the dusk and into the light. "And Rose?" She comes down two steps and looks between us. "What are you doing here?"

"What are *you* doing here?" Beau retorts, her gun unmoving, aimed.

"How did you find me?" Amber comes down the stairs, her face a map of confusion. "I thought you were someone else."

"Who?" Beau backs up, maintaining her distance, and I stick to her side like glue.

Amber reaches the bottom and glances around, nervous and twitchy. She looks bedraggled and tired, the usual power suit replaced with a tracksuit and some Uggs. Her hair is piled high. No makeup. "I don't know," she says. "I don't know who it is."

I don't like this at all. She looks fucking shifty, edgy. Who was she expecting?

"How did you know I was here?" she asks Beau, going to the window and looking down onto Miami.

"My dad offered to buy me this place."

She laughs, but it's not in humor. "He bought *me* this place." Amber faces us, noticing for the first time the vest I'm wearing. She tilts her head, moving closer, her eyes on my stomach. "Are you . . ."

I keep my mouth firmly shut, which is probably the worst thing I could do.

"You're pregnant?" Amber looks plain disgusted. It doesn't bode well.

"We're not here about me."

"Oh, well, it's all very cozy between you two, isn't it? My step-daughter and my ex's new wife."

"Stepdaughter?" Beau splutters.

"Ex?" I ask. She was never Danny's in the first place to become an ex.

"Yes, ex." Amber's edginess is suddenly gone for dust, and supremacy is back. Oh no. She is underestimating Beau. Silly woman. She casts a looks Beau's way. "Didn't you know Tom had proposed? Obviously I accepted. It's why he wanted to meet you for dinner, Beau. To tell you."

"I thought you'd split up."

"Well, we had, no thanks to you." Amber's eyes turn onto me. "Thank you for pouring poison into Tom's ear."

"Poison?" I blurt. "You mean the truth, don't you?"

Her hand lands on her chest. "I loved Tom dearly. Is that why you're here, Beau? To stake a claim on everything that's now . . . well, mine?"

Fucking hell, she's a beast of a woman. "I think we should be leaving," I declare, tugging on Beau's arm. "Beau, come on."

"Yes, run along. And enjoy the BMW." Amber smiles, and it is slap worthy. "You're welcome."

"Shut up," I snap, furious on my friend's behalf.

"Oh." She laughs. "Danny's latest whore has something to say, does she? Like your fucking opinion counts?"

I'm not standing here and listening to this bitter, twisted piece of shit devalue my marriage. I look at Beau and hate the raw fury I see. The deep breaths she's pulling to contain the monster that's trying to break free. Because, apparently, Amber knows something about The Bear. "Beau, remember why we're h—" The screens in the office catch my eye. Or rather, someone on them. I move in closer, seeing someone in the parking garage. A man. He goes to the elevator, reaches for the panel, and the doors behind us start closing.

"Beau, is that your ex?" I ask, forcing her from her frenzied trance with just the mention of Ollie. She frowns at the screens. I don't need confirmation. Especially when Ollie looks back, giving the camera his face. What the hell is he doing here?

I turn back to Amber.

But she's gone.

What?

I swing around on the spot, searching for her. "Rose!" Beau yells, just as something connects with my side and knocks me to the rug. I land with a grunt and open my eyes, reaching behind me to get the gun. No gun.

I roll to my back and come face to face with the end of my gun. My hands instinctively come up in defense.

"Stand up," Amber orders.

Heart pounding, I get to my feet and move back to Beau, who is still armed. A face-off. Amber, clearly stressed, her hands shaking where she's holding the gun, takes a step back. I know Beau could take her out in a second, but... "Remember, Beau," I say, reaching for her hand and forcing the gun down. "Remember why we're here."

"Why is that?" Amber asks. "Why you're here, why is it? You're pissed Tom left me all his money?" she asks Beau. "Or are you looking for this?" She holds up a key. "Then she looks at me. "Or is it because Danny's promised to look after me? Protect me? He was sending me to his private place somewhere."

Bull, meet red flag.

Baseball bat, meet stomach.

Heart, meet fucking knife.

Remember why we're here. Remember!

I breathe. I breathe so deeply, closing my eyes and chasing the red mist away before it ruins everything. And when I open them again, I feel so much calmer. I look Amber square in the eye.

Bang!

I gasp, Amber drops like lead, and I stare at her lifeless body on the cream rug, a pool of blood growing around her head. I look at Beau. She's staring too. "Shit, Rose," she whispers. The gun drops to the floor with a clang. Then the elevator sounds behind us and Beau snaps to life. "We have to go," she says, claiming the gun from the rug and mine from Amber's lifeless hand before pulling me to the door by the elevator. She yanks it open and we run down one flight of stairs before facing another door, this one with a panel. I hear Beau praying as she puts in the code and pulls the door. It opens, thank God it opens, and I'm dragged through and down the stairs. "Watch your feet," Beau says.

When we reach the bottom, another code is required and as Beau enters it, someone flies through the door up the stairs. We both look up as Ollie looks over the balustrade down the stairwell. He sees us. His face is a picture of distress, alarm, and anger.

Then he's flying down the stairs, and the sound of his boots hitting the concrete echoes off the walls. We run.

We run so fast.

35

JAMES

"She's turned her phone off again."

"Fuck!" I smash my palms on the steering wheel over and again, taking my frustration out on the car. I see Danny go to his phone in my peripheral vision to dial Rose again. I also see his jaw rolling when she obviously doesn't answer. "The only reason my wife would go AWOL," he seethes, taking his phone to his mouth and tapping it on his scar, "is because of her best mate, and her best mate is your girlfriend."

"Fiancée," I snap, yanking the steering wheel to the left, taking the corner fast.

"Girlfriend, fiancée, wife," Danny growls. "Ball and fucking chain. Same fucking thing." He smashes his fist into the leather. "Where the fuck are they?"

"The address where her phone was last detected," Otto says from the back, working away on his laptop. "It's a new development on South Beach. Guess who invested?"

I look up at the rearview mirror, words Beau spoke to me weeks ago coming back. *He's offered me an apartment in the new block he's building.* "How many apartments?"

"Including the penthouse, fifty."

"Look up who owns the penthouse." This is Tom Hayley we're talking about. Egomaniac. If he's going to own an apartment in a block, you bet your arse it's going to be the best one. When Otto curses, I peek up at the mirror. "Well?" I ask. *Come on, who is it? Surprise me.*

"Tom Hayley," Otto whispers, and I nod.

"For fuck's sake." Danny dials Rose again and curses again when she doesn't answer. "We need to make it to Amber before Beau."

"You've spent too much time with Brad."

"Fuck off."

Otto works his magic on the CCTV system, cutting all the cameras, before we all pile out and approach the elevator. He rips the keypad panel off the wall and plugs something in, pressing a few buttons. The elevator doors slide open. "Clear?" I ask.

"From what I can see."

Translated, can't be sure.

The tension is horrific as we travel up, and my eyes are constantly batting between Otto, Danny, and the floor counter. We all pull our weapons at the same time as the lift approaches the penthouse, jolting as it slows to a stop. I plaster my back to the wall with the others and wait until the doors are open before peeking around the edge.

Empty. Quiet. I lift a foot to step out.

"Wait," Otto blurts, stilling me. After the last time we found ourselves in this situation, it's no wonder I look down at my boots. Looking for the trip line.

"Are you kidding?" I ask quietly as he lowers and studies the space before us.

"Being cautious." He hums and rises to his feet. "We're clear."

I place my foot down out and walk slowly through the penthouse, past a study on my right, the screens on the wall black. I come to a glass coffee table and gaze around. "There's no one here,"

I say over my shoulder, as I tread across the endless parquet flooring, my boots moving gently.

Danny moves up the stairs to the mezzanine and checks, and Otto goes out onto the terrace.

"Nothing," they say in unison.

"So where the fuck have they gone?" I ask myself quietly, checking once more for signs of any life. There's nothing. It looks like the place was finished and no one's ever moved in.

36

BEAU

With my hands wrapped around the hot mug, I stare down into the coffee, still shocked, still blank, so I can only imagine how Rose is feeling. "What was Ollie doing there, Beau?" she asks, breaking the endless silence. "She said she was expecting someone. Him?"

"I don't know," I admit, looking up and around the backstreet café, flexing my stiff neck. "I used to come here with Nath." I smile sadly. "Most of the time we sat on the pavement outside because"— I shrug—"well, you know." It's getting dark now, so all of the tables and chairs have been brought inside ready for closing. We're the last in here.

Rose looks around. "It feels weird."

"What does?"

She lifts her cup to her lips and has some tea. "Sitting in a café in public having a cup of tea. Just like any normal person would." Rose's phone rings and we both stare down at it on the table. "He'll definitely have Otto installing a tracker on my phone now."

I nod and pull the key from my pocket, placing it on the table. We both stare down at it.

"What do you think it's for?" Rose asks.

I pick it up and inspect it. "It's a safety deposit key." It would have been an idea to ask Amber for more information on the key before she died, but . . . well, it didn't quite pan out that way. I slip it back into my pocket and reach for my phone, turning it on, feeling Rose look at me. "Let's go home," I say, standing. "Before we kill them with stress."

The smile of relief she gives me really does inflame the guilt. She stands and I link arms with her, leading her out to the car. "We're toast, you know that, don't you?"

"Yeah, I know that." I start the car. "But still safer with them, right?"

"You need to remove the *right* from that question."

I nod, agreeing, starting the car and pulling out as Rose relaxes in her seat, taking her phone to her ear to call Danny and put him out of his misery. Her move spikes my own, and I do the same. Except I don't get to dial James, something catching my eye in the rearview mirror.

Blue lights.

Then . . . a siren.

I let my phone slip from my hand, and I breathe in, holding my breath until my lungs are screaming as Rose looks back out of the window. "Oh fuck, Beau," she whispers, as flashback after flashback assaults me. Nath. The cops who pulled us over. The gunshots.

My foot becomes heavy on the gas, and our speed picks up. "Is your seatbelt on?" I ask.

"Yes, it's on." Rose's fingers claw into the seat as I swing a right. She doesn't protest. She doesn't yell. Because she knows we have no choice in this moment. I look up at the rearview mirror and pull a sharp left. "Fuck," Rose blurts, her palm slapping into the window.

"I'm sorry," I say, taking an immediate right, bringing her flying across toward me. "Hold the handle," I order, pointing to the top of the door. "And try not to tense too much."

She laughs and takes the handle. "My God, what the fuck are we doing?"

I look up and see the blue lights gaining, the cop car matching every turn. I screech around the next corner, back onto the main road, and put my foot down. The light up ahead changes to yellow. "Fuck!"

"Oh, God, Beau," Rose sings, both hands taking the handle, her face hiding in her arm.

I check the traffic, seeing a truck approaching the crossroad, ready to sail through and take us out. I need to beat it. If I don't, we're done. If I do, the cop car will be held up and we might stand a chance of making it back to the house alive and in one piece. "Fuck, fuck, fuck," I chant, flooring it, bracing my arms against the wheel, closing one eye.

"Beau!"

"I can make it."

"Fuck, Beau!"

I start yelling, shying away from the wheel, hiding like Rose. The sound of the truck's horn blares, along with other car. Brakes screeching, smoke rising from tires.

The truck about ready to plough into the side of us.

"Fuck!" I feel the back end of the car brush with the nose of the truck. "Oh my God!"

"Shit," Rose gasps, her hand on her chest, looking back. I peek up at the rearview mirror to see the truck in the middle of the road, a faint blue glow surrounding it from the police car behind it.

I nearly lose my breath when I see the car appear around the truck. Not giving up. "Shit," I whisper, pulling a sharp left, then a right, then another left. I screech down the bumpy road and skid out onto another main road, then back into another alleyway. I stop and look at Rose. "Out."

"What?"

"Rose, they might catch up with me. You can't be in the car when they do. That door leads into a hotel. Get Danny to pick you up."

Her face falls. "No, Beau."

I growl and get out, rounding the car and opening the door, physically removing her. "I'll be okay."

"Beau, for fuck's sake!"

"Get in the fucking hotel, Rose," I yell, and she flinches, moving back, stung. I take a few calming breaths and quickly hug her. Then I get in the car and drive off, looking down at my lap when my phone rings. It's not who I expected.

"Beau?" Ollie's voice sounds frantic with worry.

"Was that you behind me?"

"No, fuck, no, Beau!"

"Then who?" I yell, turning onto the street. "Who the fucking hell is it chasing me in a cop car?"

"I don't know!"

"You're lying!"

"Jesus Christ, I am *not* lying."

I look up and see the blue lights through the haze of my watery vision. "Is that you behind me now?" I listen carefully down the line. And I hear it. The sirens. It *is* him. I hang up and smack the steering when on a yell, then take the next turning for the freeway, heading toward MIA.

And the bank.

I park on a nearby back street and go to the front of the building, peeking through the glass doors and gazing around. It's quiet. To be expected in this part of town at this time of night.

But then I see something and move to the side to conceal myself. I recognize him. It's the guy I saw in the picture on Danny's desk and at the Minute Key. Kenny Spittle.

Didn't they shoot this piece of shit?

I pull my gun and wait, and as soon as he turns to lock the door behind him, I wedge it in his temple. He stills. Curses.

"Open up," I say.

He inhales sharply and peeks out the corner of his eye to see if it's really me.

"The Brit and The Enigma won't show up to save you this time." I force the gun farther into his temple as I pat him down, checking he's clear, before taking the briefcase in his hand and tossing it into a nearby bush.

"I'm legit," he says, sounding panicked as he pushes his way in, me following. "Do you think after what I've been through with those two I'd fuck up again? They held me in a metal container for weeks, for fuck's sake. Starved me!"

"Shut up." I lead him with my gun to the next door. "Where's security?"

"Through there." He points to a closed door, and the sound of a TV drifts into my ears. A football game.

I gaze around at the cameras pointing down on us. "How many work?"

"What? All of them."

That's unfortunate, but I haven't got time or the resources to fix that. They'll see me soon. "Open."

His shaking hands fumble over the keys until he finally gets it open, revealing more doors.

"Where's the vault?"

"Oh God, I'll go to prison!"

"I'm not here to rob you." I hold up a key. "Familiar?"

He nods and points to a door. "Oh Jesus. The vault's through there."

"Open." I demand, waving my gun. Spittle holds a key to a pad and then his eye to the scanner, and the door pings open as he starts praying while he goes through the motions of opening the vault.

When the colossal metal door drifts open, I inhale, momentarily losing my focus. A moment is all it takes. Spittle moves fast, facing me, and I fire before I have a chance to think about where I'm shooting him. Blood splatters against the wall, and I look away on a wince. "Shit," I breathe, telling myself, forcing myself to calm the hell down. I find Spittle face up, eyes open, a hole in his head. *Fuck!* I still, listening for any sounds of security coming to investigate. Nothing. I frown and step toward the door, hearing cheering from the security room, then look up and around at the cameras.

Uneasy, I take Spittle's legs and pull him to the door, using his body to wedge it open.

Then I start trying all of the boxes, looking up every time I hear a sound, pausing my search, bracing myself for a security guard to come running in. No one does. Box after box refuse to open, until . . .

The key turns, and I inhale at the sound of a lock shifting. I open the box, tense, finding a piece of paper, and with shaking hands, I unfold it.

A letter.

From my father.

And with each word, my heart slows more.

Beau, If you're reading this, you've found out something I desperately didn't want you to know.
I'm so sorry . . .

"Beau?"

I still, staring down at the words before me, frozen. The voice behind me spikes both comfort and distress.

And then a sharp stab in my arm has me dropping the paper.

And everything is . . .

Black.

37

DANNY

James screeches up outside the hotel, and I'm out before he's brought his Range to a stop, sprinting up the steps and bursting into the lobby, frantically scanning the space for Rose.

I don't see her.

I turn on the spot, my stressed sweat starting to meet the collar of my shirt. "Where are you, Rose?" I say to myself, raking a shaky hand through my hair as I stalk around, dialing her. It goes straight to voicemail. "Fuck!" Have I got the wrong hotel? I run to the reception desk and thrust my phone at the woman, showing her the screen where a photo of Rose on the beach in St. Lucia dominates the screen. "Have you seen this woman?"

The receptionist leans back, wary, her eyes jumping from the deranged man before her and his mobile. "I'm sorry, no."

"Can I help you, sir?" A man steps forward, suited and booted, looking all important. I look down at the gold badge on his blazer. The manager.

"I'm looking for someone," I say, showing him the screen. He doesn't bless it with even a look, instead raising his chin. I mentally warn him not to be difficult. My patience is non-existent. He's lucky I'm not already tearing up his hotel.

"I'm afraid guest confidentiality is something we take very seriously."

"She's not a guest," I grate, my hand squeezing my phone. It's that or this cunt's throat. "Have you seen her?"

He still doesn't look at the screen. Is he detecting the unexploded human bomb before him? The heat rises from my toes, burning the worry away and replacing it with something this prick definitely doesn't want to see in his hotel. The woman moves back as I reach for the glass jug on the counter and wrap a hand around the neck, turning it upside down. The water pours out all over the marble counter and he looks at the weapon in my hand.

No second chances. And with that thought, I draw back the jug.

"Danny."

My name breaks through the mist of fury and I still, ready to launch, and look back. James has Rose under his big arm. I drop the jug, letting it shatter everywhere, and jog over, my lungs tight, relieved. I grab her and haul her into my chest, squeezing the life out of her. "Thank God," I whisper, over and over, looking to the heavens. "Thank you, thank you, thank you."

"We need to get out of here," James says, taking the top of my arm, jerking his head back toward the entrance. I look over my shoulder and see the manager with a phone shaking at his ear. I turn Rose around, tuck her into my side, and lead her out onto the street where James has abandoned the car. We make it to the passenger side, and I release her, finally taking the time to check her over. Legs, stomach, chest, neck, face.

My eyes land on hers, just as she delivers a belter of a slap across my cheek, snapping my head to the side. "You promised to look after Amber?" she seethes.

I close my eyes and roll my jaw. It grinds, cracks, aches. "Now is not the time for your temper, Rose."

I peek up at James. I've found mine. She's fuming, but at least she's safe and well. He gets in the car, his way of communicating we should leave, and I dare to look at Rose again. Her cheeks are stained with streaks, her eye makeup is smudged, her lashes sticking together.

"Don't cry, baby," I whisper. "It doesn't suit you."

Her shoulders jerk, she lets out a ragged breath, and I haul her back into me, cuddling her, holding her, making a mental vow to never let her out of my sight ever again. It's wishful thinking, I know that. "Get in," I order, opening the back door and helping her. She shifts across the seat, and I slide in next to her.

James pulls away immediately, glancing up at me in the mirror. I nod, turning to Rose and taking her hands. "Talk to me, baby. Tell me what happened."

She looks at James and reaches forward resting a hand on his shoulder. "She loves you."

He looks away, his face pained. "Where is she?"

"I don't know."

I see his nostrils flare, watch his knuckles go white around the steering wheel. "Please talk, Rose, before I smash this town up," James says so calmly, it's pretty fucking terrifying. The Enigma. I'm seeing more of him recently than in all the time I've known James.

"We went to Amber's," Rose starts hastily, releasing her hand from his shoulder, probably from being burned by the sheer temperature of his body. "She was at the apartment that Beau's dad said he would buy for her. Hiding out, I think."

I flick my eyes to James. "Go on," I say, taking her hand as James takes a right and pulls up at the side of the road, turning in his seat to give Rose his full attention too.

"We couldn't get into the elevator, but Beau figured out the code. It was the date of her mom's memorial."

What the fuck?

The looks flying around this car are non-stop, and I have a feeling they're only going to increase.

"Amber was there." Rose looks at me with a smidge of resentment that is really fucking misplaced right now. "She said some pretty awful things to Beau."

"Like?"

"Goading her. About her dad, about the money. I tried to get Beau to leave."

Something tells me she didn't succeed. At least, not before . . . I can't think it. "And?"

"And then she called me your latest whore."

"And?" I ask, leaning back.

Rose's lip trembles as she chews it nervously. "And I shot her."

"Oh Jesus." I rake a hand through my hair, slumping back in the seat.

"*You* shot Amber?" James asks.

"Yes." Her voice wobbles. "I don't know what happened. One minute I was cooling down, talking myself out of killing her, then I opened my eyes and my hand lifted. I couldn't stop it. I shot her."

"So where's the fucking body?" James asks.

My brain slowly gets over the shock and catches up. I turn my attention to Rose. She's frowning. "We left it—"

"Rose, baby, we've just come from that penthouse. There was no body."

"But it was there on the rug! We left it and ran because—" She stops, the lines on her forehead multiplying. James and I both wait for her to find the next words, words I'm pretty fucking certain we're not going to like. "Because Beau's ex-fiancé showed up."

"What?" James blurts. "Burrows?"

"Yes," Rose whispers. "We left. He came after us."

"Fuck!" He slams his fist into the dashboard and starts his Range, pulling off fast.

38

JAMES

"Talk to me," I demand, sweating fucking fury.

"She's at Mid Bank," Otto says down the line, sounding grave.

"What the fuck is she doing there?" The bank where her mother's safety deposit box was held? The empty safety deposit box. Empty because The Bear found it before we did with a little help from the bent manager Spittle. I hang up at Otto and look at Danny in the rearview mirror. "We should never have let that prick go."

"The key," Rose says out of nowhere.

The words have me losing concentration on the road for a split second, making Danny yell and me swerve. "Fucking hell," he breathes as I miss a man on a bike by a whisker.

"A key?" I say, splitting my attention between Rose and the road, heading for Mid Bank.

"Amber had a key. Beau took it." Her eyes dart, as if she's struggling to piece together the events.

"Think hard, Rose," I say as softly as I can.

"Come on, baby," Danny says, soothingly. "We need details."

"Amber pulled a key out. Asked if that is why we were there. I was trying to get Beau to leave. I could see she was going to snap. But then I saw Ollie on the surveillance screens in the office. I was distracted. Amber barged me to the floor and got my gun."

"You had a gun?" Danny asks, proverbial steam coming from his ears.

"Yes, I had a gun." Rose's eyes narrow. "Amber told me you were going to look after her. I believe you've killed men for less where I'm concerned."

Danny can't argue with that. "And you ran," he finishes, putting aside his grievance for now. If Amber was still alive, Danny would kill her.

"Yes, we ran, but as soon as we were on the main street the cops came after us."

The cops? Or Burrows? "Anything else?"

"Beau dropped me at the hotel, and I tried to stop her, but she removed me from the car and refused to listen." Her eyes overflow again. "I tried to stop her."

I blink slowly, going back to the road and focusing on getting us to Mid Bank without killing us. I know Rose would have tried. I know Beau would have won.

I also know how much Beau loves Rose. She knows she's walking into danger and she didn't want to expose her pregnant friend to that.

God help me.

Otto makes it to the bank before we do. "Cameras are all cut," he says, falling into stride beside me. "Doors all open."

"Is she here?" I ask, getting straight to the point.

"No. Her phone's fallen out of service."

"Not switched off?" I ask, sounding robotic. It's the only way right now.

"I'm waiting for it to come back online." Otto leads the way into the bank, and I follow him, scanning the place. "Spittle's dead," he says, just as my eyes fall onto his body wedged between the door and the frame into the vault, a trail of blood leading there. "He was dragged."

I assess the scene, the blood, the pieces of Spittle's brain coating the wall.

"Two security guards through there also dead." Otto leads me into the vault, both of us stepping over Spittle's dead body. "No call has been put into the police yet." He goes on, as my eyes find the open safety deposit box on the counter.

"Beau and Rose found Amber," I tell Otto, giving him a quick, emotionless rundown. "She had a key. Beau took it after Rose shot Amber."

"*Rose* shot Amber?"

I nod. "Burrows showed up. They ran. I think he cleaned up the body."

"Why?"

"Because he thinks Beau killed her and he wants to protect Beau." I laugh under my breath, walking over to the box, wondering what the fuck was in there. Burrows's name? How the fuck did Amber come to have the key? And was that why he was at Amber's place? The man we've all hated, all wanted dead. The man who's been present yet absent. Hiding when his fucking ducks were no longer all in a row. The man with the largest reach with every criminal house . . . except us.

"Burrows?"

I look at Otto, the pieces still all rearranging as I think. Otto knows it adds up, and so many things are falling into place. "Beau's never been at risk. Not only because she's with me." For fuck's sake. I should have killed him. I should have fucking killed him! The straightest fucking cop is The Bear. And he now has Beau.

"How do you explain the Russian in the hospital who tried to kill her after she was shot?"

"Sandy," I say simply. "He was retaliating after I took out his men at the factory. Nothing to do with The Bear."

Otto steps back. "And Burrows didn't like that," he says quietly. "So he and Sandy aren't friends anymore."

"Correct." My stomach turns, my scar tingles, my fucking veins burn. "Fuck!" I roar.

"Calm down," Otto says, and I throw my head back, laughing dementedly, seeing my family home going up in flames. "James!"

"I'm fine," I exhale, pacing up and down, slowing to a stop when something comes to me. "He's too young." I say quietly, turning my eyes onto Otto.

"What?"

"Burrows. He wouldn't have even been out of college when my family were..." I swallow. "...murdered." Blown up. Burned alive. I exhale and rake a hand through my hair and watch as Otto absorbs what we should have thought about instantly.

"Fuck," he breathes. "He's not working alone."

I feel like my head is about to spin off. But who? "Where is she?" I ask, calm but not.

"We need to find this lawyer he's seeing." Otto's phone starts screaming with the sound of an alarm, and he looks down. "Shit."

"What? What is it?" I ask, not that I have to. Otto's nervous sweat speaks volumes. I fly out of the bank and throw myself behind the wheel.

"What's going on?" Danny asks from the back as Otto comes after me.

"You need to stay and clear up that mess," I say, starting the engine.

"What mess?" Danny asks.

"I'm not fucking staying anywhere." Otto runs around the front, hopping in the passenger seat. "Remember who he wants, James." Otto looks at me with a face full of fury. This is one of those times when I won't argue. "I'll call Len and Bud to come sort this." He goes straight to his phone as I wheel-spin away.

"Will someone tell me what the fuck is happening?" Danny orders shortly.

"Spittle's dead."

"Who killed him?"

"Beau." I don't question that. She's a stellar shot. She also needed to keep her escape open, hence using Spittle as a doorstop.

"Now she's at Burrows's."

"What?" Rose gasps, shooting forward in her seat, forcing Danny to pull her back.

"There was an empty box in there," I explain. "Security guards dead, cameras cut. It's Burrows." *Burrows and who the fuck else?* "She's at his place." What I don't know is whether she went there willingly, or if Burrows forced her.

"You realize this is a trap, don't you?" Danny says. "He wants us, not Beau."

"Do you want me to drop you off anywhere?" I ask, serious. I can see the mental battle he's having. His loyalty to me but his love for Rose. I don't envy him. This is the pinnacle moment in this fucking nightmare.

So I decide for him, screeching up at the curb and calling Fury, giving him the address. Rose is sobbing as she gets out, clinging to Danny like she's afraid he might abandon her. His face is impassive. But his eyes? They blaze with a hatred I can relate to. He doesn't need to speak. His icy eyes tell me everything he wants to say.

Make it messy.

He closes the door, and I pull away fast, looking at them on the roadside in the rearview mirror, Danny's arms wrapped around his woman.

I exhale, rubbing at my temple, trying to remember how it feels to have Beau in my arms. In this moment, I can't.

I return my eyes to the road, my head fucking bent.

This will be a crime of love.

But for who?

I park as close as I can to Burrows's apartment without risking being detected and jog down the street, my gun in one hand, my phone in the other. The lights are on, the whole place glowing. I creep around the back, my body hard, tense, shaking.

"The curtain," Otto whispers, nodding to a window. I look and see a slight gap, and breathe in my anticipation, looking back at Otto whose attention is on his screen. He nods. She's in here. I peek through the small sliver between the curtains.

And my heart drops into my stomach when I see Beau unconscious on the floor.

BEAU

Voices. Muffled words. A low, irritating buzz. The fridge?

Then a woman's voice.

I open one eye, just a fraction, trying to see . . . anything. Trying to make out their words. My head is ringing, my left arm dead. My eyes dart but stop when I see a pair of shoes across the room. I recognize them.

Oh God, no. How could this be?

My poor brain is in no position to compute what is happening. How it's happened. How I never knew what was right in front of me this whole time. "Beau? Beau, can you hear me?" He sounds fraught, stressed, as he comes closer, and my already racing heart gets faster and faster until I am unable to play dead anymore. I open both eyes, but my vision is far from clear, and my hearing is a whoosh of inaudible words. "Jesus, Beau." He crouches before me and strokes my hair back, and I look up to see him glancing around, his gun poised, ready to shoot. He's sweating. Breathless. I hear a noise outside the window. "Fuck," he curses, returning his eyes to me. I mumble some garbled words. I don't know if he understands them. "I'm so sorry," he says, sounding distant. Grainy.

I move fast. I don't know if it's fast enough.

Bang.

40

JAMES

I rest my back against the wall, my mind racing, feeding me instruction after instruction. I can't get them straight. Can't think clearly. I growl, my teeth gritting.

Think!

I take a deep breath, telling myself I can't go in there, guns blazing. But then a gunshot sounds, and all rationale is lost, along with my fragile temper. I roar and lift my arm, throwing my elbow back into the window, shattering it, and I'm through it soon after, numb to the sensation of glass ripping through my arm.

I scan the room and nearly fall to my arse when I see Beau on her knees, sobbing.

Burrows's head is in her lap, his eyes open, blood trickling out the corner of his mouth. His hands cover his neck, blood spilling through the gaps, pouring all over the floor and Beau.

"No," she sobs, rocking back and forth, crying her fucking eyes out. "No, no, no."

My heart splinters, my gun lowering, my useless body motionless. Clueless. She looks at me, her eyes welling, and I'm about to go to her, but I hear a noise from another room.

My body hardens again, and I follow the sound to the front. "James, no!" she yells. "Please, come back!" The front door is open, and I rush outside, seeing a woman pulling away in a Ford.

"Hey!" I yell, running out into the road, aiming my gun, trying to read the license plate. The car speeds around the corner. "Fuck!" I yell.

"James!" Beau screams, forcing me back to her. I find Otto at the door, and I reel off the license plate number as I pass him. "Find her."

"On it," he says, going straight to his phone.

I find Beau still rocking back and forth, looking down at Burrows in her lap, the noises coming from him unbearable. I should finish the fucker off. Not to put him out of his misery, but to put Beau out of hers. I slowly start to aim, get ready to shoot, my eyes passing between his and the back of Beau's head, her tears splashing all over his face.

"I'm sorry," he garbles. "I'm s-orry, I'm sorry, I'm s-sorry." They're his last words.

His eyes close and he goes limp, relieving me of the job, and I let my gun drop to my side on an exhale as Beau's sobs ramp up another notch. I can't bear to hear her cry. I dip and remove her, carrying her to a chair and sitting her down, checking her over. I see a mark at the top of her arm. A small puncture. "Beau?" I ask, wanting to shake her. She stares blankly forward, her eyes dead. Black pits of nothing. Will she recover from this darkness? I take her cheeks in my palms, desperate for her to see me. "Look at me."

She does, and I withdraw, her face expressionless. "The woman," I say.

"His girlfriend," she says robotically. "She showed up."

I frown. I thought Burrows said she was practically living here. "And?"

"I don't know. She screamed. She yelled. She ran." Her eyes find me, and I hate the infinite emptiness I see. "My dad," she says on a whisper, her voice wobbly. "My dad's name was in the box."

I exhale shakily, looking up when I detect movement by the

door. Otto looks as grave as I expect I do. *Jesus fucking Christ.* Burrows and her father?

I pull her into my chest and hug her tightly, looking up at the ceiling, cursing that motherfucker to hell and back.

It's over.

But it feels like my challenge has only just begun.

DANNY

The TV is on. I'm not watching it. Every sound in the house gets my attention. And Rose's, who's curled up in my side, pretending to relax too. It's hopeless. James and Beau got back past midnight last night. Beau looked like death. James looked like he'd been through hell.

They had, from what he told me while Doc checked Beau over and James necked a few needed vodkas. I called Higham to deal with Burrows's body. Otto has been non-stop trying to find out who this lawyer is that Burrows was seeing. The Ford was a rental. I expect he'll have a name and address shortly. Oliver fucking Burrows? The amount of times we have been in a room with that fucker.

I peek down at Rose. She's looking at the screen. Not watching though. Frankly, my time is of better use elsewhere at the moment, and I know she's thinking the same. Neither of us want to be the one to speak up.

I sigh, breaking away and getting to my knees in front of her. "As much as it's been lovely sitting here pretending to relax, I would much prefer to do this another time when I haven't got a million fucking questions on my mind."

She smiles. It's small. "I should go check on Daniel and Beau."

I nod, kiss her, and get up. "I'll be in my office." I head that way, and the moment I'm in there, Ringo pours me a Scotch. I show him my gratitude with a smack on his shoulder. Brad's shaking his head from his seat at my desk, still looking a bit shellshocked. "Where's James?" he asks.

The man with all the answers we need. "Where do you think he is?" I pace up and down, my head ringing. "Higham's sorted Burrows." Poor bloke. He'll definitely be retiring soon. "Fuck knows what Burrows did with Amber's body." That's a worry. My wife killed the ex-in-house whore, and I have no way to ensure the body is never found to protect Rose. What a fucking mess.

The door to my office opens and James walks in. He looks fucking awful. "Rose is taking some tea up," he says, going straight for the vodka. I look at Brad, who looks at Ringo, who looks at Goldie.

"How is she?" our she-warrior asks. She has more balls than any man in this room.

James laughs, increasing the uneasiness surrounding us. He turns, armed with a full glass, and toasts the air. "Mourning the death of her corrupt ex-fiancé while her current one stands here drinking himself into an oblivion wondering what the fuck this means for him."

Silence.

"What the fuck happened, James?" I ask, my brain fried. "How did Amber have a key to the box?"

He peeks up at me. "Beau found her father's name in the safety deposit box."

The collective gasps of everyone drench the room. "The fuck?" I breathe, lowering my glass as I mentally walk my way through every tiny shitty thing that's happened.

"Tom Hayley? The Bear?" Jesus, and Burrows was his little mole. The fuck? "Burrows was at Amber's for the key?"

"And Beau got there first." James drops into a chair heavily, staring forward. "He drugged her. Took her back to his place." He downs the drink as we all remain still and quiet. "His lover showed up. Disturbed him. Beau disarmed him. Killed him."

And now she's mourning him. My cheeks blow out, and I join James in supping the hard stuff. I can only imagine how livid he is. How relieved. How worried. *Lost.* It's going to take more than a break in St. Lucia to fix this shit. I get up and go to him, tentatively placing a hand on his shoulder, fully prepared for the blowback in the form of a fist to my face. "So who the fuck killed Tom Hayley?"

James laughs lightly under his breath, rubbing into his temple. "Amber. Ollie. Volodya…"

I inwardly laugh. He's right. Any one of them could have, and we'll never know for sure because they're all fucking dead. "You'll get through this."

James obviously doesn't agree, taking a glug of his drink. "I'm going to the gym." He rises, setting his glass on the desk. He needs to stand on his head for a while. Try to level himself out. He doesn't need me to tell him it probably won't work this time.

My phone rings and I pull it from my pocket as I watch James pace out of the room, all eyes following him. Something tells me that the next time I see him, he won't be James. He'll be the man we all fear. The Enigma. Even though The Bear is dead. Burrows is dead.

But James doesn't have his peace. *Fuck.* I look at the screen of my mobile. "Sandy," I say, looking up, seeing James stop at the door, his hand on the knob. "Am I talking to him?" Can I distract him with business? I doubt it—we know Sandy arranged a hit on Beau, not The Bear. Because The Bear was her fucking father.

"Someone's got to take those guns off us," Brad pipes up, looking nervously at James's back. "Chaka's going to be delivering a load more soon. We need space."

James's back rises, and he slowly turns to face us. He nods, and I answer. "Morning."

"Afternoon," he counters, making me glance at the clock on the wall. One minute past noon. "I heard there's been some developments."

I click to loudspeaker as James comes over, settling back in the chair. "News sure does travel fast in this city." I raise my brows. "How do you know?"

"Our friend Higham."

"*Our* friend?"

"You don't like sharing?"

"No, actually."

"What about selling?"

I smile and rest my arse on my desk, crossing one ankle over the other. "Depends what's on offer."

"The whereabouts of Carlo Black's remains?"

I still, the tumbler slipping from my grasp and hitting the rug. "What?"

"Since we're getting things out in the open, doing a bit of housekeeping, I will tell you now—"

"Tell me what."

"I was ordered to dig up your father."

"And you did."

"I did."

If Tom Hayley and Burrows weren't dead, I'd fucking kill them so fucking slowly, they'd be begging me to end it. "And where is he?"

"I will send you directions."

"And Beau's mother?"

"What?"

"Jaz Hayley." I eye James, who is slowly rising from his chair, his big, coiled body unfolding, looking as deadly as we all know it is. "Where will we find *her* remains?"

His extended silence does not bode well, but before I can demand an answer, the door flies open and Otto flies in. "The lawyer Burrows was seeing. She's been in Aspen since Monday. A getaway to get over a break-up. She said she and Burrows had a few casual fucks, he was uninterested, and then he suddenly wanted her there every day. She broke it off. Said he was behaving strangely. It wasn't her running away from Burrows flat."

I look at James, confused as fuck. He's staring at the floor, and he slowly lifts his gaze to mine.

"Answer my fucking question, Sandy," I order darkly.

"We only got orders to dig up your father, Black. I know nothing about Jaz Hayley's remains."

I inhale, my lips pressing together, as James's body gets taller and taller.

"I have more." Otto says, winning all of our attentions. "The rental car speeding away from the scene."

"What about it?" James asks, his voice, low, calm.

Deceiving.

"Rented under the name Dolly Daydream."

He tears out of the office on a curse.

42

JAMES

The stairs are a blur as I fly up them, my legs numb. All I can see is Beau's mum's car in the parking lot. Beau approaching warily. The fireball rising, touching the nighttime sky. I race down the corridor, the thumps of my boots and many more following me shaking the house.

I skid to a stop at our room, grabbing the door jamb to stop my body overshooting the entrance. I see Rose standing in the middle of the bedroom with a tray of tea in her hands before I see the empty bed where I just left Beau snoozing. I don't bother checking the bathroom, the terrace, any other rooms in the house.

All blood drains from my body, leaving it cold. Emotionless.

"Talk, James," Danny orders from the door, needing confirmation of the fucking crazy running amok in my head. I can't speak. Can't form the words.

"James," Rose begs, the china on the tray starting to clang together from her shakes.

My head a mess, I walk through the people behind me, down the stairs, across the lobby, out the front door, and into the driveway.

My Range Rover is missing. I look down the driveway to the gates. They're open and Bud is stomping back to the gatehouse.

I go to the first Mercedes and get behind the wheel. It doesn't make any sense. It doesn't make any fucking sense! I reach for my temple, applying pressure, forcing the relentless flashbacks away. They're unstoppable.

She hangs up, and I see Beau standing in front of the car. Frozen. No! I sprint across the car park, my heart booming, and round the front of the car, charging at her, taking her down.

We both hit the tarmac with force. She yelps, startled, as I jump up to get to Jaz.

Break out in a run.

And get blown back by the explosion.

43

BEAU

The clouds are being kind today. They roll and tumble through the sky, blending and molding into various shapes. I see a Union Jack. Handcuffs. A gun. A flame.

A face.

The ground is wet and cold beneath my back, the mud in my closed fists squelching. My heart hurts. My mind is twisted. I've never needed James so much. But never been so scared of him either. I close my eyes, escaping the cruel clouds.

I see Mom's eyes widen. See her fear as I near the car.

The impact from my side is brutal, taking me down, and I crash to the ground. I drag myself up, disorientated. The spark. The boom. I raise my arm protectively, feeling the heat hit me, take me, and my body leaves the ground, the force flinging me skyward.

"Beau Bear," she says from beside me. I keep my eyes closed, waiting for the endless darkness to swallow me. "I can't do this anymore."

Neither can I.

I open my eyes and drop my head. Funny. The emotions I expected to kill me are ... absent. "Why?" I just need answers. I just need to move on and make the life I deserve with James. I need to stop living for the ghosts.

"All I had to do was take down Spencer James." Her voice. Like in the bank, it's a comfort and a complete mindfuck. My heart is racing as fast now as it did when I read the letter my dad left for me. A letter apologizing for not being there for me. For keeping me in the dark. For trying to protect me from the unbelievable truth.

"Your father wasn't so flush back then, and us weak women not as handsomely compensated for our service." Mom shrugs, quite nonchalant. "It was the payday we needed toward our retirements." She looks at me, and her eyes on mine hit me like a brick to my face. It's like she's here but not, like my brain can't compute her presence. "Spencer James didn't just front the biggest cocaine syndicate in UK. His last deal involved the U.S. I had enough drug runners to deal with. He was a greedy fucker. Sold everything, was happy to slip into retirement and leave the rest of the world to deal with the consequences of his shit. No. I saw an opportunity, I took it. The Irish wanted him dead. I wanted him dead. I made it worth their while, they made it worth mine. I really wasn't expecting the backlash. No one on the estate was supposed to be left alive."

James. She's talking about James. Kellen James, the boy she turned into The Enigma.

She returns her eyes to the sky, and I'm so grateful. "It spiraled from there. I spent five years after the Irish ended Spencer James trying to scratch back my conscience and be the best cop. But your father started making money, and with his success came the ego. And extramarital activities. I knew I had to look out for myself. Taking backhanders was easy money." Her head tilts, almost reminiscent. "Being bent was easy. Being in control was easy. Then The Enigma showed up."

I squeeze my eyes closed, trying to squeeze away the bombardment of flashbacks. "He was on his own personal mission. That personal mission was screwing up everything. People were paying me to keep them out of cuffs and your *boyfriend* was killing them left and right."

"He wasn't my boyfriend then," I say flatly, feeling her studying me. "I was engaged. Had a great career. A mom *and* a dad."

"It's all his fault, Beau Bear," she whispers. "He fucked it all up."

"How?"

"I couldn't catch him," she grates. "I knew who he was, but I couldn't catch him. He was getting so close to finding out who killed his family. Who I was. I had to make sure that never happened."

"So you blew me up."

"No, Beau. God, no." She takes my hand, and I snatch it away on a sharp inhale, feeling like I'm being burned all over again. "I planted The Snake. Planted the message on the burner phone that said I was in danger. He was supposed to come to me first. But he came for you instead."

My God, what am I hearing? I close my eyes, trying to replay that tragic, unbearable night that's haunted me for years. What I was so sure happened is suddenly fuzzy. Unclear.

"In that moment," Mom says. "When you got too close to the car and he saved you, I had no choice but to die."

And as a result, my entire world went up in smoke. Literally. Didn't she consider the consequences for me? The pain and hurt? I feel a lump building in my throat, and it infuriates me. I sit up in an attempt to dislodge it, staring at her grave. "Who the hell have I been talking to for all these years?" I ask, staring at the empty hole in the ground where I had what was left of her buried.

"I don't know," she says. "I paid someone to make sure there was something to find in the car and make sure it wasn't identifiable." I close my eyes, breathing in, praying that when I open them, I won't be here. I open my eyes. I'm still in the cemetery. "I was so fucking angry he forced my hand," she goes on, sounding like a fucking victim. I can't bear it. "He made me die. Took you away from me. And the corruption and power spiraled and spiraled." She laughs, and *that* makes me want to hit her. "And the money came. And the need for revenge grew."

I look at her, vacant, but on the inside, I'm gawking at her like she's lost her mind. James took me away from her?

"But then he started pursuing you. Using you to get to me."

"There was no name in the safety deposit box, was there? Only James's name. *You* emptied the box."

"I needed to make it look legit."

"Have you any idea what you've done?" I ask. "Truly? The lives you've ruined?" *Including mine. Your daughter's.*

"He couldn't have you if I couldn't."

I exhale on a suppressed whimper. "He fixed what you broke." I stand and move away from her, unable to process this endless barrage of shitty facts. "You have blackmailed, murdered, blown up buildings. All just to get James?"

"Just? He destroyed my life. *Our* lives!"

"You destroyed his first!" I scream. She flinches. But she doesn't see what I see. "You blew up a restaurant when I was inside."

"You were not inside, Beau. You were on the sidewalk, I made sure of it."

"You drugged me in the bank, Mom." *Mom.* It feels like an inadequate word. *Monster.* "Why would you drug me? Take me to Ollies?" My hands find my hair and clench, trying to suppress the pain building in my head.

"God damn it, Beau, it was all for you! For us, so we can be together again."

I inhale, standing back. "You left my tracker on so James would know where to find me." *My God.* "You were going to kill Ollie and frame James. Because Ollie worked out you killed Dad and Cartwright." That's why Ollie was apologizing. His last words to me. *I'm sorry.* He was sorry for not telling me. For hiding it. For trying to shield me from the shitty truths. She was going to have James killed by lethal injection.

"Your Dad was a disgusting sack of shit. A stupid man." She throws a heavy hand up, angry by the mention of my father. It's ironic. His name used to spike the same reaction from me. Now? I don't know how I feel about him now. His last move was to try and protect me from the truth like Ollie. Does that make him a hero?

Mom looks away, like she could be ashamed. It's a joke. "I always said you were a talented cop."

"I take after my mother," I say, and she looks at me. "Unfortunately. How did Dad find out you were alive?"

"His piece of ass stumbled upon some files while she was making herself at home in *my* home. Files your father found."

"Files on what?"

"My deals with the previous mayor and my purchase of Danny Black's boatyard."

I laugh, feeling a little unhinged. "Not such a fucking good cop now, huh? Or is it not such a good criminal?"

"Beau..."

"And Amber's been running for her life because she knew Dad had been murdered."

"I had no choice, Beau Bear." She comes to me, taking my arms, shaking me like it's me who needs some sense knocking into them. "We can go. I have enough money for us. We can disappear together, me and my girl."

I shake her off and step back, hearing Ollie's words over and over. *Sorry. Sorry, sorry, sorry.* I hear him apologizing over and over for so much. "Ollie didn't deserve to die." My mind gives me a cruel flashback of the moment I disarmed him in his apartment. The moment I saw my mother behind him with a gun aimed at his back. The moment she fired, a window smashed, and James crashed in.

The moment she ran away like a coward.

I couldn't utter her name. Couldn't tell James what I'd seen. Was hoping I would wake up and find the whole awful thing had been a nightmare.

No.

It's all real.

And I'm done.

"I'm going home now," I say, passing her, raising my eyes, my heart in shards of grief. I feel like it could fall out of my chest. Break in two. But I mustn't let it. I have to keep this heart together.

For James.

For me.

I look up, and I breathe in when I see him standing a few feet away, his face wet with sweat, his hair in disarray, his stubbled face tortured. I know in this moment he's heard everything. I look back to Mom. She's staring at him. Staring like a wild animal with their eyes set on their prey.

"It's over," I say, my voice shaky. "It ends now, Mom." I hear sirens in the background, getting louder. *It's over.*

But then she moves, gunning for James, drawing her gun, and before I can register a thing, I'm moving too, with no direction or instruction. Just moving.

"Beau!" James's booming voice saturates my hearing as I crash into Mom, taking her down to the ground. We hit the ground, and I quickly get my bearings, spinning, getting Mom underneath me. I straddle her, pulling her arms back. "Jasmin Hayley, you are under arrest," I say over a sob. "You have the right to remain silent. Anything you say can and will be used against you in a court of law."

"Beau!" she yells, wriggling, forcing me to yank her arms back more.

"You have the right to speak to an attorney now, and to have an attorney present during any questioning." *Justice isn't served by death. It's served by being locked up until death. It was served by being in fear of your life on the inside.* I watch as one fat teardrop after another hits Mom's jacket and splashes up as I hold her arms in place, while she continues to struggle, the sirens close.

I look up at James. He looks traumatized. Out of his mind. I start shaking my head, my tears streaming. "I'm not okay," I whisper, making him move immediately, coming to me. I need him so fucking badly, it makes me resent my mom more, hate her harder, for being the reason I can't crawl into him now and hide from this shit.

I release her wrists for James to take over as he lowers to his knee.

It's just a fraction of time.

But it's enough.

She throws her body up, knocking me back, and spins over.

Bang!

James flies back, his chest concaving.

"No!" I pull my gun, trembling, and aim it at Mom. But my finger refuses to squeeze the trigger. I scream as she stands, pushing past me, and goes at James, firing again. His body jerks, his head snapping back. "Mom, no!"

I look at James.

All I see is love. Devotion.

Light.

I turn my eyes onto my mother.

I inhale and pull the trigger, and she flies forward, her arms shooting skyward, and falls face first into the dirt. I don't need to check. The hole in the back of her head tells me. I drop my gun, screaming to the sky, my emotions pouring out of me harder than they ever have before, jacking my body. My fists hit the ground, smash into the mud, over and over.

"Beau, baby," James wheezes, on his knee next to me, one hand wedged into the ground to hold himself up. I look up. All I see is blood. Blood and light. My lip trembles as I crawl to him, desperate, sobbing, trying to assess him, trying to find the bullet holes.

How many? Where?

"Someone help!" I scream as he drops to his shoulder and rolls to his back, struggling to breathe. "Someone help me!"

I hear screeching tires, sirens, screams.

Danny and Otto are sprinting toward us.

I hate their expressions.

Hate the crippling grief taking hold.

It's beyond excruciating, more powerful than any grief I've ever felt before.

A loss I will never get over.

44

JAMES

It has to be said, the light was blinding. And it was really fucking tempting to walk toward it. But . . .

Beau.

I could hear her need.

Feel her love.

The light on this occasion can fuck off. I didn't go through the past few months to let death take me so pathetically.

"Stop moving," she orders, flapping around the bed, pulling at the covers, throwing me filthy looks left and right.

"I'm stiff." And not in the best way.

"Doc said strict bedrest for four weeks." She gently pushes me back down, and I sigh, exhausted, unwilling, and unable to fight her.

"It's been three weeks and six days."

"Yes, and look at you," she breathes, exasperated, waving her hands up and down my broken body. "You need at least another four weeks. I'll go get Doc." She pivots, and I just catch her wrist, stopping her. I won't lie, it's fucking agony straining even that much. I grit my teeth and tug her back.

"Just lie with me for a while." I need her close. To have her near and know there is literally *nothing* in this world that can tear us apart.

Only each other.

She settles, though hesitantly, and I feel her slight body soften beautifully against me. "Are you okay?" I ask quietly.

She's quiet for a few moments, her hands stroking gently over the dressing on the side of my stomach. "I'm okay," she whispers.

I smile. *Okay.* It's ironic. Twenty years' worth of therapy shouldn't cure the kind of shit we've experienced, both together *and* alone. It probably couldn't. But I have Beau, and Beau has me.

So we're going to be okay . . . once this pain has fucked off and I've healed. I nod to myself, letting my broken body meld into the mattress, let my eyes close and know nothing will take her from me while I'm asleep.

"I love you, Beau."

"I won't ever question that."

I dose off, knowing it to be true. Peace. I've thought I've had it. When I met Beau, it teased the peripheral of my existence, tormented me, because it would never truly be mine until I'd fixed her.

I accept now, she will never be fixed. But she is most definitely mine. All mine. Her hate, her love, every broken piece of her, and that makes her as fixed as she'll ever be.

My dreams are light. My heart is so fucking heavy with love.

Peace.

Even amid the excruciating pain.

A stab of pain gets me, and I grunt, curling my body in protectively to quash it. "Fuck."

"Sorry!"

I open my eyes, groaning, not knowing whether to clench my stomach or my shoulder.

"God dammit, Brad!" Beau yells, slipping off the bed with as little disruption to me as possible.

"Do you two ever stop?" he asks, appearing at the end of the bed, looking me up and down with a scowl. "Even crippled you're insatiable."

I fucking wish. I return his scowl and try to sit up some more. And fail.

"Be still," Beau warns, her stern words making me go limp again. She takes some water from the nightstand and holds the straw at my lips. I'm in no position to contest her help. This is hideous. I latch on and slurp, noticing Brad's sling has gone.

"Fighting fit," he declares, obviously noticing I've noticed, gingerly lowering to the end of the bed. "Jerking off's still off the menu though."

I cough, and water shoots out of my nose, spraying my chest. "Fuck!" I yelp, as a tidal wave of pain rolls through me. Beau glares at Brad, who raises his hands in surrender.

"No jerking? No jokes?" He pouts. "What kind of life is this?"

I hold on to my laughter—the pain just isn't worth the lightness. "She'll kill you," I say seriously, making him smirk at Beau as she holds him in place with a look of pure filth.

"How are you feeling?" he asks. "Or is that a stupid question?"

"It's a stupid question," Beau says, collecting the bowl of water and wash cloth off the nightstand and heading to the bathroom. "But you're stupid so it figures."

I smile at her back as Brad rolls his eyes, keeping his attention pointing my way. "What—"

"If you're here to talk about work you can leave," she calls.

Brad drops his chin to his chest, exasperated. "I'm—"

"Or I'll happily walk you out."

He hitches a brow. "I should probably just leave, right?"

I nod. "Probably."

He doesn't move, the daredevil. "So, how are you feeling?"

"Like I've been shot." I grimace as I shift a fraction. "Twice." I huff, my neck hurting. "Can you just . . ." I lift my head, trying to find a firmer part of the pillow.

"What?"

"I can't . . ." I nestle into it, huffing, my neck stiff. "It's . . ."

Brad gets up and comes to me, easing the pillow out and punching it a few times. "So when are you back on your feet? Lift your head." My chin hits my chest and Brad stuffs the pillow beneath. "Better?"

"Yeah." I settle. "Tomorrow." I'll be up and about by tomorrow.

He laughs. "Doesn't look like it."

"Doc said I should be on my feet." I've just got to walk off the stiffness. "Beau's being difficult." I expect she's also got an ulterior motive.

"She's known exactly where you are for four weeks, pal. That's a luxury she's never had. I can't blame her."

I laugh under my breath, fidgeting again, uncomfortable. "It's been a fucked-up luxury for me too, knowing where she is twenty-four/seven." But now I have every confidence that she's never disappearing on me again. "Fuck this," I snap, lifting my shoulders, making Brad rush to me.

"Whoa, what are you doing?" He looks between me and the bathroom, obviously terrified of Beau's reaction. "Stay still. She'll blame me."

"Be a man," I grunt, holding my breath and gritting my teeth, working my way up to sitting.

"Be a fucking man?" he mutters, holding my shoulders, therefore stopping me from falling back to the mattress. "What should I do?"

"Brad!" Beau yells, emerging from the bathroom.

He releases me, holding his hands up like Beau's got a gun aimed at him. "It wasn't me, for fuck's sake. Why'd you blame everything on me?"

I land on my back on a yelp. "Fuck!" The pain. It fucking angers me, and in the midst of it, because it couldn't get any fucking worse,

I sit back up, hissing as I do. "Give me some of those painkillers, for fuck's sake."

Brad scrambles for the pot and tips a couple into my palm. I keep my hand out. "More?" he asks, unsure.

"More," I demand. Another two land, and I toss them into my mouth and motion for the water. Brad holds the straw at my mouth, and I slurp it down before shuffling back until I find the headboard, slumping against it. Fuck me, I'm sweating.

The door knocks, and Pearl wanders in with a tray, bringing my daily delivery of tea and toast. She's all smiles.

Until she sees Brad.

He quickly puts himself on the other side of the bed, grunting his hello, and Pearl quickly gathers herself. "Esther sent tea and toast."

My eyes jump from Pearl to Brad, happy for the distraction from my ailments. "Thanks," I murmur as Brad kicks the carpet, his hands sunken into his pockets, his eyes low.

"Welcome." She smiles and slips it onto the nightstand. "How are you feeling?"

"Like I've been shot. Twice."

She smiles awkwardly. It's nothing to do with me. It's Brad. Pearl and Anya have been in and out of my room for four weeks bringing tea, toast, water, whatever Esther's sending. Both have settled in well. Both are all smiles.

"Better," I add. "I feel better." I eye the toast. Butter. I think I must have lost twenty pounds of muscle. "Pass me a slice," I say.

"You're sitting up," Pearl says, putting a few slices on a napkin and setting it on my thighs.

"Yes, and he shouldn't be." Beau throws Brad another death glare, not that he notices, his attention still on his dress shoes.

"I have cake," Anya declares, breezing in, again all smiles. Unlike Pearl, her smile remains in place regardless of Brad's presence. "How do you say ... Limon driz?" She waggles her eyebrows.

"Drizzle," I finish for her, pointing to my lap. "Load me up."

She takes the biggest wedge and places it next to my toast. "You need fat."

"I agree," I say, opting for the cake first, wrapping my mouth around the big slice and humming my happiness. Sugar. God, that's good. Beau smiles, delighted to see me eating.

"You're sitting up!" Rose shrieks, rushing to the bed and taking my cheeks in her hands, squishing the cake in my mouth. I hear Beau laugh as she continues fussing around the bed, folding blankets, fixing curtains, brushing crumbs from my lap. Rose's eyes scan my face. "You seriously need a trim." She tugs on a bit of my beard, and I bat her away, smiling fondly at her ever-growing belly as I chew my way through my cake.

Danny strolls in, casual, suited, hands in his pockets. I cast a look to Brad. Suit. To Danny. Suit.

Nolan walks in, all smiles.

Suit.

What's going on? They've both been casual whenever they've stopped by. Casual and relaxed. In fact, the whole house has a different aura. And everyone in it. It's like the brief, fleeting moments we've all shared in St. Lucia, except in Miami. And for considerably longer than before. I can sense it, even half dead from my bed.

I suck the tips of my fingers as Danny settles on a chair, his smile mild. Relaxed.

"You need a haircut," I say, prompting him to run a hand through his dark hair that's no longer tickling his nape but resting on it.

"Well, my wife has a new salon so that shouldn't be a problem going forward."

"Oh?" I look at Rose, and she shrugs with a sneaky smile. "I've sent the girls to beauty school to finish the courses they started," she declares, smiling fondly at Anya and Pearl. "And once this baby's out of me, I'm going to business school."

I flick a discreet look at Danny, who's brushing his cupid's bow thoughtfully. I can't imagine he's loving that idea. "And I thought I would help Brad at the club," Beau declares out of the blue.

What?

I give Brad a dark look. So that's what's been going on while I'm laid up, is it? Enticing my fiancée with a job at our laundering hub? "I'm not t—"

"Unless you want me to continue smuggling your guns, of course," she adds casually, peeking up at me.

"I think this is a conversation for us to be having in private." I grab some more cake and ram it in my gob before I yell a resounding *no!*

"Coming through, coming through." Esther joins us in the room. "You're sitting up."

"I'm sitting up," I mumble through my cake, holding it up, nodding my approval. The woman can bake.

"Did someone say cake?" Otto enters, followed by Ringo and Goldie.

All suits.

"When are we going to St. Lucia?" Brad asks, breaking his silence but keeping his attention aimed on his side of the room.

"I thought you hated the lack of action?" Beau replies coyly, nibbling her lip as she fills my water up.

"Maybe The Four Seasons is in St. Lucia too." Pearl smiles sarcastically, everyone falls silent, and Brad's lip curls.

"Well, well," Doc chants, appearing through the growing crowd in my room. "How's my latest patient doing?"

"Hungry," I say, taking a piece of toast and wrapping my mouth around it. I can't get enough.

"When did you last have some pain meds?"

"Just now," I waffle as he takes my blood pressure.

"Good, good. We need to start getting you on your feet, James."

I slowly turn my eyes to Beau. She's scowling at Doc. "Yes, Doc," I say obediently, finishing my toast.

"Want some more?" Pearl asks, loading me up anyway.

"Hey, Uncle James." Daniel darts into the room with a racket in his hand, followed by the Vikings. *And* Leon and Jerry.

"Is there a party and no one told me?" I ask my crowded room.

"It's Brad's birthday," Rose declares.

"No shit."

"Shit." Brad rolls his eyes as Zinnea bursts through the middle of everyone.

"Happy birthday!" she sings, seizing Brad and planting a kiss on his cheek.

"Thirty-five today," Danny says, looking between him and Pearl, as do I. And Rose. And Beau. Even hauled up in this room, I'm fully aware of the situation. Brad seems hell-bent on ignoring it, though. It's probably wise. Fuck me, fourteen years? It's a stretch, but he is actually old enough to be her father. And perhaps that's part of the problem.

Danny clears his throat and stands. "We have a meeting with Sandy."

What? "You've not dealt with that yet?" I ask.

"We wanted our wingman," Brad adds. "Up for it?"

"Yes, I'm up for it." I need a change of scenery. Something to take my mind off this pain. "Give me five and I'll be ready." I look around the room to the endless people, literally every member of this fucked-up family. "I'm naked under these sheets."

The girls scatter like ants, all bar Beau, of course, and the men casually leave, heading down to the office. I whip the covers back and shift my legs off the side of the bed.

"No!" Beau puts herself in front of me, adamant in her stance.

I lean forward and bury my face in between her shirt-covered boobs, getting a hit of her natural smell, my hands sliding to her arse and holding it.

"James," she pleads, holding my head. "It's too soon."

"Doc said I need to get on my feet." I look up at her. "I'm walking down to the office, Beau, that's all."

"To have a meeting with a man who sent someone into my hospital room while I was unconscious to kill me."

"It's all water under the bridge," I say, making her laugh out loud. "I'm not joking." I've thought about this endlessly. I'll never be his best mate, but I have to accept that he has made moves, shared information, that has gotten us to the end. A few bullet holes to boot, but we're at the end. "It's over, Beau," I whisper. "Now we get to enjoy the light."

She shakes her head but smiles, smoothing over my face. "You're about to go downstairs and negotiate a deal on some guns."

We both accepted quite a while ago that this is our life. We just need to make it as easy as possible, and that is what we're doing. Setting the bar. Defending the bar. "We've risen," I whisper. "We cannot fall."

Her eyes scan mine, and she lowers her lips, kissing me softly. Delicately. It's the lightest kiss we've ever shared. "Come on," she says around my lips. "Before something else rises."

I jerk with my burst of laughter, hissing, wincing. "Jesus." Every muscle feels like it could snap, they're so tight. "It's too late, anyway." I take her hand and lead it to my groin, and her eyes widen.

"That *definitely* isn't happening."

I won't argue. The last thing I want to do is have sex like an old man. And that thought alone makes me determined to recover. I stand from the bed.

"Take it easy," Beau snaps, staggering back.

"I need to brush my teeth." I take one step. Another. "Good God," I hiss with each move, my muscles protesting, but they're never going to loosen up if I stay in bed rotting away. Break through the pain. It's another pain on top of my endless injuries.

But nothing compared to the agony of Beau's despair.

She walks me to the bathroom, insists on brushing my teeth, helps me into some sweats—no suit—and the whole time I watch her, fascinated by how light her dark eyes appear.

I strain to lift my arms when she helps me into my T-shirt. "You're too thin," she muses, pulling the material down my torso. She pauses at the bandages covering two new bullet wounds.

"I can put on weight," I point out, forcing her to look up at me. We stare for a long, long time. I don't know what I'm looking for. Signs that she's not okay? Because how the fuck could she be after everything that's happened? Her mum, for fuck's sake. All this time, her mum. If there's one thing I've given a lot of thought to during my time of forced convalescence, it's her mum.

"It was the payday we needed toward our retirements. I really wasn't expecting backlash of such monumental proportions. No one on the estate was supposed to be left alive. It was easy money." Slaughtering my family had been for *easy money*. She played the game well. I've always known Jaz Hayley knew who I was. Where I'd come from. What I've done. After she 'died' in the explosion the night I saved Beau, she as The Bear could never reveal that she knew who The Enigma was. Because only Jaz Hayley knew who The Enigma was. She had to move her pieces with precision and care if she was going to keep her true identity secret. Hence the safety deposit box. She devised a plan to have the box compromised so my identity would be exposed without risking her own being discovered.

Every time I've thought about it, I've wanted to scream. I've wanted to kill her. Slowly. I hate that Beau mourned her mother's death for so long. Hate that she will forever have killing her own mother on her conscience. It should have been me. But then I consider what revenge did to my soul, and how black it became. Because of Beau, hatred no longer rules me. She set me free. Allowed me to rise.

So, really, it had to be Beau to end The Bear.

Besides, I got to end The Snake and endless other Irish fuckers, so I guess it's an even playing field.

Beau feels my chest, her cheeks brightening. I take her hand, bringing it to my mouth, and kiss her ring. "I'm okay," she whispers, feeling my chest, the color in her cheeks seeming to increase by the minute.

She's okay.

Finally.

Beau leads me to the bed, sits me down, and puts my trainers on. I get an even more potent hit of the peace radiating through the house once I'm in the corridor.

Our walk down to the office is slow, but with every step, my muscles give a little more and the effort lessens. "Okay?" she asks, as we take the stairs, looking up at me.

"Okay," I reply, loving attentive Beau. Looking after me. It was never something I considered could be. Could accept. It'll be a while before I'm back in the gym, but I'm prepared to take small steps, take my time and use it wisely with Beau.

When we make it to Danny's office, she pushes the door open, and everyone looks my way. I gesture to my casual attire. "It's as good as it gets right now."

Beau helps me to the couch and eases me down. I'm a lot looser. I could have done it myself, but I'm humoring her. Mothering me suits her, and that thought alone makes me smile.

"Be gentle with him," she quips, bending over and dropping a kiss on my lips. "Behave."

"Yes, ma'am." It's also sexy as fuck. She needs to leave before I abandon this meeting and take her back upstairs. Old man be damned. "Go," I order.

She smiles and saunters out, and my eyes follow her arse until the wood comes between us. I pout, smiling to myself, planning all of the making-up sex I have to look forward to. *More.* She'll beg me for more again.

"Hello?"

I blink and look around the room. Everyone's watching me. "Get me a drink," I breathe, motioning to the full bottle of vodka on the cabinet. Goldie obliges and swiftly gets a tumbler in my hand. That first sip. Fucking heaven. I shake my head on a grimace when Brad offers me a cigarette. "What's the plan?" A newspaper lands in front of me, the front-page news quite something. I pick it up and read the article by Natalia Potter detailing the tragic death of Detective Collins at the hands of Russian ex-KGB mobster Marek Zielińska. Another newspaper lands on top of it. Another compelling front-page story. Oliver Burrows. A hero, killed in service by a bent FBI agent who was assumed dead. Beau's mother's face is next to Burrows's. "Has Beau seen this?" I ask, looking up at the date. Two weeks ago.

"Yes, she's seen it," Danny says. "In fact, she met with Natalia Potter and made sure all of the details were accurate."

I raise my brows, reading the damning report into her mother. Closure. Okay, so apparently I haven't known where Beau's been twenty-four/seven.

"I've managed to stall the second delivery from Chaka," Danny says, pulling my attention up as he pulls a pack of Marlboros from his pocket and lights up. "The Mexicans aren't happy with us."

I wince, knowing what that means. We might have lost a bear and a zoo, but there's always another enemy to replace the last. "And Sandy wants guns."

"Thank fuck," Brad says. "The bunker's bursting at the seams."

I smile, relishing another sip of vodka as Danny's phone rings and he looks down at it. "Let's see how many he wants." He answers and gives Bud instructions to bring Sandy to the office before hanging up and taking his seat at his desk, relaxing back. And the office falls silent until there's a knock at the door.

I brace myself for the murderous feelings about to descend as it swings open, but when he steps into the office, I feel . . . nothing.

"Afternoon," he says, giving everyone a moment of his eyes. "You are all here for me?"

"We're famous for our hospitality." Danny smiles around his cigarette. "Why don't you take a seat?" He motions to the chair opposite him. "Drink?"

I smile around the rim of my glass, feeling everyone else's amusement too. The Brit being all hospitable? It's a novelty.

Sandy takes a seat and nods to me. I nod back, a silent acceptance of his olive branch. "My business is out of state," he says, getting to the point.

"Are you saying you're leaving Miami?" Danny follows Sandy's lead.

He smiles. "I don't think this town is big enough for the two of us." He looks at me. "Or three."

"Four," Brad growls from the couch, making Goldie chuckle.

"It's not," Danny confirms. "So you'll be taking the guns you buy from us to . . . where?"

"Many will be sent home. Some will remain with me in New York."

"New York?" Danny muses. "The Italians have New York."

"I'm favoring the Italians over The Brit." His eyebrows rise. "Also, the Mexicans owe me. I can ensure they do not trouble you." *Interesting.* "Are we talking or not?"

Danny looks at me.

I knock back my drink. New York is far enough away from me, which means Miami is ours and ours alone.

Normality is looking more and more likely. I nod to Danny as the office door opens and Rose wanders in, looking up. She freezes. "Shit, I'm sorry," she blurts, backing out. "It can wait."

"Everything okay, baby?" Danny asks, standing from his chair.

"Yes, I forgot you had a meeting. It's about—" She pauses, her eyes drop, and she seems to pale.

"Rose?"

She smiles. It's forced. "It can wait. I'm sorry for disturbing you." The door is quickly closed, and I look at Danny. His frown is as big as mine.

"I'll be in touch," he says to Sandy, his eyes not leaving the door. "Len will see you out."

DANNY

I let Len take over at the door and run up the stairs two at a time. I saw her face. Everyone in that office saw her face. What the fuck's going on? I steam down the corridor, my walk fast and determined, and push my way into our bedroom. "Rose?" I call, listening.

I hear a noise in the bathroom. I try the handle. Locked. My chest starts to pump. "Rose," I call through the wood, my ear pressed against it, listening.

"Coming," she squeaks.

I look at the door incredulously. "Open the fucking door."

"I'm fine."

"Open the fucking door, Rose," I bellow, stress taking over. She's fucking insulting me. I look over my shoulder when I hear movement, seeing Brad and James in the room with me. "She's locked herself in the fucking bathroom," I tell them, shaking my fist into the wood. "Open the fucking door!"

"Danny," Brad says, pacifying, coming to me, leaving James to follow at a slower pace, as a horrible feeling creeps into my bones.

"What's going on?" Beau bursts into the room, looking between us all. "Where's Rose?"

"She's in there." I smack the door again. "You saw, didn't you?" I look at Brad. "Her face. You saw it, didn't you?"

"She looked . . ." Brad glances at James for help. He can't help him. James saw her face too. It was haunted.

"Is it the baby?" Beau asks, her hand over her mouth. My stress skyrockets as Beau comes to the door too, knocking a little more gently than me. "Rose, come on," she pleads. "Open the door."

I'm quickly picking Beau up and placing her to the side, and then I shoulder barge the wood. It pings open on a brief scream of protest and reveals Rose. Sitting in the corner, curled up, her face in her knees. *Oh Jesus.* My eyes naturally fall to the tile, searching for blood. Not from cuts, but from—

I can't say it. I rush over and crouch, trying to pull her hands from her face. She's rocking back and forth, her back hitting the wall constantly. "Rose, baby, please." I force her hands away. There are no tears. There's . . . nothing, actually. No expression. Nothing.

It throws me. It throws us all, the room silent as I hold her hands away from her face, searching for something. *Anything* to tell me what I'm dealing with. "Rose, baby, please talk to me."

She inhales, so calmly. "That man," she says quietly, pushing the tension in the room up to unbearable levels, as well as the stress already boiling over. Her eyes are empty as she stares at her knees. Her face expressionless. Her body hard, like a barrier has come up. Then she looks at me, and I recoil. "He raped me when I was fourteen."

I fall to my arse as everyone's inhales of shock seems to suck all the air from the bathroom, making it impossible to breathe. "No," I whisper, scrambling back, trying to put distance between us.

Beau fills that space where I'm not capable, falling to her knees and taking Rose's hands. Rose looks at her blankly. "He did, Beau," she says, on autopilot. "He came to my room." Her eyes close tightly. She's trying to hold off the flashbacks. I scramble to my feet, sweat pouring from my brow.

"Danny," Brad says calmly, holding my arm. I shrug him off, looking at my wife on the floor fighting back her past. I have to know. I *have* to know. I go to her, crouching, but I don't touch her. I can't. My hands are only capable of murder right now. Not softness.

"Could he be Daniel's father?" I ask, cold.

Beau swings a stunned look my way as Rose opens her eyes and gazes at me. She doesn't answer. She doesn't need to.

I slowly stand, every muscle involuntarily flexing, the monster inside rising. She doesn't even bother telling me to not go. I turn and walk away, burning from the inside out, my vision hazy with the rage consuming me. And Rose doesn't try to stop me.

"Danny." James reaches for me. Pointless. A cyclone couldn't stop me, let alone The Enigma at half fucking strength.

"James," Beau says, warning him.

I know he won't listen.

I march through the house feeling like my head could pop off my shoulders with the pressure, Brad and James yelling after me, pulling everyone from whatever they're doing around the house. Mum comes out of the kitchen, drying her hands on a tea towel. Those fucking tea towels. I wrench the door open and stomp down the steps. "Which one?" I shout, getting no answer to my question. I turn by the cars. "Which fucking car?" I bellow, my lungs draining, my body quaking.

"First," Ringo says, tossing a set of keys at me. I catch them and go straight to the trunk, opening and pulling out the first gun I can lay my hands on.

"Fuck, Danny, wait!" Brad yells.

I jump in and skid off, looking up at my rearview mirror. Brad's going apeshit, up in Ringo's face, fisting his suit. James is walking calmly to the next Mercedes.

I flash my lights as I approach the gates, and Bud opens them. I pass through. Slow at the entrance. Look both ways.

It doesn't take me long to decide which direction I'm going in. I spin the steering wheel to the right and floor the gas, heading toward town. I flick the stereo on. Laugh when Frankie starts singing *Relax* to me. Light up a cigarette. Focus on the road, overtaking car after car, my driving smooth and calm but really fucking fast.

I see his Bentley up ahead. Take one more, long drag of my cigarette, flicking it out of the open window collecting my gun from the passenger seat, resting it in my lap. I overtake one last car and pull in behind Sandy, flashing my lights. He starts to slow. Signal.

He pulls over at the side of the road and gets out, looking back at me. I slip out calmly, gun in hand, and walk toward him, lifting my arm, watching as his face falls into confusion.

I squeeze the trigger, but the car that screeches up behind catches me off guard, and I swing around, my finger loosening. It's not Brad or James or any of my men.

Russians.

For the first time since I left Rose in the bathroom, the fog clears. I look back and forth between Sandy and the other men, surrounded.

Outnumbered.

They all lift their guns at the same time, like Sandy's pressed the start button on his men. I inhale. Time slowing, my brain slowing with it.

The first shot catches me on my arm, knocking me back onto the bonnet of my car. The second in my thigh. The third in my shoulder. I lay on my back on the hood of the Mercedes, looking up at the blue sky, wondering . . . is this it?

Has my lack of control killed me?

I feel the tip of a gun pushing into my forehead.

I breathe in.

Close my eyes.

Bang!

"You stupid, stupid fuck!" James growls.

My eyes ping open, just in time to see his raging face before I'm yanked to the ground. "Fuck."

"You hurting?" James asks, his own face screwing up as he lifts and looks over the roof, firing.

"A bit." A fucking lot.

"Good."

A plume of dust blows up, and Brad skids down the side of the car, joining us. "You stupid, stupid fuck." He rises, fires, and drops back down to his arse next to me. "If we get out of this alive, you're dead."

"Otto flies around the back of the car, landing at my feet. I wait for what words of kindness he might throw my way. He doesn't need words; his look says enough, but he speaks anyway. "If you die, I die."

"That's very honorable of you," I wheeze, trying to lift my gun. I can't. My arm is dead.

"Not honorable, son. Just a very real threat from your mother."

"Good old Mum," I quip, my feet slipping all over the stone as I try to get up. "Where the fuck is he?" I soon drop back to my arse when bullets start hitting the side of the car.

"Driving off into the sunset." James rests back, looking up at the sky, exhausted. In pain. I'm with him.

"He got away?" I whisper, dropping my gun as Otto rises and pops off the last few men. "Why the fuck did you let him get away?" I yell, crawling to my feet and standing, watching his Bentley getting farther and farther away. "He needs to die." And I need to be the one who kills him. I snatch Brad's gun and stagger into the road, firing as I go, bullet after bullet, yelling as I do.

"The fuck, Danny?" Brad smacks the gun from my hand and gets up in my face, seething mad. "Do we all need to die too?"

I shove him away, and go back to my car, ready to go in pursuit. Fuck this shit. I am not going back to my wife until that rapist is dead.

I drop into the seat. And am quickly ejected, being hauled out and thrown to the ground. I look up at James.

Correction.

I look up at The Enigma.

And he looks far from at half strength. His finger comes up, his lips twisting. "Don't make me kick your injured arse all over this freeway, Black," he warns. "We deal with this another time. Like when we stand a fucking chance of coming out the other side alive. Now get in the fucking car."

"You dick. I got in the fucking car. You just pulled me out of the fucking car."

"Get in the fucking car!"

I do as I'm told.

Not because I'm scared.

But because he's right.

And what fucking use are we to our women if we're dead?

"You need to see Doc," Goldie says as I drag myself up the steps.

I snort. "I need to see my wife."

"You're fucking bleeding all over the place."

"No shit." And the pain. Fuck me, the pain. "Where is she?"

"In your office."

Beau comes flying out of the kitchen, her face like thunder, until she sees me virtually dragging myself along. "Shit, Danny."

"I'm fine."

"Someone get Doc," she yells, running to the door. "For fuck's sake!" She steps out, slipping her body under James's arm as he struggles along. "I'm so fucking livid," she seethes, giving me her eyes, making sure I know I'm on her shit list too.

I look down the corridor to the office. Then down my bloody body. "Fucking hell," I wheeze, clenching my side as I limp there, feeling Brad two paces behind, ready to catch me when I collapse. I really fucked myself over this time. I won't collapse. Not until I get to Rose. I take the handle, leaving blood all over the shiny knob, and push the door open.

She looks up from the couch. Takes me in. Swallows. She knew the outcome of this.

Except she doesn't.

Getting up, she comes to me, taking in my broken body, the blood, the bullet holes. Her lip quivers. "Don't cry, baby," I say hoarsely, staggering forward a little, feeling a bit light-headed. She catches me and eases me down to the couch, feeling over my jacket and shirt, looking for the bullet holes. "Doc's on his way," I assure her.

She nods, slowly lifting her eyes to mine. "Is he dead?"

I stall. Swallow. Take a deep fucking breath and use my last piece of energy before I pass out. "Yeah."

EPILOGUE

Miami — Five months later

JAMES

I'm suffocating. In this suit, in this room. "Stop fidgeting," Danny breathes from beside me pulling in his own tux. "You look like you're having second thoughts."

"I am," I admit.

"What the fuck?" Brad moves in, putting his ear closer to me. "Did you say what I think you just said?"

"Yeah, he said it," Otto confirms, throwing me a filthy look. "What the hell do you mean, you're having second thoughts?"

"We're happy as we are." I feel like such a chump, especially since it was me who pushed for this all along. But back then, I needed reassurance. I don't need it now. I needed a light to follow. I don't need to follow the light anymore. It's just . . . there.

"Suck it up." Danny smiles, his blue eyes beaming. "It's thrilling dicing with death every day."

"Speaking of dicing with death," Otto says.

"What?" Danny asks, quickly searching for his mother.

"I'm not happy about your mother doing everything around the house."

Danny bursts out laughing, offering his hand to Otto. "If you can convince her we should have a housekeeper, I might start accepting this shit between you two."

Otto snorts. "Like you have a fucking choice." He ignores Danny's hand and takes up position beside me.

I face forward, crazy nervous, and come face to face with Lawrence. I shake my head, taking in his holy man garbs. He really has taken this ordaining shit seriously. "Are you ready?" he asks.

"Nope."

His nose wrinkles. "The big scary assassin scared of a few wedding vows?"

The boys chuckle, and my stressed sweat increases. I'm pathetic. "How did you do this twice?" I ask Danny seriously.

"Lots of Scotch." He pulls out a hip flask and hands it over to me, before pulling out another for himself and swigging. "Drink up."

I do, and it's fucking glorious, the others all pulling flasks as well. I feel a tap on my shoulder and look back.

Pearl is holding up a white rose. "You forgot your buttonhole." She forces me to turn and starts fiddling with my suit jacket.

"You look lovely," I say, not just for something to say, but because she really does.

She smiles as she works. "Thanks."

"Yeah, lovely," Danny chimes in, nodding at her emerald-green satin gown. "Doesn't she, Brad?"

All eyes turn onto Brad. He's scowling. Standard when Pearl is around. "Lovely," he grunts, turning his back on her. What the fuck went down between these two? They fucking hate each other. But . . . don't.

"There." She pats my pocket and fixes the jeweled hair comb keeping one side of her red hair off her face. "You're ready."

"Am I?" I laugh, facing Lawrence again, just as he gasps, loud and dramatic, very Lawrence-esque.

"Oh, here she comes."

"Fuck," I breathe, unable to look back.

"Music, please!"

My mouth falls open when London Grammar's *Strong* starts playing, and I'm turning before I know it, searching for her. "Oh, Jesus." She floats. She fucking floats. That's how light she is. I swallow the lump in my throat, roughly wipe at my eyes, overcome by . . . everything. Her, me, this, the feelings overwhelming me.

I don't take my eyes off her. Can't.

I also can't wait for Goldie to get her to me, so I push through the men, going to her, meeting her halfway up the aisle. Her head tilts in question as I bend and pick her up. "What are you doing?" she asks.

"Taking you into the light." I move in, ready to kiss my bride already, humming when my lips brush hers.

That's as far as our kiss gets.

"Oh shit," Rose cries, winning the attention of everyone in the room. Her silver gown is taut over her bump, her long hair resting on top of it. Danny's head bats back and forth between his pregnant wife and us. "It's fine," she declares, waving a hand flippantly. "I'm fine."

Esther, looking incredible in a scarlet gown, moves into Rose's side, whispering something in her ear. Rose smiles tightly, her body definitely folding over a little. "She's in bloody labor," I breathe, setting Beau on her feet.

"No, I'm not." Rose laughs. "Braxton Hicks."

"Mom, please." Daniel passes her, going straight to Danny. "Her water broke in the bathroom this morning." He looks at his mum. "She made me promise not to tell."

Beau breaks away from me and goes to Rose, who flaps her away. "Get married," she orders.

"Where's Doc?" Danny asks, going to Rose, picking her up.

"No! I'm not leaving here until Beau's Mrs. Enigma." She virtually growls in Danny's face. "Make it happen."

"Get married now," Danny orders, jerking his head toward Lawrence. Then he smiles, big and cheesy and fake. "Please."

"I can't believe she's coming now," Beau says, pulling me toward her uncle. "I can tell she's going to be awkward like her father."

I stare down at Beau, flummoxed, feeling Danny and everyone else doing the same. "She?"

Beau's eyes widen. "I didn't say that."

"Yes," Danny says, walking forward, Rose draped over his arms. "You definitely said *she*." He looks at a timid Rose. "Do you two know what we're having?"

Silence. Rose looks at Beau with straight lips. Beau looks sorry.

"Well?" Danny presses.

A girl? Fuck me, as if this family needs a little girl.

"We truly will be outnumbered at this rate," Brad mutters, looking at Pearl but quickly looking away when she catches his eye.

"Answer me, Rose," Danny demands.

"Well, you see . . ." She nibbles her lip. Then screams in his face, making him stagger back into Ringo, who quickly steadies him. "Oh, shit, Danny!" she bellows, puffing and panting. "Hurry up!"

Lawrence starts babbling, and I don't hear a thing.

See nothing.

Only light.

It's suddenly only us.

"It's not too late," Beau whispers.

I smile. It is *way* past too late. Following Lawrence line for line, I recite his every word as instructed, never taking my eyes off Beau, and then listen intently, full of wonder, as she does the same, a small, knowing smile curving her lips.

"You may kiss your bride."

I swoop in, making the most of her mouth, eating her alive, lifting her from her feet, indulging in her. Until another scream from Rose kills the passion.

Beau, arms around my neck, looks over her shoulder at Rose. "I should go help," she says as Danny carries Rose away. She reaches into the purse dangling from her wrist and pulls out a small box. "I got this for you." She puts it in my hand, reaches up and kisses me, then leaves me standing at the aisle. "Don't open it until later."

Is she kidding? I look down, frowning as I lift the lid.

I'm quickly without the ability to breathe as I stare at two lines in the window of a white plastic stick.

"What?" I whisper, glancing up, just as Beau looks over her shoulder, smiling mildly.

And light, quite literally, explodes around her.

The Unlawful Men Series Continues with Danny & Brad in Book 5 - Coming Soon.

Sign up to Jodi's newsletter to hear as soon as information of book 5 is released.

ALSO BY JODI ELLEN MALPAS

The This Man Series

This Man

Beneath This Man

This Man Confessed

All I Am – Drew's Story (A This Man Novella)

With This Man

The One Night Series

One Night - Promised

One Night - Denied

One Night - Unveiled

Standalone Novels

The Protector

The Forbidden

Gentleman Sinner

Perfect Chaos

Leave Me Breathless

The Smoke & Mirrors Duology

The Controversial Princess

His True Queen

The Hunt Legacy Duology

Artful Lies

Wicked Truths

ABOUT JODI ELLEN MALPAS

Jodi Ellen Malpas was born and raised in England, where she lives with her husband, boys and Theo the Doberman. She is a self-professed daydreamer, and has a terrible weak spot for alpha males. Writing powerful love stories with addictive characters has become her passion—a passion she now shares with her devoted readers. She's a proud #1 *New York Times* Bestselling Author, a *Sunday Times* Bestseller, and her work is published in over twenty-five languages across the world. You can learn more about Jodi & her words at: JEM.Website